KT-404-659

'JILLY COOPER CASTS HER WITTY EYE OVER THE WORLD OF TV IN HER LATEST WORK . . . ROMPING ALONG AT BREATHTAKING SPEED, IT IS FUNNY, IRREVERENT AND EVEN MOVING'
Today

'Peopled with extravagant characters and peppered with the author's famous one-liners, here is another sure-fire winner from the Cooper stable. Written with an unflagging energy, it is sexy, stylish and totally riveting'
Options

'THE PRESSURED WORLD OF TV IS PERFECTLY SUITED TO COOPER'S GOSSIP-COLUMN SKILLS, WHILE HER POWERS OF SOCIAL OBSERVATION, HER OBVIOUS AFFECTION FOR THE COUNTRY AND FOR HER NICER CHARACTERS PLUMP *RIVALS* OUT INTO A ROUNDED, ACCOMPLISHED NOVEL'
Books

'Of her genre, Jilly Cooper is the very best, plus a jolly good read for everybody . . . a gloriously sexy rampage through the Cotswold countryside, backed by the excitement of an exceptionally well-researched account of the back-stabbing and ruthless machinations behind a television franchise battle . . . elegant, glamorous, wonderful fun'
Daily Mail

Also by Jilly Cooper

RIDERS
BELLA
EMILY
HARRIET
IMOGEN
PRUDENCE
OCTAVIA
LISA & CO
CLASS
SUPER COOPER

and published by Corgi Books

RIVALS

Jilly Cooper

CORGI BOOKS

RIVALS
A CORGI BOOK   0 552 13472 4

Originally published in Great Britain by
Bantam Press, a division of Transworld Publishers Ltd

PRINTING HISTORY
Bantam Press edition published 1988
Corgi edition published 1989

This book is set in 10/11pt Linotron 202 Goudy by
Rowland Phototypesetting Ltd, Bury St Edmunds, Suffolk

Corgi Books are published by Transworld Publishers Ltd,
61–63 Uxbridge Road, Ealing, London W5 5SA, in Australia by
Transworld Publishers (Australia) Pty Ltd, 15–23 Helles Avenue,
Moorebank, NSW 2170, and in New Zealand by Transworld Publishers
(N.Z.) Ltd, Cnr Moselle and Waipareira Avenues, Henderson,
Auckland.

Made and printed in Great Britain by
Cox and Wyman Ltd, Reading, Berks.

DEDICATION

To Annalise Kay
who is as wise as she is
good and beautiful

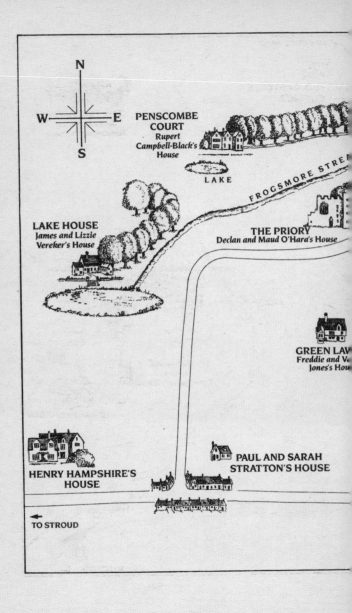

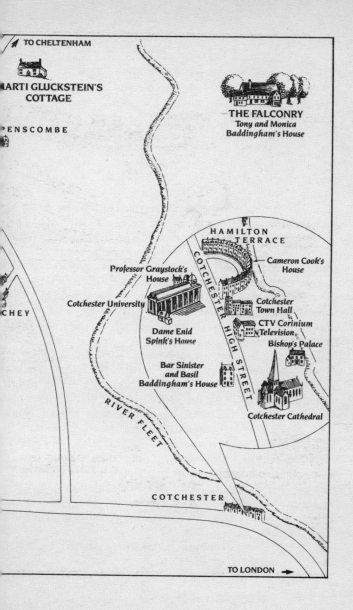

TO CHELTENHAM

MARTI GLUCKSTEIN'S
COTTAGE

PENSCOMBE

THE FALCONRY
Tony and Monica
Baddingham's House

HAMILTON
TERRACE

Cameron Cook's
House

Professor Graystock's
House

COTCHESTER HIGH STREET

Cotchester University

Cotchester
Town Hall

CTV Corinium
Television

Dame Enid
Spink's House

Bishop's Palace

CHEY

Bar Sinister
and Basil
Baddingham's House

RIVER FLEET

Cotchester Cathedral

COTCHESTER

TO LONDON →

ACKNOWLEDGEMENTS

A very large number of people helped me with this book. Most of them work in television and are exceptionally busy. They still found the time to talk to me and – particularly in the case of those from HTV – to entertain me with lavishness and generosity. All of them are experts in their own field. But as I was writing fiction, I only took their advice so far as it fitted my plot. The accuracy of the book in no way reflects their expertise. They were also all so nice to me that it was impossible to base any of the unpleasant characters in the story on any of them.

They include Georgina Abrahams, Rita Angel, William Beloe, Michael Blakstad, Roy Bottomley, James Bredin, Adrian Brenard, Doug Carnegie, Stephen Cole, John Corbett, Jenny Crick, Mike Davey, Geoff Druett, Ron Evans, Su Evans, James Gatward, David Glencross, Stuart Hall, Nick Handel, Tom Hartman, Barbara Hazell, Stan Hazell, Paul Heiney, Bruce Hockin, Alison Holloway, Patricia Houlihan, Bryan Izzard, Philip Jones, Barbara Kelly, Susan Kyle, Maurice Leonard, Barrie MacDonald, Billy Macqueen, George McWatters, Steve Matthews, Lesley Morgan, Malcolm Morris, Jack Patterson, Bob Simmons, Tom Walsh, Ann de Winton, Richard Whitely, Ron Wordley and Richard Wyatt.

Tragically, dear Eamonn Andrews, with whom I was privileged to work for four series on 'What's My Line?', died in November, after the book was finished. His utter integrity, professionalism and gentle humour were a constant source of inspiration while I was writing it.

I should also like to thank the crews, the drivers, the make-up girls and the wardrobe staff with whom I worked over the years, who came up with endless suggestions.

I must thank the people who wrote three books which were invaluable to me in understanding the extraordinarily complicated process by which television franchises are awarded. They are Walter Butler, author of *How to Win the Franchise and Influence People*, Michael Leapman, author of *Treachery? The Power Struggle at TV-am*, and Asa Briggs and Joanna Spicer, joint authors of *The Franchise Affair – Creating fortunes and failures in Independent Television*.

I am also eternally grateful to Peter Cadbury, former Chairman of Westward Television, for giving me access to his autobiography which unaccountably has never been published, to Robin Currie, of the Fire and Rescue Service HQ, Cheltenham, to Toni Westall, secretary to Captain Brian Walpole, General Manager, Concorde, and to Tim and Primrose Unwin for inviting me to some excellent hunt balls.

In addition I need to thank my Bank Manager, Keith Henderson, my publishers, Paul Scherer, Mark Barty-King and Alan Earney and all their staff at Bantam Press and Corgi, and my agent Desmond Elliott, for their faith and continued encouragement.

Three brave ladies, Beryl Hill, Sue Moore and Geraldine Kilgannon, deserve thanks and praise for deciphering my ghastly handwriting and typing several chapters of the manuscript; so does my cleaner, Ann Mills, for mucking out my study once a fortnight.

Finally, once again there are no words adequate to thank Leo, my husband, my children, Felix and Emily, and my secretary, Annalise Kay, whom I regard as one of the family, and who typed ninety per cent of the manuscript. Their collective good cheer, unselfishness and comfort over the past eighteen months knew no bounds.

Bisley, Gloucestershire
1987.

CHARACTERS IN ALPHABETICAL ORDER

RUPERT CAMPBELL-BLACK	Minister for Sport. Tory MP for Chalford and Bisley. Ex-member of the British show-jumping team.
MARCUS CAMPBELL-BLACK	His son.
TABITHA CAMPBELL-BLACK	His daughter.
CAMERON COOK	Producer/Director, NBS, New York. Later Head of Drama, Corinium Television.
CHARLES CRAWFORD	Retiring Chairman of the IBA.
JUDGE DAVEY	A member of the IBA.
OWEN DAVIES	Leader of the Opposition.
WESLEY EMERSON	Gloucester and England bowler.
SUZY ERIKSON	An American ex-girlfriend of Rupert Campbell-Black.
LADY EVESHAM	An early feminist, and non-executive Director, Corinium Television.
CHARLES FAIRBURN	Head of Religious Broadcasting, Corinium Television.
JOHNNY FRIEDLANDER	American actor and megastar.
MARTI GLUCKSTEIN	A brilliant East End accountant.
MALISE GORDON	Ex-*chef d'équipe* of the British show-jumping team.
HELEN GORDON	His wife. Ex-wife of Rupert Campbell-Black and mother of Marcus and Tabitha.
LADY GOSLING	Chairman of the IBA.
GRACE	Declan O'Hara's housekeeper.
CRISPIN GRAYSTOCK	Professor of English at Cotchester University and a disgusting lecher.
HENRY HAMPSHIRE	Lord-Lieutenant of Gloucestershire – a much less disgusting lecher.
SIMON HARRIS	Controller of Programmes, Corinium Television.

GEORGINA HARRISON	An undergraduate.
RONNIE HAVEGAL	Head of Co-Productions, NBS, New York.
HAZEL	A BBC make-up girl.
RALPHIE HENRIQUES	An undergraduate at Trinity Dublin.
IVOR HICKS	Corporate Development Controller, Corinium Television.
JILLY	Yet another Vereker nanny, but for once a dependable boot.
BEATTIE JOHNSON	Fleet Street columnist, ghosting Rupert Campbell-Black's memoirs.
GINGER JOHNSON	Financial Director, Corinium Television. No relation to Beattie.
FREDDIE JONES	A multi-millionaire in electronics.
VALERIE JONES	His wife, a nightmare.
SHARON JONES	His overweight daughter.
DEIRDRE KILPATRICK	A researcher at Corinium Television.
LAVINIA	Patrick O'Hara's girlfriend.
BILLY LLOYD-FOXE	Sports Presenter, BBC.
JANEY LLOYD-FOXE	An author and national newspaper columnist.
DERMOT MACBRIDE	A playwright and Angry Not-So-Young man.
JOYCE MADDEN	Lord Baddingham's secretary, Corinium Television.
MRS MAKEPIECE	A 'treasure' who cleans for Valerie Jones and Lizzie Vereker.
KEVIN MAKEPIECE	Her son.
TRACEY MAKEPIECE	Her daughter.
SALLY MAPLES	Head of Children's Programmes, Yorkshire Television.
MIKE MEADOWS	Head of Sport, Corinium Television.
MRS MENZIES-SCOTT	Ex-head of the Women's Institute, a member of the IBA.

GERALD MIDDLETON	Parliamentary Private Secretary to Rupert Campbell-Black.
DECLAN O'HARA	A television megastar.
MAUD O'HARA	His ex-actress wife.
PATRICK O'HARA	His son, an undergraduate at Trinity Dublin.
AGATHA (TAGGIE) O'HARA	His elder daughter.
CAITLIN O'HARA	His younger daughter.
ORTRUD	Yet another of the Verekers' comely nannies.
CYRIL PEACOCK	Lord Baddingham's PA and sometime Press Officer, Corinium Television.
THE VERY REVEREND FERGUS PENNEY	An ex-Prebendary of the Church of England, and a member of the IBA.
PERCY	Lord Baddingham's chauffeur.
PASCOE RAWLINGS	The most powerful theatrical agent in London.
BARTON SINCLAIR	Director of *The Merry Widow*.
SKIP	A beautiful American lawyer.
LORD SMITH	An ex-Secretary of the TGWU.
DAME ENID SPINK	A distinguished composer and Professor of Music at Cotchester University.
PAUL STRATTON	Tory MP for Cotchester. An ex-Cabinet Minister.
SARAH STRATTON	His ravishing second wife and ex-secretary.
SYDNEY	Rupert's driver.
URSULA	Declan O'Hara's secretary.
JAMES VEREKER	Anchorman of 'Cotswold Round-Up', Corinium Television.
LIZZIE VEREKER	His wife, a novelist.
ELEANOR VEREKER	His daughter.
SEBASTIAN VEREKER	His son.
HAROLD WHITE	Director of Programmes, London Weekend Television.
MAURICE WOOTON	A bent Gloucestershire property millionaire.

RIVALS

1

Sitting in the Concorde departure lounge at Heathrow on a perfect blue June morning, Anthony, second Baron Baddingham, Chairman and Managing Director of Corinium Television, should have been perfectly happy. He was blessed with great wealth, a title, a brilliant career, a beautiful flat in Kensington, houses in Gloucestershire and Tuscany, a loyal, much-admired wife, three charming children and a somewhat demanding mistress, to whom he had just bidden a long farewell on the free telephone beside him.

He was about to fly on his favourite aeroplane, Concorde, to his favourite city, New York, to indulge in his favourite pastime – selling Corinium's programmes to American television and raising American money to make more programmes. Tony Baddingham was a great believer in using Other People's Money, or OPM as he called it; then if a project bombed, someone else picked up the bill.

As a final bonus, neatly folded beside him were the morning papers, which he'd already read in the Post House Hotel, and which all contained glowing reports of Corinium's past six months' results, announced yesterday.

Just as he had been checking out of the Post House an hour earlier, however, Tony's perfect pleasure had been ruined by the sight of his near neighbour and long-term rival, Rupert Campbell-Black, checking in. He was scribbling his signature with one hand and holding firmly on to a rather grubby but none-the-less ravishing girl with the other.

The girl, who had chipped nail polish, wildly tangled blonde hair, mascara smudges under her eyes, and a deep suntan, had obviously just been pulled out of some other bed and was giggling hysterically.

'Ru-pert,' she wailed, 'there simply isn't time; you'll miss the plane.'

'It'll wait,' said Rupert, and, gathering up his keys, started to drag her towards the lift. As the doors closed, like curtains coming down on the first act of a play, Tony could see the two of them glued together in a passionate embrace.

A deeply competitive man, Tony had felt dizzy with jealousy. He had seldom, particularly since he had inherited the title and become Chief Executive of Corinium, had any difficulty attracting women, but he'd never attracted anything so wantonly desirable and desiring as that grubby, vaguely familiar blonde.

'More coffee, Lord Baddingham?' One of the beautiful attendants in the Concorde Lounge interrupted Tony's brooding. He shook his head, comforted by the obvious admiration in her voice.

'Shouldn't we be boarding?' he asked.

'We'll be a few minutes late. There was a slight engineering problem. They're just doing a last-minute check.'

Tony glanced round the departure lounge, filled with businessmen and American tourists, and noticed a pale, red-headed young man in a grey pinstripe suit, who had stopped his steady flow of writing notes on a foolscap pad and was looking apprehensively at his watch.

Boarding the plane twenty minutes later, Tony found himself sitting up at the front on an inside seat with a Jap immersed in a portable computer on his right. Across the gangway next to the window sat the young man in the pinstripe suit. He was even paler now and looking distinctly put out.

'Good morning, Lord Baddingham,' said a stewardess, handing Tony that day's newly-flown-in copy of the *Wall Street Journal*.

14

'Engineering fault sorted out?' asked Tony, as the engines started revving up.

Not quite meeting his eyes, the girl nodded brightly; then, looking out of the window, she seemed to relax as a black car raced across the tarmac. Next there was a commotion, as a light, flat, familiar drawl could be heard down the gangway:

'Frightfully sorry to hold you all up; traffic was diabolical.'

All the stewardesses seemed to converge on the new arrival, fighting to carry his newspaper and put his hand luggage up in the locker.

'Won't you be needing your briefcase, Minister?' asked a male steward, shimmying down the gangway.

Rupert Campbell-Black shook his head. 'No thanks, sweetheart.'

'Have a nice zizz then,' said the male steward, going crimson with pleasure at the endearment.

As the doors slammed shut, Rupert collapsed into the seat across the gangway from Tony. Wearing a crumpled cream suit, a blue striped shirt, dark glasses and with an eighth of an inch of stubble on his chin, he looked more like a rock star than one of Her Majesty's ministers.

'Terribly sorry, Gerald,' he murmured to the pale young man in the pinstripe suit. 'There was a terrible pile-up on the M4.'

Smiling thinly, Gerald removed a blonde hair from Rupert's lapel.

'I really must buy you an alarm clock for Christmas, Minister. If you'd missed that lunchtime speech, we'd have been in real stück. Good of them to hold the plane.'

'Thank Christ they did.' Looking round, Rupert saw Tony Baddingham and grinned. 'Why, it's the big Baddingham wolf.'

'Cutting it a bit fine, aren't you?' said Tony disapprovingly.

Both men required each other's goodwill. Rupert, as an MP within Tony's television company's territory, needed the coverage, whereas Tony needed Rupert's recommendation to the Government that he was running a respectable company. But it didn't make either like the other any better.

15

'Bloody good results you had this morning,' said Rupert, fastening his seat belt. 'I'd better buy some Corinium shares.'

Slightly mollified, Tony congratulated Rupert on his recent appointment as Tory Minister for Sport.

Rupert shrugged. 'The PM's shit-scared about football hooliganism – seems to think I can come up with some magic formula.'

'Setting a Yobbo to catch a Yobbo perhaps,' said Tony nastily, then regretted it.

'I was at Thames Television yesterday,' said Rupert icily, as the plane taxied towards the runway. 'After the programme I had a drink with the Home Secretary and the Chairman of the IBA. They were both saying that you'd better watch out. If you don't spend a bit more of that bloody fortune you're coining from advertising on making some decent programmes, you're going to lose your franchise.'

As Rupert leant forward so Tony could hear him over the engines, Tony caught a whiff of the scent the girl had been wearing in the Post House foyer earlier.

'And you ought to spend some time in the area. How the hell can you run a television company in the Cotswolds, if you spend all your time in London, hawking your ass round the advertising companies?'

'The shareholders wouldn't be very pleased if I didn't,' said Tony, thoroughly nettled. 'Look at our results.'

Rupert shrugged again. 'You're also supposed to make good programmes. As your local MP I'm just passing on what's being said.'

'As one of your more influential constituents,' said Tony, furiously, 'I don't think you should be checking into the Post House with bimbos half your age.'

Rupert laughed. 'That was no bimbo, that was Beattie Johnson.'

Of course! Instantly Tony remembered the girl. Beattie Johnson was one of the most scurrilous and successful women columnists – dubbed by *Private Eye* 'the First not-quite-a-lady of Fleet Street'.

16

'She's ghosting my memoirs,' added Rupert. 'We were doing research. I always believe in laying one's ghost.'

Below the blank stare of the dark glasses, his curved smiling mouth seemed even more insolent. As the plane revved up, both men turned to look out of the window, and Tony found himself trembling with rage. But not even the splendid, striped-silk-shirted bosom of the air hostess, which rose and fell as she showed passengers how to inflate their life jackets, could keep Rupert's eyes open. By the time they were airborne, he was asleep.

Tony accepted a glass of champagne and tried to concentrate on the *Wall Street Journal*. He didn't know which he resented most – Rupert's habitual contempt, his ability to sleep anywhere, his effortless acquisition of women, or the obvious devotion of the palely efficient Gerald, who was now sipping Perrier and polishing the speech Rupert was to deliver to the International Olympic Committee at lunchtime.

There had hardly been a husband in Gloucestershire, indeed in the world, Tony reflected, who hadn't cheered four years ago when Rupert's beautiful wife, Helen, had walked out on him in the middle of the Los Angeles Olympics, running off with another rider and causing Rupert the maximum humiliation.

But, infuriatingly, Rupert had appeared outwardly unaffected and had risen to the occasion by winning a show-jumping gold medal despite a trapped shoulder nerve, and going on two years later to win the World Championship, the only prize hitherto to elude him. Then, giving up show jumping at the pinnacle of his fame, he had moved effortlessly into politics, winning the Tory seat of Chalford and Bisley with ease. Even worse, he had turned out a surprisingly good MP, being very quick on his feet, totally unfazed by the Opposition or the Prime Minister, and prepared to fight very hard for his constituency.

Although scandal had threatened eighteen months ago, when Rupert's then mistress, Amanda Hamilton, wife of the Foreign Secretary, had withdrawn her patronage on finding out that Rupert was also sleeping with her teenage daughter,

17

by this time, in the eyes of a doting Prime Minister, Rupert could do no wrong. Now, as Minister for Sport, with Gerald Middleton as an exceptional private secretary to do all the donkey work, Rupert was free to roam round exuding glamour, raising money for the Olympic team here, defusing a riot against a South African athlete there. Responsibility, however, hadn't cleaned up his private life at all. Divorced from Helen, he could behave as he chose, hence his cavorting with Beattie Johnson in the Post House that morning.

Glancing at Rupert, sprawled out on the pale-grey leather seat, taking up most of Gerald's leg room, beautiful despite the emergent stubble, Tony felt a further stab of jealousy. He couldn't remember a time in his forty-four years when he hadn't envied the Campbell-Blacks. For all their outlandish behaviour, they had always been looked up to in Gloucestershire. They had lived in the same beautiful house in Penscombe for generations, while Tony was brought up behind net curtains in a boring semi in the suburbs of Cheltenham. Tony also had a chip because he only went to a grammar school, where he'd been teased for being fat and short, and because his conventional colourless father (although subsequently ennobled for his work in the war) had been considered far too valuable as a munitions manufacturer to be allowed to go off and fight, unlike Rupert's father, Eddie, who'd had a dazzling war in the Blues.

Even when Tony's father had been given his peerage, Eddie Campbell-Black and his cronies had laughed, always referring to him dismissively as Lord Pop-Pop, as they blasted away slaughtering wild life with one of his products on their large estates.

Growing up near the Campbell-Blacks, Tony had longed to be invited to Penscombe and drawn into that rackety, exciting set. But the privilege had been bestowed on his brother Basil, who was ten years younger and who, because Tony's father had made his pile by then, had been given a pony to ride and sent to Harrow instead of a grammar school, and had there become a friend of Rupert's.

As a result of such imagined early deprivation, Tony had

18

grown up indelibly competitive – not just at work, but also socially, sexually, and at all games. Spurning the family firm when he left school, he'd gone straight into advertising and specialized in buying television air time. Having learnt the form, from there he moved to the advertising side of television. A brilliant entrepreneur, who felt he was slipping unless he had a dozen calls from Tokyo and New York during Christmas dinner, by changing jobs repeatedly he had gained the plum post of Chief Executive at Corinium Television eight years ago.

Having shot up to five feet ten and lost his puppy fat in his twenties, Tony had in middle age grown very attractive in a brutal sort of way; although with his Roman nose, heavy-lidded charcoal-grey eyes, coarsely modelled mouth and springy close-cropped dark hair, he looked more like a Sicilian wide boy than an English peer. He chose to proclaim the latter, however, by wearing coronets on absolutely everything. And on the little finger on his left hand gleamed a massive gold signet ring, sporting the Baddingham crest of wrestling rams, above the motto chosen by Lord Pop-Pop: Peaceful is the country that is strongly armed.

Considerably adding to Tony's sex appeal was a hunky bull-necked body, kept in shape by self-control and ruthless exercise, and a voice deliberately deep and smooth to eradicate any trace of a Gloucestershire accent. This only slipped when he went into one of his terrifying rages, which flattened the Corinium Television staff against the cream-hessianed walls of his vast office.

In fact, it irritated the hell out of Tony that, despite his success, his fortune and his immense power, Rupert still refused to take him seriously. He would not have been so upset by Rupert's sniping if it had not echoed a warning last night from Charles Crawford, the rotund and retiring Chairman of the Independent Broadcasting Authority (or IBA as they were known). The IBA's job was to grant franchises to the fifteen independent television companies every eight years or so, monitor their programmes and generally beat them with a big stick if they stepped out of line.

19

After his programme with Rupert and the Home Secretary at Thames Television yesterday, Charles Crawford had gone on to the Garrick to dine with Tony.

'As an old friend,' said Charles, greedily pouring the cream Tony had rejected together with his own supply over his strawberries, 'I don't see what else we can do but give you a stinking mid-term report. You promised us Corinium would provide at least ten hours' drama a year for the network, and all you've produced is one lousy cops-and-robbers two-parter, totally targeted at the American market. Why can't you provide some decent programmes, like Patrick Dromgoole does at HTV?'

For a second Tony gritted his teeth. He was fed up with having Patrick Dromgoole and HTV held up to him as models of perfection. Then pulling himself together he filled up Charles Crawford's glass with priceless Barsac.

'Things are going to change,' he said soothingly. 'I've just poached Simon Harris from the BBC as Programme Controller. He's very hot on drama, and has dreamed up a terrific idea for a thirteen-parter, a cross between James Herriot and "Animal House".'

'Well that's a start,' grumbled Charles, 'but your regional programmes are quite awful too. Your territory – which you conveniently seem to have forgotten – stretches from Oxford to Wales, and from Southampton to Stratford. And you're supposed to cover the whole area. That's why we gave you the franchise.

'We also know you've been spending Corinium advertising profits, which should have been spent improving your programmes, buying up . . .' Charles ticked the list off with his fat fingers, 'a film production company, a publishing firm, a travel agency, a cinema chain, a film library, and a safari park, and what's this I hear about plans to buy an American distribution company? American, for Christ's sake.'

'That's fallen through,' lied Tony. 'It was only an idea.'

'Well, keep it that way. Finally you've got to spend more time in your area. Many of your staff have absolutely no idea what you look like. I could understand if you had to live in the middle of Birmingham or even Manchester, but Cotchester must be the most delightfully civilized town in the country. We awarded you the franchise to reflect the region responsibly, and we've given you a very easy ride up till now.'

And I've given you some bloody good dinners, thought Tony sourly, as Charles sniffed appreciatively at a passing plate of welsh rarebit.

'But when Lady Gosling takes over from me in the autumn,' went on Charles, spooning up the last drop of pink cream, 'you're all going to feel the chill cloud of higher education across the industry. Lady G believes in quality programmes and lots of women at the helm. Go on producing your usual crap, and you'll be out on your ear.'

Having brooded on this conversation and on Rupert Campbell-Black's contumely the entire flight, the only thing that managed to cheer Tony up was when the limousine that met him at Kennedy turned out to be at least three feet longer than Rupert's and twice as plush.

RIVALS

2

Tony's rule, once he got to America, was never to check
what time it was in England. To compensate for such an
unsatisfactory start to the day, he spent the next few hours
in a heady spate of wheeling and dealing, selling the format
of two sit-coms and a game show for such a large sum that it
wouldn't matter even if they bombed. It was only when he
got back to the Waldorf and found three messages to ring his
very demanding mistress, Alicia, and, checking the time,
realized that he couldn't because it was long after midnight
and she'd be tucked up in bed with her husband, that he
suddenly felt tired.

He kicked himself for agreeing to dine with Ronnie
Havegal, Head of Co-Productions at NBS, particularly as
Ronnie had asked if he could bring some producer called
Cameron Cook.

'Cameron's a good friend of mine,' Ronnie had said in his
Harvard drawl. 'Very bright, just done a documentary on
debutantes, up for a Peabody award, real class; they like that
sort of thing in England.'

With his royal-blue blazers, butterscotch tan, and streaked
hair, Tony had often wondered about Ronnie's sexual prefer-
ences. He didn't want to spend an evening avoiding buying
some lousy programme from one of Ronnie's fag friends.
Yanks always got class wrong anyway.

Christ, he was tired. Unable to master the taps in the

shower, he shot boiling lava straight into his eyes. Then, forgetting to put the shower curtain inside the bath, he drenched the floor and his only pair of black shoes.

Tony spent a lot of money on his clothes and ever since he'd seen Marlon Brando in *Guys and Dolls* as a teenager tended to wear dark shirts with light ties. The new dark-blue silk shirt Alicia had given him for his birthday would be wasted on two fags. He would keep it for lunch with Ali MacGraw tomorrow. Dressed, he fortified himself with a large whisky and put the presentation booklet of 'Four Men went to Mow', Simon Harris's new idea for a thirteen-part series, on the glass table, together with a video of possible exteriors and interiors to give the Americans a taste of the ravishing Cotswold countryside.

He was woken by Ronnie ringing up from downstairs. But when Ronnie came through the door, Tony suddenly didn't feel tired any more, for with him was the sexiest, most truculent-looking girl Tony had ever seen. Around twenty-six, she was wearing a straight linen dress, the colour of a New York taxi, and earrings like mini satellite dishes. She had a lean, wonderfully rapacious body, long legs, very short dark hair sleeked back from her thin face, and a clear olive skin. With her straight black brows, angry, slightly protruding amber eyes, beaky nose and predatory mouth, she reminded him of a bird of prey – beautiful, intensely ferocious and tameable only by the few. She gave out an appalling sexual energy.

She was also so rude to Ronnie, who was very much her senior, that at first Tony assumed they must be sleeping together. He soon realized she was rude to everyone.

'This is Cameron Cook,' said Ronnie.

Nodding angrily in Tony's direction, Cameron set off prowling round the huge suite, looking at the large blue urn in the centre of the living-room holding agapanthus as big as footballs, the leather sofas and arm chairs, the vast double bed next door, and the six telephones (with one even in the shower).

'Shit!' Her voice was low and rasping. 'This place is bigger than Buckingham Palace; no wonder you Brits need American co-production money.'

Tony, who was opening a bottle of Dom Perignon, ignored the jibe, and asked Cameron where she came from.

'Cincinnati.'

'City of the seven hills,' said Tony smoothly. 'But you must have bought those legs in New York.'

Cameron didn't smile.

'You don't look like a Lord, more like a Mafia hood. What do I call you: Your Grace, Sir, my Lord, Baron, Lord Ant?'

'You can call me Tony.' He handed her a glass.

Cameron picked up the presentation booklet of 'Four Men went to Mow'. Kicking off her flat black shoes, she curled up, looking very tiny on the huge pockmarked red leather sofa.

'What's this shit?'

'Cameron!' remonstrated Ronnie.

'Corinium's latest thirteen-parter,' explained Tony. 'We aim to start shooting in October.'

'If you get American finance,' said Cameron, sharply.

Tony nodded. 'We'll put it out early in the evening; should appeal to kids and adults.'

'Dumb title. What the shit does it mean?'

'It's the line of an English song,' said Tony evenly.

'Thought it was a series about back yards.'

'It's about four agricultural students living in a house.'

'I can read, thank you,' snapped Cameron, running her eyes down the page. 'And someone finds someone in bed with someone in the first episode. Jesus, and you're expecting this shit to go out as wholesome family entertainment in Middle America, where we haven't seen a nipple on the network for years.'

'Don't listen to Cameron,' said Ronnie. 'She needs a muzzle in the office to stop her savaging her colleagues.'

'Shut up and let me read it.'

Ronnie then proceeded to update Tony on the recent changes at NBS. 'They axed twenty people last week, good

24

people who've been there fifteen years. The new business guys are running the place like a supermarket.'

But Tony wasn't listening. He was watching this incredibly savage girl with her skirt rucked up round her thighs. Christ, he'd like to screw all that smouldering bad temper out of her.

As if aware of his scrutiny, she glanced up.

'There's too much air in this glass,' she said, holding it out for a refill.

'You're too old for TV at twenty-five these days,' Ronnie rattled on obsessively. 'I work with a guy of fifty. He lives in such constant fear of his age getting out, he keeps on having his face lifted.'

Ronnie looked desperately tired. Beneath the butterscotch tan, there were new lines round the eyes. Cameron chucked the presentation booklet back on the glass table.

'Well?' Tony raised his eyebrows.

'Schmaltz, schlock, shit, what d'you want me to say? It's utterly provincial, right, but the dialogue's far too sophisticated. If you're going to appeal to Alabama blacks, Mexican peasants and Russian Jews in the same programme, you can't have a vocab bigger than three hundred words. And I don't know any of the stars.'

'No one had heard of Tim Piggott-Smith, or Charles Dance, or Geraldine James before "Jewel".'

'They'd heard of Peggy Ashcroft. Your characters are so stereotyped. And you've got the wrong hero, Johnny's the guy the Americans will identify with. He's got drive, he comes from a poor home, he's going to make it. The Hon Will's got it already. What's an Hon anyway?'

'A peer's son,' said Tony.

'Well, make him a Lord. Americans understand Lords. And they're all far too wimpish. Americans are pissed off with wimps. We've seen too many guys crying in pinnies. You can't wear your sensitivity on your silk shirtsleeve any more.'

Tony, who'd never done any of these things, warmed to this girl.

'Go on,' he said.

'As a nation, we're getting behind the family and the strong patriarch again. There's a large part of the population that want men to reassert themselves, be more aggressive, more accountable, more heterosexual. And you've got a marvellous chance with four guys in a house together to explore friendship between men, I don't mean faggotry; I mean comradeship. It was a great Victorian virtue, but no one associated it with being gay. Today's man shoots first, then gets in touch with his feelings later.'

'Is that how you like your men?' said Tony, getting up to put the video into the machine.

'Shit no, I'm just talking about the viewers. You've got one of the guys ironing the girl's ball gown for her; yuk!'

Tony filled up her glass yet again.

'Have a look at this.'

Up on the screen came a honey-coloured Cotswold village, an ancient church, golden cornfields, then a particularly ravishing Queen Anne house.

'We plan to use this as Will's father's house,' said Tony.

'Bit arty-farty,' snapped Cameron, as the camera roved lasciviously over a lime-tree avenue, waterfalls of old roses, and a lake surrounded by yellow irises.

'Beautiful place,' said Ronnie in awe.

'Mine,' said Tony smugly.

'Don't you have a wife who owns it as well?' said Cameron, feminist hackles rising.

'Of course; she's a very good gardener.'

'Looks like fucking Disneyland,' said Cameron.

Switching off the video machine, Tony emptied the bottle into Cameron's glass and said, 'Corinium did make more than twelve million pounds last year selling programmes to America, so we're not quite amateurs. Some of the points you made are interesting, but we do have to appeal to a slightly more sophisticated audience at home.'

'We ought to eat soon,' said Ronnie. 'You must be exhausted.'

'Not at all,' said Tony, who was looking at Cameron, 'must just have a pee.'

Alone in the bathroom, he whipped out his red fountain pen and in the memo page of his diary listed every criticism Cameron had made. Then he brushed his hair and, smiling at his reflection, hastily removed a honey-roast peanut from between his teeth. Fortunately he hadn't been smiling much at that bitch.

Even in a packed restaurant swarming with celebrities Cameron turned heads. There was something about her combative unsmiling beauty, her refusal to look to left or right, that made even the vainest diners put on their spectacles to have a second glance.

Immediately they'd ordered, Ronnie went off table-hopping. 'Nice guy,' said Tony, fishing.

'Very social register,' said Cameron dismissively. 'Watch him work the room, he makes everyone feel they've had a meaningful intimate conversation in ten seconds flat.'

'Seems a bit flustered about the blood-letting at NBS.'

Cameron took a slug of Dom Perignon. 'He needs a big success. Both the series he set up last year have bombed.'

'Given him an ulcer too.'

Cameron looked at Tony speculatively.

'I guess you've never had an ulcer, Lord Ant.'

'No,' said Tony smoothly. 'I give them to other people. How do the NBS sackings affect you?'

Cameron shrugged. 'I don't mind the sackings or the rows, but now the money men have moved in, I figure I'll have less freedom to make the programmes I want.'

'How d'you get into television?'

'My mother walked out on my father at the height of the feminist revolution, came to New York hell-bent on growth. The only thing that grew was her overdraft. She was too proud to ask for money from my father, so I went to Barnard on a scholarship, and got a reporting job in the Vac to make ends meet. After graduation, I joined the *New York Times*, then moved to the NBS newsroom. Last year I switched over to documentaries, as a writer/producer. At the moment I'm directing drama.'

'Your mother must be proud of you.'

'She thinks I'm too goal-orientated,' said Cameron bitterly. 'She's never forgiven me for voting for Reagan. I don't understand my mother's generation. All that crap about going back to Nature, and open marriages, and communes and peace marches. Jesus.'

Tony laughed. 'I can't see you on a peace march. What are your generation into?'

'Physical beauty, money, power, fame.'

'You've certainly achieved the first.'

'Sure.' Cameron made no attempt to deny it.

'How d'you intend to achieve the rest?'

'I aim to be the first woman to run a Network Company.'

'What about marriage and children?'

Cameron shook her head so violently she nearly blacked her own eyes with her satellite dish earrings.

'Gets in the way of a career. I've seen too many women at NBS poised to close a deal, being interrupted by a phone call, and having to rush home because their kid's got a temperature of 104.'

The waiter arrived with their first course. Escargots for Cameron, gulls' eggs for Tony. Ronnie, who hadn't ordered anything, returned to the table, buttered a roll, but didn't eat it.

'Anyway,' went on Cameron angrily, 'what's the point of getting married? Look at the guys. New York is absolutely crammed with emotionally immature guys quite unable to make a commitment.'

'They're all gay,' said Tony. He peeled a gull's egg, dipped it in celery salt, and handed it to Cameron.

'Bullshit,' she said, accepting it without thanking him. 'There are loads of heterosexuals in New York. I know at least three. And what makes it worse, with the men being so dire, is that New York is absolutely crawling with prosperous, talented, beautiful women in a state of frenzy about getting laid.'

'Give me their telephone numbers,' said Tony lightly.

'Don't be fatuous,' snarled Cameron. 'Guys are turned off by achieving women; they make them feel inferior. What beats me is why women are so dependent on men. You see them everywhere, with their leather briefcases, and their dressed-for-success business suits, rabbiting on about independence, yet clinging onto a thoroughly destructive relationship rather than be without a guy.'

Furiously she gouged the last of the garlic and parsley butter out of her snail shells. The lady, reflected Tony, is protesting too much.

Ronnie was off table-hopping again. The head waiter was now making a great song and dance about cooking Cameron's steak Diane at the table, throwing mushrooms and spring onions into the sizzling butter. The champagne having got to Cameron's tongue, she was also spitting away like the hot fat:

'TV people have no idea what's important. Ask them about their kids, they just tell you what private schools they're enrolled in. That's a very subtle way of telling you how well they're doing. What's the point of having kids? Just as a status symbol.'

'You're a bit of a puritan at heart.' Tony filled her glass yet again. 'Your ancestors didn't come over on the *Mayflower* by any chance?'

'No, but my father was British. I've got a British passport.'

Better and better, thought Tony.

The head waiter was pouring Napoleon brandy over the steak now and setting fire to it. The orange purple flames flared upwards, charring the ceiling, lighting up Cameron's hostile, predatory face. Another waiter served Tony's red snapper, which was surrounded by tiny courgettes, sweetcorn and carrots.

'They employ one guy here to sharpen the turnips,' said Cameron, pinching a courgette from Tony's plate. For a second, she looked at it. 'Tiny,' she added dismissively. 'Like the average New York cock.' And with one bite she devoured it.

Tony laughed, encouraging her in her scorn.

'Enjoy your meal,' said the head waiter, laying the steak in front of Cameron with a flourish.

I wonder if I'm reading her right, thought Tony; anyone that aggressive must either be desperately insecure or impossibly spoilt. Maybe her mother had felt guilty about splitting up from her father, and let Cameron get away with murder.

Ronnie's sole was cold when he returned to the table, shaking his head. 'I hear you had a row with Bella Wakefield this afternoon.'

Cameron raised her eyes to the charred ceiling. 'She's so fucking useless.'

'She *is* the Vice-President's daughter.'

'She pisses me off. Every time she's got a line, which is about once a year, she teeters up on her spike heels, saying, "Cameron, what's my motivation in this scene?" So finally I flip and say: "Pay day on Friday." She went kinda mad.'

'I'm not surprised,' said Ronnie disapprovingly.

The head waiter glided up. 'Everything all right, sir?'

'Perfect,' said Ronnie, who hadn't touched his sole.

'Steak as madam likes it?'

Cameron tipped back her chair. 'If you want the honest truth, it tastes like moderately flavoured socks.'

The smile was wiped off the waiter's face. 'I beg your pardon.'

'Cameron,' hissed Ronnie.

'Like chewing my own laundry. I cannot figure why you waste such expensive ingredients producing something so disgusting. I'd rather drink the brandy straight.'

The head waiter looked as though he was going to cry.

'Would madam like something else?'

'I'll pass,' said Cameron, ostentatiously putting her knife and fork together. 'It's not even worth a doggie bag.'

RIVALS

3

As they came out of the restaurant, limos for Ronnie and Tony glided up. Cameron paused between the two.

'I haven't seen your deb programme yet,' said Tony. 'Why don't we go back to the Waldorf and look at it?'

Ronnie shook his head. 'You guys go. I'm pooped.'

Back in Tony's suite, an almost unbearable tension developed between them. Having poured large brandies, Tony removed his coat. Despite the air conditioning, he could feel damp patches of sweat forming under his arms and trickling down his spine. In silence they watched Cameron's tape. Within five minutes, Tony realized its outstanding quality.

The commentary was cut to a minimum; Cameron had let the debs and their mothers speak for themselves. But you could feel her fierce egalitarian scorn, in the way she had highlighted their silliness and pretension, and the compassion she displayed for the *noveau riche* who tried to break in, and for the wallflower who sat unfêted through ball after ball.

Despite the fact that Cameron had been vile about 'Four Men went to Mow', Tony knew when to be generous.

'They'll adore it in England,' he said at the end. 'I'll ring the Film Purchasing Committee tomorrow and insist they look at it.'

'Thanks.' Cameron got up to rewind the tape. 'I'd better go. I got up at six this morning, and you must be reeling from Concorde lag.'

With that sleek Eton crop, thought Tony, it'd be like making love to a boy. Putting out a hand to halt her he encountered a huge shoulder pad.

'Sit down. I want to talk to you. You got a regular boyfriend?'

'Until three months ago.' She sat down on the far end of the leather sofa.

'What did he do?'

'He was a threat analyst. Spent all day looking at the Soviets, and saying: "They're a threat".'

Tony laughed, edging down the sofa.

'I don't need a man to look after me,' said Cameron defensively. 'Just someone to make the sparks fly. If I'm not having a good time, I quit. Are you happily married?'

'Not overwhelmingly.'

'She a dog?'

'Not at all. It's a marriage of extreme public convenience. We get on very well when we don't see too much of each other.'

This girl is exactly what I need to wake them all up at Corinium, he was thinking. She's superbright, ambitious, aggressive. The IBA would adore the deb programme, it had quality and universal appeal; and being a woman, Cameron would appeal to the incoming chairman, Lady Gosling. Even more important, from the way she had carved up Simon Harris's treatment, she was capable of seeing what was wrong with a programme and subtly gearing it towards the American market without making it too bland. And finally, as she had a British passport, there wouldn't be the usual ghastly hassle about work permits.

'How'd you like to work in England?'

'How much?'

'Thirty grand.'

'You've got to be joking. I'm on a hundred thousand dollars here.'

'It's cheaper living in England, and we could pick up a few bills.'

'I'd have to have somewhere to live,' said Cameron, think-

32

ing longingly of the honey-coloured houses she'd seen on the video.

'We can arrange that.'

'If I'm stuck in the country, I'll need a car.'

'Of course.'

For a minute she glared at him. 'How soon do I get on the Board?'

'Cameron,' said Tony gently, 'I'm the boss of Corinium. I decide that.'

'I'll kick it around,' she said indifferently. 'You'd better sleep with me first.'

Not by a flicker did Tony's swarthy face betray his surprise. 'Why? D'you think afterwards I might not want to offer you the job?'

Cameron smiled for the first time that evening. 'No, I might not want to take it.'

Even in the bedroom she didn't stop fighting, promptly switching on the television.

'God is love,' a lady in a shirtwaister, with very long royal blue eyelashes, was saying, 'not a guy with a stick; He wants us all to enjoy ourselves.'

'And so say all of us,' said Cameron.

Tony turned off the television and, with remarkably steady hands, removed her huge earrings, and massaged the reddened lobes.

'D'you get a good satellite picture from these?'

There wasn't much else to take off. Just the yellow dress and a pair of yellow pants. Tony never dreamed that anyone with such a sinewy, well-muscled body could have such a smooth skin.

'Those Y-fronts went out with the ark,' said Cameron, throwing them in the wastepaper basket. 'I'm going to buy you some boxer shorts.'

Bearing in mind that it was eight o'clock in the morning in England, Tony thought he acquitted himself with honours.

'Mine eyes have seen the glory of the coming of the Lord,' sang Cameron as she finally climbed off him.

'Still fighting the American War of Independence,' murmured Tony into her shoulder.

But just as he was falling asleep, he realized she was rigid and shuddering beside him. Reaching down, he found her hand in her bush.

'I thought you'd come as well,' he said, outraged.

'If you figured that, Buster, you've got a lot to learn.'

'Come here, you bitch.'

Tugging away her hand, he knelt over her, kissing her navel, then very slowly progressing downwards. Lying on the floor, tangled in each other's arms, they were interrupted much later by the telephone.

It was Corinium's sales director, Georgie Baines.

'I thought you'd like the monthly revenue figures, Tony. I didn't wake you?'

'I've been up for hours.'

'You can say that again,' said Cameron, wriggling out from under him.

'They're up four million on last year,' said Georgie jubilantly. For five minutes they discussed business, then Georgie said that Percy, Tony's chauffeur, would like a word.

'Good morning, my Lord,' said Percy. 'We won the Test match by four wickets.'

Tony was almost more delighted by that than by the advertising figures. Hearing water running in the shower, he was about to jump on Cameron once more, when the telephone rang again. After that it kept ringing, ending up with a call from Alicia, Tony's beautiful and demanding mistress.

'Do you spend all your life on the telephone?' she screamed.

There was a knock on the door. Tony hung up and, wrapping a towel round his waist, went to answer it. It was the breakfast he'd ordered before going out last night.

Having signed the bill, he found Cameron in the bathroom, drying her pants with the hair dryer. She was wearing Tony's dark-blue silk birthday shirt, with one of his red paisley ties wound round her waist. Her hair was wet from the shower; she looked sensational.

'Come back to bed.'

'Can't. I've got a breakfast meeting. Got to get there early to check the room isn't bugged.'

The telephone rang again.

'You answer it,' said Tony evilly.

Cameron picked it up.

'Someone called Alicia,' she said.

'Say I'm in the shower.'

'She didn't sound very pleased,' said Cameron, putting down the receiver.

Scooping up the mini-bottles of shampoo, conditioner, bath gel, and cologne, she dropped them into her bag. Then, peeling the shoulder pads out of her yellow dress, she fixed them into the shoulders of Tony's dark-blue shirt. As she went into the bedroom, she removed a strawberry as big as a cricket ball from the grapefruit on Tony's breakfast tray.

'What are your plans?' asked Tony.

'I'm in the studios from ten o'clock onwards. I should be through around eight. And you?'

'I've got people to see. I'm lunching with Ali MacGraw – more my age group, sweetie.' He kissed Cameron on the forehead. 'And I want that shirt back.'

'You can wear my yellow dress. If I wear it, Ronnie'll know I haven't been home.' Taking a mirror from her bag, she winced at her reflection in the bright sunlight. 'He'll know it anyway.'

'I'll call you later,' said Tony.

The moment she'd gone, he showered, dressed and, having summoned one of the secretaries from Corinium's American office on 5th Avenue, dictated a completely new treatment for 'Four Men went to Mow'.

In the middle, Alicia rang and demanded who had answered the telephone.

'Your successor,' said Tony, without a trace of compassion, and hung up.

By midday he had a new and beautifully bound presentation booklet for 'Four Men went to Mow', containing a character analysis of the new hero, who was now the working-class boy and not the peer's son (who had become a lord), plus a new list of possible stars, suggested locations, story lines, and a couple of pages of simplified dialogue, all based entirely on Cameron's recommendations.

Ronnie called up as Tony was reading it through.

'How d'you like Cameron?'

'Like wasn't the operative word. What's bugging her?'

'More enfant than terrible,' said Ronnie, who wanted to do business with Tony very badly, 'but she's too ambitious for her own good, and too upfront. There's a streak of idealism which makes her scream and shout till she gets what she wants; and if you're as sexy as she is you antagonize not only women but also the men who don't get to pull you.

'Don't tell anyone I told you, but the programme controller's going to axe her last documentary, and she's been so rude to Bella Wakefield she's being taken off the series. But she's bright,' Ronnie sighed. 'Sadly they don't give a shit about talent here any more. But that's off the record.'

'We haven't spoken,' said Tony.

'As a quid pro quo, can we be the first people to see "Four Men went to Mow?" ' asked Ronnie. 'I know Cameron carved it up, but it looked great to me.'

'Of course,' said Tony smoothly.

After an exceptionally affable lunch with Ali MacGraw, who was an old friend, to discuss a long-term project, Tony strolled down to see USBC, the deadly rivals of NBS.

At the plaza of the Seagram building tourists and office workers sat on the walls, eating sandwiches and pizza, trying to woo the blazing sun down between the office blocks on to their bare arms and legs. The flowers in the centre strip of Park Avenue wilted in the heat as Tony sauntered past General Motors and the Pan Am building with their thousand glittering windows, admiring the coloured awnings outside the houses and the beautiful, loping New York girls with their briefcases, who looked back at him with flattering interest. Maybe Cameron was right about the paucity of real New York men.

The Head of Co-Production at USBC and the Daytime

Programme Controller were enchanted by the video of the honey-coloured houses and the Cotswold countryside.

'This series,' Tony told them, his deep, beautiful voice flowing on like vintage port glugging out of a priceless decanter, 'will be a cross between James Herriot and "Animal House", but in a way it's much, much more. We intend to explore real friendship between real men; not homosexuality, but that Victorian virtue, comradeship. The hero, a poor boy from a deprived background, doesn't inherit the earth or the girl, but he finds his integrity. The story, despite its depths, is simple enough to appeal to a Mexican peasant or to an Alabama black.'

Out of the corner of his eye he noticed that the extremely influential VPICDT Prog. (which stood for Vice-President In Charge of Daytime Programming) had just entered the room. Tony warmed to his subject.

'In England,' he went on, 'we are sick of wimps who wear their sensitivity on their silk shirtsleeves. The guys in our story are kind to animals and women, but they shoot from the hip first and get in touch with their feelings later. Nor would they be seen dead in an apron. Let us have men as men again, and bring back dignity and chivalry to our sex.'

Thinking he'd gone slightly over the top, Tony switched briskly to finance. 'We can do it for three-quarters of a million an hour,' he said. 'It'll be thirty per cent cheaper if we make it in England; we'll put up twenty per cent of the cost against Europe and the UK.'

Admiring the discreet blue coronet on Tony's dark-green shirt, the VPICDT Prog., who'd just been bawled out on the phone by his wife for forgetting to collect the suit she'd had altered at Ralph Lauren, reflected that Lord B had real class. And he was right – it was high time men were men again.

'Very interesting, Tony,' he said. 'We'd like to kick the idea around. You in New York for a few days?'

'Yes,' said Tony.

'Showing it to other people?'

'Of course.'

'We'll get back to you as soon as possible.'

Outside it had rained. The trees had taken on a deeper greenness. The city had the warm wet smell of a conservatory. Park Avenue was a solid yellow mass of honking taxis. Quivering with the excitement of wheeler-dealing, Tony knew he ought to ring Ronnie and show him the treatment. Let him sweat, he thought, let Cameron sweat. He went back to the Waldorf, checked out and, without leaving a forwarding address, flew to Los Angeles.

Cameron lived in an eleventh-floor apartment on Riverside Drive with a glorious view of the Hudson River. She got home at about nine after a hellish day, punctuated with screaming matches which had finally culminated in Bella Wakefield turning up on the set wearing two-inch false eyelashes and half a ton of purple eyeshadow to play a Victorian governess. When Cameron had ordered her to take her make-up down, Bella had stormed out, presumably to sob on the Vice-President's already sodden shoulder.

The moment she got in, Cameron played back her recording machine, but there was no message from Tony, not even a click to show he'd rung and hung up because she wasn't there. He hadn't left any messages at NBS either.

Cameron, however, had done her homework. As Tony had learnt from Ronnie that she was brilliant but unbalanced, she in turn had discovered that Tony was an unprincipled shit, much more interested in making money than good programmes, masterly at board-room intrigue, and so smooth he could slide up a hill. Convinced she could handle him, Cameron wasn't at all put out by this information, and decided to accept the job.

She'd always wanted to work in England and track down her English relations. She admired British television, and she'd bitterly envied all those rich girls at Barnard who'd travelled to Europe so effortlessly on Daddy's income. It would also give her a chance to get away from her mother and her mother's appalling lover, Mike. Cameron gave a shudder; she had recurrent nightmares about Mike.

She turned on the light. She would be sad to leave her

apartment, which was painted white throughout, with yellow curtains and rush matting on the polished floors. Furniture in the living-room included a grand piano, a dentist's chair upholstered in red paisley like Tony's tie, a dartboard, and a gold toe, one foot high, which had been surreptitiously chipped from the foot of a cherub in the Metropolitan Museum. Books lined most of one wall, but half a shelf was taken up with videos of the programmes she'd made. These were her identity. Cameron only felt she truly existed when she saw her credits coming up on the screen.

And now this English lord had come along and thrown her into complete turmoil because he hadn't called. Denied a father in her teens, Cameron was always drawn to older men. She was attracted by Tony's utter ruthlessness, and, despite her sniping, sexually it had ended up a great night.

Then why didn't the bastard call? Lord of the Never Rings. Collapsing on the sofa, she gazed out of the window. On the opposite bank, lights from the factories and power stations sent glittering yellow snakes across the black water. Watching the coloured Dinky cars whizzing up and down the freeway, she fell asleep.

When she woke next morning, very cold and stiff, the Hudson had turned to a sheet of white metal, with the power stations smoking dreamily in the morning mist. Perhaps Tony had only offered her a job as a ruse to get her into bed, but she didn't think he was like that. If he'd just wanted to screw her, he'd have said so. Yet when she rang the Waldorf to accept, she was outraged to be told that Tony had checked out, leaving no forwarding address.

'This guy's mighty popular,' said the operator. 'Everyone's been ringing him.'

Nor would Corinium's New York office tell her where Tony had gone, and, even worse, the morning paper had a charming picture of him coming out of the Four Seasons with Ali MacGraw.

In Los Angeles, when he wasn't spreading the word about 'Four Men went to Mow', or finalizing the deal to buy the

American distributors, which he'd had to acquire through a holding company so as not to upset the IBA, Tony thought about Cameron.

Back in New York, two days later, ignoring the increasingly desperate messages from NBS, he went to USBC and after screwing another quarter million dollars a programme out of them on the grounds that Disney were madly interested, he closed the deal.

He returned to the Waldorf, sweating like a pig, had a shower, poured himself an enormous whisky and rang Cameron. He had to hold the telephone at arm's length.

'Where the fuck have you been, you bastard?' she screamed.

'Busy,' said Tony and, when she started to give him an earful, very sharply told her to shut up and calm down.

'I've raised the cash for "Four Men went to Mow".'

'Who put it up?' demanded Cameron.

'USBC. The lawyers are thrashing out the nuts and bolts at the moment.'

'Poor Ronnie. NBS aren't going to be very happy – we didn't even get to see it.'

'Well, there you go.'

'He probably will, right out of the front door, and never come back after this. Ronnie's right – you are a shit.'

'That's no way to address your new boss.'

Cameron's heart was hammering so hard, her palms were suddenly so damp, that the receiver nearly slid out of her hand.

'Hullo, hullo,' said Tony. 'Have you thought about that job I offered you?'

'You just fuck off like that. How do I know I can trust you?'

'Give me the address. I'll be over in half an hour and we'll talk terms.'

Yet when he arrived at Cameron's flat, armed with a bottle of champagne, he was outraged to find an impossibly handsome young man lounging in the dentist's chair, holding a glass that definitely didn't contain mouthwash.

'Who the hell's he?' snarled Tony.

'This is Skip, my lawyer. He dropped by to draw up my contract of employment,' said Cameron.

'Why the hell's he wearing my shirt and tie?'

Cameron laughed. 'Since I'm moving to England, I figured he deserved a leaving present.'

RIVALS

4

On a cold Friday in February, exactly twenty months after he'd signed up Cameron Cook in New York, Tony Baddingham made an infinitely more dramatic and controversial addition to his staff. Having exchanged contracts in the utmost secrecy in the morning, he popped into the IBA headquarters in Brompton Road for a midday glass of sherry with the new chairman, Lady Gosling, to dazzle her with the secret news of his latest acquisition before setting out on the two-hour drive down to Cotchester.

Even on a raw blustery February afternoon, Cotchester's wide streets and ancient pale gold houses gave off an air of serenity and prosperity. To the north of the town, in the market square, a statue of Charles I on his horse indicated that Cotchester had once been a Royalist stronghold. Round the plinth, pigeons pecked among the straw left by the sheep and cattle sold in the market earlier in the day. To the south soared the cathedral, its great bell only muted during rush hour, the shadow of its spire on bright days lying like a benediction over the town.

Dominating the High Street was a fine Queen Anne building, once the Corn Exchange, now the headquarters of Corinium Television. Although, over the last twenty years, the building had been considerably extended at the back to include studios, dressing-rooms, an imposing new board room, and a suite of splendid offices for the directors, nothing

42

except pale-yellow rambler roses had been allowed to alter its imposing façade. On the roof the vast dark red letters CTV could be seen for miles around, letters topped by a splendid ram standing four-square, with a Roman nose and curly horns. Originally chosen as a symbol of the wool trade which once characterized the area, according to some of Corinium's more uncharitable employees the ram could now be used to symbolize Tony Baddingham's sexual excesses.

At the back of the building an entire wall of the board room consisted of a huge window looking out on to the cathedral close, water meadows and willows trailing their yellow branches in the River Fleet, a peaceful scene totally at variance with the tensions and feuds within Corinium Television itself.

These tensions had been exacerbated that particular Friday by Tony returning unexpectedly from London and calling a programme-planning meeting at three o'clock, when he knew most of his staff would be hoping to slope off early.

Tony had actually returned in an excellent mood. His meeting with Lady Gosling had been decidedly satisfactory. Simon Harris, the ex-BBC Golden Boy, and Cameron Cook had so improved Corinium programmes over the last twenty months that he was no longer seriously worried that his franchise would be taken away in mid-term. But, in case there were rival groups who might pitch for the Corinium franchise when it came up for renewal next year, he had made the decision on the way down to clean up Corinium's act well in advance.

Until that time therefore, until Corinium were officially re-selected, he was determined not only to trail some of the most glittering names in television and the arts in front of the IBA, but also to put on some really worthy regional programmes.

It was to map out ideas for these programmes that he'd called the impromptu meeting. Unfortunately half the staff were away. The Head of News was in Munich on a freebie, the Head of Documentaries was in Rome getting a prize, the

43

male Head of Light Entertainment and the comely female Head of Kids' Programmes were both away with gastric flu, which caused a few raised eyebrows, as they had been seen looking perfectly healthy the day before.

Tony took the chair, but was instantly summoned to take an urgent call from Los Angeles. The only people in the room who didn't appear terrified or at least extremely wary of him were Charles Fairburn, Head of Religious Programmes, who'd got pissed at lunchtime, and Cameron Cook, now Head of Drama.

The Head of Sport, Mike Meadows, a once-famous footballer with ginger sideboards, whose muscle-bound shoulders had grown too big for his shiny blue blazer, smoked one cigarette after another.

Simon Harris, the Controller of Programmes, who was principled and intelligent and always saw both sides of every problem, and was therefore labelled indecisive, trembled on Tony's right. He kept his hands under the table to hide a nerve rash he had scratched raw. His thin face twitched. In an attempt to gain some kind of authority he had recently grown a straggly beard. When he took off his coat – Tony always kept the central heating tropical – you could hear the rattle of the Valium bottle, and see the great damp patches under his arms.

Beyond Simon was Tony's PA, Cyril Peacock, DFC, Corinium's ex-Sales Manager, once a stocky, jolly, assertive fellow, sensational at his job. The point of a PA, however, is that he should be utterly loyal. Some Chief Executives in television buy this loyalty with money, which is dangerous, because someone else can buy it with more money. Tony bought it with fear. After making Cyril his PA, and sometime publicity officer, Tony had encouraged him to invest his savings in a company that promptly went broke. Now the terror of the Luftwaffe was someone Tony hung his coat on – a poor old dodderer in his early sixties, with loss of job and pension hanging over his head like a sword of Damocles. Tony took great pleasure in making Cyril do his dirty work – he had four people for him to fire on Monday.

On Tony's left was Miss Madden, his secretary, also in her sixties, plain, and utterly dedicated, whose chilblains were itching because of the central heating, and who never let anyone into Tony's office without an appointment except Cameron Cook, on whom she had a love–hate crush.

Finally, down the table, opposite Cameron sat James Vereker, the impossibly good-looking, beautifully coiffeured Anchorman of the six o'clock regional news programme, 'Cotswold Round-Up'.

James should have been in the newsroom getting ready for the evening's programme, but, hating to miss anything, he had muscled in on the meeting and was now using Tony's absence to rewrite the links he would have to say later on air to fit his own speech patterns.

Glancing across at Cameron, James wondered if she and Tony had rehearsed the whole meeting in bed earlier this week, turning each other on by seeing who could be the most gratuitously bloody to everyone else. He looked at Cameron's dark-brown cashmere jersey, snugly fitting the lean body, the pale-brown suede skirt, the Charles Jourdan boots and the lascivious unmade-up face, and felt a wave of loathing. Today her short hair had been coaxed upwards in gelled spikes, like a hedgehog who'd rolled in chicken fat.

James pointedly moved the arrangement of Spring flowers left over from Wednesday's board meeting up a couple of inches to obscure his view of her and, getting out a packet of Polos, handed one to Miss Madden, who went slightly pink as she accepted it.

James offered Polos to no one else. He knew who to suck up to. Properly courted, Miss Madden would sing his praises to Tony and admit him to the inner sanctum when necessary.

As Tony walked back into the room, everyone rose from their chairs except Cameron, who pointedly ignored him. Perhaps they've had a bust-up, thought James Vereker hopefully.

The good thing about Tony, reflected Charles Fairburn, Head of Religious Programmes, was that he did cut out the waffle. There was a good chance that Charles, who was going to the ballet at Covent Garden that evening, would be out of the building by five.

'I'd like to start,' said Tony briskly, 'by congratulating Cameron on being nominated for a BAFTA award. As you all know, "Four Men went to Mow" has not only been a huge network success, and sold everywhere overseas, but also because of the exceptional camera work, attracted scores of tourists to the area, and last month toppled "Howard's Way" in the ratings. We're looking for more programmes like this that project the area into the network.'

'Hear, hear,' said Cyril Peacock, his false teeth rattling with nerves.

Tony's conveniently forgotten that 'Four Men went to Mow' was my idea in the first place, thought Simon Harris bitterly. Cameron, still ignoring Tony, gazed sourly at the framed photograph on the wall of him smilingly assisting Princess Margaret to plant a cherry tree on the Corinium front lawn.

Christ, they *have* had a row, thought James.

'I'd like to give the go-ahead for a second series,' Tony went on. 'We've got the co-production money again from USBC, but I think it would be a good idea, Cameron, if you introduced perhaps a black unmarried mother into the cottage of the agricultural students to appeal to the IBA.'

Charles Fairburn suppressed a grin. The IBA were crazy about minority groups. Cameron looked outraged.

'Black unmarried mothers don't become agricultural students,' she snarled.

'There's always a first time,' said Tony smoothly. 'She could be the girlfriend of one of the four boys.'

'For Chrissake, why not have a gay shepherdess with one leg?' said Cameron.

'Why not a deaf, unemployed merry peasant?' suggested Charles Fairburn with a hiccup. 'Or a handicapped harvester?'

'That's enough,' snapped Tony.

He then went on to OK plans for an obscure Michael Tippett opera, which Cameron also scowled at, detecting

Lady Baddingham's influence (Tony's wife was crazy about opera) and a production of *Midsummer Night's Dream* as a sop to Stratford-on-Avon which was just within the Corinium boundary.

Now it was the turn of James Vereker, who, having finished re-writing his links, helped himself to a glass of Perrier and then suggested Corinium ought to show its 'caring face, Tony' and do a series on poverty and the aged.

'Jesus, how turgid,' said Cameron, glaring at him through the screen of fading daffodils. 'Of all the boring . . .'

Tony raised his hand for silence, his huge signet ring catching the light.

'Not a bad idea. We could do a very cheap pilot to impress the IBA. We don't have to make the series. Perhaps Cyril,' he smiled malevolently at his PA, 'could front it. He's been looking rather old and poverty-stricken lately.'

Cyril Peacock cracked his twitching face, trying to smile back. Thus encouraged, James suggested they should do something 'very strong, Tony' on rioting and drug abuse at Cotchester University. Swiftly Cameron swooped, the falcon Tony had trained, tearing into James:

'What a crappy awful idea,' she screamed. 'D'you want to antagonize the entire Tourist Board because everyone's scared to visit Cotchester any more? No one will want to invest money here. We're trying to boost the area for Chrissake.'

'What about a programme on the role of women in Cotchester town hall?' stammered Simon Harris, tugging at his straggling yellow beard.

'And have the town halls at Bath, Southampton, Oxford, Winchester, Stratford, et cetera et cetera in an uproar because we haven't done programmes on them,' said Cameron crushingly.

'I thought your idea, Tony, of interviewing the wives of celebrities living in the area looked a winner,' said Cyril Peacock, desperate to get back into favour.

' "Behind Every Famous Man"?' Cameron turned on Cyril furiously. 'That was my idea.'

'We could start with one of our director's wives, or perhaps,' Cyril lumbered on, 'even Lady Baddingham.'

Tony looked not unpleased. 'I think that would be a bit close to home.'

'Why not do a series on the very very rich?' said Charles Fairburn, who had not quite sobered up, 'They're far more of a minority group than anyone else. We could start with you, Tony.'

He was quelled by an icy glance from Tony, who, aware that the meeting was slightly lacking in carnage, suddenly realized that his Head of Operations, whose role was to tell creative people what they could not do, was missing.

'Where's Victor Page?' he said ominously.

'Gone to his grandmother's funeral,' said Miss Madden, her lips tightening.

'But he killed off two grandmothers during Wimbledon last year.'

'This was his step-granny,' said Miss Madden. 'His mother married twice.'

'No doubt his other step-grandmother will pop off during next Wimbledon,' said Tony, making a note on his memo pad. That would be five people for Cyril to fire on Monday.

Tony then turned to the points made during his talk with Lady Gosling that morning. There was no need to let his production staff get complacent.

'Several viewers,' he said, 'have complained about field mice copulating too long on our "Nature at Night" programme.'

Charles Fairburn, who had a round red face like a Dutch cheese, suppressed another smile. He'd better do his expenses. He hadn't been anywhere this week, but he needed some cash to buy drinks for his airline-steward friend at the ballet tonight.

'Cloakroom and gratuities £5,' wrote Charles Fairburn. 'Drinks with the Archdeacon £15.' That was pushing it; the Archdeacon was teetotal, but the Accounts Department didn't know it. They'd be shut if Tony didn't wrap up this meeting soon.

'On the kids' programmes front,' went on Tony, 'we've also had complaints about too much violence in "Dorothy Dove".'

'What kind of violence?' asked Simon Harris.

'Pecking Priscilla Pigeon and pulling out all her feathers.'

James was tempted to say his children had absolutely adored that particular episode, but decided not to. The Head of Kids' Programmes had rejected his advances at the Christmas party; he didn't owe her any favours.

'Dorothy Dove is supposed to be a symbol of peace,' said Tony.

'Peaceful is the dove that is strongly armed – or beaked in Dorothy's case,' murmured Charles Fairburn and regretted it.

'There have been complaints,' went on Tony nastily, 'about insufficient religious content in our religious programmes. I'll talk to you after the meeting, Charles, and the IBA are very unhappy about "Rags to Riches".'

Simon Harris turned dark red. It was he who had bought the format for 'Rags to Riches' from America and adapted it for the British network.

'But the ratings are sensational,' he protested.

'I know, but the IBA have pointed out that the contestants are far too glamorous and upmarket. We do need a few unemployed frumps to add a touch of reality, and please remember our ethnic minorities.'

'You can borrow my black unmarried mother,' said Cameron, shooting Tony a venomous look.

'The IBA,' went on Tony, squinting down the polished table, like a daily looking for smears, 'also feel we should have more women on the Corinium Board. After all, Lady Evesham's nearly sixty-five, so we must all wrack our brains for some powerful ladies.'

The men in the room exchanged glances of horror. Would Tony use this as an excuse to put the appalling Cameron Cook on the Board?

'And,' went on Tony swiftly, 'they feel we still haven't enough directors who live in the area.'

49

That, thought James savagely, also includes Cameron, and her exquisite Regency house on the outskirts of Cotchester.

Now Tony was saying, not without complacency, that Freddie Jones, the electronics multi-millionaire, and Rupert Campbell-Black, the Minister for Sport, who both lived in the area, would be coming in his party to the West Cotchester Hunt Ball that evening, and he would be sounding them out as possible directors.

For a second, outrage overcame the Head of Sport's terror of Tony: 'But Rupert Campbell-Black's been consistently vile about our coverage,' he spluttered. 'You'd think it was our fault Cotchester was bottom of the Third Division.'

'Good name on the writing paper. We've got to keep our local MPs sweet, with the franchise coming up,' said Tony. 'Anyway he's far too tied up with football hooligans to come to more than a couple of meetings a year, so he won't get a chance to make a nuisance of himself.'

'Don't you be too sure of it,' spat Cameron. 'Macho pig.'

Smug in the knowledge that he was the only member of the staff who'd been asked to join Tony's party at the hunt ball that evening, James Vereker couldn't resist saying, as the meeting broke up, how much he and Lizzie, his wife, were looking foward to it, and what time would Tony like them for drinks.

'About eight,' said Tony, gathering up his papers.

James could feel the laser beams of loathing and jealousy directed at him from all around the table, particularly from Cameron. That should rattle the stuck-up bitch, he thought. Since she'd been nominated for a BAFTA, she'd been getting much too big for her Charles Jourdan boots.

As Tony went out of the room, straightening the photograph of himself and Princess Margaret as he passed, James glanced at his watch. Four-thirty. He was on the air in an hour and a half and they would wrap up the programme by seven. If he had to drive the eleven miles home, bath and change, he'd be pushed for time. He'd better have a quick shower and blow dry his hair beforehand; then he could legitimately keep his make-up on – just bronzing gel, a bit of creme puff and dark brown mascara – for the ball. One got so pale in February.

He considered whether to wear his turquoise evening shirt, which brought out the blue-green in his eyes, or a white one with a turquoise bow-tie, then decided on the former. The gel might show up on the white shirt.

Wandering into the newsroom, he selected the secretary who was most in love with him and handed her twenty pages of longhand, entitled 'Poverty and the Aged: A Treatment', by James Vereker.

'I think you'll have rather fun with this one,' he told her. 'Could you centre the title in caps? I don't need it till first thing Monday morning.'

Entirely sobered up now, Charles Fairburn followed Tony into his office. He'd never get to Covent Garden and his airline steward now. But, to his amazement, Tony greeted him warmly: 'Ratings aren't bad, Charles. Wheel in the Bishop of Cotchester, a few Sikhs and a woman priest next week to talk about the meaning of self-denial and Lent; that should keep Lady Gosling happy. Look, I'm reading the lesson in church on Sunday. Rather tricky phrasing, I want to get the sense right. Could you just run through it with me?'

RIVALS

5

James Vereker drove home in his Porsche, warmly aware that 'my programme', as he always referred to it, had gone well. James Vereker's outstanding qualities, apart from his dazzling good looks, were his total egotism and chronic insecurity. In order not to miss himself on television, he had even been known to take a portable television into a restaurant. A huge local celebrity, much of whose time was spent opening fêtes and PAs' legs, he disliked going to London, or even worse abroad, because no one recognized him. When he'd worked in radio, he used to dread some crisis blowing up in Southern Europe or the Middle East in case he couldn't pronounce it.

Aware that he was dismissed as a popinjay by the editors, journalists and researchers who got 'Cotswold Round-Up' on air, and who were jealous of his inflated salary and his celebrity status, he was given to little tantrums, yet couldn't resist seeking constant reassurance. Cameron Cook had even suggested the parrot used in Corinium's Christmas production of *Treasure Island* should be given a permanent squawk-on part, telling James he was wonderful after every programme. He kept his job because he was quite good at it and because he always won the fight for viewers from the BBC.

Back at James's house, Birgitta, the children's curvaceous nanny, had just lovingly finished ironing both James's white and turquoise evening shirts, and was scenting herself and putting on make-up for James's return.

I wish Birgitta would spend slightly more time putting the children to bed, thought James's wife, Lizzie, as they swarmed into her study demanding attention. Lizzie had had two novels published and well reviewed. A third was on the way, but it was causing a great deal of morning sickness.

She and James had been married eight years, and Lizzie had supported James on her publishing salary in the early days when he was trying to break into television. Once very pretty (she had the bright eyes and long questing nose of a vole, and the shaggy light brown hair of a clematis montana clambering over an old apple tree in winter), she had recently put on too much weight.

The Verekers lived in a large messy house with a large messy garden two miles down the valley from Rupert Campbell-Black, where the Frogsmore stream hurtled into a large reed-fringed lake. They had bought Lake House, as it was called, five years ago, just after James had got the job at Corinium, when it had seemed ridiculously cheap. Viewing it in high summer, they had only seen its romantic aspect, not realizing that for at least five months of the year it was so low in the valley that it never saw the sun and would be quite inaccessible when the snows came in winter.

This mattered little to James because he spent so much time at Corinium. When the house got snowed up, he simply didn't come home for several days. But it was not good for Lizzie, who wrote there all day, eating too many biscuits to keep out the cold, or for the children who caught one cold after another, or for the nannies who found it dank and depressing, except when James was at home.

For Lizzie life turned on the children not getting ill, and nannies not leaving so that she had time to write. Unfortunately James couldn't resist pulling the prettier nannies, who invariably walked out, when he moved on to someone else. Lizzie always found out the score by reading the nannies' diaries when they were shopping in Cotchester or nearby Stroud. Birgitta, the current nanny, wrote her diary in Swedish, which Lizzie couldn't understand. But with the aid of a Swedish dictionary she was beginning to crack the code, and the word 'James' appeared rather too often. In fact you only had to see the way Birgitta perked up when James came through the door. Lizzie was used to his infidelity. She realized he needed little adventures to boost his ego, but they still upset her. She would have liked an admirer herself, but felt she was too fat to attract anyone.

Lizzie nearly had a fit when she heard James banging the front door. She'd stopped writing far too late, wrestling to get at least a draft of the first chapter down on paper. Still struggling mentally with her plot, she'd spent too long washing her hair and in the bath. Then she discovered that the long low-cut black silk ball dress which she'd decided to wear was far too tight. Not even shoe horns or the disdainful tugging of Birgitta could get her into it, so she had to wear another dress, dark red velvet to match her distraught face, and calf-length so it wouldn't conceal her ankles which had swelled up in the bath.

Finally, because she couldn't see out, she'd cut her fringe with the kitchen scissors, not realizing that Birgitta had just used them to cut rind off the children's bacon, so now her fringe stuck together and reeked of bacon. She was about to wash it again when James arrived. He hadn't been home so early in months; usually he hung around the Corinium bar mopping up adulation.

'Have a bath, darling,' shouted Lizzie, desperately trying to tone down her face with green foundation.

'I had a shower at the studios,' said James, 'so I've only got to change. We ought to leave in five minutes. How did you think my programme went?'

'Wonderful,' lied Lizzie, who hadn't watched it, starting to panic. As it was dark outside, she couldn't even make up in the car.

'I'll read you an extra story tomorrow, darlings,' she told the children as they clung whining to her on the landing. 'Or perhaps, Birgitta,' she raised her voice hopefully, 'will read you one before you go to bed.'

But Birgitta was watching James, who had decided on the white shirt after all, putting a pink carnation in his buttonhole. Poor Mr Vereker, she thought, looking so handsome in his dinner jacket, going out with such a frump. How much better would she, Birgitta, be in Lizzie's place. James, however, hardly noticed his wife's appearance. His was the one that mattered.

'You look absolutely lovely, James,' said Lizzie dutifully.

Low sepia clouds obscured the moon. As the headlamps lit up grey stone walls, acid green tree trunks and long blonde grasses, Lizzie tried abortively to apply eye liner as James described every little triumph of the planning meeting and his programme afterwards.

'Anyone interesting in our party tonight?' asked Lizzie as he paused for breath.

'Rupert Campbell-Black, Beattie Johnson his mistress, Freddie Jones.'

'Who's he?'

'Don't you ever read the papers?' said James, appalled. 'Mr Electronics.'

Oh God, sighed Lizzie to herself. I daren't ask what electronics are, and I bet I'm sitting next to him at dinner.

'And Paul Stratton and his new wife.'

'Oooh,' squeaked Lizzie. 'That's exciting.'

Three years ago, just after the Conservatives won the last election, Paul Stratton, the Tory MP for Cotchester and the very upright Minister for Home Affairs, with a special brief to investigate sex education in schools, had rocked his constituency and the entire nation by walking out on Winifred, his solid dependable boot of a wife, and running off with his secretary half his age.

Not that his constituents were prudish (having Rupert Campbell-Black in the next door constituency, they were used to the erotic junketing of MPs), but as Paul Stratton had not only used his political career to feather his nest financially, but also set himself up as a pillar of respectability and uxoriousness, constantly inveighing against pornography, homosexuality, easier divorce and the general laxity of the nation's morals, they had found it hard to stomach his hypocrisy.

'Evidently, they've bought a place in Chalford,' said James, 'and Paul and Sarah, I think she's called, are planning to spend weekends down here, re-establishing themselves with the local community.'

'I suppose Tony inviting them this evening heralds the official return of the prodigal son,' said Lizzie. 'I wonder if she's as beautiful as her photographs. I bet Rupert makes a pass at her. He's always enjoyed bugging Paul.'

'Don't be fatuous, they're only just back from their honeymoon,' snapped James, steering round a sharp bend and bringing the conversation neatly back to himself.

'I've got a gut feeling tonight is going to mark a turning-point in my career,' he said importantly. 'Tony's been exceptionally nice to me recently. And when I popped into Madden's office later this evening to find out exactly who was in the party, there was a confidential memo on Tony's desk about the Autumn schedules, which I managed to read upside-down. It appears Corinium are committed to a series of prime time interviews for the Network. I didn't dare read any more, in case Madden got suspicious, but I suspect Tony's got me in mind, and that's why he's asked us this evening.'

Tony Baddingham soaked in a boiling Floris-scented bath, admiring his flat stomach. For once the cordless telephone was mute, giving him the chance to savour the prospect of the evening ahead. One of the joys of becoming hugely successful was that it gave you the opportunity to patronize those who, in the past, had patronized you. Paul Stratton, for example. It was going to be so amusing tonight extending the hand of friendship to Paul and his bimbo wife. How grateful and subservient they'd be.

Then there was Rupert. Tony was not given to fantasy, but more than anything else in the world he longed to be in a position when an abject, penitent, penniless Rupert, who'd somehow lost all his looks, was seeking Tony's favour and friendship. The only reason Tony really wanted Rupert on his Board was in order to dazzle him with his brilliant business acumen.

In wilder fantasy, Tony dreamt of flaunting an undeniably sexy mistress, who would be impervious to Rupert's charms.

'Can't you bloody understand,' he imagined Cameron screaming at Rupert, 'that Tony's the only man there'll ever be in my life?'

Tony added more boiling water to his bath to steel himself against the arctic climate of the rest of the house. There was a running battle between Tony who liked the heat, and whose office, according to Charles Fairburn, provided an excellent dress rehearsal, both physically and mentally, for hell fires, and Monica, his wife, who regarded central heating as a wanton extravagance which ate into one's capital.

'I still feel dreadfully guilty not telling Winifred about Paul and Sarah coming tonight,' said Monica, when later, fully dressed, Tony went into his wife's bedroom and found her sitting at her dressing table vigorously brushing her short fair hair. She was wearing the same emerald-green taffeta she'd worn for the last four hunt balls, which went beautifully with Tony's diamonds, but did nothing to play down the red veins that mapped her cheeks, as a result of gardening and striding large labradors across the Gloucestershire valleys in all weathers. Yet, in a way, her rather masculine beauty, splendid on the prow of a ship or as a model for a Victorian bust of Duty, needed no enhancement.

Monica had once been head girl of her boarding school and had remained so all her life. Winifred Stratton, Paul's ex-wife, had been her senior prefect. Together they had run the school firmly and wisely, diverting the headmistress's attention away from a plume of cigarette smoke rising from the shrubbery, but gently reproaching the errant smoker afterwards. All the lower fourths had had crushes on Monica. Sometimes, even today, unheard by Tony who slept in a separate room, she cried, 'Don't talk in the passage,' in her sleep.

Known locally as Monica of the Glen because of her noble appearance and total lack of humour, she was the only woman to whom Tony was always polite, and also a little afraid. In the icy, high-ceilinged bedroom, opera and gardening books crowded the tables on either side of the ancient crimson-curtained four-poster which Tony visited perhaps once a week. But even after eighteen years of marriage, these visits gave him an incredible sexual frisson.

On the chest of drawers, which contained no new clothes, were silver-framed photographs of their three children. With her sense of fairness, Monica would never let the other two know that she loved her elder son Archie, sixteen last week, the best. Nor that she loved her two yellow labradors, and her great passions, opera and gardening, often a great deal more than her husband.

Running Tony's life with effortful efficiency, she never had enough time for these two passions, but if she was disappointed by the hand life had dealt her, she never showed it. She was not looking forward to this evening, which would involve talking until three o'clock in the morning to all those people Tony considered so important, but she would treat them with the same impersonal kindness whether they were Lords-Lieutenant or electronics millionaires. Always anxious to help humanity collectively (she did a huge amount for charity), Monica was not interested in people individually, or what made them tick or leap into bed with one another, but she was worried about Winifred. Even after she'd married Tony, and Winifred had married the much more brilliant, handsome and ambitious Paul Stratton, they had remained friends and gone to the opera and old school reunions together.

When Paul had run off with his secretary, in a scandal that rocked Gloucestershire almost as much as Helen Campbell-Black walking out on Rupert, Winifred had been utterly devastated, but like a building sapped by dry rot, one couldn't initially see the damage from outside. After Winifred had moved to Spain with her two daughters in a desperate attempt to rebuild her life, Monica missed her friendship desperately, and now, to crown it, Tony had asked Paul and Sarah to join the party tonight, and she, Monica, was expected to smooth over Sarah's first public outing in Gloucestershire.

'I just feel it's revoltingly disloyal to Winifred,' repeated Monica.

She had applied Pond's vanishing cream and face powder, and a dash of bright-red lipstick, which was the extent of her daytime make-up, and was now adding her night make-up: brown block mascara put on with a little brush.

'I swore to Winifred I'd never have that little tramp' – Monica spat on her mascara – 'over the threshold.'

Tony's brows drew together like two black caterpillars.

'Paul is still our local MP, even if he has been booted out of the Cabinet,' he said patiently. 'With the franchise coming up next year, I have to entertain whatever wife he chooses. At least I waited until after they were married.'

As Tony moved forward to do up the clasp of her diamond necklace, Monica caught sight of her husband's reflection. The red tailcoat with dove-grey facings made him look taller and thinner, and gave a distinction to his somewhat heavy good looks, but Monica hardly noticed.

'I still ought to telephone Winifred and tell her.'

'She's in Spain. Let it rest. I'd better go down; they'll be here in a minute.'

Monica glanced at her diamond watch. *Lohengrin* was about to start on Radio 3. If only she could stay at home and listen to it, she thought wistfully. As she slotted a three-hour blank tape into her radio cassette and pressed the record button, she called after Tony, 'Can you tell Victor to up the proportion of orange juice in the Buck's Fizz. We don't want everyone arriving at the town hall plastered like last year.'

RIVALS
6

An hour later, downstairs in the huge dark panelled drawing-room hung with tapestries, members of the party were beginning to unthaw and retreat from the fierce red glow of the beech logs smouldering and crackling in the vast fireplace. Lizzie Vereker, sustained by at least six glasses of Buck's Fizz, had perked up and forgotten her extra pounds and her straining red dress.

Neither Rupert nor Beattie Johnson had arrived yet, but there was plenty to gaze at. Paul Stratton's new wife, for example, was absolutely gorgeous. She had entered the room looking little girlish and apprehensive, eyes cast down, clinging to Paul's arm and hardly speaking. She was wearing a yellow silk dress which matched her thick piled-up gold hair, and a beautiful tobacco-brown fringed silk shawl covering her shoulders and wound high round her neck.

After replying in shy monosyllables to Tony and Monica's questions, she had allowed herself to be introduced to James and also to Tony's youngest brother, Bas, who was a terrific rake with black patent-leather hair, a smooth olive complexion, and a very overdeveloped little finger from twisting women round it. Now a small smile was beginning to play around Sarah's full coral lips at Bas's extravagant compliments, and the shawl was beginning to slip to reveal the most voluptuous golden shoulders and bosom. She and Paul must have been somewhere hot for their honeymoon, decided Lizzie.

Paul didn't seem to have reaped the same benefit. His dark hair, which he'd once brushed straight back, had gone silver grey and been coaxed forward, almost to his eyebrows, and in little commas over his very pink ears. Sarah, being young, had obviously encouraged him into a Paisley bow-tie and a wing collar, the points of which kept being bent over by a new double chin. His once hard angular face seemed to have softened and weakened. He still, however, had the same all-embracing smile that passed over you like a lighthouse beam, and still liked the sound of his own voice. He was now talking to Freddie Jones, the electronics multi-millionaire.

'Three million unemployed,' he boomed, 'is a Mickey Mouse figure. Didn't you see that article about that factory manager who was offering people two hundred and twenty pounds a week merely to stuff mattresses, and simply couldn't get staff? The working classes just don't want to work. They're shored up by moonlighting and the great feather bed of the welfare state.'

Paul made the mistake of thinking that someone with such capitalist instincts would automatically vote Tory. Freddie Jones listened to him carefully but didn't say anything. He was plump and jolly, with rumpled red-gold curls, round, merry grey-blue eyes, a snub nose and an air that life was a tremendous adventure. Lizzie thought he looked much more fun than anyone else.

Across the room, she noticed, James had broken swiftly away from Sarah Stratton, and was now talking to a very slim woman with dimples and short brown curls tied up by a blue bow. She was wearing a pale-blue midi dress with a full skirt and a top, of which the satin lining was the strapless bodice, and the gauze over it covered her arms down to her wrists and her shoulders and tied in a pussy-cat bow at the neck. It was the most ghastly dress Lizzie had ever seen. But the woman, who Lizzie deduced must be Freddie Jones's wife, seemed frightfully pleased with herself, and was laughing

61

away, rolling her eyes and gazing up at James's beautiful bronzed face with excessive admiration.

Apart from Sarah Stratton, Lizzie decided hazily, the men looked much more glamorous than the women this evening, gaudy peacocks in their different tail coats, red with grey-blue facings for the West Cotchester Hunt, red with crimson for the neighbouring Gatherham Hunt, dark blue with buff for the Beaufort. If he hadn't been so good-looking, James in a dinner jacket would have been outclassed.

Helping herself to another Buck's Fizz, Lizzie wandered somewhat unsteadily over to the seating plan for dinner at the Town Hall. She was sitting next to Freddie Jones. James was on Monica Baddingham's right. Maybe his predictions about his brilliant future were about to come true.

Laughing uproariously, two handsome young bloods in red coats now rushed up and started marking the seating plan with red asterisks.

'What *are* you doing?' asked Lizzie.

'Singling out the worst gropers,' said one. 'We're starting with Bas Baddingham and Rupert Campbell-Black.'

'Better put one beside my husband,' said Lizzie.

'Who's he?'

'James Vereker.'

'We were just about to.' They all collapsed with laughter.

'Have some more fizz,' yelled Monica Baddingham in her raucous voice, arriving with a jug which contained almost straight orange juice now. 'I can't think what's happened to Rupert. We'll have to leave in a sec, or we'll be late for dinner.' She drifted off.

'Do we dare put an asterisk by Tony's name?' said one of the young bloods.

'Of course,' said the other, seizing the Pentel.

Giggling, Lizzie glanced across the room to see James beckoning imperiously.

He's had enough of Mrs Jones, so he wants to palm her off on me and press the flesh, thought Lizzie.

Ignoring James, she turned back to the seating plan. Next minute James had crossed the room and seized her wrist.

'May I borrow her?' he asked coldly.

'Of course,' said the young bloods, 'as long as you bring her straight back.'

James dragged Lizzie away. 'Do pay attention when I signal.'

'I was having a nice time.'

'This is work,' hissed James. 'I want you to meet Valerie Jones. She's opening a boutique in Cotchester next month. You must go and buy something.'

Never, never, thought Lizzie sulkily, if she sells dresses like that blue thing she's wearing.

'Lizzie writes novels,' James told Valerie Jones, as if to explain his wife's scruffy appearance.

'I'd laike to wraite novels if I had the taime,' said Valerie Jones, in an incredibly elocuted voice, 'but Ay'm so busy with the boutique and the kids and moving in and we do have to entertain a lot. People are always saying, You should wraite a book, Mrs Jones, you've had such a fascinating laife.'

She screwed her face up in what she obviously thought was a fascinating smile.

Close up, Lizzie noticed that Valerie Jones had very clean nails, perfectly shaved armpits and the very white eyeballs of the non-reader and non-drinker. She was tiny and very pretty in a doll-like way, but Lizzie suddenly understood the expression: blue with cold. Valerie's china-blue eyes were the coldest she'd ever seen. The pink and white skin also concealed the rhinoceros hide of the relentless social climber.

'I'll leave you girls to get acquainted,' said James. 'Better have a word with Paul Stratton, or he'll think I'm avoiding him. We must have a dance later,' he added admiringly to Valerie. 'I bet you're as light as thistledown.'

'Seven stone on the scales this morning,' simpered Valerie.

And six-and-a-half of that's ego, thought Lizzie. 'Where d'you live?' she asked.

'At Whychey,' said Valerie.

'Quite near us,' said Lizzie. 'We're at Penscombe.'

But Valerie wasn't remotely interested in where Lizzie lived.

'And only quarter of an hour from the boutique, so Ay can

rush down there, if there's any craysis, or a special client comes in. They always ask for me.' Valerie put her head on one side. 'Ay don't know why. Ay think Ay tell people the truth. Ay mean, what is the point of selling somebody a gown that doesn't suit them? It's such a bad advertisement for the boutique.'

'Which house in Whychey?' asked Lizzie.

'Oh it's lovely; Elizabethan,' said Valerie. 'We had to do an awful lot though, ripping out all that horrid dark panelling.' Lizzie winced. 'And of course we've completely re-landscaped the garden, but it'll be a year or two before Green Lawns is the paradise we want.'

Lizzie looked puzzled. 'The only Elizabethan house I know in Whychey is Bottom Hollow Court.'

'We changed the name,' said Valerie. 'We thought Green Lawns sounded prettier.'

'Where did you live before?'

'Cheam,' said Valerie, with the flourish of one saying Windsor Castle. 'We never thought we'd find anywhere as perfect as Cheam. All our help broke down and crayed when we left. But Gloucestershire has so much to offer.'

At that moment Monica came up.

'I was just saying, Monica, that Gloucestershire has so much to offer, particularly,' Valerie raised her untouched glass, 'on a gracious evening like tonight.'

'Not if we don't get any grub,' said Monica briskly. 'We've decided not to wait for Rupert. Do either of you need a loo?'

Outside it had turned bitterly cold. Valerie came out of the house smothered in an almost floor-length mink. I hope hounds get her, thought Lizzie savagely, as she watched Freddie open the door and settle Valerie in, before going round to the driving seat.

'Isn't she a poppet?' said James. 'Knew so much about my programme.'

'Sarah Stratton?' asked Lizzie.

'No, Valerie Jones. I do hope Freddie joins the Board. We could do with a few caring wives like Valerie at Corinium.'

Lizzie was dumbfounded. Was James such a dreadful judge of character?

'What did you think of Sarah Stratton?' she asked.

'Not a lot. Didn't even know who I was. You'd have thought Paul would have briefed her.'

Off they set in convoy, cars with silver foxes on the bonnet skidding all over the road, rattling the cattle grids, lighting up the last grey curls of the traveller's joy and the last red beech leaves. Flakes of snow were drifting down as they arrived at Cotchester Town Hall.

'It's already fetlock-deep in Stow,' bellowed a woman who'd just driven up with a white windscreen. 'But of course you're a coat warmer down here.'

Cotchester Town Hall, a splendid baroque edifice, two hundred yards down on the other side of the High Street from Corinium Television, had been built in 1902 to replace the old Assembly Rooms. The huge dining-rooms on either side of the ballroom were filled with tables, packed with laughing, chattering people. But in a noisy, glamorous gathering easily the most glamorous, scrutinized table belonged to Corinium Television. The Krug was circulating (Tony was always generous when the evening was deductible) and dinner was now well underway, but Rupert and Beattie Johnson still hadn't turned up and Sarah Stratton, who should have been on Rupert's right, and Tony, who should have had Beattie on his left, were trying to hide their irritation and disappointment.

Lizzie Vereker, however, was having a lovely time sitting next to Freddie Jones. Totally unpompous, instinctively courteous, noisily sucking up his bortsch, rattling off remarks in a broad Cockney accent at a speed which must tax the most accomplished shorthand typist, he was also, despite a scarlet cummerbund strained double by his wide girth, curiously attractive.

'I don't know anything about electronics,' confessed Lizzie, taking a belt of Krug, 'but I know you're very good at them. James says you're one of the most powerful men in England.'

'My wife doesn't fink so,' said Freddie. 'It's a fallacy women are attracted to power. No one's fallen in love wiv me for years. I'd like to be tall like your 'usband. But I got my height from my muvver and my shoulders from my Dad, and the rest 'ad to go somewhere.' He roared with laughter.

At the head of the table Monica listened politely to James Vereker talking about his programme and his ideas for other programmes, and surreptitiously gazed at Sarah Stratton. Her tobacco-brown shawl had slid right off her golden shoulders now. Her piled-up blonde hair emphasized her long slender neck. The seat beside her, which should have been Rupert's, had now been taken by Bas, Tony's wicked brother, who was chatting her up like mad.

She's so beautiful, thought Monica. What chance could poor Winifred have stood?

She felt jolted and uneasy. She wished she were at home reading gardening books and listening to *Lohengrin*.

Valerie Jones had one aim in life – to rise socially. She had therefore done her homework. Knowing James was coming this evening, she had watched his programme all week so she could comment on every item. She was now sitting next to Paul Stratton, whose recent speech in the House on the proposed Cotchester by-pass she had learnt almost by heart. But Paul was less flattered by her obvious homework than James. He, like Monica, was surreptitiously watching his wife flirting with Bas, and experiencing a tightness round his heart, a jealousy never felt when he was married to Winifred.

Lizzie's and Freddie's conversation had noisily progressed to hunting.

'It was Rupert who got me going,' said Freddie. 'Put me up on a really quiet 'orse last March. I was cubbing by August, and huntin' by November.'

'Weren't you terrified?' asked Lizzie in awe.

'I needed three ports and lemons to get me on to the 'orse for the opening meet, I can tell you. But I reckoned if I fell orf I'd bounce anyway.' He roared with laughter again. 'I'm going to take up shootin' next.'

Huge oval silver plates of roast beef were now coming round.

'How's Rupert getting on with Beattie Johnson?' asked Lizzie, helping herself.

Freddie shrugged. 'Not very well. She keeps 'earing wedding bells, and we all know Rupe's tone-deaf. He said the other day he fort the relationship would last till Cheltenham.'

Lizzie giggled. 'What a typically Rupert remark. Has she finished ghosting his memoirs yet?'

'Probably providing material for the last chapter at the moment,' said Freddie. Digging a serving spoon into a creamy mass of potato dauphinoise, he gave a big helping to Lizzie, and was just helping himself when Valerie called sharply down the table, 'No tatties, Fred-Fred.'

'It's Friday,' said Freddie, the Cockney accent wheedling, as the spoon edged towards his plate.

'No tatties, I said.' Valerie's voice was pure steel.

Freddie put back the potatoes.

Looking across at Lizzie, Sarah Stratton gave her a ghost of a wink.

'You can have my roll, Fred-Fred,' she said, lobbing it across the table to him.

Valerie opened her rosebud mouth and shut it again. She knew one must behave like a lady at all times, and not brawl with one's hubby in public. Then she suddenly noticed that James, who'd ground to a halt with Monica, was looking very put out.

'What's your programme about on Monday?' Valerie asked him across the table.

Paul Stratton, on Monica's left, seized his opportunity. Turning to her, he said in a low voice, 'It's awfully good of you to take Sarah under your wing this evening. I know how close you were to Winifred.'

Monica almost choked on her roast beef. She didn't want to talk about Winifred.

'It meant so much to Sarah,' went on Paul. 'She was so worried about coming tonight.'

67

She doesn't look worried now, thought Monica, watching Sarah laughing up at Bas.

'I felt guilty at the time,' said Paul rather heartily. 'But we are all sinners, are we not? What happened to Sarah and me was part of a loving relationship. All sides behaved with dignity. I feel I can now walk down Cotchester High Street with my head held high.'

Do you indeed, thought Monica furiously.

'But one can't destroy something that's lasted twenty-five years over-night,' said Paul, spearing a piece of Yorkshire pudding. 'I still miss Win and the girls, particularly when I see old friends like you and Tony.'

He wants my sympathy, thought Monica incredulously. He's utterly destroyed my best friend, and he wants me to feel sorry for *him*.

'Do you correspond with Win?' asked Paul.

Fortunately deliverance appeared in the form of one of the hall porters, who whispered a message in Monica's ear.

'Thank you so much,' she said, and banging the table with her spoon, yelled down to Tony at the other end, 'That was a message from Rupert. He can't make it after all. Something urgent has come up.'

'Probably Rupert's cock,' said Lizzie idly, earning herself a thunderous look of disapproval from James.

'Pity,' said Sarah lightly. 'I was *so* looking forward to meeting him.'

'There'll be other occasions,' said Bas, leaning back as a waitress removed his plate.

Tony, for a minute, was unable to disguise his rage.

'Of all the fucking bad manners,' he exploded.

Rupert's defection put a considerable dampener on the evening. It was not until the syllabub had been handed round in tall glasses that Bas Baddingham, who was among other things a partner in a local estate agents, made an attempt to lighten the atmosphere.

'Has anyone else heard a rumour that Declan O'Hara's bought Penscombe Priory?' he asked.

For a second there was a stunned silence. Then all the women acted with the frantic excitement of dogs when their leads are rattled.

'I'm going on a crash diet tomorrow,' squeaked Lizzie, dropping her spoon with a clatter.

'Oh why didn't we buy a house in Penscombe rather than Chalford?' wailed Sarah Stratton.

'How much did he pay for it?' asked Valerie Jones.

'Half a million' said Bas.

There was a long pause as everyone did frantic sums to work out how much that now made their houses worth.

'That's an awful lot,' grumbled Valerie.

'But it's such a romantic house,' sighed Lizzie, 'and that lovely wild garden.'

'Hellishly cold,' shuddered James.

'And faces North,' said Valerie.

'So does Declan O'Hara,' said Sarah dreamily, earning herself a sharp look from Paul.

'Rather a lot to pay for a weekend retreat,' said James, looking put out.

To hell with impressing Rupert with the secret he'd been hugging to himself all day, thought Tony. He had a good enough audience as it was, and it was too late for any of them to leak the story to the press tonight.

'Declan's going to live here,' said Tony, looking slowly down the table. 'He's joining Corinium in September.'

There was a gasp of excitement, followed by another stunned silence.

Troublesome, tetchy, but monumentally talented, Declan O'Hara was simply the BBC's hottest property. His weekly interviews with the great and very famous went out at prime time and were avidly watched and discussed by the entire nation. Nothing like the normal chat show host, he indulged in no back slapping, nor drinking in the green room, nor bandying round of Christian names before a programme. Nor did he bounce around on long pastel sofas, cosily exchanging confidences.

His victims sat facing him, and, once on air, like a Jesuit

priest, he really listened to them, relentlessly probing with the most devastating questions and waiting so unbearably long for an answer that they invariably stumbled into a confession. To the intense disappointment of his armies of female fans, the camera was constantly trained on the person he was interviewing rather than on Declan himself.

Poor James, thought Lizzie, oh poor, poor James. That must be the series of networked interviews scheduled for the Autumn.

'How the hell did you persuade Declan?' asked Bas.

'He's fed up with the Beeb,' said Tony. 'The last straw was axing his interview with Paisley. People who saw the video said it was absolute carnage. They didn't think Paisley would go the fifteen rounds. Then they hacked great contentious chunks out of his interview with Reagan. He wants to go out live, so this kind of thing can't happen. He will when he joins us.'

'You'll never get people like Reagan coming down to Cotchester,' said Paul Stratton.

'You will for Declan,' said Freddie. 'The BBC must be as sick as a parrot.'

'They're not pleased,' Tony was purring like a great leopard now, 'but it's not exactly our job to please the Beeb.'

Clicking their tongues, the waitresses removed the untouched syllabubs.

'Declan's a bit of a pinko,' said Paul, disapprovingly.

'That's putting it mildly,' said Tony, 'but as it looks as though the socialists will be in power next year unless you lot get your act together, we can't afford to be too right wing any more.'

Trying, for James's sake, to curb her excitement, Lizzie turned to Monica. 'Have you met him?'

'They came to lunch,' said Monica. 'Declan seems a super chap.'

Sarah and Lizzie caught each other's eyes again and giggled at such a totally inadequate description.

'A bit remote,' Monica went on, 'probably shy. His wife is charming.'

'Beautiful?' asked Lizzie.

'Oh yes, exceptional.'

'Pity,' sighed Sarah, earning another scowl from Paul.

'And three utterly ravishing children,' said Monica. 'A boy of twenty at Trinity, Dublin, and two teenage girls about seventeen and fourteen.'

'With Rupert living just across the valley,' said Lizzie, shaking her shaggy head, 'Declan must be barking. He'll have to lock his wife and both daughters up in chastity belts.'

'The youngest kiddy will make a friend for Sharon, although Sharon made a lot of friends at Pony Club camp. I must get them together when the O'Haras move in,' said Valerie.

Catching Sarah's eye yet again, Lizzie decided Sarah was definitely going to be a mate.

A group of young waitresses from other tables were now hovering, wondering if it were the right moment to ask James Vereker for his autograph. Tony was also looking at James and experiencing a glow of pure pleasure. Corinium's most popular presenter was feeling all the pique and disquiet of a big fish who's been basking for years in a rock pool, then suddenly sees the fin of a shark coming over the horizon. James's exquisitely straight nose would be frightfully put out of joint by Declan's arrival. James, Tony decided, had been getting a shade above himself recently. There was nothing Tony loved more than cutting people down to size.

As liqueurs and cigars came round, Tony moved down the table beside Freddie Jones. Now Rupert had stood him up so summarily, he was even keener to get Freddie on to the Board. With satellite television in the offing, Freddie's millions and electronic expertise would be invaluable.

'When Declan arrives, we'll get him to interview you,' said Tony.

Valerie also changed places and sat next to Monica.

'What a lovely meal, Lady Anthony,' she said.

'Oh, please call me Monica.'

'Well, thank you, Monica,' said Valerie gratified. 'You may, if you like, call me Mousie. That's Fred-Fred's pet name for me. I only allow very special friends to become members of the Mousie club.'

Oblivious of Monica's look of amazement and Sarah's and Lizzie's complete hysterics, Valerie ploughed on. 'I wanted to pick your brains, Monica, about public schools. Wayne is eleven but he's extra bright, so we're thinking of Winchester or even Eton, but I just wondered if you and Tony had been satisfied with Rugborough.'

'Well, Archie's very happy there,' said Monica, her raucous voice softening. 'The only problem, if one's got a flat in London, is that Rugborough's on the Central Line and, whenever he gets bored, Archie keeps nipping home on the tube. It drives Tony demented. Archie's supposed to be doing his O-levels.'

'Our problem,' said Valerie smugly, 'is to *stop* Wayne working. Not that he's a sissy, Monica – he's really plucky at sport – but you know how important qualifications are.'

The band was playing 'Red Red Wine'. The brilliantly lit ballroom beckoned. The vast springy floor was now filling up with couples. Like a shaken kaleidoscope, the red coats of the men with their flying tails clashed gloriously with the stinging fuchsia pinks and electric blues of the women's dresses.

'I wouldn't mind if Tony'd given me an inkling beforehand,' said James Vereker furiously, as, oblivious for once of the admiring glances of most of the young girls in the room, he lugged Lizzie round the floor, 'but I looked such a pratt, knowing nothing about it, and Monica actually admitted never watching my programme. Says she prefers BBC 2. What kind of a Chairman's wife is that?'

Lizzie let him rabbit on. She felt terribly sorry for him, but it was such exciting news that Declan was moving to Corinium, and she was fascinated by what was happening on the floor.

Monica was dancing with the Lord-Lieutenant now. For

someone so mad about opera, she had no sense of rhythm. Gyrating three feet apart, they looked like two ostriches on hot bricks.

'*Red red wine*,' sang the Lord-Lieutenant over and over again, which were the only words he knew.

As the tempo speeded up, Valerie took the floor with Freddie, showing off her 'Come Dancing' skills, fishtailing, telemarquing, reversing, correcting Freddie sharply whenever he made a mistake. Freddie, his little black shoes twinkling, laughed and took it in good part.

'What on earth did you find to say to James Vereker's wife?' asked Valerie, as the band paused for a moment. 'What a mess, can't have combed her hair for weeks, and that fraightful gown.'

'Nice lady,' said Freddie firmly. 'I liked her a lot.'

Valerie gazed at Freddie as uncomprehendingly as Lizzie had gazed at James when, earlier, he'd called Valerie 'a poppet'.

'And that new wife of Paul Stratton's looks a handful,' she went on.

Freddie refrained from saying he'd love to have his hands full of Sarah Stratton.

Paul and Sarah were dancing together now. He was holding her close, his hands moving over her flawless gold back, as if testing she were real. Perhaps she'd made a special effort to look particularly stunning tonight, thought Lizzie, knowing Winifred was such a chum of Monica's.

Tony devoted the rest of the evening to wooing Freddie, but he allowed himself the treat of a dance with Sarah. She was really gorgeous, he decided. One could understand exactly why Paul let his heart rule his very swollen head and ditched Winifred, but would he ever hold Sarah? She had obviously fallen in love with Paul because he was powerful and unobtainable. Now his career had taken a nose dive in the party and he'd been sacked from the Cabinet, he was neither of these things. Nervous of losing his seat at the next election, he kept angling for Tony to offer him an executive directorship on the Corinium Board.

But Paul shouldn't have patronized Tony in the past. How much more amusing, thought Tony, to employ Paul's new wife instead. Holding her dazzlingly full and exciting body, breathing in the scent of her thickly piled-up blonde hair, trying not to gaze too openly at the beautiful gold breasts, Tony felt the stirrings of lust. If she was any good, she'd be perfect to present the new late night show. That would really put Paul in a tizz.

'It's terribly exciting about Declan,' said Sarah. 'I'm such a fan. Those programmes are like Rembrandts. Did you see the one on Placido Domingo?'

'You must come and meet him as soon as they move in,' said Tony. 'You're going to be a distinct asset to Gloucestershire.'

Suddenly Sarah looked terribly young. Even in the dim light Tony could see she was blushing.

'It was angelic of you to ask us tonight, knowing what friends you were, particularly your wife, of Winifred's. Paul's friends haven't been exactly friendly. They think I've screwed up Paul's career.'

Tony gave a piratical smile. All he needs between his teeth is a cutlass, thought Sarah.

'You've given Paul a cast-iron excuse not to be Prime Minister,' he said. 'He'd never have made it. He has neither the bottle nor the conviction.'

'You're speaking of the man I love,' said Sarah.

'I'm sorry.' Tony didn't sound it. 'I'm going to tell James Vereker to interview you for our new "Behind Every Famous Man" series.'

Sarah smiled, showing very small, white, even teeth.

'You'd do better to interview Valerie. She drives poor Fred-Fred on with a pitchfork.'

'Probably spent half the day reading etiquette books on the correct way to hold your pitchfork,' said Tony.

Back at the table, the waiter poured more Krug, but Tony put a hand over his glass.

'I'm driving to London after this,' he said. 'We're announcing Declan's appointment tomorrow, so all hell's going to break loose.'

'The Gloucestershire poacher strikes again,' said Lizzie, receiving a sharp kick on the ankle from James.

As everyone swarmed out into the High Street after the 'Post Horn Gallop' and 'Auld Lang Syne', they found a thick layer of snow on the pavements. Down the road, high above them, the Corinium red ram was already wearing a white barrister's wig of snow on his curly poll.

'Drive carefully, Tony,' called Monica, as Percy the chauffeur held open the door of the Rolls for her. 'See you tomorrow evening.' Happily she settled back in the grey seat. Soon she'd be home to at least an hour of *Lohengrin* before she fell asleep.

'Bet the old ram's making a Cook's detour via Hamilton Terrace,' said James Vereker savagely, as Tony set off for London in the BMW, waving goodbye to the last of his guests.

Tony drove towards the motorway, but, sure enough, as soon as he'd shaken everyone else off, he did a U-turn and, just as the snow started to fall again, belted back to Cotchester.

RIVALS

7

It was three o'clock in the morning but Cameron Cook was still working on the first story outline for the new series of 'Four Men went to Mow'. On Monday she'd start commissioning writers. Ones that were talented and bullyable were not easy to find.

Beyond having a shower and brushing her teeth, she'd made no preparations for Tony, no satin sheets, no black silk negligées, no Fracas – the sharp, dry scent he so adored and which he brought her by the bucket – sprayed round the room. She was wearing the same brown cashmere jersey she'd worn to the office earlier, tight black trousers and no make-up. After twenty months, the one thing that held Tony was her indifference, her refusal to jump to his ringmaster's whip.

Perhaps he wouldn't turn up at all to punish her for being so bloody at the meeting. But she was so pissed off with him going to the Hunt Ball without her, and even worse inviting that jerk James Vereker, that she'd refused to speak to him after the meeting and stormed off home. She mustn't drop her guard like that. Once Tony detected weakness, he stuck the knife in.

All the same her stint in England had been terrifically exciting. She remembered so well the July day she had arrived. Tony had met her at Heathrow and driven her straight down to Cotchester to the quiet Regency terrace to the honey-gold house he had bought her. It was the only time she'd ever known him nervous.

Inside, as they'd gone from room to room, as finely proportioned and delicately coloured as the eggs of a bird, primrose and Wedgwood blue, lemon-yellow and cream, pale green and white, with large sash windows, and pretty alcoves with shelves for china scooped out of the walls, Cameron hadn't said a word. Apart from a fully equipped kitchen and a television set in the living-room, there was no furniture except a huge brass four-poster in the upstairs attic, which spread across the whole top floor.

Cameron had opened the window and gazed out at her new back yard with its pale-pink roses, and three ancient apple trees at the end. Someone had just mowed the lawn, and, as she breathed in the smell of grass cuttings, and admired the grey-gold spire of Cotchester Cathedral rising from its bright-green water meadows, she burst into tears.

Tony, who hadn't touched her until then, thinking she hated the house, or was feeling homesick, moved forward like lightning and took her in his arms.

'Darling, what's the matter? We'll find something else if you don't like it.'

Then Cameron sobbed into his Prussian-blue silk shirt that it was the loveliest house she'd ever seen, and why didn't they christen the bed – and their love-making turned out to be even more rapturous than it had been in New York.

But that was the last time she'd displayed weakness in his presence. From the moment she'd arrived she'd had no time to consider whether she was homesick or not. When she wasn't producing and master- minding every detail of the thirteen episodes of 'Four Men went to Mow', battling with directors, designers, actors and technicians, who weren't at all pleased to have a twenty-seven-year-old American upstart ordering them around, she was furnishing the house, driving from Southampton to Stratford, from Bath to Oxford, picking up antiques, thoroughly acquainting herself with the Cotswold area and seeking new ideas for programmes.

Otherwise her life revolved around Tony. He managed to

77

spend several evenings a week with her; people noticed he'd started leaving official dinners and cocktail parties abnormally early. He also took her to all the big events in the television calendar: Edinburgh, Monte Carlo, Cannes, New York, New Orleans, where she'd justified her existence a hundred times over selling Corinium programmes and acquiring new ones.

But there was still the married side of Tony's life, from which she was so ruthlessly excluded. She had only been once to his beautiful house, The Falconry, when Monica and the children were away, and that, she was sure, was because he wanted to show the place off.

Going into the drawing-room, she had exclaimed with pleasure at the Renoir over the mantelpiece.

'Don't touch it,' screamed Tony, 'or you'll have the entire Gloucestershire constabulary on the doorstep.'

Cameron had only met Monica once or twice at office parties, or at the odd business reception. And occasionally Monica sailed into Corinium to collect Tony. The galling thing was she never recognized Cameron. In one way, Monica's lack of interest in Tony's job made it much easier for him to deceive her. In another, brooded Cameron, if you had a rival, you wanted her at least to be aware of your existence.

'Lady Baddingham is a real lady,' Miss Madden was fond of saying when she wanted to get under Cameron's skin.

Cameron liked to think Tony only stayed with Monica because the silly old bag gave him respectability, and he didn't want any scandal before the franchise was renewed.

Getting up from her desk, Cameron wandered round the living-room. It was the only room in the house she'd redecorated, papering the walls in scarlet with a tiny blue-grey flower pattern and adding scarlet curtains, and a blue-grey carpet, sofas and chairs. She had acquired a new piano in England, lacquered in red, but had brought with her from America the dentist's chair upholstered in scarlet Paisley, the dartboard, the gold toe from the Metropolitan Museum, and all the videos of her NBS programmes. Beside them on the shelf were now stacked the thirteen prize-winning episodes of 'Four

Men went to Mow' and the two documentaries Cameron had also made on All Souls' College, Oxford, and on Anthony Trollope, who'd based Barchester on Salisbury, which was, after all, within the Corinium boundary.

On the mantelpiece was a signed photograph of the four young actors who'd starred in 'Four Men went to Mow', and a huge phallic cactus, given to her as an end-of-shoot present by the entire cast. *'Darling Cameron,'* said the card, which was still propped against it, *'You're spikey, but you're great.'*

After all the screaming matches, it had been a great accolade.

Tony obviously wasn't coming, Cameron decided; she'd blown it once and for all. The weekend stretched ahead, nothing but work until more work on Monday.

For consolation, she picked up that week's copy of *Broadcast*, which fell open at a photograph of her cuddling a dopey looking Jersey cow. *'Producer Cameron Cook on location during filming of her BAFTA-nominated series: "Four Men went to Mow",'* said the caption. *'The lucky cow is on the left.'*

Going over to the window, Cameron realized it was snowing. There were already three inches on top of her car, and soft white dustsheets had been laid over the houses opposite. Snow had also filled up the cups of the winter jasmine that jostled with the Virginia creeper climbing up the front of her house. If you wanted to get to the top you had to jostle, reflected Cameron. Tony had hinted he might put her on the Board, but she knew James Vereker, Simon Harris, and all the Heads of Departments would block her appointment to the last ditch. She had interfered at all levels, criticizing every programme, and every script she could lay her hands on. She knew she was unpopular with everyone in the building. But she didn't want popularity, she wanted power and the freedom to make the programmes she wanted without running to Tony for protection.

She was so deep in thought, she didn't notice the BMW drawing up, nor that Tony was outside until he lobbed a snowball against the window. She wished he didn't look so revoltingly handsome in that red coat. Cameron detested

79

hunting, not because she felt sorry for the fox, but because of the bloody-minded arrogance of people like Tony and Rupert Campbell-Black who hunted.

'How was it?' she asked, getting a bottle of champagne from the fridge.

'Great.'

Immediately her antagonism came flooding back.

'How was Rupert?' She knew her interest would bug Tony.

'Bastard didn't turn up. But Bas had heard a rumour that Declan had bought The Priory, so I told everyone he was joining Corinium. It was OK,' he added, seeing Cameron's look of horror. 'It was too late for any of them to ring the papers. You should have seen James's face.'

Cameron grinned.

'That's an improvement,' said Tony. 'Why were you so bloody bootfaced at the meeting?'

'I had a migraine.'

They both knew she was lying. But, excited by dancing with Sarah and upsetting James, and even more by the prospect of bringing Cameron to shuddering gasping submission, Tony didn't want a row. He soon had her undressed and into the huge brass bed, now curtained with pale-grey silk, which he or rather Corinium had paid for, just as they had paid for the whole house. The excuse was that putting up visiting VIPs in Cameron's spare room would be cheaper than the Cotchester Arms, which served awful food and had no air conditioning.

'Do you do this to keep your mind off your work?' asked Tony later, as a naked Cameron straddled him in all her angry, voracious beauty.

Cameron leaned over and took a gulp of champagne.

'Who says it takes my mind off my work? I've got an idea.'

'What?' Feeling those muscles gripping his cock, Tony wondered how he ever refused her anything.

'I want to produce Declan when he arrives in September.'

Leaving Cameron at six o'clock, Tony drove up to London. He'd put on a jersey over his evening shirt, and planned to bath, shave and breakfast at his flat in Rutland Gate. As he was going up a deserted Kensington High Street, his car was splashed by another – some celebrity being raced the opposite way to Breakfast Television at Lime Grove, lights on in the back as he mugged up his notes.

Red coat over his arm, Tony let himself into his flat. For a second he thought he'd been burgled. Clothes littered the hall; bottles, glasses and unwashed plates covered the kitchen table. Then, going into Monica's bedroom, Tony discovered the naked figure of his son Archie, come home once again from Rugborough on the tube, fast asleep in the arms of an extremely pretty, very young girl.

Tony's bellow of rage nearly sent them through the double glazing. The girl dived under the flowered sheets. Archie mumbled that he was terribly sorry, but he'd thought his parents were at the Hunt Ball.

'We were,' snapped Tony. 'Now I'm going to have a bath, and I want her out of here by the time I've finished.'

At least Archie had the manners to take the girl home, reflected Tony, as he soaked for the second time in twelve hours in a boiling bath. Pretty little thing too. He'd always been nervous Archie might turn out a bit AC/DC. Having a very dominant but adoring mother didn't help, but he was pleased to see Archie following in his father's footsteps. Tony was extremely fond of his elder son. He was frying eggs and bacon when Archie returned very sheepishly.

Having bawled him out for his disgraceful behaviour, Tony said, 'Where the hell does your housemaster think you are?'

'In bed, I suppose.'

'But not whose. How old is she?'

'Sixteen.'

'Over age, thank Christ. If you ever use Mummy's bed again, I'll disinherit you. I hope you took precautions.'

'We did,' mumbled Archie. 'I'm really sorry. We were going to change the sheets.'

'Think how upset Mummy would have been.'

'We don't have to tell her, do we?' Archie's round face turned pale.

Thinking he would also have some very fast explaining to do if Monica discovered he hadn't reached the flat until eight o'clock, Tony agreed that they didn't.

'But don't let it happen again. You've bloody well got to pass your O-levels. You know how important qualifications are. Now I suppose you expect me to give you breakfast?'

RIVALS
8

Six months later, on the wettest August day for fifty years, Declan O'Hara moved into Penscombe Priory to the feverish excitement of the entire county. It rained so hard that on 'Cotswold Round-Up' James Vereker caringly warned his viewers about flooding on the Cotchester-Penscombe road. But perhaps, being Irish, reflected Lizzie Vereker the next morning, the rain made Declan and his family feel more at home.

Lizzie's children had gone out to friends for the day; her daily Mrs Makepiece was due later; Ortrud, the nanny who had replaced Birgitta in April, was upstairs no doubt writing about James in her diary. Lizzie had a rare clear day to work. But she was halfway through and very bored with her novel. Outside the downpour had given way to brilliant sunshine and delphinium-blue skies. From her study Lizzie could see the keys on the sycamore already turning coral and yellow leaves flecking the huge weeping willow which blocked her view of the lake. There wouldn't be many more beautiful days this year, reflected Lizzie. Overcome by restlessness and curiosity, she decided to walk up the valley and drop in on the O'Haras. As a moving-in present she would take them some bantams' eggs and the bottle of champagne an adoring fan had given James yesterday.

The trees in the wood that marked the beginning of Rupert's land were so blackly bowed down with rain that it was like walking through a dripping tunnel. Emerging, Lizzie wandered up the meadows closely cropped by Rupert's horses. In the opposite direction thundered the Frogsmore stream, which ran along the bottom of the valley, hurtling over mossy stones, twisting round fallen logs, shrugging off the caress of hanging forget-me-nots and pink campion, and occasionally disappearing altogether into a cavern of bramble and briar.

Coming in the other direction was Mrs Makepiece, who worked mornings for the unspeakable Valerie Jones and who was bursting with gossip. The four Pickfords' vans bearing the O'Haras' belongings had nearly got stuck on Chalford Hill, she told Lizzie, and Declan's son – well, the image of Declan, anyway – had been sighted in the village shop, asking for whisky, chocolate biscuits, toilet paper and lightbulbs, and was quite the handsomest young man anyone had seen in Penscombe since Rupert Campbell-Black was a lad.

'Will they be bringing their own staff from London?' asked Mrs Makepiece wistfully, thinking it would be much more fun working for Mrs O'Hara, who probably paid London prices and wouldn't slave-drive like Valerie Jones. Lizzie said she didn't know. Mrs Makepiece was an ace cleaner, a 'treasure'. Even the exacting Valerie Jones admitted it. Annexing 'treasures' was a far worse sin in Gloucestershire than stealing somebody's husband.

Lizzie wandered on. Having had no lunch because she was on a diet, she kept stopping to eat blackberries, which didn't count. Up on the left, dominating the valley, Rupert's beautiful tawny house dozed in the sunshine. The garden wasn't as good as it had been when Rupert's ex-wife Helen had lived there. The beeches she'd planted round the tennis court were nearly eight feet tall now. Rupert should fly a flag when he was in residence, thought Lizzie. One couldn't help feeling excited when he was at home.

Half a mile upstream, the village of Penscombe, with its church spire and ancient ash-blond houses, lay in a cleavage of green hills like a retirement poster promising a happy future. Lizzie, however, turned right, clambering over a mossy gate into a beech wood, whose smooth grey trunks soared like the pipes of some vast organ. Following a zig-zagging path upwards, which three times crossed a waterfall hurtling down to join the Frogsmore, Lizzie finally stumbled and panted her way to the top.

Across a hundred-yard sweep of lawn, which was now almost a hayfield, rose the confusion of mediaeval chimneys, pointed gables, gothic turrets and crenellated battlements that made up Penscombe Priory. On either side with the sun behind them like a funeral cortège towered great black yew trees, cedars and wellingtonias. To the left of the lawn, where once, before the dissolution of the monasteries, the nuns must have strolled and prayed, grew a tangled rose walk.

Poor O'Haras, thought Lizzie, as she hurried along it. After divorce and death, moving house is supposed to be the most traumatic experience. But, as she skirted a large pond overgrown with water lilies, round to the front of the house which faced into the hillside for shelter, she was suddenly deafened by pop music booming out of two of the upstairs turrets, and opera, she thought it was *Rheingold*, pouring out of the other two.

The old oak front door, studded with nails, was open. On the sweep of gravel outside a van was still being unloaded. Peering inside, Lizzie noticed some very smeary furniture (the O'Haras *would* be needing a 'treasure' after all), a grand piano whose yellow keys seemed to be leering at her, and several tea chests full of books.

Sprawling over the front porch was an ancient clematis which acted as a curtain for the bathroom window above and covered the doorbell, which didn't work anyway. Inside Lizzie called 'Hullo-oo, hullo-oo,' in a high voice.

Next minute a very plain, self-important black and white mongrel appeared, barking furiously and wagging a tightly curled tail.

Turning right down the hall into the kitchen, which was situated in the oldest, thirteenth-century part of the house, Lizzie found a woman, whom she assumed must be Declan's wife Maud. Ravishing, but inappropriately dressed in a pink sequinned T-shirt, lime-green tracksuit bottoms, with a jewelled comb in her long red hair, she was very slowly unpacking china from a tea chest, stopping to smooth out and read each bit of paper it was wrapped in, and drinking whisky out of a tea cup.

On the window seat, training a pair of binoculars on Rupert Campbell-Black's house, knelt a teenage girl with spiky short pink hair, a brace on her teeth and a pale, clever charming face. In her black clumpy shoes, wrinkled socks and black woolly cardigan, she looked like a tramp who'd just changed into his old clothes. Neither of them took any notice when Lizzie came in. But a very tall girl in jeans and a dark-green jersey, with a cloud of thick black hair, strange silver-grey eyes, and a smudge on her cheek, who was quickly unloading china, looked up and smiled.

'I live down the valley,' announced Lizzie. 'I've brought you some eggs and a bottle. Don't open it now. It's a bit shaken up. Put it in the fridge.'

'Oh, how really kind of you,' said the dark girl. She had a soft deep slightly gruff voice, like a teddy bear's growl. She looked very tired.

Maud, having finished reading her piece of newspaper, glanced up and gave Lizzie the benefit of her amazing eyes which were almond-shaped, sleepy, fringed with very thick dark red lashes, and as brilliantly green as Bristol glass. Deciding Lizzie was worthy of interest, she introduced her daughters Taggie, short for Agatha, the tall dark one, and Caitlin, the little redhead.

The sink was crammed with flowers still in cellophane. Sidling over, Lizzie noticed one lot was from Tony and Monica Baddingham, wishing the O'Haras good luck in their new house and a long and happy association with Corinium.

'All the nation's press tramped through here yesterday in the mud trying to interview Declan,' grumbled Maud. 'TV Times has been here all morning photographing us moving in. Two local papers are due this afternoon, and a man from the Electricity Board has been rabbiting on like Mr Darcy about the inferiority of our connections and says the whole place will have to be rewired. Have a drink.'

She extracted a mug wrapped in a page of *New Statesman*, splashed some whisky into it for Lizzie and filled up her own tea cup.

'It's a glorious house,' said Lizzie, raising her mug to them. 'Welcome. We're all wildly excited you've come to live here.'

'After yesterday's deluge, we've discovered it leaks in half a dozen places,' said Maud, 'so we shall probably have to have a new roof as well.'

'We're thinking of letting our grounds to some cows,' said Caitlin, putting down her binoculars and helping herself to a chocolate biscuit, which she proceeded to share with the black and white mongrel who was drooling on the window seat beside her.

'Moving's very disorientating,' she went on. 'Daddy's trying to work upstairs, and he's frantic because he's lost his telephone book. Taggie's lost her bra.'

'Caitlin!' The tall girl blushed.

'And I've lost my heart,' continued Caitlin, training her binoculars back on Rupert Campbell-Black's house. 'Will you introduce me?'

'He's not here that much,' said Lizzie. 'But when he is, I'm sure he'll introduce himself.'

'It's not fair,' moaned Caitlin. 'I'm going to bloody boarding school next week, and I won't get first crack at him. He's bound to fall for Taggie – or even Mummy,' she said dismissively.

There was a knock on the door and a removal man came in with a yellowing dress in a polythene bag: where did Mrs O'Hara want this put?

'My wedding dress,' said Maud theatrically, rising to her feet and holding it against her. 'Just to think, twenty-one years ago.'

'Ugh,' said Caitlin. 'It's gross. How did you get Daddy in that? But I suppose he didn't see you till he came up the aisle, and then it was too late.'

'Caitlin, hush,' chided Taggie, as Maud's face tightened with anger. 'Mummy looked beautiful; you've seen the photos.'

'Oh, put it in my bedroom,' snapped Maud, going back to the *New Statesman*.

'I'm not sure I'm going to like living in the country,' said Caitlin, fiddling with the wireless. 'No Capital Radio, no *Standard*, no second post.'

'No second post!' Taggie's gasp of dismay was interrupted by a knock on the door. Another removal man wanted to know where the piano was to go.

'On the right of the front door,' said Maud.

'Not there,' shrieked Caitlin. 'Wandering Aengus is shut in there, and that stupid bugger Daddy's let him out twice already.'

And there's Daddy, the nation's biggest megastar, thought Lizzie.

'Aengus is our cat. He's a bit unsettled,' said Taggie, smiling apologetically at Lizzie.

'Oh look,' sighed Maud, unwrapping a baby's bottle. 'That was Patrick's when he was a baby.'

Caitlin tapped the fast-emptying whisky bottle with a finger. 'And this was Daddy's when he was forty-two,' she said accusingly.

'Oh, go away,' said Maud, shooting her another dirty look.

Peering at a pile of books in the corner, Lizzie was highly gratified to see a copy of her first novel.

'I wrote that,' she blurted out.

'Did you?' said Maud in amazement, picking up the book and examining the photograph on the inside flap.

'When I was thinner,' said Lizzie humbly.

'It was really good,' said Maud. 'I thoroughly enjoyed it.'

At that moment a punk Lord Byron wandered into the room. He had flawless cheek bones, short dark glossy vertical hair, and an inch of violet shadow under his eyes, which were like Maud's only darker and much more direct; obviously the son Patrick who had so dazzled the village shop.

'Darling,' said Maud in excitement, 'this is Lizzie Vereker. She wrote this marvellous novel, and she lives down the valley, so perhaps Penscombe won't be such a cultural desert after all.'

Patrick said, 'Hullo, Lizzie,' and announced that he'd liked the book too, and where did his mother want the piano?

'In the big drawing-room.'

'Too cold; you'll never play it in there,' said Caitlin.

'Put it in the small sitting-room, then,' said Maud.

'There won't be room for anything else in there, not even a piano stool,' protested Patrick.

'Oh well, you sort it out, darling, you're so good at that sort of thing,' said Maud.

'And don't let Aengus out,' screamed Caitlin.

Patrick's reply was drowned by a bellow of rage from outside and Declan stormed in holding a piece of paper in one hand and the cordless telephone in the other. Lizzie caught her breath. She'd never expected him to be so tall and broad in the shoulders, or quite so heroic looking. He had very thick dark hair streaked with grey, and worry and hard work had dug deep lines on either sides of his mouth and round his eyes, which were as sombre and dark as the rain-soaked yew trees outside. But even with half-moon spectacles fallen down over his broken nose, a quarter of an inch of stubble and odd socks, one had to admit his force.

'This is Lizzie Vereker,' announced Maud. 'She's brought us some eggs and a bottle of champagne, and she writes lovely books.'

Declan glared at Lizzie as though she didn't exist.

'I can't find the focking A-D directory.' His Irish accent was much more pronounced than the rest of the family. 'I can't find my focking telephone book. I can't get through to Claridge's. I can't get any answer from directory enquiries in London. I've been trying for the last half-hour.'

He dialled the number again, then held out the receiver, so they could all hear the parrot screech of the unobtainable.

'Shall I try?' said Lizzie. 'You have to dial 192 for London directories in the country, and then 01 before the number.'

Two minutes later she got through to Claridge's and handed the telephone to an amazed and grateful Declan, who asked to be put through to Johnny Friedlander.

Lizzie almost fainted. Johnny Friedlander was a brilliant,

madly desirable American actor, with a well-known cocaine habit, and a penchant for under-age school girls.

'*The* Johnny Friedlander,' she mouthed at Taggie.

Taggie nodded and smiled.

Declan was put straight through, and invited Johnny on to his first programme for Corinium next month.

'I'd ask you to stay with us,' Declan went on in his world-famous husky infinitely sexy smoker's voice, 'but we're in shit order this end, and you'd do better in a hotel. We can have dinner after the programme. I'll get our contract people to talk to your people. Thanks, Johnny, I can't think of a better person to kick off the series.'

'But he's never given an interview ever,' said Lizzie in wonder, as Declan came off the telephone.

'I know. Isn't it great?' Declan suddenly smiled, a wide, slightly gap-toothed grin, which made him look much more like Taggie, and made Lizzie feel utterly weak at the knees. 'And all because you know how to use a telephone,' he went on. 'If I'd left it any later, he'd have been looped or refused point blank. I'll certainly read your book.'

He turned to Maud. 'D'you hear that, darling? Johnny's coming on the programme.'

'That's nice,' said Maud, without interest. 'Hell,' she went on, reaching the end of another torn bit of paper, 'this piece on Princess Michael is continued on page eight. Do see if you can find it, Taggie.'

She started frantically burrowing in the tea chest, throwing discarded bits of newspaper all over the floor. Taggie raised her eyes to heaven.

Lizzie turned to Declan: 'What are you writing at the moment?'

'Cheques mostly,' said Declan.

Gazing out of the window, towards the pond, he suddenly started, and grabbed the binoculars from Caitlin, nearly garrotting her with the straps.

'Grasshopper warbler,' he said a second later. 'Pretty rare for this part of the world. There are some marvellous birds round here.'

'There could be some marvellous blokes too,' said Caitlin, rubbing her neck and snatching back the binoculars to train them once more on Rupert's house, 'if they were ever at home.'

'I'm off to the public library, darling,' said Declan, attempting to kiss a still scrabbling Maud on the cheek.

'But you haven't had any breakfast or lunch,' said Taggie in distress.

'Trust you to push off leaving us to do all the work,' grumbled Maud.

'Leaving Taggie to do all the work,' said Declan with a slight edge to his voice.

After he'd gone, and Maud and Lizzie had had some more whisky, the doorbell rang.

'Probably the local paper, and your father's not here,' said Maud, who was now reading about Boy George.

But it was another bouquet of flowers, brought in by Caitlin.

'Who are they for?' asked Taggie, hope flaring then dying in her eyes, when Caitlin opened the envelope and read: *To Declan and Maura*. 'That's a new one, Mum.'

Seeing the flash of irritation on Maud's face, Lizzie wondered quite how much fun it must be to be married to such a famous man. Lizzie had experienced the same thing in a smaller way being married to James, but she wasn't stunningly beautiful like Maud. It must be awful looking like that, and having people getting your name wrong, and wanting to gawp all the time at your husband.

'Where's Grace?' said Maud fretfully.

'Not up yet,' said Caitlin. 'Said she couldn't sleep because of the quiet. I suggested the removal men should drive their vans round and round hooting under her window to remind her of the juggernauts in Fulham. Grace is our so-called housekeeper,' she explained to Lizzie. 'Patrick says she ought to join the RSPCA, she's so kind to spiders.'

'I must go,' said Lizzie regretfully.

'Have another drink,' said Maud, not looking up.

'Have some lunch,' said Taggie. 'I was just going to make some omelettes.'

'I must work,' said Lizzie. 'Thanks awfully. The children'll be home soon; it must be nearly four.'

'I'll walk some of the way with you,' said Caitlin. 'Gertrude needs a walk. Do you want to come with us, Mummy?' Her voice was suddenly conciliatory, as though she regretted cheeking her mother.

'No thanks,' said Maud vaguely. 'I must measure up some windows for curtains.'

'Curtains, indeed,' muttered Caitlin as she and Lizzie left the room. 'The only thing my mother measures with any efficiency is her length after parties.' Then, noticing Lizzie's raised eyebrows, 'I'm afraid I'm at the age when one tends to criticize one's parents a lot. Sadly one can't sever the umbilical cord gently. It has to be done with a razor blade and without an anaesthetic.'

Along a winding passage Caitlin opened a door into a large octagonal room, the base of one of the mediaeval turrets. Tall, narrow ecclesiastical windows with stained glass in the top panes provided the only interruption to shelves and shelves of books.

'Daddy's library,' said Caitlin. 'I thought, being a writer, you'd like it.'

'How lovely,' gasped Lizzie.

'I think Daddy bought the house because it already had shelves in.'

They went out of the West door on the other side of the house, past stables and a clock tower with a roof covered in ferns and dark moss, through a vegetable garden which had been taken over by nettles, and an orchard whose stunted lichened trees grew no higher than seven feet, because of the constant blasting of the winds.

'Patrick says it's going to take a fleet of gardeners to keep this place in order,' said Caitlin. 'And what with my school fees, and the re-wiring, and the new roof, and Mummy's *House and Garden* fantasies, Daddy's bloody well going to need his new salary.'

Out in the sunshine Lizzie noticed how pale and thin Caitlin was and thought a few terms playing games and eating stodge at a vigorous girls' boarding school would do her no harm. Gertrude bounced ahead, plunging into the beech wood after rabbits. Certainly, slithering down the wood was easier than climbing up.

'Is Rupert Campbell-Black as attractive as everyone says?' asked Caitlin.

'Yes,' sighed Lizzie. 'He seems to get more so.'

'They say he was very wild in his youth.'

'Well, he's had a rather extended youth.'

'And brainy.'

'Well, street bright, and very sharp with money.'

'My brother Patrick is like that. I have brains. Taggie has beauty. Patrick has both.'

'Oh you're going to be very beautiful,' said Lizzie truthfully.

'I may blossom,' said Caitlin beadily. 'But at present I am undernourished, and my teeth leave a lot to be desired. I had to make the dentist put this beastly brace on. My mother only believes in going to the dentist when one's teeth hurt.'

'And Taggie seems very efficient in the kitchen,' said Lizzie. 'Isn't *she* bright?'

'Not at all. She's dyslexic, poor darling, hardly stumbles through Mills and Boon, and she has fearful trouble with recipe books, which is a pity, as she wants to be a cook. Patrick said it was ghastly when she was small, everyone thought she was retarded because she couldn't read. Mummy shouted at her all the time, never thought of taking her to an educational psychologist.'

The wall at the bottom of the beech wood marked the end of Declan's land. Caitlin scrambled over it and held out a hand to help Lizzie.

'How beautiful,' she said, gazing at the flat water meadows and the bustling little stream. 'I can imagine mediaeval knights jousting here in the old days.'

She whistled to Gertrude who'd belted the other way, and who now rushed back, splashing and drinking in the stream.

'The ghastly thing about having brilliant famous parents,' Caitlin went on, 'is you never feel the centre of the universe, because they're so obsessed with their own lives. And if you do brilliantly at school, everyone nods sagely and says Declan's daughter, it's in the genes; and if you do badly like poor Tag, they just assume you're lazy or bloody-minded. Tag's self-confidence was in tatters when she left school.'

'But she's so beautiful,' protested Lizzie.

'I know, but she doesn't realize it. She's madly in love with Ralphie Henriques, one of Patrick's even more brilliant friends. After months of pestering, he seduced Tag at a May Ball at Trinity this year. God, look at those blackberries!' Caitlin started tearing them off the bushes with both hands and cramming them into her mouth.

'I hoped Tag would tell me *exactly* what it was like. One can't obtain one's entire sexual education from the pages of Jackie Collins, but she just clammed up, and he never rang her again. Just one postcard from Cork, and nothing since. Can you imagine doing that to Tag? That's why she waits for every post and jumps on every telephone. Patrick says Ralphie's got someone else, some pert little blonde who reads Sophocles in the original. Poor Tag can't even read English in the original.'

'What about Patrick?' asked Lizzie. 'Does he like Trinity?'

'He feels right there. He thinks my father has betrayed his roots working in England, and he also rather despises Daddy for being in television. God, these blackberries are good. Perhaps Rupert smiled at them.'

'But your father's a genius,' said Lizzie, shocked. 'Those interviews are works of art.'

'I know, but Patrick thinks Daddy ought to write books. He's been working on a biography of Yeats for years, and he used to write wonderful plays.'

'What's Patrick going to do when he leaves Trinity?'

'He'll write. He's much more together than Daddy. I know Daddy makes pots of money, but it all gets spent, and he's always having frightful rows at work. Patrick's calmer. He's a prose version of Daddy, really. And for someone with such high principles, he thinks nothing of running up the most enormous debts, which of course Mummy settles out of Daddy's despised television earnings.'

'Jolly easy to have principles when someone else picks up the bill,' said Lizzie.

'Right,' said Caitlin. 'Patrick's also a bit smug because he attracts the opposite sex so effortlessly. Do you think Gertrude will get lonely in the country? Should we get her a dog friend?'

They had crossed the stream now, to the same side as Rupert's house. Despite the lack of wind, thistledown was drifting everywhere as though a pillow had just burst. Panting up the slope, and turning in their tracks, they could just see the creepered battlements and turrets of The Priory above its ruff of beech trees, now warmed by the late afternoon sun. Climbing had also given Caitlin's pale freckled face a tinge of colour.

'Think of all those nuns living there in the middle ages,' she sighed ecstatically, 'gazing across the valley, yearning for Rupert Campbell-Black's ancestors.'

Lizzie decided not to spoil such a romantic concept by pointing out that Rupert's house hadn't been built until the seventeenth century.

'It *is* a romantic house, isn't it?' said Caitlin, still gazing at The Priory. 'Exciting things must happen to us all – even Tag – in a place like that.'

'I'm sure they will,' said Lizzie.

'I'd better go home now,' said Caitlin. 'Can I come and see you next time I'm back for the weekend?'

Lizzie floated home. What richness, what a fascinating afternoon. The prospect of new friends excited her these days almost as much as new boyfriends had when she was young. She was still bubbling over when James got home later than usual.

'What did you think of my programme?' he asked.

Lizzie had to confess she'd forgotten to watch it, because she'd dropped in and had a drink with the O'Haras.

'Did Declan say anything about me or the programme?' demanded James.

'No,' said Lizzie.

'Didn't you tell them you were married to me?' said James, utterly scandalized.

'I forgot,' said Lizzie. 'I'm awfully sorry, but there was so much going on, and the O'Haras are just *so* glamorous.'

RIVALS
9

Declan O'Hara had two obsessions in life: his work, and, rare in a profession that tends to regard a broken marriage as the only essential qualification, his wife.

He was born in a thatched cottage on a green hillside in the Wicklow mountains, where his father scratched a living from the land. When Declan was ten, his father broke his back falling from a tractor when drunk, and was thus rendered useless for heavy work, so the family moved back to Cork, his Protestant mother's home town. Here his mother proceeded to bring up Declan and his three brothers by taking endless cleaning and secretarial jobs, aided by occasional handouts from her parents. Her one joy in an exhausting life was Declan, who fulfilled his promise at school by winning a history scholarship to Trinity, Dublin. Soon he was writing poetry and plays, working freelance for the *Irish Times* and sending money home.

One evening in his second year at Trinity, he dropped into the theatre to see *The Playboy of the Western World*. Maud, with her red hair and her amazing green eyes, was the toast of Dublin as Pegeen Mike. Declan went round in a daze for three days afterwards, then sat down, wrote a play for her in a month, and posted it off. Impressed by the play, Maud asked him backstage and was even more impressed by this roaring black-eyed boy with his volcanic moods and his gift for words. The theatre put on the play for a three-month run.

It was an instant success, with Maud's extra radiance being noted by all the critics. By the sixth week she was pregnant and married Declan as soon as the play came off. Although stunned with amazement and joy that this glorious creature was his, Declan soon realized there was no way he could support her and a baby by writing plays, so he junked his academic career and got a full-time job, doing profiles on the *Irish Times*.

There was talk of Maud returning to the stage when Patrick grew older, but then Taggie came along, and then Caitlin. Habitually strapped for cash, Declan moved to television, where, although his family in Cork thought he was joining the circus, he soon became a star. Snapped up by the BBC in London, that milker of Irish talent, in a year he was writing and fronting his own programmes, culminating in a series of interviews which had promptly climbed to the top of the ratings and remained there for two years.

For not only was Declan the most natural thing ever seen on television, but, unlike other presenters and chat show hosts, he never showed off or talked about himself, and he always did his homework. To get public figures, as a result of this quiet, sympathetic, utterly relentless probing, to reveal facets of their character never seen before made for spellbinding television.

These revelations, however, did not always please the BBC who got rattled if a Sinn Fein leader appeared too attractive or a politician too unpleasant. Known as the terror of Lime Grove because of his black glooms and his sporadic bouts of heavy drinking, Declan bitterly resented interference from above. He finally walked out because the Governors, heavily leant on by the Home Secretary, pulled his interview with Ian Paisley, and because Tony Baddingham offered to triple his salary and Declan couldn't see any other way of paying his tax bill or ever clearing his overdraft.

After his early childhood in Wicklow, too, Declan had always yearned to live in the country. He truly believed it would be cheaper than London, that he would have more time to spend with his family, particularly Maud, and to finish his biography of Yeats.

Maud herself was lazy, egotistical and selfish. She idled her time away reading novels, and token scripts, spending money and talking. Playing second fiddle, on the other hand, is not an easy part. When she married Declan, she had been the star, pursued by half the men in Dublin, and the mistress of the Director. Then she had to watch Declan rise to international fame, while her career dwindled away through lethargy and terror of failure, on the excuse that she was always too busy with the children. Underneath, she was desperately jealous of Declan's success, and one reason he had never become spoilt was because Maud showed no interest in his career and was constantly mobbing him up.

There was a tremendously strong erotic pull between them, but, even after twenty-one years, Declan still felt he hadn't really won her. He was also in a Catch-22 situation. In order to support Maud's wanton extravagance he was forced to work all hours, which meant she got bored and spent more, and, to goad him, toyed with other men. Another reason Declan had moved to the country was that last year one of her toyings had got out of hand.

A week after the O'Haras moved into The Priory, Declan started work at Corinium. He didn't sleep at all the night before. It was a long time since February, when he'd accepted the job, but Maud had immediately started spending in the expectation of riches, culminating in a vast Farewell to Fulham party. Christ knew how he was to pay for that, or for all Maud's re-decorating schemes.

Nor had his friends at the BBC been backward in telling him that Tony Baddingham was a shit, or that ITV, notoriously more reactionary and restrictive than the Beeb, would be far harder to work for. In the end, too, as he had been desolate to leave Ireland, he was sad to leave the BBC, particularly as so many of the staff had come out on strike when his programme on Paisley had been axed. They had then held a succession of riotous and tearful leaving parties, finally clubbing together to give him the *Complete Oxford Dictionary of National Biography*. But all his life Declan had walked away from the safe thing – that was his instinct.

As he lay in the huge double bed, smoking one cigarette after another, watching dawn creep through the curtainless windows, Maud slept peacefully beside him. Her red hair spilled over the rose-pink pillow case, the whole of the dark-blue duvet was wrapped round her hips, and her breasts fell sideways on to a pale-green bottom sheet. Nothing ever matched in their house, reflected Declan.

He longed to make love to her to ease the panic and tension, but there was no way she'd wake before ten o'clock. She was as obsessive about sleep as he was about work. Tony had told him to roll up at eleven, but knowing work was the only way out of his black panic, Declan decided to go in early. He was expecting a pile of Johnny Friedlander's cuttings from America.

Thank God for Taggie, he thought, as he put on a beautifully ironed black and green checked shirt. Grace the house-keeper, who also never rose before ten, had an ability to singe or iron buttons off everything she touched.

As he went into the kitchen to pick up his car keys, Taggie came barefoot and hollow-eyed down the back stairs in her nightgown.

'Daddy, you shouldn't be up yet.'

'Couldn't sleep. Thought I might as well go in.'

'You must have some breakfast, or at least a cup of coffee.' When he shook his head, she put her arms round him.

'It'll be OK, I know it will. Remember you're the best in the world.'

Declan reached the Corinium Television building at a quarter to eight, just as the night security man on the car park was about to go off. Seeing a pair of vaguely familiar eyes looking over the half-open window of the absolutely filthy Mini, he raised the horizontal pole, and, having waved Declan through, went back to enjoying Page Three of the *Sun*.

Walking through the revolving front door, absolutely sick

100

with nerves, Declan found the place deserted except for a cleaner down the passage morosely pushing a mop, and a young man in pink trousers arranging roses on the marble-topped reception desk.

Aware that every other girl who worked in the building was at home washing her hair, putting on her prettiest clothes, and emptying scent bottles over herself in anticipation of Declan's arrival, the receptionist had just nipped down to Make-up to re-do her eyes before the hordes started arriving at nine.

Declan therefore waited a few minutes, admired the framed awards on the wall, which seemed all to have been won by Cameron Cook, then, still finding no one at Reception, took a lift to the fifth floor, where he eventually discovered a coffee machine and an office with his name on it at the end of the passage.

It was a splendid office with a thick blue carpet, a huge bare desk with empty drawers, two empty filing cabinets, a radio cassette, two television sets, a video machine and a large bunch of red roses, which had obviously been arranged by the pink-trousered youth. Out of the window was a marvellous view of the close, and the water meadows still white with dew. But even more marvellous on the virgin sheet of pink blotting paper lay a pile of mail including two fat airmail envelopes. Lighting a cigarette, sitting down at his desk, Declan was soon totally immersed in Johnny Friedlander's cuttings – most of them highly speculative and fictitious because Johnny never gave interviews.

The great bell of Cotchester Cathedral had tolled the hour three times when suddenly a red-faced middle-aged lady, reeking of Devon Violets, and with tightly permed hair, barged into his office, gave a squawk of amazed relief and shot out again, shrieking down the passage, 'He's here, Lord B, he's here.'

Next minute Tony Baddingham erupted into the room, absolutely purple with rage. 'Where the fuck have you been?'

Declan sat back in his chair. 'Sitting here, since about eight o'clock.'

'Why the hell didn't you tell anyone?'

'There was no one here to tell.'

With a colossal effort Tony gained control of himself and shook Declan's hand. 'Well, welcome anyway. Look, I've got most of the national press outside waiting to witness your arrival. We nearly had the police out.'

'They said you'd left home at seven-thirty,' said the lady reeking of Devon Violets, who was Tony's secretary, Miss Madden. 'We thought you might have had a car crash.'

'Or second thoughts,' said Charles Fairburn, Head of Religious Programmes, shimmying in and giving Declan a great kiss on both cheeks. 'You're not to be bloody to him on his first day, Tony. First days in an office are like birthdays. No one's allowed to be bloody to you.'

'Fuck off, Charles,' snarled Tony.

'See you later, darling,' said Charles, whisking out again, nearly colliding with an ashen Cyril Peacock.

'They're getting awfully fed up, Tony. Where the hell can the stupid fucker have got to?'

'He's been here all the time,' said Tony nastily. 'You just didn't look, Cyril. Another classical Peacock-up.'

'Oh, hello Declan. Welcome to Corinium,' said Cyril, his false teeth rattling even more violently with nerves. 'Marvellous to see you. They're all waiting for you in the car park, getting very hot.'

'Uh-uh,' Declan shook his head, looking mutinous. 'I've got nothing to say to them.'

'Well for a start you might like to refute that piece in the *Guardian* claiming you joined Corinium merely to clear your overdraft and not as a vocational choice,' said Tony with a cold smile.

'I interview people, I don't give interviews,' said Declan, not budging. 'The press made enough fuss when we arrived at Penscombe, staking us out all bloody night.'

Tony tried a different tack. 'It'll be such a thrill for all the staff,' he said suavely. 'All we want is pictures of you driving into the car park for the first time and having a glass of champagne in the board room afterwards, and then we can all get down to work.'

Declan suddenly decided he needed a drink.

'All right, I'll go and get my car.'

'You can't do that. They'll see you,' said Tony.

'Give Cyril your keys. He'll drive it round to the front, then you can drive in again.'

'It's a Mini, parked in the far corner,' said Declan.

As Declan drove his absolutely filthy Mini into the parking slot with his name on, which was between Tony's maroon Rolls Royce with the silver Corinium ram on the bonnet, and Cameron's green Lotus, there was absolutely no reaction from the crowd of reporters and cameramen. The next minute, however, there was a furious banging on the roof. Declan wound down the window half an inch. He could see a beaky nose, and a predatory mouth.

'Yes?' he said.

'You can't park here, asshole,' said an enraged female voice.

'Why not?'

'Can't you read, you fucking dumbass? This slot's reserved for Declan O'Hara.'

'Is it indeed?' said Declan softly. 'Then I've come to the right place.'

Winding up the window, he got out, towering over Cameron Cook, who gasped and stepped back as she instantly recognized the tousled black curls, the brooding dark eyes and the familiar face as battered as the Irish coastline. Shock made her even more hostile.

'Where the fuck have you been? You should have been here at eleven. It's nearly twenty past.'

'So I was, crosspatch, in my office. Nobody thought to look.'

There was a shout as the press recognized Declan and surged forward, their cameras clicking away like weaving looms, hugely enjoying the contrast between Declan's rusty banger and Tony's gleaming Rolls. From every window female staff, their clean hair flopping, screamed and cheered with excitement. Declan grinned up at them and waved.

In the Gent's, James lowered the Venetian blind a quarter of an inch and was delighted to see how old Declan was looking and that he was not even wearing a suit or a tie. Tony would not like that at all.

Outside there was almost a punch-up, as the Corinium camera crew battled to get the press out of the way, so they could get their own cameras in and film Declan's arrival for the lunchtime news bulletin.

Inside the building everyone surged forward to say hullo to Declan. The corridor was swarming with *Midsummer Night's Dream* fairies coming back from their mid-morning coffee-break. As Declan fought his way through them, shaking hands, Bottom took off his ass's head to have a better look. Next minute, Titania struggled to Declan's side, her crown askew, and kissed him on both cheeks.

'Darling, marvellous you've arrived. We must lunch later in the week. Love to Maud.'

'Wish we'd never started this fucking production,' said Tony, punching more fairies out of the way.

Mercifully he kept the press conference short: 'We are all absolutely delighted Declan's joined Corinium,' he said, when everyone had been given a glass of champagne. 'We feel he has a tremendous contribution to make, and has just the right kind of incandescent talent to revitalize our current affairs schedule.'

Declan suppressed a yawn.

'Why d'you move, Declan?' asked the very young girl reporter from the *Cotchester Times*.

'Well, to misquote Dr Johnson,' said Declan, 'we weren't tired of life, but we were a bit tired of London.'

'This Dr Johnson,' persisted the reporter earnestly, 'is he a private doctor?'

He'll crucify her, thought Cameron, waiting for the kill.

But Declan merely laughed. 'No, definitely National Health,' he said.

The press conference, in fact, was affability itself, compared with the meeting that followed in Tony's office.

As Tony, Declan and Cameron trooped past the tiny outer office where Cyril Peacock waited, grey and sweating, for Tony's reprisals after the disaster of Declan's arrival, they found Simon Harris, Controller of Programmes, lurking apprehensively in Miss Madden's office.

'I'm terribly sorry I wasn't here when Declan arrived,' said Simon, following Tony into his office. 'Fiona's had to go into hospital, so I had to take the kids to school.'

'Couldn't the nanny have done it?' snapped Tony.

'She's had to take the baby to the clinic.' Simon scratched at his eczema mindlessly.

'I'm so sorry,' Declan turned to Simon. 'Is your wife OK?'

'Multiple sclerosis,' said Simon helplessly. 'She's in for new tests.'

'I'm so sorry,' said Declan again. 'We met briefly at the Beeb.' He held out his hand.

The hand that limply gripped his was wet and trembling. Christ, he's aged, thought Declan, appalled. Simon looked awful. His eyes were unbecomingly frightened, the shoulders of his grey suit were coated in scurf.

'Well, sit down,' said Tony irritably, deliberately waving Cameron and Declan towards the squashy dark-green leather sofa which lined two walls of his vast office. Simon Harris had to make do with a hard straight-backed chair right in front of Tony. Despite the room's size, the plethora of television sets, video machines, and huge shiny-green tropical plants, plus Tony's massive empty desk and vast carved chair, made it seem unpleasantly overcrowded. A bowl of flesh-coloured orchids on Tony's desk and, despite the warmth of the day, central heating turned up like the tropical house at the zoo, increased the jungle atmosphere. Any moment Declan expected a leopard to pad out from behind the filing cabinet. As he'd already downed a couple of glasses of champagne, he wanted to go on drinking. But it was at least half an hour until lunchtime.

'After lunch, Declan,' said Tony, 'I'll hand you over to Cameron, but I thought I'd like to be in at the kick-off.'

Declan looked at Cameron in her sleeveless orange T-shirt

and her short black leather skirt. Her hair was greased back, her eyes fierce. She looks like a vulture who's spent the morning at Vidal Sassoon, thought Declan. He loathed meetings; he wanted to get back to his Johnny Friedlander cuttings.

Furious at having made an idiot of herself in the car park, Cameron was determined to regain the whip hand and weighed straight in: 'My goal is to give your programme more pizazz,' she said. 'We've chosen several possible signature tunes. Once we've decided on the right one, we can go ahead and cut a disc, which should go straight to the top of the charts with a nice profit for Corinium. But we ought to get it recorded at once. Could you listen to them this afternoon?'

Declan's eyes, which never left the face of the person he was listening to, seemed to darken.

'I know what tune I'm having,' he said flatly. 'The opening of the first movement of Schubert's Fifth Symphony.'

'Too up-market.'

'The programme's up-market. It's a great tune, and it's in the public domain, so we won't have to pay copyright. All we have to do is to record a jazzed-up version and pay the arranger.'

'Am I hearing you right?' exploded Cameron. 'This isn't fucking Radio 3.'

'No,' agreed Declan. 'But it's what I want, so we're having it.'

Cameron was spitting, but she particularly didn't want to lose face in front of Tony and Simon, so she tried another tack which would certainly have worked with James Vereker.

'I keep hearing the same complaint about your programmes.'

'What?' said Declan softly.

'The viewers don't see enough of you. We want to feature you much more in the interview, that's why we've designed a terrific set with book shelves and some really good abstracts, and this jade-green sofa.'

'No,' interrupted Declan sharply. 'I only interview people face to face.'

106

'Confrontational TV's kinda dated,' taunted Cameron.

Simon Harris opened his mouth to protest and shut it again.

'I'm not using a sofa,' said Declan firmly.

'Well, we'll argue about that later,' said Cameron.

'We will not. We'll decide now. I want two Charles Rennie Mackintosh chairs, facing each other six feet apart on pale steely-blue circular rostra.'

'Steely blue?' screeched Cameron.

'Steely blue,' said Declan firmly, 'so they rise like islands from a floor of dark-blue gloss. Then carrying on the dark blue up the bottom of the cyclorama into a limitless white horizon.'

'This is insane!' Outraged, Cameron swung round to Tony for help. 'Well?'

But Tony was calmly doing his expenses.

'It's Declan's programme,' he said smoothly. 'He knows by now how to get the best out of people.'

'How does he know until he's tried a sofa?'

'Sofa's make it look like any other chat show,' mumbled Simon.

'No one's asking you, dumbass,' hissed Cameron.

She's like a hawk not a vulture, decided Declan. She prefers her victims alive. He imagined her cruising the hillside, scanning the ground for prey, or darting down a woodland ride, scattering terrified small birds.

Squaring her shoulders, Cameron turned back to Declan. 'And we're scrapping the introductory package,' she said. 'We want you talking to camera for two or three minutes about the guest, to replace all those dreary stills and clips with a voice over.'

'The point of those dreary stills and clips with a VO,' said Declan, dangerously quietly, 'is that they concentrate the viewers' minds on the guest and set the tone of the interview. I get uptight enough as it is without having to ponce about making a long spiel on autocue. This way I can concentrate on the first questions.'

'I *must* disagree on this one,' said Tony, putting down his red fountain pen. 'The point is, Declan, that you have immense presence. It's you the viewers turn on for. You should open the programme talking to camera in a really decent suit,' he added, raising a disapproving eyebrow at Declan's scuffed leather jacket, check shirt and ancient jeans. 'It'll be up to Cameron to make you relax and be less uptight.'

Through half-closed eyes Declan looked at Cameron who was now pacing up and down through the rubber plants burning up the calories. No wonder she was so thin.

'She?' said Declan incredulously, '*She* make *me* relax?'

'We've got to be different from the Beeb,' snarled Cameron, 'or they'll just say we're serving up the same old garbage.'

'Anyway we've got three weeks to kick the idea around,' said Tony, 'and to cheer you up, Declan. I know Cameron's had a great time dreaming up people for you to interview.'

'We've checked out on all their availability,' said Cameron.

'Well, you can just uncheck them again,' said Declan harshly. 'I decide who I'm going to interview.'

Cameron stopped in her tracks, glaring at him. 'They may not be hot enough.'

Declan then stunned the three of them. He was kicking off with Johnny Friedlander on September 21, he announced, followed by Jackie Kennedy the week after.

Frantic now to keep her end up, Cameron snarled that Jackie Kennedy would just rabbit on about her boring publishing job.

'She may indeed,' said Declan, 'but she's also going to talk about her marriages, and her life as a single woman in New York.'

'You and she should have much in common, Cameron,' said Tony bitchily.

Cameron ignored him, but a muscle pounded in her cheek.

'Isn't it going to overextend your budget, flying her over?' she demanded.

Declan suddenly relaxed and gave Cameron the benefit of the wicked gap-toothed schoolboy grin: 'She's coming over on a private visit, and she'll probably stay with us,' he said.

Fifteen love to Declan, thought Simon Harris joyfully. Then it was game and first set when Declan announced that in subsequent weeks he'd be doing the French Foreign Secretary who was in the middle of a gloriously seamy sex scandal, followed by Mick Jagger, and the most controversial of the royal Princesses.

Desperately fighting a rear-guard action, Cameron said she had lined up a couple of ace researchers, who'd better get started on Johnny Friedlander and Jackie Kennedy at once.

There was a long pause. Very slowly Declan got out a cigarette, lit it, inhaled deeply, and only just avoided blowing smoke in Cameron's face.

'I do my own research,' he said softly.

'For Chrissake,' screamed Cameron, 'you can't cover subjects like this singled-handed!'

'I have done for the past ten years. For better or worse, what you've bought is not my face, but my vision – what I can get out of people.'

'It's a team effort,' hissed Cameron.

'Good,' said Declan amiably. 'Then I suggest we put your researchers on to finding some decent footage and stills.'

'We've got an excellent library,' said Simon, tugging his beard.

'Shut up!' howled Cameron.

Tony was lasciviously fingering one of the flesh-coloured orchids. Glancing round, Declan tried to analyse the expression on his face. He's enjoying it, he thought with a shudder, he's excited by seeing her rip people apart.

Noticing the disapproval on Declan's face, Tony looked at his watch.

'That was a very stimulating exchange of views,' he said, getting to his feet, 'but I, for one, need some lunch.' Then, deliberately excluding Simon, he added, 'Cameron and I've booked a table at a little French restaurant a couple of miles outside Cotchester. We hope you'll join us, Declan, and we can carry on the – er – discussion.' He smiled expansively.

Declan didn't smile back. 'Thanks, but I'm lunching with

Charles Fairburn. We worked together at the Beeb,' he added, by way of slight mitigation.

Tony was about to order Declan to cancel, then decided there would be oodles of time later to get heavy. Besides, the clash of wills had turned him on so much he had a sudden craving to take Cameron back to Hamilton Terrace for a quickie.

'What are your plans for the afternoon?' Cameron asked Declan sulkily.

'I'm going home,' said Declan. 'I've got Johnny's cuttings and all my reference books are there.'

'I trust you'll do most of your research in the building and report regularly to me and Tony,' she said. 'This is a group effort. OK? We want to be fully briefed at all times. Cock-ups occur at Corinium when no one knows what anyone else is doing.'

As she flopped down again on the green leather sofa, Declan immediately got up, as if he couldn't bear to share the same seating. From the depths of the sofa, he seemed to Cameron almost to touch the ceiling, his massive rugger player's shoulders blocking out the light, his face bleak and uncompromising. She never dreamed he'd be so dauntingly self-confident.

'I have to be left alone,' he said, speaking only to her. 'It's the only way I can operate.'

'I'm producing this programme,' she said furiously.

'Yes, but it's *my* programme you're producing.'

For a second they glared at each other, then a knock on the door made them start. Round it, like the rising sun, came Charles Fairburn's red beaming face.

'Are you through, sweeties?' he said blithely. 'Because I've come to take Declan to din-dins.'

They lunched at a very pretty pink and white restaurant off the High Street. Pretty waiters in pink jerseys and pink-and-white striped bow-ties converged on Charles.

'We've got your usual table,' they said, sweeping him and Declan off into a dark corner.

'Good boys,' said Charles. 'You know how I detest windows, they show up my red veins. Now get your little asses into gear and bring me a colossal dry Martini, and my friend here would like? Whisky is it still, Declan?'

'Bad as that, is it?' asked Declan three minutes later, as Charles drained his dry Martini and asked the waiter for another one.

'Well, I don't want to slag off the company on your first day, dear boy, but things are a shade tense.'

'Cameron Cook,' said Declan, tearing his roll savagely apart.

'Got it in one.'

'What's her position in the company?'

'Usually prostrate. She's Tony's bit of crumpet. Officially she's Head of Drama – particularly appropriate in the circs as she's always making scenes, but she's also got a finger up to the elbow in every other pie. That's how she talked Tony into letting her produce your programme.'

'Simon Harris has aged twenty years. He used to be such a whizz-kid.'

'Well, he's a was-kid now, and totally castrated. He's been threatening to have a nervous breakdown since Cameron arrived. Unfortunately he can't walk out, because he's got a second mortgage on his house, an invalid wife, three young children, and two to support from his first marriage.'

'Quite a burden.'

'Makes one feel like Midas by comparison, doesn't it?'

'Not quite,' said Declan, thinking of his tax bill.

'Well, Cameron, as you no doubt observed, jackboots all over Simon and every time he or anyone else queries her behaviour she bolts straight to Tony. The food is utterly wonderful here,' Charles went on, smiling at the prettiest waiter. 'I'll have liver and marmalade and radicchio salad. Ta, duckie.'

Declan, who liked his food plain, ordered steak, chips and some french beans.

'And we'd like a bottle of No. 32, and bring us another

whisky and a dry Martini while you're about it,' said Charles. 'Hasn't he got a sweet little face?' he added, lowering his voice.

As soon as the waiter had disappeared to the bar, however, Charles returned to the subject of Corinium: 'The entire staff are in a state of revolt. They've all been denied rises, and they're forced to make utterly tedious programmes in order to retain the franchise. James Vereker's ghastly "Round-Up" is just a wank for local councillors and Tony's business chums; and the reason why *Midsummer Night's Dream* is taking so long is that you can't get a carpenter to build a set – they're all up at The Falconry building an indoor swimming pool and a conservatory for Tony, when they're not installing a multi-gym and jacuzzi for Cameron.'

Declan grinned. Charles, he remembered from the BBC, had always had the ability to make things seem less awful.

'Nor,' added Charles, draining his third dry Martini and beckoning to the pretty waiter to pour out the claret, 'are the staff overjoyed that you've been brought in at a vast salary – yes they all read the *Guardian* yesterday – to wow the IBA. Gorgeous Georgie Baines, the Sales Director, who's stunning at his job incidentally, and whose expenses are even larger than mine, went straight in and asked Tony for a rise this morning. Tony refused, of course. Said they were paying you the market price. Depends what market you shop in, shouted Georgie, and stormed out.

'Thank you, duck,' he added as the waiter placed a plate of liver reverently before him.

Declan stubbed out his cigarette. Suddenly he didn't feel remotely hungry any more.

'Anyway,' said Charles, cheering up as the Martinis began to take effect, 'the staff like the idea of you, Declan. Christ, this liver is ambrosial. I've told them you're a good egg.'

'Thanks,' said Declan dryly.

'They all admire your work, and they can't wait to see the fireworks when you tangle with Ms Cook.'

'I already have,' said Declan, watching the blood run out

as he plunged the knife into his steak. 'Tell me about Tony.'

'Complete shit, but extremely complex. One never knows which way he's going to jump. Believes in deride and rule, plants his spies at all levels, so really we're all spying on each other. But he does have alarming charm, when it suits him. Because he's so irredeemably bloody most of the time, when he's nice it's like a dentist stopping drilling on a raw nerve.'

'What's the best way to handle him?'

'Well, he claims to like people who shout back at him like Cameron does; but, unfortunately, after a row, you and I can't make it up with him in bed, which I bet is where he and Cameron are now. Things were so much more peaceful when he spent all his time in London, but the IBA's warning him to spend more time in the area neatly coincided with his falling in love (though that's hardly the word) with Ms Cook, so he's down here making a nuisance of himself most of the time now.'

Charles suddenly looked contrite.

'You're not eating a thing, dear boy. Have I upset you?'

'Yes, but I'd rather know the score.'

'My budget has been so slashed,' said Charles, pinching one of Declan's chips, 'that I intend to interview two rubber dummies in dog collars on the epilogue tonight. Not that anyone would notice.'

'Will Tony leave Monica?'

'I doubt it. Any scandal, even a piece in *Private Eye*, is the last thing he wants with the franchise coming up. The pity of it, Iago, is that Ms Cook is very good at her job, once you dispense with all the crip-crap about checking out on your availability. I've acted as her walker at the odd dinner, when she had to take a man and didn't want to rouse Tony's ire. And she can be quite fun when she forgets to be insecure. If she had someone really strong to slap her down, there'd be no stopping her.'

'There doesn't seem much stopping her at the moment,' said Declan gloomily.

'If she gets on the Board, we're all in trouble,' said Charles, pinching another chip. 'But we have great hopes you're going to rout her, Declan; now let's have another bottle and you can tell me all about poor bored Maud, and that ravishing son of yours.'

Back at Corinium, James Vereker fingered the prettiest secretary from the Newsroom with one hand as he re-read today's fan mail for comfort with the other.

'I do really think,' he said petulantly, 'Tony might have had the manners to introduce me to Declan.'

10

A fortnight after Declan started at Corinium his younger daughter, Caitlin, went back to her new boarding school in Oxfordshire, and his elder daughter, Taggie, disgraced herself by being the only member of the family to cry.

Caitlin's last week at home coincided with her mother Maud discovering the novels of P. D. James. As a result Maud spent her days curled up on the sitting-room sofa, holding P. D. James on top of a pile of games shirts, shorts and navy-blue knickers. When anyone came into the room, she would hastily whip the clothes over her book and pretend assiduously to be sewing on name tapes. The same week Grace, the housekeeper, discovered the local pub.

As well as getting the house straight, therefore, and feeding everyone, and coping with Grace grumbling about the incessant quiet and imagined ghosts and having to drag dustbins to the end of a long drive, the task of getting Caitlin ready for school fell on Taggie.

It was not just the gathering of tuck, the buying of lacrosse sticks, laundry bags, and the New English Bible (which Declan hurled out of the window, because it was a literary abomination, and which had to be retrieved from a rose bush) and the packing of trunks which got Taggie down. Worst of all was scurrying from shop to shop in Gloucester, Cheltenham, Cotchester, Stroud and finally Bath, trying to find casual shoes and a wool dress for chapel which Caitlin didn't think gross and the school quite unsuitable.

Caitlin spent the morning of her departure peeling glow stars off her bedroom ceiling, and sticking large photographs of Gertrude the mongrel, Wandering Aengus the cat, Rupert Campbell-Black and smaller ones of her family into a photograph album, and dressing for school. On the first day back, girls were allowed to wear home clothes. By two o'clock she was ready.

'Are you auditioning for *Waiting for Godot*?' asked Declan, as she walked in wearing slashed jeans and an old dark-blue knitted jersey she'd extracted from Gertrude's basket.

By two-thirty the car was loaded. Only then did Maud decide to wash her hair and glam herself up to impress the other parents. They finally left at four by which time Caitlin was in a frenzy they were going to be late.

'Goodbye, my demon lover,' she cried, blowing a kiss to Rupert Campbell-Black's house as the rusty Mini staggered down the drive. 'Keep yourself on ice until I come home again.'

No one spoke on the journey. Declan, with his first interview in a week's time, could think of nothing but Johnny Friedlander. Maud was deep in P. D. James. Taggie and Caitlin sat on the back under a pile of lacrosse sticks, radios, records, teddy bears, with the trunk like a coffin behind them.

After three-quarters of an hour they reached the undulating leafy tunnels of Oxfordshire, and there, high on the hill surrounded by regiments of pine trees, rose the red-brick walls of Upland House, Caitlin's new school.

'My head ought to be filled with noble Enid Blyton thoughts about comradeship,' grumbled Caitlin to herself, as they were overtaken by gleaming BMWs and Volvos bearing other girls and their belongings, but all she could think was how embarrassing it was to turn up with such famous parents in such a tatty car.

As they arrived so late, all the beds near the window in Caitlin's dormitory had been bagged, and Caitlin had to be content with the one by the door, which meant she'd be the first to be caught reading with the huge torch that her mother had given her as a going-back present.

While Taggie, her fingers still sore from sewing on name-tapes, unpacked the trunk, Maud drifted about wafting scent and being admired by passing fathers. Declan sat on Caitlin's bed gazing gloomily at all those glass cubes full of photographs of black labradors, ponies and double-barrelled mothers looking twenty years younger than those in the dormitory. He wondered if he'd been mad to let Maud persuade him to send Caitlin away.

He also thought how incredibly glamorous the other fourteen-year-olds looked, drifting about with their suntans and their shaggy blonde hair, and how excited they would have made Johnny Friedlander with his penchant for underage girls.

As they left, with all the girls surreptitiously gazing out of the window to catch a glimpse of Declan, Maud did nothing to endear herself to Caitlin's housemistress by calling out, 'Don't worry, Caitlin darling, you can always leave if you don't like it.'

''Bye Tag,' said Caitlin cheerfully. 'Don't cry, Duckie. I'll be OK. Keep your eyes skinned for Rupert. I won't look while you drive away. It's unlucky.'

'She'll be all right, sweetheart,' said Declan, reaching back and patting Taggie's heaving shoulders, until he had to put both hands on the wheel to negotiate the leafy tunnels once more and was soon deep in thought again.

'Don't be silly, Taggie,' snapped Maud irritably. 'I'm Caitlin's mother. I'm the one who minds most about losing my darling baby, but I'm able to control myself,' and she went back to P. D. James.

Going to bed that night, Taggie felt even worse. In Caitlin's bedroom, she found a moth bashing against a window pane and the needle stuck in the middle of a *Wham* record, and she realized there was no one to leave the light on in the passage for any more, to ward off the ghosts and hobgoblins.

Up in her turret bedroom, which was like sleeping in a

tree top, and which creaked and leaked and yielded in the high winds like an old ship, she looked across the valley and saw at long last a light on in Rupert's house. Caitlin would have been so excited.

'Oh please God,' she prayed, 'look after her, and don't let boarding school curb her lovely merry nature.'

The O'Hara children, having been dragged up by a lot of housekeepers, and frequently neglected by their parents, were as a result absolutely devoted to one another.

Taggie, in particular, had never enjoyed an easy relationship with her mother, whom she adored but who intimidated her. Ten days late when she was born, Taggie had been a very large baby. Labour had been so long and agonizing, Maud had nearly died. Declan, insane with worry, thanked God he was a Protestant, and not faced with the painful Catholic preference for saving the baby rather than the mother. Both survived, but the doctors thought later that Taggie's dyslexia might be due to slight brain damage sustained at birth.

Maud, shattered and weakened, never took to Taggie the same way as she had to Patrick who'd been born with such ease. As a child Taggie developed normally except that she walked and spoke very late, and even when she was four was only able to manage single syllables and might have been talking Japanese.

At school in Dublin, the staff, eagerly awaiting another dazzlingly bright pupil like Patrick, were disappointed to find that Taggie couldn't read or write. She was also very clumsy and hopeless at dressing herself, putting shoes on the wrong foot, clothes back to front, doing up the wrong buttons and quite unable to tie her laces. Because she couldn't tell the time, and had no sense of direction, she always ended in the wrong classroom, bringing the wrong books, and because she was so tall, people automatically assumed she was older than her age, and dismissed her as even more lazy and stupid.

Patrick, two and a half years older, was constantly fighting her battles, but he couldn't help her in class, when the other children teased her and the teachers shouted at her, nor during those agonizing sessions at home when Maud lost her temper and screamed, but in the end got so bored that she sometimes ended up doing Taggie's homework for her.

Patrick never forgot those pieces of homework, smudged with tears of frustration, sweaty from effort, and later peppered with red writing and crossings-out from the teachers.

Early detection of dyslexia and special teaching can quickly put a child within reach or even on a level with the rest of the class. Taggie was left to flounder, constantly losing confidence, until at eleven she came to England with the family and was about to be put in a school for backward children.

In the end it was Patrick, who got a scholarship to Westminster with ease and who, acquiring a friend there with a dyslexic older sister, persuaded his parents to have Taggie tested by an educational psychologist. He pronounced Taggie severely dyslexic and said she should be sent immediately to a special school.

Maud now felt even more ambiguous about Taggie. She never told anyone what the psychologist had said to her in that brief bitter exchange after he'd seen Taggie, nor would she ever admit that she felt desperately guilty for not seeking help for the child's problems earlier.

Nor was there any way, once the condition was diagnosed, that Maud would ever have the patience and routine to spend each evening helping Taggie with her reading and learning of the alphabet. Declan was always too busy. So it was Patrick, and later Caitlin, who came to her rescue.

Five years of specialist teaching produced dramatic improvements. At sixteen Taggie wrote her first essay. She still wasn't confident in the order of the alphabet, she still read slowly and hesitantly, following the text with her finger. She had never really mastered joined up writing, and punctuation was a closed book. Her spelling was atrocious and she still didn't automatically know her left from her right, and had to think back to the kitchen in Fulham and Patrick saying: 'Window on the right, Tag, Aga on the left.'

It still took her ages to write letters or recipes, and when they moved to The Priory it took her much longer than the others to find her way round all the rooms. She also always double-checked telephone numbers, asking people to repeat them, ever since the nightmarish day when one of Maud's lovers had rung from America and asked if Maud could ring him back. Taggie had taken the number down wrong, and he'd never rung again. Occasionally, when she was drunk, Maud would bring this incident up: how Taggie had lost her the one great love of her life.

But at the end of her school career, although Taggie only managed O-levels in cooking and needlework, she left with an excellent final report: 'Taggie is a dear girl,' wrote her headmaster. 'Kind, hardworking, responsible; she deserves to do very well in life.'

Offered a place at a catering college, she preferred to learn the hard way, and worked in a restaurant belonging to a friend of her father's. After two years, coinciding with the family's move to Penscombe, he regretfully told Taggie that although he would do anything to keep her, there was nothing else he could teach her.

She cooked, he said, by instinct, by pinches, a pinch of this here, a pinch of that there. Given a barrel of self-confidence, he told Declan, Taggie could be another Escoffier.

Inspired, Taggie was longing to start her own cooking business. There must be hundreds of people in Gloucestershire who needed someone to do dinner parties, or fill up their deep freezes at Christmas or at the beginning of the school holidays. But so much of her time lately had been spent looking after the family, or crying herself to sleep at night over Ralphie Henriques. Maybe now Caitlin had gone back and Patrick was on his way to Trinity, via three weeks in France, she could get started.

The following morning did little to raise Taggie's spirits. She missed Caitlin and her acid asides dreadfully; the morning post brought no letter from Ralphie, and when Patrick rang from France, where he was staying with Ralphie's family, to report he had arrived safely, he made no mention of him. When Taggie finally steeled herself to ask how he was, Patrick had replied that he was fine.

'Doing a lot of water-skiing and drinking. But honestly, duck, I think you'd do better to cut your losses and find yourself a nice rosy-cheeked Gloucestershire farmer.'

Taggie was protesting that she didn't want a Gloucestershire farmer when Maud swanned in, enraged that Taggie hadn't told her that it was her beloved Patrick on the line, and seized the telephone.

As the alternatives that afternoon included picking apples, making green tomato chutney, or getting on Maud's nerves, Taggie decided to take Gertrude for a walk and explore the village. In an attempt to beat her dyslexia she tried to learn a new word every day and use it. Today's word was 'abhorrent'. There was certainly nothing abhorrent about Penscombe that afternoon: the wind that shook her turret bedroom last night had dropped, while the little Beatrix Potter cottages, covered in velvety purple clematis, were white in the afternoon light. A lot of Bovver boys on their motorbikes by the war memorial eyed Taggie with great interest. A nice farmer who lived down the valley asked her how they were all getting on and said they must come and have supper when the long nights began. At the village shop Mrs Banks gave her a mutton bone for Gertrude and the new *TV Times* with Declan's picture on the front, and an old lady with a blue greyhound stopped outside and exhorted her to look after the badgers who lived in the sets at the top of the Priory wood.

Cheered up by their friendliness, Taggie set out for home. She could feel the heat of the road through her espadrilles, thistledown drifted idly, and the sky was brilliant blue except for a few little violet clouds on the horizon. If only Ralphie were here with his hand in hers. Turning down the drive of yews, hollies, laurels, which almost hid The Priory from the top road, she remembered her promise to keep her eyes skinned for Rupert. She glanced across the valley, then gasped with horror as she saw a huge mushroom of brown smoke rising into the sky and realized that two of Rupert's fields on the far side of the house were on fire.

She ran down the drive to The Priory, dashed into the kitchen and unearthed the Gloucestershire telephone directory. Oh God, she must keep calm. When she panicked, her reading went to pieces, and she had even more difficulty with the alphabet.

Callan, Calvay, Cam Auto Repairs, Camamile – with agonizing slowness her finger moved down the column. There were two Campbells, one in Gloucester, another in Nailsworth, then the list moved on to Cambridge and Campden. No Campbell-Blacks. Rupert must be ex-directory, like her father.

Out of the window great clouds of smoke were belching from Rupert's red-hot flickering fields, the flames spreading ever nearer to the house. Taggie dialled 999. All the fire engines were out, explained the man at the other end, but they'd ring Cotchester. 'Don't worry, my love, we'll get one over as soon as possible.'

All the same, thought Taggie, she'd better rush over and warn Rupert. He might not be able to see the fire from the house, although he'd probably be able to smell it. It would be so awful if any of the horses got trapped in their stables. . . .

She raced across the lawn with Gertrude, slithered down the beech wood, bumping on her bottom most of the way, and ran across the water meadows; then she leapt the bustling Frogsmore, before starting the steep climb up the other side. Ripping her clothes on barbed wire, oblivious of stinging nettles and brambles tearing at her bare arms and legs, losing an espadrille on the way, she panted on, past surprised horses knee deep in lush grass, past ancient oaks and beeches, skirting the lake, tearing across Rupert's lawn, in through the french windows into a beautiful pale-yellow drawing-room, by which time she was so puffed she couldn't even shout 'Fire'.

Although the front door was open, no one was about. Returning to the garden through the french windows, her breath coming in great painful gasps, Taggie was about to run

122

towards the stables when she heard shrieks of laughter coming from the tennis court on the left of the house, which was completely hidden by a thick beech hedge. As she raced down a gravel walk putting up red admirals, gorging themselves on the white buddleia on either side, she heard another shriek of laughter.

'I can't hit a bloody thing. I should never have had so much to drink at lunch,' said a girl's voice.

'Tit-fault. Your tits were at least six inches over the line,' said a man's voice, a clipped light flat, very distinctive drawl.

'Cock fault then,' said the girl, giggling hysterically. 'You must be at least ten inches over the line.'

'You flatter me,' said the man. 'I wouldn't be if you didn't excite me so much.'

'Fire,' gasped Taggie to the beech hedge, but no sound came out.

The man was laughing now. 'We'll finish this set, and then I'll finish you off upstairs.'

Taggie raced round the beech hedge until she came to a gap.

'Fire,' she croaked.

Then, very slowly, she realized to her utter horror that a tall, blond, lean, very suntanned man, and a beautiful girl with catkin blonde hair tied up in a pink ribbon, and a golden body like distilled sunflowers, were playing tennis with no clothes on at all.

The man was serving. His body rippled with muscle as the ball scorched across the net. Dropping her racket, the girl gave a shriek and rushed to the side of the court, breasts flopping everywhere, and covered herself with a pale-pink shirt. The man proceeded to serve the second ball very hard into the far netting, then sauntered almost insolently towards the net near Taggie, over which was hanging a darkblue towel.

'Fire,' mumbled Taggie, clapping her hands over her eyes.

'What did you say?' shouted the man. 'It's OK. You can look now.'

Very gingerly, Taggie lowered her hands. He had wrapped

the dark-blue towel round his loins now. With his sleek blond hair, broad brown shoulders, and long, wickedly mocking eyes, as cornflower blue as the great expanse of sky behind him, he was quite unmistakable, from Caitlin's photographs, as Rupert Campbell-Black.

Acutely aware of her heaving breasts and sweating red face, Taggie muttered, 'Your fields are on fire.'

'They're meant to be,' said Rupert.

'Whatever for?'

'Quickest way to get rid of the stubble after the harvest.'

'But it's the most a-a-abhorrent thing I've ever heard,' whispered Taggie, utterly appalled. 'What about the r-rabbits and voles and field mice and moles and all the poor birds?'

Rupert shrugged. 'They've got legs; they can run away.'

'Not that quickly,' said Taggie furiously. 'You're a murderer.'

'I suppose,' snapped Rupert, thoroughly nettled, 'that you want me to stop ploughing my fields because it's cruel to worms, earwigs, beetles, woodlice and all the poor bugs.' He was mimicking Taggie now. 'Do you want me to give them a state funeral?'

The blonde girl giggled. She was very young, only a few years older than Taggie.

'Oh shut up!' screamed Taggie, losing her temper. 'How would you like someone to set fire to you when you were in bed?'

Rupert nodded at the blonde. 'She frequently does.'

'Don't be disgusting. You're utterly abhorrent, the sort of person who always has to be killing something; hunting, fishing, shooting.'

At that moment, a lot of dogs, back from their walk with one of Rupert's grooms, swarmed barking on to the court. There were Jack Russells, spaniels, a black labrador, and a beautiful shaggy blue lurcher, which bounded joyfully up to Gertrude, who bridled and curled her tail up even tighter.

Taggie pointed to the lurcher. 'I bet you use that for coursing,' she said furiously.

'Why don't you take that ugly brute back to its pigsty,' said

Rupert, picking up a green tennis ball and hurling it at Gertrude, 'and stop interrupting other people's innocent afternoon pleasures.'

'Don't you d-dare be beastly to Gertrude.'

Reaching for his racket, Rupert let his towel drop: 'Forty love wasn't it, darling?'

The blonde girl giggled again. But next moment the pussy-cat smile was wiped off her face as, with a manic jangling of bells, three fire engines roared up the drive.

'Fucking hell!' screamed Rupert.

Taggie gave a sob and fled back across the valley, her face flaming as much as her poor torn stung legs. Beastly, horrible, abhorrent man. Looking up in front of her she could see The Priory. Except for Declan's twelve acres, all the land in the valley belonged to Rupert. Now, thought Taggie with a shudder, it seemed to curl round The Priory like a man trapping a woman at a party, putting his hands on the wall on either side of her, so she couldn't escape.

Back home she found Maud sitting outside, wearing a big black hat to protect her white skin from the early evening sun, which had just crept round the side of the valley to admire her. She was drinking vodka and tonic and immersed in P. D. James.

'I've just met Rupert Campbell-Black,' said Taggie.

Maud glanced up and saw Taggie was puce in the face, with her black cloudy hair standing up on end in a tangled mess, her red dress ripped and her long legs and arms scratched and bleeding and covered with white nettle stings.

'My God,' said Maud, roused out of her usual languor, 'I know he's got a fearful reputation, but surely you didn't let him get that far?'

RIVALS

11

The following Sunday Monica Baddingham gave a lunch party at The Falconry to welcome Maud and Declan to Gloucestershire and launch the new conservatory built by Corinium's studio carpenters. Accustomed to going out to lunch in London where people seldom ate before two o'clock or even two-thirty, Maud and Declan didn't leave home until half past one. Declan tried to persuade Taggie to come too, but she blushingly refused when she heard Rupert might be there.

'I'm sure Monica said left at The Dog and Trumpet,' said Maud, applying a second layer of coral gloss to a pouting bottom lip.

Declan was in a vile temper. Not only had Maud made him late yet again by washing her hair at the last moment, but he had spent all morning trying to cut their hayfield of a lawn with a mower that kept choking on Gertrude's shredded mutton bones. Now they seemed to be driving half way round Gloucestershire.

'Why the hell can't you take directions down properly?' he snarled.

'He's your boss. You should have taken down the directions. Anyway it was you who wanted to move to the bloody country. Let's go home.'

'They're giving the focking party for us. Why the hell don't they put names on their houses in the country?'

126

'You don't.'

'That's because I don't want anyone to come and see me.'

Declan was also aware that, although his wife was looking a billion dollars in a very low-cut black silk dress, a green shawl which matched her eyes, black stockings and black high heels, with her shiny red hair piled under the big black hat, she was quite unsuitably dressed for Sunday lunch.

'There it is,' said Declan at last, as he drove through two lichened gate posts topped with rather newer stone rams. 'Christ, people are leaving already.'

As a dark-green BMW passed them coming the other way, the woman who was driving wound down the window:

'Love your progamme. Frightfully sorry, we've *got* to go to a christening. Welcome to Gloucestershire; you must come to dinner. Better hurry or there won't be any drink left.'

'Jesus,' muttered Declan.

The Baddinghams' splendid Queen Anne house lay in a hollow surrounded by lush parkland. The stable clock was always kept twenty minutes fast so that people might worry they were late, and be encouraged to leave early.

In huge gold letters against a black background above the second door of the porch was written: *Peaceful is the Country that is strongly armed*. In the hall, stuffed heads of deer, tiger, stag and buffalo gazed down glassily.

'My head'll be up there next,' muttered Declan as Tony came out of the drawing-room, plainly in a bait.

'Can't you ever get the time right, Declan? We've been trying to have lunch for three-quarters of an hour.'

'I'm terribly sorry,' said Maud in her most caressing tones. 'Declan and I are used to London hours.'

'Well, you'd better acquire a few rural habits. The Pimm's has run out; what d'you want to drink?'

'Oh, there you are.' Monica swept in wearing a blue cotton shirtwaister and open-toed sandals on her big bare feet. 'Taggie said you were on your way; pity you didn't bring her, I've got so many spare men. Have a quick drink, and then we'll have lunch. It's probably the last time we'll be able to

127

eat outside this year,' she added wistfully, thinking how much she'd prefer to be dividing the regale lilies.

Having given Maud a drink, she led her through the vast tapestried drawing-room out to the new conservatory, which stretched the entire back of the house at ground floor level and was crammed with statues of goddesses, iron seats painted white, lilies, palms, aspidistras and plants still wrapped, which people had brought as conservatory-warming presents.

'Beautiful,' murmured Maud, taking a huge slug of whisky.

Everyone, gathered on the lawn, turned round and stared.

'Come into the garden, Maud,' bellowed Charles Fairburn, who was already tight. Mistiming his kiss, his round red shiny face cannoned off Maud's like a billiard ball.

'Looking beautiful as usual,' he said, drawing her aside.

'You're not to monopolize her, Charles,' said Monica bossily.

'I promise I'll introduce her to everyone,' said Charles. 'Your husband's certainly been stirring things up at Corinium,' he added, lowering his voice.

'Really,' said Maud, only mildly interested.

She'd never been wild about Charles. He knew too much about her, and with such fantastic men around she didn't want to waste her first party on one who was both drunk and gay.

'Is that very good-looking man over there Rupert Campbell-Black?' she asked.

'Unfair to Rupert,' said Charles. 'That's James Vereker, Corinium's most popular presenter, drinking Perrier and working the room. He's fearfully put out by your husband joining Corinium.'

James was, in fact, absolutely furious. He'd arrived as late as he dared in order to make an entrance, then Declan had swanned in even later. Now he was trapped by three of Monica's friends who 'did an enormous amount for charity', silly old bags who all wanted him to open their Autumn bazaars and Christmas fayres for nothing. To look at Monica's toe nails, thought James in disgust, you'd have reckoned she weeded the garden with her feet; and Paul Stratton, who'd put on a hell of a lot of weight, looked ludicrous in those tight new jeans, and a denim shirt undone to the waist to reveal scanty grey chest hair. James, who'd nearly worn jeans and an unbuttoned blue shirt, was so glad he'd put on instead a new grey jersey with a pink elephant on the front, knitted by one of his adoring fans.

'Come and meet Maud O'Hara, James,' yelled Charles Fairburn.

James extracted himself from the old bags and wandered over. Maud O'Hara was certainly extraordinarily beautiful.

'Is that pink elephant on your bosom meant to reproach the rest of us for not drinking Perrier?' said Charles.

'If the cap fits, Charles,' smirked James. 'Don't you think it's a nice sweater, Maud? Sent me by a fan.' He smiled engagingly.

Charles peered at the sweater: 'Not sure about the collar.'

'It might look better if you wore a brooch,' said Maud.

James suddenly decided he didn't think Maud was beautiful at all.

'Hullo,' said Lizzie Vereker, coming over and hugging Maud, 'lovely to see you, I'm so pleased you've met James. Thank you for all that lovely whisky the other day. Are you straight yet?'

'Don't ever ask *me* that question,' said Charles with a shudder. 'What's all this about five fire engines rolling up at Rupert's house and catching him playing nude tennis with a blonde. Talk about Wobble-don.'

Lizzie giggled: 'Rupert's convinced some animal rights freak called the fire brigade because she thought he was cruel to burn his stubble.'

'Who was the blonde?' asked Charles. 'Beattie Johnson?'

'No, that finished months ago. Rupert won't say. The *on dit* is that she's the girl playing Mustard Seed in *Midsummer Night's Dream*.'

'Have you heard that Titania's so petrified of getting AIDS, she's refusing to kiss Bottom until he's had a blood test?' said Charles.

'Is Rupert here?' asked Maud, who was not interested in Corinium gossip.

'Somewhere. Probably wandered off down one of those garden glades in which everyone except Monica behaves badly,' said Lizzie.

'Speak for yourself,' said James disapprovingly.

It was certainly a beautiful garden. Rising out of a sea of lavender, roses coming up for a second pale-pink innings rampaged up the walls of the house. Pastel drifts of delphiniums, Japanese anemones, and Michaelmas daisies were sheltered from the bitter winds by yew hedges nine feet high. Two plump labradors panted on lawns as smooth as an Oxford quad. Beyond was a fish pond and a water garden, fed by the same winding River Fleet that flowed through Cotchester.

'What are you going to do about the Priory garden?' asked Lizzie.

'Get a donkey to keep down the lawn,' said Maud.

'I hope to God we eat soon,' said a harassed-looking man with a moth-eaten yellow beard, and a sleeping baby hanging from a baby sling. He was also hanging on to two frantically struggling children by the scruffs of their necks.

'There is a limited amount of time one can entertain one's kids feeding Tony's fish,' he added helplessly.

Lizzie introduced Simon Harris. All his skin seemed to be flaking in the open air, thought Maud.

'How's Fiona?' asked Lizzie.

'Still in hospital for another three weeks. It's the nanny's day off, or I'd never have brought this lot,' said Simon, as the two hyperactive horrors strained at their collars like bull terriers after a cat. 'If they get at Monica's Meissen I'm finished. I just couldn't resist a square meal,' he added pathetically.

Lizzie opened her mouth to ask him to supper, then closed it again. Simon was so boring at the moment, and she knew James, who was convinced Simon was about to get the bullet, would think it a waste of time.

The panting labradors struggled to their feet, waving their tails as Monica appeared at the conservatory door.

'Lunch,' she said. 'You stay outside with the children,' she added firmly to Simon. 'I'll get someone to bring you something out. I like children normally, but Simon's two will keep pulling the dogs' ears, and they keep knocking over my new plants,' she added in an undertone to Maud.

As Maud walked into the dining-room, Declan came towards her looking really happy for the first time that week: 'Darling, you must meet Rupert. He knows Johnny very well. He's given me some great stuff about him. It's added a totally new dimension to his character.'

Maud caught her breath. How could I ever have mistaken James Vereker for *that*, she wondered.

Rupert and Declan were both tall and broad in the shoulder, but there the resemblance ended. Declan, with his heavily lined, broken-nosed, shaggy-haired splendour, was like a battle-scarred charger returning from the wars. Rupert was like a sleek capricious thoroughbred, rippling with muscle and breeding, about to win the Derby at a canter. Yet in their great fame and their intrinsic belief (despite Declan's current self-doubts) that they were still the greatest in the world at what they did, they were the same, and therefore separate from the rest of the party. At that moment both James and Maud felt a bitter stab of envy, that Declan had been admitted so effortlessly to the same club to which Johnny Friedlander and Rupert belonged.

'Welcome to Penscombe.' Rupert kissed Maud on the cheek. 'I'm sorry I wasn't at home when you moved in, but I've been frantically busy.'

'So we hear, Rupert,' said Charles archly. 'What's this about fire engines and a burning bush?'

'Fuck off, Fairburn,' said Rupert, grinning.

'Come on, don't hold up the queue,' said Monica, beckoning from behind a long white table. 'You're getting Coronation chicken again, I'm afraid.'

Maud stood in front of Declan and Rupert, gulping down her third glass of wine and feeling totally unnerved.

'I know your house very well,' Rupert told her. 'I remember pursuing something that wasn't a fox across your haha at one

131

party. Ended up ripping the front of my trousers off on the barbed wire. How's the garden?'

'A groundsel estate, and the nettles are on the warpath,' said Declan.

'Better get those tackled professionally,' said Rupert, 'or you'll never get rid of them. I've got a man who'll do it for you.'

'What about the wood?' asked Declan.

'Forestry commission'll give you a grant for that. They'll whip out all the dead stuff and plant you new young trees as a quid pro quo for the firewood.'

'How wonderfully positive you are,' murmured Maud. 'Perhaps you can give me advice on re-decorating our bedroom?'

'Re-decorating's never been a priority of mine. Not in bedrooms,' said Rupert.

'Tuck in, Maud,' said Monica impatiently. 'And you haven't met my brother-in-law, Bas. He's dying to meet you.'

Bas was about five inches taller than Tony and decidedly attractive in a sleek, wicked, Latin way. He kissed Maud's hand, then turned it over and buried his lips in her wrist.

'Calêche,' he murmured. 'I adore it. Do you wear it all over?'

Maud laughed. 'Are you local?'

'Near enough as the helicopter flies. I can land on the palm of your hand. I've got a wine bar in Cotchester High Street,' he went on. 'Most of my evil brother's staff gather there to plot against him. No doubt your famous husband will shortly join them. You must get him to bring you in one day.'

'Don't be silly, Bas,' said Monica briskly. 'You haven't met Paul Stratton, Maud, our MP for Cotchester, nor his wife Sarah.'

She looks more like his daughter, thought Maud. With his anxious, lined, somewhat petulant face, and his brushed-forward blue-grey hair, Paul looked like one of those once-famous television personalities who eke out a middle-aged existence advising housewives to buy soap powder in television commercials.

132

Even Maud, who had a dismissive attitude to the charms of her own sex, had to admit that the wife was ravishing.

'Ah, the newly-weds,' said Bas, kissing Sarah on the mouth. 'When are you going to start being unfaithful to Paul? We're in Beaufort country here, you know, high fences and low morals.'

'Basil,' snapped Monica. 'Do stop holding up the queue. And you haven't met Freddie Jones, our electronic whizz kid have you, Maud?'

'Oh my goodness, you are smashing,' said Freddie in wonder. 'I 'ear Rupert's going to provide your 'usband with an 'orse.'

Maud felt marvellous. It was such a long time since she'd been admired by so many attractive men, so much more macho than all those wimps in London, and for once people were paying more attention to her than Declan. This dress always worked.

'Come along, Mrs O'Hara,' said Rupert, who, while Maud was busy fascinating, had loaded up two plates, acquired a bottle of white and two glasses, and put them on a tray. 'D'you want to be indoors or out?'

'Indoors,' said Maud joyfully. 'I freckle so easily.'

Rupert found them a window seat in the conservatory.

'Monica's done this rather well,' he said, looking round. 'I gather it's cost Corinium even more than your husband's first week's salary. You want to avoid this house in winter; it's the sort of place eskimos send their children as punishment.'

On cue, Simon Harris's two hyperactive monsters roared past, sending an aspidistra flying. Ten seconds later they were followed by Simon Harris, with Coronation chicken all over his beard. The baby in the sling was bawling its head off.

'Did they go this way?' asked Simon frantically.

There was a crash from the drawing-room.

'I'm afraid so,' said Rupert.

Maud wrinkled her nose as he rushed out.

'That baby needs changing.'

Rupert laughed. 'All his children do. I'd take the lot back to Harrods if I was him.'

133

Rushing almost as fast in the opposite direction came Paul Stratton searching for Sarah, who was sitting on a wall giggling with Bas.

'Paul's jeans appear to be castrating him even more than his new wife,' said Rupert, forking up chicken at great speed. 'If he bends over, his eyes will pop out.'

Maud admired the length of Rupert's pale-brown corduroyed thighs. After four large glasses of wine, she suddenly had an irresistible urge to touch one of them.

'She's beautiful, his wife,' said Maud.

'She's a tramp,' said Rupert, 'and Paul's living in Cloud Cuckold Land.'

'What's Bas like?' asked Maud, putting her chicken down on the floor untouched.

'Divine,' said Rupert. 'One of my best mates. Runs a phenomenally successful wine bar, dabbles in property, hunts four days a week in winter, plays polo all summer, and screws all the prettiest girls in four counties. Can't be bad.'

'He doesn't look like Tony,' said Maud.

'They had different fathers. After twenty-three years of utter fidelity to Lord Pop-Pop, Tony's mother fell for an Argentinian polo player. The result to everyone's amazement was Bas. Hence the name of the wine bar – the Bar Sinister.'

Maud laughed. Many men had told her that her laugh was beautiful – low, musical, joyous.

'Tell me about your children,' said Rupert, who'd finished his chicken.

'I've got a son, Patrick.'

'I'm not interested in him.'

'And a daughter of just eighteen.' Seeing Rupert's eyes gleam, Maud added hastily, 'But she's shy and retiring; doesn't go out much. And one of fourteen, who's madly in love with you; she's kept her binoculars trained on your house ever since we arrived.'

'That's nice. They're adorable at that age.'

'She's got a brace on her teeth, and going through a very plain stage,' said Maud even more hastily. 'Tell me about Freddie Jones.'

134

'He's a saint.'

'Because he buys your horses?'

'Not entirely. I've offered Declan a horse if ever he wants a day's hunting.'

'Declan rides very well,' said Maud. 'He grew up on a farm. Who's that little woman who's bending his ear at the moment, who keeps making silly faces? He looks as though he needs rescuing.'

Rupert glanced round. 'Not by me, he doesn't. That's Freddie's wife, Valerie, the Lady of the Mannerism; won't rest till she's Queen of England. Freddie unfortunately thinks she is already. Keeping down with the Joneses is an eternal problem round here.'

'You're very black and white, aren't you?' said Maud, noticing his long fingers and wishing they were unbuttoning her silk dress.

'I like people or I don't.'

Looking up, Maud gave Rupert the benefit of her most bewitching smile. The great expanse of white eyeball and the beautiful teeth (unfairly even and white after so few visits to the dentist) really did light up her face. At the same time her hair escaped from its jewelled comb and cascaded down her back.

'I hope you like me,' she murmured.

'I don't know yet,' said Rupert slowly, looking at her mouth and then her breasts. 'I like your husband very much, but you're certainly too disturbing to be living across the valley.'

Glancing through the conservatory window at Maud's pale, rapt face, Declan thought she looked far more exotic than any of Monica's orchids and felt a sick churning jealousy. Rupert had his back turned. Maud was weaving her spells again.

'*You need but lift a pearl-pale hand,*' Declan quoted to himself despairingly, '*And bind up your long hair and sigh, And all men's hearts must burn and beat.*'

Oh Christ, if only he could get away from this party, and spend a few hours on his Yeats book. And in three days he'd got to interview Johnny. He'd done his duty at this party.

He'd talked to the appallingly pompous Paul Stratton, and asked Simon Harris about his wife, and answered questions from fearful bone-headed locals about the famous people he'd interviewed, and listened to at least three women who had daughters reading English at University, who wanted to go into television, and now he was trapped by this monstrous dwarf.

'It's so wonderful to be able to stand at the bottom of one's drive,' said Valerie Jones, 'and not be able to see one's house.'

She was wearing a cricket sweater and white flannels, and rabbited relentlessly on like an obnoxious player who wouldn't stop bowling when the umpire said Over.

'We couldn't be happier with Green Lawns,' she went on smugly. 'We looked at The Priory, you know. It was on the market for ages, but it's awfully cold, and I really couldn't live in a property that didn't get sun until the evening. I must have sunshine.'

She held her silly face up to the sun. Declan longed to clout a six into it. He could see Maud was running her hand through her hair now, shaking it out. Her body was arched towards Rupert. Unnoticed by either of them, the fatter of Monica's labradors was busy gobbling up Maud's chicken.

'Even Freddie was nervous about meetin' you,' Valerie was saying. 'Ay said, don't be silly, Fred-Fred. Famous folk are just like everyone else. Most of them are on drugs, and very lonely, because all their friends have deserted them.'

'I wish some of ours would desert us,' said Declan grimly. 'That's why we moved to the country.'

In the hall Tony was throwing out Simon Harris. The elder monster had just smashed a Ming bowl.

'Was it very old?' stammered Simon, white-lipped.

'Only just over six hundred years,' hissed Tony. 'Out, OUT.'

'I'll pay for it.'

'It would take you two years' salary, which I don't think you'd like from the way you're always whining about money.

Now, bugger off, before those little bastards break the whole place up.'

'I must go,' said Rupert.

'Oh,' said Maud, put out. She wanted the afternoon to go on for ever. It was as though the sun had gone in.

'I've got to pick up my children from my ex.'

'How old are they?'

'Eight and ten.'

'You must bring them over to see us. Taggie, my daughter, dotes on children. She'd keep them out of our hair. Has your ex-wife married again?'

'Yes,' said Rupert getting to his feet, 'to my old *chef d'équipe*, Malise Gordon. He used to manage the British team when I was show jumping. Bit of a tartar, so I feel their twin rays of disapproval if I roll up late.'

At that moment Freddie Jones rolled up with two over-loaded plates of Pavlova.

''ullo my darlings; brought you some sweet.'

'Not for me, I'm off,' said Rupert.

'How's my horse getting on?' said Freddie.

'Bloody well. I think we'll run him in a two-mile chase at Cheltenham. He's ready for it.'

They were interrupted by frantic tapping on the window pane. Valerie Jones was glaring in: No dessert, Fred-Fred, she mouthed.

Lizzie Vereker took Valerie's place beside Declan: 'D'you need rescuing?'

'I did,' said Declan. 'I don't any more. She nails your feet to the floor, but I'm trained to cut across wafflers.' He shook his head. 'How's the book going?'

'Backwards,' said Lizzie. 'Are you nervous about your first programme?'

'Yes. I shouldn't be allowed out before a series starts. I get so wound up, I can't talk to anyone.'

'Good luck with Johnny,' said Rupert, pausing on his way out.

'Come and have dinner with us after the programme,' said Declan.

'Can't. I'm off to Ireland. I know we're both hellishly pushed, but let's get together soon. I'll come and look at your wood. 'Bye, darling.' He gave Lizzie a kiss.

As he crossed the deserted hall Sarah Stratton came out of the downstairs loo, reeking of Anaïs Anaïs. Glancing back towards the garden, Rupert saw that James was nose to nose with Paul Stratton, each mistakenly assuming he was furthering his own career.

'Come and feed the fish,' said Rupert, taking Sarah's hand.

He led her down a grassy ride, flanked on either side by yew hedges, to the fish pond. Stuffed to bursting by Simon Harris's monsters, the carp didn't even bother to ruffle the surface of the water lilies.

'Any repercussions?' asked Rupert.

Sarah shook her head. 'It seems funny, belting away from your tennis court with a pink dress over my head. The entire Gloucestershire fire brigade will recognize my bush, but not my face.'

Rupert grinned, and pulled her inside the thick curtain of a weeping ash. After he'd kissed her, he said: 'When are we going to finish the set?'

'Very soon, please.'

Her smooth golden face was green in the gloom; she looked like a water nymph.

'How was Maud O'Hara?' she asked.

'Seemed pretty unmoored to me,' said Rupert.

'Looks as though she'd like to tie herself to you.'

'Were you jealous?'

Sarah nodded.

'Pity your husband's summer recess coincides with mine.'

'He's never away,' moaned Sarah, as Rupert's fingers moved between her legs. 'Why don't we nip into the gazebo?'

'Got to pick up the children. I'm late already.'

'When am I going to see you?' gasped Sarah, as Rupert's other hand slid down underneath her pants at the back.

'Come to Ireland with me. I'm leaving on Wednesday afternoon.'

'I can't. My ghastly step-children are coming for a couple

138

of weeks on a trial visit. I know who it's going to be a trial to as well. Paul's going to Gatwick on Tuesday to meet them.'

'That'll give us at least five hours. Ring me at home the minute he leaves.'

'Hulloo,' called a male voice.

Frantically straightening her dress, Sarah shot out through the ash tree curtain and bent once more over the fish pond to hide her flaming face.

Wiping off her pale-pink lipstick, Rupert followed in a more leisurely fashion.

'Sarah and I were talking about horses,' he told an apoplectic Paul. 'If you're going to fork out for a groom, feed and grazing for two hunters, you're talking about at least fifteen thousand a year. Better if Sarah kept something at my yard.'

'We'll discuss it in our own time, thank you,' spluttered Paul. 'We must go, Sarah.'

Back in the conservatory, Maud was being heavily chatted up by Bas.

'Shove off, Bas,' Monica told him. 'Declan wants to go and I want two minutes with Maud.'

'I'll come and see you,' said Bas, blowing Maud a kiss.

He's very attractive, thought Maud dreamily, but not in Rupert's class.

'I'm sure you're a joiner,' said Monica, who was now busily dead-heading a pale-blue plumbago growing up a whitewashed trellis.

'No,' said Maud, 'I'm an actress.'

Very firmly, but charmingly, she managed to resist all Monica's urging that she should get herself involved in any kind of charity work.

'The children come first,' said Maud simply.

'But two of them are away,' protested Monica, 'and Taggie's eighteen.'

'But still dyslexic,' sighed Maud. 'She needs her mother, and of course Declan needs his wife.'

'But you must do something for charity,' persisted Monica.

'It's such a good way of meeting new people, and it's awfully easy to get bored in the country.'

'I never get bored,' lied Maud. 'There's so much to do to the house. I can't pass a traffic light at the moment without wondering whether yellow would go with red in one of the children's bedrooms.'

Driving home, Maud put a hand on Declan's thigh, edging it upwards. Pixillated by Rupert's interest, and Bas's extravagant compliments, hazy with drink, she felt wildly desirable and alive again.

'Let's go straight to bed.'

'What about Taggie?' said Declan.

'Say we're both tired.'

Declan curled a hand into the front of her black dress.

'They all wanted you.'

'Did you like that?' whispered Maud.

'I know how hard I've got to fight to keep you,' he said harshly and felt her nipples hardening.

Back in their bedroom at The Priory, he undressed her slowly down to her suspender belt and stockings, so black against the soft white skin.

'When did you get those bruises?' she said sharply, as he took off his shirt.

'This morning. The focking mowing machine kept stopping and I didn't.'

RIVALS

12

Gertrude, the mongrel, was walked off her feet in the next three days. When Maud wasn't drifting up and down the valley in a new lilac T-shirt and matching flowing skirt, hoping to bump into Rupert, Declan was striding through the woods, trying to work out what questions he would ask Johnny Friedlander and driving Cameron Cook crackers because he was never in when she wanted to talk to him.

Cameron's patience was further taxed by her PA getting chicken-pox, and having to be replaced by Daysee Butler, easily the prettiest girl working at Corinium but also the stupidest.

'Why d'you spell Daisy that ludicrous way?' snarled Cameron.

'Because it shows up more on credits,' said Daysee simply.

Like all PAs that autumn, Daysee wandered round clutching a clipboard and a stopwatch, wearing loose trousers tucked into sawn-off suede boots, and jerseys with pictures knitted on the front.

'It's just like the Tit Gallery with all these pictures floating past,' grumbled Charles Fairburn.

Programme day dawned at The Priory with Declan roaring round the house.

'Whatever's the matter?' asked Taggie in alarm.

'I have absolutely no socks. No, don't tell me. I've looked

141

behind the tank in the hot cupboard, and in all my drawers, and in the dirty clothes basket. Utterly bloody Patrick and utterly bloody Caitlin swiped all my socks when they went back, so I have none to wear.'

'I'll drive into Cotchester and get you some,' said Taggie soothingly.

'Indeed you will not,' said Declan. 'I'm driving into Cotchester, and I'm buying thirty pairs of socks in such a disgossting colour that none of you will ever wish to pinch them again.'

He was very tired. He hadn't slept, panicking Johnny might roll up stoned or not at all. And yesterday he and Cameron had been closeted together for twelve hours in the edit suite, putting together the introductory package, rowing constantly over what clips and stills they should use. Daysee Butler's inanities hadn't helped either. Nor had Declan's dismissing as pretentious crap an alternative script Cameron pretended one of the researchers had written, but which she in fact had toiled over all weekend. She couldn't run to Tony, who was in an all-day meeting in London, but got her revenge while Declan was recording his own beautifully lyrical script, by making him do bits over and over again because of imagined mispronunciations or technical faults or bangings outside. They parted at the end of the day not friends.

Having bought his socks, Declan arrived at the studios around five. A game show was underway in Studio 2; the Floor Manager was flapping his hands above his head like a demented seal as a sign to the audience to applaud. *Midsummer Night's Dream* had ground to a halt in Studio 1, because Cameron, dissatisfied with the rushes, had tried to impose an 'out-of-house lighting cameraperson' on the crew, who had promptly downed tools. The Rude Mechanicals, with no prospect of a line all day, were getting pissed in the bar.

Deferential, glad-to-be-of-use, Deirdre Kilpatrick, the researcher on 'Cotswold Round-Up', as dingy as Daysee Butler was radiant, was taking a famous romantic novelist to tea before being interviewed by James Vereker.

'James will ask you your idea of the perfect romantic hero, Ashley,' Deirdre was saying earnestly. 'And it'd be very nice if you could say: "You are, James", which would bring James in.'

'I only go on TV because my agent says it sells books,' said the romantic novelist. 'Oooh, isn't that Declan O'Hara? Now, he *is* the perfect romantic hero.'

Declan slid into his dressing-room and locked the door. A pile of good luck cards and telexes awaited him. He was particularly touched by one from his old department at the BBC saying, 'Sock it to them.'

'Da-glo yellow sock it to them,' said Declan, chucking thirty pairs of socks in luminous cat-sick yellow on the bed.

There was a knock on the door. It was Wardrobe.

'D'you want anything ironed?'

Declan peered gloomily in the mirror: 'Only my face.'

He gave her his suit, light grey and very lightweight, as he was going to be under the hot lights for an hour. She hung up his shirt and tie, then squealed with horror at the yellow socks.

'You can't wear those.'

'They won't show,' said Declan.

In Studio 3 two technicians were sitting in Declan's and Johnny's chairs, while the crew sorted out lighting and camera angles. Crispin, the set designer, whisked about in a lavender flying-suit. The set was exactly as Declan had wanted, except the Charles Rennie Mackintosh chairs had been replaced by wooden Celtic ones, with the conic back of Declan's rising a foot above his head like a wizard's chair: a symbol of authority and magic.

As a gesture of defiance, on the steel-blue tables which rose like mushrooms at the side of each rostrum, Crispin, the designer, had placed blue-and-red-striped glasses and carafes.

'I want plain glasses,' snapped Declan.

'Oh, they're so dreary.' Crispin pouted.

'I want them – and get rid of those focking flowers.'

'Cameron ordered them specially.'

Declan picked up the bouquet threateningly.

'Are you trying to bury me?'

'All right, no flowers,' said Crispin sulkily.

At six-thirty there was a very scratchy run-through.

'Can't you *ad lib* us through your line of questioning?' asked Cameron.

'No.'

'You must know your first question.'

'Depends on his mood.'

'May be looped, you mean. Your bloody fault, asking a junkie on the first programme.'

Declan went off and shook in the men's lavatory for half an hour. When he returned to the studio the crew were lining up their four cameras before the meal break.

'Have you heard the latest Irish joke?' the Senior Cameraman was saying. 'There was this Paddy who went into a chemist for his heroin fix.'

The crew gathered round, grinning at the prospect of more Hibernian idiocy. Halfway though the story the Senior Cameraman realized he'd lost his audience. Next moment, he was grabbed by the scruff of the neck.

'You may be the best focking cameraman in ITV,' roared Declan, 'but you'll not work on my programme if you're going to tell Irish jokes. You don't dare tell jokes about Jews and blacks or cripples any more; why pick on the poor bloody Irish?'

With a final shake, which threw the Senior Cameraman half-way across the studio, he stalked out.

'I'll report you to my shop steward,' screamed the Senior Cameraman rubbing his neck.

In the bar they were gathering to catch a glimpse of Johnny Friedlander and to support Declan by watching his programme. There was still a latent *esprit de corps* at Corinium. Someone had deliberately changed the colour on the bar television, so James Vereker's face looked like a Jaffa orange.

'What's your idea of a romantic hero, Ashley?' he was saying.

'You are, James.'

'That's very sweet of you, Ashley.' James smoothed his streaks. 'What's romantic about me?'

'Well, you're so caring, James, and you've got an inner strength like Leslie Howard.'

'Turn the sound down,' screamed a Rude Mechanical, hurling a handful of peanuts at the screen.

'Anyone seen Declan?' asked Daysee Butler, putting her top half, which had Goofy appropriately knitted on the bosom, round the door to a chorus of wolf-whistles. It was getting perilously close to transmission time.

'In the bog,' said Charles Fairburn. 'I'm surprised he doesn't move his dressing-room in there. Can't even keep down a brandy.'

'Declan,' shouted the Senior Cameraman. 'You can stop worrying. Daysee's too embarrassed to come in 'ere, but Johnny Friedlander's people have just phoned to say they've come off the M4 and they'll be wiv us in twenty minutes.'

'Thank Christ for that,' groaned Declan.

'And 'ere's a letter for you.' A piece of writing paper appeared under the door.

'*Dear Declan*, it said. '*We're sorry we was telling Paddy jokes. We won't any more, you was quite right.*'

All the crew had signed it.

'*PS. Have you heard the one about the Englishman, the Welshman and the Scotsman?*'

Declan grinned, then he glanced at his watch, and nearly threw up again. He'd be on air in less than an hour.

Johnny Friedlander arrived in a black limo which seemed to stretch the length of Cotchester High Street. He was accompanied by a publicity girl and four security men. In a second limo were four lawyers. Looking at the bulges in the security men's suits, the press allowed Johnny to be smuggled into the building without too much hassle.

From the start Johnny's visit to Corinium went off with a bang. Taking one look at the ravishing Daysee, he pulled her into his dressing-room and locked the door. The four security men stood outside with folded arms.

'Who's she?' asked Johnny's publicity girl in horror.

'A piece of ass,' said one of the security men.

'Are you quite sure she's not a reporter?'

'Couldn't report a burglary,' said Charles Fairburn, whisking past, thoroughly overexcited by so much security muscle.

In his dressing-room a pretty make-up girl with sheep in a field knitted on her bosom fussed around Declan. He wished he could lie down in her field and go to sleep.

'At least let me paint out the dark rings and give you a bit of base; you're so pale,' she murmured. 'And we'll have to do something about the beard area. You really ought to shave.'

'I'm shaking so much I'll cut myself.'

'I'll shave you.'

Next moment Cameron stormed in.

'Johnny Friedlander's barricaded himself into his dressing-room with Daysee.'

'Best place for him,' said Declan. 'At least if he's having a bang, he's not snorting coke.'

In his fifth-floor office, Tony Baddingham, even more nervous than Declan, was dispensing Krug to his special guests, who included several big advertising clients, the Mayor and Mayoress of Cotchester and Freddie and Valerie Jones. By a ghastly mischance, they had also been joined by the Reverend Fergus Penney, a former Prebendary of the Church of England. A fearful old prude constantly inveighing against sex on television, he had recently become a member of the IBA board, and was currently on a tour of the Independent television companies. Now, primly sipping Perrier, he kept peering across the corridor to the board room, where the press, assembled to watch Declan's first programme on a big screen pulled down against the far wall, were getting drunk and stuffing their faces with quiche and chicken drumsticks.

In a corner of the board room, as disapproving as the ex-Prebendary, sat Johnny's four lawyers, also sipping Perrier and fingering calculators at the prospect of litigation.

'Why the fuck d'you ask so many press?' Tony hissed to

Cyril Peacock, who knew he'd have been equally roasted if only a handful had turned up.

Nor did the fact that Tony had been entirely responsible for hiring Declan stop him now blaming everything on Simon Harris. 'You ought to be able to control Declan, Simon. That's what you're here for. He hasn't even given Cameron a running order.'

'All she needs now is a prayer sheet,' said Charles.

'Declan's my favourite telly star,' the Lady Mayoress was saying excitedly to Valerie. 'I can't wait to meet him later.'

'Oh, we know him quaite well,' said Valerie Jones, on the strength of last Sunday's lunch party. 'He always singles me out – because Ay tell him the truth. Ay think famous folk get so bored with flattery.'

A curious tension was building up through the building.

'Declan's just cut me dead,' complained James Vereker, going into the bar. 'Awfully uncool to get so uptight.'

Daysee came out of Johnny's dressing-room, looking as though she'd found the Holy Grail.

'He's having a quick shower,' she said. 'Then he wants Make-up.'

'Well, send in a boot,' said Cameron. 'We don't want him banging her as well.'

It was five minutes to blast off. The four security men had taken up their positions in the studio. In the control room the production team sat at a desk like a vast dashboard, gazing at two rows of monitor screens. On four of the monitors which came direct from the studio, Cameron could see Johnny Friedlander's carved, beautiful, degenerate face with its hollow cheek bones and Californian suntan. His fair hair was the red-gold of willows in winter, the irises of the deep-set Oxford-blue eyes were almost as dark as the pupils. Thin almost to the point of emaciation, he lounged easily in his three-thousand-dollar suit, with the sleeves rolled up to the elbow. But the air of relaxation was false.

'Why the hell did I agree to do this shit?' he drawled.

'I'm sorry,' said Declan, meaning it.

147

'Aw that's OK. I just don't feel I've got proper lines when they're my own. Rupert called, by the way. He said: "You can trust this guy, he's one of us."'

In his earpiece Declan could hear Daysee saying: 'The pink strapless is more dressy, but my holiday tan's nearly gone.'

'Can we have some level?' asked the Floor Manager. 'What did you have for breakfast, Johnny?'

Johnny laughed. 'You want to get me arrested?'

On Cameron's left, Daysee was checking different stop-watches. The moment they were on air she would forget pink strapless dresses and become as cool as a computer, timing the programme to the second.

On the right sat the vision-mixer in a red T-shirt, hands at the ready over regiments of square buttons, lit up like spangles, ready to punch up the correct picture when Cameron demanded it.

'Good luck, everyone,' said Cameron, crossing her fingers. 'Stand by Studio, stand by Opening Titles, stand by Music.'

'One minute to air,' said Daysee, clenching her stop-watch and glaring at the leaping red number of the clock. 'Twenty seconds, ten, five, four, three, two, one and in.'

Schubert's Fifth Symphony started on its jolly jazzed-up course. On the screen a rocket exploded in coloured stars above a night-lit Cotchester, and then cascaded down to form the word Declan. A great cheer went up in the bar. Tony puffed on his cigar.

'I want another gin and tonic,' said an already drunk reporter from the *Mail on Sunday*.

'Shut up,' said Johnny's four lawyers in unison, who were listening to the opening package like hawks, in the hope of finding something defamatory.

As Daysee cued Declan in, as a concession to Cameron, he swung round to talk directly to camera. For a moment his throat went dry. He's forgotten his first question, thought Cameron in anguish. Then he said: 'I welcome my first guest in this new series with the greatest humility. He is simply the best actor to come out of America in the last fifteen years.

But this is the first interview you've ever given.' He turned to Johnny, 'Why?'

'I hate publicity,' drawled Johnny. 'If all journalists were exterminated life would be just fine.'

Up in the board room a howl of protest went up from the press, who stopped filling up their drinks and started listening.

'The press detest success,' went on Johnny, 'and they screw up your sex life. However much you try not to get fed up, it pisses you off when you read lies that your latest girlfriend's been two-timing you with some Greek masseur. Every day, my exes are offered millions to tell all.'

'How d'you cope?' said Declan.

'I don't read press cuttings any more. I just weigh them; if they're light I start worrying.'

'By deliberately avoiding publicity, aren't you actually courting it?'

'Don't give me that crap,' said Johnny lightly.

And they were off, sparring, laughing, fooling about almost like two old friends discussing someone they knew and liked, but frequently disapproved of. Johnny was being absolutely outrageous now about his exploits with his leading ladies, but he drawled out his answers so honestly and engagingly that the press quickly forgave him for his earlier sniping. The lawyers were clutching their heads, but they were laughing and even the ex-Prebendary was looking moderately benign.

It's going to be all right, thought Cameron. 'Ten minutes to the commercial break, Declan,' she said into his earpiece. Following a tip-off from Rupert, Declan then said, 'And you're about to face your greatest acting challenge . . .'

Johnny raised an eyebrow.

' . . . playing Hamlet at Stratford next year,' said Declan.

Johnny looked startled. Upstairs the board room was in an uproar.

'No one knows that,' screamed the lawyers. 'The goddammed contracts haven't been fucking exchanged yet.'

'I figured I ought to have a crack at it,' said Johnny. 'Women don't get taken seriously as actresses these days until they allow themselves to look ugly and sweaty and get raped on screen. Guys still have to play Hamlet. And I like the guy. I mean he had a stepfather problem. I don't figure Claudius bumped off Hamlet's father at all. That was Hamlet's fantasy; he hated his stepfather. I hated mine.'

'Why?'

'He married my mother. I was jealous. He was a bass-tard.'

'Why?'

Tony drew on his cigar; the lawyers fingered their calculators; even the press were still.

Declan paused, waiting unbearably long. On his pale-blue island in a sea of dark blue, Johnny suddenly seemed terribly vulnerable.

'He groped my baby sister the whole time,' he said. 'So I quit. My stepfather called to say my mother was dying of cancer. I didn't believe him, so I didn't go home.' Johnny put his head in his hands. 'But she did die the next day. She topped herself. I ain't never told no one that.'

'Why did she commit suicide?' asked Declan quietly.

Johnny looked up, his eyes cavernous. 'She was jealous because my stepfather preferred my sister. Christ, what a mess.'

'Out of order,' screamed the lawyers apoplectically. The Prebendary was looking equally outraged.

'Are you worried, being American, you won't be taken seriously as Hamlet?' asked Declan.

Relieved at a change of subject, Johnny fast recovered his poise. 'He was a Dane, for Christ's sake. He didn't speak like Leslie Howard.'

In the bar James and the lady novelist exchanged caring smiles.

'It's the acting that matters,' went on Johnny. 'I could play him like JR.'

He launched into 'To be or not to be' in broad Texan; it was so funny, the cameramen could hardly keep their cameras still. Halfway through Johnny slid into Prince Charles's accent, which was even funnier; then for the last ten lines, he played it straight and was so good that Declan felt his hair standing on end. At the end, Johnny said, 'That'll be five hundred pounds, please,' in a camp Cockney accent.

'You'll be taken seriously,' said Declan.

'I can switch moods, that's why I'm a good movie actor,' said Johnny. 'But to be on stage four hours, that's something else. But then I've always lived dangerously. . . .'

Declan took a deep breath. 'Is that why you went back to America to face trial?'

'That is definitely out of order,' screamed the lawyers, positively orgasmic now at the prospect of lucrative litigation. 'We agreed he wouldn't talk about that.'

'I went back because I missed the States,' said Johnny. He still appeared relaxed, but his knuckles were white points as he gripped the arms of his chair.

'Have you always fancied very young girls?'

'Sure, if they're pretty. Most men do. This one was very pretty.'

'Did you know she was only fourteen?'

The Prebendary was about to have a seizure.

'I think you ought to have a word with the control room,' he spluttered to Tony.

'Sure, I guess it was wrong, but she was so sweet, I really cared for her. I know I screwed her, but I don't figure I screwed her up. She's very happily married with a baby now.'

'How d'you get on in prison?'

Johnny's eyes were cavernous again. 'It's not a very nice place to be. But if you're a famous movie star you're trapped anyway; going to gaol is just exchanging one kind of captivity for another. And I learnt a lot. I could burglarize your place tonight, while you were in it. And I'm shit-hot at insider trading.'

Declan stretched out his legs.

'Extraordinary coloured socks,' said the girl from the *Mail on Sunday*, pouring herself another gin.

'Did they give you a hard time inside?' Declan asked Johnny.

151

'Not really. One guy who couldn't count – he thought the girl was four not fourteen – worked me over a bit, but I made some good friends.'

'Have you never fancied older women?'

Johnny thought for a minute, then he smiled wickedly.

'No, they have droopy asses. Droopy asses are so cold in bed.'

The telephone rang in the control room.

'For Christ's sake, get him off sex,' yelled Tony. 'The lawyers are going to take us to the cleaners, and Fergus Penney's having a coronary. We'll lose the franchise if you don't shut him up.'

'It's a fucking good programme,' said Cameron, and hung up.

Then she took the telephone off the hook.

'Five seconds to the cue dot,' intoned Daysee. 'Five, four, three, two, one.' She flicked the cue switch to warn people all over the network to get ready in sixty seconds to roll in the commercials, which were, after all, the life-blood of the station.

As the End-of-Part-One caption came up, Johnny shot out of the studio, saying he must have a leak.

'You stay here,' Cameron screamed at Daysee. 'Well done, Declan.'

Johnny may not have been able to have Daysee in the break, but he had certainly taken something. In the second half he was even more outrageous, but utterly relaxed. Declan, in his wizard's chair, had only to prompt him here, jog his memory there, and curb his amazing honesty when he looked like going over the top.

The floor manager thrust the back of his hand with splayed-out fingers towards Declan to indicate five minutes more.

'I was on location in Texas,' Johnny was saying as he waved his cigarette around. 'Staying in my hotel was this glorious German girl. She gave me her room number, told me to come up in half an hour. I must have been looped. When I hotfooted upstairs later and banged on her door, someone let me in, but the room was in darkness.'

'Oh Christ,' thought Cameron. 'What's he going to say?'

'Well, I undressed and got into bed, and I reached out, and I felt a boob, like a wrinkled fig. I figured this was odd. Then moving down I found I could play Grieg's Piano Concerto on her ribs, so I groped for the light, and there were her teeth grinning at me from a glass beside the bed. I don't know which of us screamed the louder. I mean, she must have been ninety, if she was a day. I mean, under-age girls are one thing, gerontophilia's quite another.' Johnny smiled helplessly.

'Disgusting,' spluttered the Prebendary and Valerie Jones in unison.

'Anyway I shot down the bed as the security men broke in, and the old sweetie didn't give me away. I sent her a whole roomful of flowers the next morning, and,' Johnny paused wickedly – Oh Christ, thought Tony, as the Prebendary turned even more purple – 'she still sends me Christmas cards.'

The floor manager was waving a couple of fingers at Declan for two minutes more.

'Now you're going to play Hamlet, have you got any ambitions left?'

'I guess I'd like to make a happy marriage,' said Johnny seriously. 'I went to see my grandma the other day, she's been married sixty years. Now that is achievement – like building a cathedral brick by brick, a real life's work. I guess I won't achieve it, but that's what I'd like.'

'Aaaaah,' said Daysee Butler, so moved that she flicked the cue switch too early.

Now Declan was smiling and thanking Johnny for coming on the programme.

On came Schubert, jauntier than ever, up rolled the credits, but alas because of Daysee's early cue, just as Cameron Cook's name was about to come up at the end, the screen went royal blue and the Corinium television logo appeared, with the little red ram seeming to hold his horned head

153

even higher than usual. A second later they were into the commercials.

Another great roar went up in the bar and the board room. Even the crew broke into rare spontaneous applause and crowded round Declan and Johnny. Upstairs, the press raced for the telephones.

'I must talk to Declan about those yellow socks. I'm definitely going to do a fashion piece,' said the girl from the *Mail on Sunday*, pouring herself another gin.

'Great,' said Freddie Jones, 'really great. Congratulations.'

The lawyers came up and pumped Tony's hand. 'We were shitting bricks at the end, but Johnny came across great, a really nice guy, an attractive guy.'

Valerie Jones was nose to nose with the Prebendary.

'Disgraceful,' she was saying. 'My daughter Sharon is only fourteen and when one thinks . . .'

'Screw the Prebendary,' said Tony five minutes later, as he came off the telephone in his office. 'Lady Gosling thought it was terrific.'

'It was,' said Miss Madden. 'Declan wants a word.'

'That was a terrific programme. Well done,' said Tony, picking up another telephone.

'Thanks,' said Declan. 'D'you mind if we don't come up? Johnny doesn't want to see anyone. He's reached a stage when he might go right over the top. I'm taking him home for a quiet dinner.'

Through the door Tony could see the press and even the lawyers getting drunk. The Prebendary was still nose to nose with Valerie. Corinium had walked a tightrope that evening and got away with it.

'Understood,' said Tony. 'I'll talk to you tomorrow, but congratulations anyway.'

As Cameron went into the board room, everyone cheered. Tony even forgot himself sufficiently to march over and hug her. His eyes were blazing with triumph.

'Lady Gosling rang to say how much she liked it. She sent special congratulations to you.'

But Cameron felt utterly drained and despairing. Not just

because of her lost credit, but because she had produced and directed a programme in which she'd had no part. It had lived and fortunately not died with Declan.

13

Declan's first programmes for Corinium were a colossal success. The press agreed that Johnny Friedlander was the best interview he'd ever done, that the ones with Jackie Kennedy and the Princess were even better, and the ones with Mick Jagger and Harold Pinter even better than that. The programmes sold everywhere abroad, and there was even talk at the Network meetings of moving the series to seven-thirty on Thursday in an attempt to knock out 'EastEnders'. Declan sweat shirts, mugs and posters were selling faster than bikinis in June and Schubert must have looked down from heaven and been surprised but delighted to see his Fifth Symphony galloping up the charts.

Once the first programme was over Declan was much less aggressive and uptight and even drank in the bar with the crew, but he was no less intransigent about wanting his own way. Cameron smouldered and bided her time. Tony was besotted with Declan at the moment, but, knowing the nature of the two men, Cameron realized it wouldn't last.

Meanwhile, although the flood of resignations at Corinium had been arrested by Declan's arrival, Simon Harris was getting nearer his nervous breakdown and the staff were muttering even more mutinously into their glasses of Sancerre at the Bar Sinister that Cameron was about to be put on the Board.

But, to stop Cameron getting smug, Tony, ever the bubblepricker, finally invited the ravishing Sarah Stratton to lunch and arranged for James Vereker to interview her in the 'Behind Every Famous Man' series early in November. Cameron was livid and vented her rage on the rest of the staff.

The same week Sarah was due to be interviewed, Tony summoned Declan to his office.

'How's your cold?' Declan asked Miss Madden as he walked through the outer office.

'Much better,' said Miss Madden, flushing. 'How amazing of you to remember. Better hurry. Cameron's in there already.'

Cameron was lounging menacingly by the window, wearing a black polo neck, black leather trousers and spiky high heels. Declan wondered if she walked all over Tony in bed in them. The room was full of cigar smoke. Tony was drinking a brandy, but didn't offer Declan one.

'Sit down. Congratulations to both of you,' he said briskly. 'I've just heard off the record that we got our highest local rating ever for your interview with the Princess.'

Declan sank into one of the low squashy sofas, which, with his long legs, were desperately uncomfortable unless one was lying down.

Tony leant back in his chair: 'Cameron and I have decided it's time you spread your wings, Declan.'

Declan looked wary.

'We'd like you to interview Maurice Wooton this week.'

'He's not big enough,' said Declan flatly. Lord Wooton was a high-profile Cotchester property developer but of little interest nationally. 'And I'm already doing Graham Greene this week.'

'That's OK,' said Cameron. 'Do Lord Wooton as a special after the ten o'clock news on Friday night.'

'Why can't James do him?'

'James is already doing Sarah Stratton in the Famous Man slot on "Cotswold Round-Up". Besides, we want you.'

'I'm only contracted to do one interview a week.'

'Don't worry,' said Tony. 'We'll pay you extra. We just want you to get really involved in the station.'

157

'I don't have the time.' It was so hot in Tony's office that Declan could feel his shirt drenched in sweat.

'That's what researchers are for,' said Cameron, as though she was explaining to a two-year-old. 'Deirdre Kilpatrick's been working on Maurice Wooton all week. She's come up with some terrific stuff. After all,' she added tauntingly, 'a guy as great as Henry Moore wasn't too proud to employ studio assistants.'

Like a dog struggling out of a weed-clogged pond, Declan heaved himself up from the squashy sofa. 'I do my own research,' he said coldly, and walked out.

Hooray, thought Cameron, it's begun to work.

On Thursday morning Cameron rang Declan at home. It was his official day off. He'd stayed up until four in the morning reading Graham Greene. Inspired, he was determined to spend the next two days on his Yeats biography, and here was Cameron's horrible rasp ordering him to come into a meeting tomorrow at eleven o'clock.

'So we can kick some ideas around about the line you might take with Maurice Wooton.'

Declan hung up on her. When he hadn't shown up by eleven-thirty the following morning, Cameron rang The Priory in a fury. She got Maud, who said she was sorry but Declan was in bed.

'At this hour? Is he ill?'

'Not at all,' said Maud. 'He's reading.'

'Put him on.'

Declan told Cameron to go and jump in the River Fleet and that he'd no intention of coming in for any meeting. Tony then rang Declan and ordered him to come in that evening and interview Maurice Wooton. Declan, having just received an eighty-thousand-pound tax bill, which he had no way of ever paying unless he went on working at Corinium, said he'd be in later, but wouldn't submit questions beforehand.

He slid into Corinium around two o'clock, when he knew Cameron and Tony would still be at lunch, and went down to the newsroom to talk to Sebastian Burrows, the youngest, brightest and therefore most frustrated of the reporters.

'Deirdre Kilpatrick's been working like mad on your Maurice Wooton interview,' said Seb.

'Deirdre Kill-Programme,' said Declan.

Seb grinned: 'You can say that again. Maurice is emerging as a total sweetie.'

'You got any dirt on him?' asked Declan.

'He's one of Tony's best friends, isn't that enough?'

'Not quite – anything concrete?'

Sebastian's thin face lit up. 'I've got enough to send him down for ten years, but I daren't use it.'

'Give it to me,' said Declan. 'I'm going out.'

On the same Friday, Rupert Campbell-Black, having spent all week in meetings with the FA and the Club Managers trying to thrash out some suitable compromise on football hooliganism, decided he felt like a pit pony who needed a day off, and went hunting with Basil Baddingham.

Scent was very bad, however. It rained all day and the foxes sensibly decided to stay in their earths. Having re-boxed their horses, Rupert and Bas got back to Rupert's dark-blue Aston-Martin to find the windscreen covered with leaves like parking tickets. Removing their drenched red coats and hunting ties, and putting on jerseys, they drove home through the yellow gloom.

'Who shall we do this evening?' said Bas, who was feeling randy.

'No one,' sighed Rupert. 'I've got my red box to go through, and I've got to look in at some fund-raising drinks party.'

'Pity,' said Bas slyly, 'I was going to show you the most amazing girl.'

'That's different,' said Rupert. 'Where does she live?'

'Penscombe Priory.'

Thinking Bas meant Maud, Rupert said, 'Isn't she a bit long in the tooth for you?'

'No, I'm talking about the daughter,' said Bas. 'She's absolutely stunning.'

Back at The Priory, Grace, the housekeeper, who was making ridiculously slow progress sorting out the attic, stumbled on a trunk of Maud's old clothes. Maud, who had just finished her last P. D. James and was suffering from withdrawal symptoms, wandered upstairs and started trying them on. Now she was parading round in a black-and-red-striped mini which fell just below her groin and showed off her still beautiful legs.

'I remember walking down Grafton Street in 1968 in this,' she said, 'and an American clapping his hands over his eyes, and screaming: "Oh my Gard, can they go any higher?" My hair was down like this.' Maud pulled out the combs so it cascaded down her back. 'I was only twenty-four.'

'You don't look a day more than that now. Amizing,' said Grace.

'Oh, I adored this dress too.' Maud tugged a sapphire-blue mini with a pie-frill collar out of the trunk. 'I wore it to Patrick's christening. I wonder if I can still get into it.'

'Fits you like a glove,' said Grace, who was trying on a maxicoat. 'Amizing.'

As Maud admired herself in an ancient full-length mirror propped against the rafters, she heard Gertrude barking. Not displeased with her appearance, she went downstairs, then paused halfway. Below her in the hall, she could see two heads: one very dark, the other gleaming blond. Her heart missed a beat.

'Maud,' yelled Bas, 'are you in?'

'I'm up here,' said Maud with the light behind her.

Bas looked up. 'Caitlin,' he said. 'I thought you'd gone back.'

'It's me.' Maud came slowly down the stairs. 'Grice and I were being silly trying on my old clothes.'

'How old were you when you first wore that?'

'About twenty-one.'

'You look about sixteen today,' said Bas, kissing her.

'Flattery will get you an enormous drink. I assume that's what you've come for. Grice,' Maud yelled up the stairs, 'can you come down and fix some drinks? I'll go and change.'

'Don't,' said Rupert. 'I bet Declan fell in love with you in that dress. I'm quite safe,' he went on, also kissing Maud. 'Some bloody hunt saboteur sprayed me with Anti-Mate this afternoon.'

'Where's Declan?' asked Bas, as they went into the kitchen.

'Ordered in to do an extra programme,' said Maud, getting a bottle of whisky out of the larder.

'My evil brother got the screws on him already?' asked Bas. 'Have you got anything to eat? I'm absolutely starving.'

'There's some chocolate cake and a quiche in the larder,' said Maud, splashing whisky into three glasses. 'Have a look and see what you can find.'

Rupert prowled round the room. There was a huge scrubbed table in the centre of the room, with chairs down either side. Poetry and cookery books crammed the shelves in equal proportions. A rocking-horse towered over Gertrude's basket in the corner. Aengus the cat snored on some newly ironed shirts by the Aga. On the walls were drawings of Maud in *Juno and the Paycock*, and a corkboard covered with recipes and photographs of animals, cut by Taggie out of newspapers. Apart from a television set on a chest of drawers, every other available surface seemed to be littered with letters, bills, colour swatches, photographs waiting to be stuck in, dog and cat worming tablets, biros that didn't work, newspapers and magazines.

'Nice kitchen,' said Rupert.

'It's like the room described by Somerville and Ross when they were packing up before moving,' said Maud. 'Under everything, there's something.'

Valerie Jones, who dropped in half an hour later, didn't think it was a nice kitchen at all. She was shocked to find Maud showing at least six inches of bare thigh, and Rupert and Basil with their long-booted legs up on the table, all getting tanked up on Declan's whisky. Rupert was eating bread and bramble jelly and reading the problem page in *Jackie*. Bas was finishing up the remains of a mackerel mousse with a spoon. Gertrude, eyeing the remains of the quiche and the large chocolate cake, was now sitting drooling on the table on a pile of unironed sheets, which would no doubt go straight back on the beds, thought Valerie with a shudder.

Valerie herself, natty in a ginger tweed suit and a deer-stalker, said she had just been to a Distressed Gentlefolk's Committee Meeting with Lady Baddingham, and, deciding to 'straike while the iron was hot', had looked in to see if Maud had any jumble for the Xmas Bazaar next month.

'Having just moved, you must have lots of old junk to throw out.'

'Only her husband,' said Bas, starting on the quiche.

'Hush,' reproved Maud softly. 'Funnily enough, I've just been trying on all my old clothes. This was the dress I wore at Patrick's christening. The priest gathered up my skirt with the christening robes by mistake and all the congregation were treated to the sight of my red pants.'

Valerie didn't want to hear about Maud's pants. 'Then you must have lots of jumble,' she said.

'I never throw clothes away,' said Maud.

'Well, I've brought you a brochure of our Autumn range,' said Valerie, determined to turn the visit to some advantage.

'Kind,' said Maud, chucking the brochure into the débris on the Welsh dresser. 'Have a drink.'

'Ay'm driving. Have you got anything soft?' said Valerie.

'Not round here, with Maud wearing that dress,' said Rupert, cutting himself a piece of chocolate cake.

'I'll have a tea then,' said Valerie, 'and I'd love a piece of that gâteau, and those bramble preserves look quite delicious.'

'Taggie picked the blackberries down your valley; we ought to give you a pot,' Maud said to Rupert, as she put the kettle on. She felt wildly happy.

At that moment Grace walked in, wearing Maud's red and black mini.

'This is Amizing Grice,' said Maud.

'Amizing,' said Grace, gazing at Rupert in wonder. 'I'm just off to that lecture on glass-blowing at the Women's Institute, Maud,' she went on. 'See you later.'

'I didn't know there was a WI meeting tonight,' said Valerie, perplexed.

'Straight up to the pub,' explained Maud, as the front door banged.

'It's not a very good idea to be on Christian name terms with one's help,' said Valerie reprovingly. 'We don't really do it in Gloucestershire, you know.'

''Bye, Grace! Have a good evening,' yelled Rupert.

Valerie's small mouth tightened. Watching Maud pouring boiling water over a teabag, she hoped the mug was clean.

'This quiche is seriously good,' said Bas. 'And for Christ's sake leave some of that chocolate cake, Rupert.'

'Did Grace make it?' enquired Valerie. Maybe Grace was more of a treasure than she had at first appeared.

'Grace can't cook a thing,' said Maud. 'Taggie made all this. She wants to break into catering and do people's dinner parties.'

'She'd better come and work at the Bar Sinister,' said Bas. 'Darling, I wondered where you'd got to.' He swung his feet off the table and stood up as Taggie came in.

She was very pale, with her hair in a thick black plait down her back, and wearing one of Declan's red shirts above long, long bare legs.

'Hullo,' she said in delight to Bas. Then, embarrassed that he aimed straight at her mouth, turned her head slightly so he ended up kissing her hair. At that moment, over his shoulder, she saw Rupert. She gave a gasp of horror and turned as red as her shirt.

To Valerie's equal horror, Maud removed the teabag from Valerie's tea with her fingers. Then she introduced Taggie to everyone.

Smiling at Valerie, but totally ignoring Rupert, Taggie took a tin of baked beans out of the fridge and started to eat them with a spoon.

'I'm sure we've met before,' said Rupert, puzzled. 'You're not a Young Conservative, are you?' Then, suddenly he twigged and started to laugh. 'I remember now. It was at a tennis party.'

Taggie blushed even deeper.

'Brilliant quiche, stunning mousse, marvellous chocolate cake,' said Bas with his mouth full.

'Oh, it was for Daddy's supper,' began Taggie, distressed, then stopped herself. Sometimes she could murder her mother. She was about to go upstairs when Bas grabbed her hand and, sitting her down beside him, tried to persuade her to work for him at the Bar Sinister.

'It's really kind of you,' mumbled Taggie, 'but I worked in a restaurant for two years. I want to branch out on my own.'

'You can come and cook my breakfast any day of the week,' said Rupert. She looked so different from the angry child who'd screamed at him about his stubble. 'You were quite right,' he added to Basil.

Again Taggie ignored him.

'It's very good of Bas,' said Maud with a slight edge to her voice. 'Most girls would leap at a job like that. I always had to de-emphasize my career for Declan,' she added fretfully.

Taggie, however, was totally thrown. She couldn't take in what Bas was saying. She was only conscious of this horrible monster, who'd haunted her nightmares for weeks, whom she'd last seen oiled, brown-skinned, erect in every sense of the word and as totally unselfconscious of his nakedness as a Zulu chief, and who was now drinking her father's whisky and laughing at her across the table. Out of sheer nervousness, she leapt up and turned on the television.

'Pratt,' yelled Rupert, as James Vereker appeared on the screen.

Over at Corinium Television Sarah Stratton sat in Hospitality going greener (perhaps that was why it was called a green room), and wishing she'd never agreed to go on James's programme.

The appalling Deirdre Kill-Programme (as everyone called her now) had visited her at home earlier in the week and worked out lots of questions that James could ask Sarah to promote discussion and bring in James's caring nature.

Paul, furious that Sarah had been asked on, and not him, went on and on about how her high profile wouldn't help his career at the moment. He was also furious that she'd spent a fortune for the occasion on a new black mohair dress with daisies embroidered on the front and huge padded shoulders, which she was not sure suited her. Thank God Rupert was at some Tory fund-raising bash at the moment, and wouldn't watch the programme. Earlier, James had paid a fleeting visit to Hospitality to say hullo, rather like a famous surgeon in an expensive hospital, popping in before he removes half your intestine.

Ushered into the studio during the commercial break, Sarah was now sitting on the famous pale-pink sofa beside him. Catching sight of herself on the monitor, she wished she hadn't worn the mohair; it was much too hot and the padded shoulders made her look like an American footballer. On rushed the make-up girl to tone down her flushed face.

'Collar up, James,' said Wardrobe.

'I did it deliberately, Tessa,' said James. 'Thought it looked more casual. Remember to look at me, not the camera, Sarah.' She was desperately nervous, which didn't help. Glancing round at the idiot board to find out what question he was supposed to ask her first, he saw chalked in large letters: 'James Vereker can't do his programme without having a bonk first'.

'Turn it over,' hissed James, as a burst of 'Cotswold Round-Up' theme music signified the end of the commercial break.

Sarah, who had also seen the idiot board, screamed with laughter, and it was thus that the viewers had their first glimpse of her.

'Sarah Stratton,' said James, reading from the turned-over board, 'you've been married to Paul Stratton, our member for Cotchester for nearly nine months now. How do you see your role as the wife of an MP, Sarah?'

Sarah straightened her face: 'To support my husband in every possible way,' she said, gazing straight at the camera.

In the O'Haras' kitchen, Rupert turned up the sound.

'Isn't that Lizzie Vereker's husband?' said Maud. 'I like Lizzie.'

165

'She's lovely,' said Rupert. 'If she lost three stone, I'd marry her.'

'James is hell,' said Basil. 'Put him in front of a camera, you can't get him down with a gun.'

'Some viewers may find the following scenes disturbing,' said Rupert. 'Sarah's nervous. Look at the way her eyes are darting and she's licking her lips. Looks bloody good, though.'

Whatever she thought to the contrary, Sarah looked stunning on camera. She was now saying how hard it was falling in love with a married man.

'I put no pressure on Paul to leave his first wife,' she said demurely.

'Bollocks,' howled Bas. 'She carried a chisel round in her bag for years, trying to chip Paul off like a barnacle.'

'But because he did eventually leave her for me,' went on Sarah, 'and *he* made the decision, I'm branded a scarlet woman.'

'With some justification,' said Rupert. 'And her husband is as mean as the grave. It's so hard to get a drink in his house, the PM ought to make him the Minister for Drought. Which is not something anyone could accuse *you* of, Maud darling,' he added, as Maud splashed the last of the whisky into his glass.

Taggie, who was ironing sheets, was as perplexed as Rupert had been earlier. 'I'm sure I've seen her somewhere before,' she muttered, then once again went absolutely scarlet as she realized that Sarah was the beautiful blonde who'd been playing nude tennis with Rupert.

'She's quite excellent at ball play,' said Rupert, reading Taggie's thoughts. 'And *you're* going to burn that sheet.'

Furiously, Taggie went on ironing. Fortunately a diversion was created with Valerie asking how Caitlin was getting on at Upland House.

'It seems more like St Trinian's than Enid Blyton,' said Maud. 'Caitlin says they all smoke like chimneys and have bottles of Malibu under the floorboards. But I had a nice half-term report from her house mistress, saying Caitlin was a dear girl who'd settled in well, but was too easily satisfied.'

'Not something her future husband is going to grumble about,' said Rupert, who was watching Taggie. He liked making her blush.

'Caitlin's like Taggie,' said Maud. 'Watches too much television.'

'Sharon's only allowed to watch occasionally at weekends,' said Valerie smugly. 'When I was young, my sister and I made our own amusements.'

'So did I,' agreed Rupert, 'until Nanny told me it would make me go blind.'

Ignoring him, Valerie thought how much more attractive was James, with his charming boyish smile, than Rupert, who was always leading Freddie astray and making *risqué* remarks.

James, winding up Sarah's interview, asked her if she had any plans for a career.

'You must know – as a very famous man yourself,' Sarah answered admiringly, 'that wives of famous men have to take second place.'

'It is possible to be famous and caring, Sarah,' said James huskily.

'Of course,' said Sarah. 'I'm just saying if you marry someone who's been married before, you're just that little bit more anxious to make the marriage work, to *not* put your own career first – to prove everyone wrong who said it wouldn't last. So you just try harder.'

Taggie was shocked. How *could* Sarah say that, when she was busy having an affair with Rupert? It was only after a few minutes Taggie realized that Valerie was telling her all about the boutique.

'You must pop in some time,' said Valerie. 'I know it's difficult, dressing when you're so tall, but I'm sure I could find something lovely for you.'

'That's really kind,' said Taggie gratefully.

Rupert, watching Taggie, decided she really was very beautiful. It was as though someone had taken a fine black pen and drawn lines along her lashes and round the irises of those amazing silver-grey eyes. Her nose was too large, but

167

the curve of the soft pink mouth emphasized by the very short upper lip was adorable, and he'd like to see all that lustrous black hair spilling over a pillow. She must be nearly five foot ten, he reckoned, and most of it legs, and she had the gentle, apologetic clumsiness of an Irish wolfhound, who can't help knocking off teacups with its tail.

Noticing Rupert observing Taggie with such lazy, almost lustful affection, Maud felt a stab of jealousy.

'Go and get another bottle of whisky from the larder, Tag,' she said sharply, 'and clear away all these plates.'

'But it's Daddy's last bottle,' protested Taggie.

Furious, Maud turned on her. 'As if your father would deny a guest a drink in his own house.'

Trembling, Taggie switched off the iron, fetched the bottle from the larder and dumped it on the table with a crash. Gertrude was whining by the back door.

'I'll take you out, darling,' said Taggie, pulling on a pair of black gumboots.

'Do wrap up warm,' said Valerie. 'And if you want to get on in the country, you should wear green wellies,' she added kindly.

'If you really want to get on in the country,' drawled Rupert, 'you should get that dog's tail straightened.'

It was the final straw. Giving him a filthy look, Taggie went out, slamming the back door behind her.

'What's up with her?' asked Bas.

'In love,' said Maud, unscrewing the bottle of whisky. 'Some friend of Patrick's who hardly knows she exists. You know how moody teenagers are.'

Outside it was deliciously mild. The wind was shepherding parties of orange leaves across the lawn and sighing in the wood. The stream after the recent rain was hurtling down the garden. Above, russet clouds like stretched cotton wool didn't quite cover the sky. Every so often through a chink glittered a brilliant star. Still shaking, Taggie tramped down the rose walk that so often in the past must have been paced by nuns, like her, praying for deliverance.

'Oh, please God, get that horrible horrible man out of the house.'

She couldn't stop thinking of Rupert's lean oiled body, under the dark-blue jersey and mud-spattered white breeches. It was obvious her mother was wildly attracted to him; she'd seen the rapt expression, the flushed cheeks, the wild drinking so often before. And Rupert was leading her mother on, making those beastly salacious (there, at last she'd used her word for the day) remarks, and drinking all her father's drink, and eating all his supper.

Despite the mildness of the night, she shivered as she contemplated the rows ahead if Maud started one of her things. She, Taggie, would get dragged in to provide alibis. Well, she wouldn't cover up for her mother this time, she wouldn't, she wouldn't.

Her father didn't want hassle at the moment; he needed keeping calm. Turning towards the house, its great battlements and turrets confronting the shadowy garden with a timeless strength, she felt slightly comforted. Surely the house would look after them.

After 'Cotswold Round-Up', James and Sarah, both feeling rather elated, were soon cut down to size.

'What did you think of the interview, Cameron?' asked James.

'I'd rather watch slugs copulate,' snapped Cameron.

Sarah in turn rang Paul. 'Was I OK?' she asked eagerly.

'You were very clear,' said Paul. 'Have you seen Tony?'

'Yes,' said Sarah sulkily.

'Did he say anything about putting me on the Board?'

'No,' said Sarah.

'Come and have a drink,' said James, as she slammed down the receiver.

'Yes please,' said Sarah.

Soon after Taggie took Gertrude out, Valerie went home. Maud, Basil and Rupert carried on carousing. Going into the kitchen much later, Taggie was relieved to find only Bas and Maud.

'Daddy's interviewing Lord Wooton in a few minutes,' she said.

'My husband,' Maud told Basil, 'always becomes the person he's interviewing. When he did Margaret Thatcher he spent the week wearing power suits, talking about "circumstarnces", and calling me Denis in bed.'

Noticing Taggie's look of disapproval, Basil patted the chair beside him and said the interview should be interesting as Tony was pulling out every stop to get Maurice Wooton to join the Corinium Board.

Rupert returned from the downstairs loo, waving the *New Statesman*. 'Don't tell me Declan reads this,' he said in outrage.

Maud nodded. 'And actually believes it.'

'But he can't be a socialist when he earns such a vast salary.'

'I know,' sighed Maud. 'He's utterly inconsistent.'

'I expect he'd like to give some of it away,' protested Taggie angrily, 'if everyone didn't spend it all.'

'If you can't keep a civil tongue in your head,' snapped Maud, 'you'd better go to bed.' She'd never known Taggie answer back like this.

Over in Studio 3 Declan always went into himself before a programme, but he nodded when Tony came on to the floor, reeking of brandy and waving a huge cigar. Tony was in an excellent mood; two of Corinium's news stories had been used with a by-line by ITN; he'd just had an excellent dinner with Maurice Wooton, and now he'd got his way about Declan doing this interview, it was the thin end of the wedge. Declan couldn't refuse to do other specials now – Freddie Jones next week, perhaps.

'Maurice is just having a pee. He's been made-up,' he said to Declan. 'Give him a nice easy ride. He may have a reputation as a hatchet man, but he runs a huge empire, he's devoted to his grandchildren and does an enormous amount for charity. He's also delightful if you get him on to opera or his cats.'

'Just show his caring face, Declan,' said Cameron from the control room. 'And Camera 2, can you try to avoid Lord Wooton's bald patch?'

Tonight's vision mixer, sitting in front of her row of lit-up buttons, massaged her neck and opened a Kit Kat. It had been a long day. Daysee Butler fingered her stopwatch. In his earpiece Declan could hear her talking about her boyfriend: 'He's cooking supper for me tonight, cod in cheese sauce out of a packet. He's got such charisma.'

Lord Wooton was now being ushered in by the floor manager. He had plainly had too much to drink with Tony, but Make-up had toned him down with green foundation, and blacked out his greying sideboards. His revoltingly sensual face with the big red pouting lower lip was just like one of Tony's orchids, thought Declan, as he rose to his feet to welcome him.

'Very warm night,' said Lord Wooton.

'Very,' said Declan.

The introductory package, which Cameron had written, was full of nice stills and clips of Lord Wooton romping with cats, visiting children in hospital, playing cricket with grandsons, watching the first bricks of various buildings being laid, and collecting an OBE at the Palace. He was plainly delighted.

'Don't know where they dug up all those old photographs,' he said untruthfully.

'Ten seconds to end of opening package, Declan,' said Daysee from the control room.

Surreptitiously Declan removed his earpiece and put it in his pocket. His first question was sycophancy itself.

'As the leading property developer in Gloucestershire, probably the whole of the West Country, you must be proud of your achievement.'

Maurice Wooton put his hands together happily.

'One is only as good as the people who work for one, Declan,' he said smoothly. 'You must know that. I have first-rate people, hand-picked of course.'

171

'Pity you don't take better care of them,' said Declan amiably.

He then proceeded to carve Maurice Wooton up, starting with one of his managers who'd been sacked while he was in hospital recovering from open-heart surgery, then proceeding to another who'd been given no compensation when he broke his back falling off some scaffolding.

Tony rang Cameron in the control box.

'What the fuck's going on?' he roared. 'Tell him to ask Maurice about his fucking grandchildren.'

'I can't get through to him,' yelled Cameron. 'He's taken out his earpiece.'

'Well, tell the floor manager to tell him to put it fucking back in again.'

Ignoring all Maurice Wooton's spluttering denials, Declan moved on to illegal takeovers, shady deals, and then produced a just-published secret Town Hall report, which claimed that, despite a huge grant from the Council, his firm had built a block of flats cheap to faulty specifications.

Temporarily speechless now, Maurice Wooton was mouthing like a great purple bull frog.

'Another even more unattractive aspect of your business career,' went on Declan relentlessly, 'was the way you bribed three Labour councillors in the housing department at Cotchester Town Hall to give you the contract for the tower block development on Bankside.'

'This is preposterous,' exploded Maurice Wooton.

'You deny it?'

'Of course I do.'

Out of the corner of his eye, Declan could see the floor manager making frantic signals for him to replace his earpiece.

Ignoring them, he said: 'Why, then, do Councillor Bridie, Councillor Yallop, and Councillor Rogers have five thousand pounds entered on their bank statements, paid in by you from a Swiss bank account? Here are the photostats of the bank statements, the cheques, and your letters to them.' Declan brandished them under Maurice Wooton's hairy expanding crimson nostrils, then threw them down on the table. 'Thank

God there are some Town Hall officials left with integrity.'

Cameron was so insane with rage, she stubbed her cigarette out by mistake on the hand of the vision mixer, who, screaming, pressed the wrong button, which ran in telecine of a lot of very fat schoolgirls doing an eightsome reel.

'Go back to one, take fucking one,' screamed Cameron.

The schoolgirls disappeared in mid-dance to be replaced by Maurice Wooton, standing up and shouting at Declan that the whole thing was a trumped-up pack of lies, and he was going home to ring his lawyers. Next moment he'd stormed out, leaving the studio in uproar. Declan sat turned to stone in his chair.

To their great disappointment, Corinium's viewers were then treated to soothing music and a film showing close-ups of Cotchester's wild flowers, so they missed Tony roaring into the studio, so angry he could hardly get the words out.

'I've spent five years courting that man,' he spluttered. 'He was just about to join the Board and put fifteen million into our satellite project.'

Declan rose to his feet, towering over Tony.

'You should have given me time to research him properly,' he said coldly. 'I might have found something nice to ask him, but I doubt it.' And with that, he walked out of the studio.

Back at The Priory, Rupert, wiping his eyes, turned to Maud: 'That was the best television programme I've seen for years and free schoolgirls thrown in, too. After Tony Baddingham, Maurice Wooton is without doubt the biggest shit in England, and your husband is the first socialist I've ever really admired. The Corinium switchboard must be absolutely jammed, or "preserved", as dear Valerie would say, with congratulatory calls.'

At that moment the telephone rang. Rupert picked it up.

'Brilliant programme,' said a voice. 'It's the *Western Daily Press*. Is Declan in?'

'What did I tell you?' said Rupert, handing the receiver to

Maud. 'Don't look so cross,' he added to Taggie. 'I'll nip home in a minute and get your father another bottle.'

After Rupert had returned with the whisky, and he and Bas had left, Taggie watched her mother go to the hall mirror, fluff up her hair on top and smooth the dress over her hips, before sitting down at the drawing-room piano. She must be very drunk, thought Taggie, judging by the number of wrong notes.

What on earth could she give her father for supper, she wondered wearily, as she started to load the washing-up machine. Perhaps she ought to accept Bas's offer of a job, and get out and meet people. She couldn't eat her heart out for Ralphie for ever. She heard the front door bang. Going into the hall, she saw Declan gazing into the drawing-room at Maud playing Schumann in the dress she'd worn when they were first married, living blissfully on no money in Ireland. Her hair almost touched the piano stool.

Putting his hands on her shoulder, he said, 'Why did you put that on?'

'Grice and I were tidying away some of my old clothes.'

'You look beautiful.'

Schumann halted abruptly, as Declan's hands slid under the pie-frill collar. 'Let's go to bed.'

As Maud walked upstairs in front of him, his hands slid up between her bare thighs:

'Christ, you're wet.'

Maud smiled sleepily. 'I've been thinking all evening about your coming home.'

14

Tony would have sacked any other member of his staff for savaging Maurice Wooton like that. As it was he spent the weekend poring over Declan's contract with the lawyers. Unfortunately there was no clause about not presenting his victims with unpalatable truths. So in the end Tony merely wrote Declan a sharp note accusing him of misconduct and warning him that if he stepped out of line a second and third time he'd be out on his ear.

Tony's guns were further spiked by the Government immediately ordering an investigation into Cotchester Town Hall's Housing policy, and by the very favourable press coverage of the programme and Corinium in particular.

'*Corinium show their teeth at last,*' wrote the *Western Daily Press.*

'*Corinium prove they're no longer a Tory poodle,*' wrote the *Guardian.*

Hardest for Tony to take was an enthusiastic telephone call from the IBA: 'Splendid stuff, Tony. No one can accuse you of political bias now.'

The following Wednesday there was a Corinium Board meeting. Tony's temper was not improved when one of the non-executive directors, old Lady Evesham, Vice Chancellor of the local university, arrived on her bicycle in the pouring rain, just as Tony rolled up in the Rolls. Why did the stupid old bag always arrive an hour early and go nosing round the office, talking to staff and stirring up trouble? Hoping she'd go away, Tony cringed behind the *Financial Times*. Next minute she was tapping on the window. Grudgingly, Tony lowered it a few inches.

'Congratulations,' said Lady Evesham, thrusting her wrinkled, whiskery muzzle towards him. 'That interview with Maurice Wooton's the sort of thing we should be doing all the time. Routing out injustice. Man's a rogue. I shall seek out Declan and tell him so in person.'

Tony, however, had other things on his mind. In the same telephone call praising Declan's interview, the IBA had complained that Corinium still wasn't giving sufficient attention to the Southampton end of the area.

'Charles Fairburn has just finished a programme on Isaac Watts,' Tony had countered swiftly.

'Who's he?' asked the IBA's Head of Television.

'Famous philosopher, poet, teacher.' Tony hastily consulted the advance programme notes. 'Watts Square in Southampton is named after him. Wrote "Oh God, our help in ages past".'

'That's not much help in ages present,' said the IBA. 'People in Southampton will hardly regard one hour on the Sunday Godslot as good enough. We're talking about news coverage. There was nothing for example about HMS *Princess Michael of Kent* catching fire at the docks on Friday. The BBC devoted seven minutes to the story.'

'I'll look into it,' said Tony.

As a result of this conversation, Tony summoned his two most valuable executive directors, who usually worked in London but who had come down for the board meeting, into his office beforehand. Known as 'Beauty and the Beast', Georgie Baines and Ginger Johnson looked after sales and finance respectively.

Gorgeous Georgie, who had big brown eyes and even bigger expenses, was up to every single fiddle and lived in the big advertising agencies' pockets, which he lined as effectively as his own. He also made vast sums of money for Corinium. Ginger Johnson, the Beast, was a thug, with carroty hair and a beetroot face, like a particularly unappetizing winter salad. As Financial Director, he saw that the vast sums netted by Georgie were administered as remuneratively as possible. All the most important business on the agenda was always done by the three men before the board meeting.

Going into Tony's office that Wednesday, Georgie and Ginger found him looking at a map of the area.

'If we're going to hang on to the franchise,' said Tony, 'we've got to be properly represented.'

'So?' said Georgie, who'd heard this all before.

'We're going to build a studio here.' Tony jabbed the red dot of Southampton with his finger.

'Cost a fortune,' said Ginger, aghast. 'Even a small studio'll set us back five million. We don't need a studio there.'

'Nor do we want to make any more programmes,' said Georgie. 'Programmes cost too much money.'

'The IBA will love the idea,' said Tony happily. 'More programmes, more employment, better coverage. We don't have to actually build the fucking thing. But if we wave Board sanction and some provisional architect's plans under the IBA's nose, it'll keep them quiet until the franchise is in the bag.'

'I'm sure the Board won't wear it, when we're slashing budgets everywhere else,' said Ginger.

'Leave it to me,' said Tony.

Tony was at his best and his most urbane at board meetings. On his right and left sat Georgie looking beautiful, and Ginger looking ugly. Beyond them sat Simon Harris, who never spoke, and Miss Madden taking the minutes. Beyond these two, down the long elm table, sat members of the Great and the Good, including an MP for Stroud, a winner at Badminton, a famous composer who lived in Oxford, an educationalist from Stratford, a bishop, a famous footballer, and several industrialists who lived in the area, and, of course, Lady Evesham.

As the meeting got under way, everyone expressed great satisfaction at the kudos Declan's programmes had given

177

Corinium. Resolutions were then passed, budget cuts agreed. Lady Evesham then held up the meeting for at least twenty minutes. First she handed round marmite sandwiches. Having risen at six to write her biography of Emily Pankhurst, she was very hungry. Then she raised a complaint from 'an unnamed young woman researcher' – actually Deirdre Kilpatrick – who'd been denied the right to breastfeed in the newsroom.

'Oh Christ,' thought Tony, glaring at Simon Harris.

Typically, it was Simon who had given Deirdre the go-ahead to bring her baby in, because he thought bonding was all important. Deirdre had then proceeded to whip out great grey tits all over the building. As the *coup de grâce*, Baby Kilpatrick had regurgitated milk into one of the newsroom word processors just as Charles Fairburn was showing the Bishop of Salisbury round the building. Charles had promptly fainted and Tony had banished the baby.

Now Tony cleared his throat: 'I told the girl not to bring her baby in any more,' he said to Lady Evesham. 'It was quite old enough to go on the bottle, and she's got a perfectly good nanny at home. It distracted my reporters in the newsroom.'

'Surely they should be above that kind of distraction?' said Lady Evesham frostily. 'This is the twentieth century.'

'If one girl is allowed to bring her baby in, they all will.'

The famous footballer, who was given to ribaldry, then said it was always the ugly old feminist boots who wanted to breastfeed in public. If the pretty ones wanted to do it, none of the blokes would mind. He received a stony glare from Lady Evesham.

Tony, who thoroughly agreed with the famous footballer, but had to pretend to look disapproving, thought it was high time Lady Evesham resigned, and Cameron, who wouldn't stand any truck with breastfeeders, took her place on the Board.

Saying he'd look into it, Tony moved briskly on to the subject of cutting costs. He then proceeded to bore the meeting rigid with details of expenditure on stationery and calculators, and whether it was really necessary to supply the sales' staff with portable computers. Everyone glazed as he compared the merits of endless different models.

It was two minutes to one. Hearing the chink of bottles in the director's dining-room next door, everyone perked up. A delicious smell of boeuf Wellington drifted under the door.

'Well, that's all for the day,' said Tony. Then, as everyone dived for their bags and briefcases, he added, 'Except for one item that may not be on everyone's agenda: the proposed new studio in Southampton. The question of our not giving sufficient attention to the Southampton end of the territory has been raised before.'

'Hear, hear,' said the footballer, who'd once played for the Saints.

'You've all agreed the idea of a new studio in principle,' went on Tony.

The directors scratched their heads. . . . Had they? They were instantly distracted by another waft of boeuf Wellington.

'The building of the studios will create a lot of employment in the area,' said Tony briskly. 'We've got a costing which can be easily accommodated within the budget. Ginger?' He cocked an eyebrow at Ginger Johnson.

'Easily,' said Ginger.

'And you're for it, Georgie?'

'Very much so,' said Georgie, who was lost in admiration. 'Simon?'

Simon Harris had been so unnerved by the breastfeeding incident that he nodded even before Tony got his name out.

'Oh look, it's snowing,' said the footballer, distracting people even further.

'Everyone else in favour?' Tony smiled down the table.

Lady Evesham's was the only dissenting hand.

'Good,' said Tony, gathering up his papers. 'Come and have a drink everyone and meet Declan O'Hara.'

Any further thoughts about studios evaporated as they surged next door.

There was great excitement at Corinium the following Wednesday, when Dame Nellie Finegold, a friend of Lady

Evesham, and one of the last surviving suffragettes, who'd agreed to come on Declan's programme that evening, dropped dead from a heart attack.

Even greater excitement was caused when the Prime Minister, who was in Gloucestershire opening a new hospital and later dining with the Cotchester Regiment, graciously agreed to step into Dame Nellie's shoes to balance Declan's extremely favourable interview with the Leader of the Opposition the previous week. The Prime Minister, appreciating the value of preaching to eighteen million viewers, thought she could handle Declan. Her one condition, which Tony leapt at, was that Declan should submit questions first, and make an undertaking not to depart from them.

'This is our chance to nail him,' Tony told Cameron gleefully. 'If he submits questions today, we can insist he does the same for all future interviews. Then we can manipulate him to our own advantage. You've seen how lethal he can be with Maurice; just think what havoc he could cause in an election year.'

Declan looked tired and tense as he walked into Tony's office waving a sheaf of the Prime Minister's cuttings. Tipping back his chair, Tony stretched his legs and gazed consideringly at him for a moment.

'This is a big day for you, Declan.'

Declan grunted. 'I'm very much looking foward to shaking her by – ' he paused – 'the neck.'

'Now, now,' said Tony, 'let's keep it all sweetness and light.'

'The PM's only coming on the programme if she knows exactly what you're going to ask her, and no funny business,' said Cameron.

'Don't be ridiculous,' snapped Declan. 'Why should she be treated differently to anyone else?'

'Because she's the PM, dumbass, and the IBA is ultimately answerable to her, so she's got to be kept sweet.'

'Not by me she hasn't.'

'Don't be so fucking pigheaded,' screeched Cameron.

An almighty row followed, ending in Declan flatly refusing to do the interview and walking out.

Cameron and Tony exchanged glances of joy and horror – what the hell were they going to do? The Prime Minister was already in the area. She was due at the studios at seven-forty to go on air at eight. The network had been trailing Declan's dramatic change of guest since lunchtime.

'James will have to do it,' said Tony. 'But we won't announce the change of plan until just before transmission, or we'll lose the audience.'

In his office, having just re-written his links for 'Cotswold Round-Up', James switched off the wireless because he was fed up with hearing Declan's signature tune. Turning to his fan mail, he found a letter from Sarah Stratton thanking him for his standard letter thanking her for coming on the programme. Nice bold handwriting, thought James; he was sure those huge loops to the Ls meant something. During their drink at the bar, he'd decided she was very attractive, and wondered by what ruse he could see her again. But a second later, as Cameron burst into his office, his thoughts were only for one woman: the Prime Minister.

'Deirdre's working on your questions at the moment,' said Cameron. 'We've got to rush them over to the PM at Gloucester so she can look at them while she's changing. We should be able to let you have them about five. If you've got any questions to add, let Deirdre know. Here's a brief of what the PM's been up to in the last two months, but you're pretty well briefed anyway, aren't you?'

James blushed. It was the first compliment Cameron had ever paid him.

'I thought Declan was doing this interview.'

'Declan's sick,' said Cameron.

'Seriously?' said James, trying to look suitably caring.

'Not nearly seriously enough,' said Cameron viciously.

As soon as she'd gone, thanking God he'd had his hair streaked last week, James rang Lizzie: 'I'll be late. I've got to interview the PM.'

'My God! Ask her when she last got laid.'

'Don't be silly, this is for real. I'm sending a driver over for my blue suit, and could you put in my jade-green silk shirt, and the sapphire-blue tie. And could you phone the Strattons and ask them to record the programme.' He wanted Sarah to witness his hour of glory. 'I don't trust our machine one hundred per cent.'

You mean you don't trust me to remember, thought Lizzie.

Cameron, popping in to the studio later on her way to the control room, was nearly knocked sideways by Aramis.

'She's arrived. Tony'll bring her through in a minute. Are you nervous?'

'Not yet,' said James, re-plumping cushions on the pastel-pink sofa.

'Nice change from Declan,' said Cameron. 'Good luck.'

Perhaps he'd maligned Cameron, thought James, as he combed his hair for the hundredth time and removed the shine on his nose with Nouveau Beige creme puff. He used to use Gay Whisper, but had decided the name had rather unfortunate connotations.

The Prime Minister, like most women, had a weakness for charming, handsome men. Seeing her appearing through the black curtain, radiant in dark-blue taffeta, being guided over the cables and uneven surfaces by Tony, James leapt to his feet. For a second Diorella fought with Aramis. Aramis won easily.

'Welcome to Cotchester, Prime Minister. I can't tell you how privileged I feel to meet you,' said James, giving her the benefit of his beautiful aquamarine eyes, now subtly enhanced by the jade-green shirt and the sapphire-blue tie. Then, when she offered him her hand, he bowed his streaked head and kissed it reverently.

'Silly cunt,' muttered the Senior Cameraman.

'Come and sit down,' said James.

Down came the famous bottom on the pastel-pink sofa.

'I'll leave you in good hands, Prime Minister,' said Tony.

'Indeed, Lord Baddingham,' said the PM in her low voice.

The interview was pure Barbara Cartland. Aware no

182

difficult questions would be forthcoming, the PM was at her most relaxed and charming, and unbent to James as she'd never done before on television.

'Prepared only to see the steely side of your character, Prime Minister, some people make the ridiculous mistake of thinking you don't care about the unemployed or the old and poverty-stricken.'

'Mr Vereker – ' the Prime Minister's voice dropped an octave – 'if only you could realize the sleepless nights we spend worrying about hypothermia, particularly with another winter coming on.'

'How many more times is the stupid asshole going to use the word "caring",' snarled Cameron to Tony, who'd stayed with her in the Control Room.

'Hush, she's really unbuttoning,' purred Tony.

During the commercial break, the PM became positively skittish.

'They'll be into heavy petting in a minute,' said Cameron as James leant forward in sycophantic ecstasy.

At the end of the second half the Prime Minister even shed tears as she talked of her worries as a mother.

'But you are a mother to all of us,' said James, handing her his Aramis-scented handkerchief.

'Pass me the motion discomfort bag,' groaned Cameron.

'It's good,' said Tony. 'Should win her a lot of votes.'

'Ten seconds to out, James,' said Cameron, flicking on the key switch. 'Close the programme.'

'Thank you, Prime Minister, for showing us your caring face,' said James, 'and please come back to Cotchester again soon.'

As the credits went up, they could be seen laughing and joking together.

'I'm going to frow up,' said the Senior Cameraman.

'Come back, Declan,' muttered the Floor Manager, 'nothing needed to be forgiven.'

'I would love a tape of that programme, Mr Vereker,' said the Prime Minister.

Outside, a second Corinium camera crew filmed her

departure, lethargically cheered by a hand-picked crowd of Corinium staff.

'I hope we get overtime for this,' said Charles Fairburn, waving a Union Jack, as a jubilant James, Cameron and Tony accompanied the PM down the steps. Settled in her car, ready to depart to a late dinner with the Cotchester Regiment, the PM wound down her window.

'I hope Mr O'Hara feels better soon,' she said earnestly. 'This flu virus can be very pulling down.'

'About time the mighty Mr O'Hara was pulled down from his seat,' said Cameron, as soon as she had driven off.

'What a caring lady,' sighed James.

He woke next morning to find himself temporarily famous. Both the BBC and ITN picked up the interview, which was fulsomely praised the next day by the Tory press. Only the *Mirror* and the *Guardian* grumbled that James had let the PM get away with murder.

By Friday the story had got out that Declan hadn't been ill at all, but had simply refused to do the interview with the Prime Minister.

'*The Rows Begin Again*,' said a huge headline in the *Sun*.

At the BBC and around the network, people smirked knowingly. They'd known the honeymoon wouldn't last.

15

Declan was having a row about money with Maud in the kitchen when the telephone rang.

'Yes,' he snapped.

'This is Valerie Jones,' said an ultra-refined, vaguely familiar voice.

'Yes,' said Declan, who was no wiser.

'We met at Lady Monica's buffet luncheon. I was wearing a cricket jumper.'

'Oh yes,' Declan twigged – the extremely silly mid-on.

'Fred-Fred and I were wondering if you could come and dayne on December 7th, that's tomorrow week, just a few close friends. Tony and Monica Baddingham. . . .'

Declan had heard enough. He was sorry, he said, but they had a previous engagement.

Maud was absolutely furious. 'We never go out,' she stormed. 'How dare you refuse for me? I might have wanted to go.'

'It was that horrendous dwarf we met at the Baddinghams; bound to have been hell.'

'There might have been other amusing people there. How can we ever meet anyone, if you turn down everything?'

Maud's sulk lasted all day. Declan was trying to get to grips with the volatile, volcanic personality of John McEnroe, who was coming on the programme on Wednesday. Maud's black mood permeated the whole house and totally sabotaged his concentration. At dusk, unable to bear it any longer, he went downstairs and apologized.

'I'm sorry; it was selfish of me. I must work, but you go on your own. I hate it, but I've got to get used to it. Are you lonely?' he went on as Maud clung to him. 'D'you want to go back to London?'

She shook her head violently. 'I just miss my friends. I was wondering if we could give a tiny party for Patrick's birthday on New Year's Eve.'

Declan's heart sank. 'Not really, not this Christmas. We simply can't afford it.'

'It's his twenty-first,' pleaded Maud. 'He's always had such lousy birthdays, having them so near Christmas. Just the tiniest party, half a dozen couples. Taggie can do the food; it'll be good training for her. She's not getting any response from those cards.'

Declan was about to say they still hadn't paid for the Fulham Farewell when the telephone rang again. Taggie picked it up in the kitchen. Five minutes later she rushed, pink-faced with excitement, into the drawing-room.

'The most p-p-prodigious – ' her word for the day – 'thing has happened. Valerie Jones got one of my cards and she's asked me to do her dinner party next Friday. Isn't it prodigious?'

'It is, indeed,' said Declan, disentangling himself from Maud and hugging her.

'She asked us,' said Maud fretfully. 'What are you going to cook for her that we won't get?'

'I've got to go over tomorrow and discuss menus,' said Taggie.

Maud seized her chance. 'Daddy's agreed we can have a little party for Patrick on New Year's Eve,' said Maud, ignoring Declan's look of horror, 'so you can start thinking up some nice food for that.'

Taggie's already euphoric face lit up even further: 'What a prodigious idea.'

Upstairs in her turret bedroom, she clutched herself, pressing her boiling face against one of the thin, cool ecclesiastical

186

windows. If Patrick was having a party, how could Patrick's best friend not be there? She was going to see Ralphie again.

Cooking for Valerie's dinner party was Taggie's first big job, but her nerves were nothing to Valerie's. Valerie was livid with Freddie for asking Rupert, who was coming down to Gloucestershire for a constituency meeting and to present the cup at the Cotchester–Bristol football Derby. Originally he was supposed to be bringing some French actress, but she'd got stuck on location in Scotland. So Valerie'd had to find a spare woman at the last moment. She settled for Cameron Cook who had just won an American award for a documentary about arranged marriages which she'd produced last Spring. Having talked to her briefly at Declan's first programme, Valerie had no idea she was Tony's mistress.

And now Valerie wouldn't stop flapping round the kitchen tasting and criticizing everything Taggie was making – 'A soupçon more cayenne in the cucumber sauce, Agatha – ' or fretting whether they should have cheese before pudding, or who should sit next to whom.

'It says,' she announced, poring over the etiquette book, 'that the most important man should sit on my right.'

'That's me,' said Freddie, roaring with laughter.

'Don't be silly, Fred-Fred,' snapped Valerie, 'and don't pick.'

'That fish pâté's champion,' said Freddie, who'd only been allowed a small salad at lunch.

'Are you going to be all day with that dessert, Agatha?' said Valerie, beadily looking at the huge ice cream and meringue castle, around which Taggie was curling whipped cream to simulate pounding waves. 'The place is a frightful mess.'

'I promise I'll clear up in time. Everything's done but this.'

People were due at eight to eight-thirty to dine at nine. The pheasants, simmered with cranberries and ginger, had to go in at six forty-five.

'You've still got the menus to write out, one for each end

of the table,' said Valerie. 'It would be naice to have them in French.'

Taggie went pale. She couldn't even spell them properly in English; she'd always had trouble with pheasant. She started to shake.

'I'm going to check the rest of the house,' said Valerie.

The lounge looked beautiful. She'd got florists in to provide two beautiful pink arrangements. The dining-room was also a symphony in pink, with a centrepiece of roses. Valerie adored pink; it was so feminine and went so well with her mauve velvet evening gown with the flowing skirt and the trumpet sleeves. She was glad they weren't having soup – Freddie drank it so noisily. She'd worked out where everyone was going to sit. Now, standing at the end of the table, Valerie practised her commands:

'Bring in the appetizer, please, Agatha. Take away the entrée, Agatha. Bring in the dessert.'

Then there was the tricky bit, catching all the women's eyes. She glanced at alternate chairs. 'Shall we go upstairs?'

What happened if that awful Rupert read the message wrong and followed her upstairs too? He was quite capable. For safety, she'd better say: 'Shall we *ladies* go upstairs?'

'We've got a right one 'ere,' said Reg, the hired butler, who was already well stuck into the Mouton Cadet. 'Yakking away to herself in the dining-room.'

'What am I to do about this menu?' said Taggie helplessly.

'I'll help you. I'm doing French for O-levels,' said Sharon, the daughter of the house, who'd inherited her father's bulk and his sweet nature. 'I'm sure the French for pheasant is *payson.*'

Mrs Makepiece, Valerie's daily, who'd come to help with the washing up, was just raking the shagpile in the lounge, flicking away non-existent dust when Valerie rushed in and realigned the *Tatlers* and *Harpers*, leaving the *Gloucester and Avon Life* specially open at a picture of herself at the NSPCC fashion show in Cheltenham. It was seven o'clock. She'd better take a bath and change.

.

In the kitchen, Taggie finished the pudding and put the pheasants into the oven. She must remember to add chopped dill to the prawn sauce. She wished Valerie hadn't wanted things quite so elaborate. Everything was going swimmingly until Valerie came down dressed, and insisted Taggie put on a maid's black dress and a white apron which came miles above her black-stockinged knees, and then made her put her hair up. Even Taggie baulked at the white maid's cap.

'I expect you to answer the door,' said Valerie, 'supervise everything in the kitchen and wait at table.'

'You're in the army now,' sung Reg, the hired butler, now on his third bottle.

'Will you come and watch "Dynasty" with me?' Sharon asked Taggie.

'You're not watching rubbish like that, Sharon. You're to hand round nibbles and make yourself pleasant,' snapped Valerie, nearly jumping out of her skin, as music blared out from the speakers all over the house.

'It's Daddy's signature tune,' said Taggie in delight.

'Turn that horrible din down, Fred-Fred,' screamed Valerie.

'Monica loves classical music,' said Freddie.

'Oh well, leave it on, then.'

The doorbell rang. 'Go and answer it, Agatha. Put the men's coats in the downstairs toilet, and the ladies' coats upstairs in the master bedroom, and then direct them towards the lounge, where Mr Jones and I will receive them.'

It was Paul and Sarah Stratton. For a second Taggie and Sarah stared at each other, remembering their previous encounter on Rupert's tennis court. Then, with a wicked little smile, Sarah took off her red velvet cloak. Her tan had gone, but a black taffeta dress, off-the-shoulders and with a bustle, showed off her beautiful, opulent figure. Never having seen Paul before, Taggie thought he looked dreadfully old and careworn to be married to such a glowing over-excited young girl.

The next arrival was Cameron Cook, who Taggie recognized from Declan's description and tried not to hate. Declan had omitted to say she was so beautiful, and wonderfully dressed this evening in a dark-red smoking jacket and black tie with a wing collar, her hair sleeked back to show off her smooth white forehead and thick black brows. She looked straight through Taggie, and, having no coat to take, stalked past her into the drawing-room.

She was shortly followed by Tony and Monica. Tony'd been away at a conference, and for once, because he was cleaning up Corinium's act, hadn't taken Cameron with him. Now he was unflatteringly unpleased to see her. The big smile he switched on like a light bulb switched off as though there'd been a mega powercut. He always felt twitchy when Cameron and Monica were in the same room, and, even worse, Cameron, it seemed, had been invited for Rupert, his old rival. And there was Declan's bloody signature tune blaring out. He was still extremely off Declan, but his hopes of having a good bitch about him this evening had been foiled by the presence of Declan's stupid daughter.

'This music is wonderful,' exclaimed Monica.

'Come and see it in action,' said Freddie, bearing her off to witness the electronic wizardry in his study.

'Have you got any Wagner?' said Monica.

Next moment, to Valerie's horror. Siegfried's funeral march pounded deafeningly through the house.

'What the hell are you doing here?' hissed Tony to Cameron.

'I was asked,' said Cameron coldly.

'We must be very careful.'

'Of course,' said Cameron, holding her glass out to Reg for an instant refill. 'We mustn't jeopardize the franchise.'

Valerie was telling Paul about the house: 'We replaced those dreary old mullioned windows with picture windows.'

'How on earth did you get planning permission?' said Paul in horror. 'I thought this was a listed building.'

'Grade 1,' said Valerie smugly. 'Fred-Fred has friends in high places.'

'Please God, don't let the sauce curdle,' prayed Taggie in the kitchen as she added egg yolks and vinegar.

'Door, love,' said Reg, giving her a pinch on the bottom. 'You look much the sexiest of the lot.'

It was Lizzie and James, who'd plainly had a row because of Lizzie's catastrophic navigation. James loved making an entrance, but not arriving half an hour after his boss, who was looking bootfaced and standing as far away from Cameron as possible talking to Paul Stratton. James immediately gravitated towards Sarah and thought how nice it was to see Cameron out of her depth socially, and for once rather insecure.

Lizzie, who looked awful (she'd worked too late on her novel again and had not had time to wash her hair), had brought some bantams' eggs for Freddie and Valerie, and was thrilled to see Taggie: 'I know it'll all be delicious; don't worry.'

Valerie looked at her watch yet again: quarter past nine and no Rupert.

'Doesn't matter,' said Freddie, filling up everyone's glasses. 'Nice to relax on a Friday.'

'Freddie's equipment is quite staggering,' said Monica returning from the study.

Sarah caught Lizzie's eye and giggled.

Mashing the potatoes in the kitchen, Taggie was going frantic. Everything would be ruined unless they ate soon.

'Off you go,' said Reg, as the doorbell rang.

Crimson with rage and embarrassment, bending her legs to make her maid's dress look longer, Taggie answered the door. Grinning, Rupert walked into the hall. 'Called any good fire engines lately?'

'Would you like to take off your coat?' said Taggie stiffly.

'I'd much rather take off your dress,' said Rupert. 'You look like the object of all red-blooded men's fantasies. I'm late. I'd better go and make my peace.'

Valerie hid her rage less well than Taggie: 'Rupert, where *have* you been?'

Cameron choked on her champagne. Having never actually met Rupert and having been poisoned by Tony's almost pathological jealousy, she'd expected him to just be another loud-mouthed, upper-class English shit. In the flesh he was glorious, and much more American-looking than English.

Having apologized to Valerie, Rupert turned to kiss Monica.

'You haven't met Cavendish Cook, have you, Rupert?' said Monica.

'How do you do, sir,' said Rupert, admiring Cameron's smoking jacket.

'Cavendish works for Tony,' went on Monica. 'I gather you won another prize last week, Cavendish; jolly good show. I meant to watch the programme last summer, but unfortunately they were doing *Meistersinger* on BBC 2 the same night, and I was videoing that as well as watching it.'

James was in ecstasy – Cavendish Cook! There were some advantages in Monica's addiction to BBC 2 after all.

Seeing Sharon sneaking through the hall towards the kitchen, Valerie gave an eldritch screech.

'Sharon, Sharon, come in here and give Auntie Monica some nibbles. She keeps sloping off to watch "Dynasty",' she added to Monica. 'I won't have my kids watching soaps.'

'Oh I love "Dynasty",' said Monica, smiling at Sharon. 'Do tell me whether Blake and Crystal have made it up.'

Rupert walked over to James, who was still talking to Sarah.

'That was a bloody good interview you did with the PM,' he said. 'And she thought you were marvellous. Asked me for your address so she could write to you.'

James, who'd always hated Rupert, melted faster than a snowball in the microwave. Then Rupert turned to Sarah, kissing her white shoulder.

'Evening, my darling, that's an incredibly sexy dress, I don't know why you bother to wear any clothes at all. Bloody cold outside. I think it's going to snow.'

'I can never get home if it snows,' grumbled James. 'I'm thinking of installing a put-you-up in my office.'

Seeing Tony was still talking to Paul, Rupert said: 'Tony Baddingham's got a put-you-down in *his* office.'

Cameron laughed.

James, who was not going to be egged on to bitching about Tony in front of Cameron, said, 'I always feel Tony is much maligned.'

'I entirely agree,' said Rupert, draining his whisky, 'but not nearly enough.'

Sitting next to Rupert at dinner, Sarah found herself talking gibberish. The awful thing about adultery, she thought, was that one had to remember in public that one hadn't heard things that one's lover had told one in private.

'I saw your "Behind Every Famous Man" interview with James,' said Rupert, as he unfolded his napkin. 'Very good. Were you nervous?'

'Desperately,' said Sarah, blushing.

As they had discussed the whole thing and how ghastly James had been at length in bed yesterday afternoon, and because, under the table, Rupert's hand was already creeping up between the slit in her skirt, Sarah found it impossible not to giggle.

'I think I've found you a horse,' went on Rupert, giving her his blank, blue-eyed stare. Then he solemnly proceeded to describe it down to its last fetlock. As he'd also given her the same details yesterday, she found it even more difficult to keep a straight face, particularly as Paul, pretending to listen to Valerie, had ears on elastic trying to hear what they were saying.

Fortunately, distraction was provided by Taggie bringing round the fish mousse. Not remembering her left from her right, having served Monica, she moved backwards to serve James.

'Clockwise,' screeched Valerie.

There was another awful moment for Taggie when she saw Rupert and Lizzie having hysterics over the menu.

'Gingered French peasant, cravat sauce and desert château,' translated Rupert.

'Our hostess's French is slightly Stratford atte Bowe,' whispered Lizzie.

'What's that?' said Valerie sharply from the other end of the table.

For a second Lizzie caught Taggie's anguished eye, and instantly identified the author of the menu: 'Just saying how good your French is,' she said to Valerie.

Valerie nodded smugly: 'Crusty bread anyone?' she cried waving the basket. 'I will not have white bread in this house.'

'I love it,' said Freddie wistfully.

'So do I,' said Rupert. 'I'll send you a loaf for Christmas.'

Sitting opposite Tony, trying desperately not to catch his eye, Cameron longed to be able to sparkle and scintillate, but how could she with Paul Stratton on one side, watching his wife like a warder and James on the other talking about himself?

'How's your series on "Caring for the Elderly" getting on?' she asked.

James brightened. 'We think we've found a presenter at last – a Mrs Didbody. She's a seventy-five-year-old coloured lady, a widow with a daughter of fifty. Which makes her a single parent,' added James triumphantly.

'A real franchise grabber,' said Cameron, who was watching Rupert. He was easily the most attractive man she'd seen since she came to England, probably ever. It was a combination of elegance, deadpan arrogance, and a total inability to resist stirring things up. He was plainly having it off with Sarah Stratton.

'What exactly are electronics?' Monica was saying to Freddie in her piercing voice. 'What exactly d'you do?'

Cameron saw a look of fury on Tony's face, but Freddie seemed delighted by her interest.

'I make everythink really: videos, televisions, synthesizers, compact disks, floppy disks, silicon chips.'

'I always muddle up silicon with cellulite,' said Monica.

'With my computers,' went on Freddie proudly, 'scientists on the ground can place satellites in orbit. All satellites now carry my computers on board.'

'Good heavens,' said Monica. She could see now how useful Freddie'd be to Tony.

Tony was not enjoying himself. It was one of life's ironies, he thought, that at dinners like this Monica always sat next to all the brilliant achieving men, who usually didn't interest her at all (although she did seem to be having fun with Freddie), and he got stuck with their unachieving wives. Lizzie Vereker on his left looked a complete mess.

'That was delicious,' she said taking another piece of bread to wipe up the last vestiges of prawn sauce. 'Did you make it?' she asked Valerie slyly.

'Yes,' said Valerie, as Taggie was out of the room.

'How's Archie?' Lizzie asked Tony.

'Doing Business Studies for A-levels,' said Tony with a grin, 'which he thinks allows him to tell me exactly where I'm going wrong in running Corinium.'

The only time he's nice, thought Lizzie, is when he talks about his children.

'Sharon is doing *The Dream* for her O-levels,' said Valerie, ringing a bell.

Taggie, who was chopping parsley for the courgettes, threw down the knife and ran into the dining-room, tugging down her horribly short dress.

'Can you clear away the appetizer, Agatha,' said Valerie.

Returning to the kitchen with the plates, Taggie found Reg the butler, very drunk now, carving the pheasants. She wished he wouldn't cut quite such huge slices, there might not be enough to go round.

'Tender as a woman's kiss,' said Reg, helping himself to a slice. 'You're another Mrs Beeton, Agatha.'

'Oh, it does look yummy. Can I have a bit?' said fat Sharon.

'Have some later,' said Taggie, as she poured the sauce over, and scattered parsley over the courgettes. 'I must take it in.'

'I'll take round the courgettes,' said Sharon, who wanted to gaze at Rupert.

Taggie took the pheasant round the right way this time.

She noticed Rupert still had his hand inside Sarah's slit skirt, the revolting man, but had to remove it to help himself to pheasant. Was she imagining it or was he deliberately rubbing his black elbow against her breast as he did so? When she took round the potatoes, she stood as far away as possible, arching over him like a street light. As she moved down the other side of the table, his wicked dissipated blue eyes seemed to follow her, making her even more hot and bothered. Reg was taking round the Mouton Cadet now, and had reached Valerie.

'We had Sharon in 1972,' she was telling Paul, 'and we were married in, er . . .'

'Watch it,' said Reg, giving her a great nudge.

Rupert grinned broadly. Sarah and Lizzie giggled.

Valerie, knowing one must behave with dignity at all times, ignored the innuendo. 'That will be all, Reginald and Agatha. I'll ring if anyone wants second helpings.'

'We're televising Midnight Mass at Cotchester Cathedral this year,' said Tony as he put his knife and fork together. 'I'm reading the first lesson. Are you reading the second?' he asked Paul, knowing he wasn't.

'No,' said Paul, looking very put out. 'We'll be away.'

'I wonder who is reading it then,' said Tony.

'I am,' said Rupert.

'You said you were going skiing,' said an unguarded Sarah. 'I mean,' she added, looking thoroughly flustered, 'you said you'd be away at Christmas.'

There was an awkward pause.

'This pheasant is wonderful,' said Lizzie.

'I'll give you the recipe if you like,' said Valerie. 'Don't pick your bones, Fred-Fred,' she snapped, then stopped hastily as she saw that Rupert was picking his.

All the same, it was going wonderfully well, reflected Valerie later, as Taggie cleared away the cheese board. Everyone was talking like mad and seemed to enjoy the novelty of the men moving two places on. It was a good thing Rupert was sitting next to Cameron now, who'd seemed rather out of it earlier. In five minutes, Taggie would bring on the moated castle.

Turning to Cameron, Rupert thought how different she was to Sarah, as lean and hungry as Sarah was replete and voluptuous.

'I'm dying to have a pee,' he murmured, 'just for an excuse to prowl round and see what a ghastly cock-up our hostess has made of a once-ravishing house. I used to come to children's parties here.'

'I can't imagine you as a kid.'

'I always cheated at doctors and nurses.'

Across the table, he noticed Sarah deliberately flirting with James, to make him jealous perhaps or to put Paul off the scent.

To Valerie's disapproval Cameron got out a cigarette. Picking up a pink candle, Rupert lit it for her.

'You hunt with the same pack as Tony?' she asked.

'Sometimes,' said Rupert softly. 'Sometimes after the same quarry.'

Looking round at his suddenly predatory, unsmiling face, she felt a quivering between her legs. Christ, she wanted him.

'D'you want a lift home?' he said.

'No.' She could have wept. 'I brought my own car.'

'The Lotus?' said Rupert.

She nodded.

'Nice Corinium perk,' said Rupert, instantly returning to his former flippant mood. 'I see James has finally got himself a Porsche. I'll have to get rid of mine.'

'I don't know much about horses,' murmured Cameron, frantic to hold his attention, 'except my boss's wife looks like one.'

'You won't oust her by bitching,' said Rupert. Then, aware that Tony had suddenly stopped talking to Sarah and they were both listening, he said, 'There are three things you need in a horse: balance, quality and courage. Same as a woman, really.'

'I'd add intelligence,' said Cameron.

'I wouldn't.'

'Don't you like achieving women?'

'I don't like ballbreakers.'

There was a chorus of oohs and aahs as Taggie came in with the moated ice cream castle. It was the last lap. Once she'd served this, and cleared away, she could relax.

'What d'you do at Corinium?' Rupert asked Cameron, as he idly watched Taggie moving round the table. She was bright pink in the face, her tongue clenched between her teeth in her efforts to hold the pudding steady. Any make-up had sweated off. Her dark hair was fighting the pins that held it up. But nothing could disguise the length of leg, or the long dark eyelashes, or the voluptuous swell of her breasts. She was going anti-clockwise again, but most people were too plastered to notice.

'I produce Declan,' said Cameron. 'Why don't you come on the programme?'

'What?' said Rupert, dragging his thoughts back from Taggie.

'Come on the programme. I'm sure you and Declan would strike sparks off each other.'

'I don't want to,' said Rupert flatly. 'I don't need that kind of wank, and you'd never hear any chat above the rattle of skeletons tumbling out of cupboards.'

Having just served Valerie, Taggie was moving slowly round towards him.

'How d'you get on with Declan?' he asked Cameron wickedly.

'Utterly obnoxious,' said Cameron. 'He really pisses me off.'

Rupert watched Taggie to see if she'd rise.

'Very pretty,' he said, examining the pudding. 'Feel I ought to get planning permission before I dig into this. Thanks, angel,' he added, helping himself to a piece of battlement and a dollop of cream.

Ignoring him, Taggie moved round to his other side to serve Cameron.

'How on earth does Declan's wife put up with him?' asked Cameron.

'You'd better ask Taggie,' said Rupert. 'Maud's her mother.'

Cameron paled visibly. Noticing Taggie for the first time, she tried to remember what ghastly things she'd said about Declan.

'I'm sorry. I didn't realize.'

In embarrassment she helped herself to too much pudding. The whole thing swayed. Rupert could smell Taggie's body, could feel how hot, and nervous and trembling she was. Her skirt was so short. Almost without thinking, he put a leisurely hand between her thighs.

The next moment Taggie gave a shriek and dropped the very considerable remains of the pudding all over Cameron's seven-hundred-pound smoking jacket and black satin trousers.

'You stupid bitch,' screamed Cameron, forgetting herself. 'What the fuck d'you think you're doing?'

In tears Taggie fled to the kitchen.

Remembering one must behave with dignity at all times, Valerie swept an almost hysterical Cameron upstairs.

Lizzie turned on Rupert: 'You bastard,' she yelled. 'Don't you realize this was her first job? She's been trying to break into catering for months. She cooked like an angel and you had to fuck it up.'

'With looks like that,' said Rupert, retrieving pieces of broken plate from the floor, 'I wouldn't have thought a career was that important.'

'Don't be so fucking insensitive. Didn't you know poor darling Taggie's dyslexic? Can't you imagine how ghastly it is being the only unbright one in such a brilliant family?'

'Oh Christ,' said Rupert, truly appalled. 'I simply didn't know. It was entirely my fault, Freddie. I couldn't resist goosing your cook, but really you shouldn't have dressed her in such sexy clothes. I'd better go and apologize.'

'Leave her bloody alone,' said Lizzie, rushing out to the kitchen to comfort a sobbing Taggie, who was being ineffectually patted by a swaying Reg.

'Go and get a cloth and a dustpan and brush, and clear up the mess,' Lizzie told him, 'and give everyone another drink.'

'There there, duck.' She hugged Taggie.

'I'm so sorry. I wanted everything to be perfect for Mrs Jones,' sobbed Taggie.

'You mustn't worry. It was the most marvellous food anyone's had in years.' Lizzie pulled off a piece of kitchen roll to dry Taggie's eyes. 'Rupert's a bastard. He just can't resist a beautiful girl.'

'Cameron is changing into one of my ge-owns,' said Valerie, sweeping in.

'I'm so sorry, Mrs Jones,' said Taggie in a choked voice.

'I was just telling her how brilliantly she cooked,' said Lizzie.

Valerie was livid. She'd been shown up as not doing the cooking at all.

'Pull yourself together, Agatha,' she said sharply. 'Go and collect the rest of the plates, and see if Lord Baddingham and Miss Cook would like some fresh fruit, as they didn't get any dessert.'

'Cameron got her just dessert,' giggled Lizzie.

'I can't go back in there,' said Taggie aghast.

'You will,' said Valerie, 'if you want to work for me again.'

In the dining-room James was furious with Lizzie for making such a fuss over Declan's idiot daughter, and Sarah was furious with Rupert for so openly groping Taggie. She'd tried to be laid back about her affair with him, but now all she could feel was a red-hot lava of jealousy pouring over her.

Tony, on the other hand, was delighted by the turn of events. 'Child's clearly over-emotional and unbalanced like her father,' he kept saying.

'Bloody good cook,' said Freddie.

And when Taggie, very tear-stained and head hanging, brought in a bowl of peaches and grapes, Monica leaned out and squeezed her hand.

'Delicious dinner, my dear. I've got a girl's lunch next

week. Perhaps you'd like to help me out with that? Nothing elaborate, very cosy. I'll ring you tomorrow.'

Gulping gratefully, Taggie said she'd love to.

Attention was then taken off her by the return of Cameron, wearing one of Valerie's black ge-owns. It was perfectly frightful with a bow on the bum, and much too tight.

'I prefer you as a bloke,' said Rupert, wiping a blob of cream off her chair.

'I'm desperately sorry,' mumbled Taggie, as she passed Cameron, 'I'll pay for it.'

'You couldn't begin to,' hissed Cameron.

'Don't be a bitch,' said Rupert sharply. Putting a hand on Taggie's arm, he said, 'I'm really sorry, angel, it was all my fault.'

Taggie didn't say anything, but seemed to shrink away.

James sidled up to Valerie.

'One of my programmes is on in a minute. Would anyone mind if I slipped upstairs and watched it?'

'Of course,' said Valerie. 'In fact I think, ladies, we'll all go upstairs.'

Cameron got her own back by flatly refusing to go and staying to drink port with the men. Little good it did her. Tony got Freddie in a corner and persuaded him to have lunch immediately after Christmas to discuss his joining the Corinium Board, and, leaving Cameron with the frightful Paul, Rupert went off to the kitchen. Here he found Taggie loading the washing-up machine and making coffee.

'Go away!' she sobbed. 'You're the most m-m-m-malefic man I've ever met.'

''ere, 'ere,' groaned Reg from underneath the kitchen table.

16

The following Monday Declan stormed into Cameron's office without knocking. 'You were at Valerie Jones's dinner party.'

'Right,' said Cameron coolly. Inside she quailed, wondering if Taggie had told Declan how she'd screamed and sworn at her, and how earlier she'd bitched about Declan to Rupert.

'I gather Taggie tipped the pudding over you. I'm sorry,' said Declan. 'If you can't get the marks out, I'll be happy to refund you.'

'It was no big deal,' said Cameron, absolutely weak with relief. 'I took them along to the cleaners on Saturday, they'll be just fine.'

'Then we'll pick up your cleaning bill.'

'Rupert can bloody well do that.'

Declan's face hardened. 'The bastard – poor little Tag. She was distraught.'

'She did really well,' protested Cameron, feeling she could afford to be generous. 'The food was terrific, and Monica asked her to do a lunch for her.'

'I know. Monica rang on Saturday. That cheered Taggie up.'

'It was all Rupert's fault,' said Cameron, deciding to put the boot in.

'Wait till I get my hands on the bastard.'

'Why don't I ask him on to your programme?' said Cameron idly. 'That'd be a much more subtle way of burying him.'

Declan paused in his prowling and thought for a minute. It was violently against all his principles to ask someone deliberately on to the programme in order to do a hatchet job.

'He really screwed her up,' insisted Cameron, who wanted an excuse to ring Rupert.

'All right,' said Declan.

Even Tony was temporarily roused out of his anti-Declan mood. 'Bloody good idea. If Declan does a Maurice Wooton on Rupert, I'll double his salary.'

Cameron rang Rupert. 'I'm just checking out on your availability over the next few months.'

'You should have come home with me on Friday,' said Rupert.

Because he was horrendously busy and not given to introspection and would much rather spend any spare second in Gloucestershire on constituency work, or with his children or his horses, or in bed with Sarah Stratton, Rupert then told Cameron he had no intention of going on Declan's programme.

Cameron played her trump card. 'I'll tell Declan you're too chicken.'

That nettled Rupert: 'Don't be silly. All right, I'll think about it.'

And with that Cameron had to be content.

As Christmas approached Declan grew more depressed. He was totally disillusioned with Tony. He felt like a damsel in distress, who, having been rescued from the BBC by St George, had promptly been put on the game. Not a day passed without some loaded request to open Monica's Christmas Bazaar for the Distressed Gentlefolk, or draw the raffle at the NSPCC Ball (tickets seventy-five pounds each), or take part in Corinium's Pantomime to Help the Aged, or turn on the lights in Cotchester. Declan refused them all, which increased Tony's animosity and enabled James Vereker to step caringly into his shoes. The implication was the same: if you bothered to make use of our excellent research team, you could pull your weight as a member of the Corinium team.

Sapped by endless rows. Declan was aware his programme was losing its edge. He was still very high in the ratings, but he knew people were beginning to turn on in the hope he'd be better this week.

Desperate for some kind of intellectual satisfaction, he was getting up at five every day to spend three or four hours on his Yeats biography, but was too drained to make any real progress. He was also grimly aware that he wasn't paying enough attention to Maud. After a long bout of lethargy, excited about Caitlin and Patrick coming home for Christmas, she was having one of her spates of frantic energy, which invariably involved spending money. She came to the office Christmas party and charmed absolutely everyone.

Patrick arrived the next day, walking through the door slightly drunk, with four suitcases of washing.

'Is this the Priory laundry?'

'Why did you come by taxi?' asked Maud, flinging her arms round his neck.

'Because I wrote off the Golf yesterday.'

At that moment Caitlin rang from school.

'Patrick's home,' said Maud in ecstasy.

'Well he can come and collect me in the Golf, the Mini's too shaming.'

Christmas Eve saw scenes of frantic revelry at Corinium. The whole building thrummed with lust. Seb Burrows from the newsroom scaled the front of the building when drunk, and placed Charles Fairburn's Russian hat on one of the red horns of the Corinium ram. Another joker put rainbow condoms on the horns and tail of the bronze Corinium ram in the board room, just before Tony ushered in the local representative from the IBA for a Christmas drink. Secretaries with tinsel in their hair ran shrieking down the passage blowing squeakers. Just as James Vereker passed the board room door, carrying a pile of Christmas presents from caring fans out to his car, four shrieking secretaries converged on him and unzipped his flies. His trousers dropped, to reveal seasonal boxer shorts covered with Santas, just as Tony was ushering the IBA man out. Tony was absolutely livid, but not so livid as Cameron, who'd opted to work over Christmas for want of anything better to do, when she discovered Tony had dispatched Miss Madden to choose Christmas presents both for her and Monica.

'I bought two diamond bracelets,' whispered Miss Madden conspiratorially. 'I thought you might like to choose first.'

'I'll take the bigger one,' said Cameron grimly.

James was even more annoyed to find that Declan had ten times more Christmas cards than he had, and that the Christmas tree in Reception completely obscured James's framed photograph. Declan's photograph had been deliberately left unhidden for all to admire.

Despite being horribly broke, Declan sold a first edition of Trollope and gave everyone who worked on his programme, including Cameron, a Christmas pudding and a pep pill for Christmas. He also took them out to a splendid lunch at The Dog and Trumpet outside Cotchester, whose manager subsequently barred anyone from Corinium Television from ever crossing the threshold again.

As the Senior Cameraman pointed out, 'You don't need directions to go to one of Corinium's Christmas parties – just follow the blue flashing lights.'

Afterwards they all conga-ed down Cotchester High Street back to the office, where Declan found Charles Fairburn, who was meant to be organizing the live transmission of Midnight Mass from Cotchester Cathedral that evening, drinking Cointreau and doing his expenses.

Russian hat £100, wrote Charles, dinner with Dean and Chapter £80. Dinner with Chapter £100. 'The trouble with you, Declan,' he said, shaking his head, 'is that you're not creative enough in your expenses.'

In the newsroom the Corinium weather man leant out of the window at sunset, just to check that the forecast he was about to give on air of a very fine evening was correct. Next moment he received a bucket of cold water over his newly washed hair.

'It's raining, you berk,' shouted a voice from above.

Declan took a box of chocolates up to Miss Madden, who'd always been nice to him. After she'd thanked him profusely, she confided that her nephew, who was a chorister, had been chosen to sing a solo at Midnight Mass.

'My heart felt like bursting with pride, and I wanted to cry at the same time,' she said.

Cotchester by midnight, with the golden houses and the great cathedral floodlit, was at its most beautiful. The huge blue spruce just inside the cathedral gates, which was normally a glorious sight festooned with fairy lights at Christmas, was sadly bare this year, because the conservationists, headed by Simon Harris, had claimed the lights were harmful to it.

The church which was lit by candles, white fairy lights on the Christmas tree and television lights, was absolutely packed, with people hoping both to appear on television and to catch a glimpse of Declan O'Hara.

Tony read the first lesson and stumbled twice, to his entire staff's delight. Rupert read the second in his flat drawl, and hardly a girl in the congregation, except Taggie, didn't long to have him in her stocking the following morning.

'Please God, if you think it's right, give me Ralphie,' prayed Taggie.

Caitlin, taking communion, couldn't stop thinking about AIDS. But she knew one had to swallow three pints of saliva before one caught it. As she clumped down the aisle in her new black suede brothel-creepers and her wildly fashionable da-glo cat-sick yellow socks, she could have sworn Rupert was looking at her. In the long wait while everyone else took communion, Patrick, also wearing wildly fashionable da-glo cat-sick yellow socks, held out a cracker and Caitlin pulled it with a loud bang.

'I wonder if Aengus and Gertrude knelt down at midnight to honour the birth of Christ,' said Patrick, as they drove home. Far from honouring anyone's birth, sulking at being left behind, Aengus had knocked off and smashed several balls from the Christmas tree and Gertrude had opened three presents from underneath and also chewed the label off a small parcel for Taggie. Inside was the most beautiful silver pendant inlaid with amethysts on a silver chain. She gasped as she slowly read the note:

> *'Darling Taggie, I'm sorry I've been such a sod. Have a lovely Christmas. See you on New Year's Eve. All Love R.'*

'Oh it's beautiful,' she said with a sob, and fled upstairs, clutching herself in ecstasy.

Outside, the stars and the new moon seemed to be shining just for her. Ralphie had remembered after all, and in seven days she'd see him again.

RIVALS
17

By New Year's Eve the Christmas decorations at The Priory were sagging, the evergreens had brewer's droop, and Wandering Aengus, having smashed every coloured ball on the Christmas tree, had taken up crash-landing in the Christmas cards.

Outside, a force five gale, Hurricane Fiona, as Patrick had called her, was rampaging up the valley, rattling the windows, and howling down the chimneys. On the lawn a huge pink-and-white-striped marquee, heated by gas burners, wrestled with its moorings.

'Perhaps we could enter it for the Americas Cup,' said Caitlin.

'We can line all the drunks round the bottom to hold it down,' said Patrick, taking another slug of Moët.

'You'll be one of them if you don't stop knocking back that stuff,' said Caitlin reprovingly.

'It's my birthday. Everyone is entitled to behave appallingly on their birthday. *Oh, I've got the key-hee-hee of the door, never been twenty-one before.*' He was extremely happy because, unknown to his father, his mother had given him a new Golf for his birthday.

As Maud had gone off to the hairdressers and to pick up a new dress that was being altered, Patrick and Caitlin carried on doing the seating plan she had started. Taggie had tried to write names on some of the cards, but was in such a state of excitement about Ralphie's arrival that her spelling had gone totally to pot. Worried about the marquee coming down, she had gone off to ring the firm who'd put it up. Her arms ached from mashing the potato for a dozen enormous shepherds' pies. She seemed to have put crosses in a million sprouts and peeled a billion grapes for the fruit salad. The garlic bread lay like a pile of silver slugs in its aluminium foil. The turkey soup only needed heating up. The kedgeree for breakfast was in four huge dishes on top of the deep freeze, with cucumber, prawns and hard-boiled eggs, ready chopped to add at the last moment. Patrick's birthday cake, in the shape of a shamrock, rested in the fridge.

An extension lead still had to be found for the disco, a bulb was needed for the outside light, and Caitlin still hadn't written out large cards to show people where the loos were and where to hang their coats.

But things were gradually getting under control. Taggie had never felt so tired in her life. She had cooked herself into the ground, but she kept telling herself that if she got through everything and didn't grumble, God would reward her with Ralphie.

Back in the marquee, Caitlin was hastily rewriting new name cards for people Taggie had seriously misspelt.

'Monknicker Baddingham,' she giggled. 'Do let's leave that one. Put Monknicker on Daddy's right.'

'I'll put Joanna Lumley on his left. He needs some fun,' said Patrick, 'although, as it's my birthday, I ought to have her next to me.'

'Look,' screeched Caitlin. 'Utterly bloody Mummy's put Rupert Campbell-Black next to her. I'm bloody sitting next to him.'

Removing the card from Maud's right, she bore it off and placed it reverently beside hers, three tables away and behind a huge flower arrangement, so her mother couldn't spy.

'In fact – ' she scribbled Rupert's name on to a second card – 'I'm going to put him on both sides of me so there's no slip up.'

Looking at his place, Patrick noted that he was sitting next to Lavinia, his current girlfriend, and someone called Sarah Stratton.

'Oh, I'll swap her,' said Caitlin, seizing Sarah's card. 'She's ancient – at least twenty-six.'

'I was rather excited by the sound of her,' said Patrick. 'Mum said she was very beautiful and voluptuous, with a rich crumbling husband. My only answer is to marry a rich wife. I wish Pa would cut me out of his will. If I inherit all his debts, I'm finished.'

'Oh well, I'll swap Sarah back again,' said Caitlin. 'I've put Tag next to Ralphie.'

Patrick shook his head: 'I wouldn't. He and Georgina Harrison have been inseparable all term. He's bringing her tonight.'

'Well, why did he send Tag that amethyst pendant then, and apologize for being such a sod?'

'Sounds *most* unlikely. Last week he couldn't afford to buy his mother a box of handkerchiefs for Christmas, and he still owes me fifty pounds. Are you sure it was Ralphie?'

'Quite sure, the two-timing shit.'

'Shut up, she's coming.'

'I got through to the tent man; he's coming over. He says they're going all round Gloucester double-checking their erections,' said Taggie with a giggle, then turned pale as the doorbell rang.

But it was only two young pink and white Old Etonians who were doing the disco, and Maud back from the hairdressers, with her hair set in a mass of snaky curls.

'It looks lovely, Mummy,' said Taggie.

'It looks gross,' muttered Caitlin.

The telephone rang. It was Bas Baddingham.

'Darling Maud, may I bring my new new lady?'

'Of course,' said Maud. 'More the merrier. Damn,' she added as she put down the telephone, 'another really attractive spare man paired up. Who the hell's going to dance with Cameron Cook?'

'You haven't asked *her*?' said Taggie in horror, thinking of the wrecked smoking jacket. 'Daddy can't stand her.'

'How many d'you reckon are coming?' said Patrick, giving a glass of Moët to each of the pink and white Etonians, who were both staring at Taggie.

'About two to three hundred,' said Maud airily.

'But we haven't hired nearly enough plates or knives or forks or anything,' said Taggie aghast, 'or got anywhere to seat them.'

Maud turned to Patrick. 'Pop across the valley to Rupert's and borrow some,' she said.

'I didn't know he was coming too,' whispered Taggie, even more horrified. 'I thought he was away skiing.'

'He's come back specially for the party,' said Maud dreamily. 'It was too windy for him to land the helicopter but I've just seen him driving through Penscombe. Well, if there's nothing else for me to do, I'm going upstairs to paint my nails.' As she went out, running her eyes over the table seating, she caught sight of Rupert's cards on both sides of Caitlin.

Tearing one up in a rage, she put the other back on her right. 'You will not sit next to Rupert, Caitlin, you're going to sit next to Archie Baddingham and like it.' She turned back to Taggie.

'Has Grace made up the beds for all Patrick's friends?'

'Someone insulted her in the pub at lunchtime,' said Taggie. 'Introduced her as Declan O'Hara's scrubber, so she's gone to bed in a huff.'

'Well, get her up,' snapped Maud. 'At least you've got Valerie Jones's char and her two children and that butler Reg and his friends coming to help, but you better make up some more beds.'

'They can all sleep in armchairs,' said Patrick soothingly as he gathered up his new car keys. 'I'll go and borrow those plates from Rupert.'

'I've made up a bed for Ralphie in the spare room,' said Taggie, blushing.

At six-thirty Declan returned home having recorded an interview with the Bishop of Cotchester, which he was aware

211

was totally lacking in sparkle. He had been wracked with increasing foreboding during the day, as one person after another – Charles Fairburn, James Vereker, Simon Harris, Daysee Butler and then, horrors, Cameron Cook and Tony Baddingham – said they'd see him this evening. Maud had obviously got tighter than he'd realized at the Corinium Christmas party. But he never expected the frantically billowing pink and white tent on the lawn or the tables laid for two hundred people, or the disco boys checking acoustics, or the three hundred bottles of Moët on ice in various baths round the house.

Roaring upstairs, he found Maud lying on the bed naked except for a face pack and an Optrex eyepad.

'What the fuck is going on? Do you want to ruin me?' He slammed the door behind him.

In the drawing-room below, a group of Patrick's glamorous friends, who'd just arrived and were having a drink, could see the mistletoe hanging from the chandelier trembling beneath Declan's demented pacing. Then they heard Maud screaming.

'Oh dear,' sighed Caitlin, 'Daddy doesn't seem in a party mood.'

Upstairs, Taggie was frantically making up beds for Patrick's friends. Perfectly happy to sleep together in the narrowest of beds all term at Trinity Dublin, now they were sleeping in the house of one of their friend's parents, all the girls, overcome by a fit of morality, said they wanted separate rooms.

The din was increasing in her parents' room.

Maud was careful not to be too provocative. She didn't want her eye blacked. Eye-shadow and mascara were more becoming.

'*Peace on earth, and mercy mild, God and sinners reconciled,*' sang Caitlin outside the door. 'Shut up you two, you're upsetting Gertrude.'

Taggie could hear another lot of Patrick's friends arriving downstairs, crying: '*Happy Birthday.*' Running to the banisters, she could see Patrick's exquisite girlfriend, Lavinia,

212

giving him a present. She was followed by a beautiful dark girl and behind her – Taggie caught her breath – just under the mistletoe in the hall, stood Ralphie. He seemed to have got even more beautiful with his big blue eyes and blond curls.

In a panic she rushed back into the spare room, put another log on the fire, and re-arranged the Christmas roses in the blue jug beside the bed. At least they had curtains in this room, and a really comfortable bed for Ralphie – and perhaps her. Taggie clutched herself; she must not be presumptuous. There was a knock on the door.

'Come in,' croaked Taggie, hanging on to the mantelpiece for support.

The beautiful dark girl she'd seen in the hall came through the door. She was very slim and tiny, not more than five foot one.

'Oh what a lovely room,' she said, dumping a squashy bag and a black ruched dress on the bed, 'and a fire too. You are kind. Will I be able to have a bath?'

'Of course,' stammered Taggie, 'but it may not be a hot one.'

'You must be Taggie,' said the girl. 'You look just like Patrick. Oh, look at the lovely Christmas roses! You shouldn't have bothered.'

Taggie, blushing so hard she felt she could fry an egg on her face, said, 'Actually this is Ralphie's room.'

'And mine,' said the girl happily. 'I'm Georgina Harrison, Ralphie's girlfriend.'

Patrick had never seen such grief. Taggie seemed almost deranged, her whole body shuddering and shuddering with sobs.

'I can't bear it, I can't bear it, I love him so much.'

'Angel, I know you do. But really it's not on. He's frightfully shallow, and you're simply not his type. It's not anything you've done, you're just too large for him. It's like expecting a chihuahua to mate with a wolfhound. Well, not quite, but, being small, he feels daunted by tall girls. He said to me last

213

summer, "Your sister'd be absolutely heartbreaking, if only she were tiny." '

'I can't shrink.'

'Go off and nibble a mushroom.'

'Don't make jokes,' sobbed Taggie.

'Sweetheart, you've got to pull yourself together and get dressed. Mum and Dad have stopped rowing, but there's no way they can organize the grub. Mrs Makepiece has arrived with two frightful teenage children, and Grace and Reg the butler and his friends are all getting stuck into the Moët. You must go down and supervise them. Now be a good girl and dry your eyes. I'm not twenty-one every day.'

Maud had the ability to make houses look beautiful. There were no curtains on the windows, but huge fires crackled in all the downstairs rooms, which were lit by hundreds of red candles and decorated by huge banks of holly, yew and laurel. She was also totally unfazed by being a hostess, or by the frightful row she'd just had with Declan. She had certainly never looked more beautiful. The Medusa curls had dropped a little after her bath, and framed her pale face to which the heat from the fires had given a touch of colour. She was wearing a very low-cut ivy-green taffeta dress with a bustle, which brought out the witchy green of her eyes and clung to her figure. She'd lost seven pounds, hardly eating a thing over Christmas. Pearls gleamed at her wrists, her ears and her throat. If she couldn't ensnare Rupert tonight, she never would.

'New dress,' snarled Declan, tying his black tie in the drawing-room mirror.

'Oh, this old thing,' said Maud mockingly.

'The old thing's in the dress,' said Caitlin sourly.

Pinching some of her mother's scent, she had seen the bill for the dress, and really thought her mother had overdone it this time. Why did she need to spend that much money on clothes when she'd already got a man? Caitlin was worried that her father was deliberately setting out to get drunk, and even more worried about poor old Taggie. But at least at a ball with hundreds of people, Taggie might meet someone new.

'Pretend it's a job, pretend it's a job,' Taggie told herself through gritted teeth, as she stirred the great vats of turkey soup.

'Could you possibly ask Caitlin to make sure Aengus is locked in one of the bedrooms? I'm afraid he might get under a car,' she said to Mrs Makepiece's daughter, Tracey, who, dressed in the tightest of black skirts and a white tricel shirt and pearls, was upwardly mobilizing her spiky hair in the kitchen mirror. Tracey was plainly avid to have a crack at one of Patrick's friends.

Outside, Mrs Makepiece's punk son Kevin was directing cars into a nearby field, and coming in frequently to fortify himself against the cold with slugs of wine. Reg and his two friends were doing sterling work drinking and circulating drink. Grace was already pissed. 'Goodness you look tired,' she said to Taggie. 'What 'ave you been up to?'

Gertrude grew hoarse with barking as more and more people poured in. The party was plainly a success. Maud had produced a splendid mix: lots of London friends, who were knocked out by the beauty of the house and how good Maud was looking. Many of them had brought teenage children who were borne off upstairs for Malibu and coke in Caitlin's bedroom. Then there were Patrick's glamorous friends from Trinity, a large contingent from Corinium Television, and all Maud and Declan's new friends from Gloucestershire, who were thoroughly over-excited to see so many London celebs. With two hours' hard drinking before dinner, most people were soon absolutely plastered.

Bas Baddingham stunned everyone by turning up with a most beautiful wife – somebody else's.

'She left Alistair on December 12th, and was out hunting the very next day,' said Valerie Jones in a shocked voice.

Valerie could also be heard saying repeatedly that she was simply exhausted after so many parties. 'Fred-Fred and Ay simply longed for a poached egg in front of TV tonight, but we felt we couldn't let the O'Haras down,' she said to Lizzie Vereker. 'What a crush, I hope we daine soon.'

'Did you have a good Christmas?' Lizzie asked Freddie.

'Amizing,' said Freddie. 'Got some triffic presents. The staff gave me a fireman's helmet, cos I'm always rushin' about, and Rupert sent me a loaf of Mother's Pride.'

Lizzie giggled.

'Typical,' said Valerie, her lips tightening.

'And those bantams' eggs you gave us were triffic, too. You can taste the difference. I 'ad one for my breakfast this morning.' Freddie beamed at Lizzie.

'Nonsense, Fred-Fred,' said Valerie with a little laugh, 'that egg came from Tesco's.'

James, who'd skipped lunch because he was having his roots touched up, was drinking more than usual and thinking what a lot of amazingly beautiful women there were around: Joanna Lumley over there, and Patricia Hodge, and Pamela Armstrong, and Selina Scott and Ann Diamond.

Maud was looking sensational too, and there was Sarah Stratton, *not* looking as good as usual. There were black rings under her eyes, but she still exuded wantonness.

Sarah was, in fact, in a foul mood. She hadn't had any lunch either, because she'd been hunting for a dress to wear this evening. She had missed Rupert horribly over Christmas. He obviously couldn't ring her, as Paul had been home all the time, but she hadn't even had a postcard, and then in Nigel Dempster's column that morning there'd been a picture of Rupert skiing, with his arm round an incredibly glamorous French actress called Nathalie Perrault. She'd kill him when she saw him.

Where the hell was he, anyway? Who could she flirt with to irritate him? The most attractive men in the room, Sarah decided, were Declan, who was already drunk, and Declan's son, a raving beauty, who was going to be very formidable in a few years' time when he filled out. Sarah shimmied out to the marquee and, finding Rupert's place card, moved it next to hers. How dare the bastard dally with Nathalie Perrault?

Bloody Paul had read Dempster too, and made sly little digs about it all day.

Tony, to his amazement, was thoroughly enjoying the party. Shrewd enough to appreciate his vanity, Maud was treating him as the guest of honour, keeping him constantly plied with celebrities, mostly beautiful women, and introducing him to them as: 'Declan's gorgeous boss. You must get him to ask you down to Corinium, darling.' Tony was soon purring like a great leopard let loose in a goat farm.

Archie, Tony's beloved son, was getting plastered upstairs with Caitlin's friends. Poor fat Sharon Jones was desperately shy. Caitlin had introduced her to boy after boy, ordering them to look after her, but within seconds Sharon had waddled back to her increasingly irritated mother.

'I told you, go and make some friends of your own age,' hissed Valerie furiously.

Mrs Makepiece sidled up to Maud. 'Miss Taggie says we ought to eat; everything's ready.'

'We can't till Rupert arrives,' said Maud firmly. 'Tell her to wait ten minutes.'

The doorbell rang. Perhaps this was him. She went into the hall, but Declan got there first, and it was only Simon Harris barging in with the two hyperactive monsters, and the baby in a carrycot.

'Hullo, Declan,' panted Simon. 'Sorry we're late. Nice of you to invite the whole brood.' Then, seeing Declan's look of horror, he explained, 'I talked to someone called Grace, who said it'd be quite all right.'

Looking around, deciding that this was the sort of nice messy house that wouldn't mind children, Simon let go of the two little monsters. 'Where shall I put the baby?'

At that moment, Rupert sauntered through the open door with snow on his dinner jacket and in his hair, the dingy grey pallor of Simon Harris throwing his Gstaad suntan into even greater relief.

'Rupert,' said Maud joyfully, 'you made it.'

She looked so beautiful, glowing under the hall mistletoe,

that Rupert kissed her on the mouth. 'You look sensational,' he said.

'Not nearly as sensational as you,' whispered Maud. 'You must have had wonderful weather.'

'I can feel the temperature dropping here,' said Rupert, as Declan turned on his heel and stalked off towards the kitchen. 'What's up with him?'

'Oh he's just in a bait.' Maud turned to the passing Reg. 'Bring Mr Campbell-Black a bucket of whisky.'

Going back to the kitchen via the marquee, Caitlin put her place card back on Rupert's right and removed Wandering Aengus who was sitting on Valerie's plate.

'Wonderful party,' she said to Taggie who was grimly pouring turkey soup into bowls on trays. 'Rupert's arrived looking like a red Indian, so Mummy says we can eat now, and Daddy's terribly drunk.'

'Daddy's not the only one,' said Taggie. 'You should see Reg and his friends. Both Tracey and Kev have already buggered off upstairs, and good old Grace is singing "This Joyful Eastertide".'

18

Tony Baddingham was even happier at dinner sitting between Joanna Lumley and Sarah Stratton.

'I know by rights you should be on *my* right,' Maud had whispered in his ear, 'but I thought you deserved a treat.'

'Freddie and Ay'll be leaving early,' said Valerie as she went into dinner. 'The West Cotchester are meeting at Green Lawns tomorrow.'

'They're not meeting anywhere,' said Rupert. 'It's frozen solid outside, so we can all get frightfully drunk.'

He wondered what had happened to Taggie. He couldn't find her name on the seating plan.

'You're over here, next to me,' Maud called to Rupert, patting the seat beside her.

'And next to me,' beamed Caitlin, bolting up to the table and whipping away Cameron Cook's place card which was on his other side.

Maud could have murdered Caitlin, but she didn't want a scene in public.

'You better say Grace,' giggled Caitlin, who'd been at the Malibu, 'and she'll come running in singing "This Joyful Eastertide".'

It was obvious, reflected Tony with satisfaction, that Maud and Declan had had the most frightful row – probably about money. Earlier in the day Declan had very forcibly stressed that it was a tiny party, just a few friends, but there must be at least three hundred people here and by the way the Moët was being splashed about, nothing had been stinted, which was good, because the broker Declan got, the more dependent he'd be on Corinium, and the more Tony could torment and manipulate him.

Then, looking across the room at Maud's enraptured face turned towards Rupert, her elbows pressed together to deepen her cleavage, her turkey soup untouched, he decided it was more likely that Declan was upset because his wife had a thumping great crush on Rupert. This suited Tony even better, because it meant Declan would crucify Rupert even more when he interviewed him in the New Year.

Sarah Stratton, who'd stopped to say hullo to Rupert on the way in, was looking rather bleak as she sat down beside Tony.

'I'm glad we're next to each other,' he said. 'I wanted to talk to you.'

'Have you made any New Year's resolutions?' said Sarah, picking up her soup spoon.

'Yes,' said Tony, his swarthy pirate's face suddenly looking as though he was going to fight off a flotilla of rival clipper ships, 'to keep the franchise.'

'I'll drink to that,' said Sarah.

'I wouldn't mind,' said Simon Harris across the room, helping himself to a seventh piece of garlic bread, 'but Tony came roaring in today saying I'm not having fucking language like that on any fucking programme going out from my fucking station.'

'Sorry to bother you, Mr Harris,' said Mrs Makepiece, 'but your baby's crying.'

It was not surprising the baby was upset, surrounded as it was upstairs by scenes of Petronian debauchery, as teenagers smoked, drank, necked, and screamed with laughter as they opened another packet of Tampax and shot the cotton wool out like cannons.

Archie was sharing a bottle of Moët with Caitlin, who had briefly abandoned Rupert at dinner to smoke an illicit cigarette.

'What has an Upland House girl in common with a Tampax?' Archie asked her.

'Dunno,' said Caitlin.

'They're both stuck-up cunts.'

Caitlin screamed with laughter. 'Have you got a girlfriend?'

'I did,' said Archie, 'but she went off me because of my zits.'

'You mustn't worry about zits,' said Caitlin kindly. 'It means you're producing lots of Testosterone and will make a wonderfully vigorous lover later. Piss off, you snotty little buggers,' she screamed, as Simon Harris's monsters raced up and down giggling at the necking teenagers and threatening each other with one of Rupert's borrowed knives.

'My father said all your family were weirdos,' said Archie, 'but I think you're cool.'

Declan, whom Maud had put deliberately between Monica and Valerie, so he couldn't make a scene, was so drunk he was in danger of seriously jeopardizing his career. He didn't even realize Monica was talking about *Otello* until she got onto Iago.

'He's an even more evil character than Scarpia,' she was saying.

'Much more,' agreed Declan. 'Very like your husband in fact.'

'Garlic bread, either of you?' said Valerie, unable to believe her ears.

'Your husband is an absolute shit,' said Declan.

'I know,' said Monica calmly, as she tore off a piece of garlic bread. 'However, I have three children and I don't believe in divorce.'

'Nor do I,' said Declan, filling up both their glasses.

Valerie was absolutely livid when the farmer on her left said, 'You live at Long Bottom Court, don't you?' She didn't want to talk to him at all. She wanted to listen to what Monica was saying to Declan.

'You won't try and wind Tony up too much at work, will

you?' went on Monica. 'You're very good for Corinium. They need people with integrity. I'd like you to stay.'

'I'm not sure your husband would.'

'I think we'd both better stop discussing Tony,' said Monica gently, 'or we might become very indiscreet. This is a very good party. Maud's looking so beautiful.'

'Has anyone ever told you you're a beautiful woman?' said Declan.

Monica went pink. 'That's jolly well overdoing it. You really ought to eat some of this shepherd's pie. It's frightfully good.'

But Declan was looking at Maud who was gazing at Rupert. '*O heart! O heart!*' he murmured, '*if she'd but turn her head.*'

'*You'd know the folly of being comforted,*' said Monica, finishing the quotation for him. 'Don't worry about Rupert,' she went on briskly. 'Bertie Berkshire once described him as a "particularly nasty virus, that one's wife caught sooner or later", but we all get over it.'

Declan looked back at her, startled. 'Even you?'

Monica sighed. 'Even me, although Rupert had no idea. Don Giovanni must have been very like him. He can't resist the conquest, and I think, although he won't admit it, he still misses show-jumping desperately, and it's a question of constantly filling the aching void.'

'He's usually filling other people's wives' aching voids,' said Declan bitterly.

At last Maud had to stop monopolizing Rupert and turn to Declan's old boss at the BBC, Johnny Abrahams, who was sitting on her left.

'Lovely party, darling,' he said. 'Hope you can pay for it. What's up with Declan? Not working out with Tony Baddingham? I did warn him.'

'Don't be silly,' said Maud. 'You know Declan always has rows wherever he is. But look at him now, getting on like a house on fire with Tony's wife.'

'You can talk to me now,' said Caitlin to Rupert.

'How d'you do? I saw you at Midnight Mass,' said Rupert. He liked her merry face and her bright beady eyes.

'Tell me,' he went on lowering his voice, 'is your sister ever going to forgive me?'

'Ah,' said Caitlin, 'well, you haven't been very nice to her. I heard about the groping at the dinner party, which was pretty crass, and the row over the stubble burning. Taggie probably over-reacted there; she's so soppy about animals, she spends her time prising frozen worms off the paths in this weather. What really pissed her off was that you were so unkind about Gertrude.'

'Gertrude?' said Rupert, bewildered.

'Our dog. You may think Gertrude is very plain, but we're all devoted to her. Taggie's led such a sheltered life, she's never left home like Patrick and me, and she and Gertrude have never been parted.'

Rupert grinned. 'Perhaps I should have sent Gertrude a pendant instead.'

'Oh my God,' said Caitlin in horror, 'it was *you*! Because you signed it R, we all assumed it was from Ralphie. Taggie's mad about him, you see.'

'Glad I gave her a happy Christmas,' said Rupert acidly.

'But she's not happy now, because Ralphie's turned up with another woman.'

'Which is he?'

'That blond over there. Taggie likes blonds, so if you give her time . . .'

'Caitlin,' said Maud very sharply, 'go and tell Taggie to clear away the fruit salad plates. We must have Patrick's cake, or we'll be still sitting here at midnight.' She turned to Rupert. 'We've managed to get tickets for *Starlight Express* the week after next. D'you want to come?'

'Don't talk about things that happen after I go back,' grumbled Caitlin, getting up.

'Taggie, Taggie,' she squealed, racing into the kitchen, 'Mummy wants the plates cleared, then we can have Patrick's cake.'

'There isn't anyone to clear them,' said Taggie in despair. 'Both the Makepiece children have vanished, and I can't find Mrs Makepiece or Grace, or Reg, or either of Reg's friends.'

'Never mind that now,' said Caitlin. 'This is *far* more exciting. It was Rupert who sent you that pendant, because he was sorry about goosing you at Valerie Jones's.'

'There's no way we're going to get 300 slices out of this.' Taggie nearly dropped Patrick's cake. 'What did you say?'

'Rupert sent you the pendant.'

'He couldn't have,' whispered Taggie. 'I hate him.'

'No, you don't. He's really nice. Go and sit next to him. I'll try and find Reg and his mates to carry the cake in and people can eat it on their fruit salad plates. Go on, Tag.'

'Never, never,' gasped Taggie. She was deathly pale now. 'I'm going to send it back.'

Maud's plans had gone seriously awry. She had wanted them all to be dancing and she and Rupert to be standing under one of Caitlin's hundred bunches of mistletoe at midnight, but they were still sitting at the tables waiting for Patrick to cut his cake. Why on earth couldn't Taggie be more efficient?

At five minutes to midnight Declan got somewhat unsteadily to his feet, and tapped the table with his knife. 'I'm very pleased to see you all here tonight,' he said, 'and I'd just like to drink my son Patrick's health. He's a good boy and he's given us a lot of pleasure over the years.'

'And me too,' piped up Patrick's girlfriend, Lavinia, and everyone laughed and sang 'Happy Birthday' and said 'Speech! Speech!' As Reg and his mates staggered in very perilously carrying the cake, Patrick stood up. Speaking in public didn't rattle him in the least. He had all Declan's assurance:

'I'd like to thank my father and mother for having me,' he said, 'and giving me such a wonderful party, and for my sister Taggie for doing all the work, and making this wonderful cake.' For a second Maud looked furious at the loudness of the cheers. 'Thank you all for coming, and for all your presents, which I'll open later when I get a moment.'

There were more loud cheers. Then, just as Caitlin finished lighting the candles, like the dark stranger coming over the

224

threshold, Cameron Cook walked in. She was wearing an extremely tight-fitting, strapless, black suede dress, which came eight inches above her knees. Three-inch cross-laced gaps on either side from armpit to hem made it quite plain she was wearing nothing but Fracas and Mantan underneath. There was a heavy metal chain round her neck, and among the heavy silver bangles worn over her long black suede gloves gleamed Tony's diamond bracelet.

Anyone else would have looked tarty in that dress, but Cameron, with her marvellously lean, sinuous, rapacious beauty, succeeded in looking both menacing and absolutely staggering.

'Holy shit,' said Patrick into the microphone.

Everyone screamed with laughter.

'Blow out your candles,' said Caitlin.

Still gazing at Cameron, Patrick blew them out with one puff, then turned to Declan. 'Who the hell's that?'

'The biggest bitch in television,' said Declan bleakly.

'She may well be your future daughter-in-law,' said Patrick.

'Christ, I can just see her with a whip,' muttered Bas to Rupert.

'Perhaps that's what gets your brother going.'

Basil turned to Daysee Butler: 'Did you know your boss was heavily into SM?'

'Who's she?' said Daysee.

'Sorry I'm late,' said Cameron, fighting her way through the crowd to Maud's side. 'We've had a lot of hassle at work.'

'Lovely to see you at any time,' said Maud. 'Caitlin,' she added pointedly, terrified that Caitlin might start monopolizing Rupert again, 'will get you something to eat.'

'She needs a drink,' said Patrick.

Goodness, he's pretty, thought Cameron. Like Declan, but purer-looking, somehow.

'Aren't you going to cut your cake?' she said to him.

'I've got to wish,' said Patrick. Never taking his eyes off her, he slowly plunged the knife into the cake, right up to the hilt.

'I didn't have time to buy you a present,' said Cameron.

'You brought yourself,' said Patrick, slightly mockingly. 'Just what I wanted.'

Filling up his glass with champagne, he handed it to her.

'Thanks.' Taking it, Cameron drained the glass.

Just at that moment, from speakers all round the tent, Big Ben boomed out the twelve strokes of midnight. As everyone started kissing everyone else and cheering, Patrick drew Cameron into his arms and kissed her on and on and on.

At last they broke away.

'The *coup de foudre*,' said Patrick softly. 'I've waited twenty-one years for this to happen.'

'Look at Tony's face,' whispered Lizzie Vereker to Charles Fairburn with a shiver.

As the last notes of 'Auld Lang Syne' rang out, Declan could be heard saying, 'Bloody January again.'

Plates were being cleared away, tables pushed back and the marquee cleared for dancing, as the women drifted upstairs to do their faces. Telling Cameron he wouldn't be a second, Patrick went off to the kitchen to thank Taggie. Oblivious that Monica might be watching, Tony fought his way over to Cameron and seized her arm: 'What the hell are you playing at?'

Cameron winced. 'Celebrating Christmas. It hasn't been great so far.'

'I couldn't get away.'

'I guess not.'

'That dress is deliberately provocative,' snarled Tony.

'Well, if it deliberately provokes you, it's doing a great job.'

'Why are you so fucking late?'

'Titania's four months gone.'

'Shit. How d'you know?'

'Wardrobe told me,' said Cameron.

'And she's admitted it?'

'Sure.'

'Who's the father?'

'She's not sure. It could be Bottom, or Theseus or even Peter Quince.'

226

'Jesus – we'll just have to shoot round her.'

Patrick never made it to the kitchen. Declan dragged him into the library.

'For Christ's sake, Cameron's out of bounds.'

'Why?'

'She's Tony Baddingham's mistress.'

'So. Are you frightened of losing your job?'

For a second Patrick thought Declan was going to hit him.

'It's not that. You've no idea of the evil of both of them.'

'He may be, she's not. She just needs someone of her own age to play with for a change.'

'He's taught her some very unpleasant habits,' said Declan heavily.

'Like arguing with you, I suppose,' said Patrick.

'She's out of your league.'

'I don't give a fuck,' said Patrick, walking out.

'You don't have to take your clothes off to have a good time, oh no,' sang Jermaine Stewart from the disco. *'You can dance and party all night.'*

Still arguing with Tony, seeing both Monica and Patrick bearing purposefully down on her, Cameron escaped to check her face. After Patrick's kiss, she certainly couldn't have any lipstick left. Upstairs, in the only bedroom that didn't seem to be inhabited by necking teenagers, she found Sarah Stratton brushing her hair.

'Good party,' said Sarah.

'It seems so.'

'I'm glad I bumped into you,' said Sarah. 'Tony's offered me a job at Corinium. Ought I to take it?'

'Sure,' said Cameron coolly.

'You don't think he's just after my body?'

'No way,' said Cameron, who was having difficulty applying lipstick, her hands were trembling so much.

'I just wondered.' Sarah dropped her head, brushing all her hair downwards. 'Tony and Monica are an awfully weird couple, you know. Paul's ex-wife, Winifred, used to be Monica's best chum. I've often wondered if they weren't a

227

bit dykey.' Sarah tossed her head back, so her hair rose, then cascaded wildly onto her shoulders.

'Monica evidently told Winifred,' she went on, 'that Tony made such incredible sexual demands on her that she had to move into a separate bedroom. He wanted it two or three times every night. Now she restricts him to once a week, like church. Perhaps that's why he's so lecherous.'

As if in a dream, Cameron watched Sarah spray Anaïs Anaïs between her breasts, then behind her kneecaps and finally, pulling out her pants, on her blonde bush.

'Did Tony make a pass at you?' Cameron said in a frozen voice.

'Not exactly – but he was terrifically complimentary,' said Sarah. 'And I must say for an older man he's not unattractive.'

As they came downstairs James Vereker was hovering. Deliberately ignoring Cameron, he asked Sarah to dance. Oh well, thought Sarah, anything to make Rupert jealous.

'How did you get on with Tony's mistress?' asked James.

'Oh my Christ, is she?' gasped Sarah, appalled, and she told James what had happened. 'I'd better not take that job at Corinium after all,' she said finally.

'She'd certainly have it in for you,' said James. 'She has it in for any beautiful woman.' (And man for that matter, he nearly added.) 'If you came to Corinium – ' his arm tightened round her – 'I'd look after you and show you the ropes.'

'Isn't television frightfully difficult?'

'Not if you've got a teacher who really cares,' said James.

I'll kill Tony, I'll absolutely kill him, thought Cameron as, seething with rage, she went into the marquee. Both Tony and Patrick were waiting. Patrick was quicker.

'Come and dance,' he said, taking her hand. 'I'm not going to let you go for the rest of the evening, probably not for the rest of my life.'

'D'you always move in so fast?' said Cameron, laughing.

'No, I wished for you when I cut my cake.'

'You mustn't tell wishes; they might not come true.'

'Mine always do,' said Patrick calmly.

Taggie was mindlessly washing up in the kitchen when Simon Harris's little monsters returned and, saying they were hungry, broke through the clingfilm over the kedgeree and started eating it with their hands. Something finally snapped inside Taggie.

'Bugger off, you little horrors,' she screamed.

'Talking to me?' said a voice.

Rupert was standing in the doorway. He was as brown as he'd been last summer when he'd had no clothes on. Taggie went scarlet.

Rupert grinned. 'Your mother was only telling me the other day, how much you adore children.' Then, turning on the monsters, 'Go on, fuck off, you little sods. Out, OUT!'

Muttering venomously, the monsters sidled out, cramming birthday cake into their mouths as they went.

'It was the most lovely dinner,' said Rupert gently, noticing Taggie's reddened eyes. 'Will you please stop playing Cinderella and come and dance.'

'I've got too much to do, thank you, and thank you for the pendant. I didn't realize.' She stumbled on the words.

At that moment Simon Harris came in with spewed-up rusk all over his dinner jacket, carrying a bawling baby.

'Could you possibly hold her for me while I heat up a bottle?' he asked Taggie.

Of two evils, Taggie chose the prettier. 'There's a saucepan over there,' she said and, feeling Rupert's hand close over hers, she followed him into the marquee.

'I'm a very, very bad dancer,' she muttered.

'Doesn't matter,' said Rupert. 'We can sway in a dark corner.'

'*Never seen you look so lovely as you do tonight,*' sang Chris de Burgh, '*Never seen you shine so bright.*'

Taggie's hair smelt of shepherd's pie. As he drew her to him, Rupert could feel the substantial softness of her breasts, compared with the incredible slenderness of her waist. Her body was rigid with tension and embarrassment. She had absolutely no sense of rhythm at all. It was like a very slim elephant dancing at the circus.

'Did you have a nice Christmas?' asked Rupert.

'Yes.'

'Did you get nice presents?'

'Yes.'

'Come on my angel, relax.' His hands moved over her back, gentling her as though she was one of his young horses. 'Look! Gertrude's followed us. She knows I'm a rotter and she won't let you out of her sight.'

Catching Gertrude's disapproving eye, Taggie gave a half laugh, half sob.

Rupert reached down and stroked Gertrude. 'Good Gertrude, beautiful Gertrude. See, I am trying.'

'*Lady in red, Lady in red,*' sang everyone as they swayed round the floor, which were the only words they knew.

Rupert took Taggie's face in his hands. She was so tall her eyes were only just below his.

'Don't be so sad,' he murmured. 'You'll get over him.'

Taggie started. 'How d'you know?'

'Caitlin told me. You thought the pendant was from him. I'm sorry.'

'It was very kind,' said Taggie stiffly. 'I just don't accept presents from men.'

'I see. Only from boys.'

As Chris de Burgh finished and Wham started, he gripped her waist, knowing she was about to bolt.

'*Last Christmas, I gave you my heart,*' sang George Michael, '*But the very next day you gave it away.*'

Across the room Taggie could see Ralphie and Georgina dancing together. He was stroking her cheek with his hand. With a low moan, Taggie tugged herself away from Rupert. Cannoning off startled couples, she fled from the marquee upstairs to the loo to cry her eyes out once again.

Patrick danced on and on with Cameron. They didn't talk much because they were easily the best dancers in the room. Tony, grinding his teeth down to the gums, didn't dare move in with Monica looking on.

'That's the best thing I've seen in years,' said James Vereker, who was dancing on and on with Sarah.

'What?' said Sarah.

'Cameron getting off with Declan's son. At best it'll screw up Tony and Cameron. At worst it'll put Tony even more off Declan.'

Although Paul was hovering, looking thunderous, Sarah carried on dancing with James until she saw Rupert going past. Breaking away, she screamed out to him.

To keep her quiet Rupert bore her off to dance. Paul could see them rowing all the way round the floor, in that rigid-jawed way as though they'd had too many injections at the dentist.

'Why have you been deliberately ignoring me?'

'I haven't. It's just that Paul has been watching us like a Wimbledon linesman.'

'Never put you off in the past.'

'Did you have a good Christmas?'

'Of course I didn't. You obviously did, if the *Daily Mail*'s anything to go by. I don't require fidelity from my husband,' said Sarah hysterically, 'but I do from my lover.'

'Then you've picked the wrong guy, sweetheart. We've had a good time.'

Sarah looked up, aghast. 'Is it over then?'

'No, not necessarily. I'm just not prepared to offer you an exclusive.'

'Bastard,' hissed Sarah. 'I thought you were serious.'

'You were wrong, and frankly, angel, I don't think you make a very good MP's wife. Paul looks a shambles.'

In the kitchen, surrounded by undergraduates and dirty plates and glasses, Declan was declaiming Yeats:

> And the flame of the blue star of twilight, hung low
>   on the rim of the sky,
> Has awaked in our hearts, my beloved, a sadness that
>   may not die.

Cameron stood listening to him, her hand in Patrick's.

'He recites best when he's drunk,' whispered Patrick. 'Loses all self-consciousness.'

'He should do a programme on Yeats,' marvelled Cameron.

'Hardly of local interest.'

'We could do it for Channel Four.'

Upstairs, Maud was arranging her breasts in the green dress, and putting scent on her hair, and applying coral blusher to her pale cheeks. Her freckles were like a sprinkling of nutmeg tonight.

'I'm not middle-aged,' she whispered to herself. 'I'm still young and beautiful.'

'*I get no kick from champagne,*' sang the disco. '*Pure alcohol doesn't thrill me at all.*'

The message was all in the music, thought Maud. Go forth and multiply and seek love.

Going downstairs, she could hear Declan declaiming in the kitchen. She was safe for half an hour or so. Screams and shouts were coming from the direction of Caitlin's room.

The berries of the mistletoe gleamed brighter than her pearls under the hall light. It was three in the morning; soon Taggie would be serving kedgeree. As if in answer to her prayer, Maud heard Rupert's voice, 'Darling, I was looking for you.'

Taking her hand, he led her into the study where Caitlin, taking no chances, had hung more mistletoe. Rupert's hand felt so warm and dry, and the ball of his thumb was so pudgy, noticed Maud. That was the fortune-teller's clue to a passionate highly-sexed nature. It was certainly the only spare flesh on his body. Maud's heart was pounding. She must try and be distant, a little mysterious. As he turned towards her, her eyes were on a level with his black tie. She longed to caress the lovely line of his jaw. It's going to happen, she thought in ecstasy, as Rupert shut the door to blot out the screams and raucous laughter, and coming towards her, gazed deeply into her eyes.

'Angel, I've been wanting to ask you something from the moment we met, certainly from the moment I came over here with Bas after hunting. You won't be cross with me?'

'No, no,' whispered Maud. She was having difficulty breathing.

'You probably think I'm the biggest shit in the world.'

'I don't. I don't. I just think people misunderstand you.'

She could smell the faint lemon tang of his aftershave as he moved nearer.

'I'm absolutely mad,' began Rupert.

'Go on,' stammered Maud.

'About little Taggie, and she can't stand me. Could you possibly put in a good word for me?'

'Taggie,' said Maud in outrage, 'TAGGIE!'

She might have been Lady Bracknell referring to the famous handbag.

'For Christ's sake,' she screamed, 'Taggie's eighteen, you're thirty-seven. She's dyslexic, which makes her seem even younger. How dare you, you revolting letch, how dare you, how DARE you?' And, bursting into tears, she fled upstairs and locked herself in her bedroom.

She couldn't bear it, she, who'd always got anyone she wanted, being spurned under the mistletoe by the biggest rake in Gloucestershire. And for Taggie, of all people, which made it far, far worse. Almost pathologically jealous of Taggie, there was no one in the world Maud would less like to lose a man to. Was that to be her fate, growing older and less attractive, until no one wanted her?

An hour later in the kitchen Declan was still declaiming to an enraptured group.

'Christ, I wish I wasn't too tight to make notes,' said Ralphie.

'You see why he can't go on doing crappy interviews with the Bishop of Cotchester,' said Patrick to Cameron.

Cameron nodded.

•

233

A woman of so shining loveliness, [Declan was saying]
That men threshed corn at midnight by a tress,
A little stolen tress.

He looked up and saw Maud. 'A *little stolen tress*,' he repeated slowly.

For a minute they gazed at each other.

There is grey in your hair, [he began very softly]
Young men no longer catch their breath,
When you are passing.

Maud turned away, her face stricken.

Declan dropped his cigarette into the sink and, stepping over the enraptured seated undergraduates, caught up with Maud on the stairs. Not having had anything to drink for a couple of hours, he was sobering up.

'What's the matter? Did he turn you down?'

Maud nodded, tears spilling out between her eyelashes.

'I've seen it coming since September. I wanted to warn you.'

'Why didn't you then?'

Declan sighed: 'Has there ever been any point? He's no good for you. He's a traveller. It might have lasted a week, a month, then he'd have dumped you.'

He put his huge hands round her neck above the pearl choker.

'I'm sorry,' she mumbled. 'He's just so attractive.'

'I know. Hush, hush.' He raised his thumbs to still her quivering mouth. 'Let's go to bed.'

'We can't in the middle of a party.'

'What better time?'

'I've spent so much money.'

'Doesn't matter,' said Declan as they went up the remaining stairs.

'I love you,' he said softly, 'and I'm the only one of the lot of them who understands you.'

'I know,' whispered Maud.

234

Declan shut the bedroom door behind them.

Caitlin, going past, heard the key turn. Removing the sign outside the loo on which she had earlier written *Ladies*, Caitlin turned it over, wrote *Do Not Disturb, Sex in Progress*, and hung it on her parents' door.

Downstairs, the party showed no signs of winding down.

'I love yew,' said Lizzie, looking at a dark clump of greenery in the corner, as she danced round with Freddie.

'I love you,' said Freddie, giving her a squeeze. 'Honestly, on my life and at least a bottle-and-a-half of Moët.'

It was obvious that Tony wasn't going to be able to prise Cameron away from Patrick for even a second.

'We must go,' he said bleakly to Monica.

'All right,' said Monica reluctantly. 'I haven't seen Archie for hours. Where is he?'

'Upstairs, I think,' said Caitlin.

Monica swayed up the stairs, hanging onto the banisters. She hadn't drunk so much since she was a deb; it was really rather fun.

Finding several rooms heavily occupied by couples, she finally tracked down her elder and beloved son on a *chaise-longue* on the top floor, absolutely superglued to Tracey Makepiece, his hand burrowing like a ferret inside her white tricel shirt.

'Archie,' thundered Monica. 'Drop!'

Archie dropped.

'We're leaving,' said Monica, 'at *once*.'

Downstairs, she told Tony what Archie had been up to.

'Christ,' exploded Tony, 'he might put her in the club. Get him out of this bloody house as fast as possible.'

'I don't know where Declan and Maud are. We ought to thank them,' said Monica, as Archie shuffled sheepishly down the stairs.

Having witnessed the incident, Valerie gave her little laugh: 'One must learn to be democratic, Ay'm afraid these days, Monica. Sharon, of course, gets on with all classes.'

'Evidently,' said Caitlin, sliding down the banisters and

beaming at Valerie. 'She's been wrapped round Kevin Makepiece for the last two hours.'

Giving a screech close to death, Valerie bolted upstairs.

Caitlin turned to Monica, Tony and Archie with a beatific smile on her face. 'I bet Kev a pound he wouldn't neck with Sharon. I suppose I'll have to pay him now.'

'Are your parents around?' said Monica.

'I'm afraid they've gone to bed,' said Caitlin.

'Well, if you'd just tell them how very much we all enjoyed it,' said Monica.

'You may have enjoyed it,' hissed Tony, slipping on the icy drive in his haste to get to the Rolls and the frozen chauffeur, 'but frankly it was the most bloody party I've ever been to, and that child Caitlin is a minx.'

'She's sweet,' protested Archie with a hiccup.

'If you have anything more to do with any of the O'Hara children I'll disinherit you.'

About five in the morning, having behaved just as badly as everyone else, Rupert came back into the drawing-room looking for the whisky decanter, and saw a black and white tail sticking out from under the piano.

'Gertrude,' he said.

The tail quivered. Crouching down, Rupert found both Gertrude and Taggie.

'What on earth are you doing?'

'A drunk's passed out in my bed,' said Taggie with a sob. 'Every other bedroom in the house is occupied; a bloody great party, including Ralphie and his blonde are in the kitchen, so I can't wash up, the disco people haven't been paid, Mummy and Daddy have gone to bed, and I don't want to be a wallflower and cramp everyone's style.'

'You won't cramp mine. Come on.' Rupert dragged her out.

An empty champagne bottle rolled out at the same time.

'You drink all that?'

'Nearly.'

Rupert threw a couple of logs on the dying fire and then

sat Taggie down on the sofa beside him. Gertrude took up her position between them.

'It's been a wonderful party,' he said.

'It hasn't,' said Taggie despairingly. 'It's been a disaster. Patrick's got off with Lord Baddingham's m-mistress, which'll make Lord Baddingham go even more off Daddy. And Mummy's got a terrific crush on someone.' She blushed, remembering it was Rupert, and added hastily, 'I'm not sure who, and poor Daddy's got to pay for it all. I tried and tried to keep the cost down, but then Mummy went off and ordered all that champagne, and invited hundreds and hundreds of people.'

'Your father must earn a good screw from Corinium,' said Rupert reasonably.

'He does –' Taggie cuddled Gertrude like a terrified child clutching a teddy bear – 'but it's not nearly enough. He's got a massive overdraft and we still haven't paid for our leaving party in London, and he got another huge tax bill yesterday, and he hasn't paid the last one yet, and Mummy and Caitlin and Patrick won't take it seriously. They think Daddy's a bottomless pit who'll always provide.

'To produce his best work,' she went on, 'he's got to be kept calm. That's why we moved to the country for some peace and for him to finish his book. And he loathes Lord Baddingham, he thinks he's dreadfully cor – cor . . .' She blocked on the word.

'Corrupt,' said Rupert.

'That's right, and shouldn't be running Corinium at all. Daddy's so headstrong, I'm sure he'll walk out if there are any more rows, and he says the BBC won't have him back.'

Despite being drunk, Rupert appreciated it wasn't at all an ideal set-up.

'Of course the BBC would,' he said. 'Your father's a genius. He's got everything going for him.'

'Except us,' said Taggie with a sob. 'We're all a drain on him.'

'You're not,' said Rupert.

'I am. Ralphie doesn't love me. No one will ever love me.'

Rupert let her cry for a few minutes, then made her laugh by putting his black tie on Gertrude.

'I'm so sorry,' stammered Taggie, wiping her eyes on someone's discarded silk shawl. 'I'm being horribly s-s-self-indulgent.'

'You're not.' Suddenly Rupert felt very avuncular and protective as he did when one of his dogs cut its paw. He wished a visit to the vet and a few stitches could cure Taggie's problems.

'I'm going to get that drunk out of your bed and then you can go to sleep.'

'I must pay the disco – but no one seems to want them to stop – and the Makepieces. I've got the money.' She got a large wad of tenners out of the George V Coronation tin on the desk.

'I'll pay them,' said Rupert, taking the money. 'You're going to bed.'

Up in Taggie's turret bedroom, with some effort, Rupert lifted Charles Fairburn out of the bed and, lugging him down the winding stairs, put him on the *chaise-longue* recently vacated by Archie and Tracey Makepiece. As Taggie's room was like the North Pole, he returned with a duvet he'd whipped off a fornicating couple in the spare room. Taggie had got into a red flannel nightgown and cleaned her teeth. Lady in Red, thought Rupert. She had huge black circles under her eyes. She looked about twelve.

'Everything'll work out all right,' he said, tucking her in.

'You've been so kind,' stammered Taggie. 'I'm sorry I was so rude to you before, and thank you for the pendant.'

But as Rupert put out a hand to touch her cheek, Gertrude, still in her black tie, growled fiercely.

'You may have forgiven me,' said Rupert, 'but Gertrude hasn't.'

RIVALS
19

At seven-thirty the disco was still pounding. All over the house Patrick's friends, with ultra-fashionable cat-sick yellow socks over their eyes like aeroplane eye masks, had crashed out on arm chairs and sofas. Charles snored happily on his *chaise-longue*. In the small sitting-room, watched balefully by Gertrude still in Rupert's black tie, Cameron and Patrick opened Patrick's presents, throwing the wrapping paper into the fire to ignite the dying embers. Cameron had never seen such loot: gold cufflinks, Rolex watches, diamond studs, a Leica camera, a Picasso drawing, a Matthew Smith, a red-and-silver-striped silk Turnbull and Asser dressing-gown.

Patrick was like the prince in the fairy story, thought Cameron, whom each of the neighbouring kings was trying to win over with more and more extravagant presents. She thought bitterly back to her own twenty-first birthday. Neither of her parents had even bothered to send her a card.

'You'll never remember who gave you what. That's neat,' she added, as Patrick drew out a copy of *The Shropshire Lad* from some shiny red paper.

'Very,' said Patrick. 'First edition. What have you got there?'

'Silver hip flask, from someone called All my Love Lavinia. She's had it engraved. Who's she?'

'My Ex,' said Patrick, collapsing onto the sofa to read *The Shropshire Lad*.

'How Ex?'

'About two minutes before midnight last night. Listen: *When I was one-and-twenty, I heard a wise man say, Give crowns and pounds and guineas, but not your heart away.* Hope that's not prophetic. I wish Housman hadn't used the word "Lad" so often; so appallingly hearty. Who's that from?'

Cameron pulled a long, dark-brown cashmere scarf from a gold envelope. 'Georgie and Ralphie.'

'I bet Georgie paid for it – kind of them, though.'

He got up and wound the scarf round Cameron's neck, holding on to the two ends and slowly drawing her towards him.

'It's yours. Everything I have is yours,' he said, kissing her, only breaking away from her because the telephone rang.

He grinned as he put down the receiver. It was the vicar of Penscombe asking if they could turn the disco down for an hour so he could take early service.

'I must go,' said Cameron.

'You must not. I'll tell those disco boys to go and have some breakfast and then you and I are going to watch the sun rise.'

Wearing three of Patrick's sweaters, a pair of Taggie's jeans, rolled over four times at the ankle, Caitlin's gumboots, and a very smart dark-blue coat with a velvet collar left over the banisters by Bas Baddingham, Cameron set out with Patrick.

'I've shaved so I won't cut your face to ribbons,' he said.

'The wind'll do that,' grumbled Cameron.

The wind, in fact, had dropped, but a vicious frost had ermined all the fences, roughened the surface of the snow and turned the waterfall in the wood to two foot-long icicles. Gertrude charged ahead leaping into drifts, tunnelling the snow with her snout.

'Wow, it's beautiful,' said Cameron, as the valley stretched out below them. 'How much of it's yours?'

'To the bottom of the wood. The rest of the valley belongs to Rupert Campbell-Black.'

Christ, it's a kingdom, thought Cameron, looking across at the white fields, the blanketed tennis court, Rupert's golden house with its snowy roof and the bare beech wood rearing up behind like a huge spiky white hedgehog.

'We're trying to get him on your father's programme.'

'Why bother? Pa could interview him by morse code across the valley. He's the most awful stud. Evidently resentful husbands all over Gloucestershire bear scars on their knuckles from trying to bash down bedroom doors.'

'He was there last night,' said Cameron.

'Was he?' said Patrick. 'I only had eyes for you.'

They had reached the water meadows at the bottom of the wood. Here the snow had settled in roots of trees, in the crevices of walls, and in six-foot drifts anywhere it could find shelter from yesterday's blizzard. The blizzard had also laid thick white tablecloths of snow fringed with icicles on either side of the stream which ran with chattering teeth down the valley. It was deathly quiet except for Rupert's horses occasionally neighing to one another. But it was getting lighter.

'Nice scent,' said Patrick, burrowing his face in her neck. 'What is it?'

'Fracas.'

'Very appropriate. Who gave it to you?'

'Tony.'

'Why hasn't he got a neck?' Patrick hurled a snowball into the woods. Gertrude hurtled after it. 'You'd have thought with that much money he could have bought himself a neck.'

'Shut up,' said Cameron. 'Tell me, do your mother and father always slope off to bed in the middle of their own parties?'

'It's a very odd marriage,' said Patrick, pointing his new Leica at her. 'Look towards the stream, darling. My father has always seen my mother as Maud Gonne.'

'The woman Yeats was fixated on?'

'Right. Yeats fell in love with her at exactly the same age my father fell in love with my mother. Look, badger tracks.' Patrick bent down to examine them. 'Maud Gonne was a rabid revolutionary. Yeats knew he wouldn't impress her with poetry, so he got caught up in a political movement to

241

unite Ireland. Then she married John MacBride, another revolutionary. Broke Yeats's heart, but it made him write his best poetry. He claimed Maud Gonne was beyond blame, like Helen of Troy.'

'But your mother isn't a revolutionary, for Christ's sake, and she hasn't married someone else.'

'No, but she has Maud Gonne's tremendous beauty, and my father has an almost fatalistic acceptance that she's above blame and will have affairs with other men.'

'Doesn't your mother care for him?'

'In her way. I once asked her why she messed him about so much. She said that, with every woman in the world after him, she could only hold him by uncertainty.'

Cameron digested this.

'But if he only loves her, and doesn't want all these women, why can't she stop playing games and love him back?'

'That's far too easy. She's convinced that, once he's sure of her, his obsession would evaporate. So the games go on.'

'I wish they wouldn't,' said Cameron. 'It sure makes him cranky to work with.'

She sat on a log and watched Patrick write 'Patrick loves Cameron' in huge letters in the snow. Then he got out his hip flask, now filled with brandy, and handed it to her.

'You warm enough?'

Cameron nodded, taking a sip.

'Do you have a drinking problem?' she asked, as Patrick took a huge slug.

Patrick laughed. 'Only if I can't afford it. Whisky's twelve pounds a bottle in Dublin. Will you come and stay with me at Trinity next term?'

It's crazy, thought Cameron. He's utterly unsuitable and eight years younger than me, but the snow had given her such a feeling of irresponsibility, she hadn't felt so happy for years. The only unsettling thing was that he reminded her so much of Declan. They had the same arrogance, the same assumption that everyone would dance to their tune. Patrick seemed to read her thoughts.

'Don't worry, I'm not at all like my father. Being Capricorn,

I have a very shrewd business head. I may be overexacting, but I'm also cool, calculating and calm, whereas my father is very highly strung and overemotional. Capricorns also have excellent senses of humour and make protective and loving husbands.' He grinned at her. The violet shadows beneath the brilliant dark eyes were even more pronounced this morning, but nothing could diminish the beauty of the bone structure, the full slightly sulky curve of the mouth, or the thickness of the long dark eyelashes.

'Not a very artistic sign, Capricorn,' Cameron said crushingly.

'What about Mallarmé?' said Patrick. 'One of the bravest, most dedicated of poets. He was Capricorn. He knew what slog and self-negation is needed to produce poetry. He understood the loneliness of the writer. Look, here's the sun.'

Hand in hand they watched the huge red sun climbing up behind the black bars of the beech copse on the top road, blushing at its inability to warm the day.

'Looks like Charles Fairburn spending a night inside for soliciting,' said Patrick.

'God, I wish I had a crew,' said Cameron. 'D'you realize you can only afford to film sunrises in winter in this country? In summer it rises at four o'clock in the morning. That's in golden time, when you have to pay a crew miles over the rate for working through the night. Christ, I hate the British unions.'

Patrick turned towards her. 'I only like American-Irish unions. Let me look at you.'

Her dark hair, no longer sleeked back with water, was blown forward in black tendrils over her cheek bones, and in a thick fringe which softened the slanting yellow eyes, and the beaky nose. Her skin and her full pale lips were amber in the sunshine.

Patrick sighed and took another photograph. 'Even the sun's upstaged. You're so dazzling, he'll have to wear dark glasses to look at you.'

Cameron laughed. He'd be terribly easy to fall in love with, she was shocked to find herself thinking.

'How many more terms have you got?' she asked as they wandered back.

'Two.'

'What are your future goals?'

'To take you to bed when we get home.'

'Don't be an asshole! Apart from that?'

'Get a first, then write plays.'

'Just like that?'

'Just like that. I've started one already.'

'What's it about?'

'Intimidation – by British soldiers in Ulster.'

'You're crazy – neither the BBC nor ITV would touch it, particularly in an election year. Nor will the West End.'

'Broadway would, and a success there would come here.'

'Very self-confident, aren't you?'

'Not particularly. I just know what I want from life.'

He moved closer, putting his hands inside the three jerseys warming them on her small breasts.

'I want you most.'

Back at The Priory, people were beginning to surface. Bas, having put so many Alka Seltzers in a glass of water they'd fizzed over the top, was trying to find his overcoat. Caitlin was eating Alpen and reading *Lady Chatterley's Lover*. Taggie was serving breakfast to Simon Harris's monsters, trying to give the baby its bottle and comfort Simon Harris who was sobbing at the kitchen table with his face in his hands.

'Oh Patrick, thank goodness you're back,' she said. 'Could you possibly ring the doctor about . . .' She nodded in Simon Harris's direction.

'No,' said Patrick, backing out of the kitchen. 'Sorry, darling, I'm busy.'

'I'm going home to call the office and get some sleep,' said Cameron.

'No,' said Patrick, suddenly frantic. 'If we go to sleep it won't be my birthday any more and we'll break the spell.'

He took her up the winding stairs to his bedroom in the east turret, which was painted dazzlingly white, as though the snow had fallen inside. There were no carpets or curtains, and the only furniture was a desk, a chair, a green and white sofa piled high with books, and a vast red-curtained oriental four-poster with bells hanging from the tops of the posts. The view, however, was magnificent, straight across the valley and up to Penscombe. You could see the weathercock on top of the church spire glittering in the sunlight.

A volume of Keats lay open on the bed: the pages were covered with pencilled notes. Picking it up, Cameron crawled under the duvet and tried to decipher Patrick's writing. Looking up, she saw the ceiling was painted dove grey with little stars picked out in white.

If only she'd had a room like this when she was young, she thought bitterly. Patrick went off to get them some breakfast. He took longer than anticipated. Taggie was on the telephone ringing up some doctor about Simon Harris, but she ran after him and buttonholed him as he was going back upstairs with a tray, dragging him into the sitting-room, distraught that he had Cameron in his room.

'She's Tony Baddingham's c-c-concubine.'

'Is that your word for the day?' said Patrick coldly.

'No, that's what Daddy calls her. Do you want to ruin his career?'

'Tony B couldn't be that petty, firing a megastar like Pa, just because I took his mistress off him.'

'He could! He's really evil!'

'Well if he's that evil, Pa shouldn't be working for him. Now, get out of my way, sweetheart. The coffee's getting cold.'

'And I've had enough of entertaining your friends,' Taggie screamed after him.

'Bicker, bicker,' said Caitlin, looking up from *Lady Chatterley's Lover*. 'Pity it isn't Spring, then Cameron could festoon your willy with forget-me-nots. Oh my God,' she screamed, as an ashen Daysee Butler shuffled downstairs in a white towelling dressing-gown. 'It's The Priory ghost.'

Upstairs, Patrick found Cameron wearing his new red and silver dressing-gown and reading Keats. The sun shining

245

through the stained glass of one of the windows had turned her face emerald, ruby and violet like a nymph of the rainbow. Patrick felt his heart fail.

He had brought up croissants, Taggie's bramble jelly, a bunch of green grapes, a jug of Buck's Fizz and some very strong black coffee. Cameron, who'd had no dinner the night before, was starving and ate most of it. It was astonishing, thought Patrick, that she looked desirable even with croissant crumbs on her lips. But even the black coffee couldn't keep her awake for long. Patrick didn't sleep. He sat making notes on Keats, which was one of his set books, but spending more time gazing at her. In sleep her face lost all its aggression.

It was almost dark when she woke up. For a second she looked bewildered and utterly terrified.

'It's all right,' said Patrick gently. 'You're safe now.'

She got up and looked out of the window. Orion, the swaggering voyeur, was looking in at her. The great yews and cedars were black against the snow. She could hear an unearthly strangulated croaking.

'What's that?'

'Foxes barking. It's a love call. Come here.'

'Not till I've cleaned my teeth.'

Grabbing her bag she went down the landing, terrified of bumping into Declan. Instead, coming out of the bathroom she found Caitlin and Maud having a row.

'I'm nothing like Lady Chatterley,' Maud was screaming. 'Good evening, Cameron. Nothing at all.'

'You're so lucky to have a family,' said Cameron as she slid back under the duvet beside Patrick. He was still wearing a jersey and trousers.

'How many times have you been home, since you came over here?' he asked.

'I haven't.'

'Why not? One must see one's family occasionally if only to fight with them.'

The argument outside was growing more clamorous.

'My parents are divorced. My father's married again. My

246

mother lives with someone. I don't want to talk about it,' said Cameron shrilly. Suddenly she was trembling, her teeth chattering, her eyes darting and frightened.

'You must,' said Patrick. 'How can I love you properly if I don't know everything about you?'

'No!' It was almost a scream.

'Come on. It'll help, I promise.'

They argued for some minutes before she gave in.

Suddenly he reminded her again of Declan. He had the same gentle but relentlessly probing voice, the same way of never taking his eyes off her face, and almost hypnotizing her into telling him everything.

'My mother walked out on my father when I was fourteen,' said Cameron tonelessly. 'Decided she wanted to be her own person. She dabbled in a lot of things, peace marches, consciousness raising, but she wasn't sufficiently focused and when the money ran out she moved to a female commune. Took me with her, but left my dog behind, because it was male.' Cameron gave a bitter, choked laugh, 'I never forgave her for that. My father got married again, and got all tied up with his new wife. Then Mom shacked up with Mike.'

'Your step-father?'

There was a long pause.

'You could call it that. Mike was a dyke. My mother wrote a piece about coming out in the *Village Voice*. All her friends thought she was real brave. My classmates just sniggered and nudged each other.'

'You poor little baby.' Patrick took her trembling hands.

'Then Mike and Mom moved to Cincinnati and Mike got the job of City Editor on the local paper. I could have put up with her being gay, but she was a real bull dyke, more macho than a guy really, with a skin like the surface of the moon, and hip measurements in treble figures, and a beer-gut spilling over her leather belts.' Cameron shuddered. 'She had a huge motorbike and she used to take Mom on the pillion. They joined a crazy organization called "Dykes on Bikes" and roared round the country in black leather going to gay parades.'

Patrick drew her to him. He could feel the pouring sweat, the terrible fits of shivering sweeping over her.

'Go on, darling,' he whispered.

'I prayed Mike would crash and kill herself. Then, as a last straw, Mom decided their union should be blessed and went off and got pregnant by AID. Mike was mad about the idea at first, strutted round as though she was the real father. Then when the baby arrived, it was a boy, poor little sod, and she got jealous. Mom was over forty. She had a terrible labour. She was in hospital for ten days. I was alone in the house with Mike. Every night she came home plastered. Then one evening I remember she spent about ten minutes getting her key into the lock. I was trying to work in my room. I can't tell you. I've never told anyone this.' She was suddenly frantic like a cat struggling and clawing to escape. Patrick held onto her. 'It's OK. You've got to trust me. Come on, sweetheart, come on.'

'Mike yelled for me to come downstairs and fix her some supper.' Cameron's voice was toneless again, and so quiet Patrick could hardly hear her.

'I was frying her eggs and bacon when suddenly she came up behind me and started to grope me, ripping my clothes off, trying to kiss me. Ugh. She was terribly strong. I swung the pan round and hit her with it. Then I ran out into the night.'

Cameron put her fingers in her hair, rubbing the ball of her hand over and over again against her forehead, as if to blot out the memory. Patrick waited.

'I went to some neighbours. I lied that Mike had tried to beat me up. They said they'd expected it for months. They called Dad in Washington. He came the next day and took me to live with him. He'd been dying to get something on Mom and Mike and the court ruled I should stay with him.'

'What happened then?'

'It didn't work,' said Cameron wearily. 'The honeymoon wore off. My stepmother's a lawyer, my father's a diplomat; they had a young baby. They're Very Civilized People and Very Busy; they couldn't handle a savage like me. I disrupted

248

their lives, I made awful scenes, stayed out all night. They couldn't see I was crying out for someone to care. I ran away from them too in the end. I got a scholarship to Barnard, worked in the Vac to support myself, got a job on the *New York Times*, and finally moved to television. The rest is hysterics.' She gave her bitter mirthless laugh again.

'You poor darling.' Patrick pulled her back into his arms again, kissing her forehead. No wonder she was screwed up and aggressive and desperately insecure after that. He'd never felt so sorry for anyone in his life.

'Didn't you have a boyfriend to look after you?'

'Oh I screwed around like crazy, just to prove I was heterosexual. Then the AIDS scare started in the States. Then Tony came along.'

'Hardly the ideal father figure,' said Patrick.

'I'm not dependent on him,' snarled Cameron too quickly. 'I'm not dependent on anyone. The only time I feel I belong is when my credits come up on the screen.'

She was shuddering violently now, furious with herself for dropping her guard and revealing so much.

'I guess you'll run to Declan now and tell him the whole thing, so you can have a good laugh.'

'Don't be childish,' snapped Patrick. 'I'm going to look after you. I'll blot out all the bad memories, even if it takes a lifetime.'

Never taking his eyes off her face, he started to unbutton his shirt.

'It's too soon,' she whispered.

'I'm not going to fuck you,' said Patrick. 'I'm just going to hold you close. You've got to learn that someone loves you for other things besides your heavenly body, and your skills as a career bitch.'

Patrick was as good as his word. Gradually the shuddering stopped and he soothed all the tension out of her. Exhausted by so much revelation, she even slept again. At midnight she insisted on going back to her house. He was very loath to let her go.

'Let me get dressed. I'll run you home.'

'I've got my car.'

'I want to see your house.'

'That's Tony's patch.'

'Not any more. Tony's past history.'

Cameron sighed. 'I guess it's a bit more problematical than that.'

'I feel like Demeter letting Persephone go back to the underworld,' said Patrick as he fastened her seat belt. 'For Christ's sake, drive carefully. The roads are like glass. I'll ring you tomorrow. I love you.'

Hell, thought Cameron, as she drove up to the house, I must have left the living-room light on. She glanced in the hall mirror. Not a scrap of make-up. Despite the sleep, the circles under her eyes were darker than her eyebrows. Patrick had really seen her in the raw, yet she felt strangely cleansed and at peace at having told him everything. Tomorrow they'd make love. She knew it would be wonderful. The slow lazy smile of anticipation was wiped off her face when she went into the living-room and found Tony.

The videos of her programmes lay scattered over the floor. The ashtray was filled with cigar butts. The whisky bottle, which had been half-full, was empty now. Tony was a slow drinker; he must have been there hours. Cameron shut the door and leant against it, her heart crashing. With a particularly unpleasant smile on his face, Tony picked up some papers lying on the table.

'I've been looking at your contract,' he said amiably. 'D'you want to leave now or work out your notice?'

It was as though the last twenty-four hours had never existed. Here was reality. Her whole career, her only security, was crashing round her ears in ruins.

'I haven't done anything. You can't fire me,' she whispered in terror.

'I don't have to. Your contract runs out in six weeks. Such a pity you blew it.' He examined his square, beautifully manicured fingernails. 'I came round to tell you that Simon Harris gave in to his nervous breakdown and was carted off to a loony bin this afternoon on extended leave. But you know what I feel about unpunctuality and twenty-four hours is a little late to come home from the ball.'

'But I never normally see you on a Sunday,' said Cameron illogically. She seemed too stunned to take anything in.

'That doesn't mean I don't expect you to be here.'

Smiling, he picked up his glass of whisky.

'You bloody little whore,' he said softly. The next moment he'd hurled it in her face.

For a second she was speechless, as the liquid dripped down on to the suede dress.

'How odd,' she said in a strained, high voice. 'Every time I buy something new and expensive some jerk spills something all over it.' Then she lost her temper.

'You bastard,' she screamed. 'I haven't taken a weekend off in three years. I'm always at your fucking beck and call.'

'That's what I pay you for,' said Tony. His eyes were sparkling with pleasure now.

'You bloody don't. If you paid me golden time for the hours I put in for you, I'd be Howard Hughes by now. You frig around doing exactly what you like, expecting me to behave like a fucking nun, except when you require my services. Well, it's not bloody good enough.'

She sprang at him, trying to claw his face, but he grabbed her wrists. He was not bull-necked and thick-armed for nothing. As his grip tightened, Cameron gasped with pain.

'I'd put up with it,' she said through clenched teeth, 'if the relationship was remotely even. You raise hell if I date anyone else, but you're quite free to take darling Sarah Stratton out to lunch and make passes at her and offer her a job.'

Tony's eyes gleamed. 'So that's it. Who told you that?'

'She did,' yelled Cameron, desperately struggling to get away. 'And she said you still sleep with Monica.'

Tony grinned. 'She must have an excellent spy system.'

'The Old Bag system. Monica told Winifred, who told Paul, who told Sarah that, as you were always pestering her, Monica restricts you to once a week. And you told me you hadn't laid a finger on her for years. You bloody liar.'

'It's rather exciting sleeping with Monica,' mused Tony. 'There's a rarity element about it.'

'So that's why you sent Madden tripping out to James Garrett on Christmas Eve to buy us both diamond bracelets. Jesus Christ!'

Starting to laugh, Tony let go of her wrists. 'You discovered that too, did you? Poor little Cameron, you must have been festering over Christmas. Jealousy is the most destructive of emotions, you know. It hurts only oneself.'

'I hate you,' screamed Cameron, wrenching off the bracelet and hurling it at him. Missing him, it hit the window, slithering scratchily down the glass like a fingernail on a blackboard.

'Get out! I'll move out tomorrow, but leave me alone now.' She collapsed, sobbing, on the sofa. Regurgitating her past with Patrick earlier had only underlined how terrifying it was to have no security. She was a panic-stricken sixteen-year-old again, racing through the night away from Mike with nowhere to go.

Tony poured two fingers of brandy into a glass, then moved towards her, until she could feel the solidness of his thigh against hers. She resisted the temptation to cling on to it, as a child might fling its arms around a tree for comfort.

'You were jealous, really jealous,' purred Tony. 'Was that why you led that boy on?'

'Sure.'

He caught her hair, yanking her head back. 'Did you sleep with him?'

'Yes,' she muttered. Then, terrified he was going to hit her or throw the brandy into her face, 'But not the way you think, I was so goddam tired. I hadn't slept for nights worrying about everything. I crashed out on his bed.'

'And nothing happened?'

'Nothing, nothing! He's just a kid.' Oh please make him believe her.

'Did Declan know you spent the night there?'

'No, I never saw him. He never came out of the bedroom.'

With the franchise coming up this year, Tony decided, he

252

didn't really want to lose her, but he was going to enjoy torturing her a bit more.

'And you promise never to see the boy again?'

'I promise,' said Cameron wearily. 'But he may try to see me.'

'We'll have to put pressure on Declan to stop him then, won't we?' said Tony silkily, as he took off Cameron's jacket.

'That is a very disturbing dress. I'd rather you didn't wear it in public again.'

Putting his hand under the skirt, he jabbed two fingers up inside her.

Cameron winced. 'I can't, Tony, not tonight. I'm really pooped.'

'You can,' said Tony softly, 'if you want to be Controller of Programmes.'

Three days after Patrick's party Taggie was gingerly testing her heart and finding that the ache for Ralphie was much less acute than she'd expected it to be when the doorbell rang.

In the doorway stood Rupert. His suntan was already beginning to fade.

'Hullo,' he said, soulfully gazing into her eyes. 'Since your wonderful party, I haven't been able to eat a thing.'

'Oh my goodness,' stammered Taggie, her heart beginning to thump.

Rupert grinned. 'Could I possibly have my knives and forks and plates back?'

Taggie was used to unrequited love. Patrick, however, was not. Hopelessly spoilt by his mother, accustomed to attracting girls effortlessly, he couldn't believe Cameron didn't want to see him any more.

Despite Declan's tirades and Taggie's pleading, he continued to pester her with letters and telephone calls. Then, when these were not answered, he hung round the Corinium studios and outside her house.

Cameron, in fact, had hardly had time to think. As well as producing Declan's programme and coping with her new job as Acting Controller of Programmes, she had to face a virtual palace revolution from a staff outraged by her appointment.

The afternoon before he was due to go back to Trinity, Patrick rang Cameron at the office. Expecting a call from Rupert about coming on Declan's programme, Cameron unthinkingly picked up the telephone instead of leaving it to her secretary.

'Can I speak to Cameron?' said Patrick.

Cameron froze. Putting on a cockney accent, she said, 'I'm afraid she's not at her desk at the moment.'

'Where is she?' snapped Patrick. 'Lying with the Managing Director under *his* desk.'

Cameron hung up.

The telephone was ringing again as she got home that evening. Running into the hall, she snatched up the receiver. It was Rupert answering her call.

'We were talking about a date for you to come on Declan's programme,' she said with a confidence she didn't feel. 'I was just hoping to firm you up.'

Rupert laughed. 'Extraordinary terminology you use in television.'

His diary was ridiculously full, but to her amazement he said he could make a Wednesday in February, which turned out to be St Valentine's Day. He'd been so adamant he wouldn't do the programme.

'And in case I don't bump into Declan beforehand, can you ask him if he's free for dinner afterwards?'

Cameron didn't say that after Declan had taken Rupert to the cleaners she thought it most unlikely.

'That was a good party on New Year's Eve,' said Rupert. 'I saw you bopping in your suede dress. I hoped you'd jump out of your skin.'

The next moment Cameron nearly did jump out of her skin, as she felt a kiss on the back of her neck. Patrick had walked in through the unlocked door.

'Get out,' hissed Cameron, clapping her hand over the receiver.

Shaking his head, Patrick sauntered into the living-room. She caught a blast of whisky as he passed.

Talking gibberish, furious at having to wind up her conversation with Rupert so abruptly, she said goodbye and went into the living-room, where she found Patrick hurling darts at the dart board.

'Nice place you've got here. I can see why you wouldn't want to give it up in a hurry.'

'Get out,' screamed Cameron.

'Not until you tell me why you didn't ring back.'

He went up to the board, and pulled out the darts. His hands were shaking, his eyes were black hollows in a deathly pale face. He must have lost pounds; he looked terrible.

'There was no reason to call back. We had a fun day.'

'A fun day?' he asked incredulously. 'Was that all it meant to you, after the sunrise, and all you told me about your mother and Mike and you falling asleep in my arms?'

'Shut up,' hissed Cameron, looking round in terror, expecting Tony to pop up from under the piano.

Patrick picked up a huge bunch of anemones which he'd left on the dentist's chair.

'I bought you these. For Christ's sake, I love you. Can't you understand that?'

In answer Cameron snatched the flowers from him and hurled them into the fireplace. Patrick winced and turned back to the dart board. The first dart missed, crashing into the wall, the second hit the glass in the frame of one of Cameron's awards, the third hit a plate.

'Pack it in,' said Cameron more calmly. 'If Tony turns up, he'll kill us both.'

'He's a fiend. I've been checking up on him,' said Patrick, sitting down at the piano. 'He's so avaricious,' he went on between crashing chords, 'even the bags under his eyes have got gold in them, and he's corrupting you too, turning you into his pet Rottweiler to savage any of his staff he wants to reduce to jelly. You'll never get out of the Underworld if you stay with him.'

'Tony suits me,' said Cameron over the din. 'We've been together for three years, OK? My career's the only thing that matters.'

'So you agreed to drop me if he made you Controller of Programmes?'

'You flatter yourself. What can you offer me?'

Patrick's hands came down in a jumble of discords. '*I, being poor*,' he said bitterly, '*can only offer you my dreams.*'

'Stop talking like a prime-time soap.'

'You should know, you make enough of them. Can I have a drink?'

'You've had enough,' snarled Cameron. 'Tony'll be here in a minute.'

'And he'll settle you in that dentist's chair,' said Patrick scornfully, 'and say "open wide", and then it's Wham, bam, thank you, Mammon. My Christ.'

He slammed the piano lid down and got to his feet.

'Don't be obnoxious,' hissed Cameron.

On New Year's Day, when she'd sobbed in his arms, he'd seemed so strong. Suddenly now he looked terribly young and frightened. Cameron was too insecure herself to be drawn to frailty.

'I'm truly sorry,' he muttered. 'It hurts loving you, that's all. Look, I'll do anything. I'll chuck Trinity, get a job. It'll be easy with Pa's connections.'

'Always fall back on Daddy, don't you?' taunted Cameron. 'You bitch about his philistine programme, but you'll bleed him white when it suits you. Well I'm not having you bleeding *me* white. Can't you get it into your Neanderthal skull that I don't want you around?'

Guilt at the way she'd treated him made her even more brutal.

'I can't help myself,' said Patrick, going towards the door. 'La Belle Dame sans merci has me totally in thrall.'

He went to the nearest pub and drank until long after closing time. The landlady felt sorry for the beautiful, obviously desolate young man sitting there quietly gazing into space.

At midnight Patrick parked his car four houses down from Cameron's and got out. It was a punishingly cold night. Cotchester slumbered beneath her eiderdown of snow. In a sky russet from the streetlamps huge stars flickered. Icicles glittered from Cameron's gutters. In front of the house beside Cameron's green Lotus was parked Tony's bloody great dark-red Rolls Royce with the Corinium ram on the bonnet. There was a light on in the top of the house – Cameron's bedroom, guessed Patrick. He imagined Tony brutally clambering over her lovely body. The Sunday before last she'd lain in his arms, pliant as a child. He wanted to plunge one of the icicles into Tony's heart.

Wearing only a jersey and an old pair of cords, he was shivering violently now. Then he noticed that Tony's car keys were still in the dashboard. Trying the car door he found it open. The lecherous bugger had obviously been in such a hurry to get at Cameron he'd forgotten to lock it.

Easing open the door, pulling out the keys, Patrick chucked them into a nearby flower bed. They landed deep in a lavender bush, hardly scattering the snow.

At four o'clock in the morning Tony looked at his watch. 'I must go.'

Cameron didn't dissuade him. She was utterly shattered. To eradicate any memory of Patrick, Tony had recently insisted on indulging in sexual marathons. Four times that night, he thought smugly; no one could accuse him of losing his touch. Cameron daren't complain. She was also twitchy that Patrick might do something insane to rock the boat.

Hearing Tony let himself out, she was just falling asleep when she heard a key turn in the door. It was a sound that always unnerved her, reminding her of Mike. For a wild moment of dread and longing she thought it might be Patrick.

'Did I leave my keys here?' shouted Tony.

By the time they'd upended the entire house, the car and

257

the drive, screamed at each other and nearly frozen to death, the lights had come on in the houses opposite and curtains were twitching in the houses on either side. There was no way Tony could start the Rolls, or get someone to help push it out of the way. If he rang Percy, his chauffeur, it would be round the entire network in a flash, so he spent the next three hours frantically and abortively ringing round the country, trying to find another set of keys.

In the end he had to order a taxi from the station. His temper was not improved by the driver recognizing him and slyly my Lording him all the way home.

Arriving at The Falconry, he had to provide Monica with a ridiculously convoluted explanation that he'd decided to come home that night, but that his car had gone into a skid on the motorway and he'd had to abandon it. He then had to keep her in bed in the morning, so she wouldn't drive into Cotchester and see his car parked outside Cameron's house.

As it was, poor, loyal Cyril Peacock tracked down a key and removed the Rolls by midday, but by then almost the entire Corinium staff had seen the car on their way in to work and had had a good laugh. That afternoon, Cameron passed the staff noticeboard. Beneath the card announcing her appointment as Acting Controller of Programmes, someone had added the words: 'and Mistress of the Rolls'.

Later that day, Patrick rang Cameron from Birmingham Airport to say goodbye.

'Did you steal Tony's keys?' she shouted.

'Tell him to look under the lavender on the left of the front door.'

Cameron let Patrick have it. 'You stupid asshole. If Monica had come by and seen the car, you'd have landed Tony in a divorce court.'

'I thought that's what you wanted.'

'Don't be so fucking infantile.'

'I couldn't help it.' Patrick's voice faltered. 'I can't bear to think of that great toad in bed with you.'

'Get out of my life,' screamed Cameron. 'You don't know the rules.'

'I love you.' Patrick was almost crying.

'Well, I don't love you. You're a fucking nuisance. Piss off and try and do something worthwhile with your life.'

She was dead scared of telling Tony about the keys, but was amazed to find that he was grimly pleased.

'What a very silly little boy to put such a very large nail in his father's coffin.'

RIVALS
20

At the end of January the IBA formally asked for applications for the new franchises. These applications, which had to be provided not only by the fifteen incumbent independent companies, but also by any rival consortium who sought to oust them, often ran to hundreds of beautifully bound pages, giving details of finance, staffing policies, plans for future programmes and proposed boards of management.

After the applications were handed in in early May, the IBA would study them and then conduct a series of public meetings around the country, attempting to find out whether the public felt well-served by their particular local television company. After private meetings between the IBA and all the individual contenders in October and November, the franchises would be finally awarded in December.

Anticipating a long year full of lobbying and hustling, Tony Baddingham's immediate task in the New Year was to strengthen the Corinium Board. Knowing the IBA and particularly Lady Gosling's penchant for women, he intended to make Cameron a director. But he wanted to punish her as long as possible for stepping out of line with Patrick, and, as the staff were still in a state of mutiny over her appointment, he didn't want a strike on his hands in franchise year. The staff, however, had short memories. Cameron had found Simon Harris's affairs in such a shambles that Tony had quite enough excuses to dispense with his services when he came out of hospital, but that would have to be done discreetly too. Then he could appoint Cameron to the Board just before the applications went in.

Tony also had his lunch with Freddie Jones, who, heavily pressured by Valerie, was poised to join the Corinium Board. His only reservation was whether, with his electronics empire and his race horses and his hunting, he would have sufficient time. If he were a director, he wanted to do some directing.

As an added incentive to Valerie, however, Tony invited Freddie shooting the last Saturday in January, and asked some extremely grand people to shoot as well. Never having shot with Freddie before, Tony issued a warning to the other guns beforehand.

'Freddie Jones is a bit of a rough diamond, but exceptionally able. He's going to be very useful on our board, if you know what I mean. But I'm not sure how good a shot he is, so bring your tin hat.'

In the master bedroom at Green Lawns Freddie Jones lay beside his wife in the vast suede oval bed, covered with dials for quadraphonic stereo, radio, dimmer switches, razors and vibrators which Valerie used to massage her neck. They had to leave for Tony's about nine. It was now only six forty-five, which left plenty of time for sex, thought Freddie hopefully. They had already drunk two cups of tea from the Teasmade. Reaching across, Freddie put his hand on Valerie's bush, fingering her clitoris from time to time as a door-to-door salesman, not very hopeful of entrance, might press a doorbell.

Valerie sighed. She knew no wife should deny her husband his conjugal rights, but one of the joys of Freddie getting up early to go hunting every Saturday meant that she could pretend to be asleep as she did every weekday when he left for work at six-thirty.

Valerie did everything to avoid sex. She had already taken back to Jolly's of Bath the absurdly sexy black lingerie an ever-hopeful Freddie had bought her for Christmas and replaced it with some peach satin sheets for the guest bedroom. She

261

always wore woollen nightgowns buttoned up to the neck. If only she could sew up the bottom as well! The pressing finger was getting more insistent.

'D'you want to come, Fred-Fred?'

'Do you?'

'Not really. I want to be fresh for Tony and Monica.'

'Will you help me then?'

Valerie sighed again. Kneeling, she raised the red woollen nightgown, so Freddie could admire her candy pink nipples and her neatly clipped bush. She loathed watching him, but at least it stopped her getting messy.

'You're so beautiful,' sighed Freddie. 'You've got the body of a little girl.'

'Here's some tissues. Don't waste a clean towel, Fred-Fred.'

He had barely finished his lonely act before Valerie had reached up to press another switch on the bedhead which instantly sent boiling water gushing out of the 22-carat-gold mixer taps into the vast onyx and sepia marble double bath next door. Then, remembering she didn't want a flushed face, Valerie twiddled another knob to lower the temperature.

Snowdrops spread in a milk-white blur on either side of Tony Baddingham's drive. The guns, in their dung-coloured clothes, gathered outside The Falconry, pulling on gumboots and bellowing at excited dogs that whisked about lifting their legs on Monica's aconites.

At nine-thirty, just as it stopped raining, Freddie's freshly cleaned red Jaguar roared up the drive.

'Oh dear,' said Freddie, leaning out of the window and roaring with laughter at the other guns' filthy Landrovers, 'I forgot to chuck a bucket of mud over my car before I came out. Amizing, those snowdrops,' he said, clambering out. 'Just like a big fall of snow.'

He was wearing a red jersey, a Barbour and no cap on his red-gold curls. Next minute Valerie emerged from her side in a ginger knickerbocker suit, with a matching ginger cloak flung round her shoulders, and a ginger deerstalker.

'Christ,' muttered Tony to Sarah Stratton.

'It's Sherlock Lovely Homes,' said Sarah, making no attempt not to laugh. 'All she needs is a curved pipe and a spy glass.'

'What's that?' asked Valerie gaily.

'We were admiring your – er – outfit,' said Sarah quickly.

'All from my Spring range,' said Valerie, looking smug. 'Better hurry, it's selling like hot cakes.'

Tony oozed forward, exuding charm.

'You both know Sarah and Paul Stratton of course, and my brother Bas,' he said smoothly, and when he went on to introduce Valerie to the Lord-Lieutenant Henry Hampshire, two peers and a Duke from the next county, Valerie nearly had the orgasm Freddie had so longed to give her earlier. Fred-Fred must definitely join the Corinium Board, thought Valerie. It might be a Prince, or even a King, next time.

'Hullo, Valerie,' said Monica, who was wearing a green sou'wester over a headscarf. 'Would you like a cup of coffee?'

'Naughty,' chided Valerie, waving a tan suede finger. 'I said you must call me Mousie. No, I won't have a coffee, thank you.'

She didn't want to have to go to the toilet behind a hawthorn bush mid-morning in front of all the gentry.

They were about to set off when the phone rang loudly in Freddie's car.

''Ullo, Mr Ho Chin, how are fings?' said Freddie in delight. 'Grite, grite. Fifty million, did you say? Yeah, that seems about right. Look, 'ave a word with Alfredo and see if 'e wants to come in too, and phone me back. Yes, I'll be on this number all day.'

The guns exchanged looks of absolute horror, as Freddie extracted the telephone from the car, all set to bring it with him.

Tony sidled up. 'D'you mind awfully leaving that thing behind? Might put off the pheasants.'

''Course not,' said Freddie, putting it back in the car. 'If Chin can't get me 'ere, he'll ring my office.'

'D'you take your telephone hunting too?' asked an appalled Paul.

'Always,' said Freddie.

They started off up an incredibly steep hill behind the house. It was one of those mild January days that give the illusion winter is over. A few dirty suds of traveller's joy still hung from the trees. No wind ruffled the catkins. It was hellishly hard going. Valerie, wishing she hadn't worn her long johns, tried not to pant.

As it started to rain, she put up her ginger umbrella which kept catching in the branches. On the brow of the hill the guns took up their position, which they'd drawn out of a hat earlier. Except for Freddie's distracting red-gold curls, the flat caps along the row were absolutely parallel with the gun barrels. Shooting in the middle of the line between Tony and the Duke, Freddie jumped from foot to foot swinging his gun through the line like Ian Botham hooking.

The Duke, who had three daughters and was hoping for a son so the title wouldn't pass to a younger brother, was not the only gun looking at Freddie with extreme trepidation.

'I'm 'ot,' said Freddie, shedding his Barbour. Seeing the Duke's and Tony's looks of horror at Freddie's red jersey and Bas laughing like a jackass, Valerie, who'd been yakking non-stop to Sarah Stratton about puff-ball skirts, sharply told Freddie to put it back on. For once Freddie ignored her.

Suddenly the patter of rain on the flat caps was joined by the relentless swish of the beaters' flags.

'Come on, little birdies,' cooed Paul, caressing the trigger.

I hate him for being him and not Rupert, thought Sarah despairingly.

A lone pheasant came into view, high over Freddie's head.

'Bet he misses,' said Paul.

The Duke and Tony raised their guns in case he did.

But a shot rang out and the pheasant somersaulted like a gaudy catherine wheel and thudded to the ground.

Next moment a great swarm appeared, some steeply rising, some whirring close to the ground. There was a deafening fusillade and the air was full of feathers as birds cartwheeled and crashed into the grass.

The whistle blew; the first drive was over. Dogs shot off to retrieve the plunder. It was plain from the number of brace being amassed by Freddie's loader that he'd shot the plus twos off everyone else.

'Freddie Jones seems a bloody good shot,' said Bas.

'Beginner's luck,' snapped Paul, who had easily shot the least.

For the next drive the guns formed a ring round a little yellow stone farmhouse with a turquoise door and a moulting Christmas tree in the back yard.

Once more the shots rang out, once more the sky rained pheasants. To left and right, Freddie, the Duke and the Lord-Lieutenant were bringing down everything that came over. Tony fared less well. Valerie was standing behind him with Monica and her endless chatter put him off.

At the end of the drive Tony's loader, knowing the competitive nature of his boss, pinched a brace from Bas on one side and another from the Lord-Lieutenant who was gazing admiringly at Sarah.

'Those are mine!' said the Lord-Lieutenant sharply.

'Sorry,' said Tony smoothly. 'My loader's very jealous of my reputation.'

'Jealous loader, indeed,' muttered the Lord-Lieutenant.

The next drive was a long one, with the guns dotted like waistcoat buttons down the valley. Valerie was bored. Only the birds and the chuckling of a little stream interrupted the quiet. Monica, who found shooting as boring as Corinium Television, was plugged into the Sony Walkman Archie had given her for Christmas. Now she was transfixed by the love duet from *Tristan und Isolde*, eyes shut, dreamily waving her hands in time to the music and tripping over bramble cables.

Sarah was equally uncommunicative. Weekends were the worst, she reflected, because, knowing Paul was at home, Rupert would never ring. She'd only come out today for something to do. Spring returns, she murmured, looking at the ruby and amethyst haze of the thickening buds, but not my Rupert. He had been so keen, but suddenly after Valerie's dinner party he had lost interest. Was it Nathalie Perrault, or Cameron Cook, or even Maud O'Hara he was running after now? Perhaps he was just busy and would come back.

A diversion was provided by the arrival of Hermione Hampshire, the Lord-Lieutenant's wife, who looked like a sheep, had a ringing voice and appeared to be on so many of the same committees as Monica that she even merited having the Walkman turned off.

'Freddie's been shooting wonderfully,' said Monica kindly, and then started rabbiting on to Hermione Hampshire about shooting lunches.

Valerie listened to them. One could pick up lots of tips about pronunciation from the gentry. But it was confusing that Monica said 'Eyether' and Hermione said 'Eether'.

In the next field she was somewhat unnerved by some black and white cows who cavorted skittishly around, startled by the gunfire. She edged closer to Monica and Hermione.

'D'you know,' Monica was saying, 'I never spend less than forty minutes on a cock.'

Valerie was shocked to the core. She'd always imagined Monica was somehow above sex.

'I agree,' said Hermione Hampshire in her ringing voice. 'I never spend less than thirty minutes on a hen.'

'They're talking about plucking,' whispered Sarah with a giggle, 'and I don't think either of them have heard of rhyming slang.'

It was the last drive before lunch. Freddie, like a one-man Bofors, was bringing down pheasants with relentless accuracy.

'Got my eye in now,' he said, grinning at the Lord-Lieutenant.

He raised his gun as another pheasant flew towards him, then swore as it crashed prematurely to the ground.

'Sorry,' said Tony, who couldn't bear being upstaged a moment longer. 'Thought you were unloaded.'

266

This time it was carnage. The air was raining feathers. Dogs circled, loaders went round breaking the necks of the wounded.

Lucky things, thought Sarah. I wish someone would put me out of my misery.

'I love your dog,' she said to Henry Hampshire. 'I saw a beautiful springer the other day with a long tail.'

'Good God,' said Henry Hampshire, appalled, and strode off leaving her in mid-sentence.

'I thought you said you hadn't shot before,' said Tony as they walked back to the house.

'Not pheasant,' said Freddie, 'but I was the top marksman at Bisley for two years.'

Entering the garden, they passed two yews cut in the shape of pheasants.

'You couldn't even hit those today, could you, Paul?' said Tony nastily.

After so much open air and exercise, everyone fell on lunch. There was Spanish omelette cut up in small pieces on cocktail sticks, and a huge stew, with baked potatoes, and a winter salad, and plum cake steeped in brandy and Stilton, with masses of claret and sloe gin.

Freddie was in terrific form. His curls had tightened in the rain. Looking more like a naughty cherub than ever, he kept his end of the table in a roar with stories of his army career and his first catastrophic experiences out hunting.

Henry Hampshire, who had a lean face and turned-down eyes, shed his gentle paternalistic smile on everyone, even Sarah.

'D'yer really think Springers look better with long tails?' he asked her.

Sarah had a lot to drink at lunch. She looks like a Renoir, thought Tony, all blonde curls, huge blue eyes and languor.

'Have you made up your mind about joining Corinium?' he asked her.

'Yes, I'd love to. I'll come in and sign the contract tomorrow.'

'Only a three months' trial,' said Tony, who never took chances, 'but I think you'll love it. This will be a very exciting year.'

Christ, I'd like to take her to bed, he thought. Cameron was being very uptight at the moment.

'Not too worried about me getting you on the telecasting couch?' he added, lowering his voice.

Sarah went crimson. 'Cameron must have told you about that. I picked her brains, I didn't realize you and she . . . I'm sorry.'

'Don't give it a thought,' said Tony, pouring her some more sloe gin.

'No more Stilton, Fred-Fred,' chided Valerie. 'What a lovely meal, Monica.'

'Taggie O'Hara did the whole thing,' said Monica. 'I can't thank you enough for putting me on to her. She's going to fill up the deep freeze before the children come home at half-term.'

Valerie, who was feeling a little out of things because everyone was laughing at Freddie's jokes, turned to the Duke. After two glasses of claret she'd be calling him your grouse in a minute.

'We have a lovely home,' she said complacently. 'Green Lawns. I hope we shall receive you there one day. The Hunt was supposed to gather there on New Year's Day. Do you ride to hounds?'

'Well, a bit,' said the Duke, who had his own pack.

'Freddie's been asked to hunt with the Belvoir. That's the smartest pack in the country,' boasted Valerie.

Everyone except Valerie knew that Belvoir was not pronounced as it was spelt. Everyone except Tony was well-bred enough to keep their traps shut. Buy Tony was fed up with her stupid chatter.

'If you were really smart, Valerie, you wouldn't call it Belvoir. It's pronounced Beaver.'

There was an embarrassed pause.

'How long have you lived in Gloucestershire?' asked the Duke, who was a kind man.

The women went off to various loos. Freddie went off to take a telephone call from Tokyo.

'What a very amusing fellow Freddie Jones is,' said the Lord-Lieutenant.

'And very very bright,' said Tony. 'That's why I need him on my Board. Cable and Satellite isn't just about technology or delivery systems, you know; it's about marketing programmes. Freddie's a genius at marketing. Shame we couldn't include his jumped-up bitch of a wife as part of the bag.'

'Not on a cocks-only day,' said Bas.

Everyone laughed.

The guns were waiting to start off for the last two drives of the day. Freddie was still on the telephone to Tokyo. Valerie was admiring the azaleas in Monica's conservatory.

It was unfortunate that when Freddie came into the hall he found Sarah Stratton in Valerie's deerstalker giggling frantically and brandishing Valerie's tan mackintosh cape, at which Basil was pretending to charge like a bull.

'Olé,' said Tony, who was grinning in the doorway.

'It's selling laike hot gâteaux,' squealed Sarah. Then, seeing Freddie, she went very pink and asked him if he thought the deerstalker suited her.

At that moment Valerie came into the hall.

'You look delaightful,' she said excitedly. 'I've got identical ones in stock. I'll set one asaide for you.'

'I really feel I've made a breakthrough with Sarah Stratton,' Valerie kept telling Freddie as they drove home.

Having done her stuff in the morning and during lunch, Monica felt justified in staying behind in the afternoon and doing some gardening. Before she got stuck into pruning, she popped into the kitchen to thank Taggie, but found her looking absolutely miserable standing on one leg.

'What on earth's the matter?' said Monica, alarmed. 'Everything was wonderful.'

269

Taggie hung her head. 'I'm desperately sorry, Lady Baddingham, but I didn't realize it was a shooting lunch. I know it sounds p-p-priggish, but I don't app-p-prove of shooting. I think it's very cruel; all those poor pheasants, and I'd rather not cook for those kind of lunches any more. You probably won't want me to do any more cooking now. I'm so sorry, as I like working for you so much.'

Monica's face softened. 'Don't give it a thought. It was very brave of you to stick up for your principles. The shooting season's virtually over now, anyway. I quite understand, as long as you go on doing other lunches and dinner parties for me and filling up the freezer.'

When Tony came out of a meeting on Monday morning, Miss Madden greeted him with the news that Freddie had rung.

'Get him for me, would you?' said Tony.

He smiled expansively as he was put through.

'Freddie, hullo. You shot bloody well. Everyone was most impressed.'

'Thank you very much for asking us,' said Freddie.

'We must make it a regular thing next season.' Tony made a thumbs-up sign to Cameron.

'I don't fink so,' said Freddie coldly. 'I'm not joining your board.'

'Why ever not?' said Tony, astounded.

'I don't like people patronizing Valerie. I know you was all laughing at her.'

'It was a joke,' protested Tony. 'We're all devoted to Mousie.'

'I don't mind anyone laughing at me, but no one puts 'er down.' And Freddie put down the receiver.

The tragedy was that Valerie was absolutely livid with Freddie, who was not prepared to hurt her by telling her why he'd backed off. Valerie – over whose head the cracks about the Belvoir and the boutique had gone completely – ranted on and on about how Monica had become such a good friend and Tony had promised to film the boutique and put her on

'Behind Every Famous Man', and what amusing people the Duke, the Lord-Lieutenant, the Strattons, Bas and even the O'Haras were, and now she supposed all they'd do was mix with boring businessmen.

Even when Tony dispatched Sarah to the boutique to buy the cloak, the knickerbocker suit and the deer stalker, Freddie didn't relent.

RIVALS
21

Tony couldn't directly blame Declan for Freddie Jones's defection, but he blamed him for everything else: for inciting rebellion in the newsroom with his subversive lefty attitudes, for egging Charles Fairburn on to put in larger and larger expenses, for Cameron's bad temper which was no doubt caused by Declan's handsome son Patrick, for Declan's trouncing of Maurice Wooton, which had made Tony so anxious to get Freddie on the Board and waste so much time and money wooing him, only to be rejected.

It was generally agreed at Corinium that Tony had never sustained a mood of utter bloody-mindedness for quite so long, and the only way Declan could redeem himself would be to crucify Rupert Campbell-Black when he interviewed him on St Valentine's Day – a massacre Declan looked forward to with grim relish.

As he researched the programme, Declan found himself increasingly fascinated by the complexities of Rupert's character. He was obviously very good at his job. The Ministry for Sport, when Rupert was offered it, had been merely a PR post, answerable to the Ministry of the Environment, with the Home Office dealing with any major disasters like football riots.

Rupert, however, had refused to take on the job unless he was given sole responsibility for all sport in the country and any trouble that ensued. The gamble paid off. He had had

spectacular success in curbing football hooliganism, he had
raised a vast amount of money for sport, particularly the next
Olympics. He had had rows with the Teachers' Unions over
the decline of competitive sport in schools, with the Football
Association, rows with fellow ministers, even rows with the
PM. But he got things done and he cut through waffle.
Utterly sure of his own judgement, he was sometimes too
arrogant, and, having been a great athlete himself, he tended
to side with the players rather than the management, but
when he went against officials it was always because he'd
discovered a weakness in their argument. He was extremely
lucky in Gerald Middleton, his private secretary.

Declan also noted Rupert's appallingly deprived childhood,
not of material things, but of love and stability. His beautiful
mother was on her fifth marriage. His father's fourth marriage
had just come unstuck. Then there was his taking over of the
family home at Penscombe, with its four hundred acres, when
he was only twenty-one and just making the big time in
show-jumping, and soon having it running at a thumping
profit. There were the frequent rumblings in the press about
his cruelty to his horses, or at least ruthlessly overjumping
them. There was the compulsive womanizing that hardly
stopped with marriage or divorce. Even today, when he
should be setting a good example, far too many women
appeared only too anxious to say 'Yes Minister'.

Declan had spoken to Rupert's best friend, Billy Lloyd-
Foxe, now Head of Sport at the BBC, who had nothing but
praise for the way Rupert had helped him in the past, curing
him of alcoholism and virtually saving his marriage. He also
talked to Malise Gordon, Rupert's old *chef d'équipe*, now
married to Rupert's ex-wife Helen, who said Rupert's urge to
win was the strongest motivating force in his character.
'Whatever he does, he'll get to the top.' He talked to numerous exes, who all described Rupert as impossible but irresistible, not least because he made them laugh, and to several
cabinet ministers, who spoke of him with respect rather than
affection.

Everyone cited Rupert's phenomenal energy. After the

punishing hours of show-jumping he took the gruelling work load of Sports Minister in his stride. Accustomed to adulation and easy conquest on the show-jumping circuit, he had been unaffected both by the reverence and sycophancy which surrounds MPs and the brickbats thrown at them by the press and in the House. Because he was fearless and not short of money, he made a surprisingly good MP, happy to kick up a fuss on behalf of his constituency whenever necessary. Chalford and Bisley were proud. Once again Rupert had put them on the map.

This, therefore, was the man that Declan read every word written about and became obsessed with as he strode through the frozen Gloucestershire valleys, or tossed and turned in his bed at night. This was the man, he thought, as he worked out his questions, with a black, churning, sickening hatred, who could at any moment take Maud or Taggie or even Caitlin off him. On the surface Maud seemed to have got over her passion for Rupert. She had discovered Anthony Powell's novels, and was steadily reading her way through the twelve volumes of *A Dance to the Music of Time*, aided by rather too much whisky of an evening. She was very listless, but this could be attributed to the length and severity of the winter. She showed no interest in his interview with Rupert.

St Valentine's Day dawned, causing the usual flutter of excitement at Corinium Television, and giving hernias to the postmen staggering up Cotchester High Street under sackfuls of coloured envelopes.

None of these envelopes, however, were addressed to Cameron. Not that she really noticed. Since she'd taken over Simon Harris's job, she was working herself into the ground.

Not only was she still producing Declan and overseeing the production of a new series of 'Four Men went to Mow', but she was now in sole charge of Corinium Programmes, and seemed to spend her time scheduling, commissioning, arguing about budgets, or going to meetings with other Programme Controllers in London.

Patrick bombarded her with increasingly anguished letters

to which she didn't reply. Only that morning he'd sent her a huge Valentine bunch of lilies of the valley at home.

Darling Cameron [said the accompanying letter],
I am going into a decline. Decline O'Hara. I've lost so much weight my friends are convinced I've got AIDS. Having been told by you to make something of my life, you will be pleased that I have given up drink (almost) and am writing my play and working hard. The play is no longer about British intimidation in Ireland, but about a young boy in love with an older woman, who can't tear herself away from an absolute bastard. Don't worry about libel, I've given Lord Bad Hat red hair. I suppose I ought to thank you for making me experience unhappiness in love. Did you know James Joyce actually encouraged his wife to have affairs, so he could find out what it was like to be a cuckold?

'Jim' (isn't that a ghastly let down), wrote Mrs Joyce, 'wants me to go with other men, so he can write about it.' Stupid pratt, he couldn't have loved her.

My mother says my father is incredibly ratty. Are things going very badly at Corinium? Before you tear this letter up, remember it will be worth something one day, and might well keep you in lonely old age, when your ancient lover, Baddingham, has croaked. I love you and remain in darkness, Patrick.

As she left for the office, Cameron put the lilies of the valley outside the back door in case Tony came home with her after Declan's programme. Not that that was likely. Their relationship had deteriorated. They fought less, but formerly their rows had been the snapping of foreplay. Now when Tony made love to her there was a brutality and coldness never there before.

To make matters worse, Sarah Stratton, in all her radiant beauty, had joined Corinium as a prospective presenter, and her pussy-cat smile, her blonde halo of hair, her soft angora bosom and her wafts of Anaïs Anaïs, had affected the men in the building like Zuleika Dobson. James Vereker, wearing

275

a different pastel pullover every day and behaving like a lovesick schoolboy, had been nicknamed Hanker-man by the newsroom. The Head of News was taking the task of initiating Sarah very seriously indeed. Even Tony chose every opportunity to see if she was all right, summoning her to drinks in his office after work, or to join board-room lunches to impress visiting bigwigs. Cameron consequently got more histrionic and ratty with the staff.

'If Simon and Cameron are anything to go by,' observed Charles Fairburn, 'control is the one ingredient unnecessary for the job of Controller of Programmes.'

James had so many Valentines he decided to do a little item on 'Cotswold Round-Up' to thank his fans and conduct a studio discussion as to whether men were more romantic and caring than they used to be. Sarah received one Valentine card postmarked Penscombe with no writing inside. Having never had a letter from Rupert, she couldn't be sure the flashy blue scrawl on the envelope was his, but she was almost certain. Declan's Valentines arrived by the sackful, but he was too preoccupied with Rupert to open them.

Taggie had a trying day. No one sent her any Valentines. She was doing dinner for the Lord-Lieutenant that evening and had made a huge ratatouille and left it to cool overnight in the larder, only to find that Declan had put the whole lot out on the lawn for the badgers, who'd refused to touch it. Declan's only distraction these days, apart from bird-watching, was putting food out at night and crouching in a dimly-lit kitchen waiting for the foxes and badgers to turn up.

Now he was roaring round the house in bare feet, complaining once again that his utterly bloody children had swiped every single one of the da-glo cat-sick yellow socks that he had made so fashionable. Looking for a pair under Caitlin's bed, he found a vodka bottle, empty except for a cockroach, and said once again that they really must sack Grace.

'Absolutely not,' said Maud firmly. 'I need my Greek chorus.'

Declan was just leaving for the studios, weighed down with

poisoned rapiers to stick into Rupert, when Taggie came rushing into the kitchen, speechless with excitement and brandishing a vast Valentine covered in hearts, which had just arrived by special delivery, and which played 'The White Cliffs of Dover' on the xylophone every time you opened it.

'What the hell's that?'

'It's from Rupert. He's sent Gertrude a Valentine.'

'Whatever for?' snapped Maud.

'He once said she was ugly. He must have changed his mind. How gratuitously' – Taggie brought out her word for the day in triumph – 'kind of him.'

'Bloody hell,' thought Declan as he went out into the dank February drizzle. 'Not content with groping Taggie and ensnaring Maud, he's now trying to seduce my dog.'

Taggie ran after him. 'You won't give Rupert too hard a time, will you?'

Throughout the network Declan's interview with Rupert had been trailed every hour on the hour during the day. Make-up had drawn lots as to who was to attend to him. Declan tried to snatch a quiet couple of hours in his office sharpening his poisoned rapiers, but was interrupted by one member of staff after another trooping in to grumble about Tony.

'He bollocked me for not giving the reps extra bonuses in January,' said Georgie Barnes, the Sales Director. 'If I had, he'd have bollocked me for squandering Corinium's resources.'

'Last week he shouted at me because my desk was a mess,' moaned Cyril Peacock. 'So I had a big tidy out. Then, when he came in this afternoon and found me with an empty desk, he bawled me out for doing nothing.'

Charles Fairburn was furious because, for the seventh week running, his request for a hundred pounds to replace the fur hat Seb Burrows had put on the Corinium Ram at Christmas had been crossed off his expenses.

Sarah Stratton, wearing a clinging pale-grey angora dress,

sat in the newsroom with the Head of News who was showing off his muscle by demanding why the BBC had had a story at lunchtime which his reporters had missed.

'Of course "Cotswold Round-Up" is the company's flagship,' he told Sarah. 'We lose or retain the franchise according to whether or not the programme truly represents local news and views. We have to be consistent, questioning, responsible and entertaining. It's the one area where interference from Cameron or Tony isn't tolerated. The autonomy of the newsroom is undisputed.'

Beside him the internal telephone rang. Taking his hand off Sarah's knee, the Head of News picked up the receiver and turned pale.

'Of course, Lord B. I quite understand. I'll put someone on the story right away.'

Sarah smiled into her paper cup and said nothing.

On the air now, James Vereker, having thanked all his fans ver' ver' much for their caring Valentines, was interviewing a local witch who'd just made a record. She was wearing a black mini and crinkled black boots, and had huge bare mottled thighs which she kept crossing and re-crossing so James could see everything.

'I'm sure you're a very caring person, Tamzin,' said James, averting his eyes, 'but don't you think the general public has a rather more sinister idea of witches?'

'Turn him into a toad,' screamed Seb Burrows in the newsroom, throwing a paper dart at the screen.

'Wish she'd make an effigy of Tony and stick pins into it,' said Charles Fairburn.

'We could market a Baddingham pin cushion,' said Seb. 'It'd sell even better than Declan T-shirts.'

Sarah wasn't listening. Rupert will be here soon, she thought. She'd warned Paul she might be late, because Tony wanted her to help at some PR party. Tony, in fact, had asked her up to the board room to watch Rupert's interview and impress a couple of big advertisers. Rupert was bound to pop in after the programme.

278

I know he sent me the Valentine, thought Sarah, wriggling in ecstasy. He must want to come back.

Rupert, in fact, had had a very tough day. He had had an acrimonious meeting with the UEFA Committee, who were still refusing to let English soccer teams play in Europe next season. He'd had to smooth over the scandal of a Chinese ping-pong player caught shoplifting in an Ann Summers sex shop. He'd tried to persuade the Advertising Institute that there was no very good reason why a large condom manufacturer shouldn't sponsor the Rugby League Cup Final next year, and coped with the Health Authority up in arms because a famous racing driver had gone on 'Wogan' in a Marlboro T-shirt. Because all these meetings ran late, he had only had half an hour to harangue a group of headmasters on the decline of competitive sport in schools, which had been exacerbated by the teachers' strike.

Finally, just as he was leaving for Cotchester, the PM had summoned him, wanting him to lean on the British Lions to cancel their tour of South Africa to encourage the athletes to boycott the European Games next month.

Rupert lost his temper. 'Politics shouldn't be brought into sport,' he snapped. 'I'm not going to pressure anyone to boycott anything. You've absolutely no idea what it's like to be an athlete. How would you have liked it if the day you became Prime Minister, someone had ordered you to refuse the job, and you'd been almost certain you'd never get another chance? You can't force people to abide by principles you wouldn't dream of sticking to yourself.'

And the Prime Minister had dismissed Rupert very frostily, saying she hoped he'd have second thoughts on the matter.

'I feel like a football at the end of the Cup Final,' said Rupert as he collapsed into the black Government car beside Sydney, his official driver. 'Everyone's having a go at me today. Who won the three-thirty?'

They discussed racing until the Heathrow exit, then Rupert fell asleep. Sydney liked working for Rupert. He enjoyed the glamour and Rupert's erratic hours brought him spectacular overtime.

Gerald Middleton, Rupert's private secretary, sat in the back with the light on, going through Rupert's red box, streamlining as much as possible, pencilling in little notes on what action to take. Glancing at the sprawled elegant figure in front, with the head fallen sideways, Gerald fought the temptation to stroke the sleek blond hair. Rupert would never know the self-control Gerald had to exert day after day, never to betray his feelings. It must be some death wish that made him pour all his energies into Rupert's career, ensuring Rupert's rapid escalation up the political scale to the head of a far grander ministry, away from Gerald – that is, unless Rupert did something silly, like going on Declan's programme tonight.

Gerald looked at his watch. They were cutting it very fine. Just as well – Rupert wouldn't have time for too many whiskys in Hospitality beforehand.

Cameron went to the control room early. She liked to have half an hour before the programme to take a deep breath and think about what she had to do. As she closed the door, the *Jaws* theme belted out from the sound room next door. This joke had been going on ever since she was made Controller of Programmes. She found it very unfunny, but, looking though the glass windows and the vertical blinds at the guffawing sound men on one side and the vision controllers on the other, it obviously creased up everyone else.

Rupert's cool unsmiling face stared out at her from every single monitor screen, except those that would feed in stills, telecine and video tape to illustrate aspects of Rupert's life during the programme. On the studio floor they were checking the order of the stills. Up on the monitor came pictures of Rupert winning the World Cup and standing on the Olympic rostrum with his arm in a sling, of his beautiful ex-wife Helen, of Beattie Johnson and Nathalie Perrault and Amanda Hamilton, wife of the Foreign Secretary. There was Jake Lovell, Rupert's arch-rival on the circuit, and his *chef d'équipe*, Malise Gordon, who'd ended up with Helen. They looked like characters in some glamorous Hollywood mini-series. Declan was clearly hell bent on carnage.

The rest of the crew drifted into the studio after their dinner break. Daysee Butler, weighed down with stop watches and blue mascara and wearing a new pale-pink jersey with a large grey cat knitted on the front, took up her position on Cameron's left.

'Rupert'll be here in five minutes. Go and meet him, Daysee, and take him straight to Make-up,' said Cameron.

On the monitor she could already see Declan slumped in his wizard's chair. Flicking the key switch, she warned him of Rupert's arrival.

'Are you going to have a drink with him beforehand?'

'I am not.'

He looks shattered, thought Cameron. He'd lost so much weight recently. His black hair was even more threaded with grey. The violet shadows under his eyes reminded her of Patrick. But she mustn't think of Patrick.

'Just do a Maurice Wooton on him, Dec, and Tony'll die happy.'

'As long as he dies,' growled Declan, 'I don't care if he's happy or not.'

Rupert, Sydney and Gerald waited in Reception, looking at photographs of Declan, Charles Fairburn and James Vereker, who was no longer obscured by the Christmas tree.

'Fuckin' 'ell, it's Farah Fawcett Major,' said Sydney, as Daysee swayed down the royal-blue steel staircase, giving them the benefit of her bouncing strawberry-blonde hair and undulating figure.

'Can I take you straight to Make-up, Minister?' said Daysee.

'Can't you and I go to the Cotchester Arms instead?' said Rupert.

Daysee looked at her watch. 'I don't think there's time,' she said seriously. 'You're on in fifteen minutes.'

'I don't want any make-up. All I need is a vast whisky,' said Rupert.

Gerald handed Daysee some photographs.

'Here are the pix of the '76 Olympic Games.'

'Oh thanks,' said Daysee. 'I'll get Graphics to soft-mount them.'

'Sounds like a contradiction in terms,' said Rupert.

'Soft-mounting means sticking a photograph on a background from which it can easily be peeled off,' explained Daysee patiently.

'Definitely Farah Fawcett NCO,' muttered Rupert to Gerald as they follow Daysee upstairs.

'You're lovely and brown,' said the make-up girl, applying a touch of Nouveau Beige to the shine on Rupert's nose and forehead.

'Skiing last weekend,' said Rupert.

He wondered for the millionth time why the hell he'd agreed to do this interview. Partly, he knew, it was Cameron taunting him about being afraid of Declan. But, in between frantic hard work and cavorting in bed and on the ski slopes with Nathalie Perrault, he had kept remembering Taggie in floods at Patrick's party over her father's catastrophic finances.

Daysee brought Rupert a dark mahogany whisky, which Gerald immediately took to the make-up department wash basin and diluted with water.

'You haven't eaten all day, Minister.'

'Yes, Nanny,' said Rupert.

'I'd better take you down,' said Daysee.

Gerald straightened Rupert's blue spotted tie.

'For Christ's sake be careful. If he asks you anything you don't like, just say you didn't come on the programme to discuss personal matters. Don't bitch up other ministers. Try not to lose your temper.'

Rupert grinned. 'Anyone would think I was off to my first term at prep school.'

Gerald didn't smile. 'You behave like it sometimes.'

22

Large orange letters outside the studio said: No Entry When Flashing.

'I should think not,' said Rupert, draining his whisky and giving the glass to Daysee. 'Do they want me to expose myself on air?'

'Christ, he's photogenic,' said Cameron in the gallery, as she watched Rupert sit down opposite a tense, unsmiling Declan. 'Look at that jawline, and the way his eyes lengthen when he smiles.'

'Declan's nervous,' said the Vision Mixer, as the sound man tested both men for level. 'Listen to the quiver in his voice.'

In his earpiece, Declan could now hear Daysee discussing a boyfriend who was coming to dinner tomorrow.

'The recipe says lots of garlic, but I think I'll leave it out. That Rupert's dead attractive, isn't he?'

Declan looked at Rupert, lounging, so relaxed, radiating élitism and privilege with his Red Indian suntan, his beautifully cut suit and his blue silk shirt matching his insolent blue eyes. He thought of Taggie sobbing with humiliation after Valerie Jones's party, and of Maud sobbing in his arms the night of Patrick's twenty-first, and his resolve hardened.

'Either of you need a touch-up?' asked the make-up girl, whisking on with her steel basket.

'I'd love to give you one,' said Rupert.

The make-up girl blushed. Rupert leaned forward and looked at the name-tape on one of Declan's odd socks. It said Charlotte Webster-Lee.

'She's a friend of Caitlin's,' snapped Declan.

'I think I used to know her mother very well,' said Rupert. 'Is Charlotte blonde with blue eyes?'

Can't he let up for a second? thought Declan savagely.

Trouble ahead, decided Rupert, as he chatted idly with the crew about Cotchester's chances against Wandsworth United on Saturday. This man's out to bury me.

'One minute to air, Declan,' said the Floor Manager.

'Good luck,' said Cameron.

'Stand by tape,' said Daysee.

The floor manager raised his hand to cue Declan, the red light flashed on, and he was off.

'My guest tonight needs no introduction. He has been described as the greatest show jumper in the world, the handsomest man in England, the icing on the cake of the Tory party. He is, of course, the Minister for Sport, and the MP for Chalford and Bisley, Rupert Campbell-Black.'

Dispensing with the introductory package, Declan weighed straight in: 'Do you mind being described as the handsomest man in England?'

'Why should I?'

'You're not frightened of being dismissed just as a pretty face?'

'No.'

'Of being dragged into the Tory party just to add an element of much-needed glamour?'

'No, because it's not true.'

'For what other reason could you possibly have been brought in?' said Declan dismissively.

'I know more about sport than anyone else in the party,' said Rupert simply. 'Having lasted in show jumping for sixteen years on what must be the most gruelling circuits in the world, I can cope with the pressures. One day you're king of the castle in show jumping, next day you're bottom of the heap. It's helped me to be resilient about the ups and downs of politics.'

'Do you find politics as satisfying as show-jumping?'

'Of course not, but it has its compensations.'

'What are they?'

'The Olympic Fund has just passed four million and we've still got eighteen months to go. Soccer violence is down by seventy per cent. Comprehensive schools are gradually upping competitive sport and' – Rupert grinned nastily – 'England trounced Ireland at rugger last Saturday.'

Gerald, sipping Perrier in the board room, winced. That was a cheap point. Rupert shouldn't have made it.

'The Government makes two hundred million pounds a year from tax on football pools,' accused Declan, 'and yet you're asking the clubs to spend two million this year tightening up their security to reduce football violence. Why don't you give them some help?'

'With footballers earning one hundred thousand pounds a year and stars like Garry Lineker changing hands for over a million I think the football clubs can put their own houses in order.'

'Some people feel you're taking a strong line on soccer violence because it's electorally attractive.'

'Do they?' said Rupert politely.

Shit, thought Declan, I walked right into that one.

Rupert relented: 'Just because something is electorally attractive, doesn't make it wrong. I want to clean up the terraces and make them safe places for fathers to take their families again – or the game'll be drained of its support and future talent.'

Declan changed tack: 'I see from the evening paper that you're backing the British Lions tour of South Africa, thereby giving your blessing to a corrupt and evil regime.'

'Rubbish,' said Rupert, wondering if the PM was listening. 'Sport's outside politics. Athletes are so briefly at their peak, they should be allowed to compete where and against whom they like. It's bloody easy to have principles when you're not making the sacrifices.'

And so the programme went on, with nice bitchy repartee flashing back and forth, but on the whole Rupert deflected Declan's needling easily.

Then Declan said: 'You've been described as the Prime Minister's blue-eyed boy.'

'Boy's pushing it. I'm thirty-seven,' said Rupert, 'but as I've got blue eyes, I don't see how I could be anything else.'

'She seems to prefer good-looking men.'

'She'd need her head examined if she didn't,' said Rupert coldly. 'Do you prefer dogs yourself?'

'You've always got on well with women,' said Declan. 'Wasn't it Amanda Hamilton –' a large glamorous picture of the Foreign Secretary's wife appeared on the screen – 'who drew you into politics?'

'And her husband Rollo,' said Rupert quickly. 'They both encouraged me.'

Despite repeated probing from Declan, Rupert refused to give an inch on the subject of Amanda Hamilton.

'It was Mrs Hamilton,' said Declan pointedly, 'who drove you down to your first meeting with your constituency. Do you find a conflict between your ministerial and constituency duties?'

'Of course,' snapped Rupert. 'I don't have enough time to devote to my constituency. They come first; they're the people who voted me in. I've lived in the area all my life, and I don't want a bloody great motorway half a mile from Penscombe any more than they do.'

Gerald put his head in his hands.

Tony, purring with pleasure, was pacing up and down the board-room carpet. 'Rupert is beginning to lose his temper,' he said softly.

I can't help it, thought Sarah, I still love him.

'Was it merely lust for power that drove you into politics?' asked Declan dismissively.

'It certainly wasn't the money, or the free time,' snapped Rupert. 'Most ministers are hopelessly overworked. The civil service want control and pile work on to keep us quiet. Sometimes you get home at three in the morning after a session in the House, then still have to go through your box. That's when the trouble starts. You're so zonked you OK a nuclear power station in your constituency and six months later you realize to your horror what you've done. I'm very lucky. I have an exceptional private secretary in Gerald Middleton. He does all my donkey work, and wraps my knuckles if I go too far. I'm also lucky,' went on Rupert, yawning ostentatiously, 'because on the circuit I learnt to grab sleep at any time.'

'With anyone?' said Declan. He was taunting Rupert now.

'No,' drawled Rupert. 'I've always been selective.'

'That's not what your press cuttings say.'

A still of Samantha Freebody, the starlet who'd told all about sleeping with Rupert while he was married, appeared on the screen, followed by a succession of beauties including Amanda Hamilton's daughter, Georgina, Beattie Johnson and Nathalie Perrault.

'Coming to 2. We must catch Rupert's reaction after this lot,' said Cameron. 'Take 2.'

But Rupert's face was expressionless.

Declan picked up a cutting from the table: 'One Gloucestershire peer has described you as "rather a nasty virus, that everyone's wife caught sooner or later".'

'If you'd seen his wife, it's definitely later,' said Rupert lightly, but there was a muscle going in his cheek.

'With the advent of AIDS, don't you feel you should mend your ways?'

'Sure,' said Rupert. 'I'm giving up casual sex for Lent.'

Tony was getting restless, and, picking up a telephone, dialled the control room:

'Tell Declan to stop farting around and put the boot in.'

'Tony says put the boot in, Declan,' Cameron told Declan. 'Get him on to cruelty.'

Declan squared his shoulders. 'Over the past two years you've expressed sympathy for the football hooligans.'

Rupert stared at his shoes. 'Most of them probably lead appallingly dull lives during the week. Many are out of work, or just turning lathes in a factory. The terraces are their stage, their chance to vent the frustrations of the week. They generally riot because they're losing, or there's been a bad penalty at half-time.'

'You were a bad loser, weren't you?' said Declan gently.

It was the voice of Torquemada, the pale intent face of the Grand Inquisitor.

Rupert looked wary: 'What's the point of competing – except to win?'

'Even to the extent of beating up your horses?'

Rupert's eyes narrowed, but he just stared back at Declan, saying nothing.

'Look at this picture,' said Declan, showing a still of a horse so thin it was almost a skeleton.

'This was one of your horses, Macaulay. You beat him up so badly he wouldn't jump for you, so you sold him to the Middle East, where he ended up in the stone quarries.'

'That was bad luck,' said Rupert. 'I sold half-a-dozen horses to the same Sheik. One of them's at stud in America now. Two of them are still with him. The horse didn't click with him so he sold it on.'

'And your deadly enemy Jake Lovell nursed the horse back to health, and then entered it in the World Championship, and in the finals, when you all had to ride each other's horses, Macaulay wasn't very keen on having you on his back. Remember this?'

On the screen came a clip of Rupert being finally bucked off, then being chased round the ring by the maddened horse, before taking refuge in the centre of a vast jump.

'Coming to 2, take 2,' screamed Cameron, frantic once again to get the reaction on Rupert's face. But once again it was completely blank. Only his long fingers clenched round the glass of water on the table betrayed any emotion.

'He's going to walk out,' said Tony happily.

'You'd beaten up that horse so badly,' said Declan, almost in a whisper, 'that it remembered and went for you. What d'you feel seeing that clip today?'

There was another long pause.

288

'That I was in the wrong sport,' said Rupert slowly. 'With me running that fast, neither Seb Coe nor Ovett would have had a chance against me in the 1500 metres.'

For a second the two men glared at each other. Then Rupert grinned and Declan started to laugh.

'Have you got any regrets you treated your horses so badly?'

'I didn't treat them all badly or they wouldn't have jumped so well. Of course I regret it, but it helped me understand the football hooligans; poor sods out of work, their fathers out of work, often their grandfathers too. Out of sheer frustration at not winning, they resort to violence.'

'You were in work.'

'I know. There was really no excuse.'

'You treated women very badly in the past.'

Rupert shrugged helplessly. 'I liked winning there too.'

'Jake Lovell,' went on Declan remorselessly, 'was your arch rival because you bullied him at school.'

'Are we having oranges at half-time?' protested Rupert, shaking his head.

Declan smiled slightly. 'Jake Lovell finally got his revenge by running off with your wife, Helen, in the middle of the 1980 Olympics. How did you feel at the time?'

Rupert'll kill Declan in a minute, thought Gerald in panic. No one's ever dared ask him these questions.

'I was principally outraged that she should distract me and Jake, when we should have been concentrating on a team gold,' said Rupert.

'But you still got your medal, despite dislocating your shoulder, and riding with one arm.'

'That was just to show them that, even riding one man short and one man injured, we could beat the whole world.'

Prompted by Declan, Rupert went on to talk about the Olympics and Rocky, the horse he'd won a gold medal on, who still lived at Penscombe.

'I'm so cruel to Rocky,' drawled Rupert, 'that he has the entire run of my garden, and spends his time trampling over the flower beds and peering in at the drawing-room window.'

I like this man. Why I am trying to crucify him? thought Declan.

I like this man, even though he's trying to crucify me, thought Rupert.

Tony went into the next-door office to ring Cameron, so the advertisers wouldn't hear him.

'Declan's gone soft, for Christ's sake. Tell him to fucking nail him.'

'What did you feel,' Declan was asking now, 'when Helen split up with Jake and married your old team manager?'

'Well, I didn't let off fireworks. It was like one's childhood sweetheart marrying one's headmaster.'

'Do you mind her being happy now?'

'Not at all,' said Rupert in surprise. 'It's better for the children. Anyway she deserved it; she had a rough time with me.'

'In what way?'

'Show-jumping and marriage don't mix. I was never there when she needed me. When she was having Marcus I was stuck on an alpine pass. She was an intellectual and I hardly know Oscar Wilde from Kim Wilde. Then the dogs were always getting in the bed.'

'Yes,' said Declan. 'People say you were fonder of your black labrador, Badger, than of Helen.'

'I had him first,' said Rupert flatly. 'He lived with me six years after she left me. *He* never criticized or tried to improve me.'

'Is that what you want from women, uncritical adulation?' Rupert grinned. 'Probably.'

The questions were still barbed, but the animosity had gone.

'Your name's been linked since your divorce with some dazzling women. Have you ever thought of marrying again?'

'Just because I enjoy flying on Concorde doesn't mean I want to buy the plane. These questions are giving me ear-ache,' grumbled Rupert.

Out of the corner of his eye, Declan could see the Floor Manager holding up his hand for three minutes.

'When you get any free time, what's the thing you like doing best?'

Rupert put his head on one side: 'I thought this was supposed to be a family programme.'

'You must have some hobbies,' said Declan hastily.

'Hunting, shooting, fishing,' said Rupert.

'All the blood sports.' Declan's lip was curling.

'Not all. I didn't include being interviewed by you on television.'

'*Touché*,' said Declan, laughing. 'Who are your heroes? If you could choose, who would you like to meet in an afterlife?'

For a second Rupert seemed to have difficulty in speaking: 'I'd like to see Badger again,' he muttered.

'Oh, how sweet,' said Daysee, who was now revving up for her most important moment: pressing the cue switch. The Floor Manager was making wind-up signals to Declan.

'Looking back on your sixteen years in show-jumping, can you remember the hardest thing you had to do? Was it getting the first bronze, winning the King's Cup three years running, clinching the team gold in 1980, or finally winning the World Championship?'

There was another long pause.

'What was the hardest thing?' Declan urged him.

Just for a second the despair showed through on Rupert's face.

'The thing that nearly killed me,' he said bleakly, 'was giving it up.'

As Schubert's Fifth Symphony pounded out and the credits came up, Declan most uncharacteristically could be seen getting out of his chair and shaking Rupert by the hand. As soon as they were off air, Cameron came down onto the studio floor. Maybe it was because she was blinking in the unaccustomed light after the darkness of the control room, but for once her yellow eyes seemed to have lost all their aggression.

'Great programme, Declan. Best you've done for us – and

you were marvellous.' Flushing slightly she turned to Rupert. 'Declan threw you some really tough questions and you handled them so well.'

'I hope my boss thinks so,' said Rupert. 'Coming on your programme's rather like being interrogated by the IRA. I was expecting electrodes any minute.'

Cameron had amazing legs, he noticed, as she walked upstairs in front of them.

Up in Hospitality, Tony Baddingham was feeling far from hospitable, but had to restrain himself in front of his two big advertisers, who were terrific fans both of Declan and Rupert, and who felt they had just witnessed a great gladiatorial contest. With a shaking hand, the normally teetotal Gerald helped himself to a triple whisky.

'Wasn't it wonderful?' said Sarah, busily powdering her nose and undoing another pearl button of her little grey dress. 'Declan brought out a really vulnerable side of Rupert. I'm sure he just needs the love of a good woman.'

And the attention of a whole harem of mistresses as well, thought Gerald. He had disapproved very strongly of Rupert's affair with Sarah, regarding it as political dynamite. He hoped it wasn't going to start again.

But, as Rupert walked in with Declan and Cameron, Sarah rushed up and flung her arms round his neck, giving him the benefit of unsupported breasts and half a bucket of Anaïs Anaïs. 'Darling, you were wonderful, so honest.'

'Not much else I could do without walking off the set.'

'When am I going to see you?' murmured Sarah. 'Thank you so much for your Valentine.'

But before Rupert had time to answer her, Gerald muscled in.

'I'm sorry, Minister, I never dreamed Declan'd go that far.'

Rupert raised an eyebrow at Gerald's glass of whisky.

'Are we in trouble?'

'I don't know,' said Gerald. 'The press are going berserk already. I told the switchboard to say you'd left. We'll have to smuggle you out by a side door.'

Tony, having introduced the big advertisers to Rupert, went and vented his fury on Declan.

'I thought I told you to fucking well crucify him.'

'I tried to,' said Declan coldly, 'but he was too good for me,' and, turning on his heel, he headed towards the drinks.

Seeing Tony coming to give her an earful, Cameron grabbed a plate of quiche and took it over to Rupert, who, to Sarah's fury, turned away from the group to talk to her. After the tension of the interview, he was gripped by the lust that always used to overwhelm him after a big show-jumping class. In the old days he would have screwed a groom or a show-jumping groupie in the back of his lorry. Tonight he was sure he could choose between Daysee, Sarah or Cameron. Daysee was too thick, Sarah too possessive, Cameron on the other hand had a reckless, scrawny nymphomania and pulling her would have the added charm of irritating the hell out of Tony.

'Well,' he said icily, 'I had to box bloody clever to get out of that one. I suppose Tony put Declan up to it.'

'I'm sorry,' said Cameron.

Glancing up, she found she couldn't tear her eyes away.

'Being sorry isn't enough,' said Rupert softly. 'I'm going to get my own back.'

Cameron gasped. She could see Tony bearing down on them.

'I was wondering if you'd like to come on another programme? It's the third Thursday in March,' she stammered.

'And have open-heart surgery all over again without an anaesthetic? No, thanks. Besides it's Cheltenham.'

'It's not until the evening,' said Cameron quickly. 'All we'd want you to do is to judge "Miss Corinium Television" with Declan. There are some beautiful girls entered.'

'I might just be able to drag myself away,' said Rupert, 'as long as you promise me a night in the Cotchester Arms with the winner as second prize.'

'What's the first prize?' said Cameron, knowing the answer.

'A night in the Cotchester Arms with you,' said Rupert, 'and my God, I'd make you walk differently in the morning.'

It was several seconds before they both realized that a tense-looking Gerald was tapping Rupert on the arm.

'Telephone. It's the PM.'

'Oh Christ,' said Rupert. 'Back benches here I come.'

'Well done,' said the Prime Minister in her rich deep voice that always sounded like Carnation Milk pouring out of a tin. 'We were very proud of you.'

'You were?' said Rupert in amazement.

'Well, what else could you have done, faced with that spiteful little pinko? You handled him very well. That interview will do us a lot of good in the opinion polls.'

'Good God,' said Rupert putting down the telephone, 'she actually liked it.'

'Was that really the PM?' said one of the big advertisers in awe.

'Did she mention me?' said James, who'd rolled up from a Save-the-Aged fund-raising party.

'I've booked a table for us at the Horn of Plenty at nine-thirty,' said Cameron casually to Rupert. 'The cars are waiting downstairs.'

Despite her off-hand manner, Rupert noticed she was quivering with expectancy, like a greyhound ordered to sit when the woolly rabbit sets off round the track. Then he caught a glimpse of Declan, looking grey and utterly shattered. Once again he remembered Taggie's tears on New Year's Eve.

'Sweet of you,' he said to Cameron, 'but Declan and I are going back to Penscombe. We've got things to discuss.'

Aware of Tony watching her, Cameron hid her bitter disappointment. Being very young, Sarah had no such reserve. 'You can't go,' she wailed. 'We'll be far too many girls.'

'James can come instead,' said Tony smoothly. 'That's if he hasn't got to rush home to Lizzie.'

'Of course not,' said James.

'That's rather uncaring of you,' said Sarah sulkily.

'Work comes first,' said James sanctimoniously. 'And you haven't told me what you thought of my Valentine, Sarah.

I thought it was rather nice that it was sold to raise money for the Cat's Protection League.'

Back at Penscombe, two Jack Russells, a young black labrador, two springer spaniels and a blue lurcher threw themselves on Rupert in ecstasy. Once inside, Rupert whisked Gerald and Declan past tapestried hunting scenes and portraits of ancestors, only pausing to point out a huge oil painting of Badger, into the kitchen, which was low-beamed with a flagstone floor, and a window looking over the valley. As Gerald found a bottle of whisky and three glasses and Rupert investigated the fridge and the larder, Declan looked at the pictures on the wall. They were mostly paintings of dogs and horses and framed photographs of two incredibly beautiful children.

'That's Tabitha,' said Rupert, pointing to a little girl on a pony festooned with rosettes.

'She's magic,' said Declan.

'She's doing bloody well in junior classes already.'

'Does the boy ride?' said Declan, looking at the sensitive, nervous face and the huge eyes.

'No. He gets asthma, but he skis well, and he's extremely clever.' There was a slight edge to Rupert's voice.

'Can I have a look round?' asked Declan.

'Go ahead,' said Rupert.

As he wandered through beautiful pastel room after pastel room admiring the incredible pictures: a Romney, a Gainsborough, a Lely, a Thomas Lawrence, and two Stubbs for starters, and the lovingly polished furniture, he thought the whole house was like a museum, beautiful but crying out for someone to live in it, or like a horse, constantly bridled, saddled and groomed to perfection, but with no one to ride it.

Finding the library, Declan was lost in admiration. He'd never seen such books in a private house – first editions of Scott, Dickens, Trollope, Wordsworth, Keats and Shelley, and a whole set of Oscar Wilde, and other books so rare there couldn't be more than half-a-dozen copies in the country.

Half an hour later Rupert found him, oblivious of time, immersed in a first edition of *Middlemarch*.

'Supper. Christ, you can't read in this light!'

'Can I come and live here?' said Declan, shaking his head in bewildered reverence.

'Borrow anything you like whenever you want to. No one else reads them. Helen pretended to, but never seemed to get beyond the first chapter.'

Laid out on the kitchen table was smoked salmon, brown bread, gulls' eggs and half a heated-up chicken pie. Gerald had also made a tomato salad and fried some potatoes.

'It's very good of you,' mumbled Declan. 'I couldn't have faced dinner with Tony.'

'Not up to Taggie's standard, I'm afraid,' said Rupert, adding casually, 'How is she?'

'Very pleased with Gertrude's Valentine.'

'Oh, she got it?' said Rupert. 'Ironic that the first Valentine I ever sent in my life should be to a dog.'

They talked about politics, horses and sport, and then Rupert filled Declan in on local gossip, and some of the early history of Penscombe.

'I hope Penscombe waits for me,' sighed Declan. 'I've been so busy since we've lived here, I've never had a chance to explore it. I haven't even been into the local pub yet.'

It was not until they'd both got pretty drunk, and Gerald had gone to bed, that Rupert asked how things were at Corinium.

'Bloody awful,' said Declan.

'Tony?'

Declan nodded wearily. 'I seem to go from Baddingham to worse.'

'He didn't look very happy after the programme.'

'He wasn't. He wanted me to carve you up.'

Rupert grinned. 'You had a bloody good try. I know why Tony was out for my blood, but why you? Just because I'm a Tory?'

'No, for screwing up Tag at Valerie Jones's dinner party.'

'Ah.'

'And I thought you were after her at Patrick's birthday party.'

Suddenly Declan didn't want to mention Maud.

Rupert inhaled deeply on his cigar. 'Would that have been so bad?'

'She's eighteen and desperately insecure,' said Declan roughly. 'She's simply not equipped to cope. You'd break her like a moth caught in the typewriter keys.'

'Ouch,' said Rupert wincing.

'I saw them all slavering this evening,' went on Declan, 'Sarah, Cameron, that imbecile Daysee. You could have had any of them. Just spare Taggie.'

Rupert, however, was reluctant to drop the subject.

'But she seems incredibly competent. She cooked brilliantly for Valerie and she coped with your party on New Year's Eve virtually single-handed.'

'Oh, she's competent enough,' said Declan. 'You mustn't assume people with dyslexia are thick, just because they have difficulty reading and writing. Albert Einstein, Leonardo da Vinci and Thomas Edison were all dyslexic. So was General Patton. He could never learn the alphabet or his tables by heart.'

'Good God,' said Rupert in alarm. 'So we can expect to see Taggie commanding the Third Army at any minute.'

Declan grinned.

Rupert filled up their glasses with brandy.

'Is Tony really giving you a hard time?'

'Septic tankwise, I'm up to here.' Declan drew a finger across his throat.

He got up and wandered slightly unsteadily towards the window.

'Beautiful house this. Where's The Priory from here?'

Rupert pointed to the left, where, through a spiky fuzz of trees, a light was burning. 'Taggie's still awake, that's her bedroom,' he added without thinking. Then, when Declan instantly looked bootfaced, 'It's all right. I had to bodily remove some drunk from her room the night of your party because Taggie wanted to go to bed – alone.'

As Rupert joined Declan beside the window, dogs, sprawled all over the floor, sleepily thumped their tails.

'D'you know what I've always wanted to do?' said Rupert idly. 'Buy that wood below your house.'

'Pretty useless piece of land,' said Declan.

'Fifty yards to the right of the stream you could make the most perfect dry ski slope. You wouldn't see it from the road. It'd be hidden by trees on both sides.'

'How much d'you reckon it's worth?'

'About thirty-five grand,' lied Rupert.

'Seems a helluva lot,' said Declan, stroking Jack Russells with both hands.

'You could still walk through the rest of the wood if you wanted to,' said Rupert.

But Declan wasn't listening. Thirty-five grand would get me off the hook for the moment with the tax man, he thought, and pay the electricity bill and Caitlin's school fees.

'Think about it, anyway,' said Rupert. 'You also need a day off. Come out hunting on Saturday week. I'll lend you a horse.'

When Declan finally got back to The Priory, he left all the car lights on, flattened several purple crocuses on the edge of the lawn and drove slap through a flower bed.

Waiting for him on the stairs, both looking equally disapproving, were Taggie and Gertrude.

'Why,' said Taggie, 'were you so g-g-gratuitously beastly to Rupert?'

RIVALS

23

On the third Monday in March Cameron Cook had the sadistic idea of summoning the entire Corinium staff to a power breakfast in Studio 1 at eight o'clock in the morning. While they blearily consumed croissants and muesli, and orange juice (scrambled egg was considered to contain too much cholesterol), Tony gave them a rousing pep talk on how each one of them could personally help retain the franchise.

'This is a very exciting time,' said Tony heartily. '"Dorothy Dove" and "Four Men went to Mow" have yet again been nominated for BAFTA Awards. Our new series on the elderly, "Young as You Feel", starts next week. And we're delighted to announce that our new presenter is going to be Naomi Hargreaves, who, as you know, climbed Everest last year at the age of sixty-five.

'Our new networked quiz, "Master Dog", to find the canine brain of Britain, starts recording on Wednesday. The new series of "Four Men went to Mow" starts at the end of April and a performance of Michael Tippett's *Midsummer Marriage* will be recorded in Cotchester Park in early June. James Vereker's and Sarah Stratton's new afternoon programme starts on Monday week.' Tony smiled warmly at Sarah, and received a black look from Cameron. 'And we all wish them the best of luck.

'Finally, *Midsummer Night's Dream*,' Tony added with a

sigh of relief, 'is virtually in the can. We anticipate two days re-shooting, tomorrow and Wednesday, leaving Studio 1 free for "Miss Corinium Television" on Thursday.'

To put Declan down, Tony had deliberately not mentioned his programme, but now, looking round the packed studio, he discovered to his fury that Declan didn't appear to be present.

Declan, in fact, was at home, having got up at five to wrestle with his Yeats biography. Looking at the pile of scribbled notes and typed pages on his desk, he felt like Vidal Sassoon confronted by the wild woman of the West with fifty years of burrs and tangles in her hair. He wished he had Vidal Sassoon's skills. He was so tired, he hadn't had an original thought for weeks. Matters had not been helped by Grace finally walking out at the weekend because Declan had bawled her out for drinking all his whisky. Maud, furious at losing her ally and sparring partner, blamed Declan for the whole thing and was refusing to talk to him.

His black gloom was interrupted by Ursula ringing up to say she had flu.

'Poor thing. Stay in bed,' said Declan. 'Can I bring you anything?'

'No, but I'm terribly sorry, I forgot to remind you about Cameron's power breakfast,' said Ursula.

At Corinium Tony was winding up his peroration: 'I have no doubt that Corinium will retain the franchise, but I cannot remind you too strongly that this year we are on show. The IBA will not only be monitoring our programmes more closely, and examining our finances and our staff relations, but they will be looking to see how we conduct ourselves both as individuals and as a company. Any complaints from a local body, pressure group or a restaurateur will count as the blackest mark. Seb Burrows' twenty-first birthday party last week, for example, completely broke up the Beaufort room at the Cotchester Arms. If you ever have another twenty-first birthday, Seb –' Tony's big smile flashed on – 'you'll be fired.'

Realizing some sort of joke had been made, the staff tittered feebly.

'Finally I must warn you that that scourge of violence and, particularly, sex, the Reverend Fergus Penney, ex-Prebendary of the Church of England, will be visiting the station tomorrow, so for Christ's sake behave yourselves and make him feel welcome. And remember above all, appearance does matter.'

Exactly on cue, Declan walked in, deathly pale, hair un-brushed, stubble blacking his jaw, and his jersey inside out.

'I'm sorry, Tony,' he said, 'I forgot.'

'We've just finished,' said Tony coolly. 'I'm afraid you've missed the boat, but that's nothing unusual.'

'Where are you going?' shouted Cameron, as Declan turned towards the exit.

'Home,' snapped Declan, 'I've got a lot of lying down to do.'

The next day, 21st March, was the first day of Spring. The Head of News sent a crew off to photograph lambs playing in a field. James wore a new primrose yellow tracksuit to urge viewers to join his new sponsored Slim-for-Spring campaign to raise money for heart research, and Declan came in to interview Guilini. The programme, for once, was being rec-orded as Guilini was flying to New York for a concert straight afterwards.

The fair Daysee Butler, keen to do her bit for the franchise, accepted an invitation to lunch from someone almost as grand as Guilini. As it was programme day, she only sipped Perrier and ate one course of chef's salad. Her very distinguished companion, however, departed from his usual Perrier and put away a large whisky before lunch, a whole bottle of claret during, and a large brandy afterwards. He hardly touched his monkfish, but was charmed that Daysee should peel his Mediterranean prawns for him as she told him, admittedly rather monotonously, how she got every programme out on time.

On the drive back from the restaurant, which was several miles outside Cotchester, Daysee's very distinguished companion, mindful that it was the first day of Spring, pulled into a side road to admire some leaping lambs and leapt on poor Daysee. By the time he had torn half the buttons off her yellow angora jersey with the picture of Donald Duck on the front, and grabbed goatily at her thighs, laddering her stockings, Daysee was so frightened she dashed out of the car and, taking off her high heels, ran sobbing across Cotchester water meadows, across the tarmac of the car park and in through the back door of Corinium Television. Here she collided with Tony, who had lunched not wisely but too well. The sight of poor Daysee with her blonde hair awry, her mascara streaked with tears, her stockings muddy and laddered, and her yellow jersey half torn off her beautiful body, melted even Tony's stony heart.

'My dear child, what *is* the matter?'

'Someone's just tried to rape me,' wailed Daysee.

Next minute she was whisked up in the fast lift to Tony's office and ensconced on the squashy leather sofa, sobbing her heart out while Tony poured her a vast brandy.

'There, drink this.'

'I mustn't,' sobbed Daysee. 'I'll never be able to count Declan's programme out on time.'

'Nonsense! One glass of brandy won't hurt you. Anyway, it's only some tinpot conductor.'

Getting out his red silk handkerchief smelling of Paco Rabanne, Tony dried Daysee's eyes. She was really very, very pretty.

'Now, tell me who it was.'

'I c-c-can't.'

'Come on, you can trust me.' He sat down on the sofa beside her.

'It was such a shock,' whispered Daysee. 'I thought he was just interested in our programmes. I wanted to help Corinium win the franchise.'

'I know you did,' said Tony warmly. 'That's what makes it so reprehensible. Just give me his name.'

'I'd truly rather not.'

'Someone connected with work?'

Daysee gulped and nodded.

Better and better, thought Tony, mentally rubbing his hands. How wonderful if it were Declan or even James.

'If we don't get him for rape, we'll clobber him for sexual harassment,' he said, trying not to sound too eager.

Daysee shook her head in bewilderment. 'I was convinced he was just interested in my mind.'

Noticing the ten inches of thigh and the glorious depth of cleavage revealed by the torn jersey, Tony sidled down the dark-green squashy sofa and said, 'Of course he was.'

Daysee looked up, her huge eyes spilling over once more with tears. Tony put an arm round her shoulders.

'Come on, my dear, we can't allow animals like him to roam at large. He may strike again and succeed next time. Think of your female colleagues. Don't worry, I'll see your name's kept out of the papers. Now tell me who it was.' Gently he stroked her silky hair.

'It was the Prebendary,' murmured Daysee.

'What!' exploded Tony.

'The Reverend Fergus Penney from the IBA,' whispered Daysee miserably.

Instantly the solicitous smile was wiped off Tony's face. His arm jumped off her shoulders as though they were red hot.

'I don't want to hear any more about this business,' he said chillingly. 'If you value your job, don't blab about it to anyone. And I hope you've learnt your lesson, not to wear such short skirts or tight sweaters to the office in future.' With that he slammed his door in poor Daysee's face.

Still trying to be a loyal Corinium employee, Daysee tried to keep her trap shut. But Declan, noticing her reddened eyes and lack of bounce during the afternoon and being infinitely more skilled at getting confidences out of people than Tony, soon had the whole story from her with the help of a few whiskys from his office bottle.

303

'Lord Baddingham said the Prebendary was so against sex and violence,' sobbed Daysee.

'Only on television,' said Declan grimly. 'It's fine in real life.'

As he was intending to take Thursday off to go to the Gold Cup with Rupert, Declan went into the office on Wednesday to wade through a mountain of post. After the row with Maud about the telephone and drink bills which she'd hidden behind the recipe books in the kitchen, Corinium, with all its ructions, seemed the quieter place. The tax man had also called the day before to collect twenty thousand pounds, and, being told Declan was out, said he would call again next day, which was another reason for not hanging around at home. He was beginning to think there was no alternative except to sell Rupert the wood. The only thought that sustained him was that he was due for a two-month break at the end of April, but, as things were going, he'd have to spend the time off doing programmes in America to raise some cash.

He was also aware that his programmes had been very lacklustre recently. The one on Rupert had attracted huge ratings and newspaper coverage, but Declan in retrospect was bitterly ashamed of it, knowing that initially he'd let personal animosity overwhelm his detachment. Since then, the programmes had had the bite of a rubber duck.

God, he was tired. He looked at the mountain of post, a lot of it probably bills. Ursula was still away. He could smell today's special, boeuf bourguignon, flavoured from a packet no doubt, drifting down from the canteen, as could the contestants of 'Master Dog' who were barking hungrily in Studio 2.

He picked up the first memo. *The Gay and Lesbian Sub-Committee of the ACTT has been re-named the Sexuality Sub-Committee.*

On cue, Charles Fairburn drifted in, having just collected his expenses.

'Come and have a drink at the Bar Sinister.'

Declan shook his head. 'Got to deal with all this.'

'Never grumble about fan mail,' chided Charles. 'Think of poor me going off to Southampton first thing tomorrow to supervise Holy Communion for the Deaf. Have you been asked to Tony's bash for Badminton? He's put the little red ram logo on the corner of all the invites so he can offload the whole thing on expenses.'

'He won't ask me,' said Declan grimly.

'No, you are a bit out of favour, poor dear,' said Charles sympathetically, 'and you work harder than any of us. I'm expecting to get the Old Queen's Award for Lack of Industry any minute. That's better; at least you're smiling. And I'll tell you something else to cheer you up even more. In Studio 2 you'll find a lot of lovable mongrels rummaging for choc drops which have all melted under the lights, on caring James's pastel sofa. James is going to be livid when he gets back from another three-hour lunch with Mrs Stratton.'

The telephone rang. 'Corinium Waifs and Strays,' said Charles, picking it up. 'Oh, hi, Madden dear. All right, I'll send him along. Tony's leaving for London in twenty minutes, thank God,' he told Declan, 'but he wants a word with you first. I'd take the slow lift. He's in a vile mood.'

Tony, in fact, seemed in an excellent mood, purring away like a great cat about to enjoy an extended game of mouse-taunting.

'Ah, Declan. Shut the door behind you and sit down.'

As usual the central heating was turned up so high Declan felt he was having a hot flush.

'I wonder if you'd explain this.'

Tony threw Declan a picture postcard of a huge crocodile with gaping jaws. On the other side was scrawled in huge black writing: 'Here's a picture of your boss. Bloody hot here. If I don't talk to you before, I'll pick you up at The Priory at eleven o'clock. Rupert.'

There was no address or stamp.

'Who the fock opened this?' asked Declan.

'We open all mail during franchise year,' said Tony

305

smoothly. 'Just to check whether any of our staff are being propositioned by other franchise contenders.'

'This place gets more like the KGB every minute.' Declan made no attempt to hide his rage.

'I also see you've taken up élitist sports,' went on Tony, happily handing Declan the *Daily Express*, which was folded back at a picture of Rupert and Declan out hunting.

'Burying the hatchet after their recent encounter on "Declan",' read the caption.

Tony shook his head. 'You're not keeping very good company, Declan.'

'Then why has Rupert been asked to judge Miss Corinium tomorrow?'

'That's a slip-up of Cameron's. It won't happen again. There's also a piece in yesterday's *Standard* quoting you as saying you've given up hope for Lent. Not a very positive attitude. Be a bit more careful when you talk to the press in future.'

Tony got up and wandered towards the drinks cupboard.

'Like a drink?'

Declan shook his head.

'Just as well,' said Tony, pouring himself one. 'I gather you were plastered when you interviewed Guilini yesterday.' Then, as Declan opened his mouth to protest, he went on, 'I saw your old boss, Johnny Abrahams, from the BBC last night. He said they'd let you go at just the right time, that you were burnt out.'

'The bastard,' said Declan furiously. 'He's got a bloody nerve.'

'I hoped you'd take it like that,' said Tony softly, 'because I am very worried about your ratings. Only ten million for the week ending 2nd March. Cameron was at a network meeting yesterday and they're now considering what was unthinkable a few months ago, shifting your programme from peak time to shallower waters, perhaps a ten-thirty or even an eleven o'clock slot.'

'That's insane,' said Declan. 'We only got ten million because the BBC have moved "Dallas" against us. We'll get it back.'

'I doubt it,' said Tony brutally. 'Quite honestly you've lost your authority, Declan. There was a time when every interview made the front page of every newspaper. Now even the critics ignore them. You didn't make a single national last week.'

'I will next week. Bob Geldof's coming on.'

'Bit old hat – all that Aid stuff.'

Tony tipped back his chair, stretched his legs, and gazed at Declan considerately. 'I'm so sorry,' he said. 'I know how depressing it is for stars when they drop down from Number One. I do hope you're not overdoing things. Why are your hands shaking?' He looked complacently down at his own beautifully manicured hands. 'Mine don't shake.'

Declan stood up. 'That's because you don't have to work with people like you,' he snarled.

Out of the window he could see a posse of lovable mongrels scampering across the water meadows after an aniseed trail, being pursued by a panting camera crew.

Tony also rose to his feet: 'I'm trying to be sympathetic,' he said in a voice that froze even Declan's blood, 'and all I get is abuse.'

He pressed a button. Miss Madden appeared so quickly she must have been listening at the door.

'Declan's leaving,' said Tony imperiously.

Back in his office, trembling from head to foot, Declan got a bottle of whisky from the cupboard and, pouring two inches into a paper cup, drained it. The first thing that really registered in his post was a typescript and a letter from Patrick. He had finished his play and sent it to Declan to read:

Dearest Pa,
I've been poisonous enough about your stuff in the past, now I'm going to get a taste of my own medication (as Cameron would say). Please read it and tell me the truth. Give my love to Cameron, if you're still speaking. See you next week.
Love Patrick.

Patrick, Declan reflected, was a bloody sight better at getting down to things than he was. He was about to start reading when there was a knock on the door. It was Miss Madden, puce as a beetroot, bringing him a cup of coffee and two rounds of roast beef sandwiches.

'You don't eat enough.'

'You mean I'm drinking too much. That's terribly sweet of you, darling. How much do I owe you?'

'It's a present,' said Miss Madden, blushing even more deeply. 'As Lord B's gone to town and Ursula's sick, I thought you might like some help with your mail. I can polish off that lot in no time. I expect it's mostly from fans.'

'I doubt it.'

'Don't take Lord B's remarks too much to heart. He's only trying to goad you. Please don't walk out. We need you here.'

Declan was touched, and dutifully sat down and went through his post. When Miss Madden had taken it away, he felt unable to settle down to Bob Geldof's cuttings. Wandering down the corridor, he found James and Sarah recording their first afternoon programme in front of a small geriatric audience.

James was interviewing a large woman in a pin-striped suit and a monocle, who looked not unlike Thomas the Tank Engine. Insufficiently briefed, having spent far too long lunching with Sarah, he was frantically leafing through his notes to find out something about her. At last he turned up Deirdre's list of questions. Christ, she was a fucking composer. James was tone-deaf.

'A very good afternoon and welcome to Dame Edith Spink,' he said.

The audience clapped lethargically.

'May I call you Edith?'

'You may, but my name's actually Enid,' said the lady composer.

Flustered, James consulted his notes. He'd kill Deirdre after the programme.

'I'd like to say, Enid, how much I personally have enjoyed all your symphonies.'

'I've only written one,' snapped Dame Enid.

From the darkness by the door, Declan was beginning to enjoy himself. Dame Enid Spink was an extremely distinguished musician who lived on the borders of Wiltshire and Gloucestershire, and was probably only second to Michael Tippett as a composer in Britain. A notorious lesbian and a feminist, she was already furious that Corinium were doing Michael Tippett's opera this year rather than one of hers.

'You've just visited the States, Enid,' ploughed on James, 'to conduct your newest opera. Er, what do the Americans think of your work?'

'Bloody stupid question,' said Dame Enid. 'I didn't ask them all. There are about two-hundred million, you know.'

Bitch, thought James furiously, I'll fix her.

'Many critics,' he read from Deirdre's notes, 'say this latest opera of yours isn't up to standard.'

Crash came Dame Enid's hands down on her wide-apart pinstriped thighs. 'Name four,' she thundered.

'Pardon?' stammered James.

'Name four of those critics,' persisted Dame Enid.

James couldn't. Dame Enid stalked off the set.

James mopped his brow, thanking Christ the programme wasn't live. He was lucky that it was not until ten minutes later that Cameron put in an appearance and therefore entirely missed the encounter.

Now it was Sarah's turn. Her task was to interview some female rugger players and a group of lady buyers in suits with pussy-cat bows on whether it was still a man's world, followed by a studio discussion in which James would whizz round the audience with a roving mike.

Although there was already an extremely competent director, Cameron, in her role as Programme Controller, couldn't resist sticking her oar in, making an already nervous Sarah fluff her introductory patter over and over again. Now Cameron had come down on the studio floor.

'Thank you so much for spending March with us,' she told the tittering audience after the tenth take.

Sarah fluffed her patter again.

'This is really an elaborate way of handing in your notice, Sarah,' taunted Cameron to more titters. Sarah looked imploringly at James, who, sitting on the yellow sofa, suddenly seemed very interested in his cuticles. Sarah fluffed the patter again.

'If you don't pull your finger out,' Cameron told her, 'we'll be going out live.'

Declan had seen enough. 'Stop being a fucking bitch,' he yelled, marching up to Cameron.

The crew, grinning broadly, gave him a round of applause. The audience, wildly excited to see such a megastar and thinking it was part of the show, started to clap and cheer too.

'How dare you lay that number on me?' screamed Cameron over the din. 'I'm going home.'

'Put the kettle on,' the Floor Manager shouted after her. 'We'll all be round for tea in half an hour.'

Down the steps swarmed the audience, crowding round Declan, clamouring for his autograph.

'You're very like yourself,' said one lady.

'Thank you so much, Declan,' said Sarah tearfully.

'Now you can get on with the programme,' said Declan, beating a hasty retreat.

Utterly dispirited after his outburst, Declan returned to his office and, getting out the whisky bottle, settled down to read Patrick's play. As he finished it, he was equally consumed with pleasure and despair, because the play was quite simply marvellous: incredibly original, funny, very moving, slightly over the top, but possessing all the vigour and fearlessness of youth. Reading it made Declan realize once again what an utter cock-up he'd made of his own career.

Emptying the bottle, very drunk now, he wandered into the corridor, ending up in the big studio where they were shooting the last re-take of *Midsummer Night's Dream*.

Even the cardboard trees seemed to pulsate with midsummer heat and enchantment. Declan stood in the shadows, tears pouring down his face, impossibly moved by the poetry. Would *he* ever write anything good again?

Feeling a tap on his shoulder, he jumped violently. It was Cameron. Rubbing his eyes frantically, he followed her out into the corridor.

'I'm sorry I came on strong this afternoon,' she said. ' "Four Men went to Mow" starts again next month. I guess I'm uptight.'

'I guess you are,' said Declan ungraciously. 'Pick someone your own weight next time. Sarah could be very good if you don't frighten her off too soon.'

He stalked into his office, rather laboriously gathered up the pages of Patrick's play, and chucked the whisky bottle into the wastepaper basket with a clang.

'As Tony's opening people's post, I suppose he's frisking wastepaper baskets as well,' he snarled at Cameron. 'That should really convince him I'm drinking too much. I imagine it was you who told him I was drunk on the programme yesterday.'

Cameron blushed. 'No way.'

'Well, I wasn't.' He went on gathering papers together.

'What's that?' said Cameron, anxious to change the subject.

'Patrick's play.'

'Any good?'

'Exceptional. You'll be sorry one day you passed him up.'

'I'm sure you won't be,' snapped Cameron.

'No.' Declan's brooding eyes looked at her contemptuously. 'I can't imagine anything that would have filled me with more horror. He sent his love by the way.'

Cameron tried again: 'Look, I know it's screwing you up working here.'

'I'm surprised you talk in the present tense,' growled Declan, going towards the door.

'Don't forget you're judging "Miss Corinium Television" tomorrow. We want you and Rupert here by seven,' said Cameron.

'About all I'm fit for,' said Declan wearily, and walked out.

Declan was not a vain man, but if anything could have boosted his self-confidence it was that day at Cheltenham. Whenever he put his nose out of Freddie's tent to have a bet, he was mobbed, and the combination of him and Rupert together among that horse-loving, strongly Irish crowd, caused almost as much excitement as the returning winner of the Gold Cup. To add to everyone's high spirits, Freddie's horse danced home an effortless winner in the second race. Nor was it anyone's fault that, as a result of a freak snowstorm, the Gold Cup was postponed for an hour, or that Rupert had a monkey each way on the winner. Consequently Rupert and Declan got unbelievably drunk and didn't reach Cotchester until seven forty-five.

'Is this the Forest of Hard-On?' said Rupert, as he tripped over a lot of stacked-up cardboard trees outside Studio 1.

'Wrong play,' said Declan. 'They were supposed to represent Greece.'

Cameron, Tony and James, who was compèring the programme in a midnight-blue dinner jacket with a dinky rose-pink bow-tie, were all absolutely livid they were so late.

'It's a bloody disgrace,' stormed Cameron. 'There's no time to brief you. Go into my office and you'll have a chance to meet the other judges and the fifteen finalists before transmission.'

The other judges were a male pop star called Big Lil, the Mayor of Cotchester, the head of the local tourist board and a naval officer called Ron, who'd just returned from sailing round the world single-handed.

'After a girl-less ten months,' whispered Rupert, 'he'll have to be lashed to his chair.'

'We're now selecting the last seven,' Cameron told the judges. 'You should look for the kind of girl you can take anywhere.'

'In the broom cupboard, under the mulberry tree,' said Rupert.

As each girl sidled in, Tony and Cameron fired questions at them. Miss Bisley came from Cotchester. Miss Painswick from Bisley. Miss Chipping Sodbury was so well stacked she could have won a National Front award.

When Miss Wotton-under-Edge said her ambition was to run a home for homeless pussies, Rupert and Declan got serious giggles. Fortunately the room was ill-lit.

'They all talk like Valerie Jones,' said Rupert.

Having selected the last seven, they all adjourned to Studio 1, which was now organized with tables, at which sat the so-called invited audience, and the contest was on air.

The fifteen contestants then teetered on in bathing dresses and four-inch heels. Although the judges had already pre-selected their last seven, as far as the audience, the contestants and the viewers were concerned they were picking them now. Seeing the girls in bathing dresses for the first time, however, Declan and Rupert realized some of the ones they *hadn't* chosen had much better figures and legs and noisily tried to change their minds.

'You're supposed to be picking the first three now,' hissed Cameron. 'And stop making that bloody awful row.'

As Declan and Rupert rushed out to have a pee in the commercial break, Rupert grabbed a bottle of champagne from one of the tables, shoving it under his coat. Cameron, waiting in the corridor as they came out of the lavatory, shoved them into an empty dressing-room. 'Big Lil's going to sing his new single while the last seven change and you two can bloody well stay in here and behave yourselves.'

Rupert put on Bottom's head, which was hanging on a hook, and read out a notice on the wall: 'We apologize to all artistes for any inconvenience caused by accommodating them in a temporary dressing-room.'

'I am a Pees Arteeste,' said Declan, taking a swig from Rupert's bottle. Totally forgetting they were miked up, they starting discussing the contest.

'Why's James Vereker wearing red shoes?' asked Rupert.

'Must be the blood running down from all the people sticking knives in his back,' said Declan.

'What d'you think of Miss Bisley's bottom?' said Rupert from the furry depths of his ass's head.

'Terrific,' said Declan. 'What d'you think of Miss Chipping Sodbury's tits?'

'Wonderful, but not as good as Miss Wotton-under-Edge's crotch.'

'Which one d'you think Tony Baddingham's fucking?' said Declan.

'The whole lot,' said Rupert, collapsing on the bed with laughter.

Declan leant against the wall, shaking. 'And Daysee Butler will get it out to the second.'

Next minute a chalk-white sound man erupted through the door to tell them they were being overheard by everyone in the control room, including Cameron and Tony. After that Declan found events became slightly hazy. Miss Bisley was crowned Miss Corinium Television and even wept a few tears, but not enough to streak her waterproof mascara.

'I'll see you in my office in half an hour,' hissed Tony to Declan, as he ushered the Mayor and a lot of visiting VIPs upstairs.

'I won't be long,' Declan told Rupert. 'Wait in the car.'

He got his contract out of the filing cabinet in his office and took the lift to the fifth floor. He felt curiously elated.

As he stood in the doorway of the board room he heard Miss Bisley saying to Miss Painswick that Miss Cotchester's trouble was that she had an unphotogenic crotch.

Tony was talking to his VIPs, who included the Prebendary and who were all ogling the girls. Declan went up and tapped Tony on the shoulder.

'I'd like a word now.'

'Piss off.'

'Now – in your office,' said Declan, 'unless you want me to tell these creeps exactly what I think of you.'

'Do be careful,' said Miss Madden, who was sitting at her typewriter in a mauve satin dress.

Sauntering after Tony, Declan blew her a kiss.

'You look beautiful,' he told her.

'How dare you?' thundered Tony, as Declan slammed the door behind them.

'Because you're rotten,' said Declan. 'So rotten, even maggots throw you up.'

Tony went purple. 'You've flouted my authority at every opportunity,' he spluttered.

Slowly Declan walked towards him, huge, cavernous-eyed and menacing. 'Violence isn't the answer,' he said softly, 'but it's a bloody good start.'

Tony backed up against the wall, licking his lips, eyes darting, hand edging towards the intercom button.

'Don't touch me,' he croaked. 'I'll get you for GBH.'

'The H would be so fucking G,' said Declan, 'that you'd never open your big mouth again, you bastard.'

As he raised his hand, Tony cringed away until his head crashed against the framed photograph of himself and the Queen. Then he realized that Declan was holding a folded-up piece of paper.

'This is my contract,' said Declan grimly. Slowly and with great relish he tore it into tiny pieces and sprinkled it over Tony's head. Then he turned towards the door.

For a second Tony was struck dumb, but, as Declan's hand touched the door handle, he said, 'Can I take it you've resigned?'

'Indeed you can,' said Declan. 'I've prostituted myself for – ' he counted up on his fingers – 'seven months too long, and tonight I'm going to have the first night's sleep since I started working for you.'

'Has it occurred to you that you're breaking your contract?'

'I don't give a fuck,' said Declan, opening the door. 'I'm not staying here till you break me, like you broke Cyril, and Simon and half the poor mentally crippled sods in this building.'

The moment he'd gone Tony pressed the re-wind button on the tape recorder and poured himself a huge glass of brandy.

315

'Miss Madden,' he shouted, extracting the tape from the cassette, 'can you transcribe this at once? Make a dozen copies. Then sweep up these bits of paper and put them in an envelope marked Declan O'Hara's contract. What the fuck are you crying for?'

'He was a nice man,' sobbed Miss Madden. 'He always asked me about my life as though it mattered to him.'

Outside in the car park the wind had dropped and the moon was shining dimly through the clouds like a ten-watt bulb.

Rupert, still wearing Bottom's head, had finished the bottle of champagne.

'Sorry to keep you,' said Declan, getting into the car.

'How did it go?'

'I'm out.'

'Christ!' Rupert pulled off the ass's head. 'I thought you had a water-tight contract?'

'Unfortunately it wasn't whisky-tight,' said Declan. 'Let's go and get seriously drunk.'

RIVALS

24

Taggie slept fitfully, worried about her father, disturbed by a
restless Gertrude, who imagined every creak and rattle of
creeper blown against the turret windows was Declan returning. Waking at five, Taggie glanced out across the valley, as
she always seemed to be doing these days, and saw that Rupert's
lights were on. She tried not to envy her father spending a
whole day with him; he'd had such a ghastly time at work lately,
he deserved a break. Going downstairs to check if the car was
back she froze with horror to see it once more parked across a
flowerbed with all the lights on. Rushing outside, she found it
empty and stealthily started to search the house. Declan was
not in the bedroom – her mother sprawled diagonally across
the bed as though denying him access – nor in the spare room.
He wasn't in Patrick's room, or the kitchen, or either of the
drawing-rooms or the dining-room.

She was beginning to panic that he'd gone for a walk in
the wood and fallen down the ravine when she heard an
excited squeak from the library. Gertrude had found him,
still dressed, passed out cold over his desk. In his hand he
still held the pen with which he had been writing his Yeats
biography. He had knocked over a glass of whisky which had
spilt over the open page of the notebook, blurring the drunken
scrawl.

Taggie wrapped a couple of blankets round him, and put
a cushion under his head, but he didn't stir.

He woke six hours later with a debilitating hangover and an even worse sense of foreboding. Staggering groaning into the kitchen, he found Maud reading Anthony Powell upside-down and looking bootfaced. Without being asked, Taggie tore four Alka-Seltzers from their blue and silver metal wrapping and dropped them into a glass. Declan took a gulp, retched and fled from the room.

'Well,' said Maud, when he came back, even more white and shaking, 'what kept you?'

'I don't remember,' growled Declan.

The telephone rang and he clutched his head, groaning. It was the *Scorpion*, the most seamy of the tabloids. Could they speak to Declan?

'He's not here,' said Taggie quickly.

'I gather he's resigned from Corinium. D'you know where I can get hold of him?'

Taggie went pale. 'Are you sure?'

'Quite. The press office confirmed it.'

'No. He's definitely not here.' Taggie slammed down the telephone.

Declan glared at her with bloodshot eyes, sensing trouble. 'What am I supposed to have done?'

Taggie looked nervously at her mother.

'Come on,' said Declan.

'G-given in your notice.'

'Kerist! Did I really?'

'You bloody idiot,' hissed Maud. 'Ring up Tony at once and apologize. Say you were drunk.'

At that moment Ursula arrived, looking pale from her flu, but very overexcited by events. Joyce Madden had rung her in tears in the middle of the night and told her what had happened.

'I was just telling Declan to ring Tony and say he's sorry,' said Maud. 'They're bound to take him back. He's such a big star.' The contempt was undeniable.

'I'm not sure they will,' sighed Ursula.

'Sit down,' said Taggie, pulling out a chair. 'I'll make you a cup of tea.'

'Declan's got a contract,' said Maud, 'and he was far too plastered to put anything in writing last night.'

Ursula turned to Declan who was sitting with his head in his hands.

'Don't you remember anything?'

'I remember a lot of girls in bathing dresses, who were rather ugly, and Rupert dressed up as a horse, and I think I remember having a row with Tony,' he muttered.

'You did,' said Ursula. 'You gave him an earful. Then you tore up your contract and scattered it all over him and resigned.'

'Oh Jesus!' Declan opened a bloodshot eye. 'Did I really?'

'And Tony taped the entire conversation, and Joyce Madden transcribed it at once, and no doubt copies are winging their way to the IBA and the ITCA and God knows who else at this moment.'

'You stupid idiot,' whispered Maud.

Fear is the parent of cruelty. Having found Declan impossible to live with for the past few months, she had considerable sympathy with Tony. Declan's career, albeit meteoric, had always been peppered with rows. She was totally unable to appreciate the pressures he'd been under. She proceeded to be blisteringly unsympathetic.

'Well, I'm not going back,' said Declan at the end of her tirade.

'You have no choice. The BBC wouldn't touch you with a barge pole. You'll have to crawl for once.'

'Oh Mummy,' protested Taggie, putting heavily sweetened, very strong cups of tea in front of Declan and Ursula.

Declan warmed his shaking hands round the mug which had a picture of a girl whose bikini disappeared when the mug was filled with boiling liquid. Like my career, thought Declan.

'It's all your fault,' went on Maud, 'taking days off to go hunting, going on the bat with Rupert before a programme. You're like a couple of schoolboys.'

All the animosity she harboured after Rupert had rejected her and embraced Declan seemed to pour forth like scalding lava.

'I rang up Personnel and resigned too,' said Ursula importantly. 'I'm not working for a police state any more.'

Oh Christ, thought Declan, that means I'll have to pay her salary myself until she gets another job. But he put a hand on her arm.

'Thanks, darling. That was very loyal of you.'

Everyone jumped as the telephone rang. Maud picked it up. It was the *Star*. Maud could never resist journalists.

'We're a bit hazy this end,' she said. 'Declan hasn't told us anything. What happened?'

The reporter, enchanted by Maud's soft, caressing tones, told her.

'I see,' said Maud grimly. 'Where's Rupert?'

'Well, he arrived in London ten minutes late to chair a seminar on "Alcoholism in the ex-Athlete". Looked like a prime target, but he refused to comment.'

'Thanks,' said Maud. 'We'll ring you back when he comes in. How could you?' She rounded on Declan. 'Slagging off Tony when you were miked up. I thought you were supposed to be a professional.'

Declan hardly heard her. 'We'll have to sell the house,' he said bleakly.

The telephone rang again. Declan got up and seized the receiver. 'Will you fucking go away?' he screamed.

'Charming,' said a shrill voice. 'This is Caitlin, your daughter, if you hadn't forgotten, and why hasn't someone come to pick me up?'

'Oh God,' said Taggie in anguish, catching the gist. 'I thought she broke up this afternoon.'

'Well, you'd better go and get her,' snapped Maud, who had forgotten to pass on the message.

'I'm going out,' said Declan.

'Whatever for?' screamed Maud.

'To do some thinking.'

320

'Well, you'd better come up with something pretty quickly. I have no intention of selling this house.'

With four Anadin Extra, four Alka-Seltzers, a cup of strong tea and the remains of last night's whisky churning uneasily inside him, Declan set out. A mild and sunny day with a gentle breeze had followed yesterday's torrential rain, freak snow storms and razor-sharp winds. Everything sparkled. For the first time in months the birds ignored Declan's bird-table and were busy singing and courting in the trees.

Down the Frogsmore, in one day, Spring seemed to have arrived. Primroses nestled on the bank. Coltsfoot exploded sulphur yellow beneath his feet, celandines arched back their shiny yellow petals in the sunshine; even the most uncompromising spiked red blackberry cable was putting out tiny pale-green leaves.

In the fields above, he could see Rupert's horses pounding round in their New Zealand rugs, tails held high, like children let out of school. In the woods, he found the first anemones and blue and white violets. Far above him the woodpecker was rattling away at a tree trunk. He could almost hear the buds bursting open.

Why the hell had he blown it all in his fucking intellectual arrogance? All he'd had to do was to endure working at Corinium until the end of April, then in the break look around for another job. Now that he'd left in a blaze of drunken publicity with plummeting ratings, no one would want him.

He crushed a wild garlic leaf between his fingers. The smell reminded him of lunches in Soho and endlessly plotting with his cronies to make a better world at the BBC. He'd loved London, but he didn't want to go back. It was so hot that, on the way home, he took off his coat and sat down on the bank of the stream for a long time, watching the water as it glittered and squirmed with pleasure beneath the sunshine. Gertrude splashed about, and, picking up a stick, bounced up to Declan hoping he'd pull the other end; then, when he wouldn't, dropped it and licked his face.

An old man, walking his ancient Jack Russell back from Penscombe, stopped for a chat. His grandfather used to be the gamekeeper at The Priory, he said, a hundred years ago, when the land stretched for three hundred acres across the north side of the Penscombe–Chalford Road. He'd kept the place like a new pin. It was sad to see the state it had fallen into, the rotting trees and collapsing walls everywhere. Declan felt ashamed.

'You can tell Spring's come at last,' said the old man, 'because all the blackbirds are singing.'

But not for me any more, thought Declan in despair.

Then the old man peered closer. 'Didn't you used to be Declan O'Hara?' he said.

By late afternoon Taggie was shattered. Ursula, having parried the press all day, had gone home. After another terrible row with Maud, Declan had barricaded himself into the library, refusing to talk to anyone. Caitlin sat on the kitchen table with her arm round Gertrude, both watching Taggie stuffing a chicken with a mixture of apricots, sausage meat, breadcrumbs and garlic. Used to the central heating and constant chatter of Upland House, Caitlin was shivering like a whippet and gabbling away nonstop.

'There are going to be no more balls against boys' schools,' she announced. 'Last Friday we danced against Rugborough and one lot of boys took some fifth formers up on the garage roof and they were all smoking and drinking and telling the teachers to fuck off, and Miss Lovett-Standing – think of being saddled with a name like that – the gym mistress, found three condoms in the rhododendrons next morning.

'I came top in the exam on *The Mayor of Casterbridge*,' went on Caitlin. Then, seeing Taggie struggling to understand a recipe for potatoes Lyonnaise, her lips moving slowly as she read, she added kindly, 'but a sixth former who did the same paper last year told me all the answers beforehand. And two girls in the upper sixth are having abortions this holidays.'

'That's nice,' said Taggie absent-mindedly.

'Taggie, you're not listening.'

'I'm sorry. I'm so worried about Daddy.'

'He'll be OK. Someone will snap him up.'

'I don't know. He's lost all his confidence. I've never known him so down.'

'That's hangover,' said Caitlin.

Her ability to spread mess everywhere was even greater than Maud's. Her open trunk lay in the hall and lacrosse sticks, tapes, posters, rolled-up art work, wet towels, coloured files, a teddy bear and a squashy bag, overflowing with under-wear, were scattered in a trail all the way to the kitchen. She was wearing a very expensive pink T-shirt, pinched from Maud at half-term, over which all her friends had written messages in biro, a puffball skirt, laddered tights and black clumpy stompers, and was now eating muesli out of a cup with a teaspoon.

'Christ, this house is cold.'

The telephone rang again for the hundredth time. The line was awful.

'Can I speak to Declan?' said a male voice.

'He can't talk to anyone,' said Taggie hysterically.

'Is that Taggie?'

'Yes,'

'It's Rupert. How's your father?'

'Not great.' Taggie felt herself going very red, and turned her back on Caitlin. 'He walked out, you know.'

'It was partly my fault. He was in an exocet mood. I should have stopped him storming in to see Tony, but he's better out of it; it was killing him. Are you all right, sweetheart?'

The sudden gentleness in his voice made her want to burst into tears.

'I'm fine,' she mumbled.

'Well, tell him I'll be over later.'

Upstairs, Declan turned on the five forty-five news and found Tony Baddingham, with a red carnation in his button-hole, giving a press conference.

'The truth of the matter,' he was saying, 'is that Declan O'Hara tendered his resignation last night, and we accepted it.'

Stupid word 'tendered', thought Declan. There was nothing tender about it at all.

'Naturally, we're very sad to lose Declan,' said Tony, looking absolutely delighted, 'but, quite frankly, there have been a series of disagreements and there's a general feeling at Corinium that when people get too big for their boots, we'd prefer them to go off and wear out other people's carpets.'

Declan switched off and looked down at the floorboards. He hadn't got any carpets to wear out, and probably now he never would have. The telephone rang again. It was one of the Corinium shop stewards.

'Fuckin' idiot,' he chided Declan, 'you should've hung in and let him fire you.'

'I know,' said Declan almost apologetically. 'I felt I had to retain some shred of integrity.'

'Wish you'd come to us. Look, the lads want to come out. You've only got to ask. We'll black out the 'ole network for you, Declan, and get you reinstated.'

Declan was so moved he couldn't say anything for a minute. Then he said gruffly that there wouldn't be any point.

'I can't work for Tony any more, but thanks very much all the same, and say goodbye and thanks to all the boys for me.'

It was dark outside now, but a robin was singing on the bare honeysuckle outside his window. It had turned up at exactly six-thirty for the last week now, as if to cheer him on.

'*Art thou the bird whom man loves best,*' he murmured to himself, '*The pious bird with the scarlet breast, Our little English robin?*'

Tears filled his eyes. Oh God, what was he going to do?

Taggie knocked on the door and, getting no answer, walked in. She found him looking so haggard and despairing that she ran across the room, stumbling over the piles of papers and books all over the floor, and put her arms round him.

'Please don't be so sad. It doesn't matter if we go back to London. We were all happy there. You've just got to get your

324

confidence back. Rupert rang, by the way. He's coming round.'

Going upstairs to her bedroom, she was horrified by how awful she looked. She'd been so busy she hadn't had a moment to wash or even clean her teeth all day. She knew she had no chance with Rupert, that it was appallingly presumptuous, but for once she wanted to look her best when she saw him. Caitlin's welcome-home supper could wait, she decided. She was going to have a bath and wash her hair.

Caitlin wolf-whistled when Taggie came into the kitchen an hour later. She was wearing a red-and-black-striped polo-necked jersey which Patrick had given her for Christmas, tucked into black jeans which were in turn tucked into black boots. As her hair was still damp she'd tied it back with a black ribbon. She wore no make-up except smudged black eyeliner, which made her silver-grey eyes look huge and almost luminous. A hot bath and the hairdryer had given her pale cheeks quite enough colour.

'Because you so seldom bother,' said Caitlin critically, 'one forgets how beautiful you are: much more so than anyone else I know.'

'Oh, don't be silly,' muttered Taggie in embarrassment, putting the chicken into the top-right oven of the Aga.

'How soon will it be ready?'

'About nine.'

'Good, I can watch "Dynasty". Who are you going out with?'

'No one.' Taggie busied herself with draining the parsnips. 'You like parsnip purée, don't you?'

'Adore it. You haven't answered my question.'

'No one.'

'Then why are you done up like Gertrude's dinner?'

'I just felt awful,' muttered Taggie apologetically, as she threw the parsnips into the blender. 'I didn't have time to wash all day.'

'Hum,' said Caitlin beadily, as she watched Taggie add curry powder, then butter, then cream to the parsnips.

'As I just got up into yesterday's clothes, I felt I must change,' went on Taggie, even more embarrassed.

325

'Fee, fi, fo fumble,' said Caitlin, 'I smell the blood of Rupert Campbell.'

'Oh shut up,' said Taggie, turning on the blender.

Caitlin waited until she had turned it off.

'I am Campbell-Black but comely,' said Caitlin giggling. *'Rise up, my love, my fair one, and come away, For lo, the winter is past, the rain is over and gone. The flowers appear on the earth; the time of the singing of birds is come, and the turtle-necked sweater is worn in our land.'*

'Oh shut up,' screamed Taggie. Picking up Gertrude's rubber ring, she hurled it at Caitlin, missed and nearly hit Rupert, who, finding the door open, had let himself in, followed by Freddie Jones. Taggie stood rooted to the spot with horror. Gertrude went into a frenzy of outraged barking that someone had entered the house without her knowing.

'Hello, Gertrude,' said Rupert. 'How extraordinarily good you look today. Nice dog, Gertrude, well done, hurrah, what a beautiful curly tail you've got.' Bending down, he stroked the bemused Gertrude over and over again.

Taggie giggled.

'That's better,' said Rupert. He looked a bit pale after yesterday's excesses, but seemed in excellent spirits.

'Hullo,' he said to Caitlin. 'How are you?'

'Fine.' Caitlin beamed. 'I was just quoting the Bible to my sister to keep her on the straight and narrow.'

'Caitlin,' pleaded Taggie in despair, frantically concentrating on spooning the purée out of the blender to hide her blushes.

Rupert went over to Taggie and, putting a hand on the back of her neck, drew her towards him. With most women, he would have dropped a kiss on the tops of their heads, but Taggie was so tall, he was able to rest his lips for a second against her temple.

'There, angel, you mustn't worry about your papa. Frederico, the whizz kid, and I will sort him out.'

'I'll get you a drink,' stammered Taggie. 'What would you like? Daddy's in the library.'

'I'd like a Bacardi and Coke, love,' said Freddie, 'and if

Rupe 'ere can keep it down, he'd like a whisky and soda.'

'If there isn't any Malibu, I'll have a Vod and Ton, Tag,' added Caitlin.

Fleeing into the larder, Taggie paused before she got down the bottles. Unbelievingly she touched her left temple where Rupert had kissed it, then, moving her fingers to her lips, kissed them in ecstasy. What was happening to her? She wondered if Caitlin's welcome-home chicken would stretch to six.

''Ullo, Declan,' said Freddie, as they went into the library and found him slumped at his desk. 'I've just seen that fucker Tony on the news. You're well shot of the smarmy bastard.'

Sitting down on the window seat, Rupert waited until Taggie had brought in the drinks. Then he shut the door behind her and said, 'Look, Frederico and I have been talking about you for some time. To put it bluntly, both being hard-nosed businessmen, we hate to see a hot property like you being wasted.'

'We've decided to form our own independent production company,' said Freddie, 'an' employ you to make programmes for the network, Channel 4 and the overseas market.'

It took a lot of tough talking to persuade Declan they weren't just being kind. He looked at his untouched glass for a second; then a real gleam of excitement came into his eyes. 'I've got a better idea. Why don't we pitch for the Corinium franchise, and boot out Tony.'

Freddie and Rupert looked at each other. 'Aren't we too late?'

'Not at all,' said Declan. 'If we step on it. The applications don't have to be in until the beginning of May.'

'We know all the right people,' said Rupert. 'So there won't be any problems getting our Board together.'

'And we won't have any trouble getting the backing,' said Freddie, jumping up and down with excitement. 'An' I can provide you wiv all the technical know-how.'

'And I know the Corinium Programmes backwards,' said Declan, 'so we can submit better programme plans standing on our heads.'

Taggie popped her head round the door: 'Anyone want more drinks?'

Too excited to be deflected, Declan shook his head. So did Freddie, who'd hardly touched his glass. Only Rupert handed out his. 'Please, angel,' he said with a grin, 'and could I have soda this time?'

'Oh goodness, did I give you Coke? I'm really sorry, and poor Mr Jones must have had Bacardi and soda.'

'I don't think he's noticed,' said Rupert.

As Freddie and Declan got more and more excited over their plans, Rupert thought about Taggie, how she'd trembled when he kissed her, and how adorable she'd looked with her long legs in those black boots, and her hair tied back like a boy soldier. But he mustn't think about her, he told himself grimly. She was Declan's kid daughter, totally out of bounds. Wrenching his mind back, he heard Declan saying: 'In fact Tony's only trump card with the IBA is Cameron Cook, and the staff are in a state of uproar about her as it is.'

'How would it be if I seduced her on to our side?' said Rupert idly.

'We don't want *her*!' Declan exploded. 'She's a treacherous evil bitch.'

'Not once I've sorted her out,' said Rupert. 'I was always good with difficult horses. I guarantee to have her eating out of my hand in a few weeks.'

25

Overwhelmed by the day's vicissitudes, Declan went to bed and didn't emerge for thirty-six hours, waking on Saturday morning to thank God he wouldn't ever have to work for Tony again, before falling back to sleep. On Sunday he woke to a glorious day and apologized to his darling Maud for being such a bear. She apologized for being such a bitch and, after he had explained about bidding for the franchise and selling the wood to Rupert to raise some cash, they vowed that things would be better between them and made passionate, ecstatic love. Replete, tranquillized, Maud wondered why she had ever wanted to look at anyone else. Taggie, as she cooked lunch later, listened to her mother singing and playing Schubert *lieder*. She found these staggering *volte-faces* bewildering, but felt only relief that the row was over.

Rupert, having spent Saturday hunting and on constituency business, rose early on Sunday and tried out each of a new intake of horses that had arrived from Ireland earlier in the week. One dark bay mare was really exceptional, incredibly quick off the mark with a huge wild jump. In a couple of years he could have made a world-class horse out of her. He felt, as always, that reluctance to sell her on, that temptation to have one more crack at show-jumping, then put the thought sternly behind him. An election was in the offing this summer and there was the franchise to be won. He was seeing Declan and Freddie that afternoon to work out a plan of campaign. They had arranged to meet at Freddie's house because they wanted to keep their bid secret until the applications went in, and because the press were still hanging around Penscombe Court and The Priory hoping to get some juicy story about Declan's exit from Corinium.

Handing the mare back to one of the grooms, Rupert mounted his old Olympic gold medal horse, Rocky, for a ride round the estate, as he always did if he was at home on a Sunday. The pack of dogs raced ahead putting up pheasants, chasing rabbits, snuffling down badger sets and foxes' earths. Rocky loved these outings, and to prove they were both still great, Rupert put the old horse over the occasional wall and any streams or fallen logs in their path. Rupert's eagle eye missed nothing, a loose wire here, a tree blown across a fence there, which would have to be repaired before sheep were moved in, how poor or good the grass was in each field, and how the winter barley was spreading in an emerald-green haze over the rich brown earth.

In the distance he could hear Penscombe church bells ringing, and the rattle of a clay shoot. Across the valley The Priory was in shadow with the sun behind it. The beech trees in front were a crimson blur as the buds thickened. Soon the leaves would be out and he wouldn't be able to see the house any more. Taking the muddy track that wound high above the Frogsmore, he noticed the first primroses blooming happily and safely under wild rose and bramble bushes, the spiky branches keeping the predatory grazing horses and cattle away.

In their sweet pale trusting innocence, the primroses reminded him of Taggie, who, he felt, could only blossom in life if she were fiercely protected. He suddenly wished he could be those spiky powerful branches keeping away anyone who threatened her. He imagined putting her on his gentlest horse, showing her all over his land, pointing out his favourite places, then making love to her among the wild flowers, as he had done to so many other women before – but with Taggie it would be different. Christ, he must get a grip on himself and get stuck into someone else very quickly. Thank

330

goodness Nathalie Perrault was arriving this evening for a few days, and there was still the conquest of Cameron Cook to be orchestrated.

Back at Penscombe, stripped for a bath, Rupert got on to the scales and winced. Twelve and a half stone: at six feet two, no one could call him fat, but it was a far cry from the honed muscular leanness, the eleven stone, produced by eight hours in the saddle, which he'd trained down to before the Olympic Games and the World Championship. Too many dinners, too much booze, not enough exercise, he was hopelessly unfit. If he was going to seduce Cameron, he'd have to knock off a stone first – that meant no alcohol, and just meat, fish and vegetables for the next month.

When he rolled up at Freddie's house, Declan, looking ten years younger, had already arrived, and he and Freddie were poring over a book called *How to Win The Franchise*.

'The first thing we gotta do is appoint a chairman,' said Freddie.

'Better be you,' said Rupert.

'OK,' said Freddie, 'but we'll need someone respectable like a lord or a bishop or somefing as deputy chairman.'

'We must also remember,' said Declan, 'that the IBA, despite all their pronouncements about quality, are looking for applicants who won't go broke in the first eighteen months, and who'll be able to produce programmes that'll keep the company in the black over the next eight years. That's why we need a very experienced MD and a very strong Programme Controller.'

'You'd better be MD, then,' said Rupert.

'But I'm terrible with money.'

'You know about television. I'll be Financial Director, and I'll get hold of a shit-hot accountant to keep an eye on you. Sandwiched between him and me and Freddie, you can't go far wrong.'

'I've got just the man for Programme Controller,' said Declan: 'Harold White, ex-ITN and BBC. Currently Director of Programmes at London Weekend. He's bloody good.'

'I've been doing some sums,' said Freddie. 'We'll need at least fifteen million to keep the station going for the first two years, but before that we'll need at least two hundred grand up front as burn money to pay for brokers, bankers, running costs and to launch the publicity campaign.'

'Which we'll forfeit if the bid fails,' said Declan.

'Right,' said Freddie. 'Why don't we put that up ourselves? Give us some control.'

Rupert was about to agree. Then, catching sign of Declan's twitching face, said, 'Let's argue about that later. Now which do we find first, board or backing?'

'Backing's easy,' said Freddie. 'Let's get the right people first. Apart from the directors, who are actually going to run the station, we need some local millionaires, and a liberal sprinkling of the great and the good as non-executive directors.'

'Before we approach anyone, we'd better come up with a name,' said Rupert.

'I've been thinking. What about Venturer?' said Declan.

'Sounds all right,' said Freddie. 'What's it say it means in the dictionary?'

'Someone who's daring and willing to take risks, someone who's prepared to brave dangers, or embark on a possibly hazardous journey.'

In Declan's deep husky voice it sounded wonderfully romantic.

'Perfick. What we going to use as a logo?'

'I've been thinking about that too,' said Declan. 'You know that bronze I admired in your sitting-room, Rupert?' He turned back to Freddie. 'It's of a boy in an open-necked shirt and knickerbockers with bare legs. He's shading his forehead with his hand as he gazes into the distance. It's ravishing and it's got the right mix of strength and grace and vision.'

'I've seen it, it's grite,' said Freddie in excitement. 'We'll get someone to draw it; then we can put it on all our stationery and on the front of the application.'

'We'd better get T-shirts and ties and car stickers printed,' said Rupert, 'and posters too. Just imagine a poster of Taggie in a Victory for Venturer T-shirt!'

'What about a studio?' said Declan.

'Well if Tony Baddingham's prepared to sell the Corinium building, it would be much cheaper to take over that,' said Rupert. 'But, in case he turns really nasty, we'd better make contingency plans.'

Valerie Jones was absolutely livid. She never admitted reading the *Scorpion*, but the weekend fish had arrived in Saturday's edition, and Valerie couldn't miss the huge headline announcing that Declan had resigned from Corinium while getting disgustingly drunk with Rupert, and now they were both closeted together in Fred-Fred's den, and the air was thick with cigar smoke, and she was sure they were up to no good. She'd grumbled so much in the past about Freddie blasting her out with his music that he'd had the room thoroughly sound-proofed. Now she couldn't hear a word that was going on inside, even when she went outside and pretended to pull non-existent weeds out of the flowerbed under the window. How could they keep the windows closed on such a lovely day?

'Shall I take them in afternoon tea?' said poor fat Sharon, who still cherished a long-range crush on Rupert.

'No,' snapped Valerie. 'You haven't done your religious study yet. Miss Fidduck said at least an hour a day; nor have you groomed Merrylegs. What is the point of your father buying you an event horse?'

As Sharon waddled upstairs, Valerie could bear it no longer.

'Afternoon tea,' she announced ten minutes later, barging into Freddie's den with a tray.

Declan was striding up and down the room scattering cigarette ash. Freddie was whizzing round excitedly in his revolving chair. Rupert lounged on the sofa, playing with one of Freddie's executive games, which involved clashing huge ball-bearings against each other. All three of them looked up with ill-concealed irritation.

333

'What a fug,' said Valerie, dumping down the tray and throwing open the window, so all Freddie's papers blew around.

'I don't know how you can stay inside. I hope you won't be long, Fred-Fred. We're due at Sir Arthur's for cocktails at six-thirty and you promised to walk round the grounds with me beforehand.'

She turned to Rupert and Declan: 'We're opening Green Lawns to the public in July. All proceeds to the NSPCC. I'm surprised you're not opening Penscombe Court this year, Rupert,' she added, raising her voice to cover the increasing clash of ball-bearings.

'You can hardly expect the public to look at a lot of weeds,' said Rupert.

'But you've got buckets of time to get it shipshape. It seems so selfish not to raise the money if you can.' Valerie gave her little laugh.

'I'm sure the NSPCC would prefer a cheque,' said Rupert evenly.

'I don't expect Maud'll be interested in opening *your* garden,' went on Valerie, turning to Declan. 'I've just read all about your exploits in the *Sunday Express*. Tony Baddingham is quoted as saying one of the reasons you left Corinium was because you couldn't face being knocked out by "Dallas".'

As Freddie gently shooed her out, Rupert and Declan both reflected that not throttling Valerie before December would be infinitely harder than winning the franchise.

The next five weeks were frantic. Many of the bidders for franchises in other territories had spent several years perfecting their applications, raising the cash, and getting their boards together. To speed up the operation, Freddie, Declan and Rupert divided the role of recruiting officer between them.

'There's no point enlisting people who won't contribute anything,' said Declan. 'We mustn't confuse celebrity with attainment, and they *must* live in the area. Once we land a really big fish, the rest will follow.'

Hubert Brenton, Bishop of Cotchester, whom luckily Declan hadn't bitched up during his New Year's Eve interview and who was currently furious with Tony for deciding to televise Easter Communion at Gloucester Cathedral rather then Cotchester, was the first to be signed up. Declan invited him to lunch at The Priory the following week, and, as it was Lent and a Friday, Taggie cooked the most succulent Coquille St Jacques, followed by sole Veronique. Maud, with a cross round her neck and her titian hair drawn back in a bun, gravely asked the Bishop to say Grace, and pointed out the beautiful spring flowers in the centre of the table, which her children had sent her for Mothering Sunday.

Rupert, who, as part of his getting-fit-for-Cameron-Cook campaign, was off the booze, provided the most exquisite white wine. Caitlin, who, unlike poor Sharon Jones, had passed her religious studies O-level, was able to converse with the Bishop at length about St Luke, and particularly the Prodigal Son.

There was a dicey moment when she dropped her bread, butter-side down, and said 'Shit', but by then the Bishop was fortunately talking to Maud about his recent trip to the Holy Land. Fortunately, too, he'd been wandering round the Sea of Galilee last weekend and missed the newspaper reports of Declan's exit from Corinium. Over the lemon sorbet, Declan and the Bishop discussed how thrilling it would be to dramatize Lytton Strachey's brilliant essay about Cardinal Newman and Cardinal Manning, who had both lived in Oxford, which was, after all, within the franchise area.

After lunch Maud, Taggie and Caitlin discreetly withdrew, and Declan produced Rupert's venerable port.

'Not drinking?' asked the Bishop, as Rupert passed the decanter on.

'No, My Lord,' said Rupert gravely. 'I've given it up for Lent.'

The Bishop, who was very hot on sex and violence, had always thoroughly disapproved of Rupert, but perhaps at long last, after such a turbulent past, he was trying to shed his jetset playboy image and forge a more satisfying way of life.

Declan and Freddie steered the conversation round to Corinium Television and the appalling poverty of their religious programmes, and then raised the subject of their rival bid. They very much hoped the Bishop would join Venturer and become their Deputy Chairman.

'Television today,' said the Bishop warmly, 'is a key factor for the quality of life and for establishing values.'

For the past ten years, he went on, he had had special responsibilities for communication in the diocese and he saw joining Venturer as a way of extending a work that interested him greatly.

'We know busy people don't do fings for nuffink,' said Freddie, cosily. 'If we win the franchise, there'll be a very small director's fee, say ten thousand a year, which could always go to your favourite charity.'

Signing up Henry Hampshire, the Lord-Lieutenant, was even easier. Freddie and Rupert wooed him over a very expensive lunch in London. Henry, as it turned out, was absolutely furious with Tony for flogging a field ten miles from The Falconry, but only a quarter of a mile from and in full view of Henry's house, to some property developers. He was also a very old friend of Rupert's, having a wife too plain for even Rupert to have had a crack at, and had liked Freddie when they'd met shooting at Tony's.

'Any money in it?' he asked, having flogged two stone lions last week to pay a tax bill.

'Fucking fortune,' said Rupert. 'We'd need a bit up front.'

'Don't mind that,' said Henry. 'As long as you arrange for me to meet Joanna Lumley. Suppose I could always sell a Stubbs.'

'You needn't go that far,' said Rupert, shocked. 'We only want about ten grand. What about that minor Pre-Raphaelite, the one over the chimney-piece in the sitting-room?'

'Good idea,' said Henry. 'Never liked it. Silly girl lying in the water, covered in flowers. Someone should have taught her the backstroke.'

At the end of lunch, Henry tried to pay.

'No, no,' said Freddie. 'Honest, it's on Venturer.'

'Oh well, if you can get it on corsts,' said Henry.

Strong on his homework, Declan investigated the likes and dislikes of Lady Gosling, Chairman of the IBA. He also discovered that her best friend, Dame Enid Spink, was the composer interviewed so disastrously by James Vereker. Declan called on Dame Enid in her rooms at Cotchester University, where she was director of music, and found her ferociously conducting to a gramophone record of her latest opera, *The Persuaders*.

'Worst programme I've ever been on,' boomed Dame Enid, as she and Declan dipped pieces of stale seed cake into tea the colour of mahogany. 'In fact Corinium's whole attitude to music is utterly philistine. Last time the franchises came up for grabs, that treacherous little fart, Tony Baddingham, promised to finance a Cotchester Youth Orchestra. Not a penny have we seen.'

Declan said truthfully that Venturer wouldn't be prepared to finance anything except television programmes until they broke even, but he hoped Dame Enid would advise them on their music programmes.

'If you get the franchise,' asked Dame Enid, 'would you get rid of that little squirt James Vereker?'

'Indeed we would,' said Declan.

Once Dame Enid agreed, it was a piece of cake to recruit Professor Crispin Graystock, a rich left-wing English Literature don who had dry, unmanageable hair like Worzel Gummidge's dipped in soot, wild eyes and a wet formless face, and who longed to be a television star because he thought it would help sell his slim and unutterably dreary volumes of poetry.

Although he was still smarting over not being included in the new *Oxford Companion to English Literature*, Crispin

Graystock was regarded as a considerable heavyweight in the academic world.

Freddie Jones took Lord Smith, the even more left-wing ex-secretary of the Transport and General Workers Union, out to yet another very expensive lunch, where, with his mouth crammed simultaneously with lobster and Pouilly Fuissé, Lord Smith agreed to join Venturer, and provide a substantial cash investment from Union funds.

'Doesn't he feel guilty about getting involved with such a capitalist organ as Venturer?' said Rupert disapprovingly.

'Not at all. Once I told him the money to be made,' said Freddie. 'He feels television is for the people.'

Rupert, seeking a shit-hot money man, rang up Marti Gluckstein, arguably the most brilliant accountant just this side of the law.

'How'd you like to join our bid for the Corinium franchise?'

'I've already turned down four other groups,' said Marti in his nasal Cockney twang. 'I loathe television.'

'You'd have to buy a house in the area,' said Rupert. He could feel Marti shudder all the way down the telephone wires.

'I loathe the country,' said Marti.

'Don't have to live here,' said Rupert. 'Just buy a place and sell it the moment we clinch the franchise. Prices are going up so fast in the Royal triangle, you'll double your money by the time you sell it. I'll find you one.'

The prospect of making such a fast buck clinched it.

'Marti Gluckstein's a crook,' said Declan in outrage, when Freddie and Rupert jubilantly told him the good news.

'Don't be anti-semitic,' said Rupert primly.

'And he doesn't live in the area.'

'He's just bought a cottage in Penscombe,' said Rupert blithely. He was quickly learning he had to box very carefully round Declan's integrity.

Bearing in mind the IBA's obsession with minority groups, particularly ethnic ones, Declan, who knew nothing about cricket, recruited Wesley Emerson, a six-foot-five West

Indian bowler and the hero of Cotchester Cricket Club, whom he'd met at a Sports Aid drinks party.

Rupert was as outraged as Declan had been about Marti Gluckstein. 'You're crazy,' he yelled. 'It was only me and the Government stepping in with some very fast talking that stopped Wesley getting busted in New Zealand this winter. He was snorting coke on the pitch, and he's the biggest letch since Casanova.'

'I thought that was your prerogative,' said Declan coldly. 'Talk about the kettle calling the pot Campbell-Black.'

'I didn't realize we were talking about minority gropes,' snarled back Rupert.

It took all of Freddie's diplomacy to calm them down.

Basil Baddingham was the easiest of all to recruit. Rupert signed him up as they checked on the edge of a beech covert during the last meet of the season.

'D'you really want to infuriate Tony?' asked Rupert.

'How much?' said Bas, after Rupert had explained.

'Ten grand.'

'Cheap at the price. You're on,' said Bas.

Having assembled their Board of the great and the good, Venturer now needed some heavyweight production people. This had to be handled with great delicacy. Anyone worth their salt had already been approached by other consortiums. Two department heads at Yorkshire had just been sacked when it was discovered they'd joined a consortium in the Midlands. Most ITV companies, and the BBC as well, had threatened to boot out anyone found having dealings with any new franchise applicants, even in another area. As Declan was only too aware, Tony was already going through all incoming mail, monitoring telephone calls and checking through desk drawers and wastepaper baskets after dark.

Declan therefore proceeded with extreme caution, winkling out home telephone numbers and promising total anonymity. Early in April he rang Harold White, programme controller at LWT, arguably the most brilliant and innovative brain in television.

'Harold, it's Declan.'

'How extraordinary,' said Harold. 'I've been trying to get your home telephone number all day. We're bidding for Granada. You interested in joining our consortium?'

'Not really, but thanks all the same,' said Declan. 'We've just moved here, and I couldn't face another move. How about joining ours?'

One of the pledges that Venturer planned to make to the IBA was that, if they won the franchise, they would take over most of the Corinium staff below board level. But there were three people Declan was anxious to secure for Venturer in advance, in case they were lured away by another consortium.

'I want Charles Fairburn,' he told Rupert.

'He'd fight with the Bishop of Cotchester, the lazy fat poof,' said Rupert.

'Charles knows the area like the back of his handbag,' said Declan, 'and he's very bright. He's just bored out of his skull. I'd move him away from Religious Programming and put him in charge of Documentaries.'

Declan didn't recognize Charles when he rolled up at The Priory. He was wearing a false nose, a ginger moustache, a ginger felt hat with a Tyrolean feather and dark glasses.

'Can't be too careful, dear,' he said, whisking into the house. 'James Vereker spent three hours at lunchtime getting his hair streaked yet again, and Tony's absolutely refusing to believe he didn't go to an interview.'

Declan was glad he was alone with Charles when he asked him to join Venturer as Head of Documentaries, because Charles promptly burst into tears. For an awful moment Declan thought he'd insulted him.

'I'm sorry,' he muttered. 'I had a feeling you were bored with religion.'

'I am, I am,' sobbed Charles. 'You don't understand! The absolute bliss of the thought of getting away from Corinium! You've no idea how we all miss you.'

It was only then that Declan realized, despite the quips and the jokey exterior, the strain Charles must have been under for years.

'Tony demoralizes one so much, one feels one will never be good enough to work for anyone else again. I can't thank you enough, Declan. Do you think there's any chance of us getting it?'

Declan was touched by the 'us'.

'Well, a tenant whose record is good,' he said, 'stands a better chance than a new applicant of unknown potential. But Tony's record isn't exactly good, and we're getting together an incredibly strong team. Now if I tell you who they are, will you promise to keep your trap shut, because if one word of this gets out before the applications go in, Tony'll start tarting up Corinium's bid and exoceting ours.'

'Mum's the word,' said Charles wiping his eyes. 'Mummy's always been the word in fact. I wish you'd met Mummy, Declan. Now, is there anyone else at Corinium you want me to sound out?'

Declan said he was interested in gorgeous Georgie Baines, the Sales Director, and Seb Burrows from the newsroom.

'Very good choice,' said Charles approvingly. 'Both stunningly able. Seb's in dead trouble. He dug up a terrific story about a bent vet in league with one of Tony's millionaire farmer friends. Unfortunately he used hidden mikes and secret cameras without getting clearance and, when Tony pulled the programme, Seb handed it over to the BBC. If Seb wasn't Cameron's protégé, he'd be out on his ear by now. You're not interested in her are you? She's tipped for a BAFTA this week.'

Declan shook his head violently. He hoped that Rupert had forgotten about Cameron.

Rupert rang Declan that evening from London.

'We need a really good Head of Sport. How about Billy Lloyd-Foxe?'

'Excellent. I've heard nothing but good about Billy,' said Declan. 'Will you talk to him?'

The following day Rupert had a drink with his best friend

and old show-jumping partner. Billy, who was working for the BBC and very strapped for cash, looked tired and pale. Janey, his journalist wife, had just had another baby; they weren't getting much sleep at night. He absolutely jumped at Rupert's proposition, particularly when Rupert offered to treble his salary.

'You'd have to come back and live in Gloucestershire.'

'Try and stop me. You know I hate London. Might there be something in it for Janey?'

''Course there would,' said Rupert. 'How extraordinary we didn't think of her before. The IBA are dotty about women. She could have her own programme. Those chat shows she did for Yorkshire were terrific. Tell her not to write anything too outrageous in her column before Christmas. We won't know whether we've got the franchise until December.'

'What happens in the meantime?' said Billy, who felt guilty that Rupert was buying him large whiskies, and only drinking Perrier himself. 'I'd adore to join Venturer, but until you can pay me a salary, and the franchise is safely in the bag, I can't really afford to burn my boats with the Beeb.'

'It's all right,' said Rupert. 'Georgie Baines, Seb Burrows, Harold White and Charles Fairburn are all in exactly the same boat. All that happens is we attach a strictly confidential memo to our application saying we've signed up a Head of Sport, a Sales Director, a Programme Controller, etc., who are all wildly experienced, but for security reasons we can't reveal their names until we go up to the IBA for the interview in November.'

'How very cloak and dagger,' said Billy. 'I must say it'll be fun working together again.'

'We need some more women,' said Declan. 'Janey Lloyd-Foxe is gorgeous and talented, but a bit lightweight, and Dame Enid's almost a man anyway.'

'I'm going to have a crack at Cameron Cook. I'm working on it,' said Rupert, who'd already lost twelve pounds in weight.

'Not safe,' growled Declan. 'She'd shop us to Tony.'

Together Freddie and Rupert raised the money.

Rupert, in between his punishing work load as Sports Minister, had several meetings with Henriques Bros, the London Merchant Bank. He found it very difficult not drinking and sticking to his diet over those interminably long lunches, but at least it left him with a clear head. By the second week in April he'd organized a potential seven-million-pound loan.

Freddie's methods were more direct. He invited half a dozen rich cronies to lunch in his board room and got Taggie up to London to do the cooking. With the boeuf en croute he produced a claret of such vintage and venerability that a one-minute silence was preserved as the first glass was drunk.

'Christ, that's good,' said the Chief Executive of Oxford Motors.

Freddie tipped back his chair, his red-gold curls on end, his merry grey eyes sparkling: 'I can only afford to drink wine like this once a year,' he said, 'but I'd like to be able to drink it every day, and that's where all you gentlemen come in.'

By the end of lunch, having bandied the names of Marti Gluckstein, Rupert and Declan around the table, Freddie was well on the way to raising the eight million.

Jubilant, he travelled back to Gloucestershire by train and, seeing a plump lady walking down the platform, recognized Lizzie Vereker and whisked her into a first-class carriage. His mood of euphoria, he soon discovered, was matched by Lizzie's. Thanks to a wonderful new nanny, who seemed impervious to James's advances, she'd finished and delivered her new novel and the publishers loved it. It was an excuse for her to buy him an enormous drink, she said, but she didn't know if British Railways stocked Bacardi and Coke.

'Leave it to me,' said Freddie, and came back with two half-bottles of Moët.

'How's James?' he asked, as the train whizzed through Slough.

'Frightfully cross,' said Lizzie. 'People keep ringing him up asking for Declan's home number because they want him to join their consortiums. Have you seen Declan?'

'No,' lied Freddie, and wished he didn't have to. Looking at Lizzie's round, smiling face and capacious cashmere bosom, Freddie couldn't help thinking how nice it would be if Lizzie joined Venturer. She had just the right emollient quality to keep everyone happy. She had three novels under her belt and lived in the area. He gave her a lift home. Although the trees were still leafless, the wild garlic and the dog mercury were sweeping like a great emerald-green tide over the floor of the woods.

'Oh I love Spring,' sighed Lizzie. 'The bluebells will be out soon. I've only been away two days and it's like missing "EastEnders"; you suddenly discover nature's moved on another instalment without you.'

'I know I shouldn't ask,' said Freddie as the red Jaguar pulled up outside her house, 'but will you have lunch with me one day?'

'I know I shouldn't accept,' said Lizzie, 'but yes, please.'

Dropping in at The Priory on the way home, Freddie found Declan and Rupert in the library surrounded by tapes. Declan was busy writing the section of the application which would tear Corinium's programmes to shreds.

He and Rupert were now watching a tape of 'Cotswold Round-Up'. Sarah was interviewing some old lady who couldn't pay her gas bill and James was sitting on the pink sofa looking caring.

'Christ, she's pretty,' said Declan. 'She'd be dazzling if she were properly produced. We do need some more women.'

'No, no, no, no,' said Rupert. 'She really *is* lightweight.'

'What would you feel about Lizzie Vereker?' said Freddie, his voice thickening.

'Good idea,' said Declan. 'She writes very well.'

'And she's so sweet,' said Rupert, 'and it would infuriate James.'

'And she lives in the area,' they all chorused.

'Let's recruit her later in the year,' said Declan. 'She's too near to Tony and I really don't want him to know what we're up to before the applications go in.'

RIVALS
26

On the second Monday in April, Ursula, who was still working for Declan, although he could ill afford her salary, was due to lunch with her old friend Joyce Madden.

'See if you can find out Tony's whereabouts next weekend,' Rupert had asked her on the telephone beforehand.

Ursula, who loved conspiracy, came back from lunch and half a bottle of Sauternes bustling with excitement, and rang Rupert.

'Joyce told me in the strictest confidence that Tony and Cameron are off on a naughty to Madrid this weekend. Cameron's flying out on Friday afternoon. Evidently she wants some peace to polish Corinium's application before it goes off to the IBA. Tony's giving a party at The Falconry on Friday night because it's Badminton weekend and a nice excuse to ask all his posh friends paid for by Corinium. Then he's flying to Madrid on Saturday lunchtime. They're staying in the same hotel and on Sunday night Cameron's picking up some award for "Four Men went to Mow". They're both flying home on separate planes on Monday.'

'Well done, thou good and faithful servant,' said Rupert. 'Could you bear at this stage not to mention this to Declan?'

Later in the day Rupert went to a reception to welcome some visiting Russian gymnasts, during which they gave a demonstration of their skills. Watching them go into incredibly graceful contortions on parallel bar and rug, Rupert wondered whether Cameron Cook was as supple and agile as that in bed. How the hell was he to get her on her own to launch his attack? Then inspiration struck. The moment the party was over he beetled out to his Government car and rang his friend the handsome Duke, who lived at Badminton.

'Could you do me a great favour?'

'Depends how great,' said the Duke.

'You've got the Princess staying next weekend, haven't you?'

'Yes.'

'Could you possibly ask Tony and Monica Baddingham to dinner on Saturday night?'

'Do I have to? I don't mind Monica, but he's such a ghastly snob.'

'I'll knock half a grand off that Irish mare.'

'Oh, all right then.'

'I'm going away this weekend,' Rupert told Gerald Middleton next morning as they went through the diary. 'I bumped into the Secretary of State for Scotland last night, who reminded me that Hearts are playing Madrid on Saturday, and it seemed wrong that no one from our department was going.'

Gerald raised his eyebrow.

'They're the only British team in the semi-final,' said Rupert blandly.

'You're meant to be chairing a meeting opposing the Swindon/Gloucester motorway in Gloucester on Friday night,' said Gerald, who didn't approve of dates being broken.

'I know. Ring them and say I'm terribly sorry. They have my full support, but they'll have to get someone else. And can you get me a couple of presents for the wives of the British Ambassador and the Spanish Minister for Sport?'

'I hope you're not overdoing things,' said Gerald reprovingly. 'You've lost an awful lot of weight recently. Don't forget you've got a second appointment with Doctor Benson tomorrow.'

Gerald was very worried. Rupert had been edgy for the last

month, which could at first be put down to his not drinking, but this weekend he'd been really bad-tempered and two trips to the doctor in three days seemed ominous, particularly when you had screwed around as much as Rupert.

Rupert, however, rolled up at The Priory in the highest spirits the following evening to find Declan still surrounded by tapes and Basil Baddingham sitting on the edge of his desk drinking a Bloody Mary and discussing tactics.

'I was just telling Declan that I've found you a possible building in case Tony won't let us buy the existing Corinium studios,' said Bas. 'Cotchester Hall's coming on to the market in November. Why are you looking so bloody pleased with yourself?'

Rupert waved a piece of paper in front of them.

'I had an AIDS test this week and I'm clear.'

'Christ,' said Bas, examining it. 'Is there no justice in the world?'

'How long did it take you to get the results?' asked Declan.

'Forty-eight hours,' said Rupert, 'but I had to bung them.'

'I'd be far too frightened to go,' said Bas.

'I came to tell you,' said Rupert, retrieving his piece of paper, 'that I'm going away for the weekend.'

'But we've got our first Venturer meeting on Sunday,' protested Declan. 'Everyone's coming – even Harold White and Marti Gluckstein.'

'Christ, he's never been to the country in his life,' said Rupert. Then, hurriedly remembering the cottage he was supposed to be buying for Marti, asked, 'Where are you having it, at the Bar Sinister?'

'Too close to Tone,' said Bas. 'Freddie's earmarked a fantastic little pub in the middle of Salisbury Plain which no one knows and which has amazing food. The landlord just runs it for fun.'

Declan was still looking disapproving. 'You ought to be there. Meetings are essential at this stage to establish some kind of *esprit de corps*. And we'll all be tossing ideas around.'

'You know I never have any,' said Rupert.

'I thought you were chairing the motorway meeting,' said Bas.

'Had to cancel it,' said Rupert. 'If I don't spend more time in my constituency other than on Venturer business, they're going to drop me.'

'Burke only visited his constituency once in six years,' said Declan.

Rupert laughed. 'He wasn't such a berk then.'

'Where *are* you going?' asked Bas.

'To Madrid to watch some soccer.'

'Balls,' said Bas. 'You're up to something.'

'I need a break,' said Rupert. 'Man cannot live by bread alone; he needs crumpet.'

There is a moment every Spring when even the most dedicated workaholic is overwhelmed by restlessness and longs to cast clouts and wander hand in hand with a new love through the burgeoning countryside. Cameron Cook was no exception. The weather had suddenly turned so warm as she packed for Madrid on Friday morning that she was able to wander naked round her bedroom with the smell of newly mown grass drifting in through the wide-open windows. The apple trees at the bottom of her backyard were still bare, but the long grass round their gnarled grey trunks was filled with bright blue cillas, polyanthus and narcissi. Beyond the fence two mallard had nested in the rushes on the edge of the water meadows, and in the distance the willows, bowed over the river, were fringed with palest green.

Although Cameron had read that there was a heatwave in Madrid, it wouldn't catch her on the hop. She had spent several hours a week over the last month on the sun bed, baking her body to that dark smooth gold that Tony loved. She was in great shape too; her coach at the gym last night had told her that, apart from a few professional athletes, her body was the most perfect and finely tuned he had ever handled. She admired it every time she passed the long mirror. Yet only yesterday Tony had shattered her confidence once again.

In order to discuss some change in the running order, she had barged into Sarah Stratton's dressing-room yesterday afternoon and found her sharing a bottle of champagne with Tony. Sarah's gold hair was prosaically in rollers and she was sitting in a dove-grey silk petticoat which showed off her cleavage and had got rucked up to show a strip of flesh between the top of her dove-grey silk French knickers and her pale grey stockings. She was actually perfectly decently dressed and Tony was leaning against the wall six feet away from her, but there was something about the way they stopped talking when Cameron came in. Normally Cameron would have bawled Sarah out for drinking before a programme, but she couldn't with Tony countenancing it. Instead she had a row with Tony after work.

Tony was quite unrepentant.

'Poor darling Sarah, she was a bit nervous about interviewing the head of the Chamber of Commerce, in case it influenced the franchise. After all they are an important pressure group. She was asking my advice on her best line of questioning. Her great strength,' he went on, with a nasty smile, 'is that she's not afraid to show a man she's vulnerable, and she is so deliciously feminine.'

'And I'm not, I suppose?'

Tony shrugged and ruffled her spiky hair.

'No one could call you feminine, darling.'

So this morning, in a rage, Cameron, who had never worn baby-doll nighties or anything underneath her clothes other than the briefest bikini pants, rushed out and spent a fortune on matching underwear and nightgowns and negligées.

In other more subtle ways her self-confidence had been eroded recently. Ironically, since Tony had made her Programme Controller, a role she'd coveted for so long, she'd become less secure, because she spent so much time in meetings and was doing less and less of the thing she was really good at – making programmes. All the prizes she was now winning were for work done last year. The new series of 'Four Men went to Mow', starting next week, would largely be produced, directed and re-written by other people. Having clawed her way to the top, she realized, as many men had realized before her, that the view from there wasn't that great; in fact it was bloody scary. Finally, she was aware that by flexing her muscles in the office, in bed and in the gym, she was frightening guys off. In the last three years Patrick and Tony were the only ones who'd fallen in love with her, and Tony was showing every sign of getting bored.

Out on the water meadows and the cathedral close she could see office workers in shirt sleeves and cotton dresses, many of them probably from Corinium, sneaking out to early lunches, wandering arm in arm, carrying bottles to drink under the willows.

She glanced at the status symbols littered in ludicrously expensive confusion over her bed – the Charles Jourdan shoes, the Hermés scarves, the Filofax, the Rayban shades, the huge Rolex watch, the backless kingfisher-blue Jasper Conran for Sunday night's presentation – what was the point of all these spiralist trappings if there was no one to share them with? Her mood of despair lasted all the way to Madrid.

There, however, the black limo that met her at the airport and the splendour of her magnificent suite in a hotel paid for by the Spanish television authorities, gradually cheered her up.

There were two bedrooms in the suite, each with two beds, a huge living-room stuffed with antiques and lit by huge chandeliers, and an enormous bathroom with soft and hard loo paper, a hair dryer and two beautiful white towelling dressing-gowns. There was a bottle of champagne in a bucket of ice and a huge basket of fruit with pomegranates, persimmons and apples as big as grapefruit. Pink carnations floated in the finger bowls; there were flowers in every room to match the pale pink walls, and silver trays of chocolates. And this was just her suite. Tony's suite next door was identical.

'Hey diddly dee, a plutocrat's life for me,' sang Cameron, demolishing a tray of chocolates. Then she started worrying about spots. She'd better stop.

There were also telephones everywhere, even in the shower. Tony would be circulating at his drinks party now.

It brought her up with a nasty jolt that no one else in the world would like to be called by her, except Patrick and she didn't know where he was.

She strolled out on to the balcony and saw that there was a little garden restaurant below, with a summer house and floodlit lemon trees and a lawn with a fountain. The tables were filled with handsome, hawklike men with sleek black hair, and beautiful women in suits with very padded shoulders, who were all talking their heads off and having a wonderful time.

Going back into the living-room to attack a pomegranate, she noticed an etching of the Judgement of Paris on the wall. Juno and Athene, both fully dressed, were looking furious, as Venus, who was flashing an ankle and a bare boob, was awarded the apple. Venus looked just like Sarah Stratton. Cameron turned the picture to the wall. It must be tiredness that suddenly made her feel so unbelievably down again. She couldn't be bothered with supper; taking two Mogadon, she crashed out.

She got up early, spent two hours working out camera angles for the first part of 'Four Men went to Mow', then spent the rest of the morning working on Corinium's application. God it was turgid, longer than *Gone with the Wind* and infinitely less readable: all those Brownie points being notched up with promises to employ independent production companies and set up audio-visual workshops, or subsidize roving repertory companies and youth orchestras. There was also a lot of guff about grass-roots involvement and worker participation schemes. A few figures had been provided, but there was very little talk of profits.

Unable to face tinkering with it any more, Cameron lunched at the hotel, wandered round Madrid, which seemed to be packed with Scottish football supporters, then spent two hours restoring her sanity looking at the Goyas and El Grecos in the Prado. The telephone was ringing as she let herself into her suite. It was Joyce Madden.

'Lord B's terribly sorry.' Cameron could tell Madden wasn't. 'He's been trying to get you all afternoon. He's sorry but he won't be able to fly out for the awards. Something's cropped up. The Duke's asked him to dine at Badminton tonight. He says he can't refuse, particularly in franchise year. Hullo, hullo . . .' but Cameron had hung up.

She was so angry she ate all the chocolates on the silver tray. How dare he, the bastard! Standing her up for a bloody dinner party. Bloody star-fucker.

Absolutely on cue there was a knock on the door and in came a valet bringing a huge bunch of roses.

'*Sorry I can't make it, Darling,*' said the card. '*Good luck tomorrow, All love, Tony.*'

Cameron was so furious she went out and hurled the roses over the balcony, watching them whizz round and round until they landed on a mob of cheering fans.

'Bastard, fucker, asshole,' screamed Cameron at the top of her voice, then let out an enormous fart, which seemed the only way she could demonstrate her utter contempt for Tony.

'Hush,' drawled a voice, 'you'll frighten the pigeons.'

Cameron swung round and gave a gasp of appalled embarrassment.

For there, laughing his handsome head off on the next-door balcony, his face as brown as the glass of whisky in his hand, lounged Rupert.

'What are you doing here?' muttered Cameron.

'Watching Hearts win a football match. Never thought I'd get in here, but they had a last-minute cancellation, a Mr Smith.' He grinned wickedly. 'What an extraordinary coincidence to find you here. Why are you looking so bad-tempered?'

'I am bad-tempered. The TV doesn't speak English.'

'You expecting guests?'

'Not any more.'

'So that bouquet you were bombing the masses with was a peace offering from the Oily Baron?'

'You're *so* fucking perceptive,' said Cameron sulkily. Then rage overcame pride. 'Madden just called to say he can't make it. He's been summoned to dine at Badminton.'

'Probably has,' said Rupert. 'I know there's a dinner party

353

there tonight and the Princess is going. Let's have a drink. Your place or mine?'

'Mine,' said Cameron. 'Give me half an hour while I take a bath and dress.'

'I wouldn't bother.' said Rupert. 'You're overdressed as it is.'

It was all going too fast for her. What the hell was Rupert doing here? It could hardly be coincidence. He was the biggest rake in the world. No one emerged unscathed. So why was she feeling so wildly elated, washing her ears when she'd washed them that morning, and trimming her bush, and rubbing Fracas into her belly and inner thighs? As she slid into her new peach satin underwear it seemed to be caressing her in anticipation. For once she didn't need blusher, the glow came from within. Finally, she put on a pale apricot tunic, very demure and clinging with all the buttons done up, but with the hemline six inches above the knee, making her legs seem endless.

All powerful men are attractive. Men who are powerful and kind are irresistible. For once Rupert seemed to have abandoned his flip cracks and his sexual innuendoes. He appeared to be really, really interested in her career, in Corinium's programme plans and how they were approaching their application for the franchise. He was also incredibly well informed. She'd always thought he was only interested in sport and screwing.

Cameron was enjoying herself so much she didn't notice she'd drunk almost an entire bottle of champagne and Rupert had hardly touched his glass of whisky. As the boat race is usually won in the first two minutes by one crew surging ahead and taking advantage of smoother water, so the conquest of Cameron was really achieved in that first hour when she was off-guard and feeling bruised and vulnerable because Tony had stood her up. As Rupert got up to fill her glass yet again, he pointed to the mound of paper on her desk.

'What are you doing?'

'Working on the final application.'

'Anyone bidding against you?' asked Rupert, idly.

'Tony's discovered a group of Bristol businessmen calling themselves Mid-West are having a go. They claim we're too Cotchester-orientated. But I don't figure they're much cop.'

That's three of us pitching, thought Rupert, reflecting that, as Cameron Cook had such wonderful legs, spying on her was no hardship at all.

'Is Tony worried?' he asked.

'No way, but we can't afford to be complacent. Southern lost their franchises in 1980, and they didn't appear to have done anything wrong. The IBA have to make some changes to be seen to be doing their job properly.'

'What about Declan? Tony lost a network slot there. How's he going to replace him?'

'I'm not sure. Declan cost Tony so much dough, and he really zapped him out. Tony can't stand not being able to bully people. He's much less uptight since Declan walked out, but he needs a replacement. I guess he'll poach some top front-of-camera person in the next few weeks, just to distract people from Declan's departure. The media are still sniffing round.'

'Any idea who it might be?' said Rupert.

'No. Tony loves to surround himself in mystery.'

'How are you enjoying being Programme Controller?'

Cameron shrugged. 'Not as much as I expected. There's so much hassle. Admin bores me rigid. Thinking up brilliant ideas, which other people promptly screw up. I had to sack four people last week. You ever done that?'

'Frequently,' said Rupert. Christ, he thought, as Cameron rabbited on, her mouth's like a dumper. I could use her to unblock my drains.

'You should get out,' he said when she finally paused for breath. 'Any of the network companies would snap you up.'

Cameron looked at the bulky application on the desk. 'I'd like to see Corinium retain the franchise. I'll probably look around in the Autumn. Although why I hang in with that bastard, I can't think. Is it usual to be asked to dine with royalty at the last moment?'

'No,' said Rupert.

'So Tony must have known about the dinner party for ages, and didn't have the guts to tell me he wouldn't be coming out.'

'Probably didn't want you to make other arrangements,' said Rupert, emptying the bottle into her glass.

He was shrewd enough to realize that, having existed on a diet of Tony for three years, and having been flaunted at work and on the occasional jolly abroad but ruthlessly excluded from anything else, what Cameron was missing was a legitimate social life. He got to his feet.

'Well, thanks for the drink. I'm going out to dinner.'

Cameron's happiness drained away. 'Goodbye,' she said coldly, gazing at the plane trees in the square which were turning pink in the setting sun. 'Well, go on then,' she snapped a few seconds later.

'Stop sulking,' said Rupert. 'You're invited as well.'

'To a restaurant?'

'No, a private house.'

'They won't want me.'

'Yes they will. Nicky and Mary. You'll adore them. I'm just going to put on a tie.'

Next door he extracted a tape recorder the width and size of half a pencil from his top pocket, removed the tape, and put it in a secret drawer at the back of his brief case. There'd be too much noise at dinner to isolate anything interesting.

Nicky and Mary turned out to be the British Ambassador and his beautiful wife, who'd been a mad success in Madrid. They lived in a ravishing house a few miles from the centre of the town and the dinner party was just as grand as the one Tony and Monica were enjoying in England, but everyone was so friendly and easy-going and knew all about Cameron coming to Madrid to accept an award, that she instantly felt at home.

Mary, who had known Rupert at the height of his show-jumping career, was a good enough friend not to mind his totally upsetting the rigid protocol usually observed in diplomatic circles by bringing an extra guest, though it did mean a last-minute arrangement of the *placement*. At dinner Cameron sat between the Italian Ambassador and a Spanish duke, who both spoke perfect English. The gossip about royalty, politics and the jet set was sensational, but it was generally accepted that nothing would be passed on.

As Cameron ate the most delicious ravioli filled with scallop and lobster she had ever tasted, the Spanish Duke, who had slicked-back ebony hair, and hooded eyes, talked to her about the national character. 'As a people we are obsessed with death, but indifferent to it as long as the right attitude is struck. Note the matador's lack of concern for his own life. Life should be enjoyed now, not devoted to working for some distant fulfilment.'

Cameron looked at Rupert, who was seated on the other side of the table, laughing with his beautiful hostess.

Reading her thoughts, the Duke went on, 'Rupert in some ways is very Spanish, very brave, very macho, very sad underneath.'

'Sad?' said Cameron, amazed. 'Rupert?'

The Duke nodded. 'You never saw him in the show ring? It was magnificent. All the grace and courage, and apparent effortlessness of the matador. It must have been terrible for him to give it up. I thought he would drink or womanize himself to death.'

'He's made a great success of Minister for Sport,' said Cameron.

'It would hurt his pride not to make a success of anything, but he is still not fulfilled, and if the Tories lose the election, as everyone thinks they will, he'll be out of a job. He needs a great love in his life. I 'ope you are she.' He raised his glass to her.

'What was his wife like?'

The Duke kissed his bunched-up fingers. 'So beautiful, but quite wrong, nervy and not really interested in him, only what she thought he could become. You can't change Rupert, only make him more secure.'

With the Cochinillo everyone turned to talk to the person on their left.

357

'Rupert is very lucky,' said the Italian Ambassador. 'He has always had beautiful women, but seldom so clever. I believe you come to Rome next month for another prize?'

I'm having fun, thought Cameron in amazement. Tony's virtually kept me in prison for three years. For the first time since New Year's Eve with Patrick, I'm really having fun.

Rupert took her home just after midnight. They sat on opposite sides of the back of the embassy car and he made no attempt to touch her. In the darkness, she could see his profile, Spanish too with its thick slicked-back hair and forehead which ran down in a dead straight line to his nose. The only luxuriance in such a finely planed face were the wicked long blue eyes which she couldn't see in the dark, and the fullness of the lower lip. I want him she thought, helplessly; I want to be the woman who brings him fulfilment.

To their left a lot of drunken Scottish football fans were splashing about in a fountain. Above them soared the statue of Christopher Columbus.

'Can we get out and look at him?' said Cameron. 'After all, he did discover America.'

As they got out, Rupert's hair gleamed in the moonlight.

'Rupert,' screamed one of the Scottish fans. 'Look, it's Rupert.'

'No, thank you very much,' said Rupert, pulling Cameron back into the car.

Furious with herself for wanting him so badly, Cameron spoke only in monosyllables all the way back to the hotel. Totally ignoring the two smiling footmen who leapt forward to turn the revolving door for her, she shot into the elevator. In such a small space, you wouldn't have thought it possible to be so far apart, but Cameron felt her belly button touching her spine. Falling out of the elevator, she set out at a run across the patterned carpet, then, realizing she'd turned the wrong way, had to retrace her steps. What the hell was the matter with her, Controller of Programmes, mega-prize-winner, woman of substance, flapping around like a blackbird trapped in a fruit cage?

'I must be pooped,' she said in an over-bright voice. 'Thank you so much,' she mumbled outside her door, and, the moment Rupert had opened it for her, she shot inside.

Rupert made no attempt to retain her. 'Good night,' he said yawning. 'Sleep well.'

Alone in her mammoth suite, Cameron nearly went into orbit with frustration. In the mirror she could see her eyes glittering feverishly, her breath coming in great gasps, her nipples sticking through the apricot dress like thimbles. She half expected to see a pulse jumping between her legs.

She was nearly thirty. Perhaps she was losing her touch and Rupert really didn't want to sleep with her. She couldn't stand it. Ripping off the dress and the temptress's satin underwear he hadn't even seen, she went into the bathroom and turned on the cold shower, letting the icy jet blast away all the Fracas and the body lotion and the gel, and, hopefully, the desire. She turned it on so hard that it was a few seconds before she realized the telephone was ringing. No doubt it was Tony, establishing his ascendancy, so she let it ring just to worry him. After two minutes she picked it up.

'I don't see why Christopher Columbus should have a monopoly,' said a light clipped drawl. 'I want to discover America too.'

Cameron leant against the wall, feeling giddy with relief.

'Cameron.'

'Yes?'

'Who are we fooling?'

'I don't want to get hurt. Or get AIDS.'

'You won't,' said Rupert triumphantly. 'I had a test last week. I'm as clear as one of Valerie Jones's picture windows. I've got a certificate to prove it.'

'I'm amazed you haven't run off millions of copies on Ministry for Sports' stationery,' said Cameron, 'and circulated them to all interested parties.'

'Don't be bitchy. What about you?'

'I had a medical for insurance last month.'

'Tony must have bonked you since then. One could catch

359

something far nastier than AIDS from him. Now am I going to have to swing across the balcony like Tarzan or are you going to let me in?'

Rupert had cleaned his teeth and was still wearing his blue striped shirt and suit trousers. Without the camouflage of his jacket, Cameron could see how divinely proportioned he was, hunky on the shoulders, and lean and streamlined everywhere else. The golden meanie, she thought. As he came towards her, she clutched the towel round her, looking very young and vulnerable with her hair flat and wet from the shower, like a guard dog who's been uncharacteristically caught with its hackles down.

'Everyone's into prolonged courtship these days,' she gabbled. 'I don't want you to think I'm easy.'

'I don't.' Very gently Rupert took off the huge Rolex watch she'd forgotten to remove in the shower. 'I just want to see if you've got a designer cunt.'

He stopped her reply by kissing her; the towel slid to the floor.

It was a very good thing, he reflected later, that he'd lost all that weight and been jogging for an hour every morning, or he'd never have coped with the pace. Cameron was like an electric eel, knew every sexual permutation in the book, could twist herself into any position, and ordered him around like a sergeant-major.

'You are incredible,' he murmured into the back of her head, 'you'd make a matchstick feel like a cigar.'

'I need a bit more stimulation on my clitoris,' demanded Cameron.

Rupert obliged. 'In England, we pronounce it clitter-is.'

'It's *cly*-toris, and please be gentle.'

After two hours' fairly sustained screwing in both bedrooms, on the sofa in the drawing-room, under the shower, and admiring themselves in every mirror, they collapsed onto the carpet and Rupert came for the fourth and, from his point of view, final time.

'I haven't come yet,' said Cameron in his ear.

Rupert was astounded. 'What was wrong, for Christ's sake?'

'Nothing. It was the best first fuck I've ever had, I'm too uptight and too pissed, I guess.'

'Well, I'm not jumping ship till you do, so you may as well relax and stop fighting.'

Wriggling downwards, he parted her sodden bush. 'I am, after all, a member of the Cly-Tory Party,' he said in muffled tones.

RIVALS
27

Waking first, Cameron reached out and immediately realized she wasn't with Tony. Rupert had the most enormous erection, so like a Cruise missile that Cameron half expected to see lots of Greenham women camped round the bed looking disapproving and waving CND banners. Getting up, she drew back the curtain an inch. Rupert was certainly the best-looking man she'd ever been to bed with, and, despite her sniping, the best lay. Once she'd let him take over last night, everything had been perfect. She knew too that, in the space of fourteen hours, she was a different person. She'd been dependent on Tony for security but never happiness. For the first time in her life, she was in love and it terrified her.

The ring of the telephone woke Rupert up. It was Tony, all smarm, calling from his car, so the line wasn't very good. This was a good thing as Rupert started kissing Cameron all over in the middle, and so distracted her she couldn't remember anything practical, like what time the awards were or when she flew in tomorrow, or concentrate on the witty remarks Tony had made to the Princess.

'It's Tony,' she wrote frantically on the telephone message pad.

'So?' wrote Rupert.

'I'm so sorry,' gasped Cameron. 'I was working very late on the application.'

'How's it shaping?'

'Very well,' shrieked Cameron, as Rupert, grinning broadly, lunged Cruise into her. 'Look, I've got to go, I'm off to Toledo. I'll ring you before I leave tomorrow morning. You're insupportable,' she howled at Rupert, as she slammed down the telephone.

'How was the dinner party?'

Cameron grimaced. 'Said he only accepted because he felt the Duke needed his support and it was always a bit nerve-racking entertaining royalty.'

Rupert had to bury his face in her neck to stop himself laughing.

Afterwards he wanted to go back to sleep, but Cameron, who felt one shouldn't waste a minute in a foreign country, made the mistake of dragging him off to Toledo.

'You are now entering the Imperial capital,' read a large sign as they drove through the ancient city gates.

'I can think of things I'd much rather enter,' said Rupert broodily.

'Hardly Cyril Smith country,' he went on, as the official car rumbled cautiously up incredibly narrow streets, where the flowers in the window boxes on either side seemed to bend over to kiss each other beneath a thin blue strip of sky.

Cameron's hopes that Rupert might like the cathedral were soon dashed. He whizzed past the ravishing stained-glass windows, the carved pillars and the breathtaking pictures as though he was riding against the clock. A Velasquez Borgia reminded him of Tony. After gazing at a Rubens Madonna and Child for three seconds, he said they both should be dispatched to Weightwatchers. The El Grecos finished him off altogether because they all reminded him of his ex-wife's husband, Malise Gordon.

Just inside the entrance to the cathedral was a gift shop selling not only religious relics and postcards, but also flick knives, swords, guns, thumbscrews and racks. Was this symbolic of the torture Rupert was going to put her through? wondered Cameron. To cheer him up, she insisted they stop for Margueritas at a nearby bar. Rupert pronounced them

363

absolutely disgusting: neat salt water with added salt water. They'll all be at the first Venturer lunch on Salisbury Plain, he thought sourly, getting drunk and enjoying themselves. He wished he were there too.

As they were leaving Toledo, Cameron suddenly thought wistfully of Patrick and how much he would have enjoyed wandering round the city and the cathedral.

'Can we just drive up to the top and look back?' she asked the chauffeur.

The view took her breath away. The whole of Toledo sprawled out on the hillside, little houses, palaces, churches, bleached and baked over the centuries by the burning sun to the palest terracottas, roans, corals and ochres, with the occasional black-green cypress as an exclamation mark. On the right flowed the Tagus, like dark-green glass, going into a flurry of foaming water as it dropped down a level, then becoming absolutely still again, as though someone had added gelatine.

'Christ, I'd like to bring a film crew here,' said Cameron. Then she looked at Rupert's face, which was as still and cold as the dark-green water.

I've lost him, she thought despairingly. I should have let him sleep.

But, as they were driving back to Madrid, his hand along the back of the seat suddenly touched her hair. It was as though he'd sawn through the ropes and dragged her off the railroad track as the express thundered towards her.

She melted towards him. 'What's the matter?'

'I'm sorry.'

'Don't you like culture?'

'Not a lot. It's already happened, and I hate being trapped. The first time Helen and I stayed in Madrid, she went to Toledo by herself and raved on and on and on about it. I even remember her making Malise blush when she told him he was pure El Greco. She was crazy about sightseeing. I'm afraid the things I disliked in her I don't like any better in other people.'

'But you can't expect people always to do what you want.'

'I don't, but if they want to do something, I'd rather they went off and did it alone, and then not gas about it afterwards.'

'What were you doing all the time she was sightseeing?'

'I was show-jumping,' said Rupert.

When they got back to the room, they made love again, with less energy but more tenderness.

'Can I get down?' said Cameron finally as she straddled him.

'You are *able* to get down,' said Rupert, quoting his old nanny, 'but whether you *may* is another matter.'

Cameron caressed his cheek. 'Are you coming with me tonight?'

Rupert shook his head. 'Not safe. There'll be too many press.'

Despite no sleep, Cameron looked so seductive in her new kingfisher-blue backless that Rupert nearly dragged her back to bed again.

'Uh, uh.' Cameron skipped out of the way. 'I'll stagger onto the podium like John Wayne as it is. I hope I don't fall asleep in the speeches.'

As soon as she walked into the Reception she realized that it was a very good thing she'd come by herself. There was Ivor Hicks, Corinium's corporate development controller, chatting up a tough-looking Spanish woman. She also recognized people from Granada and TVS, and one of Robert Maxwell's henchmen.

'What the hell are you doing here?' she whispered to Ivor.

'Tony's after a stake in Spanish television,' said Ivor. 'The Government here's creating three new channels. Tony wants twenty-five per cent of one of them. Maxwell, Granada and TVS are after the same thing.'

Cameron sighed. 'That means less money for programmes.'

'But more security for Tony, in case he loses the franchise,' said Ivor. 'Diversification is the name of the game.'

Rupert gave Cameron half an hour. Then, seeing her going into dinner on television, he went systematically through her Filofax, dictating her future appointments into his tape recorder – and a lot of Tony's that she'd listed. Then he opened her briefcase, and removed the Corinium application. It was very bulky, like smuggling in *Lady Chatterley's Lover* when he was at Prep School.

At first the pretty girl on the reception desk told Rupert the office was closed and there was no way the application could be photostated. But Spanish guests at the hotel seldom had such blond hair, or such blue eyes, or such good teeth, or waved so many thousands and thousands of pesetas in front of her. She would see what she could do, she said. She'd have to secrete the application into the office, it might take a little time, as the manager was about. She'd ring Rupert's room as soon as it was done. Sweating, he went back upstairs and paced up and down drinking whisky. On television the awards were well underway. Stars were tottering up on to the platform wiping their eyes and thanking every member of the crew, and every madre and padre for the help they had given. What if Cameron had been on already and, overcome with lust, was belting back to him?

Going downstairs again, he met the receptionist, very flustered, but with the completed copy. It was only when he got back to his room that he realized the silly cow had put it back out of order; the sections on 'Master Dog' and 'Dorothy Dove' didn't follow on and James Vereker's afternoon programme was in the middle of Engineering specifications. It was a long and laborious task to get them in the right order, and even then Rupert wasn't sure he'd done it right. For the third time he rushed down to get the various chapters stapled together.

He was just getting back into the lift when he saw Cameron coming through the revolving door. Pressing the button, he creaked up to the seventh floor, rushed along to her room, which he'd rashly left open because he didn't have a key and double-locked it on the inside.

With trembling hands he shoved the original back in her briefcase, hoping it was the right way up, snapped the clasp and shoved the copied pages inside his jacket under his arm. The next minute there was a tantivy on the door.

'Rupert, open up,' said Cameron.

Pretending to rub the sleep out of his eyes, he opened the door. 'Sorry, sweetheart, I didn't want to be disturbed by maids replacing chocolates and turning down beds. How was it?'

'Scary,' said Cameron. 'I'll never, never be mean to any front-of-camera people again. Wasn't it awful when I dried?'

'You were sweet,' lied Rupert, 'and they were all so touched you tried to speak Spanish.'

Fortunately Cameron was a bit pissed. 'Have you eaten?' she asked.

'I wasn't hungry,' said Rupert, edging towards the door. 'In fact I've got a bloody awful headache.'

'I've got some Panadol,' said Cameron, going to her briefcase.

'I've got something even stronger next door,' said Rupert hastily. 'I'll be back in a minute.'

Back in his suite, he nearly died. He'd never had nerves like this in the old days when he was show jumping, and screwing everyone else's wives. With shaking, sweating hands, he stuffed the photostated application in the secret compartment of his briefcase.

Cameron had kicked off her shoes and was lying on the bed drinking white wine when he got back.

'Good thing you didn't come,' she said. 'There were so many people who'd have recognized you. I picked up a *Sunday Times*.'

'Thanks.'

Rupert turned immediately to the sports page, she noticed, then the smile was wiped off his face.

'Fucking hell!' He turned to the front page.

'What's the matter?'

'Riots after both semi-finals of the FA Cup,' he howled. 'Petrol bombs thrown at the police, two policemen stabbed, cars overturned and burnt, shop windows smashed, twenty people taken to hospital, forty-five arrests. Fucking, fucking

367

hell! I play hookey for one weekend and this happens.'

In a second he was on to Gerald in London.

'I've been trying to get you since yesterday, Minister.'

There were obviously other people in the room or Gerald would never have been so formal.

'Is it very serious?'

'Yes – four people are still in intensive care.'

'I'll fly back tonight.'

'I'm sorry, Minister. After all your hard work, it's a most tragic setback.'

By one o'clock, Rupert managed to get on to a private jet, arranged by the British Ambassador. He seemed to have forgotten Cameron's existence until he was leaving.

'I'm sorry to walk out on you, angel. I'm just so pissed off. I was so certain I'd pegged the violence.' He took her face in his hands. 'Look, it's been great. I won't ring you in case I get Tony, but promise to ring me. Here's Gerald's number; he'll know where to find me.'

And he was gone.

It's a beginning, thought Cameron, hanging over the balcony to see if she could catch a glimpse of him getting into his car. It was still warm. Breathing in the scent of the lemon trees rising from the little garden, she had a sudden vision of Rupert's beautiful house in Gloucestershire and all that wonderful sweep of land, and decided the only status symbol she really wanted was a Cartier wedding-ring with R C-B and CC engraved inside.

RIVALS
28

Rupert went back to England slap into a political storm. The dramatic drop in football hooliganism had been a high spot of the Tory administration. Now, after a sickening day of violence, their claims were looking very dubious. With an election in the offing, the opposition were roaring for blood and, in an emergency debate on Monday night, tabled a motion of no confidence in the Minister for Sport and howled for Rupert's resignation. Although Rupert was certain left-wing militants were behind the riots and hinted as much in the House, he couldn't prove it yet and the Government won the debate by the narrowest majority. Some of his own side were not displeased by events; Rupert had been the PM's darling for too long. The Cup Final was not until 11th May, but all Rupert's energies were now channelled into seeing the violence wasn't repeated.

He spent most of the next week trying not to lose his temper with the pack of reporters snarling at his heels as he visited the two devastated football clubs, and comforted those who'd been hurt in the riots. As a result, he didn't get down to Penscombe until late Wednesday afternoon, landing the helicopter on the lawn.

He had only been away a week, but already bluebells were flaming like Bunsen burners in his woods, and the crimson glow of the beeches had turned to a rusty terracotta as green leaves burst out of their narrow brown buds. Although brilliant sunshine and blue skies welcomed him, across the valley he could see an April shower tumbling darkly out of a huge purple cloud on to The Priory.

However angry he was, returning to Penscombe always soothed him. He was greeted by messages from Gerald that the two stabbed policemen were now off the danger list and that Cameron Cook had rung three times, leaving a number. Instead of calling her, he had a quick shower and drove over to The Priory where the rain had almost stopped, leaving a heady smell of wet earth and nettles. As he walked through the door, he was greeted by an even headier smell of frying garlic and onions. Taggie must be home, which unconsciously soothed him even more. He'd go and see her when he'd reported in. In the library he found Freddie, Bas and Charles giving a slightly unreceptive Declan tips on how to write the application.

'What a focking awful week you're having,' said Declan. 'You poor bastard. You must feel like Sisyphus.'

'I don't know who he is,' said Rupert, 'but I'm sure I do.'

'Get him a drink, Bas,' said Declan.

'Only Perrier,' said Rupert. 'I've got to fly back and vote after this. How did the first Venturer meeting go?'

The others looked at each other. Was the sun shining through the stained glass window or was Freddie blushing?

'It was somewhat hazardous,' said Declan.

'Did you all fall out?' asked Rupert, taking the Perrier from Bas, and trying to find an inch on one of the window seats that wasn't covered with books and tapes to sit on.

'Charles and Dame Enid did,' said Bas with a grin.

'Shut up,' giggled Charles.

'You tell him, Freddie,' said Declan.

'Well, we all went down to this pub on Salisbury Plain,' said Freddie sheepishly, 'which I could've sworn was always deserted, and we'd just settled into pre-lunch drinks and managed to stop Wesley Emerson offering the Bishop a joint, and got over the fact that Charles, here, turned up dressed as a woman . . .'

'Knowing the IBA's obsession with the fair sex, I thought it fitting,' interrupted Charles demurely.

'. . . when the entire nation's press arrived in three coaches to 'ave a beano before witnessing the launching of a new tank at some army base down the road.'

'Christ,' Rupert started to laugh. 'Did any of them see you?'

'Billy the Kid couldn't have emptied a saloon bar faster,' said Freddie, 'and Charles and Dame Enid got stuck trying to climb out of the Ladies'.'

'It was seriously funny,' said Bas. 'We all hotfooted it back to The Priory for a Chinese takeaway, and the whole thing seemed to bring us closer together. I must say I'd forgotten how stunningly attractive Janey Lloyd-Foxe is.'

'And belongs to Billy,' said Rupert firmly.

Through the window he could see Taggie, who'd gone out into the garden to pick some thyme from the herb garden, gazing in rapture at a rainbow. She had the most adorable bottom, he decided, which became even more adorable when she bent over the flower bed in her jeans.

'Rupert,' said Bas, 'are you still with us?'

'Looking at the rainbow,' said Rupert, hastily opening his briefcase.

'Never knew rainbows were female and five foot ten,' said Bas slyly.

'Fuck off,' said Rupert. 'Anyway, I've got a stunning bit of news to cheer you all up. I've brought you an Easter present, Declan.'

Triumphantly he chucked the two tapes and the photostat of the Corinium application down on Declan's desk.

'What's this?' said Declan, putting on his spectacles.

'Two extraordinarily informative conversations with Cameron Cook, and a photostat of the corrected final draft of Corinium's application.'

Freddie, Bas and Charles were so excited, none of them noticed Declan's look of thunderous disapproval, or that he'd dropped the application as though it was a wasp-infested pear.

'Where did you get that?' asked Freddie in awe.

'I spent the weekend in Madrid and in bed with Cameron.'

Basil's jaw clanged. 'Does my brother know?'

'Tony was due out there,' said Rupert, 'but I arranged for a chum to offer Tony an invite for Saturday night he couldn't refuse.'

Basil started to laugh. 'To meet HRH at Badminton?'

'My God, was that your doing?' said Charles in amazement. 'Tony was boasting about it to everyone.'

'So he stood up Ms Cook,' said Rupert, wandering over to the drinks table and splashing more Perrier into his glass, 'who was not overly delighted until I suddenly appeared on the adjacent balcony like *Private Lives* and took Tony's place.'

'What was she like?' asked Bas, fascinated.

'Fucks like a stoat,' said Rupert. 'In fact the end-away definitely justified the means. Although I had to endure some hellish sightseeing on Sunday before she went off to collect her prize. That was when I got the application photostated.'

'Bloody good,' said Freddie.

'You ought to join the CIA,' said Bas.

'She'll be after your blood, your untainted AIDS-free blood, when she finds out,' said Charles delightedly.

'She won't,' said Rupert. 'She hadn't a clue. Well?' He turned to Declan for approval.

But Declan was looking infinitely more thunderous than the cloud that had drenched The Priory earlier.

'You can't focking do that,' he exploded.

'Why ever not?'

'Because it's bloody dishonest.'

'I must be dreaming,' said Rupert incredulously. 'Declan dear, we're pitching for a business with a hundred-and-twenty-five-million-pound turnover, not playing fucking tiddlywinks. Have a read. You can find out exactly what Tony's up to and pre-empt it. It's the most turgid stuff, much more effective than Mogadon. Tony seems to be promising an unchecked flow of good causes and Elizabethan drama for the next ten years!'

'I'm not going to read it,' said Declan roughly. 'We're playing this thing straight.'

'Now come on, Declan,' protested Freddie. 'Think of the clout it'll give us.'

'Never cast a clout till May is out,' giggled Charles.

'Shut up, Charles,' snapped Declan. Then, turning to Rupert, who was now absolutely shaking with rage, 'I repeat, we're playing it straight.'

'Tony is evil,' hissed Rupert. 'Don't you think he'd do the same thing to you, given the chance? I thought you were out to get him.'

'Not by sinking to his methods,' said Declan coldly.

'Then what are you doing asking the Bishop to lunch, dressing Maud up like a nun and asking him to say Grace?'

'That's different.'

'It is NOT!' Rupert was furiously pacing up and down the floorboards now. 'And what are you doing poaching half Tony's staff? I'm amazed you didn't ring Tony first and ask his permission.'

'That's entirely different,' yelled Declan. 'What you've done is stolen Corinium's property. It's a criminal offence.'

'Isn't Charles Corinium's property?' yelled back Rupert.

'Ooo,' said Charles, looking excited. 'They're fighting over me.'

'Shut up,' screamed Rupert and Declan, both turning on him.

'Charles came of his own volition,' said Declan, 'but Cameron had no idea what you were up to.'

'She certainly enjoyed it,' snarled Rupert. 'Don't you go feeling sorry for her, and Jesus, the hassle I went to, getting that thing photostated. I practically had to bang the receptionist.'

'Never been a hardship for you,' said Declan icily, and, picking up the application and the two tapes, he chucked them into the wastepaper basket. Bas, Freddie and Charles winced. Rupert went very still.

'And if any of you try and retrieve them, I'll put them in the boiler,' added Declan.

'All my life I've been accused of lacking application,' drawled Rupert, 'then when I actually get hold of one . . .'

373

'It's not a joke,' roared Declan.

'I'm not laughing,' said Rupert bleakly. 'Fuck you, Declan, and screw your bloody franchise.'

'Now, wite a minute,' said Freddie, leaping to his feet.

But Rupert had walked out. In the hall he nearly sent Taggie flying. She was carrying a pile of Aertex shirts and green skirts upstairs. Caitlin was going back to school next week.

'What on earth's the matter?' she said in alarm.

'Your fucking father.'

'What's he done? Come into the kitchen.'

'It's what he won't do.' For a second Rupert debated whether to walk out, but he was so angry with Declan he had to tell someone, so he followed her into the kitchen.

'I'll get you a drink.'

'I'm not drinking. And I'll never touch a drop of your father's liquor again.'

'What's happened?' said Taggie, bewildered. Then, realizing the steak and kidney she was frying on the Aga was catching, ran across the kitchen to give it a stir.

'I've just spent all last weekend in Madrid screwing Cameron Cook,' said Rupert furiously, 'to get her on our side, and to get information about Corinium's application, and by Sunday night I not only had her eating out of my hand, but had secretly photostated the entire application.'

He was so angry, he didn't notice that Taggie's wooden spoon had stopped moving.

'What's Daddy objecting to?' said Taggie in a strangely high voice.

'He won't read it. He thinks it's taking unfair advantage. Jesus, no wonder he's broke.'

At that moment Freddie appeared in the doorway. But, seeing Rupert was talking to Taggie, he decided she'd be better at calming him down than any of them and tiptoed back to the library.

'Let me make you a cup of tea,' said Taggie.

By the time the kettle had boiled and the tea had brewed for three minutes, and Rupert had told her the whole story, she'd recovered her composure. After all, Rupert was entitled to go to bed with whom he chose, and perhaps he just did it with Cameron because he wanted to get hold of the application document, she thought hopefully, although Cameron was terribly beautiful and Patrick would be absolutely heartbroken if he found out. Oh God, what a terrible muddle.

Rupert leant against the Aga, looking moodily at a huge vase of bluebells.

'From our wood,' said Taggie, trying to lift the conversation. 'Aren't they lovely?'

Rupert was about to snap that they were from his wood now.

'Don't try to placate me,' he said coldly.

Taggie handed him a cup of tea. Then she took a deep breath. 'I think Daddy's right,' she stammered.

Rupert looked up. 'You what?' he said, unbelievingly. 'Not you, too?'

'He wouldn't feel right with himself. It's like cheating in exams. To most people it wouldn't matter, but he's got such utter integ . . . ' Taggie stumbled over the word.

'Integrity, and I haven't, I suppose.'

'Of course you have, but of a different kind. If you won the franchise because he'd spied on Tony Baddingham, he wouldn't be able to live with himself.'

'Well, he's not living with me any longer. D'you think Tony won't wheel out every trick in the book, once he finds out we're bidding against him? Your father's trying to fight a nuclear war with a pop gun.'

'It's because he disapproves of Lord Baddingham so much. He couldn't descend to his level. That's why he's bidding against him.'

'Not with me, he ain't,' said Rupert, putting down his mug. 'I'm out.'

'Oh please not,' pleaded Taggie. 'It's so lovely for them having you as part of the consortium. You've got such c-c-charisma.'

'Is that your word for the day?' snapped Rupert.

'No, it's my word for always about you,' said Taggie,

blushing crimson. 'Honestly, they think you're marvellous.'

'Funny way of showing it,' said Rupert, walking towards the door.

Taggie ran after him, her eyes filling with tears.

'Oh, please. Daddy really needs you. You and Freddie were so wonderful when he was down, I know he seems terribly clever but he's not street bright like you.'

Gazing at her, Rupert noticed how her tears and the old grey denim shirt of Declan's she was wearing emphasized the strange silver-grey of her eyes.

'Darling Taggie,' he said, his face softening, 'how can anyone refuse you anything?'

'Then you'll stay?'

Rupert shrugged. 'I suppose so . . . but I'm extremely pissed off.' He reached into his pocket and rooted out a crimson leather box. 'I got you an Easter egg in Madrid. I hope you'll like it better than the present I brought your father.'

Inside the box Taggie found a little gold egg, speckled with rubies and diamonds. She gave a gasp.

'Look further,' said Rupert.

Opening the egg, she found a tiny gold bird with ruby eyes.

'Poor thing's got conjuctivitis,' said Rupert.

'I can't believe it,' breathed Taggie. 'No one brings me presents like that. Oh thank you so so much. I love it.'

Blushing furiously again, she leant forward and kissed him on the cheek. She's the little sister I never had, Rupert told himself firmly.

'Your steak and kidney's burning,' he said.

'Are you staying for supper?'

'No, I've got to go back and vote.'

'What on?'

'Capital punishment for terrorists.'

Taggie looked horrified.

'They're not going to bring it back, are they? Daddy'd leave the country.'

In the library Freddie was tearing a strip off Declan. 'This is the big league, if you'll excuse me saying so. Rupert's a very

376

clever operator, and we can't afford to lose 'im. You've got to learn to argue wivout rancour, Declan. You can't stick your chest out all the time.'

'What do you know about it?' growled Declan.

'I've never 'ad a strike at work,' said Freddie, 'because I don't judge everyone the same. I cultivate their individual skills. You're always bangin' on about giving creative people the right atmosphere to work in. Then, when Rupert does somefink really creative, you shit on 'im.'

Watched in awed amazement by Bas and Charles, Freddie calmly retrieved the application from the wastepaper basket.

Declan gazed at him appalled: 'But, it's dishonest, for fock's sake. You wouldn't have nicked that document, would you?'

'Wouldn't 'ave 'ad the nerve,' said Freddie. 'But now we've got it, I'm certainly goin' to 'ave a little look. This is war, as Rupert said, not tiddlywinks. You don't want to be too 'igh-minded, Declan.'

By the time Sydney his driver had dropped Rupert off at Westminster, the yellow stone of the House was softened by floodlighting and Big Ben shone like a great sugar sifter against an inky blue sky.

'Only one vote,' Rupert told Sydney. 'I'm paired after that, but I've got a hell of a lot of work still to do. Can you come back about twelve-thirty?'

Nodding good evening to the policeman on the gate, Rupert went through the Member's entrance, an expression that usually made him laugh. Glancing at the monitor he saw that Owen Davies, the Labour leader, was winding up for the abolitionists. Time for a large drink . . . he was bloody tired, and he'd never had any doubts that stringing up was the answer for terrorists. But as he headed for the bar he thought fleetingly of Taggie's horror of capital punishment, and Declan's passionate disapproval, and decided to listen to the debate instead.

As he entered the chamber the Ministers of Employment and of Health moved slightly apart to make room for him on the green leather front bench.

'Owen's in barnstorming form,' whispered the Minister of Health.

Hearing a din behind him, Rupert glanced round to see Paul Stratton, who was violently pro-hanging for everything, particularly wife-pinching, looking excited for the first time in months.

'Rubbish,' Paul yelled. 'Resign, check your figures. What's the point of having British soldiers out there if we don't support them?'

Owen Davies, a brilliant orator on the dullest subject, was on magnificent form tonight. What about all those people who'd been imprisoned for terrorism, he demanded, who'd later been found innocent? How much more terrible if they'd been hanged. What evidence was there in any country that the death penalty curbed terrorism, and, conversely, didn't hanging make sainted martyrs out of the most vicious thugs?

It was great emotional stuff. But, putting aside the soft cadences, the eloquence, the Welsh voice, Rupert suddenly knew Owen was right. Every moment you could feel the spirits of the Anti-Hanging lobby rising. The Bring-Back brigade looked turned to stone. The Prime Minister, who was almost more pro-hanging than Paul Stratton, looked most bootfaced of all. Owen Davies sat down to a storm of applause.

Scenting blood, the abolitionists roared for the PM to get up. 'On your feet. Don't be bashful.'

But the PM wasn't budging. Instead, she let the Home Secretary, who was decidedly ambivalent about the merits of hanging anyway, wind up. Every time he opened his mouth, he was howled down, but he ploughed on bravely with his prepared speech, careful not to emphasize that terrorism was on the increase, but droning on about deterrents and the need to support the forces of law and order. As ten o'clock approached, the abolitionists worked themselves into the kind of frenzy only seen at Cardiff Arms Park when there's two minutes to go and the Welsh are just in the lead. Then, as Big Ben tolled ten o'clock, the noise subsided and the house divided.

The Ayes, looking tight-lipped and apprehensive, shuffled to the right. The Noes, looking elated, sauntered to the left. Without a moment's deliberation, ignoring the outraged looks of the PM, the Chief Whip and most of the Front Bench, Rupert joined the Noes. Owen Davies, turning in delighted amazement, tapped Rupert on the shoulder. 'I didn't know you were one of us.'

'I wasn't until I heard you,' said Rupert.

The Minister of Health, a pacific and gentle soul, also joined the Noes.

'We'll be on the carpet tomorrow,' he said.

'She'll have to call an election any minute,' said Rupert.

'An even tenner on 10th June,' said the Minister of Health.

'Done,' said Rupert.

Feeling suddenly shattered and not wanting a bollocking from the PM, Rupert beat a quick retreat to his office, a small room on the lower Minister's floor. Inside, the walls were covered with signed photographs of famous athletes: Pat Eddery, Ian Botham, Maradona, John McEnroe, Pat Cash, Gary Lineker, Dino and Fenella Ferranti, to name only a few. Above the filing cabinet was a picture of Wesley Emerson, the local cricketing hero who had joined the Venturer consortium, and who Rupert had saved from getting busted.

'Thanks, Rupe, Wesley Emerson,' he had scrawled in black pentel across the blue sky behind him.

I should think so too, reflected Rupert whenever he looked at the photo.

Having taken off his tie, and undone his top button, he poured himself a large whisky and soda. Christ, he was tired. He'd been on the go since five that morning and hadn't had any real sleep for a week. Making him feel even more tired was the red box full of work, the buff envelope on the blotter full of constituency letters to be signed, and the even bigger pile of mail to be read, which was probably mostly abusive letters about the football riots.

The admirable Gerald had scribbled a note: '*Gone to* Madam Butterfly. *Back about one-thirty. Ring if you need me.*'

In the corner of the room was a hard olive-green sofa, where Rupert was supposed to snatch some sleep during late-night sittings. It had never looked more seductive. If he had an hour's kip, he might work better. He had another six o'clock start in the morning. The telephone ringing made him jump.

'Rupert, it's Cameron.'

Christ, he'd completely forgotten to ring her back.

'Angel! You got home safely?'

'Well, I'm not lying in a pile of wreckage at the bottom of the Bay of Biscay.' All the insecurity and truculence had returned to her voice. It must have cost her a lot to ring.

'I'm sorry I didn't ring back. It's been frantic, and I didn't want to tread on Tony's bunions. When am I going to see you?' He suppressed a yawn.

'Christ knows,' snapped Cameron. 'Tony's taking me away for the weekend.'

'To Buckingham Palace?'

Cameron didn't laugh. 'To LA, to close a couple of deals over Easter. Then we fly straight to Cannes to meet with our various co-production partners and firm up existing relationships. I won't be back till Monday week.'

Rupert glanced at the calendar. Monday week was 22nd April. He'd be away until the 26th and the franchises had to be in on the 29th. That would give him hardly any time after she got back to persuade her to join Venturer. He ought to establish interim ascendancy over Tony by seeing her this evening.

'Where are you?' he asked.

'At home.'

'Alone?'

'Yes.'

'I'll drive down.'

'Are you crazy? D'you know what time it is?' But it was impossible for her to keep the elation out of her voice.

'I've got at least an hour's work,' said Rupert. 'The drive at this time of night should take an hour and a half. I can't afford to get done for speeding. I'll be with you about two.'

Thank God, he'd had a shower and changed at Penscombe earlier in the evening; it seemed a thousand years ago. He trusted Sydney, but not entirely, so he dismissed him and took the Ferrari, which was parked outside his Westminster flat. Torrential rain on the motorway gave way to moonlight as he reached the outskirts of Cotchester. The cathedral clock was tolling the hour; the shadow of the spire lay thick and black across the watermeadows. He was so tired he'd never be able to get it up.

Cameron, however, opened the front door with nothing on.

'I might have been the milkman,' said Rupert reprovingly.

'You're not that late,' she whispered.

As her warm, oiled and scented body twined round him, she was obviously so delighted to see him that miraculously Rupert woke up.

Bounding upstairs after her, he decided this was one relationship he would have absolutely no difficulty firming up.

RIVALS
29

Although Cameron was kept ludicrously busy selling herself and Corinium's programmes, she was shattered by how much she missed Rupert. LA was bad enough, but Cannes seemed so tantalizingly near. Every minute on the Corinium stand or on the front, or at the numerous parties, or in her hotel bedroom, conveniently next to Tony's, she expected Rupert to appear grinning like a Cheshire cat.

On her second Thursday away from him, however, her black mood was caused by rage rather than longing. One of Tony's myriad subsidiary companies, Falconry Films Inc., had made a lousy mini-series called 'Stowaway', about an aristocratic orphan who disguised herself as a cabin boy on a clipper ship and got off with the pirate captain. And now Tony had actually sailed a real clipper ship, at vast expense, into Cannes Harbour as a publicity stunt and was holding a huge bash on board. Sourly watching all the fatcat international buyers and their bikinied bimbos stuffing their faces with champagne and caviare, Cameron felt they were guzzling all the profits she'd made Corinium from 'Four Men went to Mow'.

The Mediterranean suited Tony; his olive skin had already turned mahogany. As he purred round the clipper ship in his dark glasses and discreetly coroneted black shirt, clinching deals and pinching bottoms, he looked more like a pirate king than ever.

Cameron had had plenty of time to compare Tony with Rupert while she was away. Both were reputed to be absolute shits. But, while Tony was coldly sensual, utterly venal, eaten up with envy and sadistically dedicated to putting people down, Rupert, Cameron felt, was only sharp-tongued because he was arrogant and easily bored. Apart from the day they went to Toledo, when he'd been reminded too much of Helen (which showed he was capable of deep feeling), he had been angelic and really interested not only in her as a woman, but in her career, and her programmes. She had been so touched that he'd driven all the way down to Cotchester on that last night, and that after he'd made love to her he hadn't fallen asleep as most men would, but stayed awake pestering her with questions about what she and Tony would be doing and selling in LA and Cannes.

It was a relief too that he couldn't call her, so she didn't go through the roof with expectation every time the telephone rang. Instead, at grave risk, she'd rung him twice from LA and every day from Cannes.

There was no doubt, too, that she was the flavour of the month at the festival. The third series of 'Four Men went to Mow' had already been pre-sold world wide. The Corinium publicity department had taken a full page advertisement in *Broadcast* that week, with a stunning photograph of Cameron holding a baby lamb, with the caption: '*Cameron Cook works for Corinium, meet her on stand 329*', then listing all the prizes she'd won in the last year. Everyone wanted to congratulate her and offer her work.

Back at The Priory, Declan was still working on the Venturer application, only pausing occasionally to pick up the binoculars on the window seat to check on some newly-arrived migrant bird; swallows, housemartins, whitethroats were all winging in now. Last night he had even heard the first nightingale in the wood.

'Our duty,' wrote Declan, 'is to tell the truth, to be relevant, entertaining and interesting, to monitor power and expose its abuse, to be nobody's mouthpiece.'

Christ, it was difficult not to use clichés, to be concise: *To bring the balloon of the mind that bellies and drags in the wind*, as Yeats had so perfectly put it, *into its narrow shed.*

'We will give the area a nationally recognized television identity,' he wrote. 'This we feel Corinium has failed to do. In their last application they promised to provide a new studio, a new youth orchestra, a trust fund for the arts and sciences, adequate training schemes and worker participation at board level. This they have failed to do.

'They also promised that fifty per cent of their profits after tax would go to shareholders, and the rest would be ploughed back into making programmes. This they have also failed to do.'

He was about to tackle Venturer's programme plans, when Gertrude leapt barking off the sofa, scattering papers, as Rupert and Freddie walked in.

'Christ, you're a slut, Declan,' said Rupert, looking round at the files, tapes, coffee cups and overflowing ashtrays that covered every available inch of space. 'Why don't you let Taggie tidy up a bit?'

'I'm superstitious,' grumbled Declan. 'I never tidy up between books in case I throw pages away.'

Rupert threw a copy of *Broadcast*, open at Cameron's advertisement, down on Declan's desk. 'We must have her for Venturer.'

'She's riding far too high to be interested in us,' said Declan quickly.

'She's not. She's really pissed off,' said Rupert. 'She was on to me from Cannes only half an hour ago grumbling that Tony'd blued forty-five grand hiring a boat to promote some crappy mini series not even made by Corinium.'

'We need some 'eavy-weight ladies,' said Freddie, moving the binoculars and sitting on the window seat.

'Think how useful Cameron would be for the rest of the year as a mole in the Corinium camp,' said Rupert.

'We've got Georgie and Seb and Charles,' protested Declan.

'None of them sleep with Tony,' persisted Rupert. 'We can use her to manipulate him.'

384

'More likely Tony'll use her to manipulate you.'

'No one manipulates me,' said Rupert haughtily. 'I don't mean to sound conceited, but I do know when a woman's absolutely mad about me.'

'You do sound conceited,' snapped Declan. 'She may be mad about you at the moment, but it's a long, long time from May to December, and if you get bored or start playing her up she'll bolt straight back to Tony with all our secrets.'

'Look,' said Rupert patiently, 'she's Tony's only trump card. If the IBA know from the start she's with us, it'll totally discredit him.'

'It's a risk wurf taking,' said Freddie. 'We needn't tell her too much.'

'I've got to tell her anyway,' said Rupert flatly. 'If she reads that we're pitching for the franchise in the press on Tuesday morning, she'll never forgive me and there'll be no hope of ever getting her.'

Declan shook his head. 'I want it to go on record,' he said grimly, 'that I utterly deplore the idea of using her as a mole. It's unethical and dangerous. Nor is Cameron going to be very pleased when you tell her what you've been up to already.'

Freddie scratched his curls. 'I 'aven't told Valerie yet,' he confessed. 'Been putting it off. Don't fink she'll be very pleased either.'

Valerie, in fact, was absolutely livid. Having studied her very good friend Monica Baddingham's behaviour, Valerie had decided it was upper class to be keen on gardening and she must therefore channel more of her energy into transforming Green Lawns into an absolute paradise. Wearing new gardening gloves and a tan scarf tied at the back of her very clean neck to keep her curls neat, and kneeling on a new green rubber mat, Valerie was now tackling her favourite spot, the mauve and pink garden. Fat mauve clumps of aubretia fell over the walls, candy-pink double cherries danced in the breeze above serried ranks of mauve and pink tulips. Such a pity, sighed Valerie, that none of them would be out for her

Opening in July. And then Freddie had to drop this disgusting bombshell about the franchise.

'We can't do that to Monica and Tony,' she shrieked. 'It's so unsupportive. Ay'll never hold my head up high on the Distressed Gentlefolk's Committee. Who else is behind it?'

Freddie took a deep breath: 'Declan O'Hara.'

Valerie was so cross she weeded up a purple tulip. 'That drunk – he's practically IRA, and Sharon nearly got raped at their New Year's Eve party.'

'And Rupert,' said Freddie, quailing.

'Rupert,' screamed Valerie, as purple now as the tulip she was trying to force back into the earth. 'He's a bounder. No female is safe. The evil way I saw him looking at Sharon's legs when she was wearing her tennis shorts the other day. Even worse, I found a snap-shot of him in her brassière drawer yesterday. And both Declan and Rupert are enemies of poor Tony,' said Valerie. 'Monica will be outraged.'

Like a small boy plunging into icy water, Freddie battled on: 'And Marti Gluckstein and Bas.'

'Both crooks.'

'And Arfur Smiff.'

'Common little man and a leftie,' sniffed Valerie.

'Professor Graystock and Wesley Emerson.'

'A black man,' said Valerie, incensed. 'His wife's black too. She might start poppin' into the boutique.'

'And Dame Enid.'

Valerie stamped her foot. 'That disgusting old lezzie, with Sharon in her teens. Frederick Jones, have you taken leave of your senses! You must have been plottin' this for weeks. Ay insist you drop out.'

'And Henry Hampshire and Hubert Brenton,' said Freddie.

'And what's more . . .' screamed Valerie, then stopped in her tracks as the names registered.

'Who did you say?'

Freddie repeated the last two names.

'Not *the* Lord-Lieutenant, and *the* Bishop of Cotchester?'

'Yup,' said Freddie grinning.

Dropping her trowel, Valerie leapt to her feet.

386

'Well, that does put a different laight on things. If anyone can keep Rupert in order, they can. I haven't met the Bishop's waife, but Hermione Hampshire is charming. When can I tell everyone?'

'Any time after Monday lunchtime.'

Back from Cannes, Cameron plunged into the first five days of shooting 'Four Men went to Mow'. Rupert was abroad, smoothing the path for the next World Cup in South America and playing in a Pro-Am tennis tournament to raise money for the Olympic fund, so he and Cameron didn't meet up until late on Friday.

Cameron always drove too fast. Fortunately there was little traffic on the road that Friday night as she scorched round corners and shot crossroads in her frenzy to reach Rupert. Hardly a light was on in Penscombe village, but huge, quivering stars and a full moon lit her path. The chestnuts lining Rupert's drive had reached a perfect pitch of pale greenness to welcome her. And as she screeched to a halt in front of the house, her headlights flood-lit a big white magnolia in full flower on the edge of the lawn – a thing of such unearthly incandescent beauty Cameron just gazed and gazed. I want to marry Rupert, she thought, and be as beautiful a bride as that tree.

The next moment the front door opened and the pack of dogs swarmed round the car, wagging and barking. She didn't even mind their paws scrabbling the paintwork. Rupert followed them, blond hair silver in the moonlight. Wearing a clean pink-and-white-striped shirt, reeking of expensive cologne, he had obviously just bathed and cleaned his teeth. Holding his arms out he swept her off the ground above the tidal wave of dogs.

'But they're lovely,' she cried as he put her down in the hall, and, kneeling, she hugged the dogs as they surged forward, shoving, nudging and licking her bare arms and legs in welcome.

'How strange and how nice,' said Rupert, leading her into the drawing-room. 'I never imagined you'd like dogs.'

There was a bottle of Dom Perignon on ice, which Rupert immediately opened, and a huge plate of smoked salmon and some buttered wholemeal rolls on the table.

'After a long hard day, I don't believe in screwing on an empty stomach,' said Rupert, 'and I'm certainly going to give you a long hard night.'

Cameron moved up behind him, fingering the powerful shoulders, feeling the thrust of the muscular buttocks against her belly, melting against him with lust.

'How are things at Fort Knocks-off?' asked Rupert.

Cameron shook her head. 'I feel like a mole.'

Rupert nearly spilled the champagne he was pouring. 'How d'you mean?'

'If you'd been stuck in a studio for twelve hours, you'd worry you'd never see the light again.'

'Oh, I see,' said Rupert, relieved. 'And you've got over Cannes?'

'Almost.' Cameron took a great slug of champagne. 'That's better. D'you know, I was approached by five different groups to join their consortiums?'

'Very flattering,' said Rupert, piling smoked salmon onto a roll and handing it to her. 'Anyone interesting?'

'Not bad. Unfortunately they're all pitching against companies like Granada and Yorkshire, who are virtually impregnable, and if Tony got a sniff of it, I'd be out on my ear.'

'How is he?' Rupert filled up her glass.

'Appallingly twitchy. Someone leaked the story of the clipper ship to Dempster, doubling the cost of the party.'

'Press always get things wrong,' said Rupert blandly. It was he who had fed the story. He examined his glass of whisky. 'Has the Corinium application gone in?' he asked idly.

'Yes, thank God,' said Cameron, who was shaking hands with one of the Springer spaniels. 'Tony's handing it in to the IBA tomorrow morning.'

Rupert heaved a sigh of relief. If Cameron flipped when he told her about Venturer later tomorrow, at least it would be too late for her to alter Corinium's application.

388

Slowly Cameron was taking in the beauty of the room, registering the Romney, the Gainsborough, the Stubbs and the Lely on the pale-yellow walls. Determined not to be impressed, she asked almost too aggressively, 'How can you possibly live on your own in this great barn?'

'I don't,' said Rupert. 'I've got Mr and Mrs Bodkin who look after me, and the children are often here at weekends, and there's – er – usually a house guest.'

I asked for that, thought Cameron, biting her lip.

'Don't worry.' Rupert read her thoughts. 'In order not to besmirch the memory of our last blessed encounter, I've been holding my own ever since. I suppose you've been sating yourself on Lord B?'

'Much less than before,' said Cameron quickly.

The grandfather clock struck midnight.

'D'you know what day it is now?' asked Rupert.

'1st May,' said Cameron, glancing at her Rolex.

'D'you know our local poem?' said Rupert, grinning and putting on a Gloucestershire accent:

> First of May, first of May,
> Outdoor fucking starts today.
> But as usual it do rain.
> So we fucks off indoors again.

As he moved towards her he stopped, smiling. 'Will it be too cold for you outside?'

'Not if you keep me warm,' whispered Cameron.

Outside under the moonlit magnolia he took off her clothes, slowly kissing her all over where each garment had been, until she was squirming and helpless with desire. She could feel the dew-drenched lawn under her back. Rupert's cock was really incredible. As he slid inside her, she felt all the amazed joy of a canal lock suddenly finding it can accommodate the QE2.

When she made love to Tony, she always shut her eyes. She didn't want to see the uncharacteristically untidy hair, the bulging eyes, the clenched teeth, the veins knotting on his forehead as he came. She liked him sleek and in control. With Rupert she kept her eyes open all the time because he was the stuff of fantasy, and because she didn't want to miss a second.

Deciding the ground was too hard for her, he later insisted she went on top.

'You're so beautiful,' he said, watching her transported maenad face, ghostly in the moonlight.

Lousy at accepting compliments, Cameron had to joke. 'Didn't your mother tell you off for lying on the grass?'

'I'm not lying,' said Rupert, arching his back up into her. 'I'm telling the truth.'

As Cameron opened, so did the heavens.

'But as usual it do rain,' murmured Rupert, moving in and out of her. 'D'you want to fuck off inside again?'

'Not for ages,' gasped Cameron. 'At least it'll wash off the sweat.'

She woke in Rupert's huge Jacobean four-poster to find him gone and a note beside the bed saying he was doing a morning surgery at his constituency and would be back around lunchtime.

Looking round the beautiful room with its peachy walls, corn-coloured carpet, yellow-and-pink-striped silk curtains on the four-poster and at the windows, and rose-pink silk *chaise-longue*, Cameron felt she was waking in the middle of a sunrise. It was an incredibly feminine room for a man. Then she remembered the pale-blue hall and the pale-yellow drawing-room, and decided it must all be Helen's taste. On the dressing table, amid Rupert's clutter of betting slips, silver-backed brushes, cigar packets and loose change, were photographs of his children. The girl, exactly like Rupert, had the same arrogant blue-eyed stare; the boy had very dark red hair and large dark wary eyes. Having met Rupert's pack last night, Cameron felt seven step-dogs might be an easier proposition to take on than two step-children. Helen must have been spectacular to produce kids like that. Mad on sight-seeing, she was plainly a sight herself.

Outside, through a frame of rampant, budding clematis, lay the valley, pale green except for the occasional wild cherry tree in flower, or the blackthorn breaking in white waves over the hedgerows. From an ash grove by the lake she could hear the haunting, sweet cry of the cuckoo. How could Helen have walked out on such a view and such a man?

Having showered and dressed, Cameron went downstairs. The dogs lying in the hall thumped their tails and followed her into the kitchen. There the housekeeper, Mrs Bodkin, was friendly but unfazed by her presence. Perhaps, like people in trains, she could afford to be friendly, knowing Cameron wouldn't be in situ for long. She mustn't get jealous and paranoid. Tony was turned on by rows. Rupert, she suspected, would be bored, and walk away from them.

She took some orange juice and coffee out onto the terrace. That must be Declan's house across the valley, still just visible through the thickening beech wood.

She wondered what he'd been up to since his fall from grace. How strange that on 1st January with Patrick she'd looked across at Rupert's house and thought, What a kingdom, and now, four months later, here she was.

She stopped only briefly to glance at the library and the first editions, which could be examined at length on a less lovely morning, then set out with the dogs to explore. There was a wonderful untamed beauty, rather like Maud O'Hara, about the garden. Green leaves were uncurling on the tangled old roses, the peacocks and crowing cocks once clipped out of the yew hedges were looking distinctly shaggy. The swimming-pool was full of leaves, the beech hedge round the tennis court was in need of a cut, the lawns dotted with daisies were still lit along the edges by pools of dying daffodils. Rupert and this place need a woman, thought Cameron, to cherish and sort them out.

The stables, on the other hand, were immaculate, and filled with beautiful, well-muscled horses. More horses were out in the fields. The girl grooms treated Cameron with the same we've-seen-them-all-come-and-go politeness displayed by Mrs Bodkin.

I'll show them, thought Cameron, as she set out through the beech woods. I'm the one who's going to hang in.

The ground was still carpeted with bluebells. Only when she pressed her face close could she distinguish their faint sweet hyacinth scent from the rank sexy stench of the wild garlic. The dogs charged ahead, but the shaggy lurcher called Blue kept bounding back solicitously to check she was all right, shoving his wet nose in her hand, giving her a token lick. It was all so beautiful; she had never felt so happy or so right anywhere.

She had wandered for a mile or two when suddenly she breathed in a sticky, sweet familiar scent that made her tremble. Ahead, a copse of poplars, rising like flaming amber swords, was wafting balsam down the woodland ride towards her, evoking the times she used to inhale Friar's Balsam under a towel as a child, reminding her all too violently of her mother and Mike. Instantly her euphoria evaporated. She glanced at her watch. It was half past twelve. She must get back. Grey clouds were creeping over the sun; it had become much cooler. She even felt a spot of rain. As she dropped down the wood towards the house an owl hooted. Surely it shouldn't hoot at midday? Through the trees she could see the lake grey and blank now as a smudged mirror, and as she reached the big lawn she gave a moan of horror. Last night's deluge had stripped all the petals from the magnolia, scattering them over the grass. Last night's bride was naked now.

The dogs converged, barking, as a car drew up at the front door. Cameron hoped it was Rupert, but it turned out to be a youth delivering some boxes of T-shirts, who gazed at Cameron in admiration.

'This is the first lot. Mr C-B wanted them in a hurry,' he said. 'Tell him the stickers, the posters and the badges'll be ready by Monday.'

Cameron couldn't resist having a look. The T-shirts were a beautiful cerulean blue, with a dark bronze drawing of a boy shading his forehead on the front and the words *Support Venturer* on the front and the back. They must be for some sporting event. Taking one upstairs, Cameron stripped off and put it on. It fell just below her bush. Suddenly feeling incredibly randy, she hoped Rupert hadn't got anything planned for the afternoon. As it was much colder, she shut the window, trapping a tendril of clematis which was already wilting and bruised from being trapped on previous occasions. Trying to insinuate its way into Rupert's bedroom, like her and every other woman, thought Cameron wryly.

Next minute the front door banged. Very slowly she walked downstairs. Rupert was looking at the boxes in the hall.

'They're great,' she said. 'Can I keep one?'

Rupert glanced up and froze for a second.

'Hullo, angel. Did you sleep well?'

'So well,' murmured Cameron seductively, 'that I'm ready to be exhausted again.' She lifted the T-shirt to show him her bush. Then, when he didn't react as she'd expected and come bounding up the stairs, she said, 'What is Venturer, anyway?'

Rupert's eyes seemed to have gone a darker, more opaque shade of blue and lost all their sparkle. 'Come and have a drink,' he said.

Disappointed, Cameron followed him into the drawing-room. Suddenly he seemed incredibly tense and, when she refused a drink, poured himself two fingers of neat whisky and drank it in one gulp. Then he pulled her down on to the sofa beside him.

'Look, sweetheart, this is a bit difficult, but there's something I've got to tell you.'

Cameron went white. Suddenly in that baggy T-shirt, she looked as fragile, pale and defenceless as one of the anemones that strewed the paths of Rupert's woods.

'You want to pack me in?' she whispered.

'No, no, quite the reverse.' Very gently he smoothed a tendril of dark hair behind her ear and stroked her rigid, quivering cheek.

'But you may want to pack me in. Freddie Jones, Declan and I are pitching for the Corinium franchise. We've called ourselves Venturer.'

At first she was so relieved that he wasn't trying to end the relationship she couldn't think straight.

'You and Declan? How long has this been going on?'

'Since the day after Declan walked out.'

'So turning up in Madrid wasn't only to see a football match?'

'No.'

'Or showing such interest in my career and the goings on at Corinium?'

'No.'

'Did you read the application in my briefcase?'

'I photostated it.'

She was trembling violently now and her lips were quite white.

'Don't worry,' he reassured her. 'Declan was so appalled by my skulduggery he refused to read it; so we haven't pinched anything.'

'And I suppose you arranged those riots as an excuse to fly straight home once you'd got what you wanted?'

'Uh-uh,' protested Rupert. 'Two stabbed cops, twenty-five people injured and a burnt-down stand is going too far even for me.'

'But driving down to see me before I flew out to LA and all those questions you asked me? Did you give that "Stowaway" story to Dempster?'

Rupert nodded. Truth, however devastating, was the only answer now.

'And, Christ, how much have I already told you this weekend?' whispered Cameron, looking at her watch. 'And our application's already gone in.'

Rupert had expected rage, tantrums, having his face clawed, but not this numb state of shock.

'I trusted you,' she said slowly. 'You're the first person I've trusted since I was fourteen. I thought you were so caring, you bloody Judas. This is the worst thing that's ever happened to me.'

'It isn't as awful as it seems,' said Rupert soothingly. 'I thought you were the sexiest thing on two legs the moment

I saw you. Didn't I offer you a lift home after Valerie's dinner party? I would have moved in both at Declan's party, if young Patrick hadn't been making the running, and at Corinium, if Tony hadn't been hanging about. If I hadn't fancied you to death, I'd never have bothered coming out to Madrid. I wanted to level with you but I didn't know how you'd react. We couldn't afford to let you rush back to Tony and tell him everything, in case he exoceted our bid before it got off the ground.'

Cameron leapt to her feet, tugging down the T-shirt. 'And I figured you were really interested in me. What a joke. I know how Declan detests me. He must have cracked up, and I suppose Patrick and that dumbass Taggie were in on it too. Christ, you must have been all laughing yourselves sick.'

She was crying now – angry, agonized rasping tears, and Rupert suddenly appreciated her terrible insecurity, her paranoia, her vulnerability and her terror; for the first time his heart was truly touched by her. Getting up, he tried to take her in his arms and comfort her.

'Angel, you've got it wrong. No one's laughing at you. I want you, I absolutely adore you. We all want you to join Venturer. We were just picking our moment. We've got an absolutely alpha line-up, but you'd be the jewel in our crown, and you'd be totally free to make the programmes you wanted.'

'Get out of my way!' screamed Cameron. 'I hate you! I never want to see you again!' And, diving under his outstretched arms, she bolted out of the door.

Rupert had never felt such a shit in his life. She'll have to get her clothes and her suitcase from upstairs, he thought; I can cut her off on her way downstairs. But Cameron shot straight out of the front door, and next moment he heard the wheels of the Lotus crunching on the gravel. Tony was probably still on his way down from London and Cameron couldn't rage round to The Falconry in nothing but that T-shirt, but she'd be on to him on the telephone in a flash. The early-warning system had gone off. It was just a matter of time before the H-bomb landed.

RIVALS
30

All over the country on Sunday, 2nd May, the independent companies and those consortiums who sought to oust them were assembling, colour-coding and ring-binding forty copies of their application document on A4 paper – complete with attached confidential material – to be delivered to the IBA headquarters in Brompton Road by noon the following day.

Corinium, to be on the safe side, had submitted their application the day before. Venturer, who were pushed for time, spent a wildly exciting Sunday at Freddie's house in Holland Park knocking their final draft into shape.

Everyone agreed that Declan had done a masterly job. But Freddie and Marti Gluckstein, who arrived looking like a costive lizard, felt Declan's bald and somewhat arrogant claim that 'We can find £15 million; just ring Henriques Bros' was inadequate, and were therefore considerably extending the financial section. Freddie and Lord Smith were going through the technical specifications with a toothcomb, while Harold White, Janey Lloyd-Foxe, Charles Fairburn, Dame Enid and Professor Graystock were having fun jazzing up the programme content.

Bas, having provided architects' plans for the conversion of Cotchester House into studios and offices should Tony turn nasty, was now playing chemmy with Henry Hampshire, the Lord-Lieutenant, who hadn't spent a Sunday in London for twenty-five years, and with Wesley Emerson, who had nothing really to add to the bid except his illustrious presence. The Bishop was driving up to London immediately after Evensong. Maud, who'd come for the ride, was playing the piano. Upstairs, Ursula and Freddie's secretary were frantically typing and re-typing drafts and then running okayed pages off on the word processor.

Taggie was in the kitchen. She had given everyone pâté and cheese for lunch, and was now making chicken Estragon for the celebration dinner. Four plump boiling chickens, carrots and onions were already simmering in a huge pan on the Aga. There was an extremely complicated and hazardous sauce to be made later, involving egg yolks, cream and lemon juice which might easily curdle. But at least having tramped the length of Notting Hill Gate that morning, she'd found some fresh tarragon.

From the next-door room she could hear screams of laughter.

'We must do a series on local studs called "Dongs of Praise",' Janey Lloyd-Foxe was saying. 'We can start off with Rupert; then we won't have to pay him a fee.'

'Rupert'd screw a fee out of us anyway,' said Charles.

'Well, the programme's about screwing,' said Janey.

Janey was absolutely gorgeous, thought Taggie. Rupert had said she was nearly forty, but, except for the fine pencilling of lines round her wicked dark brown eyes, you'd never have known it. Poor Billy, her husband, was abroad covering the Paris Tennis Tournament for the BBC, and Janey had turned up with the most adorable baby, who was so fat, smiling and gurgling that even the men wanted to hold her. And Janey was so blonde and beautiful, and had such wonderful brown breasts after a week in Portugal, that no one minded her breast-feeding at all.

'I've got a terrific idea for a game show,' Janey was now saying. 'You have a panel and they have to guess who the celebrity is by interviewing the cleaners who work for them. We call it "Daily Daily". Mrs Makepiece can give us some wonderful stories about James Vereker, and Mrs Bodkin would be riveting about Rupert's goings on. Mrs Bodkin used to work for us,' continued Janey, shifting the baby to her right breast. 'The first time we got a cordless telephone she found it in our bed and, assuming it was some auto-erotic device, discreetly hid it in my pants' drawer. Then, when it started ringing, Billy, who was expecting some summons to jump for Britain, went frantic trying to find it.'

Everyone screamed with laughter.

'Don't you think it's a brilliant idea, Declan?'

'No,' said Declan, who already adored Janey. 'The IBA would think it otterly ondemocratic.'

'Well, what about an English "Dallas", wife-swapping in the Royal triangle?' said Janey.

'Later,' said Declan, 'when we've got the franchise.'

They were all so bright and clever, thought Taggie wistfully. She had contributed nothing. 'An army marches on its stomach,' Declan was fond of telling her, but she was sure that everyone would have been just as happy with an Indian takeaway this evening and that her father had only suggested she did the food in order to involve her.

In the house opposite, a lot of young people were sprawled on the drawing-room carpet drinking red wine and reading the Sunday papers. It all came back to reading, thought Taggie despairingly. If she didn't keep at it, she'd lose the ability more and more, like not talking French. She *must* try harder.

She pored over the Estragon recipe in the book, but half the words were in French. Embarrassed at having to resort to a tape recorder she shut the door, so no one could hear.

She was worried about Rupert too. He'd been edgy and refused to eat anything when he'd popped in earlier, then furious because he'd forgotten to bring up the T-shirts. He'd also taken an instant dislike to Professor Graystock, whom he hadn't met before, and who had black straggly hair, like a jumble-sale crone, a wet, sensual mouth and a pale, waxy, formless face.

'Who's he in mourning for?' Rupert asked Taggie in horror.

'No one, I don't think.'

'Must be. Look at his fingernails and the inside of his collar.'

Then Rupert had pushed off, promising he and the T-shirts would be back later. Taggie was sure he didn't look after himself properly. If she made the chicken particularly nice, he might eat something this evening.

At eight o'clock the first bottle of Bollinger was cracked as they waited for the final draft to be ready. Declan had just re-written the last page to give the whole thing a uniformity of style. Ursula and Freddie's secretary were busy collating everything and Freddie and Declan were now folding up the confidential memos listing Harold White, Georgie Baines, Charles, Seb and Billy as Heads of various departments and putting these memos into envelopes.

'Pity we can't add Cameron Cook,' sighed Freddie.

'Rupert would have rung by now if he had anything to report,' said Declan, who preferred it that way.

Dame Enid and Maud, both well away, were now playing duets. The Lord-Lieutenant had lost so much money to Bas he'd probably have to sell another Pre-Raphaelite, but he couldn't have enjoyed himself more. There were so many pretty women to gaze at, and they were all such splendid chaps, and Rupert had promised he should meet Joanna Lumley very soon.

Janey, who was well stuck into the Bollinger, was breast-feeding again.

'Mother and child – a lovely sight,' said the Bishop who'd just arrived.

'So much prettier than Deirdre Kill-Programme and her disgusting brat,' said Georgie Baines to Seb Burrows.

'Please,' said Charles Fairburn faintly.

'That baby's drinking neat Bollinger,' said Bas. 'That's why it's so cheerful.'

'I hope all our burn money isn't being squandered on bubbly,' said Professor Graystock, who was on his fourth glass.

'It isn't,' said Taggie quickly. 'Rupert's paid for all of it.'

Helped by Seb, she was now putting out big plates of

chicken Estragon and rice salad. She'd worried herself sick that the sauce had gone wrong, but mercifully it had thickened as it cooled.

'That looks marvellous, Taggie. I wish you'd marry me when I grow up,' said Bas, who was now comfortably ensconced on the sofa with Janey and a full bottle.

'This tomato salad is out of this world,' said Seb, carrying the bowl in.

Taggie liked Seb. He had a good body, hunky without being fat, thick light-brown hair, short at the back and long at the front, very direct slate grey eyes and he was very nearly as tall as she was.

Then, as Big Ben struck nine, the applications were ready: forty copies of beautifully typed, ring-bound pages. On the front, beneath the clear plastic cover, was a drawing of a beautiful boy with his hand to his forehead, standing on the capitals T and U of the word Venturer against a clear cerulean background. On the back, also protected by a plastic cover, was an exquisite water-colour map of the area, painted by Caitlin, including the towns and villages, with little drawings of the relevant houses, where all the prospective Venturer directors lived, and with pale blue arrows from each of them converging on Cotchester. It had cost a lot to print, but they'd all thought it was worth it.

Everyone went mad with excitement as they sat round reading, and at last holding in their hands tangible proof that it was all really happening.

'Don't spill drink over them, for Christ's sake,' said Declan.

'It's very good, Declan,' said Harold White. 'I'd forgotten how well you write. I love the bit about "carpets being so thick and offices so sound-proofed on the Corinium directors' floor, that all one can hear is the faint rustle of nests being feathered".'

'I liked that bit too,' said Declan, blushing.

'And I love this bit about Corinium's local news programmes being presented by "pretentious pastel-clad narcissists",' boomed Dame Enid. 'That boring little fart Vereker won't like that one bit.'

'I hope that's not actionable,' said Professor Graystock primly. 'And are you quite sure there was a Roman camp at Whychey?'

'Quite,' said Declan.

'I like my cottage,' said Marti Gluckstein, examining the map at the back. 'I must come and look at it some time. Ouch!' he yelled, as Freddie kicked him sharply on the ankle.

'Sorry, but Declan thinks you spend every weekend there,' whispered Freddie.

'I do like your ideas for religious programmes,' said Janey, smiling up at the Bishop, who went very pink.

Declan saw that everyone's glasses were full, then got to his feet. 'I'd just like to thank you all for having the courage to join Venturer, and for all the hard work you've put in already. But I must warn you, this has been the easy bit. Once it's out in the open that we're pitching for Corinium, Tony Baddingham is going to do everything to discredit us and rake up dirt about all of us. Our only hope is to stick together and trosst each other.' He smiled round at everyone. 'This is a very very proud day for me. Let's all raise our glasses.'

'Victory to Venturer,' said Henry Hampshire, and amazingly, unselfconsciously, everyone followed suit.

'I shall compose a battle song for Venturer and we'll make a record,' said Dame Enid.

'I hope it's better than the song cycle she's just written,' muttered Seb to Taggie. 'It sounded more like a lot of tom cats being garrotted by knicker elastic. This chicken is just as much a work of art as your father's application,' he went on. 'Can I have some more?'

Everyone jumped as the doorbell went.

'I can't help thinking it's Tony with a pitchfork,' said Georgie Baines nervously.

But it was only the man with the T-shirts and once again everyone went wild and put them on, including the baby and Gertrude. They were baggy enough, having been ordered to Caitlin's specification, to fit Dame Enid and Charles Fairburn, and even the Bishop wore one over his dog collar. Janey wore hers just over pants to show off her long brown legs, and, after a lot of persuading, Taggie did the same.

'They're much better than Corinium's T-shirts,' said Seb in delight. 'They're custard yellow with Caring Corinium written across the front. Tony eschewed the symbol of the Corinium ram as being too libidinous.'

More champagne was drunk and food eaten. Then the photographer arrived.

'Where the hell's Rupert?' said Declan irritably.

'I think we ought to get on and get this pickie taken without him,' said Freddie in an undertone. 'Lord Smiff's shipped enough to float the *QE2* an' Wesley's on somefink else, and he's supposed to drive back to Leeds tonight for an eleven o'clock start.'

'He better go first thing tomorrow,' said Declan. 'We don't want him busted the day the applications go in.'

Bas and Janey were still nose to nose on the sofa; the baby had fallen asleep in Bas's arms.

'Line up for the photograph everyone,' shouted Freddie.

Seb dragged Taggie in from the kitchen. She loathed group photographs. She was always taller than half the men.

'You're as much a part of Venturer as anyone else,' said Seb.

Taggie sat on the sofa, Gertrude on her knee, bristling in a child's T-shirt, with Maud on one side and Janey and the baby on the other. Bas stood behind Janey. Taggie suddenly noticed his suntanned fingers caressing the back of Janey's neck and hastily looked away.

'Straighten your T-shirt, so I can see all the Venturers,' said the photographer. 'Look nice and happy please. Can you get the little dog to prick up his ears? Lovely! Smile please.'

He was still snapping away two minutes later when Taggie gave a shriek of pain as Gertrude leapt off her bare legs, barking furiously, as Rupert came through the door.

He had that same look of blazing triumph on his face, reflected Janey, that he used to have in the old days when one of his horses won a big class and he used to ride it out of the ring, giving its neck great slaps of joy. He hadn't looked like that for years.

Rupert paused in the doorway.

'Ladies and Gentlemen,' he drawled, 'may I introduce Venturer's Head of Drama.'

Taggie gave a gasp of horror; Harold White went white. Seb, Georgie and Charles nearly jumped out of the window in terror, as Rupert turned round and, putting his arm around Cameron's shoulders very much in a gesture of possession, drew her into the room.

She looked very pale and very shy, but incredibly beautiful, with her face strangely softened by love.

Maud broke the stunned silence. For months, despite Declan's denials, she had suspected Rupert of having a growing preference for Taggie. It was the one thing she couldn't have stood. Joyfully, she welcomed such a public transferring of his affections to Cameron. Rushing forward, she hugged them both.

'Congratulations, darlings. Now I'm convinced Venturer's going to get the franchise.'

'Don't look so worried,' said Rupert mockingly to the cringing Corinium contingent. 'Cameron's on the level. Her name's going to be put forward on the confidential memo like the rest of you, and she's going to stay working for Corinium until December.'

Charles decided to make the best of a bad job. 'Welcome to Venturer, sweetie,' he said, kissing Cameron.

'Fucking hell,' muttered Seb to Georgie.

'Look at the way she's looking at Rupert,' said Georgie. 'He's got her exactly where he wants her.'

'As long as he stays wanting her,' said Seb, shaking his head.

Janey's baby woke up suddenly and started bawling its head off.

'Probably got a hangover,' said Bas.

Soon the champagne was circulating again. Cameron was sitting on the sofa now, flipping through the application document with one hand, clinging onto Rupert's hand with the other.

'Why's Taggie crying in the kitchen?' Dame Enid asked Maud.

'I expect she'd like to be able to read her father's application like everyone else,' said Maud airily. 'She's dyslexic, you see.'

'Poor darling,' said Dame Enid. 'She's a bloody good cook. I'm going to have thirds.'

Seb put his arm round Taggie in the kitchen. 'You OK, babes?'

'Fine,' she muttered blowing her nose on a drying-up cloth. 'I'm just tired, I guess.'

'Your application's dazzling,' said Cameron, following Declan over to the drinks table where he was opening another bottle. 'Miles, miles better than ours. Any slight doubts I might have had about joining Venturer have been dispelled by reading it. I do hope Rupert hasn't railroaded you all into accepting me?'

'I don't want any bullying,' said Declan, glaring at her. 'One's only as good as one's work force and don't you ever forget it.'

I'm going to have to put in a lot of spade work to win him over, thought Cameron, but all that really mattered was that Rupert loved her.

Freddie clapped his hands. 'Let's get this pickie finished.'

'Come on, Cameron,' said Charles, brandishing a T-shirt.

'I'm not sure I ought to appear in it,' stammered Cameron, suddenly realizing what compromising evidence it would be.

'Put it on,' snapped Declan.

Charles slid the T-shirt over her head and once again they all lined up, George and Seb taking up their position on either side of her, with Charles standing behind.

'Straighten your T-shirts, look happy everyone,' said the photographer.

'Let's get one thing straight beside T-shirts, Miss Cook,' said Georgie out of the corner of his handsome mouth, as he beamed into the camera.

'If you shop us to Tony, we'll shop you,' said Seb as he also beamed into the camera.

'And don't forget, there are well over two hundred shopping days to 15th December,' said Charles.

As Venturer had called a press conference for the following afternoon, Declan stayed the night at Freddie's house and Taggie drove her mother and Gertrude back to Penscombe just after midnight.

Maud was plastered and went on and on about how nice Janey was, and wasn't it a turn-up for the books Rupert rolling up with Cameron, and did Taggie think Rupert had offered her marriage or to move into Penscombe or what. Taggie answered in monosyllables and fortunately, as they passed the Reading exit, Maud fell into a drunken sleep.

Taggie then proceeded to give herself a very good talking to. What the hell was she feeling so miserable about? Rupert was as far beyond her as the huge stars daisying the black lawn of sky above, and plainly as impervious to her love. It was the stupid sort of crush teenagers had on pop stars or actors, someone to dream about when you were tucked up in bed, or wandering through the woods.

Rupert had probably been kind to her because he missed his own children. The silver necklace, Gertrude's Valentine, the little Easter Egg, were all presents you might give a child, she told herself firmly. And saying that no one could resist her (Taggie wished she could memorize recipes and how to spell words as easily as she remembered every conversation she'd had with Rupert) was just the sort of thing he'd say to any girl. Cameron was beautiful, brilliant, sophisticated and tough. Taggie was sure she only disliked her because she'd upset Declan and hurt Patrick so much, but Rupert wouldn't stand any nonsense, so maybe they were well suited.

Next minute she felt a cold nose nudging her elbow and put out her hand to stroke Gertrude, who slid forward along the hand brake until she could climb onto Taggie's knee and settle down with a martyred sigh.

Taggie knew she shouldn't allow Gertrude to lie there. On

a motorway it was particularly dangerous. But she needed the comfort. She was not someone who regarded happiness as a right, but the ghastly shock of seeing Cameron and Rupert so obviously in love tonight made her realize how happy, without being conscious of it, she'd been since Valentine's Day, when Rupert began dropping in at The Priory whenever he was at home. Despite the talking to, she didn't think she'd ever felt so unhappy in her life.

31

At noon the lists closed. The information office at the IBA then had a frantic three and a half hours going through the applications and extracting the names and addresses of those involved for a press release at three-thirty.

Down at Cotchester three of the four Corinium moles made themselves scarce. Charles Fairburn drove to the Forest of Dean to spend two days in an enclosed order, ostensibly interviewing monks. Georgie flew to Manchester to see a big pet-food client. Cameron disappeared to Stow-on-the-Wold on location, leaving strict instructions that she wasn't to be interrupted. Seb Burrows, being a true journalist and hating to miss the fireworks, hung around the newsroom.

Corinium staff not involved with the Venturer bid were also kept busy. James Vereker slipped home with Sarah Stratton for an extended lunch hour. Daysee Butler, who'd been out in the evenings so much recently she hadn't watched any television, was reading the soap updates in the *Mail*, as she soaked up the sun in her bikini in the Cathedral close. Tony Baddingham and Ginger Johnson were having a celebrity board-room lunch with the French co-producers of 'Stowaway', having just sold it both to NBS and BBC. What a relief, they all agreed, they hadn't killed off the handsome pirate villain, as a sequel was already planned.

How nice it was too, thought Tony, to lunch with Europeans who still appreciated a good blow-out and decent claret, compared with the Yanks who seemed totally addicted to rabbit food and Perrier.

By three forty-five Tony was back in his office. In half an hour he would have sobered up and be wondering who to bully. Now he merely felt lecherous. All those pale-green trees and pale half-naked girls stretched out among the buttercups. The first flush and flesh of Spring always got him going. Having spent a weekend without Cameron, he decided to drop in and see her after the Chamber of Commerce dinner that night, an event which had to be endured in a franchise year.

Still feeling randy, he was about to summon Sarah Stratton to discuss her posing with a lamb for a Caring Corinium poster when Miss Madden buzzed. 'Barney Williams from the *Telegraph*, Lord B. He wants to talk about the franchise.'

'Put him on.' Tony extracted a cigar from the box on his desk and relaxed in his leather chair, preparing to be generous about Mid-West's pathetic bid.

Barney Williams came straight to the point. 'Did you know Declan O'Hara put in a rival bid?'

Tony laughed heartily. 'Is this some kind of joke?'

'I'm afraid it isn't.'

'Who else is involved?'

'Rupert Campbell-Black, Freddie Jones.'

'Whaaaat!'

It sounded like a great oak tree crashing to the ground. Even through sound-proofed doors, Miss Madden jumped in the next-door office. Then Tony was leaning on the buzzer.

'Miss Madden!' he yelled. 'Take these names down. Who else?' he asked Barney.

'Henry Hampshire, the Bishop of Cotchester, Marti Gluckstein.'

'He's never been to Gloucestershire.'

'Evidently he has a weekend cottage there. Janey Lloyd-Foxe, Dame Enid Spink, Lord Smith.'

'He can't join. He's a union member.'

'Ex-member – just. Crispin Graystock. Wesley Emerson – he's the only bit of name-plate engineering. They're all pretty heavyweight, in fact, and, oh yes, there's your brother Bas. Bit Jacob and Esau isn't it?'

Tony gave a low hiss that was almost a sigh.

'And you had absolutely no idea?' asked Barney.

'None.'

'And they're all friends of yours?'

'They were.'

'They're calling a press conference in London at four-thirty. Will you be doing the same, or can I have a quote now?'

'I've nothing to say until I've talked to my Board!'

Tony slammed down the telephone. Bastards! Traitors! Every single one of them. They'd all eaten his salt, and he'd absolutely no inkling. What kind of fucking newsroom did he have? The maddened bull's roar could be heard all down the passage.

'Ginger, Cyril, Georgie, Cameron, Charles! Come in here.'

'Georgie's in Manchester,' said Miss Madden, 'and Cameron's on location.'

'Get them back.'

Ginger Johnson thought Tony was going to have a coronary. He was magenta in the face, veins bulged like huge snakes on his forehead. He seemed to be popping out of his dark-green collar. Ginger wanted Tony's job, but not until the franchise was safely in the bag.

'What on earth's up?'

Tony was so angry as he paced up and down, fists clenched, froth flecking his mouth, he could hardly get the words out to tell him. Once he lit a cigar from the wrong end, then hurled it out of the window. Without taking the top off, he tried to pour himself a stiff whisky, then banged the bottle down.

'What have they called themselves?' asked Cyril Peacock, who was taking down the inevitable notes.

'Venturer – adventurers more likely – every bloody one of them! God, I'll crucify them! I'll take them to the cleaners!'

Ginger went to the drinks cupboard and poured Tony a large brandy. He was equally shocked at the possible loss of a £125 million turnover, but, having no personal vendettas with any of the Venturer team, he didn't feel Tony's paranoia or passionate sense of being deliberately ganged up on.

Miss Madden buzzed: 'It's the *Sun*, Lord B, and just hang on a minute . . . Beryl says the *Mirror* are on the other line.'

'Tell them Lord B's in conference and to ring back in half an hour,' said Ginger, taking the initiative. 'Don't talk to them now,' he added to Tony. 'Get your breath back. The most important thing at this stage is not to show we're rattled. Leave the mud-slinging to Venturer. We've got seven months to put the boot in. The only possible approach now is Olympian. These boring little pygmies are yapping at my heels, but I can't feel it.'

'Should we call a press conference?'

'Certainly not. They're not worth it. Why show them we're panicking?'

Downstairs in the newsroom Seb Burrows picked up his telephone. It was ITN: 'Hello, Seb. Christ, what a story!'

'What story?' said Seb innocently.

ITN told him. 'Did you know anything about it?'

'None of us did. Christ!'

'Can you interview Tony for us for the five forty-five news?'

'I'll try. I don't imagine he'll be in carnival mood.'

But, to Seb's amazement, Tony agreed. By the time the crew got up to Tony's office, every award Corinium had ever won, including the EMMYs and the BAFTAs nicked from Cameron's office, had been put on the bookshelf or hung on the wall behind Tony's head.

The earlier storm had subsided; Tony's rage was ice cold now. He had even extracted a salmon-pink carnation from the vase on the desk to put in his buttonhole.

'What's your reaction to Venturer's bid?' asked Seb.

Tony gave a big, but slightly dismissive smile: 'Well, they're good chaps, all jolly good friends of mine. I'm sure there's a lot of merit in their application, but frankly I'm more interested in the things Corinium are doing – like announcing plans for a ten-million-pound studio near Southampton, which'll mean about four hundred extra jobs, and spending two million on new equipment at Cotchester, to enable us to make even better programmes, and meet with every confidence the challenge of cable and satellite. We've won a lot of awards over the last few years.' He waved airily at the trophies glittering behind him. 'We provide an excellent local news service and make jolly good programmes, and there we rest our case.'

I'm not getting anywhere, thought Seb.

'People are saying that Declan O'Hara and your brother Basil have been deliberately plotting to oust you since Declan walked out of here last March in a blaze of publicity.'

Tony examined his nails. 'Are they?' he said with another big smile.

Ask a silly question, thought Seb, kicking himself.

'Had you any idea they were engaged in a rival bid?'

'None. I wish them luck. It would be a dull race if there were no other contenders, but it doesn't dent my confidence.'

'Which consortium, Mid-West or Venturer, worries you the most?'

'Neither. I congratulate Venturer on putting an application together at such short notice and with such secrecy. I'll be interested to see what's in it in due course.'

'And you feel no bitterness towards Freddie Jones and Rupert Campbell-Black and Henry Hampshire, who have all enjoyed your hospitality?'

'None at all,' laughed Tony, as though the idea had never occurred to him. 'Nor do Corinium have any desire to get involved in mudslinging. Let "Dorothy Dove", who recently won us a BAFTA award, be a symbol of our company, non-combative but victorious.'

The moment the camera stopped rolling the smile was wiped from Tony's face. 'Now bugger off, all of you, but come back the moment "Cotswold Round-Up" is over, Seb, and bring James Vereker with you.'

Cameron ignored Tony's summons to return at once and insisted on carrying on shooting until the four-thirty tea break. It was vital to be as bolshie as usual, or Tony would suspect something. As she drove through the angelic spring greenness with the roof down, she heard a flash on the five-thirty news that Declan O'Hara, after a mega-bust-up with Corinium in March, was now getting his revenge on Tony by heading a rival bid for Corinium. Rupert, Freddie, Dame Enid, the Bishop, Wesley, Lord Smith and Janey were also mentioned. Cameron waited in terror for her name to be tagged on at the end.

She was still in a state of shock after the weekend. When she'd run out on Rupert on Saturday, she'd gone straight home and rung Tony at home – something he'd told her never to do – and promptly got Monica. Remembering that Tony had the French co-production people over for the weekend, who were probably *Mon Dieu*-ing over Monica's fading stretch of daffodils at that moment, she'd hung up. For the next twenty-four hours she crouched shuddering in her bedroom, telephone off the hook, all doors locked, not answering the bell, going through every kind of torture at the prospect of life without Rupert. The craving had got so bad that when, on Sunday afternoon, he'd smashed the pane of her french windows at the back, let himself in, pounded up the stairs, and taken her in his arms, telling her he couldn't go on without her, the sheer relief of having him back made her agree to anything. She would join Venturer; she would stay at Corinium and spy on Tony.

'A Ms is not nearly as good as a Mole,' Rupert had told her as he'd dropped her off at Hamilton Terrace at four o'clock that morning. God knows when either of them would get any sleep.

But at last the crunch had come. All day she'd been snapping at the cast for acting badly. Now she had to give a BAFTA performance herself. At least she'd heard the news bulletin, so she didn't have to simulate complete surprise when she saw Tony.

But as she drove into her slot in the Corinium car park and read the words 'Cameron Cook, Controller of Programmes' she felt she should cross out the last three and put Traitor.

412

She reached Tony's office just before the main BBC news. The commercials, with the sound turned down, were airing on ITV. Tony, Ginger and Cyril were all watching. Cameron went straight up to Tony and put her arms round him.

'I'm so sorry, I heard it on the radio. They're all traitors, but Freddie and Bas are the worst of all.'

'Was Bas mentioned on the radio?' said Cyril, pencil poised. 'What station?'

'I don't remember,' said Cameron hastily. 'Some local bulletin, but I was switching about to see what I could find out.'

Christ, that was a near one, she thought, going to the drinks cupboard and pouring herself a stiff vodka and tonic. She'd have to be careful with the liquor too; she was so tired, other indiscretions might slip out. How the hell had Guy Burgess kept his communist affiliations a secret for so long if he was always pissed?

The BBC led on the story. Beautiful weather apart, there wasn't much news. After some introductory waffle about the contenders now circling in the paddock, they went straight over to the Venturer press conference. Not wanting him to see her face, Cameron took up her position behind Tony, leaning against the wall with her hand on his shoulder. He seemed calm enough, but she could feel the knotted tension of his muscles. A tic was leaping in his jaw and the carnation in his buttonhole had already wilted, as though poisoned by his venom.

The Venturer team looked splendid. Declan had been so hostile last night that she hadn't noticed how well he was looking, already tanned from gardening and sitting outside writing the application. Half the heavy lines seemed to have been ironed out of his face. And there was Rupert laughing with Janey, who looked amazing, bearing in mind the amount she'd drunk yesterday. Rupert had said she was the one person Cameron need never be jealous of, but she removed her hand from Tony's shoulder, in case she clutched it convulsively. Rupert looked marvellous, too. Christ, he was beautiful. Any minute, she thought, taking such a large slug of vodka that

413

it spilled down the tall glass all over her face, she'd wake up.

There was also a massive contingent of press there. People were standing on tables, fighting for space.

'Why have you pitched for the Corinium franchise, Declan?' asked the BBC.

'We want to create a company that is genuinely local,' said Declan. 'And we want to make some bloody good programmes.'

'And a fortune into the bargain?' said the *Mirror*.

Everyone laughed. Declan grinned. 'That too. Then we can afford to make even better programmes.'

Soon, however, the vitriol was flowing freely.

'Corinium have lost touch with the public and their region. They need a good shake-up,' said Rupert.

'After eight years in business,' said Freddie, 'it seems amazing that Tony B has only just decided to build a studio near Southampton.'

'I appeared on "Cotswold Round-Up" recently,' boomed Dame Enid. 'I was interviewed by some pastel-clad pansy —' she winked at Declan — 'who didn't know what the hell he was talking about. It was the worst programme I've ever been on.'

'What drew you in, Bishop?' asked the *Catholic Herald*.

'Television today is a key factor in the quality of life, in the community, in the establishment of Christian values,' said the Bishop heartily. 'I hope to play a part through Venturer in making television more uplifting and more enjoyable.' He wagged a finger. 'One doesn't exclude the other, y'know.'

Realizing the Bishop was all set to deliver a sermon, Rupert cut in, 'The Bishop feels as I do, that there's far too much sex and violence on Corinium's programmes.'

'Fucking hypocrite,' thundered Tony.

'Very much so,' agreed the Bishop. 'On "Four Men went to Mow" young people are continually going to bed with other young people and shown not to be taking precautions.'

'Corinium's drama record as a whole,' added Janey, 'is abysmal.'

414

'Bitch,' hissed Cameron in genuine outrage. 'How dare she!'

'There are, of course, good people working at Corinium,' said Declan, 'but they're hamstrung by a greedy and incompetent management.'

Tony puffed on his cigar, the knuckles of his left hand whitening as he made a dagger of the silver paper knife on his desk. Cyril's doodles became more extravagant.

'Having worked at Corinium for seven months,' went on Declan, 'I know just how bad things are.'

'Isn't that actionable?' said Ginger furiously.

But Tony held up his hand for silence as the *Star* asked Declan who Venturer were poaching from other companies.

Declan smiled again. 'We have a string of incredibly talented people who will take over as Heads of the various departments the moment we win the franchise,' he said, 'but as they're all working for ITV or the BBC, we can't tell you who they are.'

'What d'you feel about your other rival, Mid-West?' said the *Sun*.

Rupert laughed. 'Well, they were advertising for ideas for programmes in the local paper last week,' he said, 'so they must be a bit short on imagination, and as their regional trump card is a geography master who's never been to London I can't say we feel very threatened.'

The BBC, obviously feeling they'd given Venturer enough coverage, turned to the wonderful weather.

Tony immediately switched over to 'Cotswold Round-Up' who put out an outwardly impartial report about there being two contenders for the Corinium franchise, then ran Tony's interview with Seb in full. This was immediately followed by a link from James Vereker saying that Declan must have got to know Rupert when he interviewed him for Corinium.

Next the clip was run in from the programme in which Declan quoted the Gloucestershire peer describing Rupert as 'a nasty virus everyone's wife caught sooner or later'. And Rupert replying: 'If you could see his wife, it'd definitely be later.'

Finally came Declan's questions as to whether Rupert was going to mend his ways because of AIDS, and Rupert cracking back that he was giving up casual sex for Lent. Without any qualifying comment, the programme then switched to a story about playing-fields.

'That was offensive,' said Cameron furiously. 'That clip should *never* have been taken out of context.'

'The IBA won't like it one bit,' said Ginger, shaking his head.

'I didn't authorize it,' lied Tony quickly. 'I can't help it if my newsroom get a little protective and leap to my defence.'

Cameron felt sick. It was going to be much dirtier and more difficult than she'd thought. Things became worse when Seb and James rolled up after 'Cotswold Round-Up'. Tony, utterly businesslike now, said their chief object should be to dig up as much dirt on Venturer as possible and then get other people to leak the stories.

'We've got to appear whiter than white and above it all. Here's the list of their consortium.' Tony handed copies to James and Seb. 'Declan was desperately pushed for cash when he left Corinium. How's he managed to be in funds again? Investigate any IRA sympathies. His wife's a tart. See if there's any rift there.'

'Rupert's a government minister,' said Ginger. 'That's out of order for a start. He could influence the PM to lean on the IBA to give Venturer the franchise.'

'Excellent,' said Tony. 'Ring up Paul Stratton, Ginger. He detests Rupert. Get him to ask a question in the House about it. And find out who Rupert's sleeping with, Seb. It's bound to be different from yesterday. If anything moves, or rather stays still, he'll fuck it. Sarah Stratton used to sleep with him; she may still be. Talk to her.'

Seb didn't dare look at Cameron. Suddenly, he felt desperately sorry for her.

'Lord Smith likes the fleshpots far too much for a socialist,' went on Tony. 'He's got his own house with five bedrooms and a very nice car. See if he's been using union funds. Graystock's a pinko, too. Investigate any communist sympathies. He's also divorced, got a second house, and definitely sent his second child to a private school. Hang round the University, Seb, and see if he's ever fiddled with one of his students, or put one in the club.'

'Ditto Dame Enid,' said Ginger with his dry mirthless laugh. 'She's probably miffed we're doing a Michael Tippett opera this year and not one of hers.'

'That's possible,' said Tony. 'Good story to leak to the gossip columns. And the Bishop of Cotchester must have had a choirboy in his time.'

He ran his finger down the list. 'Henry Hampshire's a terrible letch; keep an eye on him. Janey Lloyd-Foxe is a whore. She left Billy for a bit and went off with one of his sponsors, and they're always broke. There's bound to be some dirt there. And Wesley Emerson's a cinch. He's always stoned or dipping his wick. We've just got to pick our moment to leak a really juicy story.'

Ginger shook his head. 'Got to be careful, there. Wesley's such a local hero, the public'll forgive him anything. He took five wickets today, only person who did.'

'Send Sarah Stratton to interview him,' said Tony. 'That should do the trick.'

James's stomach gave a terrific rumble; his extended lunch with Sarah today had not included food. 'I think we should be careful about smirching Corinium's caring face,' he said palely.

'I agree,' said Cameron, who'd also gone very white. 'Can't we just, as you said, stand on our record? We're better than them. It seems so tacky to sink to their level.'

'Don't be fucking stupid,' snapped Tony. 'This is war. I don't believe Marti Gluckstein lives in Penscombe either. Find out his alleged address and go and bung the neighbours.'

'I'll do that story,' said Seb quickly.

'Charles is a friend of both Rupert's and Declan's,' said Tony. 'He can find out what they're up to. Where the hell is he, anyway?' He turned furiously on Cyril.

'Gone to an enclosed order for two days,' stammered Cyril. 'They're not on the telephone.'

'Well, drive over and fetch him back, sunshine,' said Tony with exaggerated patience. 'If you both value your jobs, see that he rings me at home tonight after eleven o'clock.'

He opened his briefcase and took out a clean shirt and a tie. 'I've got to go to the Chamber of Commerce dinner. So bugger off, all of you. I want to talk to Cameron.'

After they'd gone Cameron couldn't stop shaking. 'It's so awful,' she kept saying.

'I think it might be rather fun,' said Tony softly. 'When the right moment comes, I'll press the destruct button on the lot of them. They've no idea what they've taken on.'

As he came towards her, his breath was foul, as though all the hatred had churned and rotted inside him. His body stank of stale sweat. Trying not to flinch when he grabbed her, Cameron said, 'I thought you were dropping by this evening?'

'I'd like to, but it's not safe. Press'll be hanging round. Venturer might even put a private dick on to me.'

He was so mad to get inside her, he broke the elastic of her panties. It was all over in a minute.

'The bastards,' he groaned. 'They've all betrayed me.'

Then he took her throat between his hands. 'If you ever betray me, I'll kill you.'

Down the High Street at Radio Cotchester the Controller of Programmes received an irate telephone call from the Managing Director who'd never been near the station since Princess Michael opened it five years ago.

'I've just heard a very favourable interview with Bas Baddingham,' he roared. 'I don't want any more crap like that on Radio Cotchester. Tell all our presenters and DJs we're backing Corinium a hundred per cent throughout this campaign. After all, Tony Baddingham owns twenty per cent of us.'

Up the High Street at the *Cotchester News* the Editor was reading tomorrow's leader: '*Tony Baddingham's words to Declan O'Hara that people who get too big for their boots should go and wear out other people's carpets must ring hollow in his ears today when the mega-star Irishman and Penscombe resident headed a bid to oust Tony Baddingham and walk on Corinium's carpets himself after 15th December. Venturer, as he's called his consortium, appears to be soundly based financially, rich in talent and determined to grasp the infinite . . .'*

The Editor had read enough and buzzed for his leader writer. 'You can't publish this! We own twenty per cent of Corinium, and Tony Baddingham owns twenty-five per cent of us. Go back and rewrite it.'

'Corinium may not be perfect,' the leader writer retyped defiantly. *'What company is? But it has now reached a level of performance far beyond that which any newcomer could achieve in a few years. Corinium has a massive expansion programme, it has won countless awards, it has all the expertise it needs, and it has Cameron Cook.'*

Then he went out and got drunk.

Cameron finally tracked down Rupert at the House after he'd voted.

'Sweetheart, are you OK?' he said. 'How's Sledge-Hammer House of Horror? Has Tony had a seizure?'

'I hate you and I hate myself,' stormed Cameron. 'How dare Janey Lloyd-Foxe say Corinium's drama was abysmal, and that bloody Bishop attacking the morals of "Four Men went to Mow"!'

'That was tactless. I'm sorry, but if we don't knock you, Tony'll suspect something. How did he take it?'

'Fine,' said Cameron. 'Very together, very positive.'

'That's not what Barney Williams told me. He said it really pulled the Krug from under Tony's feet, and that he was quite hysterical. All this expansive crip-crap about welcoming competition came much later in the day.'

Cameron wasn't interested. 'Look, Rupert, I'm not sure I'm going to be any good as a double agent.'

'What's happened?'

'Seb's got to trail you to find out who you're sleeping with.'

Rupert laughed. 'He's going to have a very boring time

then. The only person I'm sleeping or likely to stay awake with is you.'

'Are you sure?' Cameron's voice broke. 'I'm so confused. It all happened so fast. I need to see you, just to talk.'

'I need to fuck,' said Rupert. 'I want you so badly at this moment, but it'd be madness. The press are still baying round. We've got to be careful.'

'I don't think I can handle it.'

'Yes, you can. You're very brave and strong, that's what I adore about you. You're very tired too. Take a couple of Mogadon and sleep in. And sustain yourself with the thought that one day in December we'll be awarded tickets on the one surviving gravy train.'

'I thought we were only interested in making good programmes,' said Cameron disapprovingly.

'Oh well, that, too,' said Rupert.

32

Within a week the IBA had provided the press with précis of all the applications and placed a copy of each application in their library so that the public could come and look at them.

Immediately, Tony dispatched Miss Madden to the IBA to transcribe Venturer's application in her neat shorthand. Going through the revolving doors, she met Ursula, Declan's secretary, on a similar mission.

'I'm not supposed to talk to you,' said Joyce.

'Nor I you,' said Ursula.

Both agreed, however, that much time could be saved if Ursula posted Joyce a copy of Venturer's application and Joyce sent Ursula a copy of Corinium's. Then they could pretend they had transcribed and typed them themselves, and pop over to Harrods instead for a lunch of breaded plaice, fruit salad and several glasses of sweet sherry before going to the cinema.

'We mustn't discuss the franchise or I'll get sacked,' said Joyce, 'but you've no idea how demented Lord B. was when he heard Declan was bidding against him. He's really out to get him now. It's a shame we're on different sides. I always liked Declan. He was such a nice man.'

Having read Venturer's application, Tony launched his counter-offensive.

'It would be foolish to denigrate the competition,' he told the press expansively, and then proceeded to do so.

He also spent a lot of time playing his staff off against each other, having them in individually, offering them large drinks and cigars in his most urbane and disarming manner, then telling each one they were the one person he really relied on to spy on the rest. Pinned on the board was a new notice reiterating instant dismissal for any member of staff found having dealings with any of the Venturer or Mid-Week consortiums.

The Bishop of Cotchester was therefore rather bewildered when, every time he walked down the High Street or round the Cathedral close and tried to pass the time of day with any of the eight hundred Corinium staff, they bolted like squirrels up the nearest tree.

The following Sunday Declan called a Venturer meeting at The Priory. Janey and Billy couldn't make it, nor could Wesley Emerson. But Wesley had vindicated himself by already taking twenty-five wickets and wearing the Venturer T-shirt on every possible occasion.

Georgie, Seb and Charles (who was wearing a tin hat and brandishing a riot shield borrowed from Wardrobe) all turned up giggling hysterically in James Vereker's very distinctive pale-blue Porsche.

'The silly bugger left it in the Corinium car park and a second set of keys in his office,' said Georgie. 'We're going to abandon it outside your house later this afternoon, Enid, then ring up Tony and tip him off.'

'How's it going?' said Freddie.

'Tony's in a vilely twitchy mood,' said Charles, 'bugging everyone's telephones. You'd better watch out, Declan. If our chief engineer rolls up in a yellow van heavily disguised as a British Telecom mechanic, don't let him in.'

It was such a mild day they all sat outside. Apple blossom and lilac were both out and wafting their sweet fragrance. Cow parsley frothed up to meet the trailing young green leaves and white candles of the horse chestnuts round the lawn. The rushing stream was clogged with forget-me-nots and marsh marigolds, and, although the bluebells were fading, the wood was now lit up by the white flowers of the wild garlic. It was definitely a day to be in love. Rupert turned up with Cameron, who was safe because Tony had gone to Rugborough to watch Archie play cricket. She and Rupert had obviously just got out of bed. Their hair was still wet from the shower. She sat on the lawn propped against him, her hand on his thigh. They looked lean, glamorous and intensely separate.

Great excitement was caused by the arrival of the rest of the Venturer publicity material: badges, car stickers, bookmarks, peaked caps with adjustable straps at the back, which had to be taken in to fit Henry Hampshire's narrow stoat's head but let out for Dame Enid and Declan. The *pièce de résistance* was the poster. It was a blow-up from the group photograph of Taggie with Gertrude on her knee, both wearing Venturer T-shirts.

'It's fuckin' gorgeous,' said Freddie. 'Every garage mechanic will put it up in the service bay.'

'I'll have some for the bar,' said Bas.

'And I for the Close,' said the Bishop.

Both Dame Enid and Professor Graystock wanted several for the common room.

'Dirty old letch,' muttered Rupert, glaring at the Professor.

'I'll keep mine under my pillow,' said Seb, 'in case Tony drops in for coffee one evening.'

Only Cameron had been scornful when Rupert had showed the poster to her earlier.

'It's too fucking kitsch for words,' she snapped.

'I thought you might like to have a look at Corinium's rival offering,' said Georgie, unrolling a poster of Sarah Stratton cuddling a baby calf with a caption 'Corinium Cares' underneath. Her T-shirt had rather too many buttons undone.

'"Corinium Bares", more likely,' said Rupert dismissively. 'Venturer have definitely won the battle of the Crumpet. Here, let me carry that, angel,' he went on, leaping to his feet as Taggie came out with a huge chocolate cake and a plate of cucumber sandwiches on a tray.

Taggie couldn't meet his eyes, nor did she say anything when she saw the poster. It reminded her too poignantly of when she'd still been happy, when Rupert had not yet rolled up with Cameron.

After tea Declan came to the serious bit.

'For the next two months,' he told them, 'while the IBA are sifting through the applications before the public meetings begin in July, our job is to get Venturer across to the area. We got off to an excellent start. With such a dazzlingly flamboyant panel —' he grinned round at them — 'publicity has been no problem. Now we've got to get out and meet the people who matter — in the Town Halls, the Chambers of Commerce, the Rotary Clubs all round the area — and show them we're not just a bunch of dilettantes.

'We've also got to cast our net wide to cover schools, colleges, churches, young farmers, job centres, the police, sports clubs, political groups, race relations officers, etc., etc. We must let them know what we intend to do, find out how we can help them, and then sign them up as friends of Venturer. We'll collect a huge petition of names and organizations to send the IBA. But it'll have far more effect if they can also be persuaded to write a private letter to Lady Gosling giving their support.

'We must try to cover the entire area,' he went on. 'I know you're all busy and it's going to be a long hard slog, and obviously none of the Corinium moles or Billy or Harold can be seen to be doing anything.'

'I'll help,' pleaded Taggie. 'Please let me. I can drive round the area delivering handouts and telling people how good you are.'

'How can she possibly explain to anyone why they should support Venturer,' said Cameron too loudly to Rupert, 'if she can't read the fucking application?'

Seeing Taggie go crimson with mortification, Seb leapt to her defence. 'Put it on tape,' he said. 'I'll do it for you, Taggie. If I can't go round the area canvassing, it's the least I can do.'

Seb was as good as his word. Over the next two days he

not only put the most important points of the application on tape for her, but also the answers she should give to any questions.

'If they're a Leftie organization,' he explained, 'say we've got Professor Graystock, Lord Smith and your Dad in the consortium. If they're Tory, plug Freddie, Henry, Rupert and Marti Gluckstein. If they're SDP, bandy Dame Enid's name around.

'If anyone starts grumbling about sex and violence,' he went on, 'say we've got the Bishop of Cotchester and he's going to oversee all our programmes. On the other hand, if anyone says we haven't got enough sex and violence, say we've got Rupert, Bas and Wesley Emerson in the consortium.'

He coached her over and over again until her spiel was word-perfect. Taggie found him incredibly kind and patient.

'I wish I'd been taught by people like you at school,' she said wistfully.

And so the hard grind started. But as Rupert was chronically busy, and Freddie was tied up with his electronics empire, and Declan was locked into his biography of Yeats, and both professors were frantically coaching their students for finals, in the end most of the work fell to Taggie. With a car full of stickers, badges and posters, she drove round the vast area visiting everyone from trade unionists to youth leaders, from mothers' unions to arts councils, taking in every imaginable pressure group, begging them to sign her petition, to write to the IBA and best of all to come along and cheer Venturer at the public meeting in July. Because of her beauty, sweetness and passionate belief in her father's and Venturer's cause, she had surprising success.

Sometimes she was joined by the Bishop, sometimes by Dame Enid, which was great fun. Dame Enid had a convertible and they drove through the glorious Spring together with the roof down, getting brown, sucking lemon sherbets and calling an awful lot of people 'boring little farts' after they'd safely got them signed up. Driving round with Professor Graystock was less fun. He had a horrible habit of squeezing

Taggie's bare legs when he made a point, so she took to wearing trousers.

The third Saturday in May, however, was a very bad day for Taggie. She was tired because she'd been up very late doing a dinner party for Valerie Jones the night before. As she was scheduled to tour the Winchester area, which she didn't know, she'd put directions to all the places she had to visit on tape, but even so she got terribly lost and flustered.

On one of her calls she'd got the SDP muddled up with the Labour Party and started plugging Dame Enid when she should have been pushing Lord Smith and Professor Graystock. Then she'd called on a vile headmaster who'd made her tremble because he reminded her of school. 'How can Venturer help your school personally?' she asked.

'Well, get a pencil, write it down,' he said bossily.

'I'll remember it,' stammered Taggie.

'Write it down,' snapped the headmaster.

'I can't.' Taggie hung her head. 'I'm dyslexic.'

He was incredibly nice after that, giving her a glass of sherry. His eldest son who'd been killed in Northern Ireland had been dyslexic and he got out a lot of photographs to show her.

It was half past nine and getting dark when Taggie left and after ten before she managed to find her way to the gates of the local cricket club.

Perhaps they'd all gone home. But she could hear great whoops and catcalls coming from the pavilion, and, as she drew up outside, moths were bashing against the lighted windows.

Cricket – Taggie took a deep breath – that meant she had to plug Wesley Emerson's involvement and Venturer's entirely fresh approach to cricket coverage. Going through the door, she quailed. They were obviously having some all-male dinner. She couldn't see the white table-cloth for glasses. Scores of huge-shouldered men with brick-red faces and beer guts seemed to be grinning at her with unfocused lechery. A tawny giant up at the top table, fiddling with the microphone, looked vaguely familiar.

'I'm so sorry,' she stammered, clutching her stickers, posters and her petition, 'I'll come back some other time.'

'No, come in, sweetheart,' they all yelled.

A chunky dark youth rose to his feet and swayed unsteadily towards her.

'If you're from the Shalvation Army, I'm beyond shaving,' he said.

'Come back, darling,' roared the rest, as Taggie backed out through the door.

A slightly older man, who came up to Taggie's shoulders, and who seemed less inebriated than the rest, said he was the club secretary and asked if he could help.

'I just wanted to tell you about Venturer,' mumbled Taggie, 'and hoped you might sign our petition and put our stickers in your cars.'

'I'd much rather put you in my car,' said the chunky dark youth to roars of applause.

The club secretary then led her to the microphone and introduced her to the Captain, who had hard, rather unpleasant blue eyes. 'Lady wants to tell us about television,' he said.

'Well, go on then,' said the Captain nastily.

The tawny giant smiled at Taggie and sat down.

'I just wanted to tell you about Venturer television,' Taggie began in her soft growling teddy-bear voice. 'You probably know we're p-pitching for the Corinium franchise. We need your help in our campaign. We want to know how we can help you.'

'Give us a blow job, Lofty,' said a wag down the table to howls of laughter.

A bread roll sailed through the air, just missing her. Taggie blushed even deeper but ploughed on.

'Strip, strip, strip, strip,' intoned the Captain, banging on the table.

Soon the entire room took up the cry.

'Shut up, you meatheads,' yelled the tawny giant. 'Let her finish.'

Amazingly, after that they did shut up and, except for

the occasional Tarzan howl, heard her out in silence.

'I want you to know finally,' said Taggie, 'that Venturer will be providing an entirely new approach to cricket coverage. We're very interested in cricket at all levels, and er –' she froze for a second trying to remember – 'and Wesley Emerson –' she brought out the name in triumph – 'is a key member of our consortium and is specially interested in promoting cricket in schools, so you'll have some really good colts coming on in the future. Please support Venturer. Thank you very much.'

'I suppose we can now get on with the speeches,' said the Captain over the thunder of applause.

'I'm so sorry.' Taggie picked up the petition. 'Could you possibly sign this?' she asked the tawny giant who'd been so kind to her.

'Of course.' He took the petition from her. 'D'you want it signed to anyone?'

'No, no, just your name and the name of the cricket club.'

'That's a bit difficult, Lofty,' said the Captain bitchily. 'We don't play cricket, you see.'

'But this is a cricket club,' said Taggie, aghast.

'Maybe it is, darling, but this is the Winchley Rugby Club dinner and Bill Beaumont here –' he indicated the tawny giant – 'is our guest of honour and is waiting to speak to us, if you'd be so kind as to bugger off.'

Grabbing the petition, leaving the posters and the car stickers, Taggie fled sobbing into the night. How could she have been so stupid? She was absolutely no help to Venturer at all.

Her dyslexia always got worse when she was upset. As a result she got desperately lost on the way home. She couldn't read any of the unfamiliar names on the signposts, and once it got really dark she was frightened to stop the car and ask strangers the way. There were no stars, or moonlight or street lamps to guide her along the country lanes. She seemed to have been going round for hours and hours, until at last she saw a sign she could recognize: *Penscombe 2m.*

Gertrude was noisily delighted to see her, but the trail of clothes in the hall and up the stairs told her that her parents had gone up somewhat precipitately to bed. The débris of their dinner was still on the kitchen table, one of the lids of the Aga was up and Aengus had knocked over a half-full bottle of whisky which was still dripping on to the flagstones.

'Oh God,' sighed Taggie. 'Can't they ever do anything for themselves?'

The cow parsley she'd picked that morning was already shedding petals like scurf all over the Welsh dresser.

Nothing lasts, she thought in despair.

Across the valley, Rupert's house was almost blotted out by the trees. There were no lights on. He was probably tucked up in bed with Cameron. It was always when she was really tired that the longing became unbearable.

Rupert, in fact, had spent the day at the Cup Final, making the main speech at the official dinner afterwards. Despite horrific setbacks, he was the first Minister for Sport who'd tackled hooliganism head on, and when he sat down they cheered him to the rooftops.

After the dinner was over, however, he beat a discreet retreat, taking a bottle of brandy over to that other Wembley stadium, home of the Horse of the Year Show, where he persuaded an obliging groundsman with a couple of tenners to put on the lights.

Sitting in the competitors' stand, drinking out of his bottle, he proceeded hazily to relive his past glories as a show jumper. And suddenly the huge arena seemed to be filled with coloured jumps and with the ghosts of all his great horses: Revenge, Rocky, Belgravia, Mayfair, Arcturus, Snakepit and even the cussed Macaulay. He could hear the sound of the bell, the screams of the Pony Club, the roar of applause, even the voice of the commentator, Dudley Diplock, who always got the names wrong. Oh Christ, what was he to do?

Putting his head in his hands, he was overwhelmed with despair as he realized, despite his political triumphs and the buzz of pitching for the franchise and stealing Cameron from

Tony, how hopelessly empty his life was now. He hadn't got fat when he'd given up show jumping, or taken to drink, except tonight, or to boring other people with endless anecdotes about his sporting glories as so many other great athletes had. But something had died inside him.

It was nearly midnight. The government car was still waiting outside. The groundsman wanted to lock up.

'Probably fallen asleep,' said Sydney, Rupert's driver. 'He's a devil for dropping off anywhere. I'll go and wake him.'

But when Sydney tapped him on the shoulder, the face Rupert raised was so stricken and haggard, that Sydney was prompted to ask if there'd been a death in the family.

'Only myself,' muttered Rupert, chucking away the empty bottle and stumbling to his feet. 'Only myself.'

Taggie had just finished clearing up and feeding Gertrude the corned beef hash which Declan normally loved but had left half-eaten this evening, when the doorbell rang. Gertrude ran out barking as loudly as she could with her mouth full. Taggie followed, hastily kicking her mother's rather grubby bra and French knickers under the radiator. For a second she thought she must be dreaming, for there, swaying in a dinner jacket, clutching a red box, was Rupert.

'Hullo, angel. Thought I'd catch up on the gossip. Is your father in?'

'Yes, but he and Mummy have gone to bed.'

'I'm sorry. I saw a light on. Thought he might be working late.'

'Do you want a drink?'

Oh God! Suddenly she remembered. Aengus had knocked over the whisky.

'I've had enough,' said Rupert. 'I'd love a cup of coffee.'

His normally sleeked-back blond hair had flopped over his forehead, his black tie was crooked, his blue eyes crossing. Taggie realized he was absolutely plastered.

'You didn't drive down?' she said in horror.

'No, no, Syd dropped me off, Now, whatever I do I mushn't

'lose this.' Carefully he put his red box down on the kitchen table. 'My red box, my unread box. I sometimes wonder if anyone would notice if I threw the whole lot in the Thames.'

'Where have you been?' said Taggie, putting the kettle on, wondering if by some miracle he might have had a bust-up with Cameron.

'To the Cup Final.'

'Of course. You were making a speech. How did it go?'

'All right, I suppose. The speech that the department had written was so ghastly I tore it up and told a lot of blue stories instead. I hope no one was there from Corinium with a tape recorder.'

'And they liked it?'

'They seemed to. They could afford to be kind. It's probably the last one I'll make.'

'What d'you mean?' Taggie put three spoonfuls of sugar into the blackest cup of coffee and put it down on the table in front of him.

'Thanks, darling. The PM's announcing the election date as Thursday 24th June. At least I won a bet on it.'

'But you'll win,' said Taggie, sitting down at the table beside him.

Rupert shrugged. 'I'm not sure we will. The awful thing is, I don't give a bugger. I'm fed up with politics.'

'You'll feel differently tomorrow,' said Taggie.

At that moment Gertrude strolled in, looked beadily at Rupert, then, to Taggie's amazement, jumped on to his knee and gave his face a quick lick, before settling down, leaving white hairs all over his dinner jacket. Rupert stroked her and laughed.

'There are some small victories left to me,' he said.

'Was C-C-Cameron with you?'

Taggie felt it would be better if they could talk about her openly.

'No, it was much too public. Every photographer would have picked us up. Anyway, Tony's *in situ* this weekend.'

'It must be awfully difficult for you both.'

431

'Worse for her. At least I don't have to sleep with Tony. I wish she wasn't so fucking insecure. She's like a Jack Russell. One spends one's time removing her from the target of her aggression – usually oneself.'

'Patrick said she had a terrible childhood,' said Taggie. 'He didn't give any details,' she added quickly. 'Just said she'd really been through it.'

What on earth am I doing defending her, she wondered.

'I don't believe all that junk about terrible childhoods,' said Rupert. 'I've had four stepmothers and five stepfathers. You had Declan and Maud, which is even worse.'

Taggie giggled.

'We're not screwed up,' said Rupert.

That was debatable, thought Taggie.

Rupert picked up the petition. 'Look at all these names!' His eyes ran down page after page. 'Christ, you've been working hard.'

'It wasn't so good today,' said Taggie. Then she told him about the rugger club.

Rupert was absolutely furious. 'The bastards,' he howled. 'Give me their names and I'll get their ground ploughed up. But what can you expect from a lot of rugger yobbos? Poor darling, I'm so sorry. It must have been awful.'

He yawned without even putting his hand over his mouth, showing a long pink tongue, and teeth without a single stopping. Then he said, 'Why have you written L and R on the back of your hands?'

Blushing, Taggie shoved her hands under the table.

'I'll drive you home,' she said quickly.

As she started up the car, the tape came on. Frantic with embarrassment, she tried to tug it out of the machine, but Rupert's hand closed over hers like a vice.

'Leave it.'

'Turn left at the A412,' said Taggie's deep breathy voice, 'then keep going for two miles, then turn left just before the Old Mill pub, then keep going till you come to a big barn, turn right, then left up a winding road. Winchley Women's Institute is at the top on the right.'

Pulling out the tape, Rupert looked up at the windscreen, on which a large capital L and R were stuck on opposite sides.

'You poor little duck,' he said softly.

The chestnut candles were shedding their white petals along his drive, a couple of horses blinked in the gloom. As Taggie drew up in front of the house, he said again, 'You poor little duck.'

Taggie hung her head. 'I can't map-read very well. It takes me so long and signposts are difficult too, because I don't know the words. If I put it on tape it speeds everything up, and we've got so much ground to cover before July.'

Rupert couldn't bear it. What was it about Taggie that so often brought a lump to his throat?

'Angel, you can't go round on your own. Particularly not at night.'

'I don't always. Dame Enid's come with me, and the Bishop, and Professor Graystock once or twice.'

Rupert shuddered. 'That's worse than being alone.'

Enforced celibacy was not natural to Rupert. It was like asking a man who smoked sixty cigarettes a day only to smoke ten cigarettes one day a week. Denied Cameron, he was certainly not used to sleeping alone. Still very drunk, he only just stopped himself taking Taggie in his arms to comfort her, and Christ knows where that would have led to. Declan would take him apart and Cameron would bolt straight back to Tony.

Getting out of the car, however, a brilliant idea struck him. 'I'll be travelling all round the area canvassing over the next month. You can come with me and hand out Venturer posters and stickers, and paddle the Venturer canoe at the same time. We can even use the Tory loudspeaker to plug Venturer when no one from the Party's listening.'

'Is that allowed?' said Taggie in awe.

'Politics is a dirty business,' said Rupert blandly. 'The Socialists paid a lot of actors twenty-five pounds to dress up in shit order and pretend to be a dole queue for their election poster last time.'

33

Next morning Caitlin rang up The Priory, wild with excitement.

'Gertrude's in the *Daily Mail*! She looks so sweet.'

'What's she doing?' asked Taggie.

'Wearing a Venturer T-shirt and an expression of absolute outrage. She's sitting on your knee. You look nice, much better than that old tart Sarah Stratton.'

'Oh goodness,' said Taggie. 'What's the piece about?'

'The headline says: *"Rival Beauties weigh in for the Battle of the Box"*,' read Caitlin. 'They've used the two posters of you and Sarah. *"Will the blonde or the brunette pack the greater punch?"* it starts. Then there's a lot of guff about Sarah being Paul Stratton's second wife, and Corinium's latest star presenter, who pulls in three hundred fan letters a week.

'Then it goes on: *"The dark horse (or rather beauty) in the race is Agatha O'Hara, 18-year-old daughter of TV megastar Declan O'Hara, who's bidding to oust his ex-boss Lord Baddingham in the Corinium franchise fight. Agatha runs her own business"* . . . get you . . . *"cooking for the great and famous, but sadly she can no longer undertake dinner parties for her favourite client, Tony Baddingham's wife, Monica, in case state secrets slip out over the soufflé."*'

'Gosh,' said Taggie in amazement. 'Where did they get all that from? I hope Lady B isn't cross. How are you anyway?'

'All right. Fed up with revising. Can you send me some

money? And tell bloody Mummy and Daddy to write.'

'They've been really busy with the franchise and things,' said Taggie.

'Mummy's never busy with anything,' said Caitlin bitterly.

The long, hard grind of getting Venturer's message across to the people who mattered continued throughout the long, hot summer. But things were much easier now for Taggie. Several other papers reproduced the poster and, as she toured the area, people began to know all about Venturer, recognize her, welcome her and even ask her to autograph the poster.

More important, she spent much of May and June driving around with Rupert on his campaign trail. Leaving him to canvass or to rally support for other South-West Tory MPs. Taggie nipped off to visit vicars, youth clubs and Chambers of Commerce.

Rather too often for Tony Baddingham or Central Office's liking, the two campaigns merged. Rupert was not above urging people to support Venturer on the Tory loudspeaker, or sticking Venturer posters up on the van alongside those urging the public to vote Conservative. Everywhere he and Taggie went, they handed out Venturer publicity material and had great fun after dark, driving round plastering the gateposts of Corinium directors, and even the Corinium building itself, with 'Support Venturer' stickers.

To add to Tony's apoplexy, Rupert conducted the entire campaign in a blue Venturer T-shirt and twice appeared similarly clad on 'Cotswold Round-Up', and, even worse, with huge 'Support Venturer' posters on the Tory party van behind him.

Tony was quoted as saying the Venturer T-shirts had been chosen entirely by Rupert to match his blue eyes, and that no doubt the boy shading his forehead on the front symbolized all those Gloucestershire husbands trying to see where Rupert had hidden their wives. Rupert cracked back that everyone knew who the Corinium Ram was supposed to symbolize.

And so the mudslinging went on, with the local press and radio stations uniformly backing Corinium, but the National and Trade press, having scrutinized the applications and the candidates, universally agreeing that Venturer had the more exciting programme plans. Dame Enid wrote a battle song, sung by Maud, called 'Everything Venture', which to Venturer's relief didn't get into the charts.

On 24th June Labour won the election by twenty seats, with the SDP holding the balance of power. Paul Stratton lost his seat. Rupert kept his. He had, in fact, fought a brilliant campaign. Taggie's presence seemed to soothe him, so he was far less acerbic with bores and hecklers, and, as he was one of the only Tories returned with a much increased majority, Central Office had to stop grumbling about him using Tory funds and equipment to promote Venturer.

In an unprecedented move, Owen Davies, the new Labour Prime Minister, asked Rupert whether he would like to stay on as Minister for Sport if the post was made non-political. Rupert was deeply touched, but refused. He was fed up with swimming galas and ping-pong matches, and there was a big row brewing about players taking drugs at Wimbledon, which he was only too happy to hand on to his successor. He was also immediately offered a job by the International Olympics Committee, but refused that too for the moment, knowing it would mean more buzzing round the world.

He wanted a breathing space, to spend the rest of the summer at home concentrating on the yard, seeing something of his children and putting in a lot of spade work with Cameron, who was getting increasingly uptight. Falling more and more in love with Rupert, she found it almost impossible to pander to Tony's sexual needs and cope with the demanding job of Programme Controller at Corinium. While Rupert was fighting the election, he'd been constantly hounded by the press, baying for franchise gossip and trying to catch him out in some new affair, so he and Cameron had had to be doubly careful.

'All this secrecy's just like adultery, darling,' said Rupert on one of their few meetings. 'Very good training for when you're married.'

'That is the most cynical remark I've ever heard,' stormed Cameron.

'Not at all. The secret of a happy marriage is not getting found out.'

'How d'you know? You didn't have a happy marriage.'

'That's because I was always getting found out.'

As the election was over, and Tony was tied up all day in meetings in London, she and Rupert had arranged to meet at a hotel outside Henley. As they settled down to Bloody Marys and a splendid view of the Thames, a barge came chugging up stream. Two young girls in bikinis were sunbathing on deck. Cameron watched Rupert run an expert eye over them. Now he had free time on his hands, would she find it increasingly difficult to hold him? All the same, she was still not prepared to burn her boats with Corinium until Venturer had safely won the franchise, and, she had to confess, all the secret meetings with Rupert did give the affair a certain edge.

'Come on,' he said, draining his Bloody Mary and picking up the keys of their hotel bedroom. 'I want to indulge in some mole-molesting.'

But she who lives more lives than one, more deaths than one, must die. Next day, in the Corinium canteen, Daysee Butler and Deirdre Kilpatrick took their cottage cheese and kiwi-fruit salads to a corner table and didn't notice Cameron sitting next door.

At first there were the usual grumbles about bosses and crews, but just as Cameron had abandoned her shepherd's pie half-eaten and started on her yoghurt, Deirdre said, 'I don't usually read the *Scorpion* but did you see that story that Rupert Campbell-Black's having an affair with a cook?'

'Cameron Cook?' said Daysee in amazement. 'Lord B won't like that.'

'Not Cameron Cook – a cook. Declan O'Hara's daughter. She does directors' lunches and things. She's seriously pretty. Well, according to the *Scorpion*, she's been canvassing with Rupert and now they're absolutely inseparable.'

Looking down, Cameron saw she had squeezed her yoghurt so hard that it had spurted all over the table. Without attempting to clear up the mess, she walked out of the canteen into Cotchester High Street and the nearest telephone box.

Rupert was trying out one of his new, very young horses over a row of fences in the field beyond the stables. When the telephone suddenly rang in his pocket, the horse nearly took off back to Ireland. Even when he'd pressed the answer button to silence the ringing, it took all his strength to pull up the terrified animal. All Cameron could hear was a muffled thunder of hooves and expletives.

'Hullo,' Rupert said finally.

'Have you seen the *Scorpion*?'

'Yes. So what?'

'All about you and Ms O'Hara.'

'That was yesterday's *Scorpion*. They've linked me with Mary Whitehouse this morning.'

'Can't you be fucking serious?' screamed Cameron. 'Everyone's talking about it.'

'Good,' said Rupert. 'At least it keeps the heat off us.' Then, as Cameron showed no signs of calming down, he added, 'Darling, there's nothing in it, I promise you. As Taggie said in today's *Star*, "Rupert's old enough to be my father. In fact he's a friend of my father's".'

'Doesn't mean a thing – Augustus John was old enough to be a lot of girls' great-grandfather – that didn't stop him. Oh Christ . . .' she screamed as her money ran out. 'I'll call you back in a minute.'

'Please don't until you've cooled down,' said Rupert. 'I don't want both you and the horse having hysterics at the same time.'

Next time they met, it took a great deal of sweet-talking to win her round.

The next big event in the franchise battle was the public meeting held in Cotchester Town Hall at the beginning of July. Chaired by members of the IBA board, it was supposed to give the general public the chance to air their grievances about existing programme content and quiz the rival applicants about their plans. It also gave the IBA the opportunity

438

to observe the applicants in action and gauge the degree of local support.

In fact, the audience consisted mostly of Corinium, Venturer and Mid-West staff and their local supporters, members of consortiums from other franchise areas who would soon go through the same ordeal, picking up tips, local councillors whose sole object was to persuade Venturer or Mid-West that their borough was the perfect site for the new studios, members of Gay Lib, the Women's Movement and other pressure groups, and a handful of the public, only interested in gazing at Declan, Rupert and Wesley Emerson.

Much-needed rain had been bucketing down all day, but it stopped just before the meeting was due to start. Venturer arrived first. As Rupert had given them all a pep talk about being properly dressed, Declan had sulkily put on a suit and a tie.

'And you can get out of jeans,' he had snapped in turn at Taggie. 'I've hardly seen your legs since you were born.'

Taggie, having rifled through her wardrobe in despair, had rushed into Cheltenham and bought a beautiful violet dress with a scooped neckline, a nipped-in waist and flounced gypsy skirt. Newly washed, her dark hair fluffed down to her shoulder blades as though she'd beaten it with an egg whisk.

Declan, in somewhat unflattering amazement, told her she looked absolutely gorgeous. She was glad she did, when she later found that Sarah Stratton, Cameron, Daysee and Janey had all pulled out the stops. To Taggie's delight she also found the audience packed with people whose support she had sought in her drives round the area. Local councillors, race relations officers, social workers, ladies from the WI, from as far afield as Southampton, Oxford and Stratford, had turned up and now surged forward to shake her hand.

'We've still got your lovely poster up; we've written to the IBA; we've been following Venturer's programme with such interest,' they all said. 'We thought we'd come and cheer you on.'

'Remember me?' said a gaunt-looking man in a crumpled

lightweight suit, which had obviously just been unearthed from a trunk in the attic.

'Of course,' said Taggie, quite overwhelmed. 'How wonderful of you to turn up.'

It was the headmaster with the dyslexic son.

A diversion was caused when Marti Gluckstein, who'd never been to the country before, tried to enter the hall wearing gumboots, a waterproof deerstalker, a riding mac and holding an umbrella over his head.

'Don't bring that thing in here. It's unlucky!' boomed Dame Edith.

'Come on, Marti, I'll buy you a stiff drink before we kick off,' said Bas, guiding Marti back through the puddles over the road to the Cotchester Arms for a quick de-robing.

Sprinting after them, Rupert handed Bas his hip flask. 'Can you fill this up with weak rum for Wes? His attention span will never last the course unlaced.'

Wesley, having taken another five wickets that afternoon, and having just been picked for the third test, had been celebrating and was now busy signing autographs.

The next arrivals were three shiny red-faced stocky young men, who'd obviously been in the Cotchester Arms since opening time, who strode up to Taggie waving their tickets. The shortest one, who had hard blue eyes and crinkly hair, thrust a melting box of chocolates into Taggie's hand.

'Hullo, Agatha,' he said. 'Bet you didn't expect us.'

'Sorry we were a bit rowdy when you dropped in,' said the second.

'Thought we'd come and give you a bit of support,' said the third.

It was the Captain and two props from Winchley Rugger Club. Tears filled Taggie's eyes as she hugged them all. 'How sweet of you. Come and meet my father. He adores rugger.'

Declan shook them all by the hand several times. 'Treat Corinium like the Welsh at Twickenham,' he said. 'And here they come.'

A great theatrical hiss went up from the Venturer camp as

440

the Corinium mafia trooped in. They were led by Tony, very brown from Ascot. Wearing a new dark-pink and blue silk shirt, a pink tie, and a pink carnation in his buttonhole, he managed to flash his teeth at everyone in the room except Venturer. He was followed by Ginger Johnson, Georgie Baines, who'd obviously had a few to steady his nerves, Mike Meadows, Head of Sport, Charles Fairburn, Seb Burrows, Simon Harris, who'd been allowed back in a consultancy capacity to impress the IBA, and whose straggly beard had turned quite white, Cyril Peacock, false teeth rattling, sweating through his suit, and Cameron, truculent in an elongated black T-shirt which came five inches above her knees. Sarah Stratton, wearing a dress in Virgin Mary-blue, with a white Puritan collar also to impress the IBA, brought up the rear with James Vereker, whose head was held high so more people could recognize him.

'I fear the Greeks when they come bearing Presenters,' muttered Declan.

'Who's chair?' James asked Charles Fairburn as the Corinium contingent sat down in the front row.

'Dunno. Belongs to the Town Hall, I should think,' said Charles.

'No,' said James impatiently, 'who's Chair?'

'I've just told you.'

'I'm asking you, who is chairing the meeting?'

'Oh.' Comprehension dawned on Charles's round red face. 'Might be Old Mother Goose –' which was everyone's nickname for Lady Gosling – 'but I wouldn't have thought she'd have bothered to come this far.'

Cameron grabbed a seat at the end of the row by the window, as far away from Tony as possible. All she could see was one of his beautifully polished black shoes, rotating as if he were doing an ankle-slimming exercise – a sign that he was nervous. The company *in situ* always got more flak at public meetings than those seeking to oust it. Tony, frightened of ridicule, knew he was in for a bumpy evening. The entire Corinium contingent studiously ignored Venturer – the committed from distaste, the moles from embarrassment.

Henry Hampshire, however, who'd been to a drinks party, had no such reservations.

'Hello everyone,' he beamed as he came through the door. 'Hullo, Taggie darling, you're looking beautiful. Hullo, Rupert.' Then, turning to the cringing Corinium contingent, boomed, 'Oh look, there's Charles, Georgie and Cameron. Must go and say hello.'

'Hen-ree,' hissed Rupert, grabbing his arm and whispering in his ear. 'You're not supposed to know they're on our side.'

'What?' said Henry loudly. 'What's that? How d'yer mean, not on our side? 'Course they are.'

Fortunately Tony was talking to the Archdeacon and didn't hear. As Rupert tried to explain, Henry looked as deflated as an English setter who's been told he's not going on a walk, then cheered up when he saw Daysee Butler.

'Who's she? She on our side?'

'No, she's with Corinium.'

'Damn shame, pretty girl like that, and that's Sarah Stratton next to her, isn't it? She's a damn pretty girl too. Why isn't *she* on our side? Met her shooting at Tony's.'

And next moment Henry had broken away from Rupert's restraining hand and marched across the room to talk to Sarah, who introduced him to Daysee.

'Just saying to Rupert, pretty girls like you should be on our side.'

Sarah giggled: 'I don't think Tony'd like that very much. How's your Springer spaniel?'

'How incredible you remembering that,' said Henry, now beaming down on the two girls like an English setter waving his plumy tail at two bitches. 'What are you both doing afterwards?'

'Bugger off, Henry,' snarled Tony.

'Hen-ree,' Rupert dragged him off.

Fortunately at that moment a diversion was provided by Basil returning with Marti, quite soberly dressed now, and Janey Lloyd-Foxe in a pink flying-suit.

'Hullo, Rupert darling.' Janey kissed him full on the mouth. 'Sorry I'm late.'

Rupert tugged up her zip to the bounds of decency, saying, 'For Christ's sake go and distract Henry.'

Basil took Rupert aside. 'I've filled up the hip flask for Wesley.' Then, dropping his voice, he whispered, 'Those lovely lips just puckered up to meet yours were round my dick at eight o'clock this morning.'

'What?' exploded Rupert. 'What did you say?'

'You heard,' said Basil, grinning.

'How dare you,' thundered Rupert. 'She's married to my best friend.'

''Course she is, and very happily. I'm just making sure she doesn't suffer from post-natal depression when Billy's away.'

Rupert might well have hit Bas across the room if the IBA – three members of the Board and various members of their staff – hadn't trooped in and taken up their places on the platform.

'We *are* honoured,' Charles whispered to James. 'Old Mother Goose *is* in the chair. The IBA must regard the outcome as by no means certain then, if she's come all this way to have a look.'

'I can't think why you're looking so cheerful,' said James fretfully. 'Venturer's bound to offer me a job if they get the franchise. I mean I am "Cotswold Round-Up", but, as they've got the Bishop to handle religious programmes, I can't see them wanting you.'

'Who are those deadbeats over there?' Janey asked Bas.

'The Mid-West consortium,' said Bas. 'Can't think they'll bother us much.'

Rupert, having at last persuaded Henry to stop chatting up Daysee and sit down, collapsed into a seat between Taggie and Declan.

'How the hell am I going to keep this lot under control until December?' he said.

Taggie giggled: 'Henry's certainly fallen for Daysee.'

'Let me not to the marriage of true mindlessness admit impediments,' said Declan.

.

The audience were now occupying every seat in the body of the hall, with Corinium spread out along the front row and Cameron at the far end by the window. Next to her, at right-angles, on a single row of chairs, sat the Mid-West consortium, who looked a pretty moth-eaten bunch. Facing them, also on a single row of chairs, forming a square with the platform, sat Venturer.

Lady Gosling, decided Cameron, looked more like a hedge-hog than a goose, a Mrs Tiggywinkle, with small twinkling intelligent eyes, a long thin nose, a pointed chin and rather wild grey hair, held down on either side by tortoise-shell slides. She wore no make-up and, despite the warmth of the evening, was smothered in several shawls over her olive-green wool dress. The cosy exterior, however, was deceptive and hid a rapier mind. As Head of an Oxford college, Gwendolyn Gosling had taught Russian. Her fellow dons were not altogether joking when they nicknamed her 'Khruschèv'. There was shrewdness beneath the amiability, and the twinkling eyes, like the stars, gave off little warmth.

For a hideous moment at the beginning of the meeting it looked as though no one was going to ask any questions. Then a man in spectacles got up and grumbled about the reception in Gloucester. Corinium's Chief Engineer got up to answer him, and the stupor produced by engineers at public meetings allowed everyone time to collect their thoughts.

More straightforward complaints then followed from local councillors who had not yet been interviewed by James on 'Cotswold Round-Up' that coverage in their area was pitiful.

Mrs Makepiece, James's daily, then rose to her feet, and, disclaiming any connection with Corinium, said 'Cotswold Round-Up' was the best programme on telly, and why couldn't it be on seven days a week. This was greeted by bellows of 'Rubbish' and 'Offside' from Taggie's rugger players.

One of the Corinium shop stewards, who'd just screwed a two-thousand-pound rise out of Tony for all his members, as well as a fat bribe for himself, shouted from the back that he wouldn't trust Declan O'Hara's mob further than he could throw them. His claim that industrial relations at Corinium were second to none, however, were greeted by cries of 'si-down' from all over the hall.

'As Corinium fork out immediately whatever the unions demand and most of the technicians earn more than the Prime Minister, I should think industrial relations are second to none,' yelled Bas, to loud cheers from the Venturer supporters.

The Chairman of Chipping Sodbury's WI then rose to her feet and said in a ringing voice that her institute was sick to the teeth of news about Cotchester and nothing about Chipping Sodbury.

Remembering 'Miss Corinium Television', Rupert caught Declan's eye. 'She's forgotten Miss Chipping Sodbury's tits,' he whispered across Taggie.

Both men started to shake with laughter, until quelled by a cold look from Lady Gosling.

Tony rose to reply. 'I can assure you, madam,' he said smoothly, 'that, by an extraordinary coincidence, "Cotswold Round-Up" is due to visit Chipping Sodbury later this week.'

'Are we?' said James to Sarah, looking startled.

'In fact,' Tony went on warmly, 'we have super plans for the entire Cotswold area.'

'You've been here eight years. Why haven't we seen any of them?' bellowed Taggie's headmaster.

More cheers all round were counterpointed by snores from Mrs Makepiece.

'I've studied both Venturer's and Corinium's applications at the public library,' went on Taggie's headmaster, 'and Venturer's programme plans seem infinitely more imaginative. What I would like to ask Lord Baddingham is how much have his grandiose new plans for a multi-million-pound studio, for slots for every possible minority group, for cultural improvement and for spectacular entertainment been spawned by editorial inspiration or desire to hang on to his very lucrative franchise?'

Tony was about to rise and shout back over the deafening cheers, but James was too quick for him. 'James Vereker, "Cotswold Round-Up",' he announced, getting to his feet and turning sideways so he could be recognized both by the platform and the floor.

'Who's a pretty boy then?' catcalled Taggie's rugger captain.

'As anchorman of "Cotswold Round-Up," said James, 'I know I speak for each and everyone of us at Corinium from Tony Baddingham downward when I say that Corinium's ethos can be summed up in two words.'

'Bloody terrible,' said Taggie's rugger captain, to screams of laughter.

'Two little words —' James ploughed on — 'Corinium cares.'

'The only fing Tony Baddingham cares abart is making a fast buck,' shouted Freddie, to more deafening cheers.

Mrs Makepiece snored so loudly that she woke herself up. 'Let's get up a partition,' she said loudly.

Cameron knew she ought to stand up and defend Corinium, but she didn't relish getting ripped apart by Declan. She was saved by the Women-in-Broadcasting lobby, who all had moustaches and who complained that there weren't enough women in any of the consortiums. Lady Gosling nodded in agreement, and made notes.

The meeting droned on. Wesley Emerson had had a hard day in the field. No one but Rupert and Bas realized that each time his noble head nodded onto his right buttonhole he was taking a long suck of rum from a straw to Rupert's hip flask in his breast pocket.

Outside in Cotchester Park, the lime trees were in flower; their sweet delicate scent, stronger after the downpour, drifted in through the open window. Cameron watched the house martins swooping after insects, flashing their white bellies. The tennis courts were packed with people playing vigorous Wimbledon-inspired tennis. In a week or so they'd revert to their usual patball. She glanced surreptitiously across at Rupert, who was sitting next to that drip Taggie, who (whatever Rupert said to the contrary) had a thumping crush on him.

Nothing except for the occasional yawn, not even a glance

446

in her direction, betrayed the fact that Rupert had left her bed at six o'clock that morning. Cameron wondered sometimes if she'd imagined the whole thing. She was so deep in thought, she had to be nudged in the ribs by Seb to answer a question from a pale girl from Gay Lib as to whether the lesbian shepherdess who'd appeared briefly in the last series of 'Four Men went to Mow' would appear in the next one.

As Cameron sat down, the Chairman from Chipping Sodbury's WI returned to the attack. 'Nothing that comes from Corinium TV,' she said, 'is truly regional. Even Dorothy Dove speaks with a London accent.'

Another rabble-rouser, again heavily bunged by Tony, then rose to his feet.

'While we're on the subject of accents,' he sneered, 'in the first week of July four people were brutally butchered by the IRA. Do we really want an Irishman, namely one Declan O'Hara, bearing in mind his left-wing attitudes and the subversive nature of many of his programmes, to be the Chief Executive of an English television company?'

'Out of order,' screamed the Venturer contingent.

'Offside, put it in straight,' roared the rugger players.

Declan, who'd gone white, was just about to answer.

'Careful,' whispered Rupert.

'I'd like the speaker to withdraw that remark,' said Lady Gosling frostily. 'Next question, please.'

The Clean-Up Television Campaign, headed by the Archdeacon, then started slamming sex and violence, followed by the Bishop of Cotchester who said how concerned he was about his flock, and that he would be working with Venturer to reduce not only sex and violence, but the very widespread blasphemy on television. He was just getting into his stride when Henry Hampshire's ancient gardener staggered to his feet.

'I like to go to bed very early,' he grumbled. 'I do wish Corinium wouldn't put all those sexy fil-lums on so late at night, because I and the missus can never stay awake to watch them.'

447

Everyone roared with laughter, including Lady Gosling, who then clapped her hands and said it was with great regret that she had to bring this very stimulating meeting to a close as they were running out of time. They would end, she added, with a seven-minute sales pitch from each of the three contenders.

Tony rose first, deliberately turning his back on Venturer and talking half to the platform and half to the audience.

'Good evening,' he began suavely. 'I am the Chief Executive of – er –' he glanced down at his notes and everyone laughed – 'Corinium Television. We have noted,' he went on, 'the very perceptive and instructive points raised tonight, and, although we don't agree with all of them, anyone who would like a further answer to his – or indeed, her –' he smiled broadly – 'question, please write to me personally.'

'Wanker,' muttered Rupert under his breath. He folded his arms belligerently and, with the hand that was hidden, fought a violent urge to caress the side of Taggie's left breast which swelled so seductively beneath her violet dress. She looked so ravishing this evening, and she'd done so well to get all those strange but incredibly influential people to the meeting.

Firmly clenching his hand away from Taggie, he looked across at Cameron, who was gazing moodily into space with a kind of deadpan, terrorist truculence. She reminded him of the girl grooms he used to pull in the old days. He desperately wanted a fuck, but he wouldn't get Cameron tonight. Tony, overexcited by the meeting, would no doubt take advantage of that release. Rupert was finding the enforced celibacy more and more trying, and, bloody hell, what was Bas doing pulling Janey? It seemed as though he was the only person in the world behaving himself.

Having finished a rousing spiel about Corinium's long and honourable record, Tony was now paying tribute to 'the thriving, creative community' he had the privilege to lead. 'We are aware, Ladies and Gentlemen, that there is life west of Harrods, our hearts are not in "Dallas", nor is our HQ in London. Our company is run by people from the region, who have a special place in the Cotswolds and, indeed, in West

Country life. Corinium is its own man here. We will be biased, we will fight for the West, we are pledged to serve the whole community. Above all we care.'

He sat down to moderate cheers. Then it was Mid-West's turn.

A fat man with straggly white hair staggered to his feet and then took ages to find his notes. 'That's obviously the geography master who never found his way to London,' whispered Rupert to Taggie.

'I am deeply honoured,' began the fat man.

'Name, name,' yelled the audience.

'My name is Cedric Bonnington,' he mumbled. 'I hope to be Chairman of Mid-West Television.'

'Well, don't be bashful, speak up,' shouted Tony's rabble-rouser.

Sadly, Cedric didn't. In a low mumble he laboriously read out that he was very interested in all the fascinating points that had been made by the floor.

'I cannot reveal who our backers are,' he droned on, 'but very substantial funds will be available should the very talented group, whose names I also cannot divulge at this stage, win the franchise.'

'He'll probably get it,' said Georgie Baines to Seb Burrows.

'What about women?' yelled the Women-in-Broadcasting lobby.

Cedric consulted his notes. The company's Programme Controller, whose name he also couldn't divulge, he said, would be a woman of the widest experience.

'Madame Cyn,' yelled Rupert.

'Mary Whitehouse,' said Tony's shop steward.

The audience waited for more exciting revelations, and, when none materialized, egged on by the Corinium consortium, who'd all got to their feet, started to drift away. It was almost dark outside; the pubs beckoned.

'No one's going to stay and listen to Daddy,' said Taggie in anguish, and, as Declan got up to speak, people were swarming out into the High Street.

'I'd like first to answer the speaker who questioned the

right of an Irishman to run an English television company,' he began softly. 'As much right perhaps as that great Irishman, the Duke of Wellington, to command a British army.'

He spoke without notes. As people poured back into the hall again, the deep soft husky voice carried easily round the hall.

'I am proud to be Irish,' he went on, 'and, to echo the words of another great Irish patriot, Irwin Cobb, I too had an ancestor who was out with the pikes in '98. He was captured by the English and tried for treason. They hanged him by the neck until he was dead, but his soul goes marching on, transmitting to his descendants, of whom I am proud to be one, the desire to fight against tyranny whenever I come across it. I also love and honour British television. It is the best in the world. That's why I and so many of my countrymen – Eamonn Andrews, Terry Wogan, Robert Kee, Frank Delaney, Dave Allen, Henry Kelly, Patrick Dromgoole, Gloria Hunniford – are over here, learning from it and, I hope, contributing to it.

'But we still go on fighting tyranny and oppression whenever we find it. I found it in the few months I worked for Corinium. That's why I walked out, and why, with my English friends –' he turned and smiled briefly at the Venturer consortium – 'I have put in a bid to oust Lord Baddingham.'

He then proceeded to carve up Tony and tear Corinium's boring sycophantic programmes to shreds. Only at the end did he briefly outline how Venturer would be different, how they would truly both represent the area and foster local talent. 'I would like all great artists of the future to be able to say they had their first chance at Venturer.'

The audience stood up and cheered him for nearly three minutes. Stony-faced, Tony strode out of the hall. Cameron tried to follow him, but, trapped by the crowd, she watched Rupert, Declan, Taggie and the rest of Venturer, plus their supporters, jubilantly swanning off to the Bar Sinister for drinks on the house. Rupert never gave her a backward glance. Sick with desire, she wondered how much longer she could go on playing a double game.

Although the *Cotchester News* reported the meeting a rousing success for Corinium and published numerous rigged readers' letters of support, it was generally agreed that Venturer had won that round.

34

After his humiliation at the public meeting, Tony stepped up his campaign to discredit Venturer. Flipping through a list of their names the following morning, he decided his newsroom had been singularly inept in uncovering any dirt. The Bishop of Cotchester, it seemed, had neither fiddled with the collection nor with any of his more cherubic choir boys; Dame Enid had never straddled anything more exciting than her cello; Professor Graystock was recognized as an old goat, but no more so than the average don. On the other hand, Henry Hampshire was plainly capable of being led astray by Daysee Butler. Perhaps she ought to be sent off to interview him.

Nothing as yet on Rupert, except an alleged walk-out with Taggie O'Hara, which Tony didn't believe. She was far too gormless. All the same it might be a good idea to allow her to cook for Monica again. Primed with a few late-night brandies, she might become indiscreet about the moles who were joining Venturer from other companies. In addition Monica had been so outraged because Tony'd banished Taggie from the house that she'd refused to give any more dinner parties, and Tony did need to entertain some of those boring but influential local dignitaries who might otherwise drift towards Venturer.

He added Taggie's name to the list, but that didn't bring him any nearer Rupert. He made a note to track down Beattie

Johnson, who'd been writing Rupert's memoirs when Rupert booted her out last year. There must be some grievances to fan there.

Freddie Jones, Tony decided blackly, was Venturer's greatest asset. He was so solid, so dependable, so popular, so hugely successful after such a lowly start, which appealed to a crusading streak in the IBA. Ha! thought Tony, *cherchez la femme.* He buzzed Miss Madden. 'Will you tell James Vereker to come up.'

James was not happy. Even through his layers of egotism he realized he'd made a fool of himself at the public meeting. He was still miffed because no one had asked him to join their consortium, and, opening a new edition of *Who's Who in Television* that morning, he'd discovered two columns devoted to Declan and not even a reference to himself.

James brushed his hair and put on a tie. He hoped Tony wasn't still miffed about the public meeting.

Tony, however, was at his most amiable, steering James towards the squashy green sofa, when usually he made male staff perch on hard-backed chairs, telling Madden they didn't want to be disturbed, offering James a large drink.

James normally only drank Perrier at lunchtime, both for his figure and to keep his wits about him for his programme, but now he felt it fitting to accept a large Bell's, just to show that he and Tony were both males capable of holding their liquor.

'I've got a very special mission for you, James,' said Tony.

Half an hour later James returned to his office in a state of euphoria to find Sarah exuding Anaïs Anaïs and expectancy.

'Are we lunching, darling?'

'Probably,' said James. 'I've got to make a call.'

When he rang Valerie Jones, she was absolutely 'delaighted' to hear from him. 'Oh, don't mention that silly franchise. If one can't talk to one's friends,' she said. 'I was going to phone you and your – er – lovely wife –' she always forgot Lizzie's name – 'to remind you that we're opening Green Lawns to the public on Saturday, and we hoped you'd both pop in. It is looking really rather lovely at the moment.'

453

'What an extraordinary coincidence,' said James. 'I was phoning to say of course we've got your opening in our diary and we were hoping we might come and film it for "Cotswold Round-Up". We're only covering the best gardens. Tony and Monica's, of course, and the Duchess's at Badminton. Hullo, hullo, are you still there?'

'She's fainted,' said Sarah.

'Of course I am,' shrieked Valerie.

'Could I come for a recce this afternoon? Will Freddie be there?'

'He's away.'

'Good,' said James wolfishly. 'Give me a chance to get you on my own.'

Valerie's tinkle of laughter showed she was not displeased.

'What *are* you playing at?' asked Sarah as James hung up.

'Tony wants a spy in the Venturer camp. He's chosen me because he thinks I'm the one guy who can charm secrets out of Valerie.'

'The spy who came in from the cold frame,' giggled Sarah. 'Are you going to stick poison umbrellas into Valerie's garden gnomes?'

It was a muggy, still afternoon, French-grey sky on the horizon deepening to forget-me-not blue overhead. The tall seeding grasses in the hayfields were turning gold against the deep summer greens of the trees. At the bottom of the Jones's drive was a large sign saying: 'Garden Open on 13th July, to be televised on "Cotswold Round-Up". Come and meet James Vereker in person – proceeds to the Red Cross.'

Smirking, James drove up a black tarmac drive as wide as the M1. Long before he reached the house he was almost blinded by a blaze of colour. Every flowerbed was packed with serried clashing ranks of French marigolds, yellow calceolaria, royal-blue cineraria, flaming-red geraniums, billiard-ball pink zinnias and mauve asters. As he drew up in front of the house a lorry was unloading plants. Having denuded every garden centre for miles around, Valerie was now hiring four hundred scarlet salvias and three hundred yellow begonias from Rent-a-Garden.

Round the corner came a sweating youth pushing a wheel-barrow crammed with scarlet and mauve petunias. Next moment Valerie came screaming after him, brandishing a small fork.

'What are you doing, Spicer?'

'Putting them on the rubbish heap, ma'am.'

'They're meant to be planted in the wheelbarrow, you idiot. Can't you recognize creative gardening when you see it? Take it straight back to the patio.'

Then she saw handsome James getting out of his pale-blue Porsche and her face softened.

'James,' she said, holding out both her hands, 'it's been too long.'

'You're looking lovely, Mousie,' said James, taking her hands and holding them, also a little too long. 'And so's your garden.'

'It's a miracle if it is,' said Valerie. 'Our darling old gardener dropped dead last week – wasn't it maddening? – and we're having to make do with jobbing gardeners, like that idiot. No, not that way,' she screamed as another jobbing gardener was carted across the lawn slap into a bed of mauve dahlias by an out-of-control computerized mower.

When she'd finished berating that gardener, Valerie swept James round to the patio and asked him if he'd rather have iced coffee first or wander round.

James said he'd rather have iced coffee, and sat down very quickly on the hammock seat, for fear of being concussed by half-a-dozen hanging baskets weighed down by every colour of petunia. But although he coyly patted the seat beside him, once Valerie had poured the iced coffee she insisted on prowling the patio, dead-heading petunias and showing off her slim figure in the floral pink shirt-waister.

'What's happened to your poor legs?' asked James, noticing several marks on the back of her calves.

'Bites,' sighed Valerie. 'I seem fatally attractive to midges.'

'And to men, Mousie.'

Valerie smiled. She wasn't going to tell James that Henry Hampshire had promised to take Freddie and her fly-fishing, and that she'd spent all day practising on the lawn and catching the backs of her legs with the hooks.

'Tony sent his special love, so did Monica,' lied James.

'Oh, we miss them both,' sighed Valerie. 'I do wish Freddie'd never got caught up in this stupid franchise. It's all so pointless.'

'D'you get roped into meetings?' asked James, sipping his coffee and wincing because the orange marigolds and magenta petunias in a nearby tub reminded him rather too forcibly of Ginger Johnson's face.

'No, no,' said Valerie, 'but the socializing side of it's quite fun. Henry took us to As-Cot; we had cocktails with him on the way home. I was shocked by the number of weeds in his seat. But they have made rather lovely use of white buddleia in the walled garden.'

'With such interesting programme plans, Venturer must have roped in some pretty considerable production people,' said James idly.

'I hope you like our border of massed glads over there,' said Valerie. 'Bring your coffee and let's have a wander.'

Having admired every petal, every gnome, every plastic Venus de Milo, James still hadn't learned anything more about Venturer.

'Freddie used to pop into Corinium a lot,' he said as they passed a dolphin regurgitating Blue Loo into a pond. 'Does he still see any of his old friends there? I bet they're knocked-out by this lovely garden.'

'It is lovely, isn't it?' said Valerie smugly, 'but I wish we could grow rhodos in Gloucestershire.'

'Are Venturer recruiting their staff locally?' asked James. 'Who else have they signed up?'

But Valerie was off leaping across a stream to tug up some mare's tail.

'I know Tony's keeping an eye out for moles at Corinium,' fished James as Valerie joined him again.

'So are we,' said Valerie. 'Moles are Freddie's biggest worry.'

456

'Perhaps we should compare notes, Mousie,' said James.

As they were now hidden from the house by a row of yellow conifers, he slid his hand around her waist. It was nice and trim.

'Well, Freddie's been putting down Mole-Ban everywhere,' said Valerie, 'but I'm still terrified I'm going to wake up tomorrow and find mole hills all over the lawn.'

James gave up. Mousie was far too preoccupied with her plot to think about plotting at the moment. He arranged that he and the crew would arrive at about three-thirty, and asked if she could keep any Venturer T-shirts and posters to a minimum.

'Tony feels you're so special and that a lovely garden is above personalities. But we really can't use the footage on "Round-Up" if it's full of plugs for Venturer.'

As James was filming gardens all Saturday afternoon, Lizzie had planned to work on her book. Then, feeling rather old and dried-up, she rubbed a lot of skin-food into her face, only to realize she'd forgotten her neck, which is supposed to betray your age most, so she rubbed the excess skin-food down into it. Then she remembered you were supposed never to rub skin-food downwards as it made your face droop. Would her life have been different, she wondered, if she'd always remembered to rub skin-food upwards? Would James have stayed faithful to her? Unwisely, knowing it would hurt her, she snooped around in James's drawers and found a ravishing photograph of Sarah Stratton under his boxer shorts. Feeling utterly miserable, she thought how nice it would be to see Freddie Jones again. Abandoning any thought of work, she decided to go along to Valerie's opening.

As she drove through Green Lawns's electric gates, she noticed a large 'Support Venturer' sticker on the huge sign announcing that James and Corinium Television would be present that afternoon. Lizzie felt so off James that she couldn't even be bothered to peel the sticker off. In the car park she found Rupert unashamedly sticking more Venturer stickers on everyone's windscreens.

'Darling.' He kissed her. 'Divided as we are by our rival consortiums, we shouldn't consort, but do let's go round together. I need a good laugh. Mrs Jones's new rockery is like the polar bear pit at the zoo; she's been training blow lamps on her roses all night and twenty-four-hour fluorescent lighting in the greenhouse is forcing out the Christmas roses.'

Lizzie laughed. 'You can't bring that dog,' she said as Rupert let Beaver out of his car. 'Particularly if he's not on a lead. Mrs Jones will have a coronary.'

'Good,' said Rupert, locking the car. 'Look how well he's trained,' he went on as Beaver lifted his leg on a cohort of salmon-pink petunias. 'Do you think Valerie drills her flowers every morning?'

'It's just like a park,' said Lizzie as they walked towards the house.

'Unfair to parks,' said Rupert.

On the edge of the lawn a stall was selling clothes from Valerie's boutique, with the mark-up going to the Red Cross. Models, sweating in Valerie's Autumn Range, wandered aimlessly round, fanning themselves with price tags. There was not a Venturer plug in sight.

'What a lot of people,' said Rupert. 'Judging by the mob on the lawn, your husband's holding court. Let's go the other way. Isn't that hell!' He pointed to a crescent-shaped flower bed crammed with fuchsias and French marigolds that looked as if it had been dug out by a pastry cutter. 'Lady Valerie of Vulgaria's gift for self-publicity is only equalled by her appalling taste.'

As they proceeded giggling down the crazy pavement, they could hear Valerie graciously dispensing advice on the other side of the yellow conifer hedge.

'How d'you manage to grow such whopping glads?' asked a neighbour admiringly.

'I feed them with Grow-More,' said Valerie.

'She's obviously been feeding her children the same thing,' muttered Rupert as poor fat Sharon, blushing at the sight of Rupert, waddled past them.

'Hullo, Bishop,' they could now hear Valerie screaming.

'How good of you to look in. I'm about to be interviewed on TV, but you'll find Fred-Fred in the grounds.'

'It'd be grounds for divorce if I was married to her; the only person not allowed into Valerie's opening is Fred-Fred. The frigid bitch,' said Rupert, grabbing Lizzie's arm. 'Come on, buck up, let's look at the pond. I don't want to get trapped with the Bishop.'

'I thought the Bishop was on your side,' said Lizzie, panting after him.

'He is, and a god-awful bore too. He's mad about Taggie, so he keeps dropping in at The Priory unannounced, and finding Maud and Declan having a bonk, or hurling plates at one another, which, bearing in mind the Bishop's views on sex and violence, doesn't go down very well.'

'I thought it was you having a walk-out with Taggie,' said Lizzie slyly as they passed Hybrid Teas, massed in clashing colours above totally weedless beds.

Rupert raised his eyes to heaven. 'Would that I were! She's *so* sweet.'

'Why aren't you then?'

'Declan would do his nut, and she's too young.'

'Never deterred you in the past.'

'Ah, but it's franchise year.' Rupert bent down to press a Venturer sticker on the bare belly of a plastic Venus de Milo. 'And we're all having to behave ourselves, as I'm sure your husband knows. Why have you got that rash on your hands?' he asked more gently as Lizzie whipped off the same sticker.

'The doctor says it's stress-related,' said Lizzie bitterly. 'Mistress-related, more likely.' Suddenly she could bear it no longer. 'James is having an affair with Sarah Stratton. I shouldn't have told you that. You'll leak it to *Private Eye* and discredit Corinium even further.'

'Why don't you leave him? He's such a cunt,' said Rupert, putting another sticker as a figleaf over a cherub, and dragging Lizzie on before she could remove it.

'Helen didn't leave you.' Lizzie paused to examine the pond which was a mass of scarlet and yellow water lilies. 'God, isn't this hell?'

'She did in the end,' said Rupert. 'Besides, I'm not a cunt.'

They had reached the end of the garden now; cornfields the colour of French mustard and bluey-green woods stretched to the horizon. On the right, a red tractor chugged back and forth, anxious to get the hay baled and away before tonight's promised rain.

'Heaven to see some decent country,' said Rupert. 'Do you think "cunt-ricide" means murdering one's mistress?'

Lizzie laughed. 'You do cheer me up. I wish someone would murder Sarah.'

Leaving the pond, they wandered back to the house and walking under a weeping willow went slap into Freddie.

He looked very tired, and only nodded at them politely until he realized who they were. Then he jumped up and down with pleasure, giving Lizzie a big hug.

''Ullo, Rupe, 'ullo Lizzie. 'Ow are you, love? You look grite. Better not let Valerie see Beaver, Rupe, she's a bit uptight. Been dead-'eading petunias in her sleep all night; fink she's abart to dead-'ead me. I've had this bleedin' lot up to 'ere. Let's go inside and 'ave a drink. Val's doing her TV interview. Finks the sun shines out of James Vereker's arse. Oh, sorry, love –' he squeezed Lizzie's arm – 'I quite forgot he was your 'usband!'

'James thinks the same,' said Rupert, spiking another sticker on a garden gnome's fishing rod. 'I'm sure he's only here because he wants to worm secrets out of your wife, Freddie.'

Although, watching the way Freddie and Lizzie were looking at each other, Rupert reflected that Lizzie, with all her warmth and sympathy, would be far more skilled at getting Venturer's secrets out of Freddie.

Cameron had expected to spend Friday night with Tony, but he'd decided to fly to France a day early, leaving her with an unexpected free evening. Unable to get in touch with Rupert, she'd taken two Mogadon, slept alone and very well for the first time in months and woke feeling rested and happy. As

460

she wasn't due to meet Rupert until the evening, she decided to wander along and see how James was getting on filming gardens. She didn't stay long at The Falconry. The garden was too wonderful, and she didn't like such tangible proof of Monica's skills. She was surprised Tony hadn't stayed at home to crow.

By comparison Valerie's garden was utterly dreadful, but had certainly attracted large crowds, particularly round the television crew. Fighting her way through until she was blocked by a large bed of purple and salmon-pink gladioli, Cameron saw James up the other end interviewing Valerie and quickly stifled a scream of laughter. Valerie was dressed for Ascot in a yellow and white shirt-waister and a huge buttercup-yellow hat trimmed with yellow roses, but was totally unaware that someone had stuck a 'Support Venturer' sticker on her bottom.

Looking across the sea of mauve and salmon-pink, Cameron caught her breath in joy, because there, beside Freddie and Lizzie Vereker, also trying very hard not to laugh, was Rupert. As if drawn by her longing, he looked up and gave a brief grin of surprise before instantly resuming his normal deadpan expression.

'Cotswold Round-Up/Green Lawns/Take Four,' said the second assistant, snapping the clapper board.

'One only has to look at your flower beds, Valerie,' said James as the camera panned slowly in on the sea of mauve and salmon-pink, 'to appreciate what a truly caring gardener you are. Tell us your secret.'

'Well, James,' began Valerie; then her little laugh turned to a squawk of rage as the normally well-trained Beaver, suddenly seeing Cameron, who'd spent a great deal of time sharing his master's bed recently, crashed across the bed of gladioli, snapping and flattening most of them, and throwing himself on her in total ecstasy.

Just for a few seconds, to a crescendo of Valerie's squawks, Cameron and Rupert were caught on camera, absolutely collapsing with laughter, before Rupert sharply called Beaver off.

As she drove home rather tight later in the evening with James, Lizzie said, 'Cameron's the one you and Tony should be watching. I'm certain she's having an affair with Rupert.'

'Don't be ridiculous,' snapped James. 'Cameron only cares about Corinium.'

On Sunday night on his way back from France, where he'd made great strides in acquiring a stake in French television, Tony dropped in at the office to see how The Falconry garden looked on video. The cameraman had left the tape on his desk. Loosening his tie, pouring himself a large drink, Tony put the tape in the machine and lay back on his squashy sofa to watch. He was enchanted with the results. Monica had really come up trumps this year. How right he'd been not to leave her for Cameron — when one considered the ghastly shambles Paul Stratton had made of his career after he'd left Winifred. Having played back The Falconry footage twice more, he decided to have a good laugh, and ran the tape on to have a look at Valerie's garden. Having located it, he played the tape back five times, particularly freezing the frame on the last ten seconds.

Then he walked out of the building not even bothering to lock the drinks cupboard or his office door, and drove straight over to Hamilton Terrace. Cameron was not there. Letting himself in, he searched systematically through the house. In the bedroom wastepaper basket he found what he was looking for. A pile of tiny torn-up scraps of paper. No one tore paper up that small unless they wanted to hide something. And it was an added precaution, as Cameron wasn't expecting to see him until tomorrow night and by that time the daily would have emptied the basket. It took him a long time to put the pieces together because his hands were trembling so much, but finally he was able to read the words: *Venturer meeting, Henry's house, 12.30 Sunday.*

Cameron got home about midnight. Sated and reeling from Rupert, she hadn't even bothered to shower afterwards as she wanted to keep the sweat and smell of him on and inside her body as long as possible. Dropping her briefcase in the hall, she wandered into the drawing-room. The bulb that turned on by the door had blown, so in the faint light from the street lamps she groped her way across the room to turn on the light by her desk. The next minute she leapt in terror as a hand shot out, grabbing her leg just above the knee. Burglars, was her first panic-stricken thought; then, as a light flashed on, she saw Tony crouched on the sofa like a venomous toad.

'What are you doing skulking in the dark?' she stammered.

'What are *you* doing,' said Tony in a voice that utterly froze her blood, 'going to a Venturer meeting at Henry Hampshire's house today?'

Cameron's gasp of horror gave it all away: 'I-I-I had a tip-off. I went along to spy. I just hung around outside the gates, trying to see who was going in.'

'Who gave you the tip-off?'

Cameron's mind raced. 'I overheard people talking in the Bar Sinister – in the next booth.'

'You bloody liar,' hissed Tony. 'And how long has Rupert been stuffing you?'

'He isn't,' gibbered Cameron, wincing as his hand tightened on her leg. 'He's a bastard. The last person I'd shack up with.'

Tony tugged her towards him, burying his nose briefly in her groin.

'You reek of him, you fucking whore. And how come his dog knows you so well? It's all on tape, sweetheart.'

And the next moment he'd hit her across the room. She fell with a crash, catching her head on the bookshelf. Then he was on her again, picking her up by her shirt and smashing his left fist into her face. This time she crashed back into a small table, knocking over a vase of buddleia.

He's going to kill me, she thought, as he lunged at her again, kicking her in the ribs until she groaned for mercy. Yet, at the same time, another part of her terror-crazed mind was thinking that she had to get out of there before he got his hands on her briefcase which contained all her notes on the meeting, and, even worse, the names of the Corinium moles.

As he dragged her to her feet and hit her again, she managed to grab a chair and, swinging it round, caught him on the side of the head, narrowly missing his eye with one of the legs. It gave her a breathing space. Grabbing the vase of buddleia that was now leaking onto the floor, she hurled it at him and stumbled out of the room, banging the door behind her. Gathering up her briefcase, she just managed to put up the double catch on the front door, locking him in as she slammed it. By the time he'd managed to clamber out of the drawing-room window, she'd started up the Lotus and was on her way to Rupert's.

Putting her hand up to her head where she'd hit the bookcase, she could feel her hair sticky with blood. Looking in the driving mirror she saw more blood pouring out of her right eye and nearly blacked out. She had got to make it to Rupert's with the briefcase, or Tony would catch up and kill her. Somehow, in a daze of pain and sickness, constantly wiping the blood out of her eyes, she managed to reach Penscombe.

Rupert's front door was unlocked. The hall was dimly lit. Tripping over the dogs she screamed for him.

'Angel, how nice. Have you forgotten something?' he said, coming down the stairs wearing only a pair of jeans and reading *Horse and Hound*.

Then she found and switched on the main hall light and he saw her properly. Her right eye had closed up now and her upper lip was cut and terribly swollen. Her face, hair and shirt were drenched in blood.

'My Christ,' he said, appalled. 'What the fuck happened?'

'Tony found out.'

'My poor little baby.' He raced down the stairs, drawing her into his arms, feeling the stickiness of her blood-soaked hair and the frantic racing of her heart. 'The bastard, where is he? Let's get you a doctor, then I'm going round to kill him.'

'I'm OK,' mumbled Cameron. 'He had provocation. You'd

probably have done the same thing under the circs.' The next moment she passed out.

When she regained consciousness she was in Rupert's double bed, dressed in one of his shirts, with most of the blood washed off. A Doctor Benson, who was rather smooth and glamorous, had rolled up in his dinner jacket, reeking of brandy and Gold Spot, and, after examining her, assured her that her face wouldn't be marked. Having patched her up, saying she might have to have stitches in her head in the morning, he gave her a shot to sedate her.

'I don't want my head shaved,' she muttered when Rupert came back.

'Your hair's so short it's practically shaved already,' said Rupert, sitting down on the bed and taking her hands. 'I'm so desperately sorry, angel. I got you into it.'

It took all Cameron's pleading to stop him going straight round to Hamilton Terrace or even to The Falconry to beat Tony to a pulp.

'Think of the adverse publicity. It'll only trivialize Venturer's bid.'

'Nothing trivial about those bruises,' said Rupert, touching her swollen lip with his finger. 'How did he rumble us?'

'Saw the video of Valerie's opening and Beaver's crash-landing in the gladioli. And somehow he found out I was at the Venturer meeting yesterday.'

Very, very gently Rupert was stroking her cheek. Despite the pain in almost every part of her body, she had never felt safer or closer to him.

'Hell knows no fury like a womanizer scorned,' he said lightly. 'Well, he had to know some time. You'd better move in here.'

Cameron utterly despised women who cried in front of men. It was taking an unfair advantage and outraged her feminist principles. But once the tears started spilling out of her bruised eyes, she found she couldn't stop them.

'Is it such a ghastly thought?' said Rupert, taking her in his arms.

'No, no it's the nicest thought in the world. I guess I don't want to railroad you.'

'You're not. You've no idea how I hated letting you go back every time, particularly to Tony. I'm sick of never seeing you. Don't worry about your brilliant career. I'll look after you. And tomorrow, as a symbol of your new dependence, I'm going to chuck that beastly briefcase into the lake.'

Cameron managed a weak smile. 'You had better take the papers out first, or Tony'll be dropping by, using the truth drug on your duck.'

She was drowsy with dope now, so he laid her back on the pillow.

'I'll try not to get under your feet,' she muttered. 'I d-do love you – so so much.'

'I know you do.' Rupert got to his feet. 'Now go to sleep.'

'Please don't go.' She was suddenly frantic. 'You will sleep here, won't you?'

''Course I will. I'll be back in a minute. I'm just going to take the dogs out.'

Wandering mindlessly through the garden, Rupert found himself on the edge of the lake, breathing in the soapy smell of the meadowsweet, listening to the frogs croaking. There were no stars, and, glancing across the valley, he saw Taggie's turret was in darkness.

35

Valerie Jones was absolutely furious when nothing about her Opening appeared on 'Cotswold Round-Up', but not nearly as angry as Declan when Rupert told him what had happened.

'What the fock were you doing taking a dog you can't control to Valerie's opening?'

'I control my dogs a bloody sight better than you.'

'We're not talking about me. Think of the adverse publicity.'

'There won't be any. I refrained from beating Tony to a pulp.'

Declan sighed. 'And how the hell is Tony going to explain the overnight loss of his mistress and Programme Controller to his staff? Someone's going to leak the story. Pirated tapes of Beaver's flatfoot through the gladioli are no doubt circulating the network already, and it won't be long before they reach the press and the IBA.'

'It was terribly funny. I wish you'd seen Valerie's face.'

'It's not funny,' thundered Declan. 'I suppose you're used to having your character blackened but it won't do Venturer any good. The IBA don't like this kind of thing.'

He couldn't understand how Rupert could be so unrattled by such a catastrophe. He supposed he'd always lived in the eye of the storm.

'I don't know who comes out worse,' Declan went on, 'you setting out coldly and deliberately to seduce Cameron so we had a mole on our side, or Tony who beat her up. A lot of people will feel Tony was justified. He was only acting in the heat of the moment.'

'Oh, come off it,' snapped Rupert. 'Talk about making mountains out of moles. The story we leak is that Cameron and I were attracted to each other when we met, when you interviewed me in February. We resisted it because we were on opposing sides for as long as we could, but now she's moved in with me and Venturer has the best Head of Drama in the country. Christ, we're both free agents. It's Tony who's the adulterer and the mistress-basher. He won't want to make a big thing of it because of Monica and the IBA.'

A story was duly leaked and appeared in the *Mail* the next day that Cameron Cook had changed sides, moved in with Rupert and that Tony was devastated to lose his star producer. No reference was made to Cameron being Tony's mistress, or of her being beaten up by him.

Rumour, however, was rife and by Wednesday Corinium had leaked a counter-story accusing Venturer of poaching and cold-blooded enticement, and putting the blame firmly on Rupert.

'A lonely, single woman nearing thirty, worried about missing the marital boat, is in a particularly vulnerable position,' Tony was quoted as saying.

Rupert was furious. 'All we have to do is give a photograph of Cameron's bruises to the press.'

'Don't be so bloody stupid,' said Declan crushingly. 'You've no proof Tony did it and not you. It isn't as though you've exactly got a blameless reputation when it comes to beating up.'

Tony, once he had cooled down, was absolutely shattered by Cameron's defection. He'd had no idea how much both he and Corinium had come to depend on her, both as an inspiration and a sparring partner.

Discovering through his spies that Rupert would be in London opening a new sports stadium on Thursday, Tony drove over to Penscombe to see her. Surrounded by Rupert's pack of dogs, with Mrs Bodkin in the kitchen and Mr Bodkin strimming the long grass round the lake, Cameron felt safe to let him in. Dressed in an orange bikini, she still looked as though she'd just done fifteen rounds with Barry McGuigan.

Tony followed her out to the pool, which sparkled brilliant turquoise in the sunshine and was no longer filled with leaves. It killed him to see her in this beautiful opulent setting, stretched out oiled on one of Rupert's reclining chairs, guarded by Rupert's lurcher Blue, who lay by her feet panting, but growling every time Tony approached.

Immediately Tony begged her to come back, telling her for the first time how much he loved her and, when that had no effect, offering to leave Monica and marry her. He didn't even lose his temper when she told him to bugger off.

'Your job's open for you to come back whenever you want it, and here are the keys to Hamilton Terrace.' He threw them on to the table. 'The house may belong to Corinium, but it's still yours when you need it. Come and get your clothes whenever you want to. I shouldn't have beaten you up, but I love you and I just saw red.'

'Just like you did the last time I came home late after spending the day with Patrick,' said Cameron. 'Get out.'

Tony, predictably, couldn't remain nice for long. 'You know it's only a matter of time until Rupert ditches you,' was his parting shot. 'Five days, five weeks; he may even keep you five months until Venturer finally don't get the franchise; then he'll kick you out like all the rest and you'll come running back to me.'

Cameron didn't believe Tony would leave Monica, particularly during the franchise year, but at least it now meant she could pick up her clothes, her books, and, much more important, her tapes and prizes from Hamilton Terrace. She also felt privately that it was nice to have Tony as a bolthole in case Rupert started playing her up.

Rupert, in fact, couldn't have been more angelic those first few days, fussing over her, seeing she didn't get too tired, ensuring Mrs Bodkin made her delicious food (which Cameron privately thought contained far too much seasoning and fats), making love to her with surprising gentleness and subtlety, so he didn't crush her bruised ribs or her battered face.

The weather was beautiful too – long hot days, followed by short sweet nights. Cameron was happy to sleep and read and sunbathe and explore Rupert's woods and fields with the dogs. Gradually, as the black eye and the swelling on her lips disappeared, she felt she was healing inside and out.

The only drawback was Mr and Mrs Bodkin, shadowy, polite, running Rupert's life like clockwork, but always there in the background. Cameron wanted Rupert on her own, she was not used to servants. She wanted to wander round the house naked and make love in the kitchen if she felt like it. She was also inclined to treat Mr and Mrs Bodkin like Corinium minions, rapping out orders, snapping at slowness and even more at ignorance.

Even Rupert, famous for his caprice and short fuse with staff, had to pull her up repeatedly: 'Taggie O'Hara increases her vocabulary by learning a new word every day. You could start off with: please and thank you.'

Any reference to Taggie sent Cameron through the roof, so, the second week after she moved in, determined to prove to Rupert that she could cook and run a house much better than Taggie, she persuaded Rupert to give Mr and Mrs Bodkin a few days off.

'I'm better,' she insisted. 'I want to look after you. I'm going to cook you some decent food. You're getting far too much cholesterol.'

'Do I look as though it's harming me?' said Rupert, who was eating white bread and dripping sprinkled with salt as he sat immersed in the *Scorpion*.

'No, but it's futile to abuse a magnificent constitution. It'll catch up with you. And why don't you try to read the *Guardian* occasionally instead of that trash?'

'Because it uses much too long words and makes snide remarks about my party,' said Rupert.

'But objective criticism's valuable, for Chrissake.'

'Not to me. I only like people who think I'm perfect. I'd better get Mr and Mrs Bodkin back for the weekend. The children are coming on Saturday. They make a hell of a lot of work.'

'Oh, don't,' said Cameron, suddenly excited. 'Let's look after them ourselves. We'll have picnics and barbecues and all muck in. It'll be so much fun.'

Like many insecure people, Cameron was much easier to live with when she was down. After she'd been beaten up, it was her intense vulnerability that had appealed to Rupert. Wanting to protect her, he'd asked her to move in. But as she got better, her natural aggression and stridency started to reassert itself.

The day before the children were due, Cameron decided to make a big paella for dinner; the rest could be heated up for them the following day. Discovering in the middle she'd forgotten to get any saffron or squid, she dispatched Rupert to the village shop.

'I'm sure they won't stock them,' grumbled Rupert, who wanted to read *Horse and Hound*.

The kitchen wireless was blaring out Dame Enid's latest tone poem; the *New Statesman* and the *Times Literary Supplement* lay on the kitchen table all giving Rupert an unpleasant feeling of *déjà vu*. It was too much like Helen all over again.

'Well, drive into Stroud then,' snapped Cameron.

She'd forgotten what a rat race paella was to make, but she was determined to cook better than Taggie.

'And get some Parmesan as well,' she shouted after him.

The village shop had recently been converted into a tiny supermarket with shelves all round the walls, and a partition, also with shelves on both sides, running parallel to the counter. If the ubiquitous Mrs Makepiece, who did for Lizzie and Valerie and one morning a week for Maud now, hadn't been holding forth so noisily and indignantly at the head of the queue, Rupert would never have slid into the shop unobserved. Picking up a red wire basket, he chucked in some Jaffa cakes because the children liked them, and a tin of corned beef because he liked it; he couldn't find any squid, but he supposed a tin of pilchards in tomato sauce would do as well – a squid pro quo.

As he moved round to the spice shelf, Mrs Makepiece, encouraged by a chorus of clicking tongues, raised her voice. 'Declan and 'er ladyship have pushed off on some second honeymoon in the Lake District, leaving her all on her own.'

Rupert stiffened, gazing unseeingly at rows of paprika, dill and cayenne.

'All alone in that 'uge 'ouse,' went on Mrs Makepiece, 'and we all know it's 'aunted. Well, 'alf the lights fused, so Taggie went to the fuse box and read the instructions all wrong – she's disconnected, you know, the poor lamb, and she blew all the fuses, and had to shiver all night in the dark, with only Gertrude, that's her little dog, for company.'

Despite the baking heat of the day, Rupert had gone absolutely cold. Taggie might have killed herself fiddling about with that fuse box.

'She was crying her heart out this morning when I come in,' said Mrs Makepiece, egged on by the row of shocked faces. 'At first she wouldn't tell me what was the matter. Then I made us a nice cup of tea and it came out – they'd all forgotten her birthday.'

Rupert was so enraged he dropped the basket and walked straight out of the shop with the pilchards, which he had forgotten to chalk up.

The moment he got home he rang Ursula. 'Where the fuck are Maud and Declan?'

'Windermere.'

'Give me their number.'

'I promised not to; they don't want to be disturbed. This is a patch-up operation. Declan's been devoting too much time to his biography.'

'They forgot Taggie's birthday.'

'Oh, my God!'

'And you should have bloody well reminded them. Give me the number.'

Declan and Maud were out when he rang. He left a message

for Declan to ring him, saying it was about the franchise and very urgent.

Then he rang Taggie. 'Happy birthday, darling. Cameron and I are going to take you out to dinner. No, I don't want any "buts". We'll pick you up about eight.'

He was still sweating with horror at the thought of the poor little duck all alone in that big house in the dark with all those winding stairs and long passages.

'Bloody Maud and Declan,' he howled as he went into the kitchen.

'What on earth have they done now? Don't turn it off, it's Vivaldi,' protested Cameron. 'Did you get the squid?' Then, as Rupert handed her the pilchards, 'These won't do, dumbass. And where's the Parmesan and the saffron?'

'They forgot Taggie's birthday,' said Rupert bleakly.

'Well, that's not such a big thing.' Then, seeing the rage on Rupert's face, 'Haven't you forgotten your kids' birthdays?'

'No – yes, I suppose so, but Helen always remembers.'

When he told Cameron what had happened, and that they were taking Taggie out to dinner, she hit the roof. 'But it was our last night on our own. This was to be a celebration I was cooking specially for us.'

'There'll be plenty of time for that in the future.'

The telephone rang. It was Declan. Fuelled by indignation, and also because Declan had been so censorious about him and Cameron, Rupert let him have it. 'You fucking hypocrite, always banging on about tyranny and exploitation. The worst case I've seen is going on under your roof.'

'What the fock are you talking about?'

'Taggie. She works like a slave for the bloody lot of you, and all you can do is leave her alone in a huge house, with the fuses blown, and then forget her birthday.'

'Oh, my Christ,' said Declan, appalled. 'Have we really?'

'You get on the telephone the moment I ring off and say how sorry you are.'

'We ought to come back.'

'No. Cameron and I'll look after her tonight. You come home first thing tomorrow and bring her a decent present, not a crappy book of Wordsworth's poems she can't read.'

'God, I feel terrible,' said Declan. 'Now, what was this urgent thing about the franchise?'

'That was it,' said Rupert furiously. 'If she hadn't worked her ass off trailing around the area, rounding up names for your bloody franchise, we wouldn't be ahead in the race now.'

Crashing down the telephone, he poured himself a huge whisky. He was absolutely shaking with rage.

'Well, well, well,' said Cameron, chucking the wooden spoon on to the drying rice and switching off the hot plate. 'What gives with Taggie O'Hara?'

'She doesn't deserve parents like that. She's only a baby.'

'Nineteen today, to be exact. Well beyond the age of consent.'

She knew it was madness to bitch, but she couldn't help herself. 'You've got a very soft spot – or is it a hard spot – for her, haven't you? Are you nurturing some secret passion? What I want to know is where does that put me?'

Rupert looked her up and down. There wasn't a trace of tenderness in his face now.

'You're living here, aren't you?'

'At the moment.'

'Let's get one thing straight,' he said softly. 'If you want to go on living here, stop being such a fucking bitch.'

Draining his whisky, he picked up his car keys. 'I'm going to get her a present. You can ring up the White Elephant in Painswick and book a table for three at nine o'clock.'

Henry Hampshire's Springer spaniel had recently had six puppies. They'd all gone to new homes except the runt whose paw, broken when someone stepped on it, was still in plaster. The puppy had a freckled face, a bright pink mouth, crossed eyes that looked as though he'd been on the booze all night, and a stumpy tail which agitated his whole body.

'He's a great character,' said Henry. 'You can have him for a hundred pounds.'

'With a broken paw? Don't be ridiculous.'

'Plaster comes off next week. Then he'll be as right as rain. Won't stop him going all day in the field.'

'Fifty,' said Rupert.

'You've got to be joking. The others went for two hundred and fifty each. Mother was best of breed at Crufts, father won every field trial in the country.'

'Fifty,' said Rupert. 'He'll always be slightly lame.'

'Oh, all right,' said Henry. 'I had lunch with Daysee Butler today.'

'Well, you shouldn't,' snapped Rupert. 'You're bound to give away trade secrets.'

'Well, you still haven't laid on Joanna Lumley,' grumbled Henry. 'Daysee said Tony's flown to LA to search for a new Programme Controller.'

When Rupert got back to Penscombe, Cameron had washed her hair, and changed into the clinging kingfisher-blue dress she'd worn to get her award in Madrid; it had slits to sunburnt mid-thigh on both sides. She looked apprehensive, very beautiful, and came straight up and put her arms round Rupert's neck.

'I was jealous. I'm sorry.'

He breathed in Fracas, the dry bitter sexy scent she always wore; it made his senses reel.

'I'm sorry too,' he said. 'I over-reacted, but I feel so sorry for her.'

Under the blue dress he could feel Cameron's nipples stiffening. Glancing at the kitchen clock he saw that it was a quarter to eight.

'We haven't got time. It'd muss you up.'

'*You* have,' said Cameron.

Dropping to her knees, she unzipped his flies. This was one skill she knew she was better at than Taggie O'Hara.

A battered dark-green GTI was parked outside The Priory as they drove up. The front door was open; the hall was filled with clothes, books and suitcases.

'Perhaps she won't want to come out to dinner,' murmured Cameron hopefully.

475

''Course she will,' said Rupert.

It was debatable who got the worse shock, Cameron or Rupert, when they went into the kitchen and found Taggie sobbing in the arms of a tall black-haired, incredibly beautiful young man. The only difference was that Cameron instantly recognized Patrick, whereas Rupert did not. Patrick looked round, still with his arms round Taggie.

'Well?' he said icily.

Taggie glanced up, gave a gasp, then tugging herself away from Patrick, blindly snatched at some kitchen roll, frantically wiping her eyes and blowing her nose.

'I'm sorry,' she mumbled. 'Hullo, Rupert, hullo, Cameron. How are you?'

She was amazed to see Rupert glaring at Patrick with such hostility. Perhaps he resented him as Cameron's ex.

'I don't think you've met my brother Patrick, have you?' she said quickly.

'Your brother!' Instantly the hostility was gone. 'I didn't twig. It was your party on New Year's Eve, wasn't it? How did your finals go?'

'Perfectly all right,' said Patrick shortly.

Turning back to Taggie, Rupert dumped two bottles of Dom Perignon on the table beside Patrick's white carrier bag of duty free.

'Happy birthday, angel. They're just out of the fridge. Open them,' he added to Patrick, totally unaware of the look of utter loathing that Patrick was shooting in his direction.

Oh hell, thought Cameron, poor Patrick. Taggie must have told him about me moving in with Rupert.

Cutting short Taggie's stammering thanks for the champagne, Rupert seized her hand and led her out to the car. 'Come and see your proper present.'

'You d-don't have to bother,' stammered Taggie in the hall. 'I'm having a lovely birthday. Mummy and Daddy have just rung. They're bringing my present back tomorrow afternoon. They couldn't pick it up until today, and Patrick brought me back the most gorgeous Arran sweater. He's just

got back. He had so much stuff to bring after three years.'
She was rattling now, on the verge of tears again.

'Sweetheart, what's the matter?'

'I'm absolutely fine,' she said. How could she possibly explain to him that the blown fuses, the night in the dark, and the forgotten birthday, were mere irrelevancies, that it was Cameron finally moving in with him that had brought the world down round her ears.

She knew he couldn't ever be serious about someone as stupid and unsophisticated as she, but, as they'd gone round the country together, they'd become friends, and now she'd never see him again without Cameron.

'You were all on your own last night in the dark,' he said.

'Who told you?'

'Mrs Makepiece told the whole village shop.'

'It was my fault. I read the directions on the fuse box wrong.' She tried to smile. 'I seemed to spend the whole night pushing poor Gertrude round the house in front of me. Things seem to creak so much if you're in the dark.'

Rupert took her hands. 'Look, next time something awful happens, will you promise to ring me? That's what I'm across the valley for. It crucifies me to think of you all by yourself and frightened like that.'

She wouldn't look at him – all he could see was her reddened, swollen eyelids. Reluctantly he let her go.

Outside, the puppy, with its speckled paws on the car ledge, was grinning out through the open window.

'Oh, how adorable,' breathed Taggie. 'What's he done to his paw?'

'It's nearly better. He's your birthday present. I was going to buy you a guard dog, but I got sidetracked.'

Taggie was in ecstasy. No one had ever given her anything so lovely.

'Gertrude will be very jealous to begin with,' warned Rupert, as the puppy rushed off on to the lawn, quartering frantically, pursuing various cat and dog smells. 'You'll have to make a lot of fuss of her.

He noticed Taggie was still wearing jeans and an old torn red-and-white-striped shirt of Declan's.

'Aren't you going to change? We've booked a table for nine. Patrick can come too. I've never met him properly.'

Taggie blushed. 'It's terribly kind of you but we're fine on our own.'

'Don't be silly, I'm not having you cooking on your birthday.'

'Patrick and I haven't seen each other for ages.'

'You've got the rest of the summer.'

'He's going abroad tomorrow. He – er – he—'

'Yes,' said Rupert, pulling her down beside him on to the old bench on the side of the lawn.

Taggie blushed even more deeply. 'He adores Cameron, you see, and he's absolutely d-d-devastated about her moving in with you.'

'Ah,' said Rupert.

Taggie was frantically peeling paint off the bench. As the puppy bounded back to them, she gathered him up, cuddling him for comfort.

'Patrick could accept her having an affair with Tony because he thought she was doing it for her career, b-but you're different.'

'Why?' said Rupert, suddenly anxious to know the answer.

Taggie buried her crimson face in the puppy's ginger ears.

'Because one wouldn't need any incentive . . .'

'Is that your word for the day?'

'No.' She shook her head frantically. '. . . any incentive to move in with you.'

Inside, Cameron was gazing at Patrick. He's grown up, she thought. He's much tougher and more detached and less vulnerable.

'How did you really get on in your finals?'

'Got a first.'

'Have they told you?'

'No, but I know.'

He got a packet of Marlboro's out of the duty-free bag and lit himself a cigarette without offering her one. As the match flared she could see the bitterness in his face.

'I gather you've just become our next-door neighbour,' he said.

'Aren't you going to wish me joy?'

'What joy? He'll only make you miserable. Christ, you've got awful taste in men,' he added irritably. 'Tony was a disgusting thug. This man –' he couldn't bring himself to say Rupert's name – 'is like a foxhound. Can't you understand? You can't domesticate him. He'll always be hunting for something new. It's in his blood. He'll get bored with you in a few weeks, and if he doesn't, you'll get bored with him; he's the most ghastly philistine, never read a book in his life.'

'He's street-wise.'

'That expression always seems to me a euphemism for someone with extremely shady morals, which means he'll dump you sooner or later – and he'll smash your career. Tony at least encouraged that.'

'You're just jealous.'

'Not any more,' said Patrick wearily. 'I am ashes where once I was fire.'

'He's very funny. You'll like him when you get to know him.'

'I'm not going to give myself the chance. I'm going abroad tomorrow.'

Cameron was put out. She liked talking to Patrick. Now they weren't hamstrung by Tony's jealousy, she'd hoped he might grow into a friend, and that his admiration, like Tony's, would act as a spur to Rupert.

'Where are you going?'

'Australia – to work on a sheep farm. I'm not hanging round for the rest of the year seeing you all scrapping over the franchise and watching your relationship with that bastard self-destruct.'

'He isn't all bastard. Look how kind he's been to Taggie.' Cameron was fishing now.

479

'He's totally fucked her up.'

Cameron's throat went dry. 'Has he tried anything?'

'Nothing according to Tag. Just swans in in his bloody *droit de seigneur*, Lord Bountiful fashion, bombarding her with presents – silver necklaces, Fabergé eggs.'

'Fabergé eggs?' said Cameron, appalled.

'Oh, Taggie didn't know that it was. He brought her that back from Madrid. I don't know what's on offer today. A Monet perhaps, or a Henry Moore!'

'A puppy,' said Cameron in a frozen voice. 'This is it.'

The next moment Aengus shot into the kitchen, tail fluffed out like a lavatory brush, growling ferociously, and took refuge under the kitchen dresser. The puppy frolicked after him, trying to join him under the dresser, then let out a piercing shriek as Aengus caught him with a punishing right hook on his pink nose. Instantly Gertrude bustled in, the personification of outrage. The puppy bounced up to her, then let out another shriek as Gertrude bit him sharply on the ear.

'Oh Christ,' said Patrick. 'Not content with disrupting humans, Rupert has to disrupt animals as well.'

'For Christ's sake open one of those bottles,' said Cameron.

'I don't want a drink,' said Patrick sulkily.

'You'll need it. We've come to take you out to dinner.'

'Well, we're not coming. We don't want any of your fucking charity. Poor little O'Hara kids, eating their hearts out. Let's throw them a few crumbs of comfort.'

A black lock of hair had fallen over his forehead, a muscle was going in the beautiful pale right cheek. His eyes were as dark and forbidding as the depths of the huge cedar outside the window.

'Please don't hate me so much,' Cameron was amazed to find herself pleading. 'I really need a friend to talk to.'

They both jumped as the telephone rang. It was Caitlin who was staying with a friend in Newbury, ringing to wish Taggie many happy returns. By the time they had finished talking, Rupert and Cameron had left.

'How did you get rid of them?' asked Taggie.

'I told them both to fuck off and that we didn't need their charity,' said Patrick, opening one of Rupert's bottles. 'At least we can now get drunk at their expense!'

36

Cameron and Rupert had a disastrous dinner at the White Elephant after that. Rupert was outraged at being thrown out by Patrick. 'Arrogant little fucker, just like his father.'

'I thought you adored his father.'

'Not when he's playing God, or neglecting his children.'

'You certainly aren't neglecting one of them – silver neck-laces, Fabergé eggs, handicapped puppies – singularly appropriate in a franchise year.'

'Oh, shut up.'

The row continued until they got to bed, when Rupert maddened Cameron most of all by falling asleep when she was in mid-harangue. She woke next morning, feeling suicidal, to find Rupert gone. Wondering if he were already collecting his children, she went downstairs, found the paella gathering flies on the oven and chucked it out. There was a chicken in the fridge. She supposed she'd better roast it for lunch. Dispiritedly, she peeled some potatoes, put them on to par-boil, then started to make a french dressing. There wasn't any dill. If she sent Rupert off to the village shop he'd come back with nutmeg.

Outside, the sun was shining through the mist like a dog's identity disk. Cameron longed to go out to the pool and swim off her hangover. Until last night, with the Bodkins away, she had at last been able to enjoy a marvellously sybaritic few days with Rupert, swimming and sunbathing naked, brazenly tantalizing him away from whatever he was doing. She had even galloped bareback down the valley at twilight one night with no clothes on, until Rupert had caught up with her, pulled her off the horse and pulled her in the meadowsweet. Cameron had half-hoped that Taggie, on a late-night walk with Gertrude, might have caught them at it and realized that at last Rupert had found someone with a sex drive equal to his own.

But last night's row had ruined all that, and now, with the kids around, there'd be no more nude frollicking this weekend. She jumped as the dogs barked and the front door banged.

'Cameron,' yelled Rupert.

As he sauntered into the kitchen, blithe as a skylark, as though there'd been no row at all, Cameron frantically stirred the french dressing.

'We're out of dill,' she said.

'Dildos! Hardly need one of those with me around! I'm sorry I don't give you presents,' he went on, kissing the back of her neck. 'Vainly, I thought my presence was enough. Which hand will you have?'

'Both,' said Cameron sulkily.

'Telepathic,' said Rupert, uncurling his fingers.

Glittering on each palm was a diamond ear-ring, a two-inch-long chandelier, lit by little diamonds instead of crystals. Cameron was speechless. Incredulously, she ripped out the gold hoops she normally wore and hooked on the diamonds, running to the kitchen mirror, rubbing away the steam with her sleeve to have a look.

The ear-rings hung halfway down her slender neck, throwing rainbows of light on the lean, tense jawline, illuminating and softening the truculent hostile little face. Next minute Rupert's reflection appeared beside hers.

'Like them?'

In answer, she turned, kissing him with a fury and passion he'd never known in her. Cupping her face with his hands, he felt the tears sliding into his fingers. Very gently he unhooked the ear-rings.

'Shame to take them off so soon, but I must have you before I pick up the children.'

By the time they'd finished, the potatoes were too soft to roast, so Cameron mashed them instead.

Groggy with love, she waited to love Rupert's children. At half past one, trailing barking dogs, Tabitha erupted into the kitchen. Her cheeks were flushed, her eyes bright with excitement. She was clutching a huge box of chocolates.

'Mrs Bodkin! Mrs Bodkin!' She slithered to a halt in front of Cameron. 'Where's Mrs B?'

'Away for the weekend.'

'Daddy never told us. Are you the temp?'

'Well, not too temporary I hope!' said Cameron, smiling. 'You must be Tabitha?'

'Well, I'm not Marcus.' At nine, Tabitha was as blonde and as effortlessly elegant as Rupert. She stared at Cameron with the wary blue eyes of a stray kitten.

She was followed by Marcus, who at eleven was very thin, with very dark red hair, huge surprised yellow eyes, and pale delicate freckled features. He looked like a fawn liable to bolt at any minute. None of the photographs all over the house had captured their beauty, nor the way their totally different looks complimented each other.

'You must be Marcus, then,' said Cameron. 'I hope you're both hungry. There's roast chicken for lunch.'

'Not yet,' said Tabitha, grabbing an apple out of the fruit bowl. 'I'm going down to the stables.'

Marcus smiled shyly and apologetically. 'I've got a letter from my mother for Mrs Bodkin. I'd better give it to you. The chocolates were for her, perhaps you'd like . . .' His voice trailed off.

'No, no,' said Cameron, 'leave them for her.'

Helen's writing was very Vassar: '*Dear Mrs B,*' she had written, '*I hope your arthritis is better and the kids won't make too much work. Marcus's medication is in his suitcase. Please see he takes it, if he gets uptight. I enclose a list of their clothes. Could you tick them off before they come home? They lost so much last time, and can you see Tabitha learns her vocabulary, and that both do half an hour's piano practice, and say their prayers at night? I also enclose stats of their reports. Can you give them to Mr C-B? Yours sincerely, Helen Gordon.'*

Christ, she's formal, and a Born-again too, thought Cameron. Then she smiled at Marcus. 'Is Daddy on the way?'

'He's gone to the yard. Can I do anything?'

'Tell him and Tabitha lunch'll be ready in ten minutes.'

Putting on the cabbage and removing the chicken from the baking dish, Cameron started to make the gravy, and at the same time read the kids' reports. Tab's was perfectly frightful except for sport. Marcus's was brilliant. He returned to the kitchen looking apprehensive.

'They're trying out some new pony for Tab. Daddy said would half past two be OK?' Then, quailing at Cameron's expression of fury, he said quickly, 'If you don't mind I'll go and unpack.'

How, thought Cameron furiously, can I possibly keep up Taggie O'Hara standards when I get fucked about like this? Then she remembered the diamond ear-rings, and the fact that Rupert hadn't seen the kids for a few weeks, and decided not to make a fuss.

In fact they were back in forty minutes.

'I'm starving,' said Tab, heading straight for the larder. 'I thought you said lunch was ready.' She came out tearing open a packet of crisps with her teeth.

'Don't eat that. It'll spoil your lunch,' said Cameron. Ignoring her, Tab sat down at the table with *Pony* magazine.

Rupert came in with a large vodka and tonic for Cameron. 'Hullo, darling –' Cameron noticed how Tabitha looked up, eyes narrowed at the endearment – 'sorry we're late. Geoffrey Gardener brought the pony over specially. I wanted Tab to try him.'

'Any good?'

'We're going to keep him over the weekend.'

'He's called Biscuit,' said Tabitha.

'Here are the kids' reports and a letter from Helen,' said Cameron as Rupert started to carve.

'I only eat breast,' said Tab, when Rupert handed her a leg.

'Well, give it to Marcus, then,' said Rupert, who was reading the reports at the same time.

Cameron opened her mouth and shut it again. She noticed Marcus was very nervous around his father, and that, while Rupert hardly glanced at Marcus's report, he spent ages reading Tabitha's.

'"Tabitha must learn not to be so competitive at netball." What the fuck do they mean by that?' he said furiously. 'You can't be too competitive at games.'

'I should be in the netball team next term,' boasted Tab, 'and I'm easily the youngest. I don't want any,' she added to Cameron, snatching her plate away, so a large dollop of mashed potato fell on the table. Cameron's lips tightened as she scooped it up and put it on Rupert's plate.

'Or any cabbage or salad.'

'You must have veggies. I'm sure you do at home.'

'This is home.' Tabitha's blue-eyed stare was as arrogant as Rupert's. 'Isn't it, Daddy? This is home,' she repeated to Rupert, who was still reading the headmistress's report.

'Of course it is, angel,' he said, kissing her.

'Marcus's report is excellent,' said Cameron warmly.

'Ninety-five per cent for Latin, that's almost indecent,' said Rupert with an edge to his voice. Then he read on: ' "Marcus has made very good progress in Geography as he has only attended half the classes". What were you doing during the other half? Going to strip clubs?'

Marcus flushed. 'The pollen count was very high. I was off sick quite a lot of days.'

'I wish I had asthma and could bunk-off school,' said Tab, feeding the rest of her chicken to a slavering Beaver.

Rupert, having finished the reports, was now immersed in the racing pages of *The Times*.

'There's a horse called Venturer in the three-thirty,' he said to Cameron. 'We must have a bet.'

'Put a pound on each way for me,' said Tab. 'We're doing a project on snakes next term.'

'You could start off by interviewing Tony Baddingham,' said Rupert, picking up the telephone.

Now here's a chance to help Tabitha and win her confidence, thought Cameron.

'You could start off with Adam and Eve,' she said, helping herself to salad.

'The project's about snakes, not sex,' said Tab rudely.

'Eve got tempted by the snake, stupid,' said Marcus. 'That's why they left the Garden of Eden. It's a jolly good idea,' he added, kindly, to Cameron.

'My project's about real snakes,' snapped Tab.

Getting up from the table and rummaging in her squashy bag, she produced a photograph which she handed to Rupert as he came off the telephone.

'This is the pony Malise bought me. She's brilliant at cross-country because she won't stop.'

'D'you mean you've already got a pony?' asked Cameron, shocked.

'Yes, she's called Dollop the Trollop, and she shakes hooves for a polo.'

'Then why is Daddy buying you another one?'

Tabitha looked at Cameron as though she were crackers.

'Because I need at least two if I'm going on the junior circuit next summer. I can, can't I, Daddy?'

'Your mother's not crazy about the idea unless your school work picks up,' said Rupert, who was still frowning at the photograph. 'That pony's too short in front.'

Tabitha had learned to be manipulative, to play off the rivalry between her father and stepfather.

'Malise and Mummy don't want me to enter for the Pony Club Mounted Games at Wembley even if I'm picked,' she announced slyly. 'Because I'll miss a week of school.'

'Don't be bloody silly,' said Rupert angrily. 'I'll have a few sharp words with your mother.'

'Who'd like fruit salad?' said Cameron, as she cleared away the first course.

'Not me,' said Tab. 'Is there any ice cream in the freezer?'

Cameron had spent a long time that morning peeling grapes. 'If you don't like fruit salad, I'm afraid you'll have to go without,' she said sharply.

'Then I'll have another packet of crisps,' said Tab. 'I can come over every weekend this summer, Daddy, except the last week in August which is Pony Club camp.'

'Good,' said Rupert.

Oh, please no, thought Cameron. She was sure it was only out of kindness that Marcus had a second helping of fruit salad.

Fortunately, spirits were raised when Venturer won by three lengths, which meant that Rupert and Tabitha were richer by three hundred pounds and eight pounds respectively.

'Can we go into Stroud and spend it?' Tabitha climbed on to Rupert's knee, the kitten again, but this time tactile and adoring.

'Christ, no, not on a Saturday afternoon.'

'Can we watch *Amityville I* tonight?'

'No way,' said Cameron. 'It doesn't start until ten and it'll give you nightmares for months.'

'When we don't have to get up next morning Mummy always lets us watch late-night films,' lied Tab.

'Balls,' said Rupert. 'If it's that frightening, you're not watching it.'

'Can we go into Stroud and get a James Bond video then?' persisted Tab. 'And I need some pink hair spray for a punk party next week.'

'I'll take you, if you like,' conceded Cameron.

The journey to Stroud was the most successful part of the weekend. The roof of the Lotus was down and, although Marcus went white, Tab thoroughly approved of Cameron's driving.

'This is a nice car, and you go much faster than Mummy. Can I have an ice cream?'

'May I. You may if you promise to eat your supper.'

On the way back, however, Tabitha smiled sweetly at Cameron. 'You haven't got a husband, have you? Why don't you get one?'

'I'd like to,' said Cameron, thinking longingly of Rupert.

'But not my Daddy,' hissed Tabitha.

'It is absolutely ludicrous,' said Cameron to Rupert as, later, they listened to Tabitha sulkily crucifying Beethoven's Minuet in G on the drawing-room baby grand. 'This is a Saturday during the vacation *and* she's got to learn her vocabulary.'

'Helen is petrified the children will inherit my lack of brains.'

'Marcus is clearly superbright,' said Cameron. 'He's such a sweet, sensitive kid.'

'Takes after his mother,' snapped Rupert. 'Tab takes after me. My reports were much worse than hers.'

'She doesn't strike me as being dumb,' said Cameron, 'just unmotivated.'

'She looks OK,' said Rupert coldly. 'And she rides like a dream. What else matters?'

Supper was decidedly scratchy. Tab ostentatiously gave all her shepherd's pie to Beaver. Afterwards Rupert packed both children off upstairs to watch James Bond. Cameron was reading the *Guardian* in the drawing-room and feeling absolutely shattered. How the hell did mothers cope day in and day out, when piercing screams rent the air? The next minute Marcus had run into the room, waving the remote control. He had difficulty breathing.

'I don't think Tab should watch this video. It's called *For Your Eyes Only*, but it's not James Bond.'

'You got it, didn't you?' said Rupert unhelpfully.

A second later Tab came storming in and tried to grab the remote control. When Marcus held it above his head she went for him, kicking his shins and giving him a karate chop in the stomach which doubled him up.

'Stop it,' shouted Rupert, pulling her off.

'It's a lovely film,' screamed Tabitha. 'It's all about ladies licking each other.'

'I'd better come and have a look,' said Rupert.

He returned, grinning. 'Marcus was right. It's a blue film about Lesbians.' He threw the video on the sofa beside Cameron. 'We must have a watch later.'

She was wearing a sleeveless T-shirt, and he slid his hands inside caressing her armpits, then feeling for her breasts. It was ridiculous the way he could turn her to jello.

'I don't fancy your bedroom without a lock on it,' she said. 'The only safe place with this mob around is the john.'

More shrieks issued from upstairs, followed by a crash on the terrace outside. Going out through the french windows, Rupert found the remote control with all its entrails spilling out.

Cameron stormed upstairs. She'd been looking forward to watching *Dido and Aeneas* on Channel Four later, and now they'd be stuck with BBC 1.

'Why did you chuck that out of the window?' she yelled at Tab. 'I know it was you.'

'Marcus won't let me watch *Amityville*,' sobbed Tab. 'I hate him! I hate him!'

Rupert put her to bed screaming. Cameron was relieved at only having to deal with Marcus's asthma attack.

'I'm sorry about Tab,' he murmured as she finally tucked him in.

'Surely she doesn't behave like this at home?'

'Of course she doesn't. Both Malise and Mum are quite strict, so when she comes here she sort of runs wild. And she and Daddy love each other so much,' he added wistfully.

'He loves you too,' said Cameron, giving him a kiss.

Down the passage Cameron found Rupert talking to Tab, who was tucked up in bed with Paddington Bear, gloomily transvestite in the family christening robes.

'You really ought to be asleep, Tab,' she said. 'Marcus says Mummy puts your lights out at nine.'

'Marcus is a bloody sneak,' said Tabitha, yawning.

'Have you said your prayers?'

'OK.' Tab rolled out of bed. 'Dear God,' she prayed loudly, 'please bless Daddy, Mummy, Marcus, Dollop and Beaver. And please give me Biscuit, if you think that's right, God.' Then her fingers opened a fraction. She could see Cameron still hovering on the landing, hopeful of a mention. 'And please God, make Mummy and Daddy get married again, so I can come and live at Penscombe for always; make me a good girl, Amen.'

Cameron walked back to Rupert's bedroom, quivering with rage. Rupert thought it was very funny. 'Isn't she awful? She asked me earlier why I didn't sell my double bed as I didn't need it any more.'

As Marcus predicted, Tab had terrible nightmares and ended up in Rupert's bed. Turned on by the blue movie, Rupert and Cameron waited until she was asleep and then went downstairs and barricaded themselves into the dining-room.

'I've never screwed anyone in here before,' said Rupert. 'Should we put mats down in case we scorch the table?'

In fact, twelve feet of polished mahogany is not the ideal surface on which to make love. Straddling Rupert, her knees aching, Cameron took a long time. She was just capitulating to pleasure when a bright red face, as apoplectic as any Mr Barrett of Wimpole Street, appeared through the hatch.

'What,' thundered Tabitha, 'are you doing to my Daddy?'

'I'm trying to keep him warm,' replied Cameron through gritted teeth.

Things went from bad to worse the next day. Rupert went off to see his constituency secretary. Tab vanished to the stables and, despite Cameron sending repeated messages, didn't return for lunch. Grimly setting out to collect her, Cameron found Tabitha, watched by an idling trio of grooms, jumping the new pony, which ground to a halt each time it came up to a large wall.

'This pony don't jump,' yelled Tabitha.

'Think of something really nasty before take-off, and then give him a good whack,' advised one of the grooms.

Tab rode towards the wall with great determination: 'I'm going to think of CAMERON,' she howled, bringing her whip down on Biscuit's quarters. The grooms screamed with laughter, and then cheered as Biscuit cleared the wall by a foot. Tabitha leapt off the pony, cuddling him and stuffing him with pony nuts. 'Good boy, good boy.'

'Lunch, Tabitha,' said Cameron icily.

Even Tabitha looked faintly sheepish and ran on ahead back to the house.

There are a million children in England living with replacement parents, in fact one in seven is a stepchild, thought Cameron furiously, as she stalked back to the house. They can't all be awful. Just fantasy. You're doing research for a documentary on the in-coming stepmother, she told herself.

'Where's Daddy?' demanded Tab as Cameron went into the kitchen.

'Not coming back till later this afternoon.'

'I don't want any lunch till he gets back.'

'Sit *down*,' ordered Cameron.

'I will if you sit down first,' said Tab with a giggle.

Not looking behind her, Cameron collapsed heavily on to a whoopee cushion which Tab had slipped on to her chair, and which let out a succession of noisy farts. Tab screamed with laughter; even Marcus grinned. For Cameron the noise was too embarrassingly reminiscent of her encounter with their father on the balcony of her Madrid hotel.

'You bloody children, stop winding me up.'

'Don't speak to us like that,' said Tab coldly. 'You're not our mother.'

Cameron walked out of the kitchen and went and swam twenty lengths in the pool to work off her rage. Going upstairs, she discovered Tabitha must have changed at least four times that day and used the carpet of Rupert's bedroom as a dirty clothes' basket.

'Tab,' she bellowed.

'Yes.' Tab appeared from the television room, eating a Mars bar.

'Pick up your clothes, OK?'

492

'Mrs Bodkin picks them up.'

'Mrs Bodkin is not here. Pick them *up*.'

'Bloody shan't.'

Cameron moved towards her.

'Don't you touch me,' hissed Tab, her little face a mask of spite. 'Because of child molesters like you, I'm learning karate at school,' and, clenching her fist in a black-power salute, she shot under Cameron's arm, downstairs and back to the stables.

A blinding headache nudged Cameron's skull. What was the name of that silent order Charles Fairburn disappeared to the day the franchise applications went in? She took a Valium and went down to the kitchen where she found Marcus trying to clear up lunch.

He had put the roasting pan undrained in the sink so the grease floated thick and yellow on the top of the water.

'I'm sorry about Tab,' he mumbled.

'You make up for it,' Cameron said, hugging him.

'It's not all her fault,' said Marcus, fairly. 'She's used to Daddy's total attention when she's here, and Mrs Bodkin fussing over her. She looked after Tab when she was a baby, you see. When Tab says she wants lunch she's given it, and if she doesn't like it when it arrives that doesn't matter much either. She's just not used to a stranger saying, "Do this, don't do that".'

Cameron gazed at the sea of fat, feeling reproved. 'I'm sorry.'

'It isn't your fault,' said Marcus, busily sloshing water all over the surfaces as he wiped them down with a dripping dishcloth.

'I'm not around kids that much. How d'you relate to Malise?'

'OK. He's strict, but he's fair. He's very old. His grand-children are older than me.'

'Would you like your parents to get married again?'

Marcus went green. 'No, absolutely not.'

'Tab would.'

'Oh, Tab gets on much better with Daddy than I do,' said

493

Marcus bitterly. 'And if she was here she could ride all the time.

As Rupert probably wouldn't have eaten at lunchtime, Cameron decided to make him a nice dinner. Just the two of them; the kids could go to bed early. Marcus chatted to her while she cooked and, when she'd finished, offered to play the piano for her. He was just playing a Chopin impromptu quite magically when Tab charged in with Wham full blast on the wireless.

'Turn it off,' said Cameron sharply.

'Why should I?'

'Turn it *off*,' yelled Marcus, but he stopped playing and shut the piano.

Immediately Tab grinned and turned off the wireless.

'I've never been so bored in my life,' she said moodily.

Cameron's suggestion that she could unload the dishwasher was met once again with the cold blue stare.

'I'm starving. What's for supper?'

'Spaghetti hoops.'

'Yuk. What's that cooking in the oven?'

'Boeuf Provençal.'

'My favourite thing. And there are kiwi fruits in the larder. That's also my favourite thing.'

'As you haven't eaten anything I've cooked for you yet,' said Cameron coolly, 'you're going to have spaghetti hoops cooked by Mr Heinz, and then you're going to bed early. I want to spend some time with your father – alone.'

Rupert came home around half past seven, and amazed Cameron by backing her up. 'Go up to bed both of you. Cameron's looked after you all day and she needs a break. You can watch "Howard's Way".'

'Tab's been insupportable all day,' Cameron was appalled to find herself saying as soon as the children went out of the room.

Later Rupert went upstairs and Cameron toured wearily round the house, picking up kids' clothes. If she put a wash on tonight she could iron them first thing in the morning.

Rupert found Tab curled up in bed in a blue nightie, looking through a photograph album of when Helen and Rupert were married: 'Wasn't I a sweet little baby? Look at me riding on Badger's back.'

Rupert was not to be deflected. 'Why have you been so bloody to Cameron?' he said, sitting down on the bed. 'I told you to be nice to her.'

'I hate her,' said Tab calmly, 'and all the grooms hate her, and they say Mr and Mrs Bodkin hate her because she's so bossy. Even Beaver and Blue hate her.'

'Rubbish! Beaver and Blue adore her.'

'Shows how thick they are, then.'

'I told you to be nice to her,' repeated Rupert sternly.

'It's all God's fault,' said Tab, petulantly pulling the duvet up to her chin. 'I prayed specially hard to him this morning to make me really nice to Cameron, and he did absolutely nothing about it.'

Rupert thought it so funny he had to go straight off and tell Cameron. He found her in the drawing-room, rigid with anger.

'What was this doing on my side of the bed?' She handed Rupert a prayer book bound in ivory. 'Look inside,' she said shrilly.

'To my own darling Rupert,' read Rupert slowly. 'All my love, Helen. All other things to their destruction draw, only our love hath no decay.' He grinned at Cameron. 'Well, Helen certainly goofed on that one, didn't she?'

'Tab must have put it there,' hissed Cameron.

'Don't be fucking stupid. She wouldn't understand words like decay and destruction.'

'Bullshit,' screamed Cameron. 'She's the most destructive kid I've ever met, and she certainly understands "To my own darling Rupert, All my love, Helen".'

'What's wrong with that?' protested Rupert. 'Most children do want their mothers and fathers to love each other. Didn't you?'

'She's insanely spoilt.' Cameron could hear the obsessive rattle in her voice. 'Can't you see how she fawns all over you and freezes out everyone else? Your whole relationship with her is overly symbiotic.'

'I don't know what symbiotic means.' Rupert's voice was suddenly brutally icy. 'But it's fuck all to do with you how I handle my children. I suggest you read this prayer book yourself. It might teach you a little Christianity.'

'Where are you going?' she said as he went towards the door.

'To bed. I don't want any dinner. And you can bloody well sleep in the spare room.'

A minute later she heard the front door open and the dogs barking. Terrified Rupert had stormed out, she ran into the hall to find Mr and Mrs Bodkin blinking in the light, clutching their suitcases and looking sheepish.

'I hope you didn't mind us coming home a day early,' muttered Mrs Bodkin, 'but we wanted to see the children, and I thought you might need a bit of help with their meals and their washing. Mrs Gordon likes everything back in good order.'

Cameron was never so pleased to see anyone. 'Sure, it's OK,' she said. 'I shouldn't have made you have the weekend off. We've all missed you. There's some supper in the oven if you're hungry.'

The next moment she was sent flying by Tabitha tearing downstairs and throwing herself into Mrs Bodkin's arms. 'Oh, Mrs B,' she said in a choked voice, 'I'm so glad you're home. It's so horrid when you're not here.'

The next day passed without incident until the afternoon. Cameron, who knew she should have disarmed Tab by being sweet, or at least outwardly unmoved, spent the day sulking, thawing out, then sulking again. The children were due to go back to Warwickshire after tea. Rupert had bought the pony, Biscuit, for Tab, and would drive pony and two children back in the trailer.

Mrs Bodkin finished the ironing and packed the children's cases, while Rupert and the children watched *High Society* on television. Ecstatic about the new pony, Tabitha sprawled on

Rupert's knee, defiantly covering him with kisses. Cameron, determinedly doing the *Guardian* crossword, sat on the sofa as far away from Rupert as possible. They hadn't spoken since last night. The sight of Cameron's long smooth brown thighs in the shortest of khaki shorts, however, was finally too much for Rupert. As the credits came up at the end he stretched out, putting a hand on her leg.

'Don't touch her,' screamed Tab. 'It's disgusting,' and, bursting into tears, she fled upstairs. Rupert followed her to find out what was the matter. He came down shaking his head. 'It's the same old story. She wants me and Helen to get together again like Bing Crosby and Grace Kelly, so she can live here all the time.'

The following morning Rupert got a letter from Taggie: *Dear Roopurt*, she had written, *thank you for the luvly puppy. He is sweet we called him Clawdeeus becos patrick says it goes with gurtrude. they love eech other now. thank you for the shampain. Sorry we did not come out to dinner. I hope you understand. Yours sincearly Taggie O'Hara.*

Rupert wanted to weep.

'Is that from one of the children?' said Cameron, reading over his shoulder. 'They don't teach them much spelling in class. Christ, it's from Taggie. She's completely illiterate. How could Maud and Declan have produced something quite so dumb?'

37

The weekend left Cameron exhausted and with a numb sense of failure. What sort of monster was she to detest an innocent little girl of nine? Desperate for someone to dump on, she was tempted to ask Seb or even Charles Fairburn out to lunch, but decided it was too risky. Tony might easily have bugged their telephones. She longed to talk to Declan. He was so wise and she craved his approval beyond anything, but she didn't think this was the way to win it. He'd just assume she'd been treating Tab like a Corinium employee. In the end she rang up Janey Lloyd-Foxe who, stuck at home with a new baby and frantically trying to finish a book, was only too happy for any distraction. They met for lunch in London.

Janey rolled up looking stunning and fantastically brown. 'It's typing topless in the garden,' she explained. 'My bum and legs are as white as blackboard chalk because they're hidden under the table. I've got to finish this bloody book because we're desperately broke. Billy's absolutely fed up with the BBC, too. I do hope Venturer get the franchise. D'you think we will?'

'Hard to tell,' said Cameron. 'We ought to on form, but there are so many wild cards in the pack, and Declan and Rupert really aren't getting on at the moment.'

'They're both so tricky and self-willed,' grumbled Janey. 'Hello.' She beamed up at an Italian waiter who was utterly mesmerized by her brown breasts which seemed to squirm in her low-cut pink dress like day-old puppies. 'Neither of us wants to work this afternoon, so let's kick off with duo enormo vodkos et tonicos, then we can get wildly drunk and indiscreet. You are lucky not having to worry about schedules and costings any more,' Janey added, as the waiter floated back to the bar. 'It must be bliss being supported by Rupert.'

'He's not very pleased with me,' confessed Cameron, pleating the tablecloth. Then she told Janey about the weekend.

'Darling,' said Janey, taking a hefty belt of vodka, 'get one thing straight. It's not you. I told Helen yonks ago that she never need worry about Rupert marrying again because no one would take on Tab. She's adorable until she suspects anyone might take Rupert away from her, then she's Catherine de Medici crossed with all the Borgias! Mind you,' Janey went on, plunging a cauliflower floret deep into a bowl of mayonnaise, 'Tab hasn't had it easy. Helen tries to be fair, but it's obvious to anyone that Marcus is the Granny Smith of her eye. She's never got on with Tab.'

'Marcus is a really nice kid,' said Cameron. 'Why's Rupert so mean to him?'

'Jealousy. Rupert and Helen were going through one of their many bad patches when Marcus was born. Helen lavished all her affection on Marcus. Rupert started lavishing all his affection on show jumping and other women. It doesn't help that Marcus looks just like Helen, and Rupert doesn't want any reminders of her around him any more.'

'But Marcus just longs for Rupert's approval.'

'I know,' said Janey. 'It's really sad. Just as Rupert used to long for Helen's approval, but she always dismissed him as a handsome hunk and show jumping as a very second-class occupation.'

As the waiter wheeled up the hors d'oeuvres trolley Janey's eyes fell lasciviously on Mediterranean prawns, stuffed aubergine and oeuf à la Russe.

'Go on,' urged Cameron. 'It's my treat.'

'What are you going to have?' asked Janey, as the waiter piled up her plate.

'Just cold salmon and a radicchio salad.'

'Oh, that sounds nice,' said Janey. 'I'll have that next, and lots of white wine.'

'What was Helen like?' said Cameron, trying not to sound too interested as a second besotted waiter helped them to Sancerre.

'Oh, a sweet old thing really, but very earnest and high-minded, not like *us*.' Even grinning with her mouth full of tarragon-flavoured mushrooms, Janey had all the charm in the world, thought Cameron. The 'like us' seemed to unite them in a conspiracy of naughtiness and fun.

'Did she love Rupert?'

'Ish,' said Janey. 'She always disapproved of him. Mind you, he was *disgraceful* in those days. But underneath all that stunning self-assurance and sex appeal, and lack of introspection, he does need the clapping. He wouldn't be so competitive if he didn't. He's so macho, what he really needs is some very gentle, calm, submissive girl who thinks he's absolutely marvellous.'

Like Taggie O'Hara, thought Cameron savagely.

'Goodness, I shouldn't have eaten all that,' said Janey later as she put her knife and fork together. 'But I suppose I can make the excuse that I still haven't got my figure back after the baby.'

'Has Tab truly fought with all Rupert's girlfriends?' asked Cameron.

'Well, he turns them over so fast it's hard to remember,' said Janey. Then, catching sight of Cameron's face, she added quickly, 'But I'm sure it'll be different now he's met you. They liked Beattie Johnson, I think, but she was such a slut, she never imposed any régime on them, and never minded if they were frightened of the dark and wanted to get into Rupert's bed. The more the merrier as far as Beattie was concerned. I'm amazed they got any sleep with her drunken snoring.'

Knowing both Janey and Beattie Johnson had pages on national newspapers, Cameron suspected an element of professional jealousy.

'What d'you figure I should do about Tab?' she asked despairingly. 'Rupert's planning to have her over every weekend this summer.'

'He won't,' said Janey soothingly. 'He'll get distracted. But actually I think you ought to go back to work. You're far too bright to hang about all summer brooding about Tab and being Rupert's concubine.'

'It's so hard,' said Cameron. 'I've had plenty of offers, but all from companies in other parts of the country, and I don't want to leave Rupert. I've been offered loads of freelance work too, but nothing that grabs me. I guess you're right, I must do something.'

'You probably miss the bustle at Corinium, and Tony Baddingham too. I've always thought he was very attractive in a dark satanic way.'

'We were together for three years,' admitted Cameron. 'He had his moments, but he was a devil.'

'That forked tongue must have made him very good at oral sex,' said Janey wickedly.

Cameron laughed.

Having hardly touched her lunch, she put her knife and fork together. Leaning over, Janey forked up Cameron's salmon and, wrapping it in a paper napkin, put it in her bag.

'D'you mind if I take it home for my cat, Harold Evans? He's fourteen tomorrow and he loves salmon as much as he hates London.'

While Cameron was in London with Janey, Rupert went over to The Priory in an attempt to melt the dangerous *froideur* that seemed to have developed between him and Declan.

Declan, however, seemed enchanted to see him. Switching off Brahms' Fourth, and making a heavily gin-laced jug of Pimm's – 'Just the kind of focking English upper-class drink you would like!' – he took Rupert out into the garden.

'Is that the new puppy's work?' said Rupert, noticing a shredded bedroom slipper on the lawn and the flattened flower beds.

'I'm afraid so. He's been re-christened High Claudius, as

he rolled on onspeakable fox's crap yesterday, and, roshing in, leapt all over Professor Graystock who'd dropped in to drool over Taggie! At least he got rid of the Professor double quick – so he does have his advantages! It's all right,' he added hastily, misreading the sudden bootfaced expression on Rupert's face, 'he's a dear little dog – we all love him. Caitlin's taken him and Gertrude for a walk.'

He poured the Pimm's into two pint mugs, then put the jug in the shade under a nearby chestnut tree. It was another glorious afternoon. Grasshoppers scraped like toy violins in the long grass, a marbled white butterfly basked on a cushion of thyme. Through the silver trunks of the beech trees they could just see Rupert's cornfields turning gold. Even the birds were silent, worn out with feeding their young.

Declan stretched out. 'It's days like this that make that terrible long winter seem worthwhile. D'you know we've been here for nearly a year?'

'Here's to many more,' said Rupert, noticing how tired Declan was looking again. 'How's the book going?'

'All right, except that I'm constantly disturbed by my wife and daughter screaming at each other.'

'Taggie screaming?' said Rupert in surprise.

'Never Taggie. Maud and Caitlin. Maud's menopause appears to be coinciding with Caitlin's adolescence. I'm thinking of calling in the International Peacekeeping Force.'

'I could have done with them this weekend,' said Rupert, swotting an ant. 'My children were staying. Tab and Cameron were like weasels at each other's jugulars. Why can't women get on with each other? Men never fight.'

Declan laughed. 'I'd never have cast Cameron as Mary Poppins.'

Idly they discussed the franchise. Declan had recruited a very good girl from Yorkshire Television as Head of Children's Programmes. Then, heavily prompted by Rupert, he confessed he was desperately pushed again for money.

'Have you spent all that thirty-five thousand already?' said Rupert disapprovingly. 'You shouldn't keep sloping off to grope Maud in the Lakes.'

'I know, but I'd been working flat out and she's so restless. And I've just paid a massive tax bill and Patrick's fare to Australia and Caitlin's school fees for last term. And I've never seen anything like the electricity bill. Talk about electric shock treatment. Poor Tag's the only breadwinner. She's over at Monica's at the moment, filling up her deep freeze.'

'Can't she shove Tony in as well?' said Rupert, fishing a piece of cucumber out of his mug. 'I expect he'll force the poor darling to taste everything first in case she's poisoning them.'

Declan wasn't listening. His Mini, which was a 1976 model welded together by dog hair, rust and mud, which had only passed its MOT for the last few years as a result of prayer and huge sums of money changing hands, had finally given up the ghost, he told Rupert.

'You can borrow one of my cars for the moment,' said Rupert. 'In actual fact, what you need is a massive cash injection. D'you want an advance from the Venturer kitty?'

'We'll need all of that. I've got to earn it. I've spent the last week writing a script for a fifty-minute dramatized documentary on Yeats.'

'Who?'

'The Irish poet. The man I'm writing the book about,' said Declan impatiently.

'Ah,' said Rupert. Then, regaining the ascendancy, 'Doesn't sound like a money-spinner to me.'

'Will be – if it's good enough. I've sold the idea to Channel Four. And the IBA will be in raptures. Lady Gosling's half-Irish.'

Lying on his back, listening to the hum of insects and the idle cooing of the wood pigeons, gazing up at Taggie's bed-room window, Rupert suddenly had a brainwave. 'If Freddie and I put up some more money, you can afford to have Cameron produce and direct it, so we can keep it in the family.'

'Indeed you will not,' said Declan mutinously. 'Cameron and I don't get on.'

Rupert turned towards Declan, eyes squinting against the sun: 'Time you bloody learned. She really thinks you're great. She just has a communication problem. And it'll give her something to do. She's like a sheep dog, she needs work.'

'To stop her getting in your hair?' snapped Declan.

Rupert, who hadn't had any lunch, had now finished all the fruit in his Pimms and was reduced to eating the mint. 'I'm thinking of Venturer, not myself,' he said sanctimoniously, as Declan filled up both their mugs. 'We just don't want her getting restless and running back to Tony.'

'It'd mean several weeks in Ireland,' said Declan. 'We'll have to go on a recce fairly soon, and once we've cast it and fixed up the people to interview, I want to start shooting in early September. Then we'll need another week at the end of November to do the Coole woods in Autumn.'

'Perfect,' said Rupert. 'I'll be popping over to Ireland all the time from now on for the Autumn sales, so Cameron won't suffer too badly from withdrawal symptoms.'

'It's a terrible gamble,' said Declan broodingly. 'She and I never got on at Corinium; why should we get on now?'

'Because Tony won't be there putting the boot in. I promise you, Cameron really, really admires your work.'

Declan blushed slightly. 'Well, she's got to read the script before committing herself. I'm not having her working on something she doesn't like one hundred per cent.'

Cameron rang Declan later that evening, trying to keep the excitement out of her voice. 'I've just got back from London and read your script. I just love it. The characters are terrific and all the ideas for interviews are just great. The text reads so beautifully; it's superb.'

Declan was utterly disarmed by such uncharacteristic enthusiasm. For any writer, waiting for the first reaction is a nail-biting experience. Ursula, who'd typed the script out, had said she'd loved it, but then she was paid to.

'I'd just adore to do it,' went on Cameron, 'if you really figure I'm the right person?'

'Sure you are,' said Declan. 'I've just been talking to Jeremy

504

at Channel Four and told him you might be interested. He's mad about the idea.'

'You look as though you're floating on Eire,' said Rupert as Cameron put down the telephone.

'You won't mind my being away so much?'

'Yes,' said Rupert, taking her in his arms, 'of course I will, but you've got to have your freedom. I did when I was show jumping. It was the one thing that fuelled me.'

Cameron blushed. 'Do you swear it was Declan's idea I should direct it?'

'Would I lie to you?' said Rupert blandly. 'He asked me to ask you. He really admires your work. He just has a communication problem.'

'Oh, wow!' sighed Cameron. 'I feel like the first woman on the moon.'

38

Deliriously happy to be working again, Cameron threw herself into producing Declan's programme. Much of her time was spent in London or over at The Priory and she turned one of Rupert's upstairs bedrooms into a study so she could work there as well. Rupert, who'd been neglecting the yard and his business interests, and still had a full diary as an MP despite the summer recess, was also kept very busy. This suited them both; they continued to argue a lot, but sex at least was miraculous when they met. Even the children's visits seemed less of a hassle. Mrs Bodkin did all the work, and when Tabitha became unbearable, which was most of the time, instead of rowing with her, Cameron retreated upstairs to work.

On the franchise front, the IBA had now sifted through everyone's lengthy applications with a toothcomb and fired off letters to all the consortiums containing supplementary questions about programme plans, management structure, studios and general finance.

'We promised them a cross between Camelot and Utopia,' said Declan, 'and now we've got to justify it.'

The long written answer to this letter was almost as crucial in winning the franchise as the original application. Once again, therefore, the Venturer team had to get together to thrash out policy. Meetings at anyone's house were now considered too risky, as Tony had stepped up his espionage since Cameron had defected.

'I was followed down Cotchester High Street by the most ravishing piece of rough trade this morning,' said Charles Fairburn petulantly, 'but I couldn't work out if it was my lucky day or he was a member of the Baddingham KGB.'

Rupert, being such a practised adulterer, was therefore deputed to find a meeting-place where they wouldn't be found out. He chose a seedy room over a nightclub in a back street in Cheltenham.

'If this is where you bring your mistresses,' grumbled Georgie Baines when he arrived for the first meeting, 'I can see why they get fed up.'

Night after night, therefore, through the end of July and a long hot August, Declan, Freddie, Bas, Rupert, Cameron, Lord Smith, Harold White, and the Corinium Moles – when they could get away – met up to hammer out the answers. Charles Fairburn still turned up every time in a different disguise, which made everyone giggle. They needed to. Declan, deadly serious now, insisted everyone drank only Perrier until the meeting was over. They were nearly half-way through their long ordeal in the franchise fight and nervous tension was mounting.

At least they were spared the Bishop, who was spending a month in the Holy Land, and Professor Graystock, who was in Greece researching a book. But they missed Dame Enid, who'd gone on a walking tour in Wales with a woman friend, and, after 12th August, when he pushed off to Scotland to shoot, they missed the inanities of the Lord-Lieutenant. They'd all grown very fond of Henry. Janey Lloyd-Foxe, hampered by two children and a book to finish, seldom showed up. Billy was in Australia making a film about rugger for the BBC.

For Wesley Emerson, August was a wicket month. He took 8 for 42 against the Australians in the Leeds Test. Venturer basked in his reflected glory.

The letter with the answers to the supplementary questions was dispatched to the IBA at the beginning of September, by which time the franchise wives were getting very fed up. The long summer holidays were slowly grinding to a halt. The smell of moulding leaves and bonfires, the sight of huge red suns and dewy cobwebs hanging on the fences, reminded them with a pang that summer had already had its run.

Sarah Stratton, for example, not only had Paul hanging round at home, out of work and grumpily demoralized, but also his ghastly daughters who never stopped implying that Daddy would be Prime Minister now if he had stayed with Mummy, and that by going out to work Sarah was neglecting him. Sarah and James's afternoon programme was off the air for the summer. Paul and the girls watched the local news and knew that Sarah finished at seven, or even six-thirty on 'Crossroads' days. The studio was only twenty minutes from home. All were waiting bootfaced to start supper if she weren't home by eight.

Valerie Jones was increasingly irritated that Freddie seemed to be spending so much time on the stupid franchise. Completely off gardening since James had failed to immortalize her opening, Valerie had dragged Wayne and Sharon off to a villa in Portugal for a month. She'd all but persuaded Taggie to join them, and to do the cooking, until that fiendish Rupert talked her out of it, so instead they got a local slut called Conceptiona, who got so terribly on Fred-Fred's nerves (he hated foreign food anyway) that he buzzed off back to Gloucestershire saying he had too much on. As he'd been wandering round the villa with *nothing on* at all, in order to get a suntan (no doubt Rupert's fiendish influence again) this seemed very illogical.

Monica Baddingham also had, as Cameron would have said, a somewhat 'stressful' summer. There had been no discussion between her and Tony about Cameron's defection, beyond the fact that Corinium had lost a megastar and an essential weapon in the franchise battle. Privately Monica realized Tony was utterly devastated. Being humane and kindly, she felt very sorry for him, in the same way as she did for her poor distressed gentlefolk, her battered wives, her

508

stray dogs and everyone else who was the recipient of her inexhaustible charity.

It was tragic that Tony couldn't level with her. Comforting him, they might have grown closer. But at least she listened patiently to his diatribes against Declan and Rupert, and stoically accepted that he would want to sleep with her more than once a week until he found a new mistress.

Much more worrying was that Archie, her favourite child, now seventeen and not due to take his A-levels until next year, was still enjoying a most unsuitable fling with the ghastly Tracey Makepiece, whom he'd met at the O'Hara New Year's Eve party. Both Monica and Tony were terrified Archie would make her pregnant and be forced into an early marriage; or, because the Makepieces didn't believe in abortion or adoption, the baby Baddingham would be taken into the bosom of the Makepiece family and be a drain on Archie's quite insufficient pocket money for the rest of his life.

'Why the hell can't you find a girl of your own class?' roared Tony, forbidding Archie to see her any more. Archie had obviously taken no notice. One morning in early August, putting on Archie's Barbour by mistake, Monica found a letter in Tracey's loopy handwriting: '*I will love you dearest, until all the seas run dry.*' Archie had promptly been shunted off to Tuscany for three weeks.

Most despondent of all the wives, however, was Maud. No one had fallen in love with her for ages, and Declan, having been totally obsessed with the franchise, and then his Yeats programme, was now totally obsessed with both. Not wanting to leave Maud when she was so depressed, apprehensive about going to Ireland with Cameron, Declan tried to persuade Maud to make a return to acting and play Yeats's great love, Maud Gonne, in the programme, so she could come with them. Maud, terrified of failure, turned him down flatly and then detested herself for doing so. It was as though she was deliberately pushing him into an affair with Cameron.

Finally, Caitlin had been home most of the summer, full of teenage moodiness, criticizing everything Maud did, particularly her clothes, which Caitlin claimed were so out of date they should be called 'a first world wardrobe'. Maud was not amused; she'd always prided herself on being able to go to a party in a pair of Declan's pyjamas, with a jewelled comb in her hair, and look marvellous.

One morning towards the end of August Maud read a piece in the *Daily Mail* about Princess Michael entering a new golden age of maturity and confidence. She's the same age as me, thought Maud broodily, and I'm ten years younger than Joan Collins, and look how great she looks. Why am I riddled with self-doubt and about as confident as a mongrel at Crufts?

Having borrowed a hundred pounds and her new violet dress off Taggie, she decided to ignore Declan's bank balance as well and go into Cotchester and buy some new clothes. As she got ready, Caitlin wandered into her bedroom.

Even in the space of the holidays she seemed to have shot up several inches, and was as tall as Maud now. Her brace was off her teeth, she'd grown her hair and peroxided it canary yellow. Chronic sulkiness was the only thing that stopped her being incredibly pretty.

Changing her parting slightly, Maud noticed three grey hairs and tugged them out in horror.

'You'd quadruple the men after you if you had short hair or used Sun-In or a bit of gel,' said Caitlin, 'and that's Taggie's dress you're wearing.'

'When I was your age,' countered Maud, 'I had hundreds of boys after me. I can't think why you don't.'

'I'm choosey, that's why. Why don't you have your face lifted?'

Maud gazed at her reflection. Perhaps she ought to, but unable to face a filling at the dentist, she'd never cope with the pain. Anyway she'd rather have her spirits lifted. Her body looked OK still, but crêped when it was squeezed, which didn't seem very often these days. I'm over the hill, she thought with a shiver, as she started to put on her make-up. Declan will go off to Ireland – and with Cameron Cook.

'Eyeliner goes on much better if you pull your eyelids out,' said Caitlin, 'and you're not going to wear those ghastly slingbacks?'

'Better than your revolting clodhoppers,' said Maud furiously. 'It's like sharing a house with a carthorse. And what are you going to do with yourself all day?'

'I'm going to spend the morning dyeing my hair,' said Caitlin.

Cotchester was full of tourists, drifting aimlessly down the High Street, photographing the cathedral and the ancient houses, and the statue of Charles I. By contrast, Monica Baddingham, striding purposefully through the crowds, was like a powerboat chugging through a flotilla of yachts on a windless day. She detested shopping – such a time-consuming activity. But she needed batteries for her Walkman and there was a new recording of *Don Giovanni* on order which, maddeningly, hadn't arrived, and she had to pick up some scores of *The Merry Widow*.

Every year the West Cotchester Hunt put on a play which was performed to large noisy audiences in November. This year they had decided to be slightly more ambitious and join forces with Cotchester Operatic Society to put on *The Merry Widow*.

Monica had already been appropriately cast as Valencienne, a virtuous wife. Charles Fairburn had been inappropriately cast as her randy admirer Camille. Bas Baddingham was still dickering over whether to play the male lead, Count Danilo, but as yet the director, Barton Sinclair – ex-Covent Garden, no less – was still searching for someone to play Hanna, the Merry Widow. He was holding auditions in Cotchester Town Hall that very day, but was deeply pessimistic that anyone would be beautiful or stylish enough, or have a sufficiently good voice. Luck, however, was on Barton Sinclair's side. Outside the Bar Sinister Monica bumped into Maud.

'How jolly nice,' said Monica in her raucous voice as she kissed Maud. 'I've been hoping I'd run into you for ages. I wanted to say how wonderful Taggie's been. Completely saved my life cooking for all the hordes this summer. You must be so proud of her.'

511

Maud said, yes, she supposed she was.

'But she's getting too thin,' went on Monica. 'She used to be so round, soft and smiling. I hope she's not taking on too much. You, on the other hand, look splendid. How's Declan?'

'Oh, obsessed with the wretched franchise,' said Maud fretfully.

'Isn't it a ghastly bore?' sighed Monica. 'Tony can't think of anything else. But I don't see why, just because our husbands are on different sides, we can't be friends.'

It was very hot in Cotchester High Street. The cool garlic-scented gloom of the Bar Sinister beckoned.

'Nor do I,' said Maud. 'Why don't we go in and have lunch?'

'What a good idea,' said Monica in excitement. 'Plough-man's lunch, and half a pint of cider.'

Maud's aims were slightly more ambitious, and they were soon sitting down with Muscadet and crespolini.

'Oh, look, there's James Vereker and Sarah Stratton,' said Monica. 'What's Declan doing at the moment?'

'He's off to Ireland with Cameron Cook,' said Maud.

'Oh.' Monica's forkful of crespolini stopped on the way to her mouth. 'But I thought . . .'

'. . . she was living with Rupert. Yes, she is, but she's making a film with Declan in Ireland.'

Her tongue loosened by a third glass, Maud told Monica about Declan's trying to persuade her to play Maud Gonne, and how her nerve had failed. 'I couldn't face Cameron screaming at me when I didn't come up to scratch,' she confessed. 'Her sarcasm could strip furniture, and I've always found it difficult to act in front of Declan.'

Monica, at this point, became very thoughtful. 'But you would like to go back?'

'Oh yes, but at the moment I've got about as much self-confidence as a leveret at a coursing meeting.'

Monica fished in her shopping bag and brought out one of the scores of *The Merry Widow*. On the cover was a painting of a beautiful woman, with hair swept up under a big pink hat and a waist, in its swirling cyclamen-pink dress, as slender as her neck. She was raising a glass of champagne in one long purple-gloved hand. Four handsome men with black twirling moustaches were raising their glasses to her in admiring salute.

It was Maud's perfect fantasy. What did gel and Sun-In matter to that woman?

'Why don't you start with something less ambitious than Maud Gonne?' said Monica. 'We're desperate for someone to play the Merry Widow.'

'I couldn't,' faltered Maud. 'It's a very demanding part.'

'Nonsense,' said Monica briskly. 'You'd waltz it.'

'What are my two favourite women doing lunching at my restaurant without telling me?' said a voice.

It was Bas, absolutely black from a fortnight's polo in America.

'Bas,' said Monica delightedly. 'I know I'm not supposed to talk to you either, after the dreadful way you've betrayed Tony, but sit down and help me persuade Maud to audition for Hanna.'

Bas needed little persuading. Up to now he'd by-passed Maud in his amorous travels, partly because he had long-range aims for Taggie and partly because he'd realized how dotty Maud had been about Rupert at Christmas. Certainly, in the soft lighting of the Bar Sinister, she looked stunning today, and that violet dress was very becoming. It emphasized her white skin and just missed clashing with the gorgeous red hair, and all those undone buttons showed off a Cheddar Gorge of cleavage. Another bottle of Muscadet was ordered.

'Bas is toying with the idea of playing your leading man,' said Monica.

'Hopefully it'll lead to other things,' said Basil, rubbing one of his long muscular, polo-playing thighs against Maud's as he re-filled her glass.

Later, not even allowing her a cup of black coffee to sober her up, Basil and Monica frogmarched Maud down the High Street to the Town Hall where the director, Barton Sinclair, had reached screaming point, having heard ten amateur hopefuls murdering the score.

Up on stage now, the eleventh, a very made-up blonde,

who'd never see fifty again, was crucifying the Vilja song. The pianist was desperately trying to keep in time with her. A huge bluebottle buzzing against a window pane was having more success.

'She'd be too fat even if you looked through the wrong end of your binoculars,' whispered Bas to Maud. 'At least you can do better than that.'

'I can't,' muttered Maud in terror. 'That's Top G she's missing.'

As she tried to bolt, Bas's arm closed round her waist. 'Yes, you can,' he murmured. 'Just think of the fun we can have rehearsing together night after night, and it won't be all singing I can tell you.'

'Thank you very much,' said Barton Sinclair in his chorus-boy drawl.

'I sang the part in 1979,' said the blonde, teetering down the steps in her four-inch heels. 'It brought the house down.'

'Pity you weren't buried under the rubble,' muttered Barton. 'We'll be in touch. I'll be making a decision at the end of the week,' he told her. Then, waiting until she was safely out of the door, he turned to Monica. 'That's the lot, thank God. Talk about scraping the barrel organ.'

'I'm going home,' said Maud.

'Could you hear just one more?' said Monica.

Barton Sinclair looked at his watch and sighed: 'Do I have to? I was hoping to get the three forty-five back to Paddington.'

'It'll be worth getting the next train, I promise you,' said Monica. 'This is Maud O'Hara. She used to act and sing professionally.'

Barton Sinclair straightened his flowered tie, and smoothed his straggly mouse-brown hair.

'You certainly look the part,' he said.

'I haven't practised,' bleated Maud, the crespolini and the Sancerre churning like a tumble-dryer inside her.

'Try the same song,' said Barton, handing her the score. 'Take it slowly, Mike,' he added to the pianist.

'You come in on the last quaver of the fourth bar,' the pianist told Maud kindly.

Below her, Maud could see their faces: Monica's eager, flushed and unpainted, Basil's sleek and mahogany, and Barton Sinclair's London night owl and deathly pale. They seemed infinitely more terrifying than a first night audience at Covent Garden.

'I can't,' she whispered, wringing her sweating hands.

'Go on, darling,' said Bas. 'We're all on your side.'

Off went the pianist. Maud fluffed the opening.

'I'm sorry. Could we start again?'

'Of course,' said Barton.

Off went the pianist again, and Maud opened her mouth.

> *There once lived a Vilja, a fair mountain sprite,*
> *She danced on a hill in the still of the night.*

Her voice was sweet, true and hesitant, but suddenly, as she launched into the main theme, it seemed to soar out glorious and joyful, stilling the bluebottle and taking the dust off the rafters, and the four other people in the room felt the hair rising on the backs of their necks.

'A star is re-born,' whispered Monica, wiping her eyes.

'I *am* going to have a nice Autumn,' reflected Basil. 'Over forty, they're always so grateful!'

'*Vilja, Oh, Vilja, be tender and true,*' sang Maud, triple pianissimo, '*Love me and I'll die for you.*'

For a second there was silence, then her audience burst out clapping and cheering.

'*Come into Covent Garden, Maud,*' sang Basil.

'You've got the part,' said Barton Sinclair. 'The only problem is how much you're going to show up the others.'

'Thank you, Barton,' said Monica and Basil in unison.

After that they all went back to the Bar Sinister for several more bottles of Muscadet and Barton Sinclair only just made the six forty-five.

·

Tony and Declan were very apprehensive when they heard the news of such close fraternization between the rival franchise sides. On reflection, however, Tony decided he'd definitely got the better bargain. While Maud was a rattle who drank far too much, Monica drank very little and was incredibly discreet.

'Keep your trap shut and your ears open,' Tony told her. 'You may learn some interesting things.'

'I'm not pumping anyone,' said Monica firmly. 'It's simply not on. Only if anyone lets anything drop.'

'It'll be knickers if Bas has anything to do with it,' said Tony.

Declan, however, who was going to have to spend the second half of September and much of October in Ireland with Cameron, was principally relieved that Maud was so much happier. The sound of her carolling away upstairs practising her songs reminded him of the carefree days in Dublin when they were first married. Perhaps, if *The Merry Widow* were a success, she'd have enough confidence to take up acting professionally again.

Caitlin, who had now dyed her custard-yellow hair so black it almost looked blue, found her mother's euphoria even more irritating than her previous picky depression, and decided to push off to London for a few days to stay with some schoolfriends. She was going back the week after next and might as well have some fun before the prison doors clanged round her again.

She found Taggie in the kitchen fainting over a final reminder from the Electricity Board. 'I can't think why it's so high.'

'Mummy's vibrator's battery-operated, so it can't be that,' said Caitlin. 'Hullo, darling,' she added, hugging Claudius.

'He's in disgrace,' sighed Taggie. 'He's just eaten one of Mummy's new slingbacks.'

'Good thing; they were gross,' said Caitlin. 'Every Claud has a silver lining! Can you lend me fifty pounds to go to London?'

'I haven't got it,' protested Taggie. 'I've just lent Daddy a hundred pounds for a new pair of cords for Ireland.'

'At least I'll be gone for nearly a week, so you won't have to feed me,' cajoled Caitlin. 'So that's worth fifty.'

'And we haven't done your trunk yet,' wailed Taggie. 'You've grown out of everything, you need new Aertex shirts, and both your games' skirts are split.'

'Oh, sew them up,' said Caitlin airily. 'We can't possibly afford new ones if we're so poor.'

RIVALS
39

After a riotous five days in London, Caitlin rolled up at Paddington Station with just enough money for her half-fare home. Her blue-black hair was coaxed upward at the front into a corkscrew quiff. She was wearing peacock feather earrings, a black and white sleeveless T-shirt, a black Lycra mini which just covered her bottom, laddered black tights, huge black clumpy shoes, all of which belonged to various friends of hers, a great deal of black eye make-up, and messages in Biro all over her arms.

It was hardly surprising, therefore, that the man at the ticket desk refused to believe she was under sixteen. A most unseemly screaming match ensued, which first amused then irritated the growing queue of passengers behind Caitlin, who began to worry they might miss their trains home.

'My father is a very very famous man,' screamed Caitlin as a last resort, 'and he'll get you.'

'Don't threaten me, young lady,' said the booking clerk.

'It's people like you who turn liberals like me into racists,' screamed Caitlin even louder. 'You're just discriminating against me because I'm white. I'll report you to the Race Relations Board.'

At that moment Archie Baddingham, on his way home from his three weeks' banishment in Tuscany, reached the top of the neighbouring first-class queue. Hearing the din, and recognizing Caitlin's shrill Irish accent from New Year's Eve, he bought her a ticket.

'Remember me?' he said, tapping her on the shoulder.

'No, yes,' said Caitlin. 'You're Archie, aren't you? Can you lend me my fare, this stupid asshole won't believe I'm under sixteen.'

'I've got you a ticket,' said Archie.

'I can't accept a ticket from you,' stormed Caitlin irrationally. 'Your father's been absolutely shitty to my father.'

'My father's shitty to everyone,' said Archie, calmly taking her arm. 'Come on, we'd better move it.'

They only just caught the train on time, but managed to find two single seats opposite each other.

'I've never travelled first class,' said Caitlin, stretching out on the orange seat and squirming her neck luxuriously against the headrest.

Archie looked wonderful, she thought. Like her, he'd shot up and lost weight. He was wearing black 501s, rolled up above black socks and black brogues with a black polo-neck tucked into a western belt with a silver buckle, black crosses in his ears, and a brown suede jacket. His blond hair, washed with soap to remove any shine, was long at the front and cut short at the back and sides. His still slightly rounded face looked thinner because of a suntan almost as dark as his eyes.

'Why are you so disgustingly brown?' asked Caitlin.

'I've just spent three weeks in Tuscany. My parents booted me out there to get over a girl.'

'Tracey-on-the-Makepiece.'

Archie grinned, making him look even more attractive. 'How d'you know that?'

'You were superglued to her at Patrick's twenty-first.'

'So I was. Actually, I'm over her, but Dad and Mum thought I wasn't, so I thought I might as well take advantage of a free holiday. Have you been away?'

'We never go anywhere. My parents are always broke. No, it's quite OK. Nothing to do with your father. They're just hopeless with money.' There was a pause. Caitlin gazed out of the window, wondering what to say next.

'What would you like to drink?' asked Archie.

'They got any Malibu?'

'I doubt it.'

'Well, vodka and tonic, then. Can I come with you?'

The Inter-City, belting towards Bristol, swayed like a drunk as they walked towards the buffet car.

'Have you had any lunch?' asked Archie, admiring her narrow waist and slim legs which were more ladder than tights.

'No,' said Caitlin.

'I'll buy you some grub then,' said Archie.

'Been to a funeral?' said the gay barman, running a lascivious eye over Archie's black clothes.

'*Passengers are reminded that it is an offence to serve intoxicating liquor to persons under the age of eighteen,*' read Caitlin loudly, as Archie paid for everything.

'Keep your vice down,' hissed Archie.

The journey back to their seat, with each of them carrying white plastic trays of vodkas and tonics, glasses, bacon sandwiches, Mars bars, and packets of crisps, was much more hazardous. They had no hands to steady themselves against the lurching train.

'Terribly sorry,' mumbled Caitlin, going scarlet, as for the third time she cannoned off a commuter back into Archie.

'Who's complaining?' said Archie.

'Thank you so much,' said Caitlin as they sped past slow winding rivers, rolling fields, and clumps of yellowing trees. 'This bacon sandwich is the best thing I've ever tasted.'

'I'm surprised you can say that with Taggie cooking for you,' said Archie. 'Every time my father compliments my mother on the food, it turns out Taggie's made it. How is she?'

'Bit low. She's hopelessly hooked on Rupert Campbell-Black.'

'Won't do her any good,' said Archie, pouring out a second vodka and tonic for Caitlin. 'He strikes women down like lightning bolts. Anyway, he's bonking my father's ex.'

'Cameron Cook,' said Caitlin dismissively. 'She's a

crosspatch, isn't she? I can't see what men see in her. My brother was crazy about her, and now she's gone off to make a film in Ireland with Daddy. I hope they don't end up in bed. People usually do on location, don't they? I'd loathe her as a stepmother.'

'Dad was mad about her. I was shit-scared he'd leave Mum and marry her,' said Archie, breaking a Mars bar and giving half to Caitlin. 'I dread my parents getting a divorce, in case they marry again and leave all their money to their new children.'

Caitlin giggled. 'Mine haven't any to leave.'

'I hear your mother's joined the cast of *The Merry Widow*. Mum told me on the telephone that she's streets ahead of everyone else.'

'At least it's got her off my back,' said Caitlin. 'She drives me crackers: "Where are you going? Who with? Why were you so long on the telephone? Who was that on the telephone? Was it a good party? Did you meet anyone nice?" Christ! Not that she's interested.'

'My mother over-reacts,' said Archie. 'She thinks the world will end if she finds a half-eaten tin of baked beans under the sofa. And she's so embarrassing! Christ, we were at a party earlier these holidays and she suddenly asked me in a loud voice if I needed a Kirby grip.'

He raked his blond locks back from his bronzed forehead.

'It looks great,' said Caitlin, 'particularly now the sun's bleached it.'

A lot of passengers got out at Didcot, so they practically had the carriage to themselves. As the cooling towers of Didcot power station belched out unearthly white steam against a darkening charcoal grey sky, the gay barman came by with a black plastic bag, gathering up rubbish.

'I want to keep my tonic tin,' said Caitlin, grabbing it back.

As she put it in her bag, Archie examined the heart-shaped face, the pointed chin, echoed by the widow's peak, the small, beautifully shaped green eyes, the snub nose, the coral-pink mouth, sweet now it was no longer set in a sulky petulant line, the blue-black mane parted on the left, which she kept lifting with her fingers and tossing over to the right.

Glancing up, she caught him staring at her and smiled.

'That's it,' said Archie wonderingly. 'Your brace has gone.'

'So have your zits,' said Caitlin.

Archie went pink: 'I fancied you the moment I saw you.'

'What about Tracey?'

'She was just a net,' said Archie.

They were nearing Cotchester now, dense woods clinging to steep hills on each side of the line giving way to lighted houses.

Archie removed his ear-rings, putting them in his pocket, because he said his father would only make a fuss. Then blushing again, he forced a tenner into the pocket of Caitlin's clinging Lycra skirt.

'What's this for?' asked Caitlin in amazement. 'I owe *you* money.'

'For a taxi,' said Archie. 'Percy, my father's chauffeur, is meeting me, and if we give you a lift he's bound to sneak to Dad.'

'It's just like the Montagues and the Capulets,' sighed Caitlin. 'I hope we don't end up like Romeo and Juliet.'

'I'll ring you tomorrow,' said Archie, 'and hopefully we can fix an evening when all our parents are away.'

Opening his bank statement next morning, Archie nearly fainted. To make matters worse, it was his mother's birthday on Friday and he'd promised to buy her the latest recording of *The Flying Dutchman*. Normally he'd have tapped his father, who was a far easier touch than Monica, but Tony was still in Edinburgh for the International Television Festival. Besides, if Tony discovered he was financing a date with Caitlin, Archie would be crated straight back to Tuscany.

He'd been stupid to show off and buy them both first-class tickets and all that booze. If only he'd been back at school, he could have raised the cash smuggling in some booze and fags, or even porn mags, and selling them to other boys on the black market.

Nor was Caitlin the kind of girl who could be fobbed off with hamburgers and a video; she needed something special.

Grimly aware that he hadn't touched any of the ridiculous amount of holiday work he'd been set, Archie gazed gloomily at the same page of Aristophanes for twenty minutes, then threw the book across the room. If he hurried he might reach the Bar Sinister before lunch and catch his Uncle Basil before he rushed off to polo or some amorous jaunt.

He found Bas humming the Vilja song from *The Merry Widow* and taking fifty pounds out of his own till.

'Can I have a quiet word?' said Archie.

'You can have several noisy ones if you like,' said Bas. 'I thought your father had forbidden you to talk to me. Where is Rambo, anyway?'

'In Edinburgh,' said Archie. 'And please don't pump me.'

He admired his uncle, who always had the loudest tweed jackets and the prettiest girls of anyone he knew.

'Have a drink?' said Bas, taking down a bottle of Chambery and two glasses.

'Yes, please. If I work really hard in the kitchens for three days, will you let me sign the bill for dinner for two on Saturday night?'

'Are you bringing Tracey Makepiece?'

'No.'

'Good. There *are* limits. I really was on Tony's side for once on that score. Yes, you can, then.'

On Saturday night Taggie's violet dress paid its second visit to the Bar Sinister in ten days – this time with Caitlin inside it. But, with the waist jacked into nothing by a black corset belt, and the skirt turned up from mid-calf to mid-thigh by Taggie, it was almost unrecognizable. Archie, having scrubbed mussels for three days in the kitchen, and suffered agonies of doubt, like Mr Toad, that his hands would ever be unwrinkled again, felt he had really earned his date. Basil was out that evening, but all the waiters were in on the secret and gave Archie and Caitlin a table in an alcove where no one else would see them. Determined to get his wages' worth,

Archie ordered a bottle of Dom Perignon and they started off with a wine race, seeing who could drink a half-pint of champagne fastest to get things warmed up. But after that they found that they were so excited by each other's company they weren't very hungry.

'This is the most delicious thing I've ever eaten,' said Caitlin as she toyed with foie gras on radicchio. 'I can't think why I can't eat more of it.'

Archie slowly undressed a giant prawn and dipped it in dill sauce. 'Try this.'

'Gosh, it's yummy. I wish school food was like this. Nellie Newstead found a used Band-Aid in her shepherd's pie last term. Aren't you dreading going back?'

'Not if you promise to write to me.'

Caitlin looked up. God, she's sweet when she smiles, thought Archie.

'Every day, if you like,' said Caitlin.

'I've looked up the distance between Rugborough and Upland House,' said Archie. 'It's only about forty miles. A mate of mine's passed his test, so we'll drive over and take you out one Sunday; and it'll be half-term soon.'

Archie was wearing a dinner jacket over black baggy trousers and a grey and white shirt over a Sisters of Mercy T-shirt. He looks incredibly cool, thought Caitlin lovingly.

As if in a dream, she watched his sunburnt hand closing over her white one; his palm felt so warm and dry that suddenly she longed for him to touch her all over.

Archie ordered another bottle of champagne.

'You really shouldn't,' protested Caitlin. 'It's frightfully expensive in restaurants, and I already owe you for my ticket and my taxi.'

'You can pay me in kind,' said Archie, gently stroking the inside of her wrist. 'A pound a kiss. No, I won't be able to afford it, a penny a kiss.'

'*Da mi basia mille,*' sighed Caitlin.

'What's that?'

'Catullus. Give me a thousand kisses.'

'Are you frightfully clever?'

'Of course, that's why I chose you.'

They screamed with laughter; suddenly the stupidest things seemed funny. Archie thought he should try and be poetic too.

'Your eyes are the same colour as beech leaves in spring,' he said, gazing into them. 'You're like a little wood nymph.'

'A dry-ad,' said Caitlin, taking a swig of her champagne. 'Nothing very dry about me.'

'What are we going to do after this?' said Archie, getting out a packet of Sobranie. 'Did you say your parents are both away?'

'Daddy's in Edinburgh, probably killing your father, but Mummy might be back from her rehearsal, although she seems to be getting later and later.'

'There's no one at home,' said Archie. 'I'll get them to get us a taxi.'

It was only when she got up to walk out of the restaurant that Caitlin realized how drunk she was. It's like InterCity all over again, she told Archie. Only by grabbing her arm did he prevent her cannoning off every table.

He kissed her all the way back to The Falconry. Caitlin, who'd spent three days practising kissing the palm of her hand, found Archie's mouth a great deal more exciting.

And when they were ensconced on Monica's huge flowered chintz sofa, having both carefully removed each other's ear-rings, Archie discovered that Caitlin's small, incredibly springy white breasts were far more thrilling than Tracey Makepiece's. It was just a question of preferring nectarines to melons. And her waist was so tiny, once he'd removed the black corset belt, that he was terrified he might snap her in two. But nothing could exceed her enthusiasm.

'I do hope I'm not too pissed to remember every minute of this tomorrow,' she said.

'Have you ever been to bed with anyone before?' Archie mumbled into the gel-stiffened straw of her hair.

'Never. Have you?'

'Yes.'

'Lots?'

'About two and three-quarters.'

'A man of experience,' sighed Caitlin in ecstasy.

Undoing a few more buttons, Archie, who was down to his Sisters of Mercy T-shirt now, kissed his way down her shoulder until he was sucking her right nipple. He was also wrestling with his conscience as to whether he ought to take her to bed. He wanted to like mad, but he was pissed enough to botch it, and she was certainly so pissed she might easily regret it in the morning. He had a condom in the breast pocket of his dinner jacket, which was hanging over the chair. But if he got up to get it, it might destroy the mood. But again it was unlikely they'd have an empty house to themselves for months.

As her little hands slid inside his T-shirt, he found his hand, as if magnetized, creeping up her legs.

'I'm climbing your ladders to paradise,' he whispered.

The next minute he jumped out of his skin as a great white light shone in at the window.

'Holy shit,' said Archie.

'Ooh,' squeaked Caitlin in excitement, 'it's a close encounter.'

'Bloody sight too close!' said Archie. 'It's my father flying in from Edinburgh.'

It was too late to make a bolt for it. With lightning presence of mind, Archie turned on a side light, plugged a tape in the video, pressed twelve on the remote control and did up Caitlin's buttons.

'I'll ring for a taxi as soon as I can and take you home. We'll just have to try and bluff it out.'

The next minute James Vereker's new pilot on 'Keeping Fit for the Elderly' burst on to the screen.

Tony, fortunately, had been hosting a very successful dinner for the IBA and, after several belts of brandy on the way home, was in a mellow mood. It soon became even mellower when he found his favourite son in the drawing-room with an enchantingly pretty little brunette. She looked vaguely familiar, but Tony was too vain to put on his spectacles, and by no stretch of the imagination could she be called Tracey Makepiece.

526

'This is Caitie,' said Archie heartily. 'I was just going to ring for a taxi to take her home.'

'Where does she live?' said Tony.

'Chalford,' lied Archie.

'I'll take her,' said Tony expansively. 'No distance at all. Let's all have a drink.'

'Caitie's tired,' said Archie desperately.

'She doesn't look it,' said Tony, admiring Caitlin's flushed cheeks and glittering green eyes. 'There's a bottle of Moët in the fridge.'

Shoving Caitlin's corset belt under a pink-and-white-striped cushion, Archie reluctantly left the room.

'Why are you watching this tape?' asked Tony as a lot of geriatrics with purple faces started doing press-ups.

'I love Corinium's programmes,' said Caitlin dreamily. 'I adore "Master Dog". We've got two dogs, one's very thick, one's brilliant. I'm sure she'd win.'

'You'd better give me a ring in the office next week,' said Tony. 'We're always looking for bright dogs.'

'I'm going back to school.'

'Where d'you go?'

'Upland House.'

Better and better, thought Tony in delight; the girl was a lady.

'D'you know my niece, Tonia Martin?'

'Frightful slag,' said Caitlin. 'She nearly got sacked last term for having boys in her room. She's got a terrible reputation at Stowe, too.'

Tony was enchanted. His sister's daughter was always being held up as a paragon of virtue.

'And d'you by any chance know Caro McKay? Teaches Biology, I think.'

'Of course. She teaches me.' Caitlin beamed. 'Ghastly old dyke. She and Miss Reading live in a two-bedroom house with a spare room.' She screamed with laughter. Tony joined in.

Once Caitlin got an audience, there was no stopping her. Archie was torn between hysterical laughter and total panic

527

as she regaled Tony with one scurrilous story after another about the daughters of his friends and colleagues.

After the bottle was finished, Tony insisted on driving her home. The only way Tracey would have got out of the house, reflected Archie, would have been in a hearse. Bitterly ashamed of himself, he funked going with them; he couldn't face the return journey.

It was a lovely night. A butter-coloured moon was gliding in and out of threatening blue-black clouds, gilding their edges. Mist was rising. There was a smell of dying bonfires and wet leaves.

'What a heavenly car,' said Caitlin, playing with the electric windows.

'How long have you known Archie?' asked Tony.

'About nine months. I don't mean to suck up, but I do think you've brought him up well. He's so considerate.'

Tony purred. 'He is a nice boy. Wish he'd work a bit harder. Have you taken your O-levels yet?'

'Last term.'

'Get a few?'

'Eleven,' said Caitlin simply. 'You seem more pleased than my mother,' she added bitterly a minute later.

Archie's father, she decided, was really, really nice. Extra-ordinary how her father and Tag got everything wrong. He was soon saying she might like to come to the Hunt Ball if she could get off school, and even suggested skiing in the Christmas holidays.

'Oh, I'd love to,' said Caitlin.

As they neared Penscombe, she noticed the car telephone. 'Oh, how lovely, you are lucky. Can I use it?'

'Of course,' said Tony.

The length of Caitlin's slender white thighs on the black leather seat reminded him almost unbearably of Cameron. He'd been hoping he'd bump into her at Edinburgh, but she hadn't shown up. Without thinking, Caitlin rang The Priory. It was two o'clock in the morning and no one answered for ages.

'Hullo,' murmured a sleepy voice.

'Taggie, darling,' said Caitlin, 'did I wake you?'

Tony nearly ran into a wild rose bush. Suddenly the temperature in the car dropped below zero.

'What did you say your surname was?' said Tony as Caitlin put back the receiver.

'O'Hara,' said Caitlin in a small voice.

'Declan's daughter?'

'Yes.'

'What the fuck are you playing at? Did your father put you up to this?'

'Oh, please don't tell him,' gasped Caitlin. 'He'd be furious.'

'Not any more furious than I bloody am,' roared Tony. 'The little snake! I'll murder Archie when I get home.'

'Oh, please don't!' Caitlin, who'd had a great deal too much to drink, burst into tears.

'For Christ's sake,' exploded Tony.

'I like you so much,' sobbed Caitlin, 'and I thought you liked me.'

'I do,' said Tony in exasperation, handing her his blue spotted handkerchief, reeking of the inevitable Paco Rabanne. 'I just can't stand your father.'

'*The fathers have eaten sour grapes,*' sniffed Caitlin dolefully, '*and the children's teeth are set on edge.*'

'And you're not going to tell Declan that you're going out with Archie?'

'Christ, no,' said Caitlin. 'I don't want to get butchered in my prime.'

Tony did a lot of thinking as he drove home. When he turned on the light in Archie's room, he found him huddled under the duvet, with his pyjamas buttoned up to the neck, desperately pretending to be asleep. Not for the first time, however, Tony astounded his son.

'You can go on seeing that girl as long as you try and find out as much as you can about Venturer.'

'That's immoral,' said Archie, shocked.

'Don't be bloody wet,' said Tony brutally. 'D'you want Corinium to lose the franchise?'

'No.'

'Or for me to forfeit four hundred thousand minimum a year?'

'No,' said Archie.

If he was rich, he reflected, he wouldn't have to scrub mussels for three days every time he wanted to take Caitlin out to dinner. One day she would live in The Falconry with him. His father was right, he decided, blood was thicker than water. If Declan didn't get the franchise, he, Archie, would look after Caitlin.

40

Taggie had a very wearing September. Getting a besotted and reelingly untogether Caitlin packed up and back to Upland House was bad enough, but dispatching Declan to Ireland was even worse.

As the departure date drew nearer, he grew increasingly reluctant to leave Maud or his precious franchise, which was just coming up to the boil.

Maud was plainly revelling in *The Merry Widow*. Declan was glad, but was her euphoria slightly over the top? And was it really necessary for her to have a bath, wash her hair and pinch yet more of Taggie's clothes before every rehearsal? And when she carolled the words '*All the world's in love with love, and I love you,*' over and over again from the Southern Turret, who were they really aimed at? As the yellow woods turned gold and the swallows seemed to postpone their departure, and even the huge red suns sunk more slowly into Rupert's woods in order to hear Maud's exquisite notes floating down the valley, Declan prayed she wasn't leading her leading man on too much.

Maud herself was much happier after Caitlin had gone back to school. No one was quicker on the draw than a teenager in love, which ruled out any illicit incoming telephone calls for Maud. But now it seemed Cameron Cook was always in the house, monopolizing the telephone and Declan, and not being deferential enough to Maud, the arrogant bitch. Anyone would think they were going off on a six months' polar expedition rather than three silly weeks on location.

Maud also bitterly resented Cameron treating Taggie like a slave. Only this morning, on the eve of departure, Perry O'Donovan, who'd been cast as Yeats, wanted Cameron to call him back, and Taggie had taken the number down wrong.

'Don't keep apologizing,' screamed Cameron, running out of breath after five minutes of invective. 'Just get it right in future.'

The only person allowed to exploit and scream at Taggie, reflected Maud, should be Maud herself.

The eve of departure, in fact, was full of spats, and now at dusk Declan was in the library firing off last-minute instructions to Freddie, who was just back from Portugal again, and Rupert, who was just off to Virginia for a few days. Between them they would probably run things far more smoothly than Declan. The appalling Professor Graystock had also dropped in, returned from his working holiday in Greece to get ready for the new university year, and was, as usual, swilling Declan's whisky. Dame Enid had just come down from upstairs, after going through Maud's *Merry Widow* score with her and making some extremely helpful suggestions.

'She'll be totally irresistible,' Dame Enid told Declan as she accepted a large pink gin. 'Wish I were playing her leading man.'

Cameron sat in the corner going through her lists for tomorrow with half an ear on the meeting. She'd checked that everyone – actors, wardrobe, make-up, and crew – knew where to meet her and Declan at Birmingham Airport; she'd double-checked that the air-conditioned coach would be waiting to take them to Sligo by early evening, and that the hotel overlooking the bay would be expecting them for dinner.

Glancing across the room at Rupert, who was gazing moodily out of the window at Claudius chewing a library book, she knew that he was bored. There was nothing he loathed more than other people's waffle. He'd been affectionate enough recently, but slightly detached; perhaps he always distanced himself before a separation. She hated the thought of him going to Virginia on his own. She couldn't imagine American women leaving anything as beautiful or as explosively macho alone. She'd lived with him for sixty-eight days and – she glanced at her watch – eighteen hours, and she still wanted him continually.

'Now, you all know that I'm on the end of the telephone,' Declan was saying. 'By the time I get back we should have the date for our IBA interview. Then we can start having dry-runs. I've booked Hardy Bisset to coach us. He's ex-IBA so he's witnessed the interviewing process from the other side. 'There's also a permanent exhibition on the history of television at the IBA,' he went on. 'Parties of school-children and tourists visit it every day. I think you should all try and have a look at it before the interview so you at least know something about the business you're intending to run. Go in, in ones or twos, or it'll look too obvious. We must get Wesley, Marti, Bas and particularly Henry along there, or they'll make complete pratts of themselves at the interview. I think that's all.'

He ran his hands through his hair and leaned back in his chair surveying the chaos on his desk in despair.

Rupert turned away from the window. 'When d'you reckon Yeats'll be finally in the can?' he said.

'For Chrissake, dumbass,' screamed Cameron, 'I've told you a hundred times, it's pronounced "Yates".'

Declan raised a disapproving eyebrow. Dame Enid was much more up front. 'You haven't learned to pronounce the word "hostile" yet, young lady,' she snapped, 'but you certainly manage to be it most of the time.'

'Thank you, Enid. The age of chivalry is not entirely dead,' said Rupert lightly, but his face had lost all expression.

Oh, God, thought Cameron, I shouldn't have said that.

'The answer to your question,' said Declan to Rupert, 'is sometime in December. We'll have to edit and do all the VOs when we get back.'

'I hope you've got in the story about Yeats cutting his precious fur coat in half because he didn't want to disturb a cat who was sitting on it,' said Dame Enid. 'Must have been a good bloke to do that.'

'Or the time that he signed a lot of cheques "Yours sincerely, W. B. Yeats",' said Professor Graystock, determined not to be upstaged. 'Or even the story . . .' he began.

Rupert had had enough – fucking intellectuals. He walked out of the library, out of the front door, and down the garden. Migrating arrows of birds were flapping down the valley. There had been a storm at lunchtime; roses were pulping and disintegrating; tobacco plants prostrated themselves like palms before his feet. Beyond the garden, in one of his fields, the grass had been flattened by the deluge, as though a herd of elephants had been having a gang bang.

Half a dozen young steers grazing there had recently been joined by a Guernsey cow and a little chocolate-brown calf, which a grateful neighbouring farmer had sent Rupert as an early birthday present. Now he could see the steers pushing the baby calf away and drinking her mother's milk. With her long-legged gawkiness, her big eyes and long fringed eyelashes, the calf reminded him of Taggie. He looked at the mother's pink udder with its four teats. Perhaps Cameron would pronounce them 'tates'. Fucking intellectual. He'd get the mother and calf moved to a field of their own tomorrow.

Instead of returning to the library, he went round to the kitchen and found Taggie listening to pop music and trying to iron a great pile of Declan's shirts and read a recipe at the same time.

'*Dashing away with a smoothing iron, she stole my heart away,*' said Rupert.

Taggie gave a start. 'I don't see how anyone could steal anybody's heart away when they're ironing,' she mumbled. 'One gets so red in the face.'

'And you're about to singe that shirt,' said Rupert.

Hastily Taggie upended the iron. 'You're just the person I wanted to see. Sarah Stratton wants me to do a dinner party for her the week after next, and she's given me this recipe all in French, and I can't make head nor tail of it.'

Rupert, who'd had plenty of experience of Sarah's writing, took the piece of paper and reeled off the recipe.

'Oh marvellous! Could you read it out to me?' said Taggie, grabbing a pencil.

Rupert was about to take the pencil, saying it'd be much quicker if he scribbled it down himself. Then he remembered something he'd read recently about encouraging dyslexics. Very slowly, making sure he didn't get too far ahead, resisting the urge to touch Taggie's white neck, revealed in all its vulnerability as her black ponytail fell sideways, he read it out.

'You are brilliant,' sighed Taggie as she finished. 'No one else could translate it. Daddy doesn't read French, nor Mummy, nor even Cameron.'

Suddenly Rupert felt ten feet tall again. What a bugger he had to fly to Virginia tomorrow, but he desperately needed a new stallion and he hoped to get in a few days' hunting. He was about to make a firm date for dinner the moment he got back when the repulsive Professor Graystock wandered in.

'Ah, Taggie,' the Professor's formless mouth widened, showing crooked yellow teeth. 'I'm frightfully hungry; only had time for a bowl of soup at lunchtime. Could I have something to eat? Nothing fancy, simple repast, bread and cheese will be quite sufficient.'

Disgusting old goat, thought Rupert with a shudder, typical leftie with his second house, and no school fees to pay, bumming off anyone he regarded as capitalist. Taggie tried to smile. The Professor gave her the creeps, too. He still never missed an opportunity to squeeze her, or gaze at her breasts, or make *risqué* remarks.

'Cameron's looking for you, Rupert,' said the Professor pointedly. 'She wants to go home.'

Rupert took no notice and went on stroking Aengus, who was stretched out by the Aga.

Mouth watering, the Professor watched Taggie put out a

loaf of wholemeal bread, some Brie and Cheddar, and half a pound of butter.

'Any celery?' he asked. 'I'm partial to celery. With Father in Ireland and Mother rehearsing all the time, you're going to be rather lonely, Taggie. Perhaps you'll come over one evening to the campus and cook supper for a lonely old man?'

'She's working every night,' snapped Rupert. 'Someone's got to keep this doss house in whisky.'

'No need to over-react, dear boy,' said the Professor, cutting a doorstep of bread and spreading it thickly with butter. 'I've got an intellectual poser for you both. What would you have done –' he leered at Taggie – 'if you'd discovered, as I did last term, your most brilliant first-year student – guaranteed to get a first – in bed in college with a naked girl? Would you have sent him down?'

'If she'd been pretty,' said Rupert coldly, 'I'd have confiscated her.'

Cameron felt twitchy as she packed. She was still kicking herself for showing Rupert up in front of the others, but she got so uptight before she went on location. It was a million times worse than before a period. At the bottom of her bags she'd packed a book on coping with stepmotherhood. When she came back from Ireland, she was determined to get it together with Marcus and Tab. Wandering into Rupert's dressing-room, she found him also packing. He was catching Concorde in the morning.

'I love you,' she said, putting her arms round him. 'You will fly out to Ireland when you get back from the States, won't you?'

'Of course,' said Rupert, as he hastily flipped a book called *Overcoming Dyslexia* under a pile of shirts.

For a man so confident in business matters, Freddie Jones was surprisingly timid in matters of the heart. For months he had longed to ring up Lizzie Vereker, but only screwed up the courage the day Declan and Cameron left for Ireland.

'How about lunch today?' he said, wading straight in.

'Where's Valerie?' asked Lizzie.

'In Portugal.'

Because she had the curse, two large spots, dirty hair, hairy legs, unpainted toe nails, needed a hundred years to go on a crash diet and had been caught on the hop, Lizzie said no, she was frantically busy. Then felt absolutely miserable. 'What about next week?' she asked hopefully.

'Valerie'll be home,' said Freddie despondently.

'Well, ring me anyway,' said Lizzie.

All week Lizzie was very absent-minded. She spilt red wine over a review copy which she hadn't reviewed, and which James intended to give to his mother for a birthday present. On Thursday morning she kept filling up cups of coffee with cold water and even swallowed a conditioning pill herself which she'd intended to give to the dog. Perhaps she'd go barking mad. She knew she ought to be working on her new book, but all she could think about was Freddie. Distracted and miserable, she walked in the pouring rain down to the lake. A moorhen was summoning her chicks into the rushes with a strange fluted call. The beeches trailed their red leaves in the raindrop-pitted water. Suddenly Lizzie heard shouting from the french windows. It was Jilly, her treasure of a nanny, who seemed even more of a treasure when she said Mr Jones was on the telephone.

''Ullo,' said Freddie. 'Fort you might like to go for a picnic?'

'But it's pouring,' said Lizzie joyfully.

'We could 'ave it indoors at Green Lawns.'

'Where's Valerie?'

'At the Nearly New Sale for the Distressed Gentlefolk.'

Anticipating adultery was rather like going to the doctor, mused Lizzie as she painted her nails, washed her hair, bathed and shaved and cleaned her ears. Then she rubbed body lotion into every centimetre of her body – one really had to get oneself up.

The only problem was that she had forgotten that the Corinium Television gardener (one of James's perks) came that morning. He must have been amazed to see so many gallons of soapy water gushing into the bathroom drain, and to see Lizzie emerging so startlingly painted and scented at midday, to announce that she was off to the Nearly New Sale and then going on to do some shopping, so would he weed the main herbaceous border, which she had already thanked him profusely for weeding last week. She'd even rung James to tell him she was going to the sale and to ask if he needed anything in Cotchester.

Lizzie had had no intention of going to bed with Freddie that day. She wouldn't have if she hadn't bought a lovely blue tweed skirt for a pound at the clothes stall and passed Valerie noisily manning the produce stall on the way out.

'Look,' cried Lizzie, waving the skirt, 'look at my lovely bargain.'

'You'll never get into that!' said Valerie crushingly. 'That used to be Sarah Stratton's.'

Valerie was looking very Sloane, Lizzie decided, in a pale-blue cashmere jersey, dark-blue stockings and Gucci shoes, with her hair drawn off her forehead in a velvet bow.

'Do you know what that absolute swine Tony Baddingham is threatening to do?' Valerie went on, lowering her voice. 'Build twenty homes on a field next to our grounds. It'll ruin our view. I mean, we *are* designated an area of outstanding natural beauty.'

'He won't get planning permission,' said Lizzie.

'Probably will, with all those bribes he offers. Tell James to absolutely refuse to interview any of the Planning Committee on "Cotswold Round-Up". So embarrassing when Monica and I are such close friends.'

Valerie's beady eyes fell on Lizzie's purse. 'Now what are you going to buy? I'm sure James likes beetroot slices in vinegar. I'll give you a penny off.'

'I'll buy that coffee cake; it looks delicious. How long are you stuck here for?' asked Lizzie.

'Until four o'clock,' said Valerie crossly. 'Someone has to hold the fort.'

'It's the fort what counts,' murmured Lizzie.

•

'I fort you was never coming,' said Freddie as he opened the door. In the kitchen was a bottle of Dom Perignon on ice and a huge plate of smoked salmon. Freddie had picked Rupert's brains about seducing techniques.

'The ideal picnic,' sighed Lizzie. 'I brought us some coffee cake for pudding.'

They stayed in the kitchen, in case they messed up the cushions poised on their points on Valerie's settees. Briefly they discussed the franchise.

'D'you think you'll get it?'

'I know we will,' said Freddie. 'Now let's talk about us. I want to see a great deal of you, Mrs Vereker, but it won't be easy wiv Tony Baddingham, an' Valerie, an' James breaving down our necks.'

'James won't be,' said Lizzie.

'Where is he at the moment?'

'Inside Sarah Stratton, I should think.'

They both roared with laughter and, for the first time, Lizzie found she didn't mind. She liked everything about Freddie, she decided – the way his eyes turned down at the corners, and his beer gut, and the damp patches under his arms because he was so nervous, and the way he smoked with his cigar between finger and thumb to eke it out, and coiled into the palm of his hand as though he was still hiding it from the foreman, who was probably now called Valerie.

As a writer, she told herself firmly as Freddie led her upstairs, one has to experience life. All the same she didn't think she would have gone to bed with Freddie on that first day, and certainly not in Valerie's bedroom, if she hadn't found four of her favourite books in the spare room bookshelf, which she'd lent to Valerie when she'd had flu and which Valerie'd sworn she'd given back to Lizzie.

When they got upstairs Freddie initially seemed far more interested in showing off his gadgets – the eight-horsepower jacuzzi and the bath which turned on by remote control and regulated the water from the bed, which was huge and oval, with its great dashboard of buttons at the head.

'Shall we sleep in it,' whispered Lizzie, 'or hi-jack it and fly it to paradise?'

'You do say the loveliest fings,' said Freddie, drawing her close. His paunch slotted in below her splendid breasts, so it was very easy for them to kiss.

'What music would you like?' asked Freddie.

'Brahms's Second Piano Concerto,' said Lizzie.

Next moment, incredibly, it flooded through the room. 'I must have a pee first,' said Lizzie, wading through the shagpile to the bathroom.

'I'll get undressed,' said Freddie.

Lizzie washed herself with Valerie's flannel, but not too much, in case she rubbed away all the lubrication. She wanted Freddie to know how excited she was. For a second she examined the lips of her labia, just peering out of her bush, like a wrinkled old tortoise, then shoved them inside. How could men possibly find women beautiful down there? Would her opening be prettier than Valerie's? she wondered.

Coming out, she opened the wrong door and nearly went into the linen cupboard. Goodness it was tidy, as though it had been laid out with a set square. Adultery certainly taught you about other people's houses. She expected Freddie to be completely undressed by the time she got back, but he had so much jewellery to remove that she beat him to it.

'I've dreamed and dreamed of this moment,' said Freddie as he stretched out beside her. 'Ever since we first met at that 'unt ball, eighteen monfs ago. I fort, what a lovely lady.'

'I'm so fat,' sighed Lizzie.

'You're not,' said Freddie. 'It's much more fun climbing Everest than the foothills.'

Lizzie put her hand on his cock. 'And it's so nice to see software becoming hardware.'

'And I'm going to declare this an area of outstanding natural beauty,' said Freddie. Reaching for his glass of champagne on the bedside table, he emptied it into her bush and proceeded to lick it all off. After Mousie's fragility, he reflected as he climbed on top of her, it was like having a wonderfully sturdy cob between your thighs.

540

'I hope you're using a Condom Perignon,' mumbled Lizzie half-laughing and half-crying with pleasure as he entered her.

Brahms's Second Piano Concerto was her favourite piece of music, but from then on she forgot its existence until the last ecstatic bars of the final Allegretto.

'You're absolutely perfick,' whispered Freddie. 'You're the big fing in my life now.'

'I love you,' said Lizzie.

'And I love you,' said Freddie.

Afterwards they had another bottle and ate all the coffee cake, and longed to make love again, but decided it was too risky. To establish an alibi, Lizzie then went shopping in Cotchester, so drunk and happy she could hardly get the clothes back on the hangers. Coming out of the chemist, having bought a huge guilt present of Aramis for James, which she thought she might give to Freddie, she heard a car tooting.

Not being vain, she didn't even turn round when it went on tooting, and only did so when Tony Baddingham lowered his electric window and yelled out to her.

Keeping her mouth tight shut so he wouldn't catch the champagne fumes, wondering if he could see the words 'adulterer and traitor' branded on her forehead, she edged towards him.

'You're looking great,' said Tony smoothly. 'Really great. Must have been a good holiday. What have you been buying?'

'Scent for James,' said Lizzie.

'How very nice,' said Tony. 'And it isn't even his birthday! You're a good wife, Lizzie. Look forward to seeing you on Saturday week.'

'Saturday?' said Lizzie, bewildered.

'Sarah Stratton's dinner party,' said Tony. 'We'll have a good talk then.'

Back at Lake House, Lizzie rushed upstairs, washed off all her make-up and scent, removed the nail polish from her toes and got into her old clothes in case James came home early.

Fortunately he was very late, so she was able to watch almost the entire production of *Midsummer Night's Dream* by herself. It was magical, despite Titania's bulge, and must have won Corinium a lot of Brownie points in the franchise battle. Throughout the performance, Lizzie kept thinking of Freddie, and how cuddly and sweet and kind he'd been, and how she wanted him to make love to her over and over again.

'Funny goings on at Venturer,' said James in a pleased voice, pouring himself an uncharacteristic drink the moment he got in. 'Evidently Cameron's pushed off to Ireland with Declan, and I've just seen Bas coming out of the Bar Sinister with Maud.'

Funny goings on everywhere, thought Lizzie dreamily, what with James and Sarah, and her and Freddie, and Rupert probably still hankering after Taggie. It was as though they'd all been affected by Puck's mischievous witchery like the mortals and Titania in *Midsummer Night's Dream*. James fell asleep the moment his head touched the pillow.

'I am the mistress of a very nice man,' wrote Lizzie ecstatically in her diary before she turned out the light.

41

The first Saturday in October Taggie overslept. Working late, she hadn't got to bed until four. She was just making a cup of coffee when Wandering Aengus, mewing horribly, padded in with a live fieldmouse in his mouth.

'Beast,' yelled Taggie, hurling a dishcloth at him. She missed, but Aengus was so startled he dropped the fieldmouse, which took refuge under the dresser.

Having shut the enraged and growling cat in the larder, Taggie managed to rescue the mouse with a dustpan and brush and put it in a cardboard box. Dressed in only the briefest nightie and gumboots, she carried the box across the lawn to set it free at the edge of the fields. Very gently she tipped it out, but the poor little thing didn't move; perhaps it had died of shock. Next moment she nearly died too. Coming towards her out of the blue mist across the dew-drenched field on a big, sweating dark-brown horse, rode Rupert. As he raised his hat, Taggie put her finger to her lips and showed him the mouse which was still motionless.

'Aengus caught it,' she whispered. 'D'you think it'll survive?'

Rupert privately thought a quick shove with his boot would put the mouse out of its misery, but, knowing this would upset Taggie, said it might just be frozen with fear, and why didn't they leave it for a bit. Gazing at Taggie's nightgown and gumboots, he asked her if she was going out. Taggie went crimson and said she'd been doing a late dinner party. There was a long pause. Casting desperately round for something to say, Taggie mumbled that it was a nice day.

'Very. I've been cubbing,' said Rupert.

'Oh, poor little things,' said Taggie in horror. 'Did you kill any?'

'No,' lied Rupert. 'I brought you these,' he went on, producing some huge mushrooms out of his riding-coat pocket.

'Oh, aren't they beautiful?' Distracted, Taggie examined their pleated pink undersides, 'How really kind. Thank you so much.'

Anyone would have thought he'd given her another Fabergé egg, thought Rupert. Stammering furiously, she asked him if he'd like some breakfast.

'I hoped you'd say that. I'll drop off my horse and come back.'

Taggie raced upstairs and was appalled to see that her nightie had a huge tear, her eyes were full of sleep, and her mascara was all smudged. Frantically she washed, put on an old pair of black sawn-off cords and a dark-brown T-shirt which seemed to be the only things Maud hadn't pinched, and started cooking breakfast. She steeled herself to the possibility that Rupert would get caught up in some drama at the yard, or at home, and forget to return; or that Maud, smelling frying bacon, would come down and join them. But he was back in a quarter of an hour with a bottle of champagne for Buck's Fizz, and Maud stayed upstairs, perfecting a song called 'Jogging in a one-horse gig'.

'She really is working at it,' said Rupert, edging the bottle open with his thumbs.

'It's wonderful. She's so much happier,' said Taggie, thinking how black and luscious the white mushrooms had gone, and tipping most of them onto Rupert's plate.

'I hope Tony Baddingham and your father don't bump into each other on the first night,' said Rupert as the cork flew through the window into the long grass outside, 'or either your mother or Monica really will be a merry widow!'

He picked up the *Guardian* which had a grim front-page story about the rocketing AIDS figures. Thank God he'd had that test.

It was such a lovely day, they had breakfast outside on the peeling white bench. Despite the warmth, the cedars, wellingtonias and yews flanking the house were already full of orange leaves from the nearby horse chestnuts, and the ground was littered with conkers. Lavender, roses, and evening primroses still bloomed on, bravely waiting for the first frost.

'I've never felt such hot sun in October,' said Rupert, taking off his jersey. 'With a few more leaves off the trees, I'll be able to see your house again.'

'How was America?' asked Taggie, dividing her bacon rind between a slavering Gertrude and Claudius.

'Good,' said Rupert, deciding not to mention four magnificent days hunting in Virginia. 'I've found a marvellous stallion, and a brood mare for Freddie. Which reminds me, I saw Freddie's red Jaguar parked outside Mrs Vereker's house while "Cotswold Round-Up" was on the air last night. If he's going to err and stray, he ought to find a more discreet car.'

Taggie giggled. 'Lizzie's so nice, isn't she?' she said, breaking a sausage in half for the dogs.

'She certainly deserves some fun. James treats her like an old wheelchair he can fall back into in old age. This breakfast is quite marvellous. Why are you giving all yours to the dogs?'

'I don't usually eat breakfast,' mumbled Taggie, taking a slug of Buck's Fizz.

Rupert ran his eyes over her. 'You're losing weight. I'll have to start adding molasses and carrots to your oats.'

'*Jogging in a one-horse gig, any time of night or day,*' sang Maud from upstairs, '*Careless of the weather, very close together, lovers fall in love that way.*'

Rupert raised his eyebrows and filled up Taggie's glass.

Please God, she prayed, make this moment go on for ever and ever. The next moment Gertrude had joined them on the bench seat on Taggie's side, not giving herself enough room, so Taggie had to move closer to Rupert.

'Well done, Gertrude,' said Rupert, grinning. 'You really are on my side.'

Taggie's heart seemed to be beating completely out of time to Maud's singing. Frantically, she stroked Gertrude.

'Heard from your father?' asked Rupert.

'No,' stammered Taggie. 'Have you heard from Cameron?'

'Not recently.'

There was another long pause. A conker plummeted on to the shaggy lawn. Laughing and watching her, Rupert waited.

'You mustn't worry about Daddy and Cameron being on their own together for so long,' Taggie finally blurted out. 'I know Daddy's wildly attractive, but he is utterly obsessed with Mummy.'

Rupert was about to deny that he was remotely worried about Cameron. Instead he removed a long dark hair from her shoulder and put it in his shirt pocket.

'I dreamed about you last night.'

'You did?' said Taggie in amazement. 'Was it nice?'

'Lovely, and extremely disturbing.' He trailed the back of his fingers down her arm. Taggie quivered and stopped stroking Gertrude.

'It's the last night of the Horse of the Year Show tonight,' went on Rupert. 'Tabitha's in the final of the mounted games. It's a good evening. Why don't you come with me? We could have dinner afterwards.'

Taggie nearly wept. 'Sarah Stratton's giving a dinner party. I've got to work.'

'Pity,' said Rupert lightly.

Gertrude stuck her nose under Taggie's trembling hand, jerking it upwards, urging Taggie to stroke her again. Gertrude and me, thought Rupert.

'The Baddinghams and the Verekers are going, so they'll all talk about the franchise. I'll probably be made to stay in the kitchen,' babbled Taggie.

'Well keep your ears open and put a pint of arsenic in Tony's whisky. They certainly won't get Buck's Fizz like this tonight. Paul's so mean he makes it with Babycham.'

Damn, damn, damn, thought Taggie as she followed him to the door.

'I'm off to the Tory Party Conference next week,' said Rupert, getting into his car. 'I'll ring you when I get back. That was a lovely breakfast, thank you. By the way,' he added ultra-casually as he drove off, 'I hope you noticed I didn't burn my stubble this year.'

In a complete daze Taggie finished off the Buck's Fizz. Rupert had dreamt about her, *and* he'd asked her out, *and* he hadn't burnt his stubble. The whole thing was desperately confusing. She ran upstairs and looked out of her window. It was true. Instead of charred patches all over the valley, his cornfields were still yellowed by stubble, or reddy-brown after being ploughed up. She couldn't possibly be the reason, but it was so nice of him to say so.

There were so many things she ought to do, picking apples, planting the indoor bulbs, getting in the geraniums. There were large bowls of picked mulberries and blackberries reproachfully gathering fluff in the fridge, waiting to be turned into jam. And she must make some tomato chutney, not to mention painting the bench and mowing the lawn.

Suddenly she heard an enraged mewing from the larder. She'd forgotten Aengus. She couldn't even get cross that he'd eaten half the turbot mousse she'd made for the first course this evening. At least when she went out to search for the fieldmouse it had run away.

By the time she'd reached the Strattons' house she'd sobered up. Paul was still out playing golf. Sarah was in a panic because she wanted everything to be perfect for Tony, her boss, and even more so for James.

'Giving a dinner party is far worse than going on television,' she moaned. 'Look, I know it sounds horrendously Valerie Jones, but do you mind pretending I've done the cooking tonight? Especially the main course, which is a particular favourite of a friend of mine,' added Sarah, going pink. 'If anyone rings, pretend you're our daily, Mrs Maggs.'

Then, leaving Taggie with a mile-long list of instructions, she swanned off to Bath to buy a new dress.

At least everything was tidy, the table laid and the house clean. Taggie got out the French recipe that Rupert had translated for her. An hour and a half later, she was getting on well. The beef daube was sizzling in the oven, the pudding was in the fridge and just needed whipped cream and sugared violets, and she'd done the vegetables earlier. All she had to do was to make another fish mousse. Perhaps she'd just better double-check the beef.

'Oh, my God,' she said aghast as she licked the spoon. She tried again from the other side of the dish, and then the centre, where it was even worse. She must have been so distracted by her encounter with Rupert that she'd added a tablespoonful of salt instead of sugar. She tested the sugar in the glass bowl and went green. It was definitely salt.

The beef was quite inedible, absolutely impregnated with salt, and she'd used up all the other ingredients. It was after five and she'd never get to Cotchester in time. She gave a whimper of horror. She'd wrecked Sarah's party and she knew Sarah could be extremely difficult if things didn't go right.

The telephone rang. Oh God, she sobbed, I've got to remember to be the daily. Trembling, she picked up the receiver.

'Hullo,' crackled a voice from a car telephone.

'Mrs Stratton be shopping, thank you very much. Who be you?' mumbled Taggie.

Rupert laughed. 'That is the worst Gloucestershire accent I've ever heard. How's it going?'

Taggie burst into tears. 'It was James's favourite recipe and she's supposed to have made it for him,' she sobbed.

'Cheer up or you'll cry more salt into the beef,' said Rupert calmly. 'Get on with the fish mousse. I'll be over in half an hour.'

He arrived twenty-five minutes later. He screeched the Aston-Martin to a halt in a cloud of dust and nearly tipped Beaver and Blue, who were sitting on the back seat, through the windscreen, then he sauntered into the kitchen with a huge casserole dish containing boeuf Bourguignon for twelve from Luigi's, the local five-star restaurant in Cheltenham.

'Oh, you're lovely,' said Taggie, flinging her arms round his neck.

'Hands off! We've no time for dalliance!' said Rupert briskly, as he emptied the Bourguignon into one of Sarah's big bowls and chucked Taggie's salty remnants into Luigi's casserole dish. 'Don't tell Paul and Sarah what happened,' he added. 'Just pretend this is how the recipe turned out. They'll all be too pissed to notice, anyway. I'd better beat it, or she'll be back from shopping and start accusing me of bugging the room.'

Still stammering her thanks, Taggie followed him out to the car. An owl was hooting. A semi-circle of orange moon was rising out of the sycamores.

'The moon was a mandarin segment, as Valerie Jones would say,' said Rupert.

'I can't ever begin to thank you,' bleated Taggie.

Rupert pulled her towards him, dropping a kiss on her cheekbone.

'Oh yes, you can, angel. Just wait till I get back from Blackpool.'

The patron saint of cooking guided Taggie that evening. The food was positively ambrosial, and Sarah took all the credit, particularly for Luigi's boeuf Bourguignon, which was so tender you could cut it with a spoon.

'D'you remember that daube we had at the White Elephant at Painswick?' whispered Sarah to James as they went in to dinner. 'Well, I wrote to them for the recipe and I've made it for you tonight.'

Putting on his horn-rimmed spectacles to have a closer look across the table, Tony Baddingham decided he hadn't been wrong about Lizzie Vereker. Whether it was the Marbella sun or a stone off, or just some new inner contentment, she looked sensational.

The talk during dinner was mostly of the rocketing AIDS figures. They also drank to 'Master Dog' which was edging up on 'EastEnders' in the ratings; but they waited until Taggie was safely out of the room to discuss the franchise.

'There are some quite fascinating developments,' Tony said tantalizingly, 'but I'm not prepared to leak them until November, when it'll be nearer the IBA meetings and people are properly back from their holidays and reading newspapers again. And then, my God, Venturer will wish they'd never tried to take us on.' He paused as Taggie came in with the salad.

Not that she would have taken anything in that night. In the kitchen she was frantically trying to watch the Horse of the Year Show, hoping to catch a glimpse of Rupert. At least she saw Tabitha in the mounted games – utterly adorable and so like Rupert as she jumped up and down waiting for the baton, then grabbing it and scorching up the arena. The finals were just coming up when Sarah summoned Taggie to clear away the pudding.

By this time Tony was banging on about AIDS again.

'By the year 2000, unless we get our act together in this country, we'll have sixteen million cases. The message from America is loud and clear, affairs are *passé*.' He gazed down the table. 'Monogamy and fidelity in marriage are in fashion again. It's vital that everyone is made aware of the dangers of AIDS. It's up to us at Corinium to set the ball rolling.'

James felt that Sarah had been so very very caring to go to all that trouble with the daube that, in the hall after dinner, he was foolish enough to behave in a thoroughly unmonogamous fashion and be caught by Tony not only kissing her, but putting his hand inside her new silk dress.

On Monday morning Tony summoned James to his office. 'I've been thinking a lot about our conversation about AIDS on Saturday night,' he began briskly. 'I've decided it's time for you to have your own series, which we'll almost certainly sell to the network.'

'That's very good of you, Tony,' said James.

'I want to make a series examining all aspects of marriage,' went on Tony.

'Financial, dual careers, how much housework should the caring husband do,' rattled off James excitedly. 'Sex, rows, decorating the house.'

'That's right,' said Tony. 'We could perhaps even introduce children and the pressures they put on a marriage. But basically the whole series will be aimed at couples who are getting behind marriage again, who want to avoid AIDS by staying with the same person for the rest of their lives. We'll call it "How to Stay Married".'

'With the AIDS panic, it'll be a real franchise-grabber,' said James excitedly.

'Exactly,' said Tony urbanely. 'And I want you and a very charming lady not far from your heart to front it.'

'I don't even have to guess, Tony,' said James warmly, 'but d'you really feel she's experienced enough?'

'More important,' said Tony, who was enjoying himself, 'she's a natural. She's not too obviously glamorous, but she's got just the right kind of lovely warm bubbly personality that'll make couples talk and trigger off a really good audience reaction.'

James bowed his head. 'I know Sarah will appreciate the very great honour you're bestowing on her, Tony, both to combat AIDS and to help Corinium retain the franchise.'

'I'm not talking about Sarah, you berk,' said Tony icily. 'I mean your wife, Lizzie, and if you value your job, the less you see of Mrs Stratton over the next three months the better.'

Taggie spent the next week dreaming of Rupert. She knew he loved and lived with Cameron, who would be back in a week or so, but she couldn't help herself. On Thursday she watched him on television at the Party Conference making a brilliant speech saying that the Tories must get off their fat backsides and start thinking positively about unemployment and the way it directly affected hooliganism and rioting in the inner cities. Taggie, detecting Declan's influence, felt very proud.

On Friday night a slight distraction was provided by Caitlin coming home for a long weekend, with her black hair dyed white at the front, still utterly besotted with Archie.

'He went into the town and brought eighty cans of beer back in a taxi and smuggled them in and sold them to the other boys on the black market in order to buy me this gorgeous jersey. I haven't taken it off since he sent it me, so please can you wash it tonight, and my black jeans so I can wear them tomorrow? Archie's taking me out to lunch. What's Mummy doing for the rest of the day?'

'Rehearsing, I think,' said Taggie.

Exactly on cue, Maud wandered in, looking radiant. 'Hullo, darling, how's school?'

'Ghastly. Anyone with layered hair is being sent home, so I'm going to get mine layered on Monday.'

'I've bought some apples,' said Maud, waving a large paper bag at Taggie. 'They're so cheap in the market.'

And they cost nothing in the orchard, thudding on to the grass every two minutes, Taggie wanted to scream. She wanted to murder her mother sometimes.

'That's a nice jersey,' said Maud, looking at Caitlin. 'Where did you get it?'

'It was a present,' said Caitlin noncommittally. 'You will wash it carefully, won't you, Tag? How's *The Merry Widow*?' she asked her mother.

'Oh, exhausting, but fun,' said Maud, pouring herself a large whisky. 'I – er – thought I might go to the cinema with some of the cast tomorrow night,' she added casually. 'Taggie's cooking. Will you be all right on your own, Caitlin?'

'Brilliant,' beamed Caitlin. 'Stay out as long as you like. I've got masses of work. Have dinner and make a night of it. I've got to read *Antony and Cleopatra* and write an essay on *Streetcar Named Desire*. I think it's extraordinary that they shut us up in single-sex schools and then give us these amazingly erotic set books.'

By the time Taggie had cleared up supper and washed and ironed Caitlin's jersey and jeans and put them in the hot cupboard it was two o'clock in the morning. Admittedly her progress had been slowed up by constantly looking out of the window to watch for Rupert's helicopter landing on the lawn, or his car coming up the drive. But there was nothing. Perhaps he'd gone to Ireland to see Cameron after all.

It seemed she'd hardly fallen asleep when she was roused by an hysterical Caitlin. 'That bugger Mummy used all the water, so I can't wash my hair or have a bath, and even worse she's gone off in my new jersey and jeans. And now I can't wear it for Archie, and he'll never believe I haven't lost it, like Desdemona's handkerchief. I hate, hate, hate her, bloody old cow, and she's bound to split my jeans.'

'I'll run you into Cotchester and buy you something else,' said Taggie. 'I got paid in cash yesterday.'

'It's no good,' screamed Caitlin. 'I wanted Archie to see me in his jersey. I'll kill her, I'll absolutely kill her.'

Nothing Taggie could say would calm her down.

'I'll ring up Rupert and see if you can have a bath there,' said Taggie in the end.

Throat dry, heart thumping, hands drenched in sweat and trembling, Taggie misdialled the number three times in her nervousness. When Rupert didn't answer immediately, she nearly put the telephone down.

'Hullo.' He sounded irritable and very sleepy.

'It's Taggie.'

'My darling.' His voice softened.

'I'm desperately sorry,' she began. Then, stammering worse than ever, she explained what had happened, but didn't mention Archie's name. 'Could I possibly rush Caitlin over to wash her hair and have a bath?'

'Of course,' said Rupert, 'as long as we can all have it together.'

Rupert hadn't shaved when they arrived. He was wandering around in bare feet, having obviously just put on the white shirt and the black dinner-jacket trousers he'd been wearing last night. He looked bugeyed.

'I won't stop,' mumbled Taggie, desperate not to impose on him. 'I'll pick Caitlin up in an hour, OK?'

Rupert pulled her into the house. 'Don't be boring. As I'm

such a notorious reprobate, you ought to stay and chaperone Caitlin.'

Caitlin promptly started raging on about Maud. 'Bloody old cow, nicking all the water, and my seducing kit. What does she want with it? I bet she's up to someone, the old tart. It's high time my father came home.'

'Cait-lin,' remonstrated Taggie, going pink. 'Rupert hasn't got all day. I thought you wanted to be ready by twelve. Go and have a bath.'

Grinning, Rupert took Caitlin upstairs and showed her where everything was. Taggie glanced at some photographs of Tabitha at Wembley which were lying on the kitchen table.

'Aren't these gorgeous?' she said, as Rupert came back. 'I saw a bit of it on television at Sarah Stratton's, but I missed the final. Did her team win?'

'No, but they came third, and she did well. *Horse and Hound* described her as a "chip off the old Campbell-Black"; which was nice.'

'Marvellous,' said Taggie. 'Am I in your way?' she asked as Rupert paused on his way to the fridge.

'No, I just like standing behind you. I know you'll spring to her defence, but your mother is an absolute disgrace. Swanning off with all Caitlin's clothes at her age. Maud's trouble is that she wants to have her cake and eat it, and make trifle out of it as well.'

Taggie giggled, but she said, 'I know, but it's such a relief that she's happy and working again. She might even start doing it professionally, and she's so beautiful,' Taggie sighed. 'It's hardly surprising all the cast's in love with her.'

Rupert privately deduced that Maud must be in love with one of the cast to have lost enough weight to get into Caitlin's jeans, but merely said, 'I've got a hangover. Let's have a drink.'

'I mustn't,' said Taggie, 'or I'll make another cock-up of cooking tonight.'

'Don't say you're working again?' said Rupert, appalled. Taggie nodded dolefully.

'Jesus,' said Rupert. 'I'd better make a date with you for *next* October.'

'I'm so sorry,' stammered Taggie, hanging her head, 'It's n-not that I wouldn't love to.'

'I've got an idea,' said Rupert. 'My children are coming over this afternoon. Why don't you come out with us for the day tomorrow, and help me entertain them?'

'I'll make a picnic,' said Taggie, suddenly excited.

'No, you won't. For once you're not going to cook a thing.'

With both Maud and Caitlin plundering her wardrobe, Taggie was at her wit's end as to what to wear. Feeling desperately guilty, with the Electricity Board, the television hire firm, the village shop, and God knows who else baying to be paid, she blued, or rather greyed, Friday lunchtime's cash wages on a pale-grey cashmere polo-neck which brought out the silver-grey in her eyes and clung to her in all the right places. There was no more money, so she'd have to wear her old black cords.

Next morning Maud whizzed off very early to yet another rehearsal. Caitlin, who nobly said she'd dogsit and read *Antony and Cleopatra*, hustled Taggie out of the house.

'You look delectable. Randy Rupe won't be able to keep his hands off you. Don't hurry back. I'm quite OK on my own –' she smirked wickedly – 'or, almost on my own. The Hon Arch will be dropping by *plus tard*. Or Marble Arch, as I call him, now he's lost his suntan.'

Tabitha, amid the swirling pack of dogs, answered the door looking belligerent. She was wearing a pink sweater embroidered with blue flowers and a blue puff-ball skirt.

'Hullo,' said Taggie in delight. 'I recognize *you*; you were on television last Saturday. You were wonderful, and what a beautiful clever pony. He was much the fastest. What's his name?'

'Biscuit,' said Tabitha coldly.

'Can I see him?'

'He's at my other house.'

'Oh, what a shame. I've brought him some carrots.' Taggie

rummaged round in a carrier bag, 'and I've made you some fudge.'

'Thank you,' said Tab, looking slightly mollified. 'Can I have a bit now?'

'I don't see why not. I like your puff-ball skirt. I wanted to get one, but my knees are far too knobbly.'

'Mummy says hers are, too,' said Tab. 'Perhaps they're not suitable for grown-ups.'

Stroking the dogs, Taggie sat down on one of the stone seats inside the porch.

'What's your name again?' said Tabitha.

'Taggie. It's really Agatha, isn't that awful? Tabitha's so much nicer. My parents call me Tag, sometimes, which sounds just like Tab, doesn't it? I expect when Marcus shouts Tab we'll both go charging into the kitchen to see what he wants and bump into each other in the doorway.'

Tabitha stared at her consideringly, and suddenly she smiled.

'And you're nine and a quarter?' said Taggie.

'Yes,' sighed Tab, pushing her blonde hair out of her eyes. 'Can't you see my wrinkles?'

Taggie giggled. 'Still, it's awfully young to be in the Mounted Games. Were you the youngest?'

'Yes,' said Tab. 'If you come back to Warwickshire with us tonight you can see Biscuit. We've got a foal here. Would you like to come and see it?'

'Yes, please,' said Taggie.

The front door opened; it was Marcus. 'Hullo,' he said. 'Daddy wants to know where you've got to.'

'She's talking to me, stupid,' said Tab. 'She's brought you some fudge.'

'Tag,' bellowed Rupert from the kitchen, 'where are you?'

'Here,' said Tab and Tag in unison. Then they both looked at each other and burst out laughing.

Taking Taggie's hand, Tabitha dragged her into the kitchen. 'Can she come back to Warwickshire with us this evening and see Biscuit?' said Tabitha.

Rupert, who was drinking black coffee and reading the racing pages of the *Sunday Times*, looked surprised.

'Of course she can. I thought you'd kidnapped her.'

'She's brought us fudge, and carrots for Biscuit, and a big bottle of cough mixture,' said Tabitha, unpacking the carrier bag.

'It's sloe gin,' said Taggie, blushing. 'I made it yesterday. You mustn't drink it for three months.'

'Thank you, angel,' said Rupert, kissing her on the cheek. 'I hope I don't have to wait that long for you,' he murmured in an undertone.

'Come *on*, Taggie,' said Tabitha impatiently. 'I thought you wanted to see the foal. This fudge is smashing.'

They had lunch in Cheltenham in an up-market hamburger bar. The children, who insisted on sitting on either side of Taggie, had huge milkshakes. Rupert, who complained he had alcohol shakes, ordered a carafe of red.

'That jersey suits you,' he said approvingly to Taggie. 'How d'you manage to keep it out of Maud's clutches?'

Taggie blushed. 'I slept with it under my pillow.'

'We're doing a "Messiah" at the end of term,' announced Tabitha, sucking air noisily from the bottom of her milkshake. 'There are going to be two trumpets and a drum, and real fathers in the chorus. I'm in the altos. They're much naughtier because they're mostly boys, silly twits.'

'D'you like singing?' asked Taggie.

'No. Mrs Brown takes us. She's just got married. She takes us for history too. She was reading a book called *Improving your Home* in class this week.'

'She was reading a book about drains in our class,' said Marcus.

'And that's what I pay your school fees for,' grumbled Rupert. 'I wish they'd organize a sponsored walk to Save the Parents.'

Having ordered, he looked across at Taggie, who was talking to Marcus about conkers.

'We used to roast them slowly in the oven to harden them up.'

557

'We soak them in vinegar,' said Marcus.

'My sister Caitlin used to put them in the hot cupboard and they always fell down behind the boiler and went mouldy. We've got masses at The Priory if you want any more, but I expect you've got hundreds already.'

Christ, she's sweet, thought Rupert, noticing the way the grey cashmere moulded the full breasts.

'Mary had a little lamb and surprised the midwife,' said Tabitha to her father.

'Really,' said Rupert absent-mindedly.

'Mary had a little lamb and surprised the midwife. It's a joke.'

'Ha, ha,' said Rupert, filling up Taggie's glass.

'Why d'you always say ha ha and not mean it? Can I have a packet of Frazzles?'

'No,' said Rupert. 'Here's your lunch.'

'Can I have punk hair like Cameron?' said Tabitha, picking bits of mushroom out of her salad and putting them round the edge of her plate.

'No.'

'Why not?'

'Because I don't like short hair.'

'You've got very nice hair,' said Marcus to Taggie, blushing scarlet as he bit into his hamburger.

'Yes,' agreed Rupert. 'She has.'

Tabitha gazed dreamily into space. 'Mrs Bodkin must have slept with Mr Bodkin an awful lot of times.'

'What on earth makes you think that?' asked Rupert in amazement.

'She told me she'd had four miscarriages,' said Tab.

Taggie didn't dare look at Rupert. She thought she had never been happier in her life. Suddenly the most ordinary things – a hamburger smothered in tomato ketchup, the mural of the village street round the wall, with its milk cart and postman – were illuminated because she was with Rupert and these adorable children.

'Everything all right, Meester Campbell-Black?' asked the Manager.

'Perfect,' said Rupert. 'Could we have another carafe of red?'

'I would like to congratulate you,' went on the Manager, looking round rapturously at Marcus, Tab and Taggie. 'I never knew you haff three such beautiful children.'

RIVALS
42

After lunch, they went for a walk in Rupert's woods. It was ridiculously mild. Insects moved leisurely in the rays slanting through the thinning beech trees, like specks of dust caught in the light from a projector. Birds sang drowsily, orange leaves drifted down on to already orange paths. The squirrels, stupefied by the sun, were fooling around on the ground instead of gathering nuts.

'What are you singing at school?' asked Taggie.

'"Green grow the rushes-oh,"' said Tab.

'*I'll sing you three-oh,*' sang Marcus.

'*What is your three-oh?*' sang back Tab.

'*Three for the rivals, Two, two the lily-white boys, Clothed all in green-o,*' replied Marcus, his pure treble echoing through the soaring cathedral of beech trunks. Then both children took up the chant:

'*One is one and all alone, And ever more shall be so.*'

'Lovely,' sighed Taggie.

'Three for the rivals sounds like Corinium, Venturer and Mid-West,' said Rupert.

He used up a couple of reels of film, then, exhausted after a strenuous week at Blackpool, fell asleep under a chestnut tree, while Taggie played games with the children.

'D'you know,' she said, drawing them away down the ride so they wouldn't wake Rupert, 'that every time you catch a falling leaf, you get a happy day? Let's see if we can catch thirty, so we can give Daddy a really happy November when he wakes up.'

'Easy peasy,' said Tabitha, leaping forward as a yellow sycamore leaf pirouetted through the air towards her, then, caught by a puff of wind, dummied round her and fluttered to the ground.

'It's harder than it looks,' panted Marcus, reaching out as a twig of ash leaves floated tantalizingly out of his grasp. 'Would those have counted as seven?'

'Not really,' said Taggie.

'Bugger,' screamed Tab, as she just missed a beech leaf.

'Hush,' said Taggie. 'We mustn't wake Daddy.'

Silently they raced round the wood trying to suppress their screams of joy whenever they managed to catch a leaf. After a particularly piercing yell, when Tab tripped over a bramble cable but managed to hang on to a wand of chestnut leaves, Rupert woke up; but he pretended to be asleep. Watching Taggie, gambolling long-legged over the beech leaves, ponytail flying, looking, as the Manager had thought, not a day over fourteen, he was suddenly kneed in the groin with longing.

'Here you are, Daddy,' said Tabitha, her hands full of leaves, 'a whole happy month for you.'

Rupert, who privately thought that the only thing that could make him happy at the moment was a whole month in bed with Taggie, said thank you very much.

'Can we go and see the new Woody Allen?' asked Tabitha.

Rupert looked at his watch: 'It's nearly four o'clock. You'll be very late back.' The last thing he wanted to do was to go to the cinema.

'We can go on our way home,' pleaded Tabitha.

'We've done our homework,' said Marcus.

Rupert turned to Taggie who said she'd adore to see it; anything to prolong the day with Rupert.

'I'm going to sit next to Taggie,' said Tabitha, seizing her hand.

'I'm going to sit next to her too,' said Marcus, taking her other hand.

'If she sits on my knee, you can both sit next to her,' said Rupert.

Severely jolted, he felt it was increasingly necessary to make a joke about the whole thing.

The Woody Allen was extremely funny, but Taggie hardly took any of it in, she was so aware of Rupert slumped in the seat beyond Tabitha gazing totally unmoved at the screen. How awful for Rupert being left by Helen and losing these heavenly children, living alone by himself in that big house.

'*One is one and all alone and ever more shall be so,*' sang Tabitha as they drove home.

Taggie felt Rupert's loss far more acutely when she met Helen, who was simply the most beautiful woman she'd ever seen, with huge serious yellow eyes and long red hair drawn back in two combs from her freckled face, and incredibly slim ankles and wrists. She had the same colouring as Maud, reflected Taggie, but while Maud cavorted untrainably through life like a red setter bestowing her favours indiscriminately, Helen would be far more fastidious and sparing with her affections. Helen was like a red deer. If you tamed and won the confidence of anything so delicate and nervous, you'd feel incredibly proud.

But before she had much time to observe Helen or her husband, Malise, who seemed very old, Taggie was dragged off to the stables by Tabitha to meet Biscuit and Dollop. Then she had to see Marcus's room and then Tabitha's room, both extraordinarily tidy (in fact, the whole house was incredibly tidy for a Sunday evening), by which time it was well past the children's bedtime.

Back in the drawing-room, Taggie found Helen tapping her beautifully shod foot and looking at the clock, and Rupert standing in front of an unlit fire, holding an empty glass and looking absolutely glazed.

'What would you like to drink?' Malise asked Taggie.

Taggie glanced at Rupert, who almost imperceptibly moved his head in the direction of the door.

'Nothing, thank you very much,' she said.

'We must go,' said Rupert. 'I've got to get this child home.'

So the day was to end just like that. Taggie suddenly felt suicidal. Malise, seeming to sense her depression, said, 'Helen and I are tremendous fans of your father's. I do hope he gets the franchise. Corinium's programmes are absolutely ghastly.'

'Oh, *The Dream* was excellent the other night,' protested Helen. 'Marcus said Cameron Cook had something to do with that, Rupert. You must bring her over sometime. I'd love to discuss the production with her. It was a most original interpretation. They set it in Victorian England and had some fascinating parallels between Queen Victoria and John Brown and Titania and Bottom.'

Rupert stifled a huge yawn.

'I think Taggie and Rupert want to go, darling,' said Malise gently, putting his arm round Helen's shoulders.

He has the most charming smile, thought Taggie. I can see why she finds him attractive, but not compared with Rupert, and he is *terribly* old. The children came to see them off.

'Promise, promise, we can see you next time we come over,' said Tabitha, clinging to her like a monkey.

'Thank you so much for the fudge,' said Marcus.

'Rupert is awful,' said Helen, having packed the children upstairs to have baths. 'That girl must still be at school.'

'She's a bit older than that, but not much,' said Malise, straightening the Sunday papers. 'D'you know, she gives me the same ghastly sense of foreboding I had when I first met you?'

'I hope you haven't fallen in love with her too,' said Helen, somewhat too archly.

'No. One just knows he's going to break her heart,' said Malise grimly, 'and feels powerless to do anything about it.'

'He may have mellowed,' said Helen. 'She's the first girl he's ever brought here, and the kids obviously adore her.'

Malise shook his head. 'He's like a hound. You can't domesticate him. Hunting'll always be in his blood.'

Rupert was very quiet on the drive back to Penscombe. Taggie, feeling utterly miserable because the day was almost over and the Aston-Martin seemed to be gobbling up the miles, assumed he was merely depressed because his ravishing wife and children didn't live with him any more. Rupert, however, for the first time in his life, was battling seriously with his conscience.

Taggie was Declan's teenage daughter; he was committed to Cameron, who was already paranoid about Taggie, and there were deadly serious things like franchises to be won.

Then, in the light from a street-lamp in Cheltenham, he caught sight of Taggie. Everything seemed to turn upwards, her nose, her long sooty eyelashes, her adorably short upper lip, and those beautifully soft breasts, which he'd dreamed of the other night. His conscience lost.

'Would you like some dinner?'

'Oh yes, please,' said Taggie joyfully. 'If you're sure you're not too tired and I look smart enough?'

'Never, never get smart,' said Rupert. 'I loathe done-up women.'

'They're such adorable children,' said Taggie. 'And so beautiful. Not surprising really with such a beautiful mother.' In the darkness of the car, now they were out of the town, it seemed easier to talk. 'Is it absolutely agony every time you see her again?'

'Agony,' said Rupert soulfully. Then, shooting a sideways glance at Taggie, he explained, 'Because she bores the fucking tits off me.'

Taggie gave a gasp of shocked laughter.

'I can't think how the hell I stayed married to her for seven years. While you were upstairs, she gave me the entire plot of the Italian film they'd seen that afternoon, and, if Malise hadn't shut her up, we'd have had a five-act analysis of *Midsummer Night's Dream*. How he puts up with it!'

'He seems very nice,' said Taggie, 'but he's almost like a grandfather to the children.'

'Thirty years older than Helen,' said Rupert, 'but he's made her very happy.'

'And what happened to you after she walked out?' asked Taggie.

'Oh well, I had one or two fish of my own I was frying at the time,' admitted Rupert. 'But the fat began to spit too much, so I backed off. Then I had a long stint with an engaging tramp called Beattie Johnson, and then a few games of tennis with Sarah Stratton.'

'Oh God,' moaned Taggie.

Rupert laughed. 'I'm half-tempted to stop the car and see how much you're blushing. Were you terribly shocked when you saw us?'

'Yes, no, yes,' mumbled Taggie. 'More for Gertrude, really. She's led such a sheltered life. It must have been awful all those fire engines turning up.'

'We were bloody lucky,' said Rupert. 'Cameron tells me that the Corinium newsroom give the Cotchester Fire Brigade so much booze at Christmas that invariably the firemen tip them off and keep their hoses running until the television crew arrive. Sarah and I in the buff would have been a sensation on "Cotswold Round-Up".'

Taggie giggled. She didn't like to tell him how much in the last few months the memory of his oiled, mahogany-tanned, wonderfully constructed body had haunted her dreams.

The White Elephant at Painswick was packed and taking last orders, but still managed to find a corner for Rupert. Taggie fled to the loo. All she had in her bag was a defunct mascara wand, a comb, some scent and a picture of Claudius. If only she could clean her teeth. She made do with soaking the roller towel, rubbing some soap on it, rubbing her teeth, then rinsing her mouth out with water. Then she de-tangled her hair and put it back in its ponytail.

When she got back to the table, Rupert, realizing she

would be totally floored by the French menu, had ordered a bottle of Pouilly Fumé and smoked salmon and scrambled eggs for both of them.

'And you're going to eat the lot.'

At first they discussed the children.

'I wish they got on better with Cameron,' sighed Rupert, 'but, being totally unused to children, she makes neither extra beds nor allowances.'

It was good that they could talk about Cameron naturally now, thought Taggie, suddenly longing to touch the fan of fine lines at the corner of Rupert's eyes. Perhaps she could become his long-term confidante, and even when he was eighty, he'd come roaring over to The Priory and tell her he'd met some marvellous new fifty-year-old. At least it'd be better than not seeing him.

'Does it still upset you going to the Horse of the Year Show when you're not winning all the cups any more?' she asked tentatively.

'Yes,' he said. 'That's why I wanted you to come along last week –' he took her hand – 'to hold *my* hand. I don't think I realized at the time how desperately I minded giving up. Just stopping overnight after the World Championship, burying myself in politics, refusing to recognize I was suffering from withdrawal symptoms far worse than any junkie. There's so little time to think while you're show jumping. Even on those interminable drives there was always Billy to yak to, or some horse to natter about, always something to look forward to, a prize to be won, someone else's time to be beaten, a horse to be sorted out, a girl to be laid. I suppose I never gave myself time to grow up, and when Helen buggered off I blocked that out too.'

Still holding her hand, he looked into her loving, infinitely understanding and sympathetic eyes. Christ, he'd never admitted things like this to anyone, not even Billy. Then she asked the same question: 'Does it still hurt seeing Helen?'

Rupert shrugged. 'I got bored with hating her, I guess. The only thing that really irks me is that Malise succeeded where

I failed. I can't honestly say I've ever made any woman happy, or not for very long.'

'You make me very happy,' said Taggie gruffly.

For a second they gazed at each other and he watched the colour mounting in her cheeks.

'I'd like to try,' he said softly. 'I'll just pay the bill and we'll go.'

As he drove her slowly back to Penscombe, Chris de Burgh was singing 'Lady in Red' on the car radio. It was such a beautiful night. The moon was hiding behind a vast ebony cloud shaped like a yew tree, tipping its edges with silver; the rest of the pearly grey sky was threaded with stars. A few windows were still lit up in the village like cardboard cut-outs.

Just before he reached the right turn up the long chestnut avenue to Penscombe Court, Rupert slowed the car down almost to a standstill and raised a finger to Taggie's cheek.

'Are you quite sure, angel?'

He could feel her cheekbone rubbing frantically against his finger as she nodded. Totally adrift with love, she had no thought of refusing.

'Fucking hell,' howled Rupert, as they drew up outside the house. Parked outside, beside Taggie's car, was a Lotus. In the moonlight it could have been any dark colour.

Cameron, thought Taggie in horror.

But the girl who came out of the front door had thick lustrous hair, as golden yellow as the sycamore leaves swirling across the gravel. It was Sarah Stratton. Sobbing, she threw herself into Rupert's arms.

'I must talk to you.'

'I must go,' said Taggie.

'No, don't,' said Rupert sharply. Then, realizing what he was saying, added, 'Well, it is a bit late. We'll check through the rest of those names tomorrow, and we'll tackle the southern part of the region later in the week.'

'Oh, the fucking franchise,' screamed Sarah.

Leaving time only to squeeze Taggie's hand and say he'd

ring her tomorrow, Rupert took Sarah into the drawing-room, where she collapsed sobbing on the sofa. The temperature suddenly seemed to have dropped several degrees. The house felt horribly cold and empty without Taggie and the children.

It was a few minutes before he could get any sense out of Sarah. Evidently James Vereker had given her the bullet.

'Tony ordered him to. He said everyone was gossiping about me and James, and it doesn't do Corinium's reputation any good in a franchise year. Jesus, and when you think of the way he was carrying on with Cameron.'

'*Was* is the operative word,' said Rupert, pouring Sarah a glass of brandy. 'There's no prude like a reformed rake.'

'I know James loves me,' sobbed Sarah hysterically, 'but that shit Tony offered him the carrot of his own thirteen-part series on staying married, and ordered him to front it with Lizzie. Tony's convinced the IBA will adore the idea, what with all this panic about AIDS.'

Rupert whistled. 'That's quite shrewd.'

'So James and the podgy frump have to present a lovey-dovey united front until the franchise is in the bag, and James is going to go along with it.'

'Ambition should be made of sterner stuffing,' said Rupert idly. 'And how's Lizzie taking it?'

'Oh, lapping it up, I should think,' said Sarah viciously. 'Must be the first time anyone's slept with her in yonks.'

Hum, thought Rupert. 'Well, you'll just have to be a bit more discreet until after 15th December,' he said.

'That's what I said, but James is refusing even to have a drink with me. If I talk to him in the passage at Corinium, he scuttles off like a daddy longlegs. He won't even gossip during the break in "Round-Up". I know he's vain and ambitious, but I love him. I can't live without him.' Her voice rose to a shriek.

Slumped on the sofa, in a rucked-up amber mini-skirt, and a saffron yellow jersey, with her tousled tawny hair and her tear-streaked face, Sarah should have been the epitome of desirability. But, comparing her hard, petulant, demanding little face to Taggie's, so sweet, so infinitely kind and gentle, Rupert wondered how the hell he'd ever fancied her.

'I can't live without him,' Sarah repeated shrilly. 'I'll never get over it.'

'I hate to point it out,' said Rupert, 'but you said exactly the same thing to me after Christmas, and you've got over me pretty thoroughly, and no doubt when Paul thought he ought to do his duty and stay with Winifred you said the same thing to him.'

'You can't compare the two,' said Sarah furiously. 'I've just spent a whole weekend with Paul,' she added with a shudder.

'Paul's palled, has he?' said Rupert, topping up her glass.

'I can't stand living with him a moment longer. He won't stop pawing me,' wailed Sarah. 'And he's so old. I mean he's nineteen years older than me. It was all right when I started working for him. I was twenty and he was thirty-nine and he seemed so wonderfully forceful and dynamic and experienced. But now I'm twenty-nine and he's forty-eight, and his body's going, and he looks all grey and rumpled when he wakes in the morning, and he wears cornplasters and snows scurf on his suits, and he's always clearing his throat and picking his nose behind the FT and peering at me over his spectacles.' Sarah's voice rose to a screech again as she catalogued his crimes. 'I can't stand it.'

Mindlessly, Rupert patted her heaving shoulder, as he bleakly worked out that the age gap between him and Taggie was exactly the same, or would be when he was thirty-eight next month. Gradually Sarah stopped crying.

'The one thing that puts men off is scenes,' said Rupert. 'You'll just have to grin and not bare it until 15th December. Everyone's going to be behaving in a pretty tense way for the next two months. I honestly can't see James and Lizzie's rapprochement lasting very long, and at least if you concentrate on your career at Corinium you'll be able to support yourself. You won't be able to afford two hunters, a Lotus and Jasper Conran dresses if Tony kicks you out, which he will do if you don't leave Vere-karing alone.'

Sarah sat up and rubbed the mascara from under her eyes.

'I suppose I'd better seduce Tony, but he's got one cloven hoof in the grave too. You and Cameron are so lucky – being near in age.'

Then her eyes narrowed. 'And while we're on that subject, what were you doing rolling up with the Galloping Gormless just now?'

Rupert's mind raced. He'd got to kill that rumour stone dead. If Sarah told Tony he'd been out with Taggie, Tony'd make sure it went straight back in a wildly exaggerated form to Cameron.

'I had the children for the weekend,' he said carefully. 'Cameron's away, so Taggie was helping me amuse them. She's nearer their age.'

'Well, that's a relief,' said Sarah. 'I thought for one ghastly moment you were after her as well. I mean, she's simply not up to it. Very sweet and all, but not very bright. A bit loco, James thinks. The last thing she needs is a lascivious old ram like you. You'd crucify her. Anyway you're far too old. It'd be just like Paul and me in a few years' time.'

It was like a dentist hitting a raw nerve with a high-speed drill. Rupert never dreamed remarks could hurt him quite so much. Mercifully he was saved by the telephone. Then the dentist seemed to hit another nerve.

'Christ, I've missed you,' said Cameron's seductive rasp. 'Sorry I haven't called, but we've been up to here. Perry O'Donovan's such an asshole, and he can't stand Esther McDermott. She's an asshole too, and they've both had such rows with Declan, he's walked off the set twice.'

'So it's all going as planned,' said Rupert.

As Cameron rattled on about the cock-ups and frustrations of filming, all he could hear was prison doors clanging shut on him.

'So we've managed to finish a day early,' she said finally.

'God, what a bore,' said Rupert who hadn't been listening.

'Sweetest, this is a terrible line, I said I'll be coming home a day early. Declan and I are flying in tomorrow.'

'Great,' said Rupert, feeling sick. 'I'll come and meet you.'

'No, I've got the car at the airport. I'll see you late

570

afternoon, and darling,' her voice dropped huskily, 'I've been celibate for three weeks. We've got a lot of catching up to do, so cancel any appointments for the rest of the day. I love you.'

'Me too,' said Rupert automatically.

'Good,' said Sarah, as Rupert put down the receiver and went and poured himself a large whisky. 'An absolute bastard like you needs an utter bitch like her to keep you in order.'

After she'd left, Rupert couldn't face going to bed. He took the dogs into the garden. As they weaved about snuffling and barking after badgers and masochistically lifting their legs on rose bushes, he looked across the valley. The moon had set; black clouds covered the sky; a chill wind was shepherding beech leaves irritably across the lawn; The Priory was in darkness, except for one light in Taggie's bedroom. Rupert almost wept. He longed to ring her now to explain why he wouldn't be ringing her tomorrow, or any day after that, but he didn't dare in case he weakened.

Sarah was right. He was too old, too shop-soiled, too reprobate. He'd only bring her unhappiness. Besides, Cameron was coming home tomorrow and he couldn't jeopardize the franchise by risking her running back to Tony. It was his fault; he'd gone into the whole thing with his flies open. Not only had the prison door clanged shut, but he could hear a huge key turning for ever in the lock.

One is one, and all alone, and ever more shall be so, he thought despairingly.

43

Across at The Priory, by some lucky chance, a starry-eyed but slightly sheepish Maud swanned in at five to twelve just in time to take a telephone call from Declan saying he was coming home tomorrow. Cameron would drop him off and, bar fogs or airport strikes, he would be with her by twilight.

All next day Taggie waited for Rupert to ring, and by some vicious twist of fate, as she cleaned the house and cautiously dusted and hoovered round the chaos of precious papers in her father's study and put clean sheets on her parents' bed, the telephone rang incessantly. But it was only Archie ringing once again to say goodbye to Caitlin, or members of the cast ringing for Maud, or every member of Venturer ringing to ask whether Declan was back. Each time, Taggie pounced on the telephone, and each time, like a stray dog dumped bewildered on the motorway hoping each passing car might be her master returning, when it wasn't Rupert she slunk back in utter despair. And as the day ebbed, so did her hopes. Once Cameron was home, he wouldn't ring.

The weather had changed too, and as the grey skies closed in on the October afternoon, the black tracery of ivy fretted against the casement windows and sharp bitter winds swept the leaves from the lime walk and drove them in withered heaps along the dry gravel paths. However many jerseys she put on, however much she raced about the house, Taggie was still cold, while upstairs Maud oiled and scented herself for Declan's return, no doubt leaving a horrible mess both in the bathroom and bedroom, which Taggie had just cleaned.

In the kitchen, having put some green tomato chutney to cook on the Aga, Taggie was trying to find a place on Caitlin's incredibly skimpy pants to sew a name tape. Caitlin, having scattered breadcrumbs all over the dresser, dumped papers and magazines on the table, left the orange juice carton out and her scrambled-egg pan unwashed in the sink, was now peeling an orange.

> *Give me to drink mandragora,*
> *That I might sleep out this great gap of time*
> *My Archie is away* [she moaned].

'One day you'll be sewing the name Caitlin Baddingham and a coronet on my pants. Don't you think I'll make a good Lady Baddingham?' She dropped a deep curtsey. 'I'm going to bunk out of school next weekend so I can see him.'

'I wouldn't,' said Taggie, breaking off a thread with her teeth. 'You'll get expelled and it's bound to get in the papers. Oh, for God's sake,' she snapped, as Caitlin dropped her orange peel on the table, 'can't you ever throw anything in the bin?'

'Don't nag,' said Caitlin. 'When I grow up I'm going to live in a really messy house.'

'What happens when you meet a fantastic man at a party and want to bring him back for a cup of coffee afterwards?'

'I'd go to his house,' said Caitlin. 'How can I live without Archie till next weekend?'

How can I live without Rupert for ever? thought Taggie, getting up to give the tomato chutney a stir. She jumped as Gertrude and Claudius rushed in and leapt on to the window-seat, bristling furiously. They were followed by Maud in a big fluffy pink towel.

'What on earth are you cooking?' she demanded in outraged tones.

'Tomato chutney,' said Taggie, through gritted teeth.

'What a disgusting smell to welcome home your poor

573

father, and there are cows in the garden doing great splattering cowpats all over the lawn and the paths, which is even worse. They must be Rupert's. Ring him up and tell him to take them away.'

'You ring him,' screamed Taggie. 'I can't do everything.'

'Temper temper,' said Maud, exchanging surprised glances with Caitlin. 'Well, I certainly haven't got time to ring. Someone's got to be ready to welcome him.'

'Scrubbing off other men's fingerprints,' said Caitlin scornfully, as Maud flounced off upstairs.

She put a hand on Taggie's shoulder.

'You OK?'

'N-not really.'

'Is it Rupert? Did you have a lovely day?'

Taggie nodded. 'But Sarah Stratton was waiting for him when we got back, so I came home. He said he'd ring, but . . .' Her voice trailed off. She stared at the great congealing brown mass of onions, brown sugar and tomatoes. Her mother was right. It was a repulsive smell.

'I'll ring him about the cows,' said Caitlin. 'That'll remind him.'

But when she got through, Rupert was on the other line and the secretary said she'd send the farm manager over at once to remove the cows.

'Rupert's probably terribly busy,' said Caitlin consolingly. Then, as the telephone rang, 'There, that'll be him now.'

'You answer it,' gasped Taggie. Please God make it be Rupert, she whispered over and over again into the vat of chutney.

'Hullo, Upland House Bakery. Which tart would you like to fill?' said Caitlin. 'Oh Archie, darling, I won't survive either.'

She was interrupted by frantic barking. Gertrude and Claudius shot off the window-seat, taking the cushions with them, and rushed into the hall as a car crunched on the gravel.

'My father's just got back. He'd lynch me if he knew I was talking to you,' said Caitlin hastily. 'I'll write tonight. Love you madly. *Ciao*.'

Fighting back the tears, Taggie went out to welcome Declan. He looked wonderful, incredibly suntanned from filming outside and much less tired. He was about to hug her when she was sent flying by Maud, a tornado of Arpège and desire, wearing Taggie's new grey cashmere jersey. Throwing herself on Declan, she buried her face in his chest so that he shouldn't see the guilt flickering in her eyes.

'Darling, you're so brown and handsome,' she murmured. 'I've missed you every single minute.'

Caitlin, lounging in the doorway, whistled, then she quoted sardonically:

> When my love swears that she is made of truth,
> I do believe her, though I know she lies.

Declan was too delighted to find Maud in such good spirits to take in what Caitlin was saying. 'Cameron's outside,' he said. 'Come and say hullo while I unload the car.'

Taggie's heart sank as Cameron came through the door. Like Declan, she looked wonderful. Her face seemed even softer, her hair less severe. She was wearing a cream silk shirt tucked into brown suede jodhpurs above tight, shiny brown boots. Either it had been a highly successful shoot or she was obviously over the moon about seeing Rupert again.

Ignoring Taggie and Caitlin, she went straight up to Maud and hugged her. 'Ireland was terrific, but we sure missed you. If you'd been playing Maud Gonne, we'd get an Emmy. Esther McDermott was just awful. But Declan was such an inspiration. His sarcasm can bruise, but, wow, it makes you grow.'

'Really,' said Maud, not altogether enthusiastically.

Taggie, unable to take any more, went out to the car, where she had no difficulty in picking out her father's battered roped-together leather case from Cameron's Louis Vuitton. On the second journey she picked up a couple of carrier bags.

'No,' said Cameron sharply, appearing in the doorway. 'Those are gifts for Rupert and the kids. I must show you what I got Tabitha, Maud.'

575

She produced a little leather pony, with a girl rider, and bridles and saddles that came off.

'Isn't it neat?'

'Lovely,' said Maud without interest.

Cameron had bought a beautifully illustrated book of Irish legends for Marcus, and a pair of gold cuff links for Rupert, which she insisted on showing to Taggie.

'I'll get his crest put on later,' she said. Taggie stared at her dumbly.

'Very nice, I'm sure,' said Caitlin tartly. Then, looking at Cameron's jodhpurs, 'Are you going for a ride?'

'I sure am,' said Cameron with a sudden lascivious smile. 'After three weeks away I need one, and not on the back of a horse. I'm off, Declan,' she yelled into the house, 'I'll call you as soon as I know when we can see the rushes.'

'Bitch,' screamed Caitlin at the departing Lotus. Taggie shook her head. Cameron was the one who Rupert belonged to.

Taking a bottle of duty-free whisky, Declan and Maud went up to bed. Taggie also went up to her room, and, with trembling hands, tried to hold Caitlin's binoculars still as she looked across the valley to Penscombe Court. Enough leaves had come off the trees now for her to see lights on downstairs in the kitchen and the drawing-room. Then, like a firefly lighting up the almost leafless chestnut avenue, she saw Cameron's Lotus storming up Rupert's drive. In an unbearably short time another light went on, which Taggie knew from Tabitha's guided tour of the house yesterday was Rupert's bedroom. No one bothered to draw the curtains.

Taggie collapsed on the bed. What was that expression her father was always quoting? 'The heart transfixed upon the huddled spears.' She knew what it meant now. Two minutes later there was a bang on her door.

'Go away,' she groaned.

Caitlin walked in with the dogs, who leapt on to the bed, frantically trying to lick away Taggie's tears.

'You got over Ralphie; you'll get over Rupert,' said Caitlin.

'Anyway you may not have to. He's got to keep that bitch sweet until after the franchise.'

'Bugger the franchise,' sobbed Taggie. 'What would you do if you saw Archie and some woman in bed?'

'I'd light a cigarette, have a drink and go and stuff my face,' said Caitlin. 'Look, I hate intruding on your grief, but the tomato chutney smells even more disgusting burning, and as those carnal beasts won't emerge from their bedroom before morning, I'm afraid you'll have to take me back to Uplift House.'

'*There's a pauper just behind me and he's treading on my tail*,' groaned Declan the following morning as, reeling from hangover and too much sex, he went through the pile of final reminders and endless requests from charity organizations for his time, his money or 'one of his very personal things'.

'Why don't you send them all a lock of your hair?' suggested Ursula.

'I'd be bald in a week.'

'It's only because you're a household name that people mistakenly assume you're rolling,' said Ursula soothingly.

'I'll be a poorhouse-hold name at this rate.' Declan winced as he bent down to retrieve an unopened letter that had fallen under the table among the débris of biros and pencils chewed up by Claudius. 'This looks more interesting.'

The letter was from the IBA telling Venturer that their interview would be at ten o'clock on 29th November at the IBA headquarters at 80 Brompton Road.

Declan immediately swung into action and called a Venturer meeting the following week. The room over the nightclub in Cheltenham was considered too risky, so a suite was booked in an obscure Bloomsbury Hotel. For security's sake, a large board in the lobby announced in white plastic letters that the O'Hara, Black & Jones Drainage Co. Sales Conference was being held in the Virginia Woolf Suite on the fourth floor. The whole of Venturer turned up except Dame Enid, who had a concert in New York, Janey Lloyd-Foxe, whose baby had gastric flu, and Bas who had ostensibly been caught up in some crisis at the Bar Sinister.

Cameron took special trouble with her appearance, wearing a new very waisted red silk suit with padded shoulders, a very plunging neckline and an extremely short skirt. This was because she was meeting Rupert's best friend, Billy Lloyd-Foxe, for the first time. He'd been away making a film on rugger for the BBC for the past three months and Cameron was determined to make a good impression. She needn't have worried. Billy came up to her straight away with that famous smile which had been described as 'able to beam into millions of homes without the aid of satellite'.

'Hullo, gosh, I've been longing to meet you,' he said, kissing her. 'I'm mad about "Four Men went to Mow". Janey's taped all the episodes for me. It's exactly how Rupe and I used to carry on before we were married. It was just starting in Australia when I left, and being marvellously received.'

He was extremely attractive, Cameron decided. His light-brown hair had gone greyer and he'd thickened out since his show-jumping days, but he had such a young face, and his turned-down eyes were so merry you didn't notice the broken nose or the doubling chin. He also had a sweetness and an air of life being hilarious, but at the same time a little bit too much for him that had endeared him as much to the BBC viewers as to everyone in the sporting world. Janey was mad to mess him around, thought Cameron. She wondered if that was why Bas wasn't here today.

Rupert and he seemed to know each other so well, they slipped into familiarity like a pair of old bedroom slippers, arguing about horses, finishing each other's sentences, howling with laughter at each other's jokes. It was nice to see Rupert happy again, thought Cameron. His fuse had been very short since she got back. She suspected, although he denied it, that he hated being in opposition – a shadow minister of his former self.

'When you come back to Penscombe, we're bloody well going to start a racing stable,' Rupert was saying in an undertone.

'I thought we were going to run a television station,' said Billy.

'We are, but with the revenue coming in, we'll have access to a hundred and twenty-five million a year. Just think what we can do with that.'

'Good God,' said Billy in amazement. 'Christy may be able to go to Harrow after all. I must have a drink.'

At that moment Declan tapped a large mahogany table in the centre of the room and asked everyone to sit down on the row of chairs lined up on the opposite side.

'Where's the bar?' asked Rupert.

'No one's having anything to drink until we've finished,' Declan said firmly.

Wesley's face fell. Billy turned pale. 'What is this, a concentration camp?'

'Concentration –' Declan smiled thinly – 'is what we're after tonight. If you're all swilling booze and getting up to get each other drinks, you won't take in what I'm saying. There's Perrier if anyone wants it.'

'Now I know why it's called a dry run,' said Billy sulkily. 'Come and sit by me,' he said to Cameron, patting a chair. 'At least I can cheer myself up gazing at your legs.'

Cameron looked like a cross between Joan Collins and Donald Duck, Billy decided, frightfully glamorous but somewhat high-powered.

'I'm frightfully hungry. Can we at least ring for some sandwiches?' said Professor Graystock, deliberately pressing against Cameron's breasts and having a good look as he leant over to pinch one of Billy's cigarettes.

'Later,' said Declan.

Billy, Harold White, Seb Burrows, Georgie Baines and Sally Maples, the children's editor Declan had recruited from Yorkshire Television, then jumped out of their skins when an unknown man in spectacles with a crew cut and a purposeful expression walked in.

'It's all right,' said Declan soothingly. 'This is Hardy Bissett. He used to work for the IBA and knows exactly what sort of questions they'll ask us at the interview. He's going to drill us over the next few weeks.'

'Who's that turgid old crone in the portrait over the mantelpiece?' Billy whispered to Cameron.

'Virginia Woolf,' whispered Cameron.

'I'd do anything to keep her from my door!' said Billy. 'What did she do for a living – belly dancing?'

'A fine writer,' said Professor Graystock reprovingly.

Declan found Hardy a chair beside him on the other side of the table. Then he said, 'The IBA meeting, as you all know now, is fixed for 29th November. The good thing is that Corinium's meeting is the afternoon before, so there won't be any problem for those of you who have to go to both meetings.'

Everyone jumped again as a fat man waddled into the room wearing a stocking over his head, waving a blue plastic toy gun, saying, 'This is a shoot-out.'

Then he peeled the stocking off with a broad grin and said, 'Boo!' It was Charles Fairburn.

'Oh, for fock's sake, Charles,' exploded Declan. 'This is serious. I was just explaining that ours and Corinium's meetings are on different days, so you won't bump into Tony and Ginger Johnson coming out of the IBA as you go in. But please think up excuses to be out of the office on the 29th well in advance. We want as many of you there as possible.'

'Are you sure no one will see us?' asked Sally Maples nervously. 'We've all been threatened with the sack again this week.'

'So have we,' said Billy.

Declan shook his head. 'All you have to do is to drive into the underground garage at the back of the IBA – you needn't go near the front at all – and you'll be whisked up to the eighth floor.

'By now,' he went on, 'the IBA will have digested our applications and answers to the supplementary questions, and noted our performance at the public meeting. They will obviously have some idea as to whom they want to award the franchise. But have no doubt, the interview on the 29th is key. Just as important as a viva to an undergraduate taking finals.'

'I wouldn't know about that,' murmured Billy.

'I'm now going to hand you over to Hardy,' said Declan, sitting down, 'who'll take you through the dry run.'

Hardy Bissett, despite his bristly crew cut, had an air of officialdom which unnerved them all. Getting to his feet, he tapped the table with a biro: 'This is exactly the kind of table you'll sit along during the interview, except the IBA table is oval-shaped. Facing you will be the twelve members of the Authority, with Lady Gosling in the centre. None of them know anything much about television. They are worthy public figures, academics, business people. One of them, Mrs Scott-Menzies, for example, is the ex-Chairman of the WI. Another used to run the Post Office. Another is an ex-Labour Minister of Education. Yet another, whom I think you've come across, Declan, is the Reverend Fergus Penney, a disgusting old goat who was once a Prebendary of the Church of England.

'It is essential for you to memorize all their names. All important people in their own field once, they tend to be vain and enjoy recognition. Behind them during the meeting will sit half a dozen officials who work for the Authority, who know *all* about television. They do not speak during the interview, but they brief before and advise afterwards, and will be watching you all like hawks.'

Billy mopped his brow. 'It sounds most alarming,' he sighed.

'God, that man's disgusting,' thought Rupert, as Professor Graystock pinched yet another of Billy's cigarettes.

As if reading Rupert's thoughts, Hardy Bissett said, 'One of the crucial things at the interview is to appear to like and admire each other and prove you are not merely a star-studded bunch after a quick buck, but actually capable of forming a workable and amicable team. As you will be sitting in an almost straight line and will not be able to catch each other's eyes, it is also crucial to work out in advance who will field

581

what questions. Freddie perhaps should answer any technical questions, the Bishop should deal with religion, Dame Enid with music, Charles the arts, and so on.

'It is also vital that everyone has their say. One excellent consortium lost the breakfast franchise a few years ago because their chairman, a newspaper editor, answered all the questions quite brilliantly, thereby convincing the IBA that they would be too much of a one-man band.

'All right.' He clapped his hands together. 'Enough waffle. To begin with I'll fire questions directly at individuals. Later on in rehearsals we'll get to the stage when I can fire a question in the air, and the appropriate person will leap to answer it. Now remember, the interview will last at least an hour.'

'I won't if I don't get a drink,' grumbled Billy.

'Shut up,' snapped Hardy Bissett. He turned to Henry Hampshire. 'I'm interested to know why as Lord-Lieutenant you decided to join the Venturer consortium?'

For a second, Henry mouthed helplessly like a goldfish. 'Because Rupert told me I'd make a fortune,' he said, 'and that he'd introduce me to Joanna Lumley.'

Everyone screamed with laughter except the Bishop, Declan and Hardy Bissett.

'Which Rupert hasn't done yet, what?' said Henry, delighted at the reaction.

'This is meant to be a dry run,' said Hardy icily. He turned to Wesley. 'How d'you intend to retain the cultural traditions of the ethnic minorities in your area, Mr Emerson?'

Wesley looked blank. 'Don't know, man. Declan promised me a fortune too, but he didn't say anything about Joanna Lumley.'

Billy wiped his eyes. 'This is wonderful,' he whispered to Cameron.

Like a terrier, Hardy Bissett caught Billy off guard. 'As Venturer's head of sport,' he asked sharply, 'how d'you intend to revolutionize Corinium's sporting coverage?'

'Er-hum,' said Billy helplessly. 'Making programmes is a bit like sex. I do it all the time, but I'm afraid I never talk about it. Programmes are living things, particularly sport,' he went on apologetically. 'They seem to materialize as you go along.'

'Very lucid,' said Hardy so sarcastically that Billy went crimson. He then turned to Professor Graystock. 'I wonder, Professor, if you might be able to provide us with a more serious answer to the question I asked Wesley?'

The Professor cleared his throat. 'At Venturer we would naturally give the ethnic minorities the chance to develop their own programmes in their own way,' he said in his fulsome drone. 'This will keep alive the cultures and traditions which would otherwise be neglected as the minorities become fully integrated into the population.'

'Excellent, Professor,' said Hardy. 'That's more like it, although you could have gone on to specify some of the programmes and had a crack at Corinium's abysmal record at the same time.'

He turned to Freddie. 'Have you got a definite policy towards industrial relations?'

Freddie looked somewhat apprehensively at Rupert. 'I and my Managing Director, Declan, and my Financial Director, Rupert, are all firmly committed believers in industrial democracy.'

'Are we?' said Rupert in amazement.

'Shut up,' hissed Cameron. 'Will you and Billy stop taking the piss.'

Sulkily Rupert got out the *Evening Standard* and surreptitiously started reading his Scorpio horoscope, which was all about career opportunities and staying cool in the face of provocation. Then, because he read Taggie's horoscope as automatically as his own these days, his eyes moved up three places to Cancer.

'*As there is a new moon this week,*' wrote Patric Walker, '*you are probably wondering where the next blow will fall and feel everyone is against you.*'

Oh the poor little duck, thought Rupert, suddenly overwhelmed with longing and protectiveness. She'd been so adorable the other day. He never dreamed he'd miss her so much.

'Rupert,' snapped Cameron. 'Hardy wants to know if we've got an employment policy.'

'Yes,' said Rupert coolly. 'We'll employ very good people. We'll pay them extremely well to work, and if they don't we'll tell them to fuck off.'

The Bishop and Professor Graystock exchanged pained glances. Declan's bitten fingernails drummed on the table.

'Slightly too simplistic,' said Hardy Bissett acidly. 'I hope someone else has something a little bit more illuminating to say on the subject.'

At the end of half an hour Hardy called a halt.

'That was absolutely appalling,' he said bluntly. 'Declan, you're fielding too many questions – can't say I blame you with these morons – and getting totally carried away by your own blarney. So are you, Bishop.' The Bishop turned purple. 'You're both far too long-winded. The rest are much too short. You should be answering the questions in a sentence, and then immediately using the subject to dive into another area where you want to make a point. The object is to put across Venturer's message and make your pitch whatever questions you're asked.'

'Christ,' said Billy to Rupert as the Professor nicked yet another of his cigarettes, 'it's like one of those terrible nightmares of being back at school. Who is this fink on my right who talks like a British Telecom technical manual?'

'Professor Graystock,' said Rupert. 'Declan brought him in. He's a disgrace.'

'We'll have another half-hour session,' said Hardy Bissett. 'Then we'll have a drink.' He turned to Freddie. 'Mr Jones, how did the idea for Venturer originate?'

Freddie scratched his curls.

'Well, it was like this, Rupert an' me 'ad both 'ad an up-and-downer wiv Tony Baddingham over different fings. Declan was having a rough time of it. Tony's a fug, make no bones abart it, got a board made up of professional account-ants, who use profits for anyfing other than making programmes; won't take risks; that's why their share of the ratings is dropping. Anyway, Declan 'ad a barney wiv him and walked out. Rupe and I both fink Declan's terrific; he's a real man of stature; could become the Lord Reef of ITV, so we decided to pitch for the franchise.

'We all live in the area,' he went on. 'Rupe's lived there all 'is life. Declan, Cameron and I are comparative newcomers, more like Cafflic converts, so we love it wiv a passion, and we just feel it's being shabbily represented by Corinium.'

'Well done,' said Rupert. But once again the Professor and the Bishop exchanged pained glances.

After that Harold White and Cameron were both excellent on programme plans, Georgie was brilliant on advertising, and Seb marvellously bitchy about the newsroom and 'Cotswold Round-Up'. But at the end Hardy Bissett was just as scathing.

'Look at you,' he said mockingly, 'cringing on the back of your seats trying to make yourself invisible to an examiner who might ask you the awkward question. You've got to sit forward, be eager and positive, bursting with enthusiasm.'

'Gimme a drink, then,' murmured Billy.

'But it was better than last time,' went on Hardy. 'You've got just over a month to get your act together, and if we keep going over the same ground night after night –' Billy and Rupert exchanged looks of horror; Freddie glanced at his watch – 'you're bound to improve. It's obvious our moles won't be able to make every evening. But I'm glad to say most of them, not all –' Hardy glared pointedly at Billy – 'acquitted themselves well and are obviously less in need of coaching than the rest of you. I congratulate you, Declan, on your poaching skills. Just don't get rumbled, any of you, between now and December.'

When they'd all got drinks, Declan gave them a brief progress report. 'You needn't be too disheartened by our abysmal showing today. Elsewhere things are looking good. The most dramatic bit of news is that Mid-West have pulled out. They can't raise the cash evidently, so their Geography master will probably never get to London now.' He grinned. 'This means it's a two-horse race – just us and Corinium.'

Everyone was wildly excited by this information, except Rupert. Two two the rivals now, he thought bitterly. Why did everything remind him of Taggie?

'I've also heard off the record that the IBA have had at least three thousand letters from local organizations pledging their support for Venturer,' Declan went on. 'Tony was also supposed to appear on a programme on Radio Cotchester this week, with me and the West of England man from the IBA, but he's backed off because he claims a programme interspersed with pop records is not the right vehicle for serious discussion, i.e., he's got cold feet.

'The story's been leaked to tomorrow's papers. Finally Ladbroke's make us five to four on today, so we're on our way.'

'So am I,' said Freddie, going towards the door.

Rupert followed him. 'Where are you going?'

'To a meetin',' said Freddie, looking shifty.

'With Mrs Vereker?' said Rupert. 'For Christ's sake be careful. Sarah Stratton rolled up at my house in hysterics the other day, saying James had been told to back off and concentrate on Lizzie, as they're going to make this marriage series together.'

'I know,' said Freddie. 'Makes fings very difficult. That's why Lizzie and me's meeting up here.'

'It's a bloody good story,' said Rupert. 'Corinium presenter ordered to give up his presenter mistress and concentrate on his wife in order to win franchise. The *Scorpion* would adore it.'

'No!' said Freddie, appalled. 'It'd hurt Lizzie, and hurt her kids to have their father's name plastered all over the papers.'

'Frederick, dear,' said Rupert patiently, 'it's a good story, I said. It'll discredit Corinium and make a complete mockery of the marriage programme if everyone knows it's a sham. D'you want to win this franchise or not?'

Freddie shook his head stubbornly. 'Not if it 'urts Lizzie. Anyway, you're barking up the wrong tree, mate. Fact that

Tony's told James to drop his mistress and concentrate on making his marriage work will only score Brownie points with the IBA. Besides, if the papers start sniffin' round James, they might easily cotton on to Lizzie and me.'

Rupert sighed. 'If Declan and I can behave ourselves, I can't think why you can't.'

As soon as Freddie had gone, the Bishop and the Professor, who was clutching a huge whisky in one hand and a vast plate of smoked salmon sandwiches in the other, closed in on Rupert.

'Could we have a word?' said the Bishop.

'We're a bit concerned about Freddie Jones,' said the Professor with his mouth full.

'Charming chap, of course,' said the Bishop smoothly. 'Definitely one of nature's gentlemen, but a little bit of a rough diamond.'

'Rough diamonds are a consortium's best friend,' said Rupert lightly, but there was a deterrent steeliness about his eyes.

'Ha, ha,' said the Bishop heartily. 'However, as I was saying, Crispin Graystock knows several members of the IBA who we'll be meeting on the 29th. I myself am not unfamiliar with quite a few of them either. Mrs Menzies-Scott is an old friend, and of course I've exchanged views with the Prebendary. We just feel that Freddie Jones is not quite the right vehicle to put Venturer's message across.'

'What d'you mean, vehicle?' snapped Rupert. 'Freddie's not a van!'

'Well, someone who talks about Lord Reef and Cafflic converts and refers to Tony Baddingham as "a fug" –' delicately the Professor mimicked Freddie's accent – 'and extols the joys of "miking vast sums of money", will hardly go down very well with the IBA.'

'To be frank,' said the Bishop, 'poor Freddie can hardly string a sentence together.'

'Freddie is a star,' said Rupert furiously. 'He's far the most genuine person Venturer's got. He runs one of the most successful companies in the country and he's got the common touch.'

'A very common touch,' said the Professor, stuffing two more sandwiches into his face and gargling them down with a huge slug of whisky.

'All we're suggesting,' said the Bishop soothingly, 'is that Freddie Jones may be very much at home on the shop floor, with businessmen, even with the press, but not with the clergymen, academics, ladies of the Women's Institute and senior statesmen he's going to encounter on the 29th.'

'We feel very strongly that he should stick to technical specifications, take more of a back seat and perhaps take a few elocution lessons,' added the Professor.

'I know an ex-actor who lives in Will-is-den,' said the Bishop, taking Rupert's stunned silence as assent, 'who's worked absolute miracles with somewhat – er – provincial young curates, who have difficulty taking services and giving sermons.'

'I've never heard such a bloody awful idea in my life,' exploded Rupert. 'D'you want to castrate Freddie, to take away all his spontaneity and bounce? And coming from two jumped-up ex-grammar school boys who talk about "Will-is-den", and "substarntial involevement" makes it all the more laughable. Do you want Freddie to talk like a fucking toastmaster?'

'I beg your pardon?' thundered the Bishop, turning puce.

'And for someone who calls himself a Christian and another a practising socialist, you're both a bloody disgrace,' added Rupert.

'I hope you'll withdraw that remark,' spluttered the Professor, showering Rupert with whisky-soaked crumbs.

'Sausage rolls, anyone?' said Cameron, coming over and shoving a plate between them. 'What on earth's the matter?'

'The Bishop and the Professor have just pointed out that Freddie is a social embarrassment to Venturer and should take some elocution lessons,' said Rupert furiously and stalked out of the room.

It took all Cameron's and, later, Declan's tact to calm the

Bishop and the Professor down. Both threatened to resign, demanded Rupert's resignation or at least most humble apologies, and were only placated by a large and very expensive dinner at the Gay Hussar.

It was two-thirty in the morning before Declan got home to Penscombe, but he found Taggie still up laying out apples in an upstairs spare room. With all the bills flooding in, it might be all they had to live on soon.

'How did it go?' she asked.

'Awful, but Hardy Bissett says it's always ghastly to begin with. He'll knock them into shape. Billy Lloyd-Foxe turned up.'

'Is he nice?' said Taggie.

'Enchanting,' said Declan. 'Exactly the right kind of person to calm everyone down. With the last fence in sight, they're all getting incredibly twitchy.'

Then he told Taggie about Rupert's row with the Bishop and the Professor.

'Rupert was right. Poor Freddie,' said Taggie indignantly.

'He was not,' said Declan. 'Winding up other members of the consortium at this stage is insane. Keeping the Bishop sweet is absolutely crucial. Rupert was flip and obstructive the whole way through the meeting. I don't know what's got into him, or how poor Cameron puts up with him.'

It was poor Cameron now, reflected Taggie grimly.

'She was fantastic at the meeting,' Declan went on, with unexpected warmth. 'The more I see of her, the better I think she is. In fact all the moles distinguished themselves, even Sally Maples, once she got over her nerves. And Charles keeps everyone's spirits up. And Billy, as I said, just has an enchanting personality, which is bound to endear us to the IBA. I hate to sound over-confident –' he reached over and touched the skirting board – 'but if we don't do anything bloddy silly between now and December, our chances of getting the franchise must be focking good.'

44

In the first week in November Tony Baddingham called a press conference. He looked on top of the world, the scarlet poppy in his buttonhole adding just the right note of concerned sobriety to offset the hedonistic effect of a splendid Los Angeles suntan.

He had been in LA, he told the waiting army of reporters and cameramen, to sign up a brilliant new woman programme controller who would start in the new year.

'Assuming you win the franchise?' asked ITN.

'There's no doubt about that,' said Tony smugly.

'Is she better than Cameron Cook?'

'I have no doubt about that either,' said Tony even more smugly.

He went on to say that Corinium had set aside sixteen million pounds next year for new programmes and pledged to have 'an even fresher and more responsible approach to covering the region'.

'The old fox is up to something,' muttered the *Mail on Sunday*. 'He didn't get us here just for this crap.'

'What about advertising?' asked the *Observer*.

'Revenue may be down,' Tony replied smoothly, 'but so is the advertising revenue of all the ITV companies.'

It had been a bad summer for advertising, he explained, because the weather had been so good, but this had boosted

Corinium's leisure interests, so shareholders could expect excellent mid-term results in December.

'Why weren't you prepared to face Declan O'Hara on Radio Cotchester?' asked the *Scorpion*.

'Because Corinium prefer to rest on their laurels and not indulge in vulgar abuse and –' Tony lowered his voice, so the journalists had to crane forward to catch what he was saying – 'Declan O'Hara might not have been quite so happy to face me had he been aware that I know everything he's been up to.'

'Here it comes,' said ITN, as Tony very slowly got out a cigar and made a great play of cutting off the end before lighting it.

'Declan O'Hara,' he went on slowly, 'has been poaching my staff. This summer he enticed Cameron Cook away, but as early as May he had signed up my sales director, Georgie Baines, my religious editor, Charles Fairburn, and my finest news reporter, Sebastian Burrows. I'd like also to warn the BBC, London Weekend, and Yorkshire Television, that Billy Lloyd-Foxe, Harold White and Sally Maples –' Tony enunciated the names particularly carefully so all the journalists could get them down – 'are also signed up and poised to move to Venturer in the most unlikely event of them winning the franchise.'

There was a stunned silence.

'How the hell did you find all this out?' asked the *Mail on Sunday*, almost sent flying by the unseemly dash for the telephones.

'I wouldn't be chief executive of Corinium if I didn't know everything that was going on in my own company,' said Tony grimly, 'and I intend to keep it that way for many years to come. Unlike Venturer,' he added dismissively, 'whose security is even worse than MI5.'

For twenty-four hours Tony left the three Corinium moles to sweat, and the whole Corinium building in a turmoil of rumour and speculation. James Vereker, for one, was absolutely furious on initially hearing the news. How dare Declan

591

ignore him and sign up Charles, who was nothing but a fat drunken fag, or Seb, who was infinitely junior to James in the newsroom, or Georgie, of whose longer eyelashes James was inordinately jealous? Then James's fury turned to pleasure, as he realized that all three moles would be for the high jump. He even gave several interviews to the nationals, saying he was utterly disgusted by their disloyal, uncaring behaviour, and that he felt huge sympathy for Tony Baddingham in his hour of desertion.

James was therefore not the only member of Corinium's staff hanging round the newsroom waiting for fireworks the following morning, after word whistled round the building that Tony had sent for Georgie Baines. Seb was demented with worry, thinking of the loan he'd wheedled out of his bank manager for a new Ferrari. Charles could only take another gulp of claret and think greyly of his five-figure overdraft and the mortgage he'd just taken out on a tumble-down cottage near Penscombe.

Half an hour later Georgie Baines staggered into the news-room making agonized faces and clutching his bottom as though he'd just been given twelve of the best. Then, very slowly, he drew the latest Corinium Company Report out of the seat of his trousers, then roared and roared with laughter.

'Tony gave me an absolute bollocking,' he told his amazed audience, 'said if I have any more dealings with Venturer, he'll sue me for breach of contract, but it's made him realize how much I'm worth to Corinium. So he's doubled my salary, and made me Deputy Managing Director – so you better all behave yourselves, my darlings.'

'Oh, how sweet,' said Daysee Butler, bursting into tears.

'You're not joining Venturer then?' asked Seb.

'Not for the moment,' said Georgie. Then, rubbing his hands, 'And now that I'm deputy MD I'm going to start getting heavy. Off with his head!' he yelled, pointing at a very discomforted James Vereker. 'And don't you go giving any more interviews to the press about me and disloyalty, you little twerp.'

Muttering about being seriously misquoted, James bolted

out of the newsroom, whereupon everyone cheered and started opening bottles to celebrate.

Seb was summoned ten minutes later and received more or less the same treatment.

'Tony's sending me to the New York office for six months to get me out of the way,' he said. 'Then, if I behave myself, I can come back. I suppose it's better than the sack.'

'Much, much,' said Charles Fairburn, draining his bottle of red. Feeling vastly relieved that he wasn't going to be out on his ear, Charles too obeyed a summons from above.

'*Mea culpa*,' he said in mock seriousness, winking at Miss Madden as he sauntered into Tony's office.

Five minutes later he was back in the newsroom, trembling like a great white blancmange. Everyone stopped their revelling.

'Whatever's the matter?' said Georgie, who'd been tangoing in and out of the desks with Daysee Butler.

'I've been sacked,' whispered Charles. 'On the spot, and he's not giving me any redundancy money because I was warned three times.'

Over at the BBC, at London Weekend and Yorkshire Television, Billy Lloyd-Foxe, Harold White and Sally Maples, all ashen and trembling and mindful of their overdrafts and their dependants, denied any involvement with Venturer and were all suspended from programme-making pending further investigation, and warned that the most tenuous contact with Venturer would mean the sack.

The story was front page in every paper for several days. Declan and Rupert, as the best-known members of Venturer, were blamed for enticement, which no one minded about very much, and lousy security, which, however, reflected very badly on their management skills. Worst of all, Venturer was now left without a sales director, a programme controller, a children's editor, a sports editor, and a head of news, until Seb, enraged by the cavalier sacking of Charles Fairburn, told Tony to stuff his New York job and resigned as well. This was all very high-minded of Seb, but now meant that

593

Venturer's fast diminishing kitty was faced with paying both his and Charles's salaries. Seb would have no difficulty finding another job, but, at fifty-one and a notorious piss artist, Charles was far more of a problem.

Venturer, meanwhile, had been thrown into complete pandemonium. On the afternoon of Tony's putsch, Rupert, Freddie and Declan met up at The Priory.

'There must be a countermole, or how could Tony have found out all these things?' said Declan. Freddie, however, was scrabbling under Declan's desk. Then he took Declan's telephone apart.

'Bugged,' he said bleakly. 'I'll get my men in at once to sweep the room and check all the phones. It's possible the 'ole place is bugged. They'd better do your phones as well, Rupe.'

Declan was appalled. 'Christ knows how much Tony has found out, then.'

'If he smashes Venturer, he finks he'll get Cameron back,' said Freddie. 'I said we was dealing with a villain. He's out to bury us.'

'But how the hell did his men get in here to bug the telephone?' said Rupert. 'The dogs would frighten anyone away, and there's always someone in the house.'

As Taggie was out doing a dinner party in Cheltenham, Declan sent for Maud. 'Has anyone called to check the telephones lately?' he asked.

'Yes,' said Maud, 'someone from British Telecom came last Friday; such a delightful young man. He said his mother's favourite opera was *The Merry Widow*. He heard me rehearsing and made me sing the Vilja song over and over again.'

'What was he doing here?' asked Declan wearily.

'His department had been notified that we'd been overcharged, so he was checking all the telephones to see if they were using up too many units,' said Maud beaming. 'He said they might be able to give us a rebate. I quite forgot to tell you.'

Declan put his head in his hands.

'How long was he here?' he groaned.

'About three hours,' said Maud.

Rupert and Freddie exchanged glances of horror. If it hadn't been so terrible, it would have been funny.

'That was your bugger,' said Rupert.

'D'you mean to say all that time he was bugging our house?' said Maud indignantly. 'And I gave him three cups of tea with sugar and a Penguin.'

'I'm sorry,' sighed Declan after she'd gone, 'I'm not making excuses for her, but I don't think it's quite as simple as that. Tony knew about *all* the moles, but I've never rung Billy on this telephone. Rupert's always been the one to get in touch with him. And because I was ultra-conscious of security, I've always made a point of directly contacting all the moles from a callbox outside Penscombe, so the calls couldn't be traced back. Anyway, if the telephone was only bugged last Friday, I rang everyone about the dry run before that. I've got a horrible feeling someone tipped Tony off.'

'All right,' said Freddie, sitting down heavily on a lot of tapes, 'let's go through the list of possibilities. Taggie was working at Sarah Stratton's a fortnight ago and the Baddinghams and the Verekers were both there.'

'Don't be bloody silly,' snapped Rupert, who was pacing up and down the room. 'Of course it's not Taggie. She's entirely responsible for all those letters being sent to the IBA and what the fucking hell's she got to gain by leaking secrets to Tony?'

Freddie raised his eyebrows. 'No need to overreact. She could have just let somefink slip to Sarah over the dishes.'

'And how d'you know the Verekers and the Baddinghams were at the Strattons the other night?' said Rupert, still furious. 'I suppose Lizzie told you. Lizzie's much more likely to have told Tony.'

'Lizzie's nothing to do with us,' said Declan irritably. 'Do keep to the point, Rupert.'

'Lizzie's something to do with Freddie,' persisted Rupert. 'You could easily have talked in your sleep.'

Freddie turned dark red. 'There's nuffink going on there.'

'Hum,' said Rupert.

Declan looked disapproving. 'Is there?' he said icily.

Freddie shuffled his feet. 'I'm very fond of Lizzie. I haven't told her anyfing.'

Declan then admitted that Maud had told him Caitlin had been out once with Archie Baddingham, but they were just a couple of kids, and he was quite certain Caitlin knew nothing of importance. Anyway she was back at school now.

'Caitlin knows everything,' said Rupert. 'She doesn't miss a trick, and she might easily have seen Sally Maples or Harold.'

'They've never been to the house,' said Declan. 'I suppose one of the moles could have turned countermole.'

'More than their life's wurf,' said Freddie, shaking his head. 'If they shopped us, they automatically shop themselves. Georgie is the only one it might have been, and he was far too upset when Tony broke the news yesterday. I expect Tony's got the thumbscrew on him now, getting the rest of Venturer's secrets out of him.'

'What about Maud?' said Rupert. 'She's always hanging around with Monica.'

'When did my wife ever take the slightest interest in the franchise? She doesn't know a thing,' said Declan bitterly.

'Valerie's got a soft spot for James Vereker,' suggested Rupert.

Freddie sighed. 'Valerie's like Maud, simply not interested.'

'Much as I'd like to suspect the Bishop and Professor Graystock,' said Rupert, 'they're far too motivated by greed and self-interest to shop us, and the same goes for Marti.'

'Not if Tony made it worth their while,' said Declan. 'I wouldn't rule them out.'

'Well, Basil's in the clear,' went on Rupert, 'and I honestly think Wesley and Henry are too thick, or in Wesley's case too spaced out to remember anyone's names anyway. But I suppose they're possibilities.'

'Everyone's a possibility,' said Declan bleakly, 'and finally there's Cameron. She's my choice. I've had my doubts about her all along.'

'Balls,' said Rupert irritably. 'She's far too obsessed with us winning the franchise and, since she came back from Ireland, with making movies with you.'

'And frankly,' said Freddie, 'she's far too smitten by our Rupe.'

When Declan said nothing, Rupert protested: 'Cameron's got a lot of faults, but she's basically honest. That's why she so loathed carrying on with Tony and Corinium while she was sleeping with me.'

'I've always suspected she was treacherous,' said Declan. 'How do we know she hasn't been spying for Tony from the very beginning?'

'Don't let's get Le Carré-ed away,' said Rupert. 'We'll just have to keep an eye on her.'

'We'll have to keep an eye on everyone,' said Declan grimly.

In an atmosphere of sniping and growing suspicion, Venturer carried on preparations for the IBA interview. There were secret communications with Georgie, Billy, Harold and Sally, arranging that they would join Venturer if and when the franchise was won – it no longer seemed a certainty – but there was no way they could be present at the IBA meeting on 29th November. Night after night without them, therefore, Hardy Bissett fired endless questions at the rest of the consortium, until they were word perfect, and answered almost without thinking. Then he accused them of being too glib.

One evening Charles Fairburn, desperately trying to hide his anxiety about being fired, turned up dressed as Lady Gosling in a grey wig, half-moon spectacles, and hundreds of shawls, and proceeded to lay everyone in the aisles by answering questions in a high soprano until Hardy sharply slapped him down.

But the questions rolled on: 'How d'you hope to promote interest in scientific matters in your schedule? What is your attitude to training schemes? How will you ensure equal opportunity for women in your company?'

'By screwing every one of them,' answered Rupert.

'Don't be bloody flip,' yelled Hardy. 'You can be funny, but never flip, and, with a female chairman, never never be funny about women.'

Rupert was bored and fed up. Why the fuck couldn't they tell the truth, that they just wanted to make good programmes and a lot of money, and dispense with all this flannel? He was relieved when Cameron and Declan set off to Ireland for a final week's shooting. He needed some space and time to think. He spent most of the week they were away in London on political work and keeping the rattled Venturer backers happy. Outside his office the last of the plane leaves were drifting down, reminding him unbearably of Taggie. He still had the thirty leaves she and the children had given him. They hadn't brought him much bloody happiness. He steeled himself not to ring her up, or drop round. He was truly terrified how much he wanted to.

45

When Rupert didn't take advantage of Cameron's week away to ring her, Taggie wanted only to retreat into her turret room in utter despair. But, alas, Monica had asked her to do the food for the first night party for *The Merry Widow* next Saturday, and when she wasn't cooking and freezing in both senses of the word (now the cold weather had set in, The Priory was absolutely arctic) Taggie was calming down or boosting the morale of an increasingly demanding and nervous Maud. Corinium were showing highlights of the first night and Maud was counting on Declan getting back from Ireland in time. She couldn't face such an ordeal alone.

In addition the press were on the prowl for a story. Both Venturer and Corinium consortiums were turning out in force and dinner jackets for the first night. The newly sacked Charles Fairburn was playing Monica's lover, Declan's exquisite wife was making her stage comeback, and her leading man was the handsome Bas who was on opposing sides to his loathed brother Tony. With Declan due back from Ireland, with Rupert Campbell-Black's live-in lover, who was also Tony's ex, it was clear that there were endless possibilities for fireworks. 'Cotchester', wrote Nigel Dempster slyly, 'are celebrating Guy Fawkes Day ten days late this year'.

The Merry Widow dress rehearsal on Friday afternoon was disastrous. The presence of the television crew on a dry run threw the entire cast. Tempers flared, lights dimmed too early, lines were fluffed or forgotten. The television director decided to put two cameras in the dress circle and in the two boxes on either side of the stage, so they wouldn't have to take out any stall seats. The technicians stood around yawning, one sound man even fell asleep and snored loudly throughout the second act. James Vereker (Cotchester's dusty answer to Humphrey Burton, according to Charles Fairburn) would be presenting the programme.

'Just as well we bombed early,' said Barton Sinclair, *The Merry Widow*'s director, but he seemed far from happy.

Over in County Galway Cameron and Declan were at the end of their last day's filming. Declan, in a dark-blue fisherman's jersey and jeans, his thick black hair lifting in the gentle west wind, was speaking to camera.

'*Hallow this spot,*' he began softly. '*Here once stood the proud white Georgian house which belonged to Lady Gregory. Here for the last thirty years of his life, Yeats spent every summer and most of his winters. That's a long time to put up with not the easiest of house guests —*' Declan smiled briefly — '*even bearing in mind the number of servants large houses employed in those days. Here in this tranquil, ordered household, Yeats's genius was able to blossom on and on like a rose right into the winter of his days. "I doubt," said Yeats, "if I'd have done much with my life, but for Lady Gregory's firmness and care."*'

'Cut!' shouted Cameron. 'That was excellent. We'll now do close-ups of the copper beech on which he carved his initials, and then straight down to the lake for the last shot. We'd better hurry. The sun'll set in three-quarters of an hour.'

Twenty minutes later Declan was standing on the shore of the lake with a huge blood-red sun sinking gradually behind the coloured trees and casting a warm glow on his face.

'*While Yeats stayed at Coole Park,*' said Declan, bending down and picking up a pebble and sending it spinning across the still water, '*he wrote his poetry in a room looking towards this lake, a time lovingly remembered in his poem "The Wild Swans at Coole".*' He began to quote softly:

The trees are in their autumn beauty,
The woodland paths are dry,
Under the October twilight the water
Mirrors a still sky . . .

Oh, that husky, heartbreakingly sexy voice, thought Cameron, feeling the hairs lifting yet again on the back of her neck. She could go to the stake for Declan at times like this. They'd been so lucky with the weather too. Enough leaves still hung from the trees to pretend it was October, but one hard frost would have stripped them in a day.

The crew, going out to get plastered at an end-of-shoot party, tried to persuade Declan and Cameron to join them, but because they were both tired and faced a late night at *The Merry Widow* tomorrow, they opted for a quiet dinner at the hotel. Afterwards they sat alone in the bar. Apple logs cracked merrily in the grate, giving off a sweet cider smell. Occasionally the flames flared, lighting up Declan's face, as he sat immersed in the *Galway Post*, his whisky hardly touched.

Cameron was happy to watch him, memorizing every tiny black bristle of stubble, every deeply trenched line on the battered, craggy Western hero face. Without seeing the rushes, she knew they had made a great programme. Schemes were afoot for other programmes, but this first would always be the most exciting. Exploring and luxuriating in each other's talent, she had learnt so much from him already. Despite the fact that all the crew were at times victims of his almost feudal caprice, he certainly inspired devotion. He allowed no insubordination. Only that morning he'd roared at the sound man for giving the hung-over PA a Bloody Mary for breakfast. He was irascible, with an extremely short fuse, and got so wrapped up in the work that he frequently upset people, but he was so mortified afterwards and so ready to apologize, that they always forgave him, not least because he had more charm than anyone Cameron had ever met.

Tomorrow, she thought, putting another log on the fire,

she'd return to Rupert and reality, or was it unreality, with both of them following their separate careers in that huge house with nothing in common except the franchise, only coming together literally for sex in that huge pink and yellow silk-curtained four-poster.

She wanted to marry Rupert more than anything in the world, to tame and hold such a beautiful man, and have access to all that wealth and privilege. Rupert was her fix, but she was frightened how increasingly she was drawn to Declan. Together they could make an amazing team. He would understand her far better than Rupert, and she would look after him, and sort out his money problems far more efficiently than that parasitic, feckless, hopeless Maud. And what would happen to her and Rupert if they lost the franchise?

Declan looked up and smiled: 'I'm neglecting you. How's your drink?'

The barman had wandered off to talk to Mrs Rafferty about some cows, or it might be cars (Cameron had difficulty with the Irish pronunciation), and had left the whisky bottle and a jug of water on the table for them.

Cameron was even learning to like whisky without ice; she'd be saying dustbin and petrol soon.

As Declan filled her glass she said, 'This time in a month, we'll know if we've won. I was just wondering if there was life after franchise for me and Rupert.'

The dark brooding eyes bored into her. 'I'd like to think there was. I've grown very fond of you both.'

'Honest?' stammered Cameron.

'Honest. Under all that bitching and stridency, you're as soft as thistledown. The only problem is that you may be too good at your job for Rupert. He needs a wife to come home to, not one to come home with.'

'A little stately home maker,' said Cameron bitterly.

'Partly. He must be the dominant Tom. You'd compete with him, and I'm not sure he could handle you becoming a big star.'

Then, suddenly, out of the blue, never having mentioned

602

it before, he asked: 'Why were you so focking awful to Patrick?'

Cameron gasped. 'I guess I liked him too much. I was scared. He was so attractive, so élitist, so certain, yet so magnificently unprepared for the knocks that life was bound one day to give him. And Tony was pathological about any competition. All I cared about then was getting to the top, so I could have the space and freedom I needed. There was no way a penniless student could be part of my future goals. I didn't figure he had sufficient weight.'

'Patrick has more weight than anyone,' said Declan, 'and he's more together. I wish you'd read that play.'

'And I knew how violently you disapproved of me and Patrick,' said Cameron slyly.

'Indeed I did,' Declan grinned. 'But I know you better now. He'd suit you better than Rupert. And he wouldn't mess you about.'

But it's you I want, thought Cameron, resisting a terrible urge to reach out and touch Declan's hand, and then drag him up the black polished winding stairs to her hard narrow bed.

Wondering if she was crazy to jeopardize what had certainly been their most intimate conversation yet, she said: 'Maud messes *you* about enough.'

'Maud,' said Declan, topping up his glass, 'is a dramaholic. That's why she devours novels, soap operas and newspapers like a junkie. Occasionally her heroine-addiction spreads to real life, and she has to live out one of these romantic plots. It never lasts very long.'

'Has she got something going at the moment?'

Declan looked out of the window at the moon, peering through the bars of an elder tree like a prisoner. Then he drained half his whisky in one gulp.

'Yes,' he said harshly, 'Bas.'

'Doesn't it crucify you?'

Declan shrugged. 'Adultery isn't the only kind of infidelity. I'm unfaithful to her each time I get locked into work. I can't help myself any more than she can. And if you marry someone like Maud you accept the conditions that beautiful people are the blood royal of humanity and not governed by the same rules as ordinary mortals.'

'She's not that beautiful,' protested Cameron, glancing at her own extremely satisfactory reflection in the mirror above the fireplace.

'She is to me,' said Declan simply.

Cameron wanted to shake him. 'How can you be sure one of these men won't come along one day and walk off with her altogether?'

'She doesn't go after other men for sex,' said Declan arrogantly. 'She knows she'll never better what she has with me. She does it for excitement, flattery and the relief from the loneliness anyone who lives with a writer has to endure.'

Cameron got up to examine a horse brass, pulling her big black leather belt forward with her thumbs so he could appreciate the slenderness of her waist.

'Have you ever cheated on her?' she muttered into the flames.

'No.'

'Have you ever wanted to?' she whispered to his reflection in the mirror.

'Yes,' said Declan simply. 'All this week.'

Cameron stayed motionless by the fire until the heat from the flames became too strong. 'Then it wasn't just me?'

'It's going on location,' said Declan flatly. 'When you create something you both know is special, it seems natural to have some kind of consummation.'

'One devoutly to be wished,' said Cameron fiercely.

'And ludicrously prevalent in television,' said Declan. 'It happens on shoots all the time.'

'Not like this,' pleaded Cameron. Turning, she went up to him. Idly he reached out and fingered the huge low-slung silver buckle of her belt.

'It'd complicate things,' he said roughly. 'At a time we don't need complications. Maud would disintegrate; I can't afford to fall out with Rupert. I can't afford anything at the moment.'

'Don't joke. It's too important,' hissed Cameron, moving her legs between his, pressing her groin forward against the palm of his hand. She felt Declan tremble.

'We'd be so good together, let's go upstairs now,' she urged. They both jumped as the barman returned.

'Not much wind tonight,' he said blithely, 'but what there is is blowing terrible hard.'

'You look frozen,' said Declan. 'Sit down and have a drink.'

Fuck fuck fuck, or rather no fuck, Cameron screamed inwardly, as the barman collected a glass and sat down between them.

'You'll be being a bit of a writer, Declan,' he said. 'Did ye know there's another of your kind living not ten minutes from here? Anglo-Irish, name's MacBride.'

Declan froze, like a dog hearing a rabbit in the undergrowth. 'Dermot MacBride, he lives here?'

'Came in the other night. Said he'd just finished a play, but he didn't think anyone'd be interested. Thought they'd all forgotten him.'

'Him!' said Declan incredulously. 'Do you forget Ibsen or Miller? Have you got his address?'

'I've his number,' said the barman. 'He wanted some manure for his garden.'

'Name's familiar,' said Cameron.

'The angriest of all the angry young men,' said Declan, 'and easily the most unpleasant, and the most talented. He made a bomb from his first play, then the second was so venomous and obscene no one would touch it. He took umbrage and vowed never to write another word. Christ, it's like a new novel from Salinger. Give me the number,' he said to the barman, 'I'm going to ring him.'

'But it's half past eleven,' protested Cameron.

Declan was back, ecstatic, ten minutes later. 'He'd gone to Dublin. I rang him there. I'm going to see him at eleven tomorrow morning.'

'Cutting it a bit fine,' said Cameron. 'The flight's at one. Maud,' she added bitterly, 'would totally disintegrate if you missed it.'

605

'I'll see him alone,' said Declan. 'He's not keen on women. I'll keep a taxi waiting and meet you at the airport.'

He put his hand on her head, briefly stroking her hair: 'We'd better go to bed, we've got an early start in the morning.'

As Saturday wore on, Maud was increasingly in need of Declan. To fill in time, she went to the hairdressers, and even had a manicure, but her hand shook so much the manicurist had trouble getting the polish on. She also bought good luck cards for the rest of the cast, and some champagne in case by some miracle anyone came backstage to see her afterwards.

Arriving at the theatre, she gave a gasp of terror at the huge lights on metal stands trained on the main entrance, ready to film the arriving celebrities, and huge cables running from these and from the cameras inside the theatre to a variety of OB vans. She felt even sicker at the sight of a make-up caravan, a mobile dressing-room for James, and a double-decker catering bus for the technicians.

Even though the town hall was less than 300 yards from the Corinium Television building, union rules required all these facilities.

Going into her dressing-room, Maud gasped again, but this time with delight, because she'd never seen so many flowers – from the family, and Rupert and Cameron, and the Vere-kers, and the Joneses and the Baddinghams, and so many of her friends in London. There were also scores of good luck cards, and a telex from darling Patrick in Brisbane. But so much good will made her feel even more nervous. What happened if she let them all down?

She looked at her watch: five o'clock. She needed twenty minutes alone with the script to absorb the notes Barton had given her yesterday. Then her make-up would take an hour, by which time Declan would be here, and he could do up her dress and her jewellery and they could have a quiet hour together. But, as she tried to concentrate on the script, she was interrupted by the arrival of more and more flowers, and by Monica popping in to see if she were all right, and by Bas who'd brought her a fluffy stuffed black cat which miaowed good luck when you pressed it. Maud was enchanted.

'And we've got time to rehearse "Love Unspoken" just once more,' she said.

'Let's rehearse it lying down,' said Bas, who'd just come back from hunting and was feeling randy.

'Not before a performance,' said Maud, shocked. 'I couldn't possibly concentrate.'

'Well I'm not risking you going down on me with chattering teeth,' said Bas. 'So I'd better buzz off back to the Bar Sinister and pay the wages. We're doing a roaring pre-theatre trade.'

As Taggie carried great saucepans of chicken Marengo in through the stage door, she could see people gathering in the foyer hoping for returns. The advance publicity and the possibility of the audience appearing on television had made it a total sell-out.

As she fell over cables and bits of scenery, she could hear, behind every dressing-room door, the cast warming up like the record department at Harrods. She felt simply terrified for her mother. Once she'd unloaded the stuff, there wasn't much to do. The puddings were cold. The salads only needed dressing and she had just to put the chicken, the mashed potato and the garlic bread in the oven to heat up.

If the ovens were turned on low during the interval, everything would be ready, in case anyone was frightfully hungry, by the final curtain. Thank goodness Monica had provided plenty of people to help serve and wash up. As she came in with the last chocolate meringue cake, the telephone was ringing by the stage door.

'Maud O'Hara,' shouted the doorman.

'My mother,' said Taggie. 'Shall I take it and see if it's urgent?'

It was.

'Maud,' said the all-too-familiar, seductive rasp.

'No, it's Taggie.'

'Your fucking father's missed the plane.'

607

'Oh, my God, are you sure?'

''Course I bloody am, I was on it,' snapped Cameron. 'The next one doesn't land until nine forty-five. I've arranged for a car to pick him up and bring him straight to the theatre.'

'But M-Mummy'll die. She's been going through our leaking roof with nerves all week.'

'Tranq' her till we get there,' said Cameron. 'I've got to change, and then Rupert and I'll be over.'

With a sinking heart, Taggie knocked on Maud's door.

'Declan,' said a low excited voice.

Maud, wearing only a sliding emerald-green towel now, sat at the brilliantly lit mirror, different eyeshadows littering the shelf in front of her, as though a paintbox had been upended. She had just spent forty minutes on her eyes. Huge, gold-green, hypnotic, impossibly seductive, like two separate works of art, they seemed almost too dominant for the heart-shaped, delicately flushed face.

'You look beautiful,' said Taggie nervously. 'And what wonderful flowers.'

'Where's Daddy?' demanded Maud. 'He should have been here five minutes ago. Is he parking the car?'

Taggie took a deep breath, and was almost asphyxiated by the heady smell of fuchsias and jasmine. 'I'm sorry, he missed the plane,' she said. Then, as Maud opened her mouth to scream, 'But he'll be here for the end of the last act and the party. He didn't mean to.'

Going into hysterical sobs, Maud put her hands up to her eyes and deliberately smeared the make-up all over her face, neck and shoulders. Taggie winced. It was like seeing the Mona Lisa slashed with a razor.

'I don't believe it,' sobbed Maud. 'He can't do this to me. The one night I need him. He did it on purpose because he was jealous. He doesn't like me having the limelight.' Her voice rose to a screech. 'I can't go on, I can't.'

Hearing the din, Monica rushed in wearing only her petticoat with one eye made up, demanding what was the matter.

'You *must* go on,' she said in a shocked voice. 'Don't be so jolly wet and selfish. They're all coming to see you.'

'He did it on purpose,' screamed Maud, rocking backwards and forwards. 'If it had been an act of God like an engine fault or fog I could have forgiven him, or even a crash.'

'Oh don't say that,' said Taggie, turning pale.

'And you can shut up,' yelled Maud. 'You and your father are just the same, never think of anything but your bloody work.'

'That's jolly unfair,' said Monica.

There was something almost obscene about Maud's daubed screaming face and neck, and her bare shoulders and breasts as the towel slipped downwards.

Monica yanked it up round her, tucking it in, as Barton burst in. But neither Monica's rallying exhortations, nor Barton's hair-tearing, nor Charles's jokes could shift Maud. Finally they all lost their tempers and shouted at her like some operatic trio admonishing a wrong-doer, and Cameron, who'd heard a great deal too much in praise of Maud recently, was only too happy to make it a quartet when she arrived.

'For Chrissake, Maud,' she screeched, 'you can't let the cast and the audience down. Don't be so fucking unprofessional.'

'I'm not going on,' Maud screamed back. 'And why did Declan miss that plane?'

'He went to see . . .' began Cameron, then realizing she couldn't mention Dermot MacBride in front of Monica who might tell Tony, 'to see someone very important about the franchise.'

It was like a spark from the fire landing in a box of matches. Maud went berserk.

'All he thinks about is his fucking franchise,' she screamed, her face a shuddering grotesque coloured pulp of rage and misery, and, turning on her flowers, she started to tear them apart, pulling off the heads and then the petals and throwing them on the floor.

'Shouldn't we slap her face?' said Cameron longingly.

'Stop it, Maud,' said Monica angrily. 'That's wanton and destructive.'

'I don't care,' screamed Maud, ripping apart poor Taggie's yellow roses.

In despair, Taggie went out into the passage and ran slap into Rupert, who was no doubt about to add his own particularly vicious brand of invective. Behind him members of the cast and the Corinium television crew were peering curiously out of doors and round corners.

'Where is she?' said Rupert grimly.

'Oh, please. They're all shouting at her. They don't realize how frightened she is.'

Rupert paused, weighing up the options, then, like a wand fleetingly restoring her happiness, he touched Taggie's cheek with his finger: 'Go and get a large brandy, angel. I'll sort her out. Shut up the lot of you,' he yelled, as he went into the dressing-room.

'We'll have to play the understudy,' said Barton despairingly, 'even though she's fifteen stone and about to draw her pension.'

The floor was entirely carpeted with petals now.

'She won't go on,' said Cameron contemptuously.

'I'm not surprised with you lot yelling at her,' said Rupert. 'Get out, everyone.' And he slammed the door on them.

Rupert sat down on the bed and pulling Maud into his arms, gently stroking the silken shoulders, letting her cry, until gradually the sobbing and shuddering ceased.

'There,' said Rupert encouragingly. 'There's a brave girl.'

'He wanted me to go to Ireland with them and play Maud Gonne,' said Maud in a choked voice.

'I know.' Rupert went on stroking her.

'I wanted to do it so badly, but I funked it. I didn't want to fail again, particularly in front of Cameron. I'm sure she's having an affair with Declan. I kept imagining them meeting secretly after a day's shooting, and discussing how terrible I'd been.'

'You're a dick,' said Rupert gently.

'Declan fell in love with me the first time he saw me acting. I wanted him to fall in love with me all over again tonight.'

'Declan adores you. He's never looked at anyone else.'

'Then why isn't he here?' Maud's voice grew shrill again. For a second Rupert thought he'd lost her.

'He went to see Dermot MacBride.'

'*The* Dermot MacBride?'

Rupert nodded. 'He's written a new play. Declan felt if Venturer could tell the IBA we'd bought an option, it would really give us the edge.'

Maud quivered with rage. 'I loathe the franchise,' she said tonelessly.

'Declan's only obsessed with it because he sees it as the one way he'll get you out of your financial mess. You don't want to sell The Priory, do you?'

Maud shook her head violently: 'Could it come to that?'

'It almost has,' said Rupert.

There was a knock on the door.

'I don't want to see anyone,' said Maud hysterically.

Rupert wrapped the towel round her again. But it was only Taggie with an enormous brandy for Maud and an equally huge whisky for Rupert.

'Thanks, sweetheart.' He took them from her. 'Now beat it.'

Maud took such a huge gulp that she choked. Rupert didn't tell her he suspected Declan had deliberately missed the plane because his nerve had failed and he couldn't bear seeing Maud humiliated. Nor did he say that the press were howling like jackals outside and that, if she didn't go on, the publicity, with both her and Declan letting everyone down, would be devastating for Venturer.

'I'm disappointed,' he said idly. 'I heard you practising at The Priory so often. I wanted to hear it for real, and see the others make absolute tits of themselves by comparison. Look, you've had a shock, why not get back into your jersey and jeans and finish that brandy.'

There was a long, long pause.

'Better not,' said Maud shakily, putting down her glass, 'or I'll start forgetting my words. I'd do better with a drop of oil to get me through all those skylarking bits.'

Rupert said nothing, but, reaching for the huge blue tin

of cleansing cream, he took off the lid, gouged out a white blob and very slowly began to smear it over Maud's face, blurring away the ravages.

'How did you know to use that?'

'I've watched enough actresses take their make-up off in my time.'

'Most of mine's come off on you,' said Maud, suddenly contrite, as she noticed his hopelessly streaked evening shirt.

'Treat it as war paint,' said Rupert. 'Later I'll be doing battle with Tony.'

Docile as a child, Maud let him remove all the smeared make-up: 'You won't leave me?'

'I'll stay with you the entire evening, but I have to admit making up your face is beyond even my skills.'

Outside, Barton looked at his watch for the hundredth time. It was ten past seven. The press were howling for a decision. The understudy was already changed. If only he could make an announcement that the performance was starting late at least it would keep the audience happy.

'If she weren't going on,' said Cameron, 'Rupert would have come and told us.'

'He was always good at boxing difficult horses,' said Bas, who had changed into his stage clothes and was now raring to go in and comfort Maud.

As her door opened, everyone surged forward. Coming out, Rupert put a finger to his lips, then made a thumbs up sign: 'Has anyone got any eyedrops?'

'Mine are by appointment to the Queen Mother,' said Monica, diving into her dressing-room to get them. 'They jolly well make your eyes sparkle.'

46

Out in the foyer, Tony was now welcoming the Mayor and Mayoress and the Reverend Fergus Penney from the IBA, who was visiting Cotchester for the performance.

'I have to warn you there may be hold-ups,' purred Tony happily. 'Declan O'Hara, who usually misses the boat, has missed the plane this time and failed to turn up on the night of his poor wife's famous comeback. She's gone to pieces and is refusing to go on, so the understudy is waiting in the wings. I'm afraid one really can't rely on Venturer,' he added to Fergus Penney, 'but at least we can all pass the time pleasantly enough having a glass of champagne.'

Steering them through a door marked *Private*, he found his latest acquisition wearing a new black and gold dress to complement her newly streaked hair and getting stuck into the Bollinger.

'Can I introduce Lizzie Vereker,' said Tony warmly. 'I told you she and James are fronting our new series to discourage the spread of AIDS: "How to Stay Married", didn't I, Fergus?' he added to the Prebendary, who was now licking his thin lips at the sight of Lizzie's curves.

'Norman and I could give you a few tips on that,' said the Mayoress. 'We're celebrating our forty-fifth next week.'

'You must come on Lizzie's programme then,' said Tony, raising his glass. 'Cotchester's most distinguished married couple.'

I can't bear it, thought Lizzie, allowing her glass to be filled up. In this dress she felt as though she'd been gift-wrapped at Harrods. She longed to get out into the foyer and see if Freddie had arrived. Because of James's new uxoriousness and a general tightening up of security, she and Freddie had only managed to talk on the telephone this week.

Outside in the auditorium Sarah Stratton was spinning out the signing of autographs. Anything not to be trapped in the middle of the second row with Paul and thus not able to accost James as he came past. James, absolutely livid at being mistaken for the manager by some enraged theatregoer whose seats had been double-booked, was now trying to explain the extremely complicated plot of *The Merry Widow* to the viewers.

The Bishop, mingling with his flock and pressing the flesh, misconstrued Freddie's abstractedness as animosity and wondered darkly whether Rupert had passed on his remarks about Freddie being a rough diamond.

As the five-minute bell went, Tony glanced at his watch. Seven thirty-five. Bugger, they were hardly going to be late at all. At least they could rely on the understudy to be perfectly awful.

'I think we'd better find our seats,' he said.

Charles, wearing pantaloons so tight he felt he was standing inches above the ground, peered through a chink in the thick Prussian-blue velvet curtains, as he and Monica and the chorus, all in evening dress, waited in the wings to go on.

'It's absolutely packed,' he reported in a hollow voice. 'People are standing at the back and in the side aisles. The première of "The Messiah" in Dublin was such a sell-out that the men were told to leave off their swords. Pity that people weren't frisked at the door today. I bet your husband's carrying a long knife, Monica dear. No, it's no use looking reproving, he's given me the bullet, I can say what I like,' and, turning, he stuck a rather green tongue out through the curtains as Tony came in.

Taggie helped Maud pile up her hair with two *diamanté*

combs and zipped her into her slinky black ball dress. Then, leaving Rupert and Bas to do up her jewellery, she slipped into her seat. There were only two empty seats between her and Cameron, but they should have been inhabited by Rupert and Declan, so the gap seemed wider than the Atlantic. Judging by Cameron's set profile it was obvious that she was seething because Rupert wasn't beside her, particularly as a smirking Tony had just rolled up with the Mayor and was sitting directly behind them.

Cameron was seething even more that, after not seeing her for three months, Tony should catch her when she'd only had a few minutes to change and hadn't showered or washed her hair. She was wearing the smoking jacket which Taggie'd tipped dessert over last year and which didn't evoke very happy memories either. It definitely needed clean hair and very dramatic make-up to carry it off. She felt horribly butch. Dame Enid, who was conducting the orchestra in a dinner jacket, had been giving her some very hot looks, but at least she didn't look as awful as Taggie, who must have lost a stone and was wearing a dreadful brown dress that was just the wrong length and made her look completely flat-chested.

There was a gap on Taggie's left too. Where the hell was Caitlin? wondered Taggie. She'd arrived by taxi half an hour ago and, despite promising to behave, had promptly disappeared.

All round, Taggie could hear the roar and sizzle of anticipation as the lights went out and the orchestra started. The cameramen, who'd been forced into dinner jackets by Tony, took up their positions behind their cameras, the soundmen made a final check of the microphones, as Caitlin, apologizing profusely, clambered along an irritated row of people and collapsed panting by Taggie's side.

'Do up the buttons of your shirt,' said Taggie furiously. In the row behind, from the other side, having kicked the Mayoress in the varicose veins and trodden on the Prebendary's bunions, the Hon Archie, the bow of his black tie under his left ear, collapsed panting beside a bootfaced Tony.

Next moment Tony's bootfaced expression turned to one

of apoplexy: 'How dare you wear a made-up tie?' he hissed, as the Prussian-blue velvet curtains creaked back on the Pontevedrian Embassy in Paris. The Ambassador was giving a ball, and the guest of honour about to arrive was the Merry Widow.

After a rousing opening number by the chorus, it was Monica's and Charles's turn. Monica, playing the ambassador's beautiful ex-actress wife, couldn't act for toffee. But by tackling the part with the same breezy competence with which she ran charity committees or bathed labradors, she gave the rest of the cast a much-needed confidence. And Charles looked so sweet in his tight pantaloons, swearing eternal and extremely camp devotion, that it was rather like a skittish Billy Bunter getting off with the head girl.

'*My marriage is sacred to me,*' warbled Monica, to the smirks of the audience, who all knew she was married to Tony.

'*If marriage is sacred to you,*' sang back Charles, lasciviously stroking her bare arm, '*there's not very much I can do,*' to even more smirks from the audience, who nearly all knew Charles was gay. And they liked it even better when his moustache fell off and he nearly split his pantaloons bending over to pick it up.

'What a lot of gold fillings Monica's got,' whispered Caitlin to Taggie, 'and, waving that baton, Dame Enid looks as though she's playing Stickie with Gertrude. When's Mother Courage coming on?'

'Any minute,' said Taggie, who was praying.

Maud, clinging to both Bas's and Rupert's hands, stood shivering like a whippet in the wings. Although her black velvet dress was Turn-of-the-Century in fashion, Basil, for some reason, was dressed as a Regency buck. The longest legs in Gloucestershire were set off by gleaming black boots and pantaloons, the cut of his slate-blue coat would have had Beau Brummel in raptures and his sleek black hair had been coaxed forward into Byronic curls. He looked the perfect Georgette Heyer hero.

'You look gorgeous,' he whispered to Maud.

'So do you,' said Maud, whose teeth were chattering loud enough to provide the castanets in the orchestra.

'You'll be all right,' said Rupert, patting her shoulder.

And suddenly she was. There was no more need of Rupert's presence; she was really keen to get on stage. She must gather the audience into the play and say every line exactly right. She was only nervous because she was a young provincial widow, a little shy but heartbreakingly beautiful, about to be launched on Parisian society.

There was a terrific roll of drums, a tantivy of horns, and she glided into the glittering ballroom, standing deliberately under the huge chandelier so all her jewels sparked and the audience could take in the beauty of her body in the tight black dress, and her pallor which only set off her red lips and her brilliant red hair.

'*Gentlemen no more,*' sang Maud, pianissimo.

'*I've never seen the Spring going to a ball before,*' sang a swooning French aristocrat, played by the bank manager of Lloyds, Cotchester. '*You throw us into ecstasies, lovely lady.*'

And for once the words were believable. Now Maud was singing again, the exquisite voice hitting F sharp as clear as a bell.

'Shit,' murmured Caitlin. 'She's fucking good.'

'Oh, thank God,' breathed Taggie. 'It's going to be all right.'

I can't bear it, thought Cameron. She'd dismissed Maud as a sluttish, middle-aged parasite with unfashionably long hair, who dressed like a tramp, and here she was bringing the entire audience to their feet at the end of her first number.

Bas's entrance stepped up the excitement even more. He had a glorious, slightly husky voice and added just the right touch of rakish Latin glamour.

'Shit,' said Caitlin again. 'Lucky Mummy. He's *dead* attractive.'

The sexual tension between him and Maud was incredible, particularly when offset by Monica and Charles, who, stepping up the camping, got more and more like Dignity and Impudence. Having dispatched all the competition, Bas was

617

left alone on the stage with Maud at the end of the first act.

'*Music so sweet*,' he crooned softly, dancing round and round her, tempting her into his arms, '*speaks to the heart and the feet.*' And finally, triumphantly, he swept her into a waltz.

Elegant, incredibly romantic, they revolved under the chandelier until the curtain came down to a deafening roar of applause and a fusillade of bravoes.

After the first act, even though there was the Vilja song and several big numbers to come, Maud felt nothing but relief. It didn't matter that Declan hadn't turned up. She even sent Rupert back to his seat. She felt totally insulated. She'd been so petrified, and concentrated so hard on getting that first act perfect, that now she felt on automatic pilot. All trace of tears had gone. And although Charles almost stole the show when he bent down to retrieve his moustache yet again and his trousers split to reveal pink boxer shorts covered in pale-blue teddy bears, it was Maud's night. When the final curtain came down she was cheered to the rooftops, taking curtain call after curtain call, as the whole audience, even Tony, were on their feet, yelling and clapping like promenaders.

Rupert turned to Taggie. 'We did it,' he said triumphantly.

'No,' she said. 'You did it.'

'Don't cry,' said Basil, as he and Maud took their final bows.

'You were better than anyone could have dreamed,' said Barton Sinclair, pale beside the made-up actors, as he kissed Maud's hand and, to roars of applause handed her a huge bouquet of flowers that appeared through the curtains.

'I saw *The Merry Widow* in Paris,' said Valerie Jones petulantly to Professor Graystock. 'It was quite a different opera. But then it was performed by professionals.'

'I wouldn't call *Die Lustige Witwe* opera,' said the Professor, showing off that he knew the German title, 'but I did think Maud O'Hara was marvellously in voice.'

'I'd like to meet Maud O'Hara,' said the Prebendary. 'She seems an interesting person.'

'You shall in a minute,' said Tony cosily.

Maud rushed back to her dressing-room to change out of her gold last-act dress into a blue silk suit she'd bought for the occasion. After that it was bedlam, people pouring in and out, hugging, kissing and congratulating her. The champagne went in a flash. The press bombarded her with questions, but she was not to be drawn on the subject of Declan. 'My husband's in Ireland on business,' she said firmly. 'He'll be here later.'

At the party everyone kept coming up and saying how marvellous she'd been, but she still felt curiously detached, as though nothing could dent her now.

'I wonder if you'd like to have lunch one day,' said the Prebendary, his voice thickening. 'Now I'm in the autumn of my life, I enjoy the company of lovely women.' He was furious when the Bishop came up and joined them, with a plate piled high with Taggie's food.

'Evening, Fergus, you look very fit. Good to see Venturer pulling their weight this evening. Maud, my dear, you were absolutely splendid, such good tunes too, nice to see my flock enjoying it so much. Can I get you some refreshment?'

'I'd love another drink,' said Maud.

'Well, go and get her one,' said the Prebendary irritably.

'Here's a waiter coming,' said the Bishop, not budging. 'I must tell you about my recent trip to the Holy Land, Fergus.'

The Prebendary didn't want to hear about the Holy Land one bit, particularly when Maud excused herself. She was just going over to thank Rupert once again when she felt a warm hand on her back.

It was Tony. '*Even the ranks of Tuscany could scarce forbear to cheer,*' he said softly. 'Couldn't you hear me yelling like a schoolboy?'

'Was it really all right?'

'Stupendous. There wasn't a man in the audience who wasn't madly in love with you. I'm sorry your husband didn't make the grade. But then making the grade has never been one of his specialities, has it?'

'Unfortunately he takes the franchise as seriously as you,' said Maud bitterly.

'Ah,' said Tony with an evil smile. 'But the difference is, he's not going to win.'

'Maud, my dear,' said Monica, bringing forward a distinguished-looking man in a leather jacket with greying hair. 'I didn't tell you before, but this is Pascoe Rawlings.'

Maud's jaw dropped. Pascoe Rawlings was simply the most powerful theatrical agent in London.

'Were you in the audience?' said Maud.

'And in total raptures,' said Pascoe, drawing her out of the shadowy corner and under the naked light bulb hanging in the wings and examining her face carefully. 'Yes, close-up you're even better. Look, Jonathan Miller's casting *A Doll's House*. Can you have lunch with me very early next week?'

The party was, in fact, a great success. James spent the evening holding Lizzie in front of him like a riot shield to ward off the advances of Sarah Stratton, and only let her go because he wanted to be introduced to Pascoe Rawlings. The next moment Freddie had whipped Lizzie behind one of the huge cardboard pillars which had stood in the Pontevedrian ballroom.

'This is a pillar of unrespectability,' said Lizzie.

'I love you,' said Freddie desperately.

'And I love you. James is going to London tomorrow night.'

'What time will the children be asleep?'

'By nine,' said Lizzie, 'even if I have to drug them.'

'I'll be there at nine-firty,' said Freddie.

In her mother's dressing-room, on a floor of wilting petals, Caitlin lay in Archie's arms and had no need of words.

Taggie spent the evening removing plates, keeping out of Rupert's way and sticking up for her father. It was not just Tony who thought he'd behaved appallingly.

'So unsupportive,' snapped Cameron.

'He ought to have his knuckles rapped,' said Monica, 'but in a way that storm of grief seemed to enhance her performance.'

620

'I always said you can never trust the Irish,' said Valerie Jones.

'D'you think Declan's coming back tonight?' whispered Bas in Maud's ear at midnight, 'because if he isn't . . .'

Everyone stopped talking as Tony tapped his glass with a spoon.

'On behalf of Corinium Television,' he said suavely, 'I'd like to thank our Mayor and Mayoress and, of course, you, Prebendary, for being here this evening. I want to congratulate Barton and all the cast of *The Merry Widow* for a truly splendid performance, but most of all I think we should praise Maud O'Hara, who, under the most difficult circumstances –' he smiled at Maud – 'was without doubt the star of the evening.'

Exactly on cue, Declan walked in. He was deathly pale and still wearing yesterday's jeans and dark-blue jersey. But such was his presence that, as usual, he made everyone else seem like pygmies.

Charles Fairburn, who was pissed, gave a very theatrical hiss. 'Hullo, Declan dear, I'm surprised you haven't popped up through a trap door in a great puff of sulphur and brimstone.'

'Good morning, Declan,' drawled Tony, ostentatiously looking at his watch, 'you're late. Four and a half hours late to be exact. What kept you? I do hope you're not as late as this when you go to the IBA on Friday week, or there's even less chance of Venturer winning the franchise.'

Declan ignored him and walked up to Maud.

'I'm desperately sorry, darling,' he said. 'I hear you were sensational. I knew you would be.'

Indignation overcame Monica's normal good manners: 'You knew nothing of the sort, you beastly man, you ought to be hung, drawn and quartered. She was absolutely super, but no thanks to you. You wait till you see the video.'

'There was a good reason,' said Declan, not taking his eyes off Maud, 'but as I don't like some of the company you're keeping this evening, I'll tell you later. Let's go.'

'But she's the guest of honour,' said Monica furiously.

Just for a second everyone expected Maud to slap Declan's face. Instead she reached up and hugged him.

'Poor darling,' she said, 'you *must* be tired. Thank you all –' marvellously theatrically, the big star now, she turned slowly round, smiling at everyone in the room – 'for a lovely, lovely party.'

Then, taking Declan's arm, she dutifully followed him off the stage.

Caitlin, who'd just emerged from Maud's dressing-room with Archie, shook her head. 'I'll never understand that couple,' she said.

On the way out Maud and Declan passed Rupert and Cameron. 'Rupert saved me,' said Maud, ignoring Cameron, whom she had not forgiven for her abuse earlier.

'I know,' said Declan, 'Taggie told me on the way in.'

Briefly he took Rupert aside. 'Look, I'm sorry I focked everything up, but Dermot MacBride insisted I sat down and read the whole play. I didn't realize his mother was from Gloucestershire and the play's all about his childhood just outside Stroud. He's giving it to us, with an option on the next play. I'm going to fix a price with his agent tomorrow. It's a focking good play.'

'It better be,' said Rupert icily. 'You nearly paid for it with a far higher price than money.'

47

Six days later the Gatherum, which was the neigbouring hunt to the West Cotchester, held their hunt ball in Henry Hampshire's beautiful mouldering Elizabethan house. This was the last time the two consortiums would meet before their encounters with the IBA next week, and once again the whole place seemed to divide like the Dreyfus case. At one table sat Freddie and Valerie, Henry Hampshire, very much on his best behaviour as host and in the presence of his wife Hermione, Declan and Maud and Rupert and Cameron. Bas was turning up later with some ex-mistress, whose husband was conveniently in America.

Two tables away sat the Baddinghams, Ginger Johnson and his wife, Georgie Baines, with his long eyelashes cast down, and his wife, Paul and Sarah Stratton, and James and Lizzie Vereker. Although some of the women in both parties exchanged occasional banter and smiles, the men of one side studiously ignored those of the other side.

Maud appeared to be the only member of the Venturer party in tearing spirits. The two subsequent performances of *The Merry Widow* on Tuesday and Wednesday had been just as successful. She had had hundreds of letters and telephone calls of congratulation, and yesterday she had lunched with Pascoe Rawlings, who was arranging for her to audition as soon as possible for *A Doll's House*. Tonight she looked stunning with her red-gold hair piled up, and an old-gold taffeta dress which looked suspiciously new, turning her green eyes a tigerish yellow. No doubt when Bas arrived, after the success of *The Merry Widow*, the band could be prevailed upon to play a quick waltz, and Bas would sweep her on to the floor.

Cameron, who'd been editing the Yeats rushes all week, and working hard with Declan on additional programme plans to present to the IBA next Friday, looked thin and drawn. She was worried Declan seemed suddenly distant. There was none of the intimacy they'd achieved in Ireland. Tonight, obviously hating being so near Tony, he was pale and edgy. As the only member of the party in a dinner jacket rather than a red coat, his black lowering presence seemed to accentuate Venturer's gloom and tension.

Cameron was even more worried about Rupert, who had gone increasingly into his shell since she'd come back from Ireland. He also looked desperately tired. The new Socialist majority was so tiny that the Tories were determined to contest it to the full on every vote, which meant endless late night sittings. The interminable IBA rehearsals, even though both Henry and Wesley were word perfect now, were also taking their toll. Even Freddie didn't seem his usual bouncy self. Only Valerie was appallingly unchanged.

'What are you doing, Fred-Fred?' she screeched, as Freddie started crawling around under the priceless Jacobean table.

'Lookin' for bugs.'

'You're more laikely to find woodworm,' said Valerie disapprovingly. 'I can't think why Henry and Hermione don't junk all this nasty dark stuff and invest in some decent Repro. And have you seen the state of the place?' Valerie had already had a prowl round some of the bedrooms, the long gallery and the grand staircase with its heraldic leopards. 'All the plaster's peeling. There's so much damp, and you should have seen the moths flutter out when I touched the drapes in Hermione's bedroom.'

'Didn't you realize this is a moth sanctuary?' said Rupert gravely. 'You know Henry is Venturer's conservation expert.'

Valerie looked at Rupert sharply. She was never sure if he wasn't mobbing her up.

'Actually I wanted to pick your brains,' she said, lowering her voice, 'about Fred-Fred's birthday. There was an article in *The Times* yesterday saying the latest thing in the hunting field is to have a brass flask of sherry attached to your saddle.'

'Sounds hell,' said Rupert with a yawn. 'The only thing I want attached to my saddle is my bum.'

At that moment Tony paused in front of the Venturer table – surveying them with amusement.

'I see the devil has cast his net,' he said loudly.

'If the holes in his net were as big as your mouth, we'd all escape,' drawled Rupert.

Everyone at the surrounding tables howled with laughter and Tony retreated discomforted.

'And Ladbroke's has us at 2–1 on today,' Rupert yelled after him.

Valerie turned to Cameron. 'You're looking a bit washed out. I don't think black's really your colour – too deadening. Why don't you pop into the boutique and buy something naice for all the Christmas functions coming up?'

'What's the difference between a shop and a boutique?' asked Henry, who'd got bored of welcoming people.

'They sell exactly the same stuff, but a boutique is about five times as expensive,' said Rupert.

Valerie looked very boutique-faced as Rupert turned his back on both of them.

People were sitting down at their tables now and the waitresses were beginning to carry plates of smoked trout down the aisles. Looking round, Rupert noticed the place was absolutely crawling with beautiful, only-too-available women. It was just the sort of evening he once would have revelled in, getting drunk and off with half of them, behaving atrociously, not a cordoned-off four-poster untested. What the hell was the matter with him? He didn't even want to sleep with Cameron any more.

'Where's Taggie?' asked Valerie, picking up her fork. 'No, leave your bread roll, Fred-Fred.'

'Dog-sitting,' said Maud, holding up her glass for more Muscadet. 'I don't know what's got into her at the moment, she's so lethargic. I tried to persuade her to come this evening, but she wouldn't. She hadn't got a partner. When I was her age I had hordes of boys chasing after me.'

'When all this franchise business is sorted out, we must all put our heads together and find her a decent guy,' said Cameron.

'Don't be fucking silly,' snapped Rupert. 'You can't find people for other people. Taggie's perfectly capable of finding someone herself.' He put his fork down, his trout hardly touched, and, refusing wine, asked the waiter to bring him a bottle of whisky.

Across at the Corinium table, Sarah Stratton plonked herself down beside James.

'You shouldn't be here,' he hissed, giving her the sort of look delphinium growers reserve for slugs. 'The High Sheriff's wife is supposed to be sitting there.'

'I shifted the place cards,' hissed back Sarah. 'You don't want to sit next to that old bag.'

'But you've totally ruined Monica's placement,' said James in outrage. 'And that means Tony's got to sit next to the High Sheriff's wife, which he won't like one bit.'

'Serve him right for trying to split us up. I love you.'

'Keep your voice down.' James looked furtively round.

'I'll talk even louder if you don't let me stay. Surely you must have a programme in your marriage series on coping with temptation? Well, you can bloody well research it tonight.'

Home at The Priory, Taggie, having dispatched her parents to the ball, was wondering forlornly what to do for the rest of the evening. The only decent film on television was Italian, and she wouldn't be able to read the subtitles fast enough to get the gist of it. It was a vicious night. The wind was howling round the windows, trying to get in out of the cold. The snow was falling steadily, already lining the window-ledge and bowing down the evergreens. At least there was a nice fire in the little sitting-room. Gertrude, Aengus and Claudius were all stretched out in front of the blaze. The logs came from their wood, or rather it was Rupert's wood now; everything seemed to come back to him.

How will I ever get through my life without him, she thought hopelessly, when I can't even face a much-longed-for free evening?

She jumped at a sudden pounding on the door. The bell was still blocked up with loo paper to discourage creditors. Outside was Hazel, one of the make-up girls from the BBC, who'd once worked on Declan's programme and become a great family friend. Flakes of snow like brilliants in her hair gave her an added glamour. She'd been doing a job in Bristol and was on her way home.

'Everyone's out except me,' apologized Taggie, 'but come in and have a drink.'

'What a lovely house, really Gothic,' said Hazel in awe as they went into the sitting-room.

'Not too large,' she squawked, as Taggie poured her a vodka and tonic. 'I've got to drive back to London.'

'You must stay the night,' urged Taggie. 'You can't drive in this weather and Daddy'll be d-devastated to have missed you.'

'I can't believe Caitlin's taking O-levels. She was such a wee little thing,' said Hazel twenty minutes later. 'And Patrick got a first, and he's as tall as your Dad. I do hope your Dad gets the franchise. We're all rooting for him at the Beeb. Tony Baddingham's such a shit.'

The telephone rang. It was Bas. 'Taggie, babe, you're coming to the ball.'

'I can't,' squeaked Taggie. 'I've got someone here.'

'Well get rid of them. Annabel, my date, has been out all day with the Belvoir, and the snow's too bad for her to drive down, and anyway, she's bushed. So I've got no one to go with and I can't think of anyone more delicious than you.'

'I haven't got anything to wear.'

'Fret not, I'll be over in an hour with some frocks.'

'I've been asked to the Hunt Ball,' said Taggie in awe.

'Wonderful,' said Hazel excitedly. 'I'll dog-sit. Go and wash your hair and have a bath. I'll make you up. You'll come up beautifully.'

Bas, naughty as his word, arrived an hour later with a back seat loaded up with ball dresses.

'Where did you get them?' asked Taggie incredulously.

'Corinium's wardrobe department,' said Bas. 'Their security is atrocious.'

'What a gorgeous man,' murmured Hazel enviously, 'and I've had some heart-throbs through my fingers in my time.'

'This dress is made by B-A-L-Main,' spelt out Taggie slowly. 'What happens if I put my foot through it?'

'Try the crimson one,' said Bas. 'It's much the best colour for you and at least it won't show up the red wine that's bound to get poured over you.'

'It's awfully low-cut,' said Taggie dubiously.

'All the better,' said Hazel, checking the Carmen rollers. 'Hurry up and decide. I want to do your hair.'

Back at the ball, dinner was over and dancing had begun. It was a measure of Monica's niceness that no one else but she knew that Valerie had auditioned and been turned down for both Maud and Monica's parts in *The Merry Widow*. Still smarting from the rejection (she would have been *so* much better than Maud), Valerie was now determined to demonstrate her dancing skills and had dragged a reluctant Freddie on to the floor. She was soon bawling him out.

'Can't you concentrate for one minute, Fred-Fred? I said fish-tail not telemarque.'

Through a swirling herbaceous border of red coats and brilliantly coloured dresses, Freddie could see Lizzie in fuchsia pink being humped round the floor by James, who'd at last managed to shake off Sarah.

As they passed Tony sitting at the Corinium table, James deliberately pressed his cheek and his body against Lizzie's.

I can't stand it, thought Lizzie wretchedly. She'd imagined it would be better seeing Freddie tonight, than not seeing him at all, but it made everything much, much worse.

Watching across the room, Freddie wanted to punch James

on his perfectly straight nose, and then whisk Lizzie upstairs on to a moth-infested four-poster and tear off her fuchsia dress and kiss her all over.

'Fred-Fred,' screeched Valerie in his ear, 'are you tipsy? This is a foxtrot.'

Declan danced with Maud, who was well away. Over his shoulder she glanced at her gold watch. Bas was very late. At the Venturer table it was plain to Cameron, watching Rupert pour another large whisky, that he was deliberately setting out to get drunk. People kept pausing to say hullo, but, seeing the set expression on his face and the sinister glitter in his eyes, they didn't stay long. Cameron, acutely conscious of Tony two tables away talking in lowered tones to Ginger Johnson and watching her every move, tried to talk to Rupert. A slow anger rose in her when he only answered in monosyllables.

Why make it so obvious that you've absolutely no interest in me, she wanted to scream. Was he deliberately goading her to go back to Tony?

'The next dance is definitely mine,' said Henry to Cameron.

'Oh, good. Here's Bas at last,' said Maud, pinning up a tendril of hair at the back.

'Good Lord,' said Henry in wonder, his glass of wine poised halfway to his lips. 'What a stunning girl!'

'Annabel Kemble-Taylor's hardly a girl,' said Rupert, who had his back to the floor. 'Half Leicestershire's been up her.'

'She is pretty. Most dramatical,' said Freddie, putting on his spectacles. 'Blimey, it's Taggie.'

Rupert swung round and caught his breath. There, undulating across the floor, rouged, lipsticked, her eyes vast and black-lined with kohl, black hair a mass of snakey ringlets, her shoulders, far creamier and lusher than Maud's, rising out of a ruched crimson dress with a bustle, was indeed Taggie. Everyone was turning round to gawp at her. Basil, who'd been slowly stalking her for fourteen months, looked beside himself with pride.

629

'You look like a Christmas cracker,' he whispered in her ear, as he fingered the ruched dress, 'and, my God, I can't wait to pull you.'

Taggie giggled. She was slightly overwhelmed by how different Hazel had made her look and the sensation she seemed to be creating. Her only aim was to please Rupert. She wanted to show him that she had at last grown up. But as he stared at her, his face totally unsmiling, her courage failed and she gave the dress a desperate tug upwards. Then, just as she and Bas reached the Venturer table, the band started again.

'Lady in Red,' said Basil in delight. 'How appropriate.' And, taking Taggie's bag from her and dropping it in front of Rupert in a curiously insolent gesture, he swept her onto the floor.

'I can't dance,' pleaded Taggie, half-laughing. 'I truly, truly can't.'

'You can with me,' said Bas, putting his hand round her waist. 'This is a nice slow one to start with. This song could have been written for you, you are so so beautiful. '*Never seen you looking so lovely as you do tonight,*' he sang, *never seen you shine so bright.*'

'I find all this lipstick a bit strange,' said Taggie.

'Don't worry, I'll kiss it all off later.'

Taggie blushed. He was at least five inches taller than her, and so supple and strong, and with such a Latin sense of rhythm, that Taggie was soon following him perfectly in time.

'You dance beautifully,' he said, laying his cheek against her hair.

'I can do it,' said Taggie excitedly. 'I can really dance.'

'*The lady in red is dancing with me,* sang Bas gazing deep into her eyes, '*There's nobody here, just you and me.*' What a good thing Annabel had such an exhausting day with the Belvoir.'

'*Lady in red, Lady in red,*' sang Taggie dreamily and tunelessly, not knowing any of the other words. 'It is a most gorgeous song.'

'And you're the most gorgeous girl,' said Basil, french-kissing her shoulder.

'Very fast man across country, Bas,' said Henry approvingly.

'Very fast man on the dance floor,' said Freddie. 'Don't they go well togevver?'

Maud was looking extremely wintry. Cameron was watching Rupert. His face was like marble, but the tendons on the back of his hand, which was clenched round his glass, were like underground cables. He never took his eyes off Taggie as she and Bas moved round the floor. Then, suddenly, as the music stopped and Bas bent his otter-sleek head and kissed Taggie on her crimson mouth, his hand tightened on the glass so convulsively that it shattered. Amazingly he didn't cut himself, but there was glass everywhere.

'My Auntie was so superstitious,' said Valerie, as a waitress rushed in with a dustpan and brush, 'that if she broke something precious she'd rush down to the bottom of the garden and smash two jam jars to break the run of bad luck.'

'As Rupert's heart's just been broken as well,' said Cameron viciously, 'we only need smash one more thing.'

'Shut up,' snarled Rupert, pouring a slug of whisky into a nearby wine glass.

Declan shot him a warning look. Nor were matters improved by Bas arriving at the table with Taggie.

'Haven't I done well?' he said smugly. 'Annabel dropped out, so the understudy took her place. I knew you'd be pleased, Maud darling,' he added blithely as he bent down to peck Maud's gritted cheek. 'You were just complaining yesterday Taggie never had any fun.'

'You look absolutely perfick,' said Freddie.

'Where did that gown come from?' asked Valerie accusingly.

'Corinium wardrobe department,' said Basil, lobbing Freddie's roll at Georgie Baines at the next table. 'Suits her, doesn't it?'

'She looks great,' said Declan proudly. 'But make sure it isn't bugged.'

'All the bug would pick up is the hammering of her heart because she's with me,' said Bas, squeezing Taggie's hand.

Taggie glanced shyly across at Rupert, who was now looking at her with complete indifference. Suddenly she felt utterly deflated. Even with every stop pulled out, there was no way she could win him. But there was little time to fret. Next minute a thoroughly over-excited Henry had whisked her off to dance. They were just circling decorously when the band broke into 'Rock around the Clock'.

'Ha ha ha,' said Henry, suddenly galvanized like an over-adrenalized tarantula. 'I know this tune. There's life in the old dog yet.' And he flung Taggie across the floor with great energy.

Every time he twirled her round he nearly pulled her out of her cracker dress. He'll discover a paper hat and a motto in a minute, she thought as she frantically tugged it up again. As soon as the band stopped, a young blood swooped and asked her to dance, and then another, and another. Each one took her telephone number and said they'd ring her.

Great excitement, because it was regarded as highly symbolic, was caused at the Corinium table when Tony won a portable television on the Tombola.

'He won't be needing that much longer,' growled Declan, who was getting increasingly worried about Rupert.

Freddie had also vanished, ostensibly to fetch Valerie some lemon squash, but he'd been away for three-quarters of an hour, and James Vereker could be seen hunting everywhere for Lizzie as he tried to escape from Sarah. Bas claimed another dance with Taggie and persuaded the band to play 'Lady in Red' again. As he and Taggie danced past them, all the band stood up in salute to her beauty.

Rupert was three-quarters of the way down his bottle of whisky when he was tapped sharply on the shoulder by one of his more forceful lady constituents.

'I know this isn't the time, but could we have a word about the Swindon–Gloucester motorway?'

632

She had a face the colour and texture of corned beef and it was now very close to Rupert's.

'Bugger the motorway,' he said.

The corned beef seemed to engorge and darken like the interior of black pudding.

Getting to his feet, leaving her mouthing apoplectically, Rupert reached the dance floor just as Taggie and Bas were coming off. Grabbing Taggie's hand, he dragged her back onto the floor. Alone in the centre, they gazed at each other. Slowly Rupert examined the huge, blackened, almost feverish eyes, the trembling ruby mouth, the quivering white breasts hardly covered by the crimson ruching. Adoring the way she looked normally in old clothes, with hardly any make-up, he detested this new grown-up, glamorous Taggie.

'What's the matter?' she stammered, stepping back as though scorched by the disapproval in his eyes. 'I hoped you'd l-l-like it.'

'You look like a complete tart,' he said viciously, 'and as you're with Bas, you're obviously going to behave like one.'

Taggie gave a gasp of horror as, turning on his heel, Rupert walked straight back to the table.

'What was that about?' taunted Cameron. 'I thought you liked little girls with bust measurements bigger than their IQs.'

'I like them better than fucking American smart asses,' snarled Rupert.

Spitting with fury, passing heraldic shields, suits of armour and antlers of several kinds of deer, Cameron fled to the Ladies. Rupert was a bastard, an utter asshole. But as she looked at her reflection in the ancient, dusty mirror, which should have flattered her, she couldn't blame him for neglecting her. She looked awful, and the black dress she'd thought so sophisticated and understated had understated her so much she was practically invisible. Why the hell hadn't she worn her black suede dress? Savagely she daubed her cheekbones with blusher and emptied the remains of a bottle of Jolie Madame – what a singularly inappropriate name – over her wrists and neck.

Coming out into the long gallery, she saw Tony emerging from behind a suit of armour and went sharply into reverse. He was too quick for her. Grabbing her wrists, he drew her into an alcove behind a huge urn filled with blue hyacinths. She tried to wriggle away, but he was too strong for her. Oh, why did that sweet, heady smell make her almost faint with longing?

'I've missed you,' he said, as he regained his breath. 'I've never stopped missing you. I need you. Corinium needs you. Come back to us.'

'Don't be fucking infantile,' hissed Cameron. 'After the dirty trick you've pulled on us?'

'I'm going to bury Venturer,' he said evilly, 'and you'll go under too. You've just no idea what I've got up my sleeve.'

Cameron tried not to appear fazed: 'You'll never get away with it. The IBA knows you're as bent as hell.'

'By the time I've finished with Venturer I'll look like a shining white angel.'

Drawing her towards him, he slowly fingered her rib cage, then pressed the ball of his hand up against her breast, at the same time running the other hand equally slowly over her bottom. It was an act of assessment – not of lust.

'Dear, dear,' he sighed, 'you used to have such a beautiful body. Now you could do a commercial for famine relief.'

'Don't be disgusting.'

'I'm just sad you've lost your looks.' The hand still rotated on her bottom. She shuddered, unable to stop the squirming, helpless, revolted longing. Tony always did this to her.

'I've been working, for Chrissake.'

'You always thrived on work. You're having Rupert trouble. I watched you tonight and last Friday.'

Suddenly Cameron realized what the scent of the blue hyacinths reminded her of – the much fainter smell of bluebells in Rupert's wood the first weekend she spent at Penscombe.

'He's got the hots for Taggie O'Hara, hasn't he?' gloated Tony. 'Everyone's talking about it.'

In the distance the band was belting out 'Mac the Knife'. It was as though Tony was turning it in her heart.

'Bullshit,' she said with a sob, and fled away from him, hearing his laughter following her all down the long gallery.

Cameron was so distraught, she didn't see Declan standing in the shadows of a high tallboy. Worried about her scrap with Rupert, he'd come looking for her, wanting to comfort and steady her. He was about to call out. The next moment he froze as he saw a man emerging from behind the urn. The glint of his huge signet ring as he smoothed his hair, and the almost orgasmic expression on his face as he passed, made him instantly recognizable.

Declan went straight back to the Venturer table, but found only Maud and Freddie.

'You was so dramatical in *The Merry Widow*,' Freddie was saying.

'Was I really?' said Maud, looking very happy.

'What's hup?' said Freddie in alarm as he saw Declan's face. Sitting down, Declan came straight to the point.

'I've just seen Cameron talking to Tony.'

'Just saying 'ullo.'

'No, it was a long and very intimate conversation. She was in tears when she left him. He looked delighted with himself.'

'Shit,' said Freddie. 'It's Rupert's fault. He's been diabolical to Cameron all evening.'

'What's much, much worse is that she and I have been working on the Dermot MacBride deal and the Royal Shake-speare negotiations all week. If she leaks those to him we're stymied.'

'I still don't fink she's like that,' said Freddie. 'They was probably just reminiscing.'

'We're off,' said a voice.

It was Bas with his arm round a somewhat tearstained Taggie.

'You've only just arrived,' said Maud hysterically.

'I know, but we've got somewhere else to go on to,' said Bas.

Suddenly there was a shriek of excitement as Henry rode a horse into the ballroom and round the floor, followed by hounds. He had snow on his shoulders and his black hat, and all the hounds had snow on their faces and their frantically wagging sterns. Everyone came rushing in to cheer them. There were terrific view holloas, as a hound trotted calmly up to the Corinium table and lifted its leg on the back of Tony's chair.

'Wish that dog was a member of the IBA,' said Freddie.

By the time the hounds had gone, Cameron and Rupert were back at the table. Rupert, Declan noticed, had snow on his hair too and was shivering uncontrollably. Maud, too, seemed suddenly terribly upset, particularly when Valerie pointed out how keen Bas seemed on Taggie.

'Much better for him to find someone nearer his age,' she said smugly. 'Where are they, anyway?'

'Gone,' said Declan.

'Where?' asked Rupert, looking up sharply.

'I don't know.'

'Get your coat,' said Rupert to Cameron.

He was waiting in the hall, glaring at a buffalo whose eyes were as glassy as his own, making no effort to conceal his impatience.

'It's not easy extracting one's coat from underneath a heaving husband and someone else's wife,' snapped Cameron.

Outside, the snow was already four inches deep. As the long dresses of departing guests trailed over the white lawn, flurrying flakes seemed to blur the great house and a party of whooping young bloods, all no doubt with Taggie's telephone number in their breast pockets, engaged in a snowball fight. Cameron felt she had gone back four hundred years.

'I'll drive. You're drunk,' she said to Rupert as they reached the car.

Careful, she told herself, as the Aston-Martin slid all over the road like Thumper on the ice, he's reached that pitch of drunkenness that will erupt into violence at any minute. Having been beaten up by Tony, she was terrified of it happening again. But as they drew up outside the front of Penscombe Court, Rupert waited until she got out of the car, then slid across into the driving seat and set off in a tremendous flurry of snow.

Sobbing uncontrollably, Cameron let herself into the house and, shouting at the dogs to get out of her way, went straight to Rupert's office and started searching. In the bottom drawer of his desk, under the lining paper, she found what she was looking for – that impossibly ill-spelt and ill-punctuated letter Taggie had written Rupert, thanking him for Claudius, and two photographs of her running in the wood. She stiffened when she saw the second. Rupert's kids were there as well as Taggie. They were holding her hands and laughing. The leaves were flame-red on the beech trees, so it must have been autumn, and Tab was wearing her puff-ball skirt, so it must have been this year. Shit – and they all looked so happy. It must have been while she was away in Ireland. That was why Rupert had been so reluctant to have the kids over since, and insisted on taking them out on his own, in case they babbled on about Taggie. That was almost the worst thing, that she had utterly failed with the children, where Taggie had succeeded. Also under the lining paper, which she couldn't interpret, was a pile of faded leaves.

Rupert knew he was far too drunk to drive, but he didn't care. Anyway, he had always jumped horses when he was pissed with that much more dash and brilliance. Unable to stop himself, he drove straight into Cotchester and parked outside the Bar Sinister. The roofs of the honey-coloured houses were completely hidden with snow now. Flakes were landing like huge polar bears on his bonnet, almost obscuring his vision, but not so much that he couldn't see the lights in the flat above. Bas was plainly at home.

Christ – why had he been such a shit to Taggie? She'd looked so fucking gorgeous and he'd detested it because he wanted to keep her as his little teenager. At the back of his mind he'd expected her to be always there. Rationally he knew he must never make a play for her, that one day she'd find some nice dull kind boy of her own age to take care of her. But he hadn't thought the whole thing through, or realized he'd be driven into a maddened frenzy of jealousy because she'd been stolen from under his nose by the second worst rake in the county who was probably expertly initiating her into the pleasures of the flesh at this moment.

He slumped on the steering wheel, groaning. He wanted to break down the door, to kill Bas, to drag Taggie back to The Priory like a father out of a Victorian melodrama. In his misery he didn't even feel the cold. Gradually the snow obscured the entire windscreen and he had to turn on the engine to start up the wipers, when suddenly the balcony doors opened and Bas and Taggie came out. She was wearing Bas's red coat. Winding down the window, Rupert could hear her cries of joy at the beauty of the snow. Next moment Bas had gathered up the snow along the balcony rail to make a snowball and handed it to her, but she only managed to chuck it a few yards down the ghostly whitening street.

'Tell you never played cricket at school,' said Bas fondly.

Then, drawing her close by the lapels of his coat, he slowly kissed her. They were so preoccupied, they didn't even notice Rupert. Totally sobered up, he drove back to Penscombe.

The rest of the weekend was like the Phoney War. Rupert and Cameron were perfectly polite to each other. She worked on the franchise, he was off to Rome on Sunday for a meeting with the International Olympics Committee, but would be home on Wednesday night.

The only time she saw him with his guard down was when she caught a glimpse of him watching a Lassie film in the study. He was clutching Beaver and the tears were running down his cheeks.

638

48

After lunch next day, having scraped the frozen snow off the bird table and fed the birds for the fourth time, Declan had great difficulty getting out of his drive to visit Freddie. The gritters had been at work on the main roads, but the side lanes were murder. For once the beauty of the black and white landscape held no charms for him. He passed several cars, totally submerged, which must have been abandoned last night, and a farmer frantically trying to dig out some sheep before dusk. The sky was a dull mustard yellow, promising more snow. What would happen if none of the Venturer consortium could get up to London for the IBA meeting? Freddie's drive had already been lavishly gritted.

'I sent the Council a grittings telegram,' he said with a huge laugh. 'In fact I bunged them a few tenners so they made a detour past the 'ouse.'

He poured Declan a large brandy and took him into his study. The house was blissfully warm after The Priory. Outside, Valerie's garden had never looked more beautiful, totally hidden by snow, the gaudy colours wiped out, the vast rockery transformed into a mini-Andes, the garden gnomes and the plastic cherubs fluffed out into creatures of fable. Even the serried ranks of hybrid teas had become a white army hoisting up fistfuls of snow. If Valerie moved to the Arctic, reflected Declan, she might become an arbiter of garden taste, a Vita Sackville-North.

Freddie was in terrific spirits, brandishing the *Telegraph* with a piece on the forthcoming franchise struggle.

'It says four incumbent companies are vulnerable and names Corinium as one of them. It also says: "*Venturer, Corinium's rival must be reckoned a considerable creative and management force.*" Then it goes on to say: "*Corinium are strongly challenged, and as a result their shares are selling at a substantial discount to assets.*"'

'I don't understand what that means,' said Declan.

'Don't matter. It's good, believe me. We're on our way, boy.'

'What are we going to do about Cameron and Tony?'

Freddie chewed on his cigar. 'I can't believe she's turned.'

'I don't want to, but we still haven't discovered who leaked the names of the other moles to Tony.'

'How was she in Ireland?' asked Freddie.

'Wonderful,' said Declan wistfully.

'Well then, my guess is that she's dotty about Rupert, and when he started giving 'er the runaround last night, Tony seized his chance and accosted her on the way back from the Ladies.'

Declan thought it was more complex. To bolster her chronic insecurity, Cameron had to have a man in her life, and after that last night in Galway, when she'd made such a definite play for him, he didn't think she was Rupert's exclusive property any more. He was also furious how much seeing her with Tony had upset him.

'We've fought this fight absolutely straight up to now,' said Freddie.

'Except for Rupert seducing Cameron in the first place.'

'But so much is at stake now,' Freddie went on, 'that we'd better put a private detective on Tony and get Rupert to slip a tiny bug into Cameron's 'andbag.'

The snow was falling again, flakes tumbling down dark against the muddy yellow sky, then getting lost to view as they reached ground level.

'Better not involve Rupert at this stage,' said Declan. 'If he realizes she's been hobnobbing with Tony, he might get really rough and send her scuttling back to Tony for good. Anyway, she's got a dozen bags. Rupert's bound to bug the wrong one, and he's off to Rome for three days tomorrow.'

'OK,' said Freddie, stubbing out his cigar and getting to his feet. 'We'll start wiv a private detective on Tony. I know an ace one. Leave it wiv me.'

Declan sensed that Freddie was anxious to get rid of him. 'Where's Valerie?' he asked.

'Visiting her sister in Cheam.'

'Do you want to come over for supper?'

Freddie shook his head. 'It's not really a night to go out, thanks. I've got an 'ell of a lot of work to do. I keep forgetting I'm the Chief Executive of a public company.'

Committing adultery, Freddie reflected ruefully after Declan had gone, made one tell an 'orrible lot of lies. James Vereker was spending the night in London at another Corinium dry run. Lizzie's nanny was away for the weekend. He must remember to ring Valerie before he left, so she didn't ring and find him not at home.

As he arrived at Lizzie's, he felt glad that the steadily falling snow would cover any wheel tracks by morning. Lizzie was looking out for him, so no doorbells should wake the children.

She welcomed him in a primrose-yellow silk dressing-gown, rosy, warm and Floris-scented from the bath. The lights were low in the bedroom, but a fire burned merrily in the grate. Reflected tongues of flame lasciviously licked the ceiling. Making a mental note to throw away the evidence first thing in the morning, Lizzie said there was a bottle of Moët to be opened. Instead, Freddie opened her silk dressing-gown and felt his heart stop. Lizzie was wearing just black high heels and a black corset which pushed up her breasts, moulded her waist and stopped just above her damp blonde bush, except for four black suspenders holding up black fishnet stockings.

'You are the loveliest fing I've ever seen,' murmured Freddie. 'Come live wiv me, and be my love. Leave it on,' he added as Lizzie started unhooking.

Kneeling down, he removed her high heels and, kissing

her instep, slowly kissed his way up until he could bury his face in the soft marshmallow of her thighs. Lizzie bent down to take off his jersey and shirt, feeling his stomach muscles tauten as she unbuckled his trouser belt. There was a huge mirror on the ceiling. James adored to watch his own reflection when he made love. Beside his lithe and taut bronzed beauty, Lizzie had always felt like a Beryl Cook lady. With Freddie she felt slim and beautiful and wanted to watch the whole thing.

'I never rated swucksont-nurf before,' said Freddie happily.

The snow had grown two inches on the window ledge. Freddie had grown several inches and diminished again. The logs had died in the grate before Lizzie leaned up on her elbow smoothing the red-gold curls on his chest.

'I love you,' she said softly, so as not to wake him.

Freddie opened an eye. 'I meant it when I said come live wiv me and be my love,' he said.

The following Tuesday morning James Vereker had a rare and intimate breakfast with his five-year-old daughter Eleanor. Usually James fled the din of little children in the morning and either had his muesli, prunes and herbal tea in bed or breakfasted at the Corinium canteen after a work-out in the gym. This week he and Lizzie were recording their second programme in the series on the way children enrich and restrict a marriage. James had already written his script which began: 'As a caring parent, I . . .' and was now, in between reading the Guardian, doing a little research into fatherhood.

Sebastian, Ellie's brother, who'd already got soaked making a snowman and nearly drowned testing the ice on the lake, was upstairs having his clothes changed by Jilly, the dependable boot of a nanny. Lizzie was working. Ellie was eating a boiled egg, dreamily dipping buttered toast soldiers into the yolk.

'I hope you'll watch "Round-Up" tonight,' James said to her. 'We're visiting the zoo and filming a new polar bear cub, which is called James after me.'

'I saw Freddie bare the other night,' said Ellie dreamily.

'I don't think I know Freddie Bear,' said James. 'Do the BBC make it, or is it one of ours?'

'I saw Freddie bare,' repeated Ellie.

'I heard you,' said James patiently. 'Is it a new cartoon?'

'No – Freddie bare. He was on the bed with Mummy. They were struggling.'

James put down his spoon. 'I beg your pardon?'

'I wanted a drink of water, so I went into Mummy's room. Freddie and Mummy were in bed. Freddie was bare, but Mummy was wearing long socks with her bottom hanging out.'

James went very red in the face.

'Are you trying to tell me that Mummy was in bed with someone – er – someone who wasn't Daddy?'

'Yes,' beamed Ellie. 'Freddie with the big tummy. He's nice, he brings us Smarties.'

'You're not to make up wicked fibs,' said James furiously. 'Jilly!' he yelled for the dependable boot. 'It's time the children went to school.'

Lizzie had the effrontery to giggle when James confronted her.

'It's not funny,' thundered James.

'No, it isn't. Oh dear, I hope the poor darling isn't totally put off sex for life.'

'Is that all you can say? What about me?'

'Nothing would put you off sex for life,' said Lizzie.

'Stop being frivolous. I cannot believe you'd cheat on me with that dreadful, overweight, common little man.'

'Freddie is a very nice man,' said Lizzie.

'He's totally dishonourable and so are you.'

'What about all *your* affairs?'

'They're finished,' said James sanctimoniously. 'And being in the media one is inevitably the target of certain attentions. Anyway, it's different for men.'

'Don't blame Freddie then.'

'Freddie,' said James, working himself up into a fury, 'is a member of the rival consortium. I feel utterly betrayed. It's like fraternizing in the war.'

'Well, I'm not having *my* head shaved,' screamed Lizzie.

'And what's this about wearing long socks and your bottom hanging out?'

Lizzie giggled again. 'It must have been my fishnet stockings and my corset.'

'You dress up like a prostitute! Whatever for?'

'To excite him,' said Lizzie simply.

'You never bothered to do that for me,' said James indignantly.

Lizzie watched James catch sight of himself in the mirror. Smoothing his hair, he composed his features into an expression suitable for a wronged husband. He's just the wrong husband, she thought.

'I suppose you realize,' said James nastily, 'Freddie's only been running after you to worm Corinium secrets out of you. I shall have to tell Tony of course. We have to report anything suspicious. He'll be delighted to have something on Mr Squeaky Clean at last. I shan't blame you. I'll say being somewhat unsophisticated and unused to male attention, you fell for it.'

'I've heard enough,' said Lizzie furiously. 'Freddie is the most honourable man I've ever met. After you junked Sarah, because Tony ordered you to clean up your marital act, she went screaming round to Rupert and told him everything.'

James winced.

'Rupert was all set to give the story straight to the *News of the World*. It would have been a goody: "*Corinium stud ordered to give up mistress by boss in order to present image of idyllic marriage to viewers and IBA.*" There were plenty of Corinium people, including Sarah, who'd have enjoyed shopping you to the press. And the whole thing would have been a lovely black blot on Corinium's escutcheon. But Freddie wouldn't let Rupert do it. Unlike Tony, he feels that sort of thing is below the belt. He didn't want mine, or the children's names, dragged in; said it wasn't fair having them branded as the offspring of an adulterer — and a pratt,' she added as an afterthought.

'You uncaring bitch,' spluttered James.

'And what is more,' continued Lizzie coldly, 'if you breathe a word about me and Freddie to anyone, I'm leaving you, and then your silly marriage programme's going to look even sillier.'

The moment James left the house, Lizzie burst into tears. She was still crying when Jilly the dependable boot got back from the school run. In the end Lizzie told her the whole story.

'I'd no idea poor darling Ellie came into our bedroom that night.'

'She'd have screamed if she'd been frightened,' said Jilly comfortingly. 'She was perfectly happy on the way to school on Monday; only interested in whether the lake would be frozen enough to slide on.'

She picked up a table which James had knocked over as he rushed from the room.

'If it comes to a split, I'd like to stay with you. You're the best boss I've ever had, and I love the kids. I don't mind taking a cut in salary if things get hard. There, there, there's no need to start crying again.'

Freddie was just going into a board meeting when Lizzie rang him.

'I'll come and get you.'

'No, no,' said Lizzie. 'We've got to lie low. I don't want to give Tony any ammunition at this stage. Venturer doesn't need it, and think of Valerie, Sharon and Wayne. We'll just have to play safe and not see each other till after 15th December.'

'That's over a fortnight,' said Freddie aghast.

'Well, we must try, anyway.'

Freddie was utterly distracted at the meeting. When an outside director congratulated him on the new billion-pound deal with the Japs, he looked blank. When another informed him that the ex-Chairman, General Walters, had died of a heart attack, Freddie said, 'Triffic news. Keep up the good work!'

Outside in the beautifully kept company gardens, the sun, like a huge red Christmas bauble, was setting down the side of a large yew tree. Freddie shivered at the thought that the sun might be setting on his relationship with Lizzie. Then one of his secretaries summoned him from the meeting. There was a call, she said, on his very, very, very private line whose number was only known to Lizzie – and now the private detective. It was the latter ringing: he'd seen Tony and Cameron go into the Royal Garden Hotel early that afternoon. They'd spent ninety minutes in the Residents' Lounge. He'd walked through twice and there'd been no one else there.

Freddie's heart sank. He told the detective to keep on tailing Tony and immediately rang Declan, who was utterly shattered. They both decided, however, that if Cameron had spilled any more beans, it was too late to muzzle Tony now. If, as was just possible, she hadn't, she was still too important a trump card with the IBA to be frightened off.

They decided to wait until Rupert returned from Rome tomorrow before tackling her.

Next morning, after a restless night, Declan woke up to more snow, and, not wishing to risk either car, walked down to the village shop to get the papers. Yesterday at The Priory, they'd had a power cut and frozen pipes. Today the washing machine and the tumble dryer were kaput, and it was warmer out than in. Three-foot icicles hung from the faulty gutters. The evergreens lining the drive were bent double by the snow. Every blade of grass edging the road was rimed with frost and burned with a white heat of its own.

The traffic was crawling so slowly that Declan didn't bother to put the dogs on leads. Gertrude, a bit lame from the hard ground, still rushed into every cottage front garden and barked at the snowmen. Claudius, encountering his first snow this year, was wild with excitement, plunging into drifts, leaping to catch the snowballs Declan hurled for him. As Declan passed the white church, he sent up a prayer that Venturer might win. On such a beautiful day, one couldn't fail to be optimistic. But as he walked into the village shop Mr Banks, who was a great newspaper reader, waved *The Times*.

'Lord Baddingham's been blowing his own trumpet again.'

Declan felt his throat go dry, his stomach churned.

'Page five,' went on Mr Banks, handing the paper to Declan.

' *Baddingham Set for Victory*,' said the headline. There was a very nice picture, taken from above and at a slight angle to reduce the heavy jowl. Tony was smiling and showing excellent teeth. The interview had been written by a well-known financial journalist.

As he was so confident of retaining the franchise, Tony had told him, he was only too happy to reveal Corinium's plans for next year. They were very happy to welcome three new directors on to the Board, all production people, including Ailie Bristoe, who'd just spent three years in Hollywood and who would be Director of Programmes. They were also very excited about their new networked thirteen-part series on marriage which, Tony predicted, would turn James and Lizzie Vereker into big stars.

It was safe enough stuff. Declan sat down on the snow-covered window-ledge outside the shop, obscuring the postcard advertisements for lost gerbils, daily women and second-hand carrycots in the window.

Corinium, he read on, had also made arrangements with the Royal Shakespeare to televise special productions of whatever Shakespeare plays children in the area would be taking for O- and A-levels each year. Then they would offer the videos for sale. They'd also be filming Johnny Friedlander's *Hamlet*, which had been postponed until the summer.

Shit, thought Declan in horror, those were both Cameron's ideas. But most exciting of all, he read on, was that Corinium had signed up a new play by Stroud-born playwright, Dermot MacBride, with an option on the second. There followed a lot of guff about MacBride's towering genius, and how happy

Tony was to welcome this lost son of Gloucestershire back into the fold.

'We paid a lot for MacBride,' Tony had admitted.

But, as the financial journalist pointed out, the publicity value alone would be worth thousands of pounds to Corinium.

'Please don't obscure my advertisement,' said a shrill voice. 'I'll never get a cleaner that way.'

Looking up, Declan discovered an old lady with a red nose glaring at him. Looking down he saw Gertrude and Claudius sitting at his feet, shivering miserably. Slipping and sliding, falling over twice, moaning with rage, Declan ran home to The Priory.

'Look at fucking that!' He brandished *The Times* under Maud's nose. 'Tony's bought Dermot MacBride's play. Cameron must have leaked it to him.'

'I always thought she was untrustworthy,' said Maud, who was plucking her eyebrows.

Declan's hands were so cold it took him a long time to dial the number of Dermot MacBride's agent.

'We had a deal. What the fuck are you playing at?'

'The contract hadn't been signed,' said the agent defensively. 'My duty is to get the best deal for my authors. Tony offered three times as much as you.'

'You could have come back to me. I'd have matched his offer.'

'He said if I talked to you the deal was off.'

'That's the last deal I'll ever do with you,' roared Declan.

'Never mind. I'm retiring at Christmas.'

Through the window, Declan watched the Priory robin furiously driving a rival robin away from the bird table.

'How did Tony know about our deal?'

'Dunno. He phoned about five yesterday. I spoke to MacBride. We exchanged contracts this morning. It'll buy a few gold watches for me.'

The moment Declan put down the telephone, Freddie rang.

'Have you seen the *Cotchester News*? There's a bloody great picture of you an' me, an' Rupert, an' Basil, an' 'Enry – all in our red coats out huntin' wiv big grins on our faces, wiv a caption: *"Do you want these butchers to run your television station?"*'

'That's libellous,' howled Declan. 'Have you seen *The Times?*'

'Yes,' said Freddie grimly. 'Unfortunately that's not.'

'I'm not waiting for Rupert to get back,' said Declan. 'I'm going round to have it out with Cameron right now.'

But when he got to Penscombe, Mrs Bodkin told him Cameron had gone out and wasn't expected back until evening. Guilt, thought Declan in a fury.

Cameron got home around eight that evening. She knew she shouldn't have played truant, but, having brooded agonizingly about Rupert since the hunt ball, she felt she had to get out of the house. The heavy frost had made the white valley look so beautiful that morning. Why should I give up all this without a fight? she had thought. Rupert was an alpha male, he was exceptionally handsome, funny, very rich, clever in a totally different way to herself, and, now that she'd given him six months' intensive training on pleasing a woman rather than automatically pleasing himself, spectacular in bed.

A great believer in positive action, she drove into Cheltenham to the branch headquarters of 'Mind the Step', a support group for step-parents and step-children, which had just opened. Cameron figured the subject would not only make a good programme, but might help her love Rupert's children and understand her own tortured relationship with her mother and Mike. She had a long talk with the organizer, who then gave her several names and addresses. Driving round Gloucestershire, Cameron was amazed how many people welcomed her in. At their wits' end, hemmed in by snow and coping with step-children at home for several days, they were only too happy to talk to someone.

Listening to the shrill invective, to half-hearted attempts at love, to occasional genuine affection, to grown women blaming their own step-mothers for lack of love, which prevented them in turn loving their own husbands and children, Cameron forgot her own miseries. She decided it would make a marvellous programme and was already pre-selecting the people to interview.

Like Declan on his way to the village shop that morning, she returned to Penscombe with a feeling of optimism. She found messages from Mrs Bodkin that Rupert had rung twice, Freddie three times and Declan four.

Going into the kitchen, she poured herself a large vodka and tonic and decided to scribble down some ideas for the 'Step' programme while it was still in her head. Searching for a biro on the kitchen shelf, she found the yellow sachet that had been included with the flowers that Tony had sent her after he beat her up, which you were supposed to add to the water to make the flowers last longer. Stabbed with sudden misery, she wished she could sprinkle the sachet on Rupert to prolong their relationship.

With a lurch of apprehension, she heard the dogs barking in the hall. Not Rupert, the welcome wasn't clamorous enough, but it was obviously someone they knew. She went into the hall.

'Declan!' Her face lit up. 'Sorry I didn't call back. I've had a great idea for a programme.'

'On treachery?' asked Declan bleakly. 'You're an expert on that subject.'

'What are you talking about? Do you want a drink?'

'No thanks.' He followed her into the drawing-room. 'You seen *The Times*?'

'Haven't seen any papers. I've been playing hookey.'

Declan picked up *The Times* from the table. It took him ages to find the right page.

'Here.' He thrust it at her.

'What a crazy photo of Tony,' she said, settling down on the sofa for a good read. 'They've made him look almost benign. Oh my God,' she whispered a minute later, the laughter vanishing from her face. 'I don't believe it. How the fuck did he find out?'

'You tell me.'

650

Something chilling in his tone made her look up in alarm. He had moved close and seemed to tower above her, his legs in the grey trousers rising like two trunks of beech trees, the massive shoulders blocking out the light, and, in his deathly pale face, the implacable ever-watchful eyes of the Inquisitor.

Cameron shivered. 'What d'you mean?'

'I saw you plotting with Tony on Friday night.'

'He was waiting for me when I came out of the john, for Chrissake.'

'So Freddie and I had him followed.'

Cameron's eyes flickered.

'You're not going to tell me you and Tony were talking just about cucumber sandwiches for an hour and a half in the Royal Garden yesterday afternoon,' said Declan.

Cameron suddenly looked the picture of guilt.

'Sure I saw him. We had tea. I needed advice on, on –' she flushed scarlet – 'a personal matter.'

'You gave him all our programme plans, just as last month you told him the names of all the moles. No doubt he's got lots of other info about Venturer up his pinstriped sleeve for the meeting tomorrow.'

Cameron looked furious and terrified now – the hawk cornered by her captor about to strike.

'I didn't tell him anything.'

'You bloody liar,' thundered Declan. 'How long have you been spying for him? Ever since the beginning, since Rupert got his legover in Madrid?'

'How could I possibly spy for Tony?' she screamed. 'He beat me up, for Chrissake. This –' she waved *The Times* piece at Declan – 'sabotages everything we've worked for. Someone else leaked it.'

'Why did you bother to go to London on the worst day of the winter?' snarled Declan.

Blue, the lurcher, who'd been hovering nervously, jumped up on the sofa beside Cameron and, glaring at Declan, started to whine querulously at him. The other dogs licked their lips. Beaver slunk out of the room.

'Blue believes me,' pleaded Cameron. 'Why the fuck should

I come to Ireland, and work so hard on the programme plans, if I was spying for Tony? He's given my old job to Ailie Bristoe.'

'That's a front.'

'Bullshit,' said Cameron furiously. 'Is this some kind of a nightmare? Are you back at Corinium? Am I your guest tonight? Where's the fucking thumbscrews and the rack, or do you use electrodes and knee-capping like the fucking IRA?'

Grabbing her arm, Declan yanked her to her feet.

'No one else knew about Dermot MacBride. How much else have you told him?'

Ignoring the low growl from Blue, he started to shake her like a rat.

'You arrogant, pig-headed Irish asshole,' yelled Cameron. 'Why don't you believe me?'

Maddened because she'd let him down, violent because he felt guilty about wanting her so much, Declan slapped her very hard across the face. The next minute Blue leapt at him, burying his teeth in Declan's arm.

'Leave!' screamed Cameron. 'Leave, Blue.' Grabbing the dog's collar she tugged him off, then, almost carrying him back onto the sofa beside her, collapsed sobbing into his shaggy coat.

Pulling himself together, Declan lit two cigarettes, but, as he handed one to Cameron, Blue gave another ominous growl.

'It's OK, boy,' gasped Cameron.

She wiped her eyes frantically on her sleeve, then took the lighted cigarette. Inhaling deeply, she felt she was drawing the fires of hell into her lungs. Blue struggled up on his front paws and licked her face.

'My only friend,' she said tonelessly. 'You'd better have a tetanus jab,' she added to Declan.

Massaging his arm, Declan retreated to a respectable distance in front of the empty fireplace.

'OK, what was the personal problem? And why Tony?'

'I know he's a shit, but sometimes I figure he's the only person in the world who truly cares for me.'

'After beating you up?'

Cameron fingered her reddened cheek and shrugged. 'Seems to be catching.'

'I'm sorry.'

Cameron took a deep breath. 'I saw Tony because Rupert doesn't love me any more, and I can't handle it.'

'Just because he was bloody-minded at the ball,' said Declan scornfully. 'We're all uptight at the moment.'

Cameron's lip was trembling again. 'Rupert doesn't give a shit about the franchise. All he cares about is Taggie.'

'Taggie?' said Declan, flabbergasted. 'My Taggie? Are you out of your mind?'

'He saw her when we were in Ireland. In his bottom desk drawer, under the lining paper, he's hidden pictures of her with his kids.' Cameron gave a sob. 'And he's also kept some totally illiterate thank-you letter she sent him.'

Declan was utterly appalled.

'Rupert and Taggie,' he growled so furiously that Blue started rumbling back at him, like rival storms across a valley. 'I'm not having that profligate bastard laying a finger on Taggie.'

'But it's OK for him to finger me,' hissed Cameron, 'I'm only a mole.'

Earlier that afternoon Rupert had flown in from Rome and gone straight to his office in Whitehall. Ignoring a long list of telephone messages, he signed his letters, gathered up the rest of the post, made sure he was paired for the Finance debate that evening and set out for Gloucestershire. Slumped in the corner of a first-class carriage with his hand round a large Bell's, he looked at the snowy landscape turned electric blue in the twilight. Even in London it wasn't thawing. It had been a wasted visit to Rome. He'd made no contribution to the International Olympics Conference. He hadn't been able to sleep, or eat, or think straight, he was so haunted by the image of Taggie and Basil on the Bar Sinister balcony, or of Taggie's gasping with pleasure in Basil's expert embrace.

He tried to concentrate on the *Standard*, but beyond the

fact that Corinium shares had unaccountably rocketed, and Patric Walker forecast a stormy day for him tomorrow, and warned Cancers, which was Taggie's sign, to ignore all outside influences, he couldn't take anything in. Sitting opposite, an enchanting blonde was eyeing him with discreet but definite interest. Glancing at her slim knees above very shiny black boots, Rupert reflected that by now, in the old days, he would have bought her a large vodka and tonic and been investigating the prospect of a quick bang at the Station Hotel, Cotchester – if not at Penscombe. What the hell was happening to him? His secretary in London had given him a carrier bag of Christmas cards to sign for constituents and party workers. Wearily he scribbled *Rupert Campbell-Black* in a few, but not *love*, not for anyone in the world except that feckless Taggie.

Unknown to him, Taggie was slumped, shivering and equally miserable, in a second-class carriage down the train. She'd been doing an early Christmas lunch for some overseas sales reps in Swindon which had seemed to go on for ever. She always found train journeys unnerving, having to read all the strange station names and the platform directions and the train times. Today by mistake she'd got on a train going back to London and had to get off and wait in quite inadequate clothing on Didcot station for half an hour.

As Declan had taken the new Mini, Maud had borrowed Taggie's car to buy a new dress for her audition for *A Doll's House* tomorrow. She'd promised to meet Taggie at Cotchester if Taggie rang and told her what train she was coming on. But when Taggie had tried to ring her at Didcot there was no answer.

Rupert thought he was dreaming when he saw Taggie ahead of him on the platform at Cotchester. The snakey curls had dropped; she was back to her old ponytail. As she walked up the steps of the bridge, he noticed a man behind admiring her long black-stockinged legs. Fucking letch; Rupert wanted to kill him. As she turned to hand in her ticket, under the overhead light bulb he noticed the black shadows under her eyes. Too much sex, he thought savagely.

No one was there to meet her; there were no taxis; the telephone box didn't work. Peering out through the square glass panes, Taggie's legs nearly gave way beneath her as she saw Rupert getting into his car. Rushing out into the street, she waved at him. There was a moment of blind hope as she thought he waved back as he stormed past spraying snow all over her, but he was only adjusting his driving mirror.

The only answer was to walk into Cotchester and find another telephone box, or perhaps ask Bas to run her home. Why the hell hadn't she worn boots? She wasn't thinking straight at the moment. The icicles glittered from the station roof as she went past. Ahead she could see the white spire of Cotchester cathedral glinting in the moonlight with all the coloured windows lit up by a service inside. The next minute a car skidded to a halt beside her.

'What the hell are you doing?'

'Trying to find a telephone box to ring Mummy,' she muttered through furiously chattering teeth. Her lips were a livid green, her nose bluey-brown in the orange street light.

'Get in,' said Rupert. Viciously he punched out the number he knew so well. He let the telephone ring for two minutes. There was no answer.

'Mummy's on the toot as usual,' he said. 'I'll run you home.'

'Oh please don't bother.'

'It's not exactly out of my way,' he said sarcastically.

The frozen snow twinkled like rhinestones in the moonlight. Once they'd got out of Cotchester on to the country lanes there was only room for single-line traffic between the huge polar drifts. They didn't speak for a few miles, then, glancing sideways, Rupert saw the tears pouring down her face.

'What the fuck's the matter now?'

'I thought we were friends.'

'Then why did you go to bed with Bas?'

'I didn't. I meant to, because I was so miserable about you. I thought if I got some really good experience, you might fancy me a bit, but when it came to the crunch, I couldn't do it. I love you too much.'

Rupert stopped the car, pulling it into a gateway.

'I'm desperately sorry,' sobbed Taggie, groping in her bag for a paper handkerchief. 'I know it must be boring having every woman you meet in love with you. I didn't want to be one of them. I've tried so hard to get over you. Work doesn't help at all. It's just that you've been so kind looking after us, sorting Mummy out the other night and getting all that food when I made an up-cock at Sarah Stratton's dinner party, and giving me all those lovely things, and buying the wood for far more than it's worth.'

'Who told you that?' said Rupert, appalled.

'Ursula did. She saw Daddy's bank statement. It was the only good thing in it. I'm sorry for being such a drip.'

Rupert raised clenched fists to his temples in a superhuman effort not to reach out for her. Taggie mistook the gesture for sheer horror at being propositioned by yet another girl.

'I'm sorry.'

'For Christ's sake stop apologizing.' Rupert started speaking very slowly and deliberately as if he was addressing some loopy foreigner. 'Look, it wouldn't work. I'm terribly fond of you, Tag, but I'm far too old. Remember that hamburger bar manager who thought you were my daughter? I've never been faithful to anyone for more than a few weeks, and I'm not going to ruin your life by having a brief fling with you.'

'My life's ruined already,' sobbed Taggie, who'd soaked one paper handkerchief and was desperately searching in her pockets for another.

'You'll get over me,' said Rupert, handing her his.

'Like that five-bar gate in front of us,' said Taggie helplessly.

What made it worse was that the car got stuck and they had to push it out and Taggie slipped over and Rupert picked her up, then almost shoved her away, as though she was white hot, so desperate was his longing to take her in his arms.

The Priory was in darkness when they got back.

'Tell your father I'll ring him later,' said Rupert, cannoning off a low wall in his haste to get away.

Across the valley he could see lights on in his house. He

couldn't face Cameron at the moment. If only he could dump on Billy, but it was Wednesday and Billy would be at the television centre presenting the sports programme. Mindlessly he drove back to Cotchester and parked outside Basil's flat.

One look at Rupert's set white face was enough. Bas poured him a large whisky.

'Taggie said there wasn't a leg-over situation.'

'There wasn't,' said Bas. 'Not through lack of trying on my part. She is utterly adorable, but she utterly adores someone else, you lucky sod.'

Rupert drained his whisky.

'I'm not going to do anything about her.'

'Why ever not?' said Bas incredulously. 'It's on a plate.'

'I'm too old, shopsoiled, evil . . .'

'Oh, don't be so fucking self-indulgent. All these histrionics and tantrums are just the last frantic struggles of the lassooed bronco. You've never been in love before. It's really very nice, if you stop fighting it. Everyone's got to hang up their condom sometime. Taggie'd be worth it.'

'I don't want to talk about it.'

'OK,' said Bas, filling up their glasses.

'Am I interrupting you?'

'Not excessively. I was just looking at the books. The Bar's had a staggering year, thanks to all those malcontents from Corinium drowning their sorrows and plotting my big brother's downfall. Won't be so good next year, with you and Freddie and Declan running things. They'll all be working so hard, they won't have time for a lunch hour. D'you really think we'll get it?'

''Course we will,' said Rupert, thinking he really didn't give a fuck any more.

Bas shook his head. 'Tony gave a bloody good interview to *The Times* this morning. Came across as Mr Caring.' He threw the paper in Rupert's direction.

Rupert ignored it. 'Did she really say she loved me?'

'Yes, she did, which I find extraordinary, knowing you as I do.'

657

Rupert shook his head in bewilderment.

'It's never, never hit me like this before either. I'm still not going to do anything about it.'

RIVALS

49

Up in London that night the fourteen directors and senior staff of Corinium Television had an extremely successful final dry run before their meeting at the IBA the next afternoon. Tony, in a new dark-blue pin-stripe suit paid for by Corinium, was in coruscating form.

'They can have one drink,' he told Ginger Johnson beforehand, 'and then not one drop until we've been round the course – and I'm going to grill them.'

No one at the meeting tomorrow, he said, was to speak until he'd introduced them. There was now, as a result of recent hiring and firing, a most satisfactory preponderance of ex-production people on the Board who would do most of the talking. The money-men, like Ginger and Georgie Baines, who brought in the vast advertising revenue, would keep a low profile. In fact it would be better if the word 'profit' were not mentioned at all. All the men had had hair cuts.

'No doubt,' muttered Sarah Stratton to James Vereker, 'there will be a nail inspection in the morning.'

Afterwards they all dined wisely but not too well at the Carlton Tower, where they were staying overnight. No shellfish was allowed, nor liqueurs after dinner. Everyone was very impressed with Ailie Bristoe, the new Programme Controller, who'd flown over from Hollywood for the occasion, and seemed as beautiful as she was bright. James Vereker, in particular, thought she looked very caring.

'I'm surprised Tony hasn't put the women in separate hotels,' grumbled Sarah, as they were all sent up to bed early.

'Be sure to order a *Scorpion* for tomorrow,' was Tony's parting shot. 'You'll all find it very interesting reading.'

Back in Gloucestershire, Declan finally stormed out of The Priory around ten o'clock, having failed to get a confession out of Cameron. Utterly devastated that he and Freddie could possibly think she was the mole, Cameron was slumped on the sofa, still cuddling Blue when the telephone rang. It was some girl, saying Rupert wouldn't be back until the morning, but he sent his love. There was a terrific din in the background and the girl sounded as though she was ringing from a bar. Bastard, thought Cameron, but she was too proud to ask where he was. As she put the telephone down it rang again.

'Can I speak to Rupert Campbell-Black?'

'He's not here.'

'Is that Cameron Cook?'

'This is she.'

The voice thickened and became oily as though it was asking for extended credit.

'This is the *Messenger* here. Wondered what you feel about Rupert's memoirs in the *Scorpion*.'

'I don't know what you're talking about.'

'Rupert's really done it this time. Bloody bad timing on the day before your IBA meeting.'

Cameron had had a long day and was not connecting well but gradually it sank in that Beattie Johnson had finally got her revenge on Rupert by telling all to the *Scorpion*. Not only, according to the *Messenger* reporter, had she produced every kind of salacious detail about her two years with Rupert and the unbelievably kinky things they'd got up to, but, even worse, revealed intimate details of his sex life with other women, including Helen.

'Oh my God!' whispered Cameron. 'Does he mention me?'

'Not yet, sweetheart,' said the reporter, who'd already seen and admired Cameron's photograph, 'but you may be in Saturday's instalment. They're trailing the spread that's going out on Friday, the morning you go to the IBA. It's all about Rupert's affair with Amanda Hamilton, wife of the shadow Foreign Secretary. Very pretty lady, evidently she liked being spanked.'

Cameron groaned.

'And there's a particularly damaging bit tomorrow,' said the reporter, who was beginning to enjoy himself. 'I'll read it. Beattie writes: "*I always felt Rupert was unnaturally close to fellow show jumper Billy Lloyd-Foxe. Rupert admitted that when they were in Kenya, he, Helen and Billy and his journalist wife Janey (who left Billy for nine months soon after they were married) had a naughty foursome. Did Helen (who started an affair with Jake Lovell shortly after this incident) discover the true nature of Rupert's sexual preference that night?*"'

'I don't want to hear any more,' screamed Cameron, slamming down the receiver. It rang again. It was the *Sun.*

'Go away,' she screamed.

Immediately she'd put down the receiver, she dialled out.

'Fuck off, all of you,' snarled a voice.

'Declan, it's Cameron. Have you heard about Rupert's memoirs?'

'Yes,' said Declan, 'and I don't know where the fuck to get hold of him.'

'Nor do I,' sobbed Cameron.

The juggernauts rumbling along Cotchester High Street woke Rupert next morning to the worst hangover in recorded history. Moaning, he pulled the blankets over his head. There was a knock on the door.

'Bugger off. I feel terrible.'

'You're not going to feel any better when you read this,' said Bas, handing him a Fernet Branca and the *Scorpion,* which Rupert read in silence.

'The dirty bitch,' he said softly. 'She said she'd get me in the end.'

It was as though some terrible monster from his past had put a hand up from a manhole and dragged him down into the mire and slime below. He went straight to the lavatory and threw up.

'Lend me a toothbrush, and then a telephone,' he said to Bas. He was put straight through to Freddie.

'Look, I've only just seen the *Scorpion*. I'm ringing up to resign.'

'Don't be daft,' said Freddie.

'I've got to. There are two more days to go, and it's bound to get worse. Unless I pull out, there's no way you'll get the franchise.'

'Don't be rash, mate. We won't be much good at running a TV station if we can't ride out somefink like this. Got to stick togevver. Come over 'ere and we'll sort out the best plan of action, but you're not resigning.'

'Up to me really,' said Rupert. 'I must see Cameron, and then I'll be over.'

Arriving at Penscombe, he found cars parked all the way up his drive, and the gravel in front of the house completely hidden by journalists, photographers and television crews. Corinium had even had the temerity to send a mobile canteen. Stony-faced, greyer than the trampled snow, Rupert got out of his car.

'Fuck off, the lot of you,' he snarled as they all surged forward. 'I've got to talk to my lawyer.'

'What about the franchise?' asked the *Mail on Sunday*.

'Come on, Rupe,' said the *Star*. 'Give us a quote. We've waited all fucking night.'

'I've got nothing to say. I'll put my dogs on you if you don't beat it.' Fighting his way into the house, he slammed the door behind him.

'Well, well, well,' said Cameron from halfway up the stairs.

She wore no make-up, and her hair was sleeked back from her face which was deathly white.

'I'm sorry,' began Rupert.

'Fuck off,' screamed Cameron, as a photographer appeared at a side window. Racing downstairs, she drew the curtains.

'Come upstairs,' said Rupert.

They went into his bedroom, the set for so much of the

662

action in the first instalment of the memoirs. Almost as though the great four-poster would contaminate her, Cameron gave it a wide berth and went over to the fireplace.

'How could you?' she whispered. 'Have you told people those sort of things about me?'

'Never, never,' said Rupert. Suddenly dizzy, he slumped on the flowered chintz-covered chair in front of Helen's old dressing table. 'Beattie was a special case. The thing that turned her on was stories of my screwing other women. She must have had a tape recorder running under the bed the whole time.'

'Then you did say those things. They're disgusting, insupportable.' She shuddered. 'You realize your career's finished? You'll be kicked out of the party. I hope you've already resigned from Venturer. And I suppose Saturday's instalment will be all about your touching designs on Taggie O'Hara. How the great rake was reformed and approached his waiting bride with a tenderness which was all the more careful, the more considerate because he knew the depths of her apprehension – Ker-rist!' Her voice rose to a screech.

Rupert looked at her incredulously. Expecting the exocet from the front, he was suddenly being torpedoed from underneath.

'You're in love with her, aren't you?' said Cameron.

Rupert looked across the valley at his white fields. He'd always seen them as arms protecting Taggie. Now they seemed like a great predatory polar bear, crushing The Priory to death.

He turned back to Cameron.

'OK,' he said flatly, 'I do love her. If I'm honest, I've loved her ever since New Year's Eve, probably long before that. I'm desperately sorry, I know I've dealt you a marked card. I'm much too fond of you to kid you along any longer, just for the sake of the franchise, that you and I are going to end up together.'

Cameron opened her mouth to yell at him, but Rupert raised his hand for a second's more silence.

'I didn't know a thing about these memoirs coming out – not that you'd want me anyway after reading them – but I want you to know that I was intending to level with you today about Taggie.'

For a second Cameron seemed to sway with frenzy, like a viper about to strike, then she screamed: 'You won't get her. Declan knows about it too, and there's no way he'll let you ever get your filthy depraved hands on his darling daughter.'

'I know there isn't,' said Rupert. 'This –' he picked up the *Scorpion* and wearily dropped it in the wastepaper basket – 'has finally done for us.'

'Serve you fucking right,' yelled Cameron. 'I'm getting out of here, and I never want to see you again.'

She rushed downstairs out of the front door, then kicked and punched her way through the waiting journalists, sending several of them leaping for safety as the Lotus stormed down the drive.

'Nice quiet girl,' said the *Mail on Sunday*, picking himself out of the snow.

Arriving at Green Lawns, Rupert found Freddie and Declan desperately trying to salvage the IBA meeting. As a result of Rupert's memoirs, two of the major financial backers had pulled out and Professor Graystock had resigned. As Rupert went into Freddie's study, the Bishop rang up:

'I'm afraid in the light of Rupert Campbell-Black's quite appalling revelations, I shall have to withdraw my support for the Venturer bid.'

'You can't,' said Freddie, aghast. 'The meeting's tomorrow morning. Your not being there will really tip the scales. I fort the Church of England were supposed to forgive sinners.'

'I have to set a good example to my flock,' said the Bishop and rang off.

'Lily-livered bastard,' said Freddie furiously. 'We're well shot of 'im.'

'He'd have impressed the IBA,' said Declan bleakly, who couldn't look Rupert in the eye. Was it because of Taggie or the memoirs?

'Then I must resign,' said Rupert. 'It's the only honourable thing to do.'

'No, you won't,' said Freddie. 'It don't add up. Beattie Johnson was a slut, but she 'ad a good 'eart. I don't fink she'd 'ave written those fings wivout considerable financial inducement. Seb Burrows has got nuffink to do at the moment. I'm going to put him on to the story and see what he can dig up. And can't we slap an injunction on the *Scorpion?*'

Rupert shook his head wearily. 'I wish we could, but I'm afraid it's all true. Although, it's appallingly slanted. The only wrong thing is that Billy and I aren't gay. Seven-eighths of it was never, never meant for publication, but she was such a fucking good listener, and you know I can never resist making people laugh. We were together for two years, for Christ's sake.'

'How's Cameron taken it?' asked Declan harshly. 'She was in a terrible state last night. Thinks you and she are kaput.'

Rupert slumped on the sofa, putting his head in his hands. 'We are. I've just told her.'

Declan lost his temper. It was like an earthquake and a volcano erupting at the same time.

'Can't you ever keep your fucking trap shut? First you tell everything to Beattie Johnson, then you have to give Cameron the boot. Don't you realize this'll screw up any final chance we have of getting the franchise? No Bishop, no professor, no financial backing, no Cameron – she'll bolt straight back to Tony and tell him everything she hasn't told him already.'

'What d'you mean?' Rupert looked up, the bloodshot eyes suddenly alert.

'Haven't you read *The Times* yet?'

'Bas muttered something about it last night, but I forgot to read it.'

'Cameron leaked all our plans to Tony on Tuesday.'

'Don't be ridiculous.'

'We put a private detective on to Tony. They spent an hour and a half together in the Royal Garden.'

'So?' said Rupert. 'They were having a bunk-up. Cameron's straight, I swear it.'

'So do I,' said Freddie.

'Well, it's purely academic now, since Rupert has seen fit to kick her out.'

'I'm sorry, Declan.'

'It's not bloody good enough.'

Unshaven, putty-coloured, his shirt on its second day, his suit crumpled, Rupert looked so desolate and so ill, slumped on the sofa, that Freddie went over and put a hand on his shoulder.

'Could 'appen to anyone. You'll come out of it.'

'Venturer won't. I've done for the lot of you.'

At that moment Valerie marched in.

'I've read every word of your disgusting memoirs,' she screeched. 'I don't want you in the house. You might give Wayne or even Fred-Fred some horrid disease.'

'Shut up,' snapped Freddie. 'He's 'ad enough punishment. Now just bugger off and bring us some black coffee.'

Feeling he was such an irritant to Declan, Rupert left soon after that. Holing up in Bas's flat, he spent the rest of a nightmare day on the telephone, trying to resign from the party, from his constituency and from the International Olympics Committee. To his frustration no one would accept. The Leader of the Opposition, for example, was amazingly sanguine:

'Wait until the franchises have been awarded,' she said. 'That tramp Beattie Johnson took me to the cleaners just before I became leader – slanted the whole interview. Jolly nearly cost me the job. The Amanda Hamilton business is unfortunate, I grant you, but Rollo's only Shadow Foreign Secretary at the moment, and you haven't done anything illegal. There's been absolutely no security leak, and it isn't as though you were married when you were in office. Just hang on a bit.'

Amanda Hamilton, on the other hand, was absolutely

gibbering with anger when Rupert rang her. Rollo was intending to sue, she said.

Malise Gordon, by contrast, was icy cold with rage that Helen's name had been dragged into it.

'I'm not excusing what's happened,' said Rupert, 'but I was very raw when Helen left me. Beattie lived with me for two years. Naturally I confided in her about my marriage, it never entered my head she'd shop me. None of the stuff that's been printed was intended for the memoirs. Will you tell Helen how desperately sorry I am? I did tell Beattie hundreds of good things about her, which she conveniently forgot to put in.'

'I'm sure that'll be a great comfort to Helen,' said Malise acidly.

'Look, I'm going abroad immediately after the IBA meeting tomorrow,' said Rupert. 'I won't be back for Christmas. I must see the children before I go.'

'I don't think that's at all a good idea,' said Malise crushingly, 'and I know Helen won't either. Tab's far too young to understand, and I doubt if Marcus will ever speak to you again after the things you said about his mother. The press are howling round the place; your presence would only exacerbate things. Just bugger off and leave us all alone.'

'I must explain –' just for a second Rupert's voice faltered – 'that whatever's happened, I still love them. For Christ's sake, Malise.'

'You can always write,' said Malise, and hung up.

Rupert sat slumped for a long time. Then he borrowed two hundred pounds in cash from Basil's till, a piece of writing paper and an envelope.

'*Darling Taggie,*' he wrote, '*I'm sorry I was bloody the last two times we met. Of course we're still friends. One day you'll find some nice boy who's worthy of you, and he'll be the luckiest sod in the world. In the meantime could you spend the enclosed on Christmas presents for Marcus and Tab. You'll know instinctively what they'd like. Thank you for everything. God bless you . . . Rupert.*'

Shoving the cash and the letter in an envelope, he gave it to Bas to deliver to The Priory.

Towards nightfall, over at Green Lawns, Freddie and Declan were just trying to prevent another backer pulling out when the private detective rang on another line. He had something too important to tell them over the telephone. He'd be straight round. He turned out, to Declan's surprise, not to be some seedy unfrocked cop in a dirty mac, but a delightfully understated, mouse-haired young Wykehamist with an innocent pink and white face. Nor did he beat about anyone's bush.

'Tony Baddingham spent yesterday afternoon in a Stow-in-the-Wold motel with a woman. I've got pictures of them arriving separately and then leaving together, and exchanging kisses in the car park.'

He threw the pictures down on the table. Fascinated, Freddie and Declan got up to have a look. In the first photograph the woman had her black coat collar turned up and was wearing a black beret, dark glasses and her hair tied back. In the second, coming out of the motel, her coat was unbuttoned, she was laughing, holding the dark glasses and the beret in one hand, with her glorious red hair trailing down her back. In the third, she was kissing Tony in front of Taggie's car.

'Is this some kind of a joke?' hissed Declan.

'I'm afraid not,' said the private detective. 'I'm awfully sorry, Mr O'Hara. After they'd gone I talked to the reception-ist. After I'd bunged her, she admitted they'd been there several times before. She showed me the register – they'd signed in as Mr and Mrs Jones. The girl remembered Mrs O'Hara because she was so beautiful.'

Declan started to shake. It was like seeing the first stroke of the woodcutter's axe going into a great oak tree, thought Freddie.

'But it was Bas, not Tony,' muttered Declan.

'Bas must have been a front,' said Freddie.

'Look how upset she was the other night when Taggie

668

turned up with Bas,' said Declan, frantically trying to convince himself.

'That's because she's jealous of Taggie,' said Freddie wisely. 'It was only later she got really upset, which was when you told us you'd just seen Cameron with Tony – and she did know all about Dermot MacBride and the Shakespeare plays.'

'I don't believe it,' muttered Declan. 'She wouldn't. I must find her.' He stumbled towards the door.

'For Christ's sake, drive slowly,' warned Freddie.

As Declan walked into The Priory Maud came out of the drawing-room with a glass of champagne in her hand. She was wearing a black polo-neck jersey, a black coat, black stockings, black flat shoes and a black beret on the back of her head. She was very pale, she wore no lipstick, but her skin had a glowing luminosity and her eyes were huge and dreamy. Declan thought she had never looked more beautiful, and suddenly knew she was as guilty as hell.

'Darling – I got it!' she said ecstatically.

'What?'

'The part – Nora – in A *Doll's House*. We start rehearsing immediately after Christmas and they're paying me four hundred a week, so our money worries are all over.'

How little she knows about anything, thought Declan – how can a child have done such terrible things?

'Where's Taggie?' he asked.

'Cooking supper, I think. You don't seem very pleased for me, darling.'

As if in a dream he led her into the drawing-room, shutting the door and then opening it again to let in Claudius and Gertrude. Gertrude had a Bonio sticking out of the side of her mouth like a pipe. She could sit there for hours, saliva hanging in festoons. Declan leant against the door for support, watching Maud put a log on the fire. Despite all Maud's grandiose plans for The Priory, there were still no curtains at the windows which were as black as her clothes.

'How long have you been having an affair with Tony?' he asked almost conversationally.

669

Maud's face went as blank as a digital clock in a power cut.

'I don't know what you're talking about.'

'Don't prevaricate. I've got evidence.' Declan threw the photographs down on the sofa. Slowly Maud examined them.

'Rather good, that one.' She took a leisurely sip of her champagne. 'I might use it as a publicity photograph.'

'How long's it been going on?'

'Since September.'

'So you told him everything?'

Maud shrugged: 'I really don't remember. We found so much to talk about.'

This can't be happening to me, thought Declan. I don't feel anything. It's as though we're discussing two characters in a play.

'But why Tony? Bas I can understand, but not –' for the first time he betrayed any emotion – 'not that filthy venomous toad.'

Maud looked at him for a moment, her hand gently stroking Claudius's ears.

'Because he was kind, because he listened to me, because he was interested in me as a person – not just as a hole between two legs.'

Her sudden uncharacteristic coarseness shocked Declan almost more than her betrayal.

'Tony!' he said in amazement, 'kind?'

Suddenly Maud flipped. 'You're so obsessed with your fucking franchise,' she yelled, 'you don't know anyone else exists, except when you want to fuck them. You couldn't even forget it for one moment to get back for my first night, when I really needed you. Christ – I needed you! And then swanning in and ordering me away from my own first-night party.

'I was only fooling around with Tony until then. It was only after that that it got serious. He arranged for me to meet Pascoe Rawlings. He saw that a car delivered me to Pascoe's office last week and brought me back. He fixed for me to be driven to the audition today, and even though he'd got his

IBA meeting this afternoon, he still rang me this evening to see how I'd got on. You'd even forgotten I was going.' She laughed; it was a horrible sound without any merriment. 'The great interviewer, so praised for his judgement of character and his consideration to the staff, who doesn't know a thing about his own wife.'

'Can't you understand that he's using you?' said Declan slowly. 'The only thing that turns Tony on is acquisition. You've just lost us the franchise, and you were going to stand by and let me blame Cameron.'

'Serve her right – arrogant little bitch,' cried Maud hysterically.

Outside in the hall Taggie could hear her mother's screams getting louder and louder. Oh God, her father didn't need upsetting any more when he had the IBA meeting in the morning. Next moment the drawing-room door burst open.

'I'm leaving you,' screamed Maud.

'Come back,' roared Declan.

'Never, and don't send Ursula looking for me at the Lost Property Office, because I won't be there.' She shot past Taggie and out of the front door, banging it so hard the whole hall rattled.

Taggie ran to open it. Outside it was snowing again. She watched Maud drive off in her car, hell for leather, down the drive.

'What on earth's the matter?' she said, turning to Declan, who was standing as if blasted white by lightning.

'She was the mole.'

Taggie gave a gasp. 'She couldn't be. She can't have meant to.'

'She did,' said Declan in a voice of utter despair, 'because I neglected her. It's all my fault. I blamed Cameron last night and Rupert today, and just now I blamed her. But through my focking obsession and hubris I've brought us all down.'

50

For Rupert next morning the press was crucifixion – ranging from highly moralistic pieces about the chronic Tory failure to keep their noses clean to double-page spreads with pictures charting the rise and fall of the Tory party golden boy. The tabloids had dug up several of Rupert's more bitter exes, who, having done a great deal more than kiss, were now only too happy to tell. The seamiest tabloid of all had a huge frontpage headline: '*Campbell-Blackguard*,' above an enchanting picture of Tabitha.

'*In the playground of exclusive Bluebell's school (fees £1,500 a term),*' ran the copy, '*a little child sobs alone. In a voice hardly above a whisper, Tabitha Campbell-Black told the Scorpion:*

'"*I don't mind my friends not playing with me any more, but I don't want Daddy to die of AIDS.*"'

'This is the final fucking limit,' howled Billy Lloyd-Foxe, hurling the *Scorpion* across the room. 'I'm coming with you to the IBA.'

'The Beeb will sack you if they find out,' said Janey, who was painting her nails because it was less hassle than cleaning them. 'And as I turned down a hundred grand yesterday to tell all about our life with Rupert, and this suit cost nearly as much, I don't think you can afford to.'

'I don't care,' said Billy mutinously. 'Rupert's my best friend, and anyway since Beattie implied I was gay yesterday, I shall certainly be snapped up by Radio 3.'

At Freddie's house, the remnants of the Venturer consortium gathered before the meeting. With no Bishop, no Professor, no Cameron and none of the moles, their numbers were utterly depleted and their bid in tatters. The second day of Rupert's memoirs was even worse, with intimations of under-age school girls. Freddie had spent half the night trying to persuade a demented Declan that they'd got to shop Tony, not just for seducing Maud and bugging their houses, but because Seb was working on excellent evidence that Tony had bribed Beattie Johnson to sing to the rooftops, just at a time when it would be most damaging to Venturer.

But like Wellington at Waterloo refusing to turn the guns on the enemy commandant, Declan refused to let anyone condemn Tony. He didn't want Maud's name dragged into it. He was clearly still suffering from shock. He looked terrible.

'A black ram is tupping my white ewe,' he kept saying over and over again, 'and it was all my fault.'

Rupert, who arrived with Bas, didn't look much better, but at least he'd got a grip on himself. The meeting had to be got through. There were people not to be let down, there would be the rest of his life to mourn for Taggie and probably his children as well. Helen had rung this morning, saying she was applying for a court order to deny him access.

Even Henry Hampshire arrived walking wounded, wearing a dark suit with uncharacteristically flared trousers, and with his leg in plaster.

'Horse put its foot down a rabbit hole,' was all he would say about it.

''Morning.' He went up to Rupert, who was huddled on the sofa trying to keep down a cup of coffee. 'Enjoying your memoirs; great stuff.' He lowered his voice. 'I had a crack at Mandy Hamilton myself twenty years ago. God, she was pretty. Might have made more progress if I'd known she liked having her bottom smacked.'

Rupert managed a pale smile. 'At least it kept you out of the papers.' Then, also lowering his voice, he added, 'Look,

I don't think there's any chance now of us getting the franchise. Tony's now odds on and we've gone way out.'

'Better have a bet then,' said Henry, limping towards the telephone. 'Anyway, I've had more fun in the last six months than I can ever remember. We'll have to bid for another area next time.'

Dame Enid arrived next, resplendent in a pinstriped trouser suit with an even wider white stripe than Tony's, a bright blue tie, and an Al Capone hat.

'Stick 'em up, it's a shoot out,' said Marti Gluckstein, who came with her. He was dressed in a lurid green Norfolk jacket and knickerbockers, and sucking on a pipe.

'Did you get that at Valerie's boutique?' said Bas, then hastily shut up in case Freddie overheard.

'Thought I ought to appear as the country squire,' said Marti. 'Where's the Bishop?'

'Pulled out, I'm afraid,' said Freddie, handing him and Dame Enid cups of coffee.

'Good riddance, pompous old fart,' said Dame Enid, helping herself to sugar. 'Can't you pull a rabbi out of a hat to replace him?' she added to Marti.

Marti smirked. 'For you, my dear, anything.'

'Crispin Graystock's pulled out too,' said Freddie.

'Well, thank God we've got rid of the two worst wafflers,' said Dame Enid philosophically. 'Graystock's got complete verbal diarrhoea.'

'Which reminds me,' said Henry, hobbling off at great speed towards the lavatory, 'had the most ghastly trots all night. Sure I'm going to botch my answers.'

The moment he arrived, Lord Smith went straight up to Rupert. 'Really feel for you, lad,' he said. 'But everyone regards the *Scorpion* as fiction. That Beastly Johnson did me over once. Took down what I said, but twisted it like barley sugar. I've got a message from Alf Smithers. Chairman of the FA,' he added, by way of illumination, when Rupert didn't react.

'I know,' said Rupert flatly. 'He was my cross.'

'He's not cross now. Told me to wish you luck today. Said

you were the best Sports Minister they've ever 'ad. They all wish you'd come back. What's up with Declan?'

'Wife trouble,' said Rupert.

'Happens at franchise time,' said Lord Smith. 'When we bid for the Midlands eight years ago, the wives got so fed up, they was all at it – even mine.'

'Only two more to come,' said Freddie, trying to cheer up his own and everyone's spirits. 'And 'ere they are,' he went on, as Seb and Charles came through the door.

'We're going to have a fuller house than you thought,' said Charles. 'I've just seen Billy, Janey, Harold White and Sally Maples getting out of a taxi.'

Freddie had tears in his eyes as he welcomed them. 'You shouldn't have come. It's totally out of order,' he said. 'I know what you're risking, but I won't say I'm not bloody pleased to see you.'

Declan seemed hardly to notice, but Rupert's jaw quilted with muscles when he saw Billy. 'You're fucking insane,' he said roughly.

'I like "lorst" causes, as Henry would say,' said Billy cheerfully. 'Anyway, I brought you luck at the LA Olympics. And you brought me luck, too. If I hadn't done the commentary for the BBC, they'd never have given me a job.'

'Which you're about to lose.'

As the hands of the clock inched past nine-thirty, they decided that there was no point waiting any longer. Cameron wasn't coming.

'Pity,' sighed Hardy Bissett, going round straightening ties. 'Now, don't forget, no sniping – solidarity is all. Sit up straight. Burst with enthusiasm. You're bursting a little too much, Janey darling.' He did up two buttons of her shirt. 'Although, on reflection, if you're sitting anywhere near the Prebendary, undo them again and press your elbows together.'

It was still bitterly cold when they set out for the IBA in their cars. The snow in the park was the colour of dirty seagulls. In High Street, Ken. the shop windows with their jolly snowmen, spangled Christmas trees and mufflered bright-eyed tots hurling snowballs were at variance with the sullen sky outside, and the shoppers shuffling blue-lipped and bad-tempered along the slushy pavements.

Janey's scent was making Rupert feel sick. In a greengrocer's shop, he noticed, they were already selling mistletoe, the one thing he wouldn't need this Christmas.

'Oh look, there's Father Christmas,' said Janey, pressing a button to lower the window, as the car swung round The Scotch House into Brompton Road.

'Please Santa,' she called out to him, as he marched alongside the car, 'will you put a franchise in my stocking?'

'Ho, ho, ho,' said Father Christmas, hoisting his sack onto his back and batting his long black eyelashes at Janey. 'For a pretty little girl like you, I just might.'

'My Christ,' said Janey, with a scream of laughter, as he turned right in front of the car and strode purposefully across the road through the revolving doors of the IBA. 'It's Georgie Baines.'

'I wish I'd thought of that,' said Charles petulantly. 'I wanted to come as Gwendolyn Gosling again, but I thought I'd better play it straight.'

To avoid the press, and preserve the utmost security, the convoy of cars turned right down Lancelot Place, entering the IBA from the back by the underground car park. From here their passengers were whisked up to the eighth floor and, although the moles nervously looked for reporters in every dark corner, they were all safely led along the corridor and installed in an empty office.

'I feel like a courtier waiting for an audience with Louis XIV: "Please don't banish me to my estate in the Loire, Sire",' said Charles, as he peered out of the window on to another IBA block of offices, where every secretary seemed to be clutching paper cups of coffee and reading Rupert's memoirs.

'God, I'm nervous,' said Henry, mouthing the answers to possible questions. 'D'you think I should say brilliant wild life "photographer" or "cameraman"?'

'Cameraman,' said Billy. 'Photographer is press, and we don't like them very much at the moment.'

'I wish I could take in a calculator,' said Marti in a hollow voice.

'D'you think they'll shine lights in our faces?' asked Janey.

'They didn't yesterday, but then Corinium has a better track record,' said a voice. It was Georgie Baines, who'd shed his Father Christmas disguise and was now wearing a dark suit and fluffing up his dark curls.

Everyone crowded round him in delight.

'Of course! You went in yesterday afternoon with Corinium,' said Freddie.

'Wearing a different tie,' said Georgie.

'How long were you in there?' asked Seb.

'Exactly an hour,' said Georgie.

'What was it like?'

'Falling off a log. Not one difficult question. Tony's star is definitely in the ascendant, that's why I'm here. I've always believed rats should desert a rising shit.'

'How did you manage to get away?' asked Janey, removing a last bit of white beard from Georgie's chin.

'Tony thinks I'm at Saatchi's.'

A female IBA official was going spare trying to organize everyone's entrance into the board room in a pre-ordained order, so the Authority would know who they were.

'I expected eleven people,' she said in bewilderment. 'There seem a great many more. I know who you are,' she said to Janey, 'and you,' she said to Rupert, keeping her distance, 'and you,' she turned to Declan, looking perplexed as though she hardly recognized him.

'Are you the Bishop of Cotchester?' she asked Marti as she consulted her notes. Everyone giggled. 'And I wasn't expecting you, Mr White, or you, Billy, or you, Miss Maples, and certainly not you *again*, Mr Baines.'

'Well we're all here,' said Harold White. 'We belong to Venturer.'

'Have you all got your two photographs?'

Everyone duly produced them.

'Had to go into Woolworths to get it taken,' announced Henry. 'Never been there before. Rather a lark.'

The female official scratched her head in despair: 'And where's Cameron Cook?'

'Not coming, nor the Bishop, nor Professor Graystock. They've dropped out,' said Freddie helpfully. 'Nor Wesley Emerson. He's still wiv us, but he's playing in a test match abroad.'

'No, I'm not,' said a voice deeper than the Caribbean Sea.

It was Wesley in a Support Venturer T-shirt and an England blazer. He was greeted with screams of delight. Dame Enid thumped him on the back till he pleaded for mercy.

'How did you manage to get away?'

'Pulled a muscle, man,' said Wesley, grinning from ear to ear. 'But I haven't slept all night, so I hope there's no tricky questions about ethnic minorities.'

Rupert took him aside. 'You really are fantastic,' he said.

Wesley grinned. 'I read all that shit about you, man. Same thing happened to me; thought we ought to show a united front.'

'I really think I've got you all sorted out,' said the IBA lady. 'I'll just check that Lady Gosling's ready.'

After that there was a dreadful quarter of an hour wait.

'It's just like standing outside the headmaster's study,' said Seb. 'Are we going to have to run round the pitch fifty times or get six of the best?'

'Amanda Hamilton'd like that,' said Charles. Then, seeing the bleak expression on Rupert's face, 'Oh come on, Rupert, one's got to laugh.'

Rupert, who'd been thinking of Taggie, didn't really think one did have to.

'Must go to the lavatory,' said Henry.

'Will you all come in, please?' said the IBA lady.

'Good luck, everyone,' said Freddie.

'Remember the old bat who isn't Lady Gosling is Mrs Menzies-Scott, ex-chairman of the WI,' hissed Georgie.

•

The twelve members of the authority, flanked by six senior staff from the IBA, were already seated along one side of the beautifully polished oval table, as Venturer filed in and took up their places opposite them.

In the centre sat Lady Gosling in a thick brown tweed suit and a bottle-green cardigan. Despite the warmth of the room, a thermal vest could be seen peeping above her brown check shirt. Mrs Scott-Menzies of the WI, who'd been foolish enough to wear a rust angora jersey, had already turned puce in the heat. Other members of the panel included such worthies as the ex-Labour Minister for Education, who gave Lord Smith the ghost of a wink, a Welsh Judge Davey, a Catholic bishop, the Prebendary, who had an expression of extreme distaste on his face, several dons, two ex-chairmen from public companies, and Lady Barnsley, late of the White Fish Authority, who was alleged to have an orgasm every time she saw a celebrity. Handbag rammed protectively against her groin, she was now gazing at Rupert with a mixture of terror and excitement. Three other Authority members, who'd been avidly reading the memoirs, hastily shoved them away as Venturer came in.

'I wish I'd brought my autograph book,' whispered Judge Davey, who was generally regarded as the group wag.

Freddie sat in the middle facing Lady Gosling, flanked by Rupert and Declan. On Rupert's right, as obvious and disfiguring as a lost front tooth, was a space where Cameron should have been. Janey was up the end of the table, with only Henry beyond her, so he could stick out his plaster leg. The Prebendary sat opposite them, gazing at Janey with pursed lips. Surreptitiously, she undid a couple of the buttons of her grey silk shirt. It was like dining at Lady Margaret Hall, she thought as she looked at the worthy unpainted faces of the women opposite. She wished she'd soft-pedalled her eye make-up.

Henry was gazing out of the window at Knightsbridge Barracks. 'Used to work there,' he announced in a loud whisper. 'You'd never believe there was a squash court on top.'

Lady Gosling, who had not winked at her friend Dame Enid, greeted them with the utmost coolness.

'I'm sorry you were kept waiting so long. It was because of the very considerable changes in the numbers attending. I see all the so-called "moles" –' one could feel her fastidiously putting quotes round such a slang word – 'have decided to show up, despite the threat of dismissal, and we certainly weren't expecting you,' she added to Wesley. 'We gathered you were playing in a test match.'

Wesley gave her the benefit of his heavenly banana-split smile.

'I was, Mrs Menzies-Scott.'

'Gosling,' hissed Janey.

'I'm sorry, Mrs Gosling, I got injured. And coming to this meeting seemed more important. After all, we'll be running a television company for a long long time.'

'Hum,' said Lady Gosling. 'Somewhat hubristic of you. And where are the Bishop and Professor Graystock?'

Freddie cleared his throat.

'Er, they've withdrawn because of a conflict of interests.'

'One can understand that,' said Lady Gosling heavily. 'And Cameron Cook?'

Freddie opened his mouth.

'I'm here,' said a voice behind him. 'I'm so sorry, Lady Gosling, my cab ran into another car in the Old Brompton Road.'

It was Cameron in her scarlet silk suit, bringing a wonderful warmth and colour into the room. She was very pale beneath her blusher, and wearing tinted glasses, but totally self-possessed. Sliding into the seat beside Rupert, she very deliberately put a hand over his, then smiling down the row said once again: 'I'm so sorry, everyone.'

'You little beauty,' said Freddie under his breath.

Cameron's arrival seemed to pull Venturer magically together. The first questions were about finance and technical specifications, and initially fielded by Freddie. Then, like a tigerish scrum-half, he passed the ball out to his wings,

Rupert, Bas, Lord Smith, Marti, and Georgie Barnes, who'd arrived with a pile of revenue forecasts.

Freddie in fact was the life and soul of the application. A born showman, puffing on his cigar, giving occasional infectious roars of laughter, he exuded honesty, energy and huge enthusiasm for the task.

The Prebendary, who was still looking beady, didn't throw Wesley on ethnic minorities, but, seeing him yawning, asked him why he personally wished to oust Corinium as the franchise holder.

'I live in the area, man,' drawled Wesley. 'I'm absolutely fed up, like everyone else in this consortium, with having to watch such God-awful programmes.'

Even Lady Gosling suppressed a smile, and nodded to Lady Barnsley, who rather nervously asked if the applicant's programme plans were based on its view of the characteristics and needs of the franchise area. It was a sod. There was a long pause.

'Almost entirely,' said Cameron. 'We all know and love and live in the area, so we want to put something back, and give it a regional identity. We want to make friends with the viewers, to make them feel part of one great Venturer family.

'But our approach would be the same if we were pitching for any area in the British Isles. Great television comes from telling people the truth, from entertaining them so well they don't realize they're being educated. We want to make documentaries and dramas that tackle the problems we all face, coping with unemployment, loneliness, adolescence, being in love. Even –' she smiled, testing the age group of the panel – 'with the traumas of having one's grandchildren to stay over Christmas.' The panel smiled warmly back.

'Cameron can hardly say this for herself,' chipped in Charles, 'but I'd just like to add that with her and Declan, we have the most exciting team to hit the screen since Ivory and Merchant. They've both been in Ireland making a film on Yeats for Channel Four. I saw the uncut version last week. It is utter magic and will bring Yeats's poetry and the beauty of the Irish countryside to millions of new viewers. It would be nice to think they could do the same for the Cotswold area.'

Lady Gosling nodded sagely, noticing, however, that Declan was gazing blankly into space and taking no part in the proceedings.

Everyone drank a great deal of Highland Spring water. Dame Enid and Charles were superb on the arts; Billy charmed all the panel on sport; Janey had some wonderful ideas for women's interests; Seb made them laugh on news coverage, saying that the Corinium Head of News was so idle, he consulted his opposite number at the BBC every morning, so they could both cover the same local events, and there would be absolutely no danger of either of them being bawled out for scooping the other.

Henry started off brilliantly when Judge Davey asked him about his involvement in the consortium. He was just waxing lyrical on capturing the wild life of the area on film, and appearing to scratch his plaster for the third time, when Janey suddenly realized he was pulling up the flare of his trousers and reading the whole thing off his plaster and got the most frightful giggles. Terrified that the Prebendary, who was sitting next to Henry, would take his eyes off her bosom for one second and see what Henry was up to, Janey nudged Henry sharply in the ribs.

'Ouch! – shrews, voles, badgers,' ended Henry lamely, dropping his trouser-leg and thus losing his impromptu autocue.

'I love badgers,' said Lady Barnsley, looking very excited. 'We've got some in our wood.'

'Have you really?' said Henry. 'So have we, and so has Declan actually. I passed two big chaps having a fight in my drive the other night. They were so preoccupied, I managed to get really close up.'

'Did you really?' said Lady Barnsley.

Lady Gosling, however, had had enough about badgers. She looked straight at Declan, who was still slumped in his chair totally unrecognizable from the dazzlingly charismatic, self-confident demagogue who'd laid into Tony Baddingham at the public meeting.

'Who is going to run the company?' she asked him.

'I'm chairman,' said Freddie, when Declan didn't answer. 'I intend to devote at least one day a week to Venturer if not more. 'Enry's non-executive deputy chairman, Rupert'll handle finance and admin with Harold. Declan and Cameron will oversee programmes. Georgie will be in charge of sales. Charles, Janey, Sally, Billy and Seb will all be Heads of various departments. Marti, Bas, Lord Smiff, Dame Enid an' Wesley will be non-executive directors. But they'll all act on a consultancy basis, and add to the smooth running of the company.'

'But who is really going to run the company?' persisted Lady Gosling.

No contribution was clearly forthcoming from Declan, so Rupert looked at Lady Gosling squarely. 'I am,' he said.

'I would have thought,' said Lady Gosling icily, 'that your very limited business experience doesn't include the creation of new companies. It's a tough skill to acquire.'

'When I was twenty-one,' snapped Rupert, 'I started my own show-jumping business, which has now developed into a yard, which turns over ten million a year. I'm also an MP, and on top of all this I ran an extremely successful sports ministry for four years. I shall also have the constant and incredibly able advice of all my directors, particularly Harold, who's been in charge of LWT's programmes for the last few years.'

'The entire Board would support Rupert as Chief Executive,' said Bas.

All of Venturer murmured their assent except Wesley who was sleeping peacefully.

'He did come on an overnight flight,' explained Janey, giving him a nudge.

'Howzat,' said Wesley, waking up.

Lady Gosling looked with infinite disapproval from Wesley to Declan, to Rupert to Billy, then up the table to Janey. 'Don't you feel there are too many celebrities, too many prima donnas in your consortium? Can you honestly convince us that Venturer will be able to stick effectively together as a team?'

'Yes,' said Rupert evenly, once more looking her straight in the eye. 'It hasn't been an easy week with my so-called "memoirs" coming out, but except for the Bishop and the Professor, we're all here, aren't we?'

Lady Gosling dropped her eyes first.

Glancing at the clock on the wall, Cameron could see they'd been in there an hour and a half. Was that a good sign, or did the IBA merely want to prove Venturer's inferiority beyond doubt? Knowing nothing about Maud's affair with Tony, she had also realized there was something seriously wrong with Declan. He hadn't contributed to the discussion at all. By now he ought to be revving up for his final peroration, tearing Corinium limb from limousine, but he was saying nothing.

She looked down the row, at Janey and Billy radiating panache and glamour and high spirits when she knew how desperately broke they were, at Charles who had no future if Venturer went down, at Georgie, Sally and Harold, who'd certainly jeopardized their careers, at Henry dreaming of bosoms and badgers, at Wesley who'd flown thousands of miles to support them and probably jeopardized his test career as well, at Rupert who, despite the devastating blows that had been dealt him that week, had performed so incredibly bravely, and back to Declan, who had taught her humanity. They were her friends, the people she most wanted to work with.

Lady Gosling looked at her watch, and poured herself a glass of Highland Spring. 'Well, we've listened to you all, and studied your bulky application. Has anyone anything else to say?'

There was a long agonizing pause:

'I have,' said Cameron, getting to her feet, as slim and brave in her red suit as the young Portia.

'Ladies and Gentlemen, last week at one of the northern

684

television stations a young Head of News hanged himself.'
She glanced along the row of shocked reproving faces. 'Sure,
we've all been fed the official story that he had domestic and
financial problems. The truth was he couldn't handle all the
pressures in the run-up to the franchise awards. He was being
so bullied to get so many different lobbies, local worthies,
friends of his Managing Director on to his programme to
impress you, the IBA, so that his lousy bosses could keep
their franchise and go on making a fortune. This is a tragedy
and a disgrace,' went on Cameron fiercely, 'and an appalling
indictment on the whole IBA and ITV system. We in production should not feel we've got to put on worthy uplifting
boring programmes every eight years in order to impress you
and retain the franchise. We should make good programmes
all the time.'

She turned, pointing to the framed document on the wall,
giving the IBA its own coat of arms and motto: 'Your motto
is *Servire populo*. But you're not serving the people if you're
encouraging the companies to make programmes that please
you, which you feel the people ought to watch, rather than
what they want to watch. I worked for Tony Baddingham
for four years,' she went on bitterly.

'And produced some very good uplifting programmes that
weren't boring,' said Lady Gosling dryly.

Cameron grinned. '*Touché*.' Then instantly she became
serious again. 'But that was because Tony Baddingham was
inordinately fond of me and gave me *carte blanche* to ride
roughshod over all the staff, and also gave me an unlimited
budget, while cutting the budgets of all other programmes to
nothing. Morale at Corinium was and is absolutely rock
bottom.

'Declan O'Hara –' she looked at Declan, pleading with
him to glance up or react in some way – 'is one of the all-
time greats of television. But when he was at Corinium, he
was very nearly broken by Tony, who forced him to interview
people of total insignificance, big businessmen, local dignitaries, people whose influence he believed he needed to win the
franchise. Fortunately Declan escaped and formed Venturer.

685

I've spent the last two months working with him and learnt that you don't need to terrorize people, or reduce them to hanging themselves, to make good programmes. Once you've got the authority, if you'll forgive the pun, you get far more out of people by kindness and interest in their welfare.'

The Welsh judge put on his spectacles for a better look at Cameron. Really she was a most astonishingly attractive girl. She could read for the Bar if ever she got fed up with television.

'ITV audience figures are plummeting,' went on Cameron accusingly, 'because so many of the programmes are so awful, and because most of the companies are run by accountants who aren't prepared to take risks any more. Why spend ten million on a serial which may fail, when for peanuts you can buy a quiz from another company?

'Venturer's going to change all that. We're going to revitalize ITV and not only make really good programmes right across the board, but also change the scheduling of the whole network so it's based on an exact analysis of what the public wants. At the moment it is simply a ragbag of whatever happens to be lying around, or fits in with the resources of the contributing company. We know what difficulties lie ahead. We know we can't produce profitable results if we have to make continually uplifting programmes. We'll need your help, understanding and guidance all along the way. But I promise you, unlike Corinium, we are not April when we woo, and December when we wed. I'm sorry, I've gone on too long.' She collapsed back into her chair, embarrassed.

It was some comfort that Rupert put his hand over hers with real pride.

'Normally your chairman would sum up at this stage, but I think we've all heard quite enough about Venturer's policy from Miss Cook,' said Lady Gosling. 'Thank you all for coming.'

After all the effort it was a very curt dismissal. Feeling utterly despondent, Venturer filed out of the room. Even worse, as they were smuggled out of the underground car park they went slap into the press, who were out in force clamouring to get a quote from Rupert about the memoirs. Fortunately they concentrated on getting pictures of him and didn't notice the rest of the moles cringing inside the convoy of cars.

For want of anything better to do, they all went back to Freddie's for a wake. On the way there, Janey, Billy and Freddie told Cameron about Declan and Maud.

'But the IBA ought to be told,' stormed Cameron. 'Someone's got to wise them up what an absolute bastard Tony is.'

'You made a pretty good job of it just now,' said Freddie. 'And Declan won't hear of it.'

As soon as he got to Freddie's, Rupert took Cameron aside.

'Thank you for turning up, sweetheart. You were absolutely marvellous.'

Cameron shrugged. 'If you can get a gold with a dislocated shoulder, I can talk too much with a broken heart.'

'Christ, I admire you.'

'I'd so much rather you'd loved me,' said Cameron sadly.

For a second Rupert lowered her dark glasses, and winced to see how red and swollen from crying her eyes were.

'I'm so sorry, angel. You know you can stay on at Penscombe as long as you like. I won't be there for the next few weeks.'

'Where are you going?' asked Cameron, suddenly frantic.

'America, this afternoon. The only hope is to get the hell out of England until the dust settles.'

'So you won't be back for Christmas?'

Rupert shook his head wearily. 'What Christmas?'

'Or for the IBA verdict on the 15th?'

'The result's a foregone conclusion. Couldn't you feel the tidal waves of disapproval and distaste emanating from those tweed bosoms throughout the interview? We haven't a hope.'

'Probably not,' said Cameron, glancing at Declan who was now slumped in a chair, shivering uncontrollably with an untouched glass of whisky in his hand. 'But Declan's going to need a lot of support in the next few days.'

'Not from me,' said Rupert bitterly. 'The best thing for all the O'Haras would be to have me out of their hair.' He looked at his watch. 'I'd better be off.'

'Can I ask you just one favour?' said Cameron. 'Could I possibly keep Blue?'

The doorbell rang and they both jumped thinking it might be Taggie. Freddie's secretary answered it and the next moment a man marched into the room. For a second Cameron thought she was hallucinating, for it seemed as if the old Declan, the forceful, confident, aggressive, clear-eyed, sun-tanned Declan, whom she remembered so clearly that first day he arrived at Corinium, had just walked through the door. Then she realized it was Patrick, thickened out, weathered and bronzed from five months working on a sheep farm. He'd obviously come straight from the airport, and being Patrick, even in a family crisis, had bothered to buy duty free whisky and cigarettes. He'd need them both over the next few days.

Near to tears, Declan rose to his feet. Ignoring everyone else in the room, Patrick went over and put his arms round him.

'It's all right, Pa,' he said gently, 'I rang home first. Taggie told me about Mum. It was a terrible thing for her to do, but she had reasons. It'll be all right. It's you she loves. She'll come back.'

He was like the father comforting the child.

'She sabotaged the franchise,' groaned Declan, 'and it was all my fault.'

'Rubbish,' said Patrick. 'The responsibility for that lies elsewhere.'

He let go of Declan and turned towards Rupert, his face hardening. 'You deliberately set out to seduce Cameron because you wanted her on Venturer's side, didn't you? Well that's for fucking *her* up.' The next moment he'd smashed his fist into Rupert's right jaw and, as Rupert reeled sideways, caught totally by surprise, Patrick hit him again on the right eye with his other fist. 'And that's for fucking up Taggie,' he added, as Rupert crashed to the ground.

In the press over the weekend there was endless speculation

as to which of the wronged husbands named in Rupert's bonk-statement (as the memoirs were now known), had given Rupert the black eye.

RIVALS

51

The next two weeks were terrible for Venturer. Deeply guilty that his utter failure to pull himself together at the meeting had finally cost them the franchise, Declan went home to Penscombe. Taggie and Patrick made sure he was never alone, as he seemed to sink deeper and deeper into depression, constantly vacillating between loathing Maud for betraying him and longing to have her back. There was no word from her; she seemed to have totally vanished.

Patrick, displaying patience and understanding way beyond his years, spent hours talking to his father: 'Taggie said Mum was absolutely gibbering with terror before *The Merry Widow*. It was such a colossal distance from obscurity back to the limelight. A little amateur production perhaps to you, but to her it wasn't just an extra step to cross the Frogsmore, but a vast leap over a five-hundred-foot-deep ravine. She needed you so desperately to witness her triumph or catch her if she fell.'

'I know,' groaned Declan. 'Because I always had to fight so hard to keep her, I never realized how much she needed me.'

'And you know she lives any part she plays. In her head she's now become poor bullied Nora in *A Doll's House*, marching out with a slammed door on an insensitive tyrannical husband. She wanted to hit back, to slam the door on your figures.

'And finally you mustn't underestimate the influence of Tony Baddingham. I know the effect he had on Cameron. He is pure Iago. He only had to point out how brilliant, beautiful and sexually voracious Cameron was; how you were spending more and more time with her; how could the two of you *not* be having an affair? You know what an imagination Mum has. This was even more immediate than P. D. James. Imagine, too, the appalling things he must have said about you, and finally the escape from poverty he offered her: new dresses, new jewels, furs, no more brown envelopes, or creditors at the gate, even warmth.' Patrick shivered. After the Australian summer The Priory central heating left a great deal to be desired. 'And he was around all the time, and you were away, or preoccupied with the franchise or Yeats, and Mum was probably turned on because the whole thing was so utterly *verboten*. All he had to do was to switch on his electric carving knife, dip it in washing-up machine powder and turn it in the wound.'

Declan winced: 'I can understand all that, but deliberately to hand over all our secrets.'

'She may not have done,' said Patrick. 'Taggie was out a lot cooking. Tony probably came to the house. The plans were on your desk. Your writing isn't *that* indecipherable.'

'D'you think I should go round to The Falconry and kill him?'

Patrick gave a wintry smile. 'I wouldn't. You know how Lady Gosling abhors violence.'

Taggie, who was kept enormously busy cooking for parties and filling up people's deep freezes for Christmas, made heroic attempts to be cheerful, but she worried Patrick far more than Declan. Never one to grumble, she refused to discuss Rupert, but Patrick knew she was bleeding to death inside.

Outside, the weather was frantically warmer, the snow thawed in patches, leaving fantastic shapes, a sea horse there, a camel here. All down the valley the streams that tumbled into the Frogsmore were still frozen into dirty grey glaciers. Wandering numbly through the fields with the dogs, Taggie only noticed the flattened tufts of thick tawny grass sticking up through the snow, like the heads of a thousand Ruperts slain in battle.

'*Too long a sacrifice,*' quoted Patrick bitterly, thinking too of his own situation, '*can make a stone of the heart.*'

Cameron, mercifully, was still very busy editing Yeats (Declan had lost all interest in the project), and setting up the programme on stepmothers which Channel Four had commissioned. She popped over on several occasions to cheer Declan up, but managed to avoid times when Patrick was at home. Patrick didn't know if she'd gone back to Tony, or whether Tony was looking after his mother. He and Taggie decided it would be better to do nothing until after the franchise results were announced.

Sunday, 15th December was D-Day. The form was that from nine o'clock onwards, in an atmosphere of high drama and secrecy, the existing managing directors of all the commercial television companies would roll up at the IBA in their limos at quarter of an hour intervals. Driving past the battalions of reporters, photographers and camera crews, they would be ushered once again into the building from the underground car park and be whizzed up in the lift to yet another empty office. Here, not unlike the suitors in *The Merchant of Venice*, they would be handed a sealed envelope from Lady Gosling and then be left alone to open it and learn if they had held onto their franchise, or whether, as in some instances, they had to merge with their rivals. Allowed a few minutes to digest this information, they would then be summoned to Lady Gosling's office for a brief word of congratulation or commiseration. Afterwards they would leave the building by the back door or by the front, having sworn not to reveal a word of the results to the press. After all the existing contractors had been seen, the contenders, who hoped to depose them, would come in one by one after lunch and endure the same procedure.

At four-thirty Lady Gosling would call a press conference to announce the results, which would simultaneously be rushed to the Stock Exchange and the Home Secretary, who would inform the Prime Minister.

Tony Baddingham was so certain he had retained the Corinium franchise that he'd taken a suite overnight at the Hyde Park Hotel.

Expectation had been boosted by front-page forecasts in most of the Sunday papers of a definite Corinium victory. The Krug was therefore flowing at a reception for the press and for all Tony's Corinium supporters, as he left for his twelve o'clock appointment with the IBA.

Tony was relieved the contenders weren't being seen until the afternoon. He would need police protection if he met Declan in the lift. He preferred to gloat over Venturer's utter humiliation at a distance.

It was a bitterly cold grey day, with an icy wind, which razor-cut the face far more effectively than any East End villain. Rather than walk the two hundred yards from the Hyde Park Hotel to the IBA, Tony made Percy drive round the park and approach 80 Brompton Road from South Kensington. Innumerable cameramen and journalists were mingling on the pavement with the Christmas shoppers as his Rolls drew up.

Never one to resist publicity, Tony decided to go in through the front door and let Percy take the Rolls round to the car park. There was a frenzy of activity and popping of flashbulbs as he got out. Tony had always kept a high profile; most of the press recognized him. Posing for thirty seconds in his Garrick tie and new £900 suit, he told the grey forest of microphones that he didn't believe in jumping the gun, but he was confident, quietly confident, that he'd still be in business that afternoon, before scurrying through the revolving doors of the IBA.

'Arrogant focker,' snarled Declan who was watching ITN at Freddie's house. 'Don't talk about guns in my presence, you bastard.'

'Don't watch it,' said Patrick, switching off the television. 'It'll only upset you. You ought to change soon, and have a shave.'

'What's the point of looking pretty for a firing squad?'

The door bell rang. Declan started. Why did he pray each time it might be Maud?

'I'll answer it,' said Freddie.

Freddie's heart was heavy. He knew there was no hope of Venturer getting the franchise, but he'd tried to keep everyone's spirits up for the last two weeks and tried even harder to be a good husband to Valerie. In return Valerie hadn't even bothered to come up to London today, she so detested failure. But as Freddie peered through the spyhole, he felt his heart expand in joy and gratitude, for there, her face as red and purple with cold as a mandrill's bottom, stood Lizzie. Never was a door opened so fast. As he drew her into the house out of the sight of any lurking press, she fell into his arms.

'You shouldn't be here,' he mumbled incoherently.

'I know I shouldn't,' said Lizzie, 'but James is being so smug, and I couldn't sit around drinking Tony's champagne. I thought it would poison me.'

At Tony's house in Rutland Gate, totally oblivious of the franchise affair, with only thought for one another, Caitlin O'Hara and Archie Baddingham met up on the first day of the school holidays.

'Are you sure it's safe,' asked Caitlin as they went into Monica's bedroom, 'and your father won't descend down the chimney like Father Christmas?'

'No, they'll be whooping it up all day at the Hyde Park,' said Archie. 'And poor Mum will spend her time fending off kisses from ghastly drunken hangers-on like James Vereker. I'm sorry your father hasn't got it.'

'It's a shame,' said Caitlin. 'He worked jolly hard. So did Tag.'

'I'll support you,' said Archie, putting a bottle of Sancerre and two glasses on his mother's bedside table. 'Look, are you sure you want to go through with this, and wouldn't rather wait until after we're married?'

Caitlin, who, despite her habitual air of unconcern, was

trembling like an earthquake, shook her head. 'Most people sleep together first these days, just to find out whether they're sexually compatible. Anyway, I reached the age of consent last week. It's awfully tidy in here.' She looked round in amazement. 'You ought to see my parents' bedroom. D'you think we ought to put a red towel underneath us? It'd be so awful if I bled all over your mother's sheets.'

'What time is it?' whispered Archie.

'One forty-five,' said Caitlin, looking at the flickering red figures of the digital clock. 'Why?'

'I want to remember what time the most important thing in my life took place,' said Archie, as he unbuttoned her black cardigan.

He looks terrible, thought Taggie, as she brushed Declan's dark-blue suit and straightened his tie. The new Harvie and Hudson green-and-blue-striped shirt Cameron had bought him last week in honour of the occasion was already too big. In the last fortnight the thick black hair had become almost entirely silver, and despair and grief had dug even deeper trenches on his forehead and on either side of his mouth.

The clock struck two.

'Car's here, Declan,' called Freddie from the hall.

'Good luck,' said Taggie, hugging him. 'It'll be over in half an hour.'

One by one the members of Venturer shook Declan's hand and wished him well. Billy gave him the faded four-leaf clover he'd worn in his boot when he'd won the show-jumping silver in Colombia. Henry Hampshire gave him a piece of white heather, foisted on him by a gypsy outside Harrods that morning. Rupert had sent a telex from LA. Professor Gray-stock and the Bishop of Cotchester were no doubt at this moment enjoying their second helpings of roast beef in Gloucestershire. Everyone waved to Declan as he set off.

'Majestic though in ruin,' said Patrick ruefully.

'Not yet,' boomed Dame Enid. 'Don't be so defeatist, boy.'

•

The media went berserk as Declan's car drew up. It had been a long, cold, somewhat boring day. Not admitted inside the IBA for reasons of security, they had spent their time belting the hundred yards between the front of the building and the back, desperate to get a story. Managing Directors of television companies are enormously powerful but not always very well-known men. One camera crew had had the embarrassment of asking their own Chief Executive what television company he worked for. Another crew wasted a lot of film on their own press officer.

But everyone knew Declan. Many of the crews had worked with him, and loved him, and wished he could have won. The Christmas shoppers, battered by the cold and each other, knew him too, and cheered and mobbed him. It took him several minutes to fight his way across Brompton Road and, as he went in through the revolving doors, a fat woman gave him a piece of holly for good luck. Coming the other way was Johnny Abrahams, his old boss at the BBC who'd put in a bid to oust Granada.

'How did you do?' asked Declan.

'They told us to go home,' said Johnny despondently.

Declan was taken up in the grey steel lift to the eighth floor and ushered into a large office which said 'Members' Viewing Room' on the door. Inside, a lot of maroon chairs were lined up in front of a large screen. The grey telephone in the corner was dead. A smell of turkey drifted down the passage, the aftermath of Lady Gosling's festive lunch. Out of the window he could see Knightsbridge and the north-east corner of Harrods, strawberry roan against a sullen grey sky with its coloured flags fretted by the icy wind.

He looked down at the piece of holly which still had two red berries. It was nice that all those people had been pleased to see him. Perhaps one day, when he'd got this mockery of a franchise behind him, he might work again. He wondered what Maud was doing; probably celebrating at the Hyde Park Hotel with Tony by now. Directly below him was Lancelot Place. It was ironic that he was the Arthur who'd promised the IBA Camelot, and Tony was the Lancelot who'd stolen his Guinevere. Oh Christ, he groaned, how could he possibly ever do anything in life without her?

'Mr O'Hara.'

Declan started violently, looking round stupidly. A kind-faced woman in spectacles had walked through the door with a tray full of envelopes and handed a white one and a larger brown one to him.

'Your envelopes. Best of luck.'

'Thank you,' muttered Declan.

He waited politely until she'd gone, then shoved them in his coat pocket. Like bills, he never believed in opening unpleasant things. Out of the window he saw a group of horses and riders jingling back to the stables at Hyde Park, back to oats and a warm straw bed. Christ, how peaceful in life to be a horse. And how beautiful they were. He'd have to put The Priory on the market immediately, but he might get a day or two's hunting before he left.

'Mr O'Hara.'

'I'm sorry. I was just leaving.'

'Would you come upstairs and have a word with Lady Gosling?'

'Not much point really. Nice of her to bother, though.'

'She asked me to collect you,' said the bespectacled woman firmly.

Lady Gosling sat in her office, behind a huge desk. The Director General and his deputy sat on the sofa. The room was full of smoke. They'd obviously all had a good lunch.

'Good afternoon, Mr O'Hara.' Lady Gosling rose slightly, holding out her thin freckled hand.

Declan held out his, realized he was still holding the bit of holly, and blushed.

'Rather premature to celebrate,' said Lady Gosling dryly. 'I should sit down if I were you.'

Declan mumbled he would prefer to stand.

'Well,' she began sternly. 'There were certainly some patchy moments in your bid. Freddie Jones obviously has an exceptional grasp of finance, and Cameron Cook was first class. What a very bright, courageous girl. And, of course, some of your programme plans are extremely interesting.'

What's she going on about? thought Declan wearily. It was like a condemned man being told that he's got a really sympathetic hangman.

'Some of the publicity, on the other hand, has been perfectly frightful,' went on Lady Gosling fiercely. 'And your security left a lot to be desired. However, we were impressed by this.' She handed Declan some sheets of paper.

At the top of the first were three typewritten lines. It was a little time before Declan's tired eyes could make out what they said.

'We, the undersigned, wish to state we would like to support Declan O'Hara's bid for the Corinium franchise. He makes the kind of television we believe in, and in the brief time he was at Corinium we were all impressed by his utter integrity and kindness to staff at all levels. If his consortium were awarded the franchise we would all like to work for him.'

Slowly, slowly, Declan's eyes travelled down the list of names: Georgie Baines, Cyril Peacock, Daysee Butler, Deirdre Kilpatrick, Mike Meadows, then on to PAs, tea girls, secretaries, production buyers, designers, security men, receptionists, best boys, gaffers, producers, sparks, riggers, researchers, make-up girls, engineers, floor managers, directors, commissionaires, canteen ladies, sound men, vision mixers. He turned the page. The list went on in three columns down to the bottom of the next page, and then down to the bottom of the next and swam before his eyes.

Declan turned towards the window. The horses had all gone in. He pressed his hands to his eyes, his great shoulders shaking.

'That's a most impressive document,' said Lady Gosling gently. 'I should frame it and look at it if ever you feel low.'

Declan turned to her, frantically rubbing his eyes.

'I'm sorry to let them down,' he said in a choked voice. 'It was good of you to show it to me.'

'On the contrary,' said Lady Gosling. 'You haven't let them down at all. Why don't you open those envelopes.'

698

Still clutching his piece of holly, Declan's hands were trembling so much, he tore the white envelope and had to piece the letter together.

'Dear Mr O'Hara,' he read incredulously, 'We have great pleasure in telling you that the Venturer Consortium has been awarded the Corinium franchise.'

Declan read the letter three times in silence. Then he opened the brown envelope, which contained contractual details.

'I wouldn't bother to try and absorb those at the moment,' chipped in the Director General, also in a slightly unsteady voice, 'but it's all good news. Well done.'

In silence Declan shook hands with them, then presented the piece of holly to Lady Gosling and walked out of the room. Totally forgetting Freddie's driver waiting in the underground car park, he took a lift to the ground floor. Outside the building the press surged forward.

'How d'yer do, Declan?'

Then, seeing he was fighting back the tears, they divided and let him through as he walked unsteadily off in the general direction of Holland Park.

Gathered round the radio, because there was no television news till six o'clock, the Venturer consortium pounced on every bit of news. A great cheer went up when the reporter said that Tony Baddingham had been seen driving away from the building looking stony-faced.

'Perhaps we haven't come to another wake, after all,' said Freddie, in amazement. 'Let's have a drink anyway.'

'Maybe the IBA want us to merge in some way with Corinium,' suggested Cameron.

'Count me out then,' said Charles. 'I'd rather stay on the dole.'

They all jumped as the wireless crackled.

'The latest news on the franchise front,' said the commentator, 'is that Declan O'Hara has just come out of the IBA building in tears, so I'm afraid things look bleak for Venturer. He's just walked through the crowds and was last seen heading towards South Kensington tube station like a man in deep shock.'

Cameron looked at Patrick. 'That's that, then.'

'That bugger Baddingham's beaten us after all,' said Dame Enid furiously. 'I'm bloody well going to tell Gwendolyn Gosling how he enticed Maud away and bribed Beattie Johnson. I don't give a damn what Declan says, we must be able to appeal.'

'I don't fink we can,' said Freddie wearily. 'The decision's final.'

'Nothing's final,' said Dame Enid briskly.

Taggie went white. 'You don't think Daddy will do something silly?'

'Of course not,' snapped Cameron, because she had thought the same thing and was frightened too.

Lizzie took Freddie's hand. 'I'm so sorry, darling.'

Freddie shook his head, near to tears too, unable to speak.

Next minute Freddie's chauffeur rang from the car: 'I 'eard the bad news on the radio, Mr J. I've picked up Mr O'Hara at South Ken.'

'Is he OK?' said Freddie.

'Well, he's not making much sense, but I'll bring him back to Holland Park.'

Ten minutes later Declan walked into the drawing-room. For a second he looked like a thundercloud, so they all knew finally there was absolutely no hope. Then for the first time in weeks, he gave his wicked schoolboy grin: 'It's all right, my darlings. We got it.'

There was a stunned silence, followed by an explosion of cheering; everyone was hugging each other. Janey burst into tears, so did Charles. Dame Enid and Billy were wiping their eyes.

'Fuckin' 'ell,' yelled Freddie, jumping up and down.

'Good Lord,' said Henry.

Taggie suddenly found herself hugging Cameron. 'We got it,' they both screamed simultaneously.

'Are you quite, quite sure?' said Bas incredulously. 'Can we see the proof?'

Grinning broadly, Declan got the torn white letter out of his pocket. Everyone crowded round to have a look.

'Bloody hell, it's true,' said Janey, giving a whoop of joy and hugging Billy. 'We can move back to Penscombe.'

'I'm going to be the next Trevor MacDonald,' shouted Wesley.

'I might even keep my cottage after all,' said Marti.

'What decided them finally to give it to us?' Cameron asked Declan over the Tarzan howls and the deafening fusillade of champagne corks.

'Mostly you,' said Declan, putting an arm round her shoulders. 'They thought you were marvellous, and they adored Freddie, but it was everyone,' he went on, raising his hand for silence. 'It was all of you turning up at the IBA that finally swung it. A case of everyone ventured, everything won. In the end, none but the brave deserved the franchise.' He wiped his eyes. 'I'm so proud and happy for us all.'

'So am I,' said Henry, who'd been laboriously doing sums on the back of an envelope, 'I had one thousand pounds on us at 2–1.'

'Christ,' said Bas. 'You can almost buy Joanna Lumley for that.'

Everyone screamed with laughter and started hugging everyone else all over again.

Over at Rutland Gate, Caitlin lay in Archie's arms.

'Are you sure that was all right,' he asked her for the hundredth time, as he stroked her flat white belly.

'Of course it was.'

'I thought guys were supposed to go off girls the moment they'd had them, but I love you more than ever. You're so beautiful. Did it hurt very much?'

Caitlin giggled: 'One has to suffer to be beautiful. And we've got the whole holidays ahead of us. Have you got masses of work to do?'

'Yes,' said Archie.

'So have I. We can do it together.'

'Are you hungry? I am. I'll see if there's anything in the larder.' Archie got up. Naked, still slightly plump, but to Caitlin entirely beautiful, he peered through the curtains. At three-thirty, it was getting dark.

'Holy shit,' said Archie. 'My mother's just getting out of a taxi.'

Frantically Caitlin kicked the bottle under the bed, put the two glasses in the bedside cupboard, dragged on her jeans, her black cardigan and her boots, and shoved her shirt, bra, pants and socks into her carrier bag. Archie turned off the bedroom lights.

Going into the drawing-room a minute later, Monica found Archie and Caitlin sitting on either side of an empty fireplace. Caitlin was reading *Country Life* upside-down.

'Hullo, Mummy,' said Archie heartily, getting up and kissing her. 'I thought you'd be at Dad's celebration piss-up. I was about to join you.'

'It's been cancelled,' said Monica numbly. 'We've lost the franchise.'

'What!' exploded Archie. 'We couldn't have. All the papers said it was in the bag.'

'They were wrong. For security, the IBA leave MI5 standing.'

'My God, I'm sorry.'

Caitlin couldn't take it in. 'D'you mean Daddy's got it?' she said slowly.

'I don't know.' Monica looked at Caitlin dazedly. 'I suppose so.'

Still in her fur coat and headscarf, she sat down very suddenly on the sofa, stared at her rough gardening hands, with their huge diamonds, and burst into tears. Archie, who'd only seen his mother cry once years ago when one of her labradors had to be put down, was utterly helpless. It was like watching the *Titanic* sink.

'I just feel so sorry for him,' sobbed Monica. 'I know he's done dreadful, dreadful things, left no stone unturned to try and win the franchise, but he wanted to beat Rupert and Declan so very badly.'

Rushing across the room, Caitlin put her arms round Monica.

'I'm so sorry. I'm delighted for Daddy of course, but it's like the Boat Race. Someone's got to win, but it doesn't stop it being horribly, desperately, publicly humiliating for the crew who don't. There, please don't cry. Get her some brandy,' she ordered Archie. 'Will you be terribly poor?'

'No,' gulped Monica, 'I don't think so. Tony's got all his other companies. It's just that he minded so much, and it's such a shock. He was so certain.'

Struggling to her feet, desperately wiping her eyes, saying she must find a handkerchief, she stumbled off to her bedroom.

Thinking of the unmade bed, Archie and Caitlin looked at each other in horror.

'I must be going senile,' gulped Monica when she returned, wiping her eyes and blowing her nose. 'I could have sworn I made my bed this morning.'

'You've been under a terrific strain,' said Caitlin sympathetically. 'My father topped up a whisky and soda with milk the other day.'

'But I never leave it unmade,' whispered Monica. 'I can't afford to go to pieces. Tony's going to need so much support.'

She made a face like a little girl drinking medicine as she took a gulp of the brandy.

'I'll go and make it for you,' said Caitlin. 'That'll make you feel better. Then Archie and I are going to get you some lunch.'

In the middle of Venturer's amazed and joyful celebrations, the telephone rang. Dame Enid picked it up. Not bothering to put her hand over the receiver, she yelled: 'It's the boring old fart for you, Declan.'

'Congratulations, Declan,' said the Bishop of Cotchester heartily. 'Delighted you've finally got the franchise. With the festive season nearly upon us, I've been pondering much on the nature of forgiveness. I think, on balance, my flock will understand if I overlook Rupert Campbell-Black's lamentable behaviour. I would like to reconsider my position *vis-à-vis* Venturer.'

A beatific smile spread over Declan's face: 'Flock off,' he said, and hung up.

Cameron sat on the sofa cuddling Blue.

'A penny for your thoughts,' said Patrick, sitting down beside her. 'Although, now you've won the franchise, I suppose they're much more expensive than that.'

Cameron grinned: 'I was thinking how odd it is to feel so wildly happy when one's heart is breaking.'

'It's relief,' said Patrick, filling up her glass, 'to discover you're going to survive after all.'

He glanced across at Taggie who, with a fixed smile on her face, was gathering up glasses like a zombie.

'I'm not sure my sister is.'

'What's she got to complain about?' said Cameron bitterly. 'Rupert loves her.'

'She hasn't got a clue he does,' said Patrick, 'and he's not going to do anything about it. He's probably out on the tiles at some Hollywood orgy at this moment, busy forgetting her. Freddie and Pa have been trying to get through to him all evening, but there's no answer.'

Cameron looked at her watch.

'It must be breakfast time in LA,' she said.

52

Over in California Rupert was slowly going out of his mind with misery. Leaving England had made everything far, far worse. He couldn't eat or sleep. He must be dying if he didn't even want to drink. All he could do was long for Taggie. He'd never dreamed anything could hurt so much.

'Rupert,' said Suzy Erikson, his beautiful hostess, as they breakfasted by the pool, having just come in after an all-night party, 'I've been talking to you for twenty minutes, and you haven't heard a single word.'

'I know. I'm sorry.'

'I've also trailed all the most glamorous women in Hollywood in front of you for the past fortnight and you've paid no attention to any of them.'

'I know. I'm sorry about that too.'

'Still brooding about your Irish teenager?' said Suzy, plunging a spoon into her melon. 'Go home and screw her. It's the only way you'll get her out of your system.'

Rupert looked at his cooling cup of coffee. 'I can't, I mustn't fuck her up,' he repeated dully. 'Apart from Billy, she's the only genuinely good person I've ever met.'

'That seems rather a good omen,' said Suzy. 'Billy's the only person you've ever been faithful to, and the only one you haven't fucked up either.'

As Rupert got up to prowl up and down the terrace, Suzy thought how much weight he'd lost and how really ill he looked. Having some years ago been desperately in love with him, she'd always longed to see him brought to his knees. But now, so abject was his despair, she could only feel sorry for him.

'I want to look after her,' he was saying. 'She's the only person who's ever made me want to find a dragon and slay it for her sake, although,' he added with a half-smile, 'she wouldn't appreciate it. She doesn't like cruelty to animals at all.'

'Good thing she didn't know you in the old days,' said Suzy. 'Have you got a picture?'

Rupert walked back to his chair and extracted a creased snapshot from the inside pocket of his boating jacket, which was hanging over the back of the chair. It was one he'd taken in the woods. Taggie was pink-faced from catching leaves with the children.

'Not a great beauty, is she?' said Suzy with a certain satisfaction. Rupert snatched back the photograph.

'She is,' he said icily. 'She's the most beautiful girl I've ever seen.'

'Hum,' said Suzy. 'Well, if you think that, you have got her badly.'

An extremely tense silence was broken by the telephone.

'Someone called Declan O'Hara for you,' said Suzy. 'He seems kinda drunk.'

Rupert steeled himself for abuse.

'We've got it, we've focking got it,' yelled Declan.

'You what?'

'Not just us – you as well. We've focking got the franchise.'

Judging from the shrieks and whoops, there was the most terrific party going on in the background. Rupert wished, after the initial passionate relief, he could feel more excited and respond appropriately to Declan's almost incoherent ecstasy. Then he talked to Freddie, who was calmer but equally euphoric, and briefly to Cameron who sounded pretty overexcited as well. Then Declan snatched back the telephone.

'Isn't it focking marvellous? You'd better come back soon,

706

and we can find out if we know how to run a television company – what's that? Oh Taggie says to wish you a Happy Christmas.'

Switching off the telephone, Rupert walked to the edge of the shimmering pale-blue pool and looked up at the snowy peaks of the Santa Monica mountains that rose like one of Taggie's puddings. He wondered if the snow had thawed at Penscombe.

'I'm going home,' he said.

'To propose to your pink-faced Amazon?'

Rupert shook his head violently. 'No, no. I just think if I was in the same country as her, it might hurt less.'

The journey home was hell. All the air hostesses fluttered round him, plying him with champagne and delicious things to eat, which he left untouched. By some ghastly irony, the film was the Woody Allen which he'd seen with the children and Taggie. He took in as little of it as he had the first time. He tried to sleep, but it was as though he was destined to watch eternal television with Taggie's face on all four channels. He dropped off for a few minutes as the plane flew over Ireland, but dreamed of her and woke in utter desolation to find she wasn't there.

Heathrow at seven-thirty on a raw December morning was still dark.

'Good morning, Mr Campbell-Black,' said the passport man, who didn't even get a nod.

As he waited for his luggage, Rupert watched the carousel going round. It was the last circle of hell, he reflected, for people who never got the person they wanted in life. His heart was so heavy, he'd have to pay excess baggage on it. As he went through the green door at Customs, he thought of all the times in the old days when he'd sauntered through carrying dope or illegal currency in the bottom of his boots. Now he had nothing forbidden to declare but his hopeless love for Taggie.

Once through the barrier, he looked wearily round for his driver, but no one came forward. Christ, that was all he needed. He set off towards the telephones, passing a fleet of people brandishing cards with names on. Suddenly a particularly large placard caught his eye. On it was painted in huge letters: Roopurt Cambel-Blak. Only one person could spell that badly! He must be going mad. Then, below the placard, he saw a pair of very long, very slim legs in familiar faded jeans. The legs were shaking frantically, so was the placard. Rupert, finding too that his legs would hardly hold him up, walked towards it. Very gently he pushed it down, seeing first the mane of black hair, then two silver-grey eyes, then the deathly white face, and the desperately trembling mouth he'd dreamed of kissing for months now.

'Oh Tag,' he said despairingly.

'I can't help it,' she sobbed. 'I'll do anything. I'll drive you around. I'll look after your children. I'll cook, clean your house, muck out your horses, weed your garden. I just want to be near you. I can't bear it any longer.'

The next moment the placard crashed to the ground and Rupert had taken her face in his hands, feeling the contrast between the softness of her cheeks and the frantic tension of her jaw. And just to prove to himself she was real, he wonderingly kissed her lips, and her wet salty eyes, and then her forehead.

'I'm such a selfish bastard,' he muttered into her hair.

'I'm used to selfish people,' sobbed Taggie. 'I'd be lost without them.'

'And what about the memoirs?' There was so much uncertainty and despair in his voice that Taggie drew slightly away from him. Then she laughed despite her tears. 'I couldn't read them. That's one advantage of being dyslexic.'

Rupert started to laugh too, and then, taking her in his arms, gave her a kiss that, everyone gathered round said afterwards, should for length and passion have gone straight into the *Guinness Book of Records*.

'I love you,' he gasped as he came up for air. 'I've never loved anyone like I love you.' Then, aware that she was still trembling, added, 'It's all right, darling,' and suddenly he knew that it was and he'd never let her go again.

'Mr Minister,' said a voice, 'I mean, Mr Shadow Minister.'

Glancing round, Rupert saw they were surrounded by press. Holding Taggie close, he whispered, 'Where's the car?'

'Outside, just through the door.'

'We'll make a dash for it.'

On the motorway he managed to shake off the reporters, took an exit into some Royal Berkshire countryside and pulled up with a jerk in a lay-by. Then, removing both their seat belts, he turned to face her, taking her hands.

'I want you to know . . .' it was he who was stammering now . . . 'that I only joined the fucking consortium because of you. In fact, I only came back from Gstaad for your rotten brother's twenty-first because I wanted to have a crack at you. I only let myself be intervie.ved by your father because I thought he'd think me a wimp if I didn't, and I might be able to ingratiate myself with him. I only bought his bloody wood for that ludicrously inflated price because I love you. The only reason I didn't move in months ago was because in the one unselfish gesture of my life (and Christ, it was the most difficult), I thought it was unfair to foist my sodding bloody-minded nature on you. No one could have had a more appalling past.'

Taggie put up a hand to his lips to halt him. 'I don't care about your past,' she said shakily. 'All I want to be is your future.'

It was not long before the car had misted up completely, and Rupert stopped kissing her and wrote, 'I adore you. Will you marry me?' on the windscreen.

And underneath Taggie wrote, 'Yes pleese.'

Back on the motorway it was light now, and Taggie could see how grey and thin Rupert looked, and how blackly shadowed he was under the eyes.

'I just can't wait to feed you up,' she wailed.

Looking ahead, she saw the pallid full moon, which like a sympathetic friend had peered in at different windows of her turret bedroom throughout the night as she paced the floor boards wondering whether or not she should go and meet

Rupert. Now, clearly dying to go to bed, the moon kept on bobbing round clumps of trees or above the frozen white downs, as if just managing to keep awake to see how the story ended. Silently, thankfully, Taggie made a joyful thumbs-up sign as the moon finally disappeared from view.

'How did you screw up the courage to come and meet me?' asked Rupert, putting his hand on her thigh as they turned off the motorway.

'I went to see the children and gave them your presents yesterday afternoon. I was so desperate, it was the nearest I could get to you. They were so sweet, and Malise and Helen were really nice. They asked me to stay to supper, and after the children went to bed, I talked to Malise. He said he and Helen had over-reacted about the memoirs, and he was sorry, and how happy Helen had made him, and he was thirty years older than her, and he told me to go for it.'

'Really?' said Rupert in amazement. 'Good for Malise.'

'Where are we going?' asked Taggie, snuggling up to him.

'To ask your father's permission. If he won't give it, we'll have to elope, but I don't want it hanging over us.'

'You'll have to see Mummy as well.'

'She's back!' said Rupert in outrage. 'When, for Christ's sake?'

'The day before yesterday, the evening we got the franchise.'

'That figures,' said Rupert dismissively. 'Realized she'd backed the wrong horse.'

'No,' said Taggie. 'She saw Daddy crying on television when he came out of the IBA. You know how emotional he is, and she thought it was from unhappiness because he'd lost it, and felt so sorry for him that she rushed back and turned up at Freddie's house in the middle of the celebrations, just after Daddy'd rung you in fact. It was so odd. I'm not boring you?' she added quickly.

'You never, never bore me,' said Rupert, touching her cheek.

'Well, d'you know what Mummy said when she first saw him? Such a strange remark that I remembered it. She said:

"My Oberon! what visions have I seen! Me thought I was enamoured of an ass." Patrick says it comes from *Midsummer's Night Dream*. Anyway, they were both crying and fell into each other's arms, and disappeared into Freddie and Valerie's bedroom.'

'Pa and Ma for the course,' said Rupert, shaking his head.

Taggie giggled. 'It was a bit embarrassing. Hordes of press and television people turned up to interview Daddy and photograph him about getting the franchise, and he'd locked himself in with Mummy. So Freddie and Cameron had to field all the questions.

'And then, even worse, Valerie arrived. She'd beetled up from London the moment she'd heard Venturer had won to get in on the act, and she found everyone plastered, and Freddie kissing Lizzie Vereker on the sofa. So she stormed off to bed, and she couldn't get in because Mummy and Daddy were in there already.'

'Christ, we'll never behave like that, will we?' said Rupert putting his hand over hers. 'Still, I'm glad they're back together again.'

All the same Rupert was surprisingly nervous about confronting his future father-in-law. He needn't have bothered. When he went into the library Declan was poring over all sorts of leaflets for electronic equipment, spread out on the table.

'Rupert. Great to see you, good of you to come back so quickly. Come and look at this stuff. We're going to bid for satellite next.'

Rupert took a deep breath. 'I actually came back to ask for your daughter's hand in marriage, Declan.'

'Have you? Declan peered over his spectacles at Taggie. 'I thought you might. Well, she certainly looks happier than she's done for the past nineteen years, so I'd better say yes. We've got a hell of a lot to do here. Can you start work before Christmas?'

'No, I bloody can't. I'm going to be on my honeymoon over Christmas.'

711

'So soon. Can't you wait till the Spring and go to Paris? Maud and I went to Paris. I'd better call her and we'll have a drink. Good thing you didn't turn up yesterday, we were all so hungover, you might not have had such a genial reception. Maud!' he yelled up the stairs.

Maud wandered down, looking pretty wretched after her prolonged disappearance, but with plenty of her old insouciance, and embraced them both.

'She's obviously so glad to be home, she wouldn't have minded you marrying the cat,' Rupert said to Taggie afterwards.

A bottle of champagne had been opened, when Patrick marched in, looking like a thundercloud.

'Oh Christ, here comes Frank Bruno,' said Rupert, ducking behind Taggie.

'I've just heard the news on Radio One,' said Patrick coldly. 'I suppose none of you has had the decency to tell Cameron.'

'Oh dear,' said Declan. 'I'll ring her.'

'It's my responsibility. I'll do it,' said Rupert.

'I'll do it,' said Patrick heavily.

He took the telephone into the drawing-room next door and dialled the number of Cameron's house in Hamilton Terrace. She took a long time to answer.

'I've just heard,' she said in a flat voice.

'It must hurt, I'm very sorry.'

'You needn't be,' snapped Cameron. 'Why should I care if your sister's finally got him, when it's all over between him and me?'

'Still hurts,' said Patrick reasonably. 'Not much fun seeing someone get a clear round on a horse you were bucked off by. I'll be over later.'

'Whatever for?' Cameron's voice was shrill with hostility. 'I'm going out.'

'You stay where you are.'

Cameron collapsed on her bed. She had nowhere to go anyway. She supposed her house belonged to Venturer now. Outside, the shoppers were trailing argumentatively home in the rain, weighed down by Christmas presents. Then, like a frozen pipe that suddenly bursts with a thaw, Cameron, for the first time since Rupert left for America, gave way to tears.

Around five-thirty, when there seemed nothing left to weep out of her system, she tried to pull herself together, took Blue for a quick desolate walk across the water meadows and had a bath. At half-past-six and seven she was interrupted by carol singers. At a quarter-past-seven she was disturbed by two men with a van, who said they had some stuff to deliver.

'What stuff?' snapped Cameron.

'Six tea chests full of books, records and some clothes.'

'Don't be fucking stupid! You've got the wrong house! Take it away!' she screamed.

At that moment Patrick walked purposefully through the door, carrying two squash rackets and a portable typewriter under one arm and a large ginger cat under the other.

'I don't like cats, nor does Blue,' snarled Cameron.

'You will,' said Patrick soothingly. 'Just give me five minutes,' he added to the van driver, as he pushed Cameron into the sitting-room and shut the door behind him.

'What the bloody hell are you playing at, and what's all that shit they're delivering?'

'I'm moving in,' said Patrick, putting the ginger cat down. Immediately Blue bounced up to the cat, dropping gracefully down on his front paws, head on one side. The cat hissed, tail like a Christmas tree, and took a fierce swipe at Blue's nose. Blue gave a yelp and retreated between Cameron's legs.

'They'll get used to each other,' said Patrick, 'just like we will.'

'We bloody won't.'

'Yes, we will. I love you.'

'You can't any more. I've been such a bitch,' said Cameron, going very pale. 'Anyway, I love Rupert.'

'No you don't, or you wouldn't have gone to bed with my father in Ireland.'

'I didn't,' stammered Cameron.

'Yes, you did on the last night, and he felt so guilty about it afterwards, that's why he didn't get back for Mum's play.'

'Don't you mind?' said Cameron, appalled. 'It's practically incest.'

'It is not. It's you I'm interested in, and, anyway,' said Patrick with more than a touch of Declan's arrogance, 'as I'm a much younger, more beautiful, more together, about to be much more successful version of my father, it's perfectly logical that you should fall in love with me.'

'You're a toy boy,' said Cameron as his hands tightened round her waist.

'I'm not. I'm a man of substance. The BBC have just bought my first play and commissioned another. I'm going to write a kid's play called "Noddy in Toyboyland".'

Cameron grinned. 'You'd better cancel the contract, and I'll produce them both.'

'Nope,' said Patrick firmly. 'I never mix business with pleasure, and you, my dear, dear love are only pleasure.'

'I love Rupert,' wailed Cameron.

'Don't be silly,' said Patrick, drawing her close to him.

'Well, perhaps I don't,' said Cameron bewildered, as a few minutes later they were interrupted by a loud knock on the door.

'Can we unload the stuff now, sir?' said the driver.

Patrick looked at Cameron questioningly.

'Oh well, I guess you bloody well can.'

As the men stumped out to the van, Patrick smiled down at her: 'I just want to check out on your availability for the next thousand years.'

'I've never seen such a change in Taggie,' said Caitlin to Archie next morning. 'She keeps giggling all the time, and grinning from ear to ear, and she's suddenly got terribly protective. Rupert's been asleep for twenty-four hours in the spare room, and the most amazingly important people have rung up, and she hasn't let any of them talk to him.'

'That's nice,' said Archie, kissing her. 'They say love hits you with even more of a thunderbolt when you're old.'

Rupert woke to blue skies and birds singing outside, a fire in the grate and total panic inside. He had no idea where he or Taggie was. Then suddenly he became aware of something warm and furry, and realized Gertrude was lying in the small of his back. Slowly the events of yesterday reasserted themselves and he felt so happy he nearly went back to sleep again. Next minute the door opened very cautiously.

'I'm awake,' said Rupert.

'You did sleep well,' said Taggie in delight as she put down the breakfast tray piled with orange juice, coffee, croissants and home-made apple jelly.

'Because I felt safe for the first time in my life. Come here.' Rupert patted the bed, and when he kissed her, she smelt equally of toothpaste and her mother's scent.

Afterwards he stroked her face incredulously. 'I still can't believe I'm going to spend the rest of my life with you.'

'Nor I you,' sighed Taggie.

'I was going to bring you bacon and eggs,' said Taggie, spooning a pip out of the orange juice, 'but I thought if you hadn't been eating, it might be too rich for you.'

Then she giggled. 'A girl from the *Daily Mail* rang up just now.'

'What did she want?' asked Rupert, thinking how wonderfully it suited her to be so happy.

'She said, "How did you first meet your fiancé and what was he doing?" I couldn't say you were playing nude tennis with Sarah Stratton, so I said Basil brought you round for a drink. And the Leader of the Opposition rang twice. Evidently the Government's fallen and there's going to be an election. She wants you to ring her urgently. I said you were asleep.'

Rupert's eyes gleamed. 'I've got a feeling you're going to be far, far more use to me than I ever dreamed. We'd better get married at once. I'm allergic to the word fiancée; even you can't glorify it.'

'I certainly can't spell it,' said Taggie.

Later, downstairs, they discussed marriage plans.

'I suppose it'll have to be Cotchester Registry office,' said Maud, who was thinking about her wardrobe.

'I got married in a registry office the first time round,' said Rupert. 'As it's the real thing this time —' he raised Taggie's hand to his lips and kissed it — 'we thought we might get married in church. I'm sure we can find some trendy parson in London who won't mind my being divorced.'

'I've got a better idea,' said Declan, reaching for his telephone book.

'Tabitha's going to be a bridesmaid,' said Taggie to Caitlin. 'Would you like to be one too?'

'Only if I can wear jeans,' said Caitlin.

Declan, having for once dialled the right number, was put straight through to the Bishop of Cotchester. He immediately apologized for being so shirty on the telephone the other day and wondered whether the Bishop would reconsider coming on to the Venturer Board after all.

After some huffing and puffing about having to take a stand over Rupert Campbell-Black's disgusting memoirs, the Bishop said he would be delighted, and wrote down the date of the first board meeting.

'There's just one other thing,' said Declan. 'My daughter, Taggie, is getting married and her one wish is to be married by you in Cotchester Cathedral.'

Taggie turned crimson. 'It isn't true!' she squeaked, looking at Rupert who had started to laugh.

The Bishop once again told Declan that he'd be delighted. He'd become extremely fond of Taggie in the past year.

'Just the simplest service,' said Declan. 'Only family and very close friends and, of course, all our Venturer supporters.'

'Splendid, splendid,' said the Bishop. 'And who is the very, very lucky young man?'

'Well, I'm just coming to that,' said Declan.

THE END

RIDERS

BY JILLY COOPER

'Sex and horses: who could ask for more?' *Sunday Telegraph*

If you thought you knew what to expect of Jilly Cooper – bursts of restless romance, strings of domestic disasters, flip fun with the class system – RIDERS will come as a pleasurable surprise.

A multi-stranded love story, it tells of the lives of a tight circle of star riders who move from show to show, united by raging ambition, bitter rivalry and the terror of failure. The superheroes are Jake Lovell, a half-gipsy orphan who wears gold earrings, handles a horse – or a woman – with effortless skill, and is consumed with hatred for the promiscuous upper-class cad, Rupert Campbell-Black, who has no intention of being faithful to his wife, Helen, but is outraged when she runs away with another rider.

Set in the tense, heroic world of show-jumping, Jilly Cooper's novel moves from home-country gymkhanas through a riot of horsey events all over the world, culminating in the high drama of the Los Angeles Olympics.

'Blockbusting fiction at its best'
David Hughes, *The Mail On Sunday*

'I defy anyone not to enjoy her book. It is a delight from start to finish' Auberon Waugh, *Daily Mail*

0 552 12486 9

OTHER JILLY COOPER TITLES
AVAILABLE FROM CORGI BOOKS

☐ 10427 2	Bella		£2.50
☐ 10277 6	Emily		£2.50
☐ 10576 7	Harriet		£2.50
☐ 11149 X	Imogen		£2.50
☐ 12041 3	Lisa & Co.		£2.50
☐ 10717 4	Octavia		£2.50
☐ 10878 2	Prudence		£2.50
☐ 12486 9	Riders		£4.50
☐ 11525 8	Class		£3.50